The
MX Book
of
New
# Sherlock
# Holmes
## Stories

Part XLIX
The True Sherlock Holmes:
England's Greatest Hero
(1880-1888)

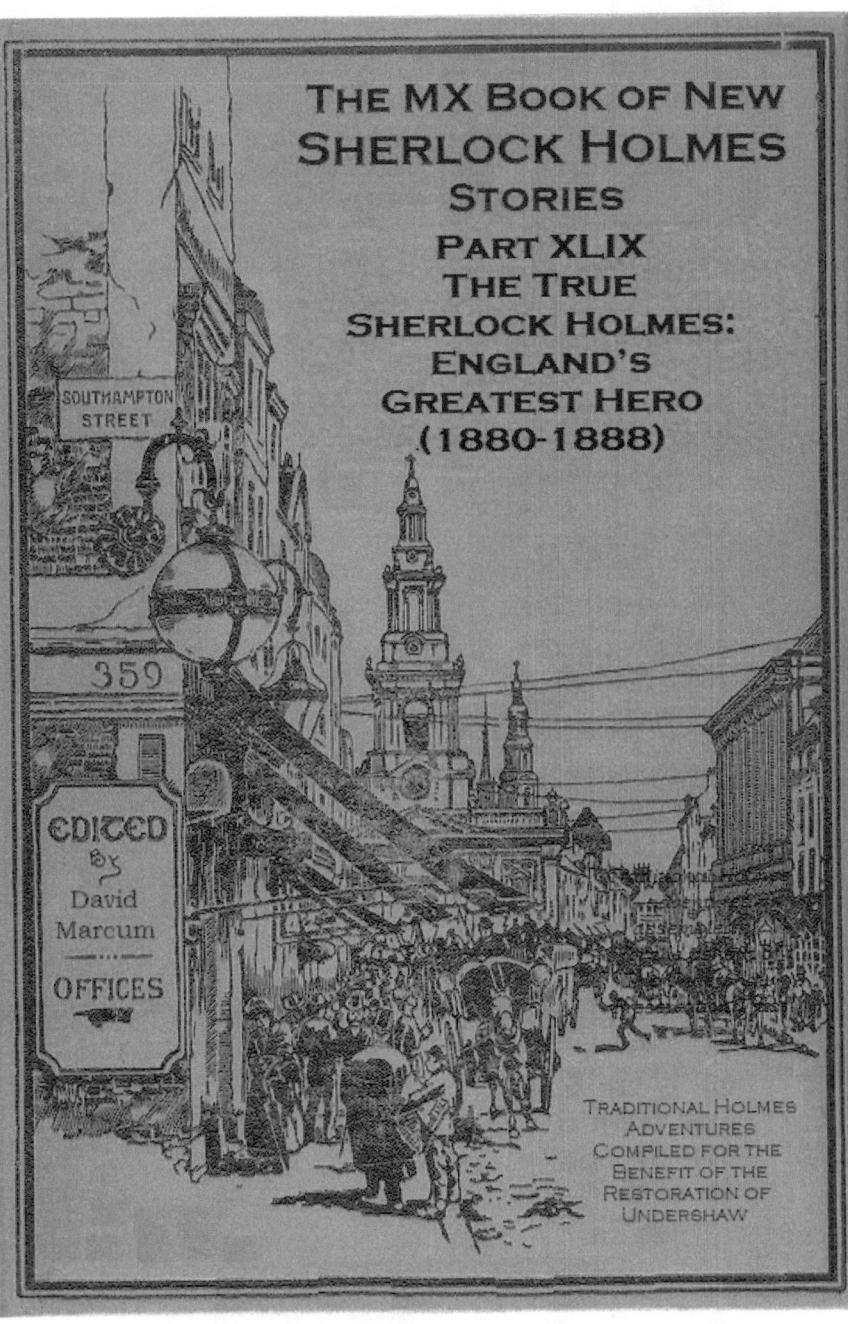

# THE MX BOOK OF NEW SHERLOCK HOLMES STORIES

## STORIES

## PART XLIX
## THE TRUE
## SHERLOCK HOLMES:
## ENGLAND'S
## GREATEST HERO
## (1880-1888)

SOUTHAMPTON
STREET

359

EDITED
By
David
Marcum

OFFICES

TRADITIONAL HOLMES
ADVENTURES
COMPILED FOR THE
BENEFIT OF THE
RESTORATION OF
UNDERSHAW

ISBN Hardback 978-1-80424-683-2
ISBN Paperback 978-1-80424-684-9
AUK ePub ISBN 978-1-80424-685-6
AUK PDF ISBN 978-1-80424-686-3

Published in the UK by
**MX Publishing**
335 Princess Park Manor, Royal Drive,
London, N11 3GX
www.mxpublishing.co.uk

David Marcum can be reached at:
*thepapersofsherlockholmes@gmail.com*

Cover design by Brian Belanger
*www.belangerbooks.com* and *www.redbubble.com/people/zhahadun*

*Internal Illustrations by Sidney Paget*

# CONTENTS

## Foreheads

Editor's Foreword: A Thousand Cunning Windings      1
     by David Marcum

Foreword      21
     by Bonnie MacBird

"Let me recommend this book . . . ."      23
     by Roger Johnson

An Ongoing Legacy for Sherlock Holmes      26
     by Steve Emecz

A Word from Undershaw      28
     by Emma West

The Reader (*A Poem*)      43
     by Kevin Thornton

## Adventures

The Adventure of the Four Knaves      45
     by Deanna Baran

The Adventure of the Flagitious Sire      59
     by David Marcum

The Adventure of the Madman's Sister      88
     by Tom Turley

The Carpetbag Case      113
     by Brenda Seabrooke

*(Continued on the next page . . . .)*

The Adventure of the Prized Possession      132
     by Tracy J. Revels

The Single Shoe      150
     by Stuart Douglas

The Case of John Bull vs Brittania      169
     by Roger Riccard

The Widow      183
     by Marcia Wilson

The Arlington-Fisher Affair      224
     by Mark Mower

The Luxton Tragedy      241
     by Tracy J. Revels

The Mystery of the Missing Body      256
     by DJ Tyrer

The Problem at Arnsworth Castle      270
     by Jane Rubino

The Etherege Case      289
     by Hugh Ashton

The Youngest Client      306
     by Gordon Linzner

The Mystery of the Medical Misdiagnosis      319
     by Will Murray

The Adventure at the Art School      342
     by Stephen Herczeg

*(Continued on the next page . . . .)*

The Adventure of the Distracted Detective                    363
    by Shane Simmons

The Adventure of the Headless Saint                          375
    by Tracy J. Revels

The Case of the Australian Atlases                           393
    by Paul Metcalfe


*About the Contributors*                                     417

**These additional adventures are contained in**

**Part L – The True Sherlock Holmes:**
**England's Greatest Hero (1889-1896)**

The Enigmatic Friendship (A Poem) – Jim Hawkins
The Adventure of the Twentieth Gun – Mike Adamson
Antoinette's Apparition – P.C. Shumway
The Adventure of the Intrepid Follower – Arthur Hall
Eyes of Wood, Judging – Marcia Wilson
The Sharpshooter's Revenge – P.C. Shumway
The Indiscriminate Paragraph – David Marcum
The Mystery of the Caroline Crown – Brett Fawcett
The Case of the Vanishing Adders – Ian Ableson
The Case of the Ghazi Genie – Paula Hammond
The Claws of Qift – John Linwood Grant
The Devil's Bridge – John Lawrence
The Second Strand – Tim Newton Anderson
The Adventure of the Twice-Murdered Man – Tracy J. Revels
The Murano Musician – Richard Gillman
A Yuletide Mystery – Alan Dimes
The Case of the Covent Garden Medium – Paula Hammond
The Adventure of the Tattooed Men – Arthur Hall
The Adventure of the Tallowed Cadavers – I.A. Watson
The Incident of the Poisoned Shipping Magnate – Sean M. Wright and
DeForeest B. Wright, III
The Adventure of the Black Diamonds – Ashley Williford

**Part LI – The True Sherlock Holmes:**
**England's Greatest Hero (1897-1901)**

Finding Holmes (A Poem) – Christopher James
The Case of the Three Cufflinks– Steve Lockley
Pease Poison Cold – Marcia Wilson
The Adventure of the Vanished Uncle – Arthur Hall

*(Continued on the next page . . . .)*

Murder in Grasmere – David MacGregor
The Case of the Bryniau Witch Tower – Paula Hammond
The Mystery of the Authentic Mystic – William Todd
Sherlock Holmes and the Female Detective – Susan Knight
The Case of the Puzzled Postman – Naching T. Kassa
The Uncle's Cryptic Clue – David Marcum
The Adventure of the Amnesiac – Dan Rowley and Don Baxter
The Adventure of the Murderous Clown – Tracy J. Revels
The Killing of Lady Grace Everley – Paul Nash
The Box – Robert Stapleton
A Puzzle in Porphyry – DJ Tyrer
The Adventure of the Fearful Printer – Arthur Hall
The Prophecies of the Brahan Seer – Paul D. Gilbert
The Clockmaker's Fate – Mike and Arianna Fox
The Wages of Loyalty – Mike Adamson
Death of an Uncommon Man – Geri Schear
The Adventure of the Long Arm – Alan Dimes

**Part LII – The True Sherlock Holmes:
England's Greatest Hero (1902-1923)**

Sherlock Holmes: The End? (A Poem) – Joseph W. Svec III
The Adventure of the Disgraced Baron – Derrick Belanger
Holmes the Hunter – Susan Knight
The Adventure of the Live Burial – Shane Simmons
Phantom of the Operetta – Tim Newton Anderson
The Ambassador's Dilemma – Peter Coe Verbica
The Adventure of the Dreaming Dragon – Josh Reynolds
The Disappearing Detective – J. Lawrence Matthews
The Adventure of the Unfinished Case – John McNabb
The Interrupted Retirements – Don Rowley
The Adventure of the Longest Case – I.A. Watson
The Clue of the Undamaged Stones – David Marcum

*(Continued on the next page . . . .)*

The Sound of the Grand's Piano – Paul Hiscock
The Adventure of the Fearless Postman – Andrew Salmon
The Adventure of the Cheapside Secret – Steven Philip Jones
The Adventure of the King's Code – Mike Chinn
His Longest Case – Martin Daley
The Bohemian Corporal– Orlando Pearson
The Riddle of the Sphinx – Liz Hedgecock
The Case of the One-Armed Crabbe – Roger Riccard
The Mystery of the Graveyard Angel – Adrian Middleton
The Adventure of the Wonderful Things – Craig Janacek
*Epilogue*: A Travel-Worn and Battered
           Tin Dispatch Box – David Marcum

# The MX Book of New Sherlock Holmes Stories
## Parts I – LII (2015-2025) contain the following:

## PART I: 1881-1889
Foreword – Leslie S. Klinger
Foreword – Roger Johnson
Foreword – David Marcum
Sherlock Holmes of London (A Verse in Four Fits) – Michael Kurland
The Adventure of the Slipshod Charlady – John Hall
The Case of the Lichfield Murder – Hugh Ashton
The Kingdom of the Blind – Adrian Middleton
The Adventure of the Pawnbroker's Daughter – David Marcum
The Adventure of the Defenestrated Princess – Jayantika Ganguly
The Adventure of the Inn on the Marsh – Denis O. Smith
The Adventure of the Traveling Orchestra – Amy Thomas
The Haunting of Sherlock Holmes – Kevin David Barratt
Sherlock Holmes and the Allegro Mystery – Luke Benjamen Kuhns
The Deadly Soldier – Summer Perkins
The Case of the Vanishing Stars – Deanna Baran
The Song of the Mudlark – Shane Simmons
The Tale of the Forty Thieves – C.H. Dye
The Strange Missive of Germaine Wilkes – Mark Mower
The Case of the Vanished Killer – Derrick Belanger
The Adventure of the Aspen Papers – Daniel D. Victor
The Ululation of Wolves – Steve Mountain
The Case of the Vanishing Inn – Stephen Wade
The King of Diamonds – John Heywood
The Adventure of Urquhart Manse – Will Thomas
The Adventure of the Seventh Stain – Daniel McGachey
The Two Umbrellas – Martin Rosenstock
The Adventure of the Fateful Malady – Craig Janacek

## PART II: 1890-1895
Foreword – Catherine Cooke
Foreword – Roger Johnson
Foreword – David Marcum
The Bachelor of Baker Street Muses on Irene Adler (A Poem) – Carole Nelson Douglas
The Affair of Miss Finney – Ann Margaret Lewis
The Adventure of the Bookshop Owner – Vincent W. Wright
The Case of the Unrepentant Husband – William Patrick Maynard
The Verse of Death – Matthew Booth
Lord Garnett's Skulls – J.R. Campbell
Larceny in the Sky with Diamonds – Robert V. Stapleton
The Glennon Falls – Sam Wiebe
The Adventure of *The Sleeping Cardinal* – Jeremy Branton Holstein

*(Continued on the next page . . . .)*

The Case of the Anarchist's Bomb – Bill Crider
The Riddle of the Rideau Rifles – Peter Calamai
The Adventure of the Willow Basket – Lyndsay Faye
The Onion Vendor's Secret – Marcia Wilson
The Adventure of the Murderous Numismatist – Jack Grochot
The Saviour of Cripplegate Square – Bert Coules
A Study in Abstruse Detail – Wendy C. Fries
The Adventure of the St. Nicholas the Elephant – Christopher Redmond
The Lady on the Bridge – Mike Hogan
The Adventure of the Poison Tea Epidemic – Carl L. Heifetz
The Man on Westminster Bridge – Dick Gillman

## PART III: 1896-1929
Foreword – David Stuart Davies
Foreword – Roger Johnson
Foreword – David Marcum
Two Sonnets (Poems) – Bonnie MacBird
Harbinger of Death – Geri Schear
The Adventure of the Regular Passenger – Paul D. Gilbert
The Perfect Spy – Stuart Douglas
A Mistress – Missing – Lyn McConchie
Two Plus Two – Phil Growick
The Adventure of the Coptic Patriarch – Séamus Duffy
The Royal Arsenal Affair – Leslie F.E. Coombs
The Adventure of the Sunken Parsley – Mark Alberstat
The Strange Case of the Violin Savant – GC Rosenquist
The Hopkins Brothers Affair – Iain McLaughlin and Claire Bartlett
The Disembodied Assassin – Andrew Lane
The Adventure of the Dark Tower – Peter K. Andersson
The Adventure of the Reluctant Corpse – Matthew J. Elliott
The Inspector of Graves – Jim French
The Adventure of the Parson's Son – Bob Byrne
The Adventure of the Botanist's Glove – James Lovegrove
A Most Diabolical Plot – Tim Symonds
The Opera Thief – Larry Millett
Blood Brothers – Kim Krisco
The Adventure of The White Bird – C. Edward Davis
The Adventure of the Avaricious Bookkeeper – Joel and Carolyn Senter

## PART IV – 2016 Annual
Foreword – Steven Rothman
Foreword – Richard Doyle
Foreword – Roger Johnson
Foreword – Melissa Farnham
Foreword – Steve Emecz
Foreword – David Marcum
Toast to Mrs. Hudson (A Poem) – Arlene Mantin Levy

*(Continued on the next page . . . .)*

The Tale of the First Adventure – Derrick Belanger
The Adventure of the Turkish Cipher – Deanna Baran
The Adventure of the Missing Necklace – Daniel D. Victor
The Case of the Rondel Dagger – Mark Mower
The Adventure of the Double-Edged Hoard – Craig Janacek
The Adventure of the Impossible Murders – Jayantika Ganguly
The Watcher in the Woods – Denis O. Smith
The Wargrave Resurrection – Matthew Booth
Relating To One of My Old Cases – J.R. Campbell
The Adventure at the Beau Soleil – Bonnie MacBird
The Adventure of the Phantom Coachman – Arthur Hall
The Adventure of the Arsenic Dumplings – Bob Byrne
The Disappearing Anarchist Trick – Andrew Lane
The Adventure of the Grace Chalice – Roger Johnson
The Adventure of John Vincent Harden – Hugh Ashton
Murder at Tragere House – David Stuart Davies
The Adventure of *The Green Lady* – Vincent W. Wright
The Adventure of the Fellow Traveller – Daniel McGachey
The Adventure of the Highgate Financier – Nicholas Utechin
A Game of Illusion – Jeremy Holstein
The London Wheel – David Marcum
The Adventure of the Half-Melted Wolf – Marcia Wilson

## PART V – Christmas Adventures

Foreword – Jonathan Kellerman
Foreword – Roger Johnson
Foreword – David Marcum
The Ballad of the Carbuncle (A Poem) – Ashley D. Polasek
The Case of the Ruby Necklace – Bob Byrne
The Jet Brooch – Denis O. Smith
The Adventure of the Missing Irregular – Amy Thomas
The Adventure of the Knighted Watchmaker – Derrick Belanger
The Stolen Relic – David Marcum
A Christmas Goose – C.H. Dye
The Adventure of the Long-Lost Enemy – Marcia Wilson
The Queen's Writing Table – Julie McKuras
The Blue Carbuncle – Sir Arthur Conan Doyle (Dramatised by Bert Coules)
The Case of the Christmas Cracker – John Hall
The Man Who Believed in Nothing – Jim French
The Case of the Christmas Star – S.F. Bennett
The Christmas Card Mystery – Narrelle M. Harris
The Question of the Death Bed Conversion – William Patrick Maynard
The Adventure of the Christmas Surprise – Vincent W. Wright
A Bauble in Scandinavia – James Lovegrove
The Adventure of Marcus Davery – Arthur Hall
The Adventure of the Purple Poet – Nicholas Utechin

*(Continued on the next page . . . .)*

The Adventure of the Vanishing Man – Mike Chinn
The Adventure of the Empty Manger – Tracy J. Revels
A Perpetrator in a Pear Tree – Roger Riccard
The Case of the Christmas Trifle – Wendy C. Fries
The Adventure of the Christmas Stocking – Paul D. Gilbert
The Adventure of the Golden Hunter – Jan Edwards
The Curious Case of the Well-Connected Criminal – Molly Carr
The Case of the Reformed Sinner – S. Subramanian
The Adventure of the Improbable Intruder – Peter K. Andersson
The Adventure of the Handsome Ogre – Matthew J. Elliott
The Adventure of the Deceased Doctor – Hugh Ashton
The Mile End Mynah Bird – Mark Mower

## PART VI – 2017 Annual
Foreword – Colin Jeavons
Foreword – Nicholas Utechin
Foreword – Roger Johnson
Foreword – David Marcum
Sweet Violin (A Poem) – Bonnie MacBird
The Adventure of the Murdered Spinster – Bob Byrne
The Irregular – Julie McKuras
The Coffee Trader's Dilemma – Derrick Belanger
The Two Patricks – Robert Perret
The Adventure at St. Catherine's – Deanna Baran
The Adventure of a Thousand Stings – GC Rosenquist
The Adventure of the Returned Captain – Hugh Ashton
The Adventure of the Wonderful Toy – David Timson
The Adventure of the Cat's Claws – Shane Simmons
The Grave Message – Stephen Wade
The Radicant Munificent Society – Mark Mower
The Adventure of the Apologetic Assassin – David Friend
The Adventure of the Traveling Corpse – Nick Cardillo
The Adventure of the Apothecary's Prescription – Roger Riccard
The Case of the Bereaved Author – S. Subramanian
The Tetanus Epidemic – Carl L. Heifetz
The Bubble Reputation – Geri Schear
The Case of the Vanishing Venus – S.F. Bennett
The Adventure of the Vanishing Apprentice – Jennifer Copping
The Adventure of the Apothecary Shop – Jim French
The Case of the Plummeting Painter – Carla Coupe
The Case of the Temperamental Terrier – Narrelle M. Harris
The Adventure of the Frightened Architect – Arthur Hall
The Adventure of the Sunken Indiaman – Craig Janacek
The Exorcism of the Haunted Stick – Marcia Wilson
The Adventure of the Queen's Teardrop – Tracy Revels
The Curious Case of the Charwoman's Brooch – Molly Carr

*(Continued on the next page . . . .)*

The Unwelcome Client – Keith Hann
The Tempest of Lyme – David Ruffle
The Problem of the Holy Oil – David Marcum
A Scandal in Serbia – Thomas A. Turley
The Curious Case of Mr. Marconi – Jan Edwards
Mr. Holmes and Dr. Watson Learn to Fly – C. Edward Davis
*Die Weisse Frau* – Tim Symonds
A Case of Mistaken Identity – Daniel D. Victor

## PART VII – Eliminate the Impossible: 1880-1891

Foreword – Lee Child
Foreword – Rand B. Lee
Foreword – Michael Cox
Foreword – Roger Johnson
Foreword – Melissa Farnham
Foreword – David Marcum
No Ghosts Need Apply (A Poem) – Jacquelynn Morris
The Melancholy Methodist – Mark Mower
The Curious Case of the Sweated Horse – Jan Edwards
The Adventure of the Second William Wilson – Daniel D. Victor
The Adventure of the Marchindale Stiletto – James Lovegrove
The Case of the Cursed Clock – Gayle Lange Puhl
The Tranquility of the Morning – Mike Hogan
A Ghost from Christmas Past – Thomas A. Turley
The Blank Photograph – James Moffett
The Adventure of A Rat. – Adrian Middleton
The Adventure of Vanaprastha – Hugh Ashton
The Ghost of Lincoln – Geri Schear
The Manor House Ghost – S. Subramanian
The Case of the Unquiet Grave – John Hall
The Adventure of the Mortal Combat – Jayantika Ganguly
The Last Encore of Quentin Carol – S.F. Bennett
The Case of the Petty Curses – Steven Philip Jones
The Tuttman Gallery – Jim French
The Second Life of Jabez Salt – John Linwood Grant
The Mystery of the Scarab Earrings – Thomas Fortenberry
The Adventure of the Haunted Room – Mike Chinn
The Pharaoh's Curse – Robert V. Stapleton
The Vampire of the Lyceum – Charles Veley and Anna Elliott
The Adventure of the Mind's Eye – Shane Simmons

## PART VIII – Eliminate the Impossible: 1892-1905

Foreword – Lee Child
Foreword – Rand B. Lee
Foreword – Michael Cox
Foreword – Roger Johnson
Foreword – Melissa Farnham

*(Continued on the next page . . . .)*

Foreword – David Marcum
Sherlock Holmes in the Lavender field (A Poem) – Christopher James
The Adventure of the Lama's Dream – Deanna Baran
The Ghost of Dorset House – Tim Symonds
The Peculiar Persecution of John Vincent Harden – Sandor Jay Sonnen
The Case of the Biblical Colours – Ben Cardall
The Inexplicable Death of Matthew Arnatt – Andrew Lane
The Adventure of the Highgate Spectre – Michael Mallory
The Case of the Corpse Flower – Wendy C. Fries
The Problem of the Five Razors – Aaron Smith
The Adventure of the Moonlit Shadow – Arthur Hall
The Ghost of Otis Maunder – David Friend
The Adventure of the Pharaoh's Tablet – Robert Perret
The Haunting of Hamilton Gardens – Nick Cardillo
The Adventure of the Risen Corpse – Paul D. Gilbert
The Mysterious Mourner – Cindy Dye
The Adventure of the Hungry Ghost – Tracy Revels
In the Realm of the Wretched King – Derrick Belanger
The Case of the Little Washerwoman – William Meikle
The Catacomb Saint Affair – Marcia Wilson
The Curious Case of Charlotte Musgrave – Roger Riccard
The Adventure of the Awakened Spirit – Craig Janacek
The Adventure of the Theatre Ghost – Jeremy Branton Holstein
The Adventure of the Glassy Ghost – Will Murray
The Affair of the Grange Haunting – David Ruffle
The Adventure of the Pallid Mask – Daniel McGachey
The Two Different Women – David Marcum

## Part IX – 2018 Annual (1879-1895)

Foreword – Nicholas Meyer
Foreword – Roger Johnson
Foreword – Melissa Farnham
Foreword – Steve Emecz
Foreword – David Marcum
Violet Smith (A Poem) – Amy Thomas
The Adventure of the Temperance Society – Deanna Baran
The Adventure of the Fool and His Money – Roger Riccard
The Helverton Inheritance – David Marcum
The Adventure of the Faithful Servant – Tracy Revels
The Adventure of the Parisian Butcher – Nick Cardillo
The Missing Empress – Robert Stapleton
The Resplendent Plane Tree – Kevin P. Thornton
The Strange Adventure of the Doomed Sextette – Leslie Charteris and Denis Green
        *(Introduction by Ian Dickerson)*
The Adventure of the Old Boys' Club – Shane Simmons
The Case of the Golden Trail – James Moffett
The Detective Who Cried Wolf – C.H. Dye

*(Continued on the next page . . . .)*

The Lambeth Poisoner Case – Stephen Gaspar
The Confession of Anna Jarrow – S. F. Bennett
The Adventure of the Disappearing Dictionary – Sonia Fetherston
The Fairy Hills Horror – Geri Schear
A Loathsome and Remarkable Adventure – Marcia Wilson
The Adventure of the Multiple Moriartys – David Friend
The Influence Machine – Mark Mower

## Part X – 2018 Annual (1896-1916)
Foreword – Nicholas Meyer
Foreword – Roger Johnson
Foreword – Melissa Farnham
Foreword – Steve Emecz
Foreword – David Marcum
A Man of Twice Exceptions (A Poem) – Derrick Belanger
The Horned God – Kelvin Jones
The Coughing Man – Jim French
The Adventure of Canal Reach – Arthur Hall
A Simple Case of Abduction – Mike Hogan
A Case of Embezzlement – Steven Ehrman
The Adventure of the Vanishing Diplomat – Greg Hatcher
The Adventure of the Perfidious Partner – Jayantika Ganguly
A Brush With Death – Dick Gillman
A Revenge Served Cold – Maurice Barkley
The Case of the Anonymous Client – Paul A. Freeman
Capitol Murder – Daniel D. Victor
The Case of the Dead Detective – Martin Rosenstock
The Musician Who Spoke From the Grave – Peter Coe Verbica
The Adventure of the Future Funeral – Hugh Ashton
The Problem of the Bruised Tongues – Will Murray
The Mystery of the Change of Art – Robert Perret
The Parsimonious Peacekeeper – Thaddeus Tuffentsamer
The Case of the Dirty Hand – G.L. Schulze
The Mystery of the Missing Artefacts – Tim Symonds

## Part XI: Some Untold Cases (1880-1891)
Foreword – Lyndsay Faye
Foreword – Roger Johnson
Foreword – Melissa Grigsby
Foreword – Steve Emecz
Foreword – David Marcum
Unrecorded Holmes Cases (A Sonnet) – Arlene Mantin Levy and Mark Levy
The Most Repellant Man – Jayantika Ganguly
The Singular Adventure of the Extinguished Wicks – Will Murray
Mrs. Forrester's Complication – Roger Riccard
The Adventure of Vittoria, the Circus Belle – Tracy Revels

*(Continued on the next page . . . .)*

The Adventure of the Silver Skull – Hugh Ashton
The Pimlico Poisoner – Matthew Simmonds
The Grosvenor Square Furniture Van – David Ruffle
The Adventure of the Paradol Chamber – Paul W. Nash
The Bishopgate Jewel Case – Mike Hogan
The Singular Tragedy of the Atkinson Brothers of Trincomalee – Craig Stephen Copland
Colonel Warburton's Madness – Gayle Lange Puhl
The Adventure at Bellingbeck Park – Deanna Baran
The Giant Rat of Sumatra – Leslie Charteris and Denis Green
        *(Introduction by Ian Dickerson)*
The Vatican Cameos – Kevin P. Thornton
The Case of the Gila Monster – Stephen Herczeg
The Bogus Laundry Affair – Robert Perret
Inspector Lestrade and the Molesey Mystery – M.A. Wilson and Richard Dean Starr

## Part XII: Some Untold Cases (1894-1902)

Foreword – Lyndsay Faye
Foreword – Roger Johnson
Foreword – Melissa Grigsby
Foreword – Steve Emecz
Foreword – David Marcum
It's Always Time (*A Poem*) – "Anon."
The Shanghaied Surgeon – C.H. Dye
The Trusted Advisor – David Marcum
A Shame Harder Than Death – Thomas Fortenberry
The Adventure of the Smith-Mortimer Succession – Daniel D. Victor
A Repulsive Story and a Terrible Death – Nik Morton
The Adventure of the Dishonourable Discharge – Craig Janacek
The Adventure of the Admirable Patriot – S. Subramanian
The Abernetty Transactions – Jim French
Dr. Agar and the Dinosaur – Robert Stapleton
The Giant Rat of Sumatra – Nick Cardillo
The Adventure of the Black Plague – Paul D. Gilbert
Vigor, the Hammersmith Wonder – Mike Hogan
A Correspondence Concerning Mr. James Phillimore – Derrick Belanger
The Curious Case of the Two Coptic Patriarchs – John Linwood Grant
The Conk-Singleton Forgery Case – Mark Mower
Another Case of Identity – Jane Rubino
The Adventure of the Exalted Victim – Arthur Hall

## PART XIII: 2019 Annual (1881-1890)

Foreword – Will Thomas
Foreword – Roger Johnson
Foreword – Melissa Grigsby
Foreword – Steve Emecz
Foreword – David Marcum
Inscrutable (*A Poem*) – Jacquelynn Morris

*(Continued on the next page . . . .)*

The Folly of Age – Derrick Belanger
The Fashionably-Dressed Girl – Mark Mower
The Odour of Neroli – Brenda Seabrooke
The Coffee House Girl – David Marcum
The Mystery of the Green Room – Robert Stapleton
The Case of the Enthusiastic Amateur – S.F. Bennett
The Adventure of the Missing Cousin – Edwin A. Enstrom
The Roses of Highclough House – MJH Simmonds
The Shackled Man – Andrew Bryant
The Yellow Star of Cairo – Tim Gambrell
The Adventure of the Winterhall Monster – Tracy Revels
The Grosvenor Square Furniture Van – Hugh Ashton
The Voyage of *Albion's Thistle* – Sean M. Wright
Bootless in Chippenham – Marino C. Alvarez
The Clerkenwell Shadow – Paul Hiscock
The Adventure of the Worried Banker – Arthur Hall
The Recovery of the Ashes – Kevin P. Thornton
The Mystery of the Patient Fisherman – Jim French
Sherlock Holmes in Bedlam – David Friend
The Adventure of the Ambulatory Cadaver – Shane Simmons
The Dutch Impostors – Peter Coe Verbica
The Missing Adam Tiler – Mark Wardecker

## PART XIV: 2019 Annual (1891 -1897)

Foreword – Will Thomas
Foreword – Roger Johnson
Foreword – Melissa Grigsby
Foreword – Steve Emecz
Foreword – David Marcum
Skein of Tales (*A Poem*) – Jacquelynn Morris
The Adventure of the Royal Albert Hall – Charles Veley and Anna Elliott
The Tower of Fear – Mark Sohn
The Carroun Document – David Marcum
The Threadneedle Street Murder – S. Subramanian
The Collegiate Leprechaun – Roger Riccard
A Malversation of Mummies – Marcia Wilson
The Adventure of the Silent Witness – Tracy J. Revels
The Second Whitechapel Murderer – Arthur Hall
The Adventure of the Jeweled Falcon – GC Rosenquist
The Adventure of the Crossbow – Edwin A. Enstrom
The Adventure of the Delusional Wife – Jayantika Ganguly
Child's Play – C.H. Dye
The Lancelot Connection – Matthew Booth
The Adventure of the Modern Guy Fawkes – Stephen Herczeg
Mr. Clever, Baker Street – Geri Schear
The Adventure of the Scarlet Rosebud – Liz Hedgecock

*(Continued on the next page . . . .)*

The Poisoned Regiment – Carl Heifetz
The Case of the Persecuted Poacher – Gayle Lange Puhl
It's Time – Harry DeMaio
The Case of the Fourpenny Coffin – I.A. Watson
The Horror in King Street – Thomas A. Burns, Jr.

## PART XV: 2019 Annual (1898-1917)

Foreword – Will Thomas
Foreword – Roger Johnson
Foreword – Melissa Grigsby
Foreword – Steve Emecz
Foreword – David Marcum
Two Poems – Christopher James
The Whitechapel Butcher – Mark Mower
The Incomparable Miss Incognita – Thomas Fortenberry
The Adventure of the Twofold Purpose – Robert Perret
The Adventure of the Green Gifts – Tracy J. Revels
The Turk's Head – Robert Stapleton
A Ghost in the Mirror – Peter Coe Verbica
The Mysterious Mr. Rim – Maurice Barkley
The Adventure of the Fatal Jewel-Box – Edwin A. Enstrom
Mass Murder – William Todd
The Notable Musician – Roger Riccard
The Devil's Painting – Kelvin I. Jones
The Adventure of the Silent Sister – Arthur Hall
A Skeleton's Sorry Story – Jack Grochot
An Actor and a Rare One – David Marcum
The Silver Bullet – Dick Gillman
The Adventure at Throne of Gilt – Will Murray
"The Boy Who Would Be King – Dick Gillman
The Case of the Seventeenth Monk – Tim Symonds
Alas, Poor Will – Mike Hogan
The Case of the Haunted Chateau – Leslie Charteris and Denis Green
        *(Introduction by Ian Dickerson)*
The Adventure of the Weeping Stone – Nick Cardillo
The Adventure of the Three Telegrams – Darryl Webber

## Part XVI – Whatever Remains . . . Must Be the Truth (1881-1890)

Foreword – Kareem Abdul-Jabbar
Foreword – Roger Johnson
Foreword – Steve Emecz
Foreword – David Marcum
The Hound of the Baskervilles (Retold) (*A Poem*) – Josh Pachter
The Wylington Lake Monster – Derrick Belanger
The *Juju* Men of Richmond – Mark Sohn

*(Continued on the next page . . . .)*

The Adventure of the Headless Lady – Tracy J. Revels
*Angelus Domini Nuntiavit* – Kevin P. Thornton
The Blue Lady of Dunraven – Andrew Bryant
The Adventure of the Ghoulish Grenadier – Josh Anderson and David Friend
The Curse of Barcombe Keep – Brenda Seabrooke
The Affair of the Regressive Man – David Marcum
The Adventure of the Giant's Wife – I.A. Watson
The Adventure of Miss Anna Truegrace – Arthur Hall
The Haunting of Bottomly's Grandmother – Tim Gambrell
The Adventure of the Intrusive Spirit – Shane Simmons
The Paddington Poltergeist – Bob Bishop
The Spectral Pterosaur – Mark Mower
The Weird of Caxton – Kelvin Jones
The Adventure of the Obsessive Ghost – Jayantika Ganguly

## Part XVII – Whatever Remains . . . Must Be the Truth (1891-1898)

Foreword – Kareem Abdul-Jabbar
Foreword – Roger Johnson
Foreword – Steve Emecz
Foreword – David Marcum
The Violin Thief (*A Poem*) – Christopher James
The Spectre of Scarborough Castle – Charles Veley and Anna Elliott
The Case for Which the World is Not Yet Prepared – Steven Philip Jones
The Adventure of the Returning Spirit – Arthur Hall
The Adventure of the Bewitched Tenant – Michael Mallory
The Misadventures of the Bonnie Boy – Will Murray
The Adventure of the *Danse Macabre* – Paul D. Gilbert
The Strange Persecution of John Vincent Harden – S. Subramanian
The Dead Quiet Library – Roger Riccard
The Adventure of the Sugar Merchant – Stephen Herczeg
The Adventure of the Undertaker's Fetch – Tracy J. Revels
The Holloway Ghosts – Hugh Ashton
The Diogenes Club Poltergeist – Chris Chan
The Madness of Colonel Warburton – Bert Coules
The Return of the Noble Bachelor – Jane Rubino
The Reappearance of Mr. James Phillimore – David Marcum
The Miracle Worker – Geri Schear
The Hand of Mesmer – Dick Gillman

## Part XVIII – Whatever Remains . . . Must Be the Truth (1899-1925)

Foreword – Kareem Abdul-Jabbar
Foreword – Roger Johnson
Foreword – Steve Emecz
Foreword – David Marcum
The Adventure of the Lighthouse on the Moor (*A Poem*) – Christopher James
The Witch of Ellenby – Thomas A. Burns, Jr.

*(Continued on the next page . . . .)*

The Tollington Ghost – Roger Silverwood
You Only Live Thrice – Robert Stapleton
The Adventure of the Fair Lad – Craig Janacek
The Adventure of the Voodoo Curse – Gareth Tilley
The Cassandra of Providence Place – Paul Hiscock
The Adventure of the House Abandoned – Arthur Hall
The Winterbourne Phantom – M.J. Elliott
The Murderous Mercedes – Harry DeMaio
The Solitary Violinist – Tom Turley
The Cunning Man – Kelvin I. Jones
The Adventure of Khamaat's Curse – Tracy J. Revels
The Adventure of the Weeping Mary – Matthew White
The Unnerved Estate Agent – David Marcum
Death in The House of the Black Madonna – Nick Cardillo
The Case of the Ivy-Covered Tomb – S.F. Bennett

## Part XIX: 2020 Annual (1882-1890)

Foreword – John Lescroart
Foreword – Roger Johnson
Foreword – Lizzy Butler
Foreword – Steve Emecz
Foreword – David Marcum
Holmes's Prayer (*A Poem*) – Christopher James
A Case of Paternity – Matthew White
The Raspberry Tart – Roger Riccard
The Mystery of the Elusive Bard – Kevin P. Thornton
The Man in the Maroon Suit – Chris Chan
The Scholar of Silchester Court – Nick Cardillo
The Adventure of the Changed Man – MJH. Simmonds
The Adventure of the Tea-Stained Diamonds – Craig Stephen Copland
The Indigo Impossibility – Will Murray
The Case of the Emerald Knife-Throwers – Ian Ableson
A Game of Skittles – Thomas A. Turley
The Gordon Square Discovery – David Marcum
The Tattooed Rose – Dick Gillman
The Problem at Pentonville Prison – David Friend
The Nautch Night Case – Brenda Seabrooke
The Disappearing Prisoner – Arthur Hall
The Case of the Missing Pipe – James Moffett
The Whitehaven Ransom – Robert Stapleton
The Enlightenment of Newton – Dick Gillman
The Impaled Man – Andrew Bryant
The Mystery of the Elusive Li Shen – Will Murray
The Mahmudabad Result – Andrew Bryant

*(Continued on the next page . . . .)*

The Adventure of the Matched Set – Peter Coe Verbica
When the Prince First Dined at the Diogenes Club – Sean M. Wright
The Sweetenbury Safe Affair – Tim Gambrell

## Part XX: 2020 Annual (1891-1897)
Foreword – John Lescroart
Foreword – Roger Johnson
Foreword – Lizzy Butler
Foreword – Steve Emecz
Foreword – David Marcum
The Sibling (*A Poem*) – Jacquelynn Morris
Blood and Gunpowder – Thomas A. Burns, Jr.
The Atelier of Death – Harry DeMaio
The Adventure of the Beauty Trap – Tracy Revels
A Case of Unfinished Business – Steven Philip Jones
The Case of the S.S. Bokhara – Mark Mower
The Adventure of the American Opera Singer – Deanna Baran
The Keadby Cross – David Marcum
The Adventure at Dead Man's Hole – Stephen Herczeg
The Elusive Mr. Chester – Arthur Hall
The Adventure of Old Black Duffel – Will Murray
The Blood-Spattered Bridge – Gayle Lange Puhl
The Tomorrow Man – S.F. Bennett
The Sweet Science of Bruising – Kevin P. Thornton
The Mystery of Sherlock Holmes – Christopher Todd
The Elusive Mr. Phillimore – Matthew J. Elliott
The Murders in the Maharajah's Railway Carriage – Charles Veley and Anna Elliott
The Ransomed Miracle – I.A. Watson
The Adventure of the Unkind Turn – Robert Perret
The Perplexing X'ing – Sonia Fetherston
The Case of the Short-Sighted Clown – Susan Knight

## Part XXI: 2020 Annual (1898-1923)
Foreword – John Lescroart
Foreword – Roger Johnson
Foreword – Lizzy Butler
Foreword – Steve Emecz
Foreword – David Marcum
The Case of the Missing Rhyme (*A Poem*) – Joseph W. Svec III
The Problem of the St. Francis Parish Robbery – R.K. Radek
The Adventure of the Grand Vizier – Arthur Hall
The Mummy's Curse – DJ Tyrer
The Fractured Freemason of Fitzrovia – David L. Leal
The Bleeding Heart – Paula Hammond
The Secret Admirer – Jayantika Ganguly

*(Continued on the next page . . . .)*

The Deceased Priest – Peter Coe Verbica
The Case of the Rewrapped Presents – Bob Byrne
The Invisible Assassin – Geri Shear
The Adventure of the Chocolate Pot – Hugh Ashton
The Adventure of the Incessant Workers – Arthur Hall
When Best Served Cold – Stephen Mason
The Cat's Meat Lady of Cavendish Square – David Marcum
The Unveiled Lodger – Mark Mower
The League of Unhappy Orphans – Leslie Charteris and Denis Green
        *(Introduction by Ian Dickerson)*
The Adventure of the Three Fables – Jane Rubino
The Cobbler's Treasure – Dick Gillman
The Adventure of the Wells Beach Ruffians – Derrick Belanger
The Adventure of the Doctor's Hand – Michael Mallory
The Case of the Purloined Talisman – John Lawrence

## Part XXII: Some More Untold Cases (1877-1887)

Foreword – Otto Penzler
Foreword – Roger Johnson
Foreword – Steve Emecz
Foreword – Jacqueline Silver
Foreword – David Marcum
The Philosophy of Holmes (*A Poem*) – Christopher James
The Terror of the Tankerville – S.F. Bennett
The Singular Affair of the Aluminium Crutch – William Todd
The Trifling Matter of Mortimer Maberley – Geri Schear
Abracadaver – Susan Knight
The Secret in Lowndes Court – David Marcum
Vittoria, the Circus Bell – Bob Bishop
The Adventure of the Vanished Husband – Tracy J. Revels
Merridew of Abominable Memory – Chris Chan
The Substitute Thief – Richard Paolinelli
The Whole Story Concerning the Politician, the Lighthouse, and the Trained Cormorant –
        Derrick Belanger
A Child's Reward – Stephen Mason
The Case of the Elusive Umbrella – Leslie Charteris and Denis Green
        *(Introduction by Ian Dickerson)*
The Strange Death of an Art Dealer – Tim Symonds
Watch Him Fall – Liese Sherwood-Fabre
The Adventure of the Transatlantic Gila – Ian Ableson
Intruders at Baker Street – Chris Chan
The Paradol Chamber – Mark Mower
Wolf Island – Robert Stapleton
The Etherage Escapade – Roger Riccard

*(Continued on the next page . . . .)*

The Dundas Separation Case – Kevin P. Thornton
The Broken Glass – Denis O. Smith

## Part XXIII: Some More Untold Cases (1888-1894)
Foreword – Otto Penzler
Foreword – Roger Johnson
Foreword – Steve Emecz
Foreword – Jacqueline Silver
Foreword – David Marcum
The Housekeeper (*A Poem*) – John Linwood Grant
The Uncanny Adventure of the Hammersmith Wonder – Will Murray
Mrs. Forrester's Domestic Complication– Tim Gambrell
The Adventure of the Abducted Bard – I.A. Watson
The Adventure of the Loring Riddle – Craig Janacek
To the Manor Bound – Jane Rubino
The Crimes of John Clay – Paul Hiscock
The Adventure of the Nonpareil Club – Hugh Ashton
The Adventure of the Singular Worm – Mike Chinn
The Adventure of the Forgotten Brolly – Shane Simmons
The Adventure of the Tired Captain – Dacre Stoker and Leverett Butts
The Rhayader Legacy – David Marcum
The Adventure of the Tired Captain – Matthew J. Elliott
The Secret of Colonel Warburton's Insanity – Paul D. Gilbert
The Adventure of Merridew of Abominable Memory – Tracy J. Revels
The Affair of the Hellingstone Rubies – Margaret Walsh
The Adventure of the Drewhampton Poisoner – Arthur Hall
The Incident of the Dual Intrusions – Barry Clay
The Case of the Un-Paralleled Adventures – Steven Philip Jones
The Affair of the Friesland – Jan van Koningsveld
The Forgetful Detective – Marcia Wilson
The Smith-Mortimer Succession – Tim Gambrell
The Repulsive Matter of the Bloodless Banker – Will Murray

## Part XXIV: Some More Untold Cases (1895-1903)
Foreword – Otto Penzler
Foreword – Roger Johnson
Foreword – Steve Emecz
Foreword – Jacqueline Silver
Foreword – David Marcum
Sherlock Holmes and the Return of the Missing Rhyme (*A Poem*) – Joseph W. Svec III
The Comet Wine's Funeral – Marcia Wilson
The Case of the Accused Cook – Brenda Seabrooke
The Case of Vanderbilt and the Yeggman – Stephen Herczeg

*(Continued on the next page . . . .)*

The Tragedy of Woodman's Lee – Tracy J. Revels
The Murdered Millionaire – Kevin P. Thornton
Another Case of Identity – Thomas A. Burns, Jr.
The Case of Indelible Evidence – Dick Gillman
The Adventure of Parsley and Butter – Jayantika Ganguly
The Adventure of the Nile Traveler – John Davis
The Curious Case of the Crusader's Cross – DJ Tyrer
An Act of Faith – Harry DeMaio
The Adventure of the Conk-Singleton Forgery – Arthur Hall
A Simple Matter – Susan Knight
The Hammerford Will Business – David Marcum
The Adventure of Mr. Fairdale Hobbs – Arthur Hall
The Adventure of the Abergavenny Murder – Craig Stephen Copland
The Chinese Puzzle Box – Gayle Lange Puhl
The Adventure of the Refused Knighthood – Craig Stephen Copland
The Case of the Consulting Physician – John Lawrence
The Man from Deptford – John Linwood Grant
The Case of the Impossible Assassin – Paula Hammond

## Part XXV: 2021 Annual (1881-1888)

Foreword – Peter Lovesey
Foreword – Roger Johnson
Foreword – Steve Emecz
Foreword – Jacqueline Silver
Foreword – David Marcum
Baskerville Hall (*A Poem*) – Kelvin I. Jones
The Persian Slipper – Brenda Seabrooke
The Adventure of the Doll Maker's Daughter – Matthew White
The Flinders Case – Kevin McCann
The Sunderland Tragedies – David Marcum
The Tin Soldiers – Paul Hiscock
The Shattered Man – MJH Simmonds
The Hungarian Doctor – Denis O. Smith
The Black Hole of Berlin – Robert Stapleton
The Thirteenth Step – Keith Hann
The Missing Murderer – Marcia Wilson
Dial Square – Martin Daley
The Adventure of the Deadly Tradition – Matthew J. Elliott
The Adventure of the Fabricated Vision – Craig Janacek
The Adventure of the Murdered Maharajah – Hugh Ashton
The God of War – Hal Glatzer
The Atkinson Brothers of Trincomalee – Stephen Gaspar

*(Continued on the next page . . . .)*

The Switched String – Chris Chan
The Case of the Secret Samaritan – Jane Rubino
The Bishopsgate Jewel Case – Stephen Gaspar

## Part XXVI: 2021 Annual (1889-1897)

Foreword – Peter Lovesey
Foreword – Roger Johnson
Foreword – Steve Emecz
Foreword – Jacqueline Silver
Foreword – David Marcum
221b Baker Street (*A Poem*) – Kevin Patrick McCann
The Burglary Season – Marcia Wilson
The Lamplighter at Rosebery Avenue – James Moffett
The Disfigured Hand – Peter Coe Verbica
The Adventure of the Bloody Duck – Margaret Walsh
The Tragedy at Longpool – James Gelter
The Case of the Viscount's Daughter – Naching T. Kassa
The Key in the Snuffbox – DJ Tyrer
The Race for the Gleghorn Estate – Ian Ableson
The Isa Bird Befuddlement – Kevin P. Thornton
The Cliddesden Questions – David Marcum
Death in Verbier – Adrian Middleton
The King's Cross Road Somnambulist – Dick Gillman
The Magic Bullet – Peter Coe Verbica
The Petulant Patient – Geri Schear
The Mystery of the Groaning Stone – Mark Mower
The Strange Case of the Pale Boy – Susan Knight
The Adventure of the Zande Dagger – Frank Schildiner
The Adventure of the Vengeful Daughter – Arthur Hall
Do the Needful – Harry DeMaio
The Count, the Banker, the Thief, and the Seven Half-sovereigns – Mike Hogan
The Adventure of the Unsprung Mousetrap – Anthony Gurney
The Confectioner's Captives – I.A. Watson

## Part XXVII: 2021 Annual (1898-1928)

Foreword – Peter Lovesey
Foreword – Roger Johnson
Foreword – Steve Emecz
Foreword – Jacqueline Silver
Foreword – David Marcum
Sherlock Holmes Returns: The Missing Rhyme (*A Poem*) – Joseph W. Svec, III
The Adventure of the Hero's Heir – Tracy J. Revels
The Curious Case of the Soldier's Letter – John Davis
The Case of the Norwegian Daredevil – John Lawrence
The Case of the Borneo Tribesman – Stephen Herczeg
The Adventure of the White Roses – Tracy J. Revels

*(Continued on the next page . . . .)*

Mrs. Crichton's Ledger – Tim Gambrell
The Adventure of the Not-Very-Merry Widows – Craig Stephen Copland
The Son of God – Jeremy Branton Holstein
The Adventure of the Disgraced Captain – Thomas A. Turley
The Woman Who Returned From the Dead – Arthur Hall
The Farraway Street Lodger – David Marcum
The Mystery of Foxglove Lodge – S.C. Toft
The Strange Adventure of Murder by Remote Control – Leslie Charteris and Denis Green
        *(Introduction by Ian Dickerson)*
The Case of The Blue Parrot – Roger Riccard
The Adventure of the Expelled Master – Will Murray
The Case of the Suicidal Suffragist – John Lawrence
The Welbeck Abbey Shooting Party – Thomas A. Turley
Case No. 358 – Marcia Wilson

## Part XXVIII: More Christmas Adventures (1869-1888)

Foreword – Nancy Holder
Foreword – Roger Johnson
Foreword – Steve Emecz
Foreword – Emma West
Foreword – David Marcum
A Sherlockian Christmas (A Poem) – Joseph W. Svec III
No Malice Intended – Deanna Baran
The Yuletide Heist – Mark Mower
A Yuletide Tragedy – Thomas A. Turley
The Adventure of the Christmas Lesson – Will Murray
The Christmas Card Case – Brenda Seabrooke
The Chatterton-Smythe Affair – Tim Gambrell
Christmas at the Red Lion – Thomas A. Burns, Jr.
A Study in Murder – Amy Thomas
The Christmas Ghost of Crailloch Taigh – David Marcum
The Six-Fingered Scoundrel – Jeffrey A. Lockwood
The Case of the Duplicitous Suitor – John Lawrence
The Sebastopol Clasp – Martin Daley
The Silent Brotherhood – Dick Gillman
The Case of the Christmas Pudding – Liz Hedgecock
The St. Stephen's Day Mystery – Paul Hiscock
A Fine Kettle of Fish – Mike Hogan
The Case of the Left Foot – Stephen Herczeg
The Case of the Golden Grail – Roger Riccard

*(Continued on the next page . . . .)*

## Part XXIX: More Christmas Adventures (1889-1896)

Foreword – Nancy Holder
Foreword – Roger Johnson
Foreword – Steve Emecz
Foreword – Emma West
Foreword – David Marcum
Baskerville Hall in Winter (A Poem) – Christopher James
The Sword in the Spruce – Ian Ableson
The Adventure of the Serpentine Body – Wayne Anderson
The Adventure of the Fugitive Irregular – Gordon Linzner
The Father Christmas Brigade – David Marcum
The Incident of the Stolen Christmas Present – Barry Clay
The Man of Miracles – Derrick Belanger
Absent Friends – Wayne Anderson
The Incident in Regent Street – Harry DeMaio
The Baffling Adventure of the Baby Jesus – Craig Stephen Copland
The Adventure of the Second Sister – Matthew White
The Twelve Days – I.A. Watson
The Dilemma of Mr. Henry Baker – Paul D. Gilbert
The Adventure of the Injured Man – Arthur Hall
The Krampus Who Came to Call – Marcia Wilson
The Adventure of the Christmas Wish – Margaret Walsh
The Adventure of the Viking Ghost – Frank Schildiner
The Adventure of the Secret Manuscript – Dan Rowley
The Adventure of the Christmas Suitors – Tracy J. Revels

## Part XXX: More Christmas Adventures (1897-1928)

Foreword – Nancy Holder
Foreword – Roger Johnson
Foreword – Steve Emecz
Foreword – Emma West
Foreword – David Marcum
Baker Street in Snow (1890) (A Poem) – Christopher James
The Purloined Present – DJ Tyrer
The Case of the Cursory Curse – Andrew Bryant
The St. Giles Child Murders – Tim Gambrell
A Featureless Crime – Geri Schear
The Case of the Earnest Young Man – Paula Hammond
The Adventure of the Dextrous Doctor – Jayantika Ganguly
The Mystery of Maple Tree Lodge – Susan Knight
The Adventure of the Maligned Mineralogist – Arthur Hall
Christmas Magic – Kevin Thornton
The Adventure of the Christmas Threat – Arthur Hall
The Adventure of the Stolen Christmas Gift – Michael Mallory
The Colourful Skein of Life – Julie McKuras

*(Continued on the next page . . . .)*

The Adventure of the Chained Phantom – J.S. Rowlinson
Santa's Little Elves – Kevin Thornton
The Case of the Holly-Sprig Pudding – Naching T. Kassa
The Canterbury Manifesto – David Marcum
The Case of the Disappearing Beaune – J. Lawrence Matthews
A Price Above Rubies – Jane Rubino
The Intrigue of the Red Christmas – Shane Simmons
The Bitter Gravestones – Chris Chan
The Midnight Mass Murder – Paul Hiscock

## Part XXXI: 2022 Annual (1875-1887)
Foreword – Jeffrey Hatcher
Foreword – Roger Johnson
Foreword – Steve Emecz
Foreword – Emma West
Foreword – David Marcum
The Nemesis of Sherlock Holmes (A Poem) – Kelvin I. Jones
The Unsettling Incident of the History Professor's Wife – Sean M. Wright
The Princess Alice Tragedy – John Lawrence
The Adventure of the Amorous Balloonist – I.A. Watson
The Pilkington Case – Kevin Patrick McCann
The Adventure of the Disappointed Lover – Arthur Hall
The Case of the Impressionist Painting – Tim Symonds
The Adventure of the Old Explorer – Tracy J. Revels
Dr. Watson's Dilemma – Susan Knight
The Colonial Exhibition – Hal Glatzer
The Adventure of the Drunken Teetotaler – Thomas A. Burns, Jr.
The Curse of Hollyhock House – Geri Schear
The Sethian Messiah – David Marcum
Dead Man's Hand – Robert Stapleton
The Case of the Wary Maid – Gordon Linzner
The Adventure of the Alexandrian Scroll – David MacGregor
The Case of the Woman at Margate – Terry Golledge
A Question of Innocence – DJ Tyrer
The Grosvenor Square Furniture Van – Terry Golledge
The Adventure of the Veiled Man – Tracy J. Revels
The Disappearance of Dr. Markey – Stephen Herczeg
The Case of the Irish Demonstration – Dan Rowley

## Part XXXII: 2022 Annual (1888-1895)
Foreword – Jeffrey Hatcher
Foreword – Roger Johnson
Foreword – Steve Emecz

*(Continued on the next page . . . .)*

Foreword – Emma West
Foreword – David Marcum
The Hound (A Poem) – Kevin Patrick McCann
The Adventure of the Merryman and His Maid – Hal Glatzer
The Four Door-Handles – Arianna Fox
The Merton Friends – Terry Golledge
The Distasteful Affair of the Minatory Messages – David Marcum
The Adventure of the Tired Captain – Craig Janacek
The Grey Man – James Gelter
The Hyde Park Mystery – Mike Hogan
The Adventure of the Troubled Wife – Arthur Hall
The Horror of Forrest Farm – Tracy J. Revels
The Addleton Tragedy – Terry Golledge
The Adventure of the Doss House Ramble – Will Murray
The Black Beast of the Hurlers Stones – Roger Riccard
The Torso at Highgate Cemetery – Tim Symonds
The Disappearance of the Highgate Flowers – Tracy J. Revels
The Adventure of the New York Professor – Wayne Anderson
The Adventure of the Remarkable Worm – Alan Dimes
The Stone of Ill Omen – Mike Chinn
The Commotion at the Diogenes Club – Paul Hiscock
The Case of the Reappearing Wineskin – Ian Ableson

**Part XXXIII: 2022 Annual (1896-1919)**
Foreword – Jeffrey Hatcher
Foreword – Roger Johnson
Foreword – Steve Emecz
Foreword – Emma West
Foreword – David Marcum
Of Law and Justice (A Poem) – Alisha Shea
The Crown of Light – Terry Golledge
The Case of the Unknown Skull – Naching T. Kassa
The Strange Case of the Man from Edinburgh – Susan Knight
The Adventure of the Silk Scarf – Terry Golledge
Barstobrick House – Martin Daley
The Case of the Abstemious Burglar – Dan Rowley
The Blackfenn Marsh Monster – Marcia Wilson
The Disappearance of Little Charlie – Tracy J. Revels
The Adventure of the Impudent Impostor – Josh Cerefice
The Fatal Adventure of the French Onion Soup – Craig Stephen Copland
The Adventure of the Subversive Student – Jeffrey A Lockwood
The Adventure of the Spinster's Courtship – Tracy J. Revels
The Politician, the Lighthouse, and the Trained Cormorant – Mark Wardecker
The Gillette Play's the Thing! – David Marcum
The Derisible Dirigible Mystery – Kevin P. Thornton

*(Continued on the next page . . . .)*

The Ambassador's Skating Competition – Tim Symonds
What Came Before – Thomas A. Turley
The Adventure of the Art Exhibit – Dan Rowley
The Adventure of Peter the Painter – David MacGregor
The Valley of Tears – Andrew Bryant
The Adventure of the Tinker's Arms – Arthur Hall
The Adventure of the Murdered Medium – Hugh Ashton

## Part XXXIV: "However Improbable . . . ." (1878-1888)

Foreword – Nicholas Rowe
Foreword – Roger Johnson
Foreword Steve Emecz
Foreword – Emma West
Foreword – David Marcum
However Improbable (A Poem) – Joseph W. Svec III
The Monster's Mop and Pail – Marcia Wilson
The Wordless Widow – Gordon Linzner
The Mystery of the Spectral Shelter – Will Murray
The Adventure of the Dead Heir – Dan Rowley
The Body in Question – Tim Newton Anderson
The Adventure of the False Confessions – Arthur Hall
His Own Hangman – Thomas A. Burns, Jr.
The Mediobogdum Sword – David Marcum
The Adventure of The Sisters McClelland – James Gelter
The Mystery of the Vengeful Bride – DJ Tyrer
A Fatal Illusion – Paul Hiscock
The Adventure of the Newmarket Killings – Leslie Charteris and Denis Green
        *(Introduction by Ian Dickerson)*
The Possession of Miranda Beasmore – Stephen Herczeg
The Adventure of the Haunted Portrait – Tracy J. Revels
The Crisis of Count de Vermilion – Roger Riccard
The Adventure of Three-Card Monte – Anisha Jagdeep
The Adventure of the Armchair Detective – John McNabb

## Part XXXV: "However Improbable . . . ." (1889-1896)

Foreword – Nicholas Rowe
Foreword – Roger Johnson
Foreword Steve Emecz
Foreword – Emma West
Foreword – David Marcum
The Widow of Neptune (A Poem) – Christopher James
The Devil of Dickon's Dike Farm – Margaret Walsh
The Christmas *Doppelgänger* – M.J. Elliott
The Terror of Asgard Tower – Paul D. Gilbert
The Well-Lit Séance – David Marcum
The Adventure of the Deadly Illness – Dan Rowley and Don Baxter

*(Continued on the next page . . . .)*

Doctor Watson's Baffled Colleague – Sean M. Wright and DeForeest B. Wright, III
The Case of the Deity's Disappearance – Jane Rubino
The Tragedy of Mr. Ernest Bidmead – Arthur Hall
The Adventure of the Buried Bride – Tracy J. Revels
The Adventure of James Edward Phillimore – Alan Dimes
Soldier of Fortune – Geri Schear
The Mystery of the Murderous Ghost – Susan Knight
Mycroft's Ghost – The Davies Brothers
The Terror of Trowbridge Wood – Josh Cerefice
The Fantastical Vision of Randolph Sitwell – Mark Mower
The Adventure of the Paternal Ghost – Arthur Hall
Pit of Death – Robert Stapleton
The Jade Swan – Charles Veley and Anna Elliott
The Devil Went Down to Surrey – Naching T. Kassa
The Dowager Lady Isobel Frobisher – Martin Daley
The Confounding Confessional Confrontation – Kevin P. Thornton
The Adventure of the Long-Distance Bullet – I.A. Watson

## Part XXXVI: "However Improbable . . . ." (1897-1919)

Foreword – Nicholas Rowe
Foreword – Roger Johnson
Foreword Steve Emecz
Foreword – Emma West
Foreword – David Marcum
The Mythological Holmes (A Poem) – Alisha Shea
The Adventure of the Murderous Ghost – Tracy J. Revels
The High Table Hallucination – David L. Leal
The Checkmate Murder – Josh Cerefice
When Spaghetti was Served at the Diogenes Club – John Farrell
Holmes Run – Amanda J.A. Knight
The Adventure of the Murderous Gentleman – Arthur Hall
The Puzzle Master – William Todd
The Curse of Kisin – Liese Sherwood-Fabre
The Case of the Blood-Stained Leek – Margaret Walsh
The Bookseller's Donkey – Hal Glatzer
The Adventure of the Black Perambulator – Tracy J. Revels
The Adventure of the Surrey Inn – Leslie Charteris and Denis Green
        (Introduction by Ian Dickerson)        )
The Adventure of the Traveller in Time – Arthur Hall
The Adventure of the Restless Dead – Craig Janacek
The *Vodou* Drum – David Marcum
The Burglary at Undershaw – Tim Symonds

*(Continued on the next page . . . .)*

The Case of the Missing Minute – Dan Rowley
The Peacock Arrow – Chris Chan
The Spy on the Western Front – Tim Symonds

**Part XXXVII: 2023 Annual (1875-1889)**
Foreword – Michael Sims
Foreword – Roger Johnson
Foreword Steve Emecz
Foreword – Emma West
Foreword – David Marcum
The Adventure of the Improbable American – Will Murray
The Return of Springheeled Jack – Brenda Seagrove
The Incident of the Pointless Abduction – Arthur Hall
The Adventure of the Absent Crossing Sweeper – Steven Philip Jones
The Adventure of the Disappearing – Dan Rowley and Don Baxter
The Abridge Disappearance – David Marcum
The Adventure of the Green Horse – Hugh Ashton
The Adventure of Woodgate Manor – Sonya Kudei
The Incident of the Mangled Rose Buses – Barry Clay
The Sandwich Murder – DJ Tyrer
The Adventure of the Wandering Stones – Mark Wardecker
The Charity Collection – Paul Hiscock
The Catastrophic Cyclist – Tom Turley
The Adventure of the Sketched Bride – James Gelter
The Adventure of the Downing Street Demise – Brett Fawcett
The Continental Conspiracy – Martin Daley
The Belmore Street Museum Affair – Bob Byrne
The Adventure of the Furniture Collector – Tracy J. Revels
The Serpent's Tooth – Matthew White

**Part XXXVIII: 2023 Annual (1889-1896)**
Foreword – Michael Sims
Foreword – Roger Johnson
Foreword Steve Emecz
Foreword – Emma West
Foreword – David Marcum
The Muddled Monologue – Ian Ableson
Bad Timing – Gordon Linzner
The Adventure of the Living Terror – Craig Janacek
The Adventure of the Predatory Philanthropist – I.A. Watson
The Affair of the Addleton Giant – Margaret Walsh
The Adventure of the Faithful Wolfhound – Tracy J. Revels
The Texas Legation Business – David Marcum
Death at Simpsons – David MacGregor
The Adventure of the Reluctant Executioner – Arthur Hall

*(Continued on the next page . . . .)*

The Norwegian Shipping Agent – Sonya Kudei
Lucky Star – Jen Matteis
A Matter of Convenience – Geri Schear
The Spectral Centurion – Charles Veley and Anna Elliott
The Hyde Park Blackmailer – Peter Coe Verbica
The Adventure of the Counterfeit Uncle – Michael Mallory
The Adventure of the Seven Sins – Tracy J. Revels
The Adventure of the Fourth Key – Carlos Orsi
The Adventure of the Deathstalker – Susan Knight
The Keeper of the Eddystone Light – Tim Newton Anderson

## Part XXXIX: 2023 Annual (1897-1923)

Foreword – Michael Sims
Foreword – Roger Johnson
Foreword Steve Emecz
Foreword – Emma West
Foreword – David Marcum
The Case of the Curative Cruise – Dan Rowley and Don Baxter
The Totten Wood Mystery – William Todd
The Case of the Hesitant Client – Naching T. Kassa
A Study in Eldritch – Naching T. Kassa
The Stanhope Orphan – Ember Pepper
The Adventure of the Rainsford Inheritance – Alan Dimes
The Adventure of the Terrified Urchin – Arthur Hall
The King of Spades – Peter Coe Verbica
A Touch of the Dramatic – Jane Rubino
Two Goodly Gentlemen – Paula Hammond
The Adventure of the Folded Overcoat – Tracy J. Revels
The Third Baroness – Kevin Thornton
The Adventure of the Elusive Assassin – Arthur Hall
The Adventure of the Lost Alliance – Tom Turley
The Adventure of the Substitute Murder – Arthur Hall
The Case of the Lighthouse, the Trained Cormorant, and the Frightened Politician –
        Leslie Charteris and Denis Green *(Introduction by Ian Dickerson)*
The Curious Circumstances of the Imitation Ripper – David Marcum
The Adventure of the Petulant Queen – Shane Simmons
The Sketchy Blackmailer – Roger Riccard
The Green Honey – Chris Chan
The Case of the Disfigured Lieutenant – John Lawrence

## Part XL: Further Untold Cases (1879-1886)

Foreword – Tom Mead
Foreword – Roger Johnson
Foreword Steve Emecz
Foreword – Emma West
Foreword – David Marcum

*(Continued on the next page . . . .)*

The Case of the Cases of Vamberry Burgundy – Roger Riccard
The Adventure of the Aluminium Crutch – Tracy J. Revels
The Most Winning Woman – Liese Sherwood-Fabre
Mrs. Farintosh's Opal Tiara – Brenda Seabrooke
A Case of Duplicity – Gordon Linzner
The Adventure of the Fraudulent Benefactor – Mike Adamson
The Adventure of the Dead Rats – Hugh Ashton
The Laodicean Letters – David Marcum
A Case of Exceptional Brilliants – Jane Rubino
The True Account of the Dorrington Ruby Affair – Brett Fawcett
The Adventure of the Old Russian Woman – Susan Knight
The Adventure of the Silver Snail – Alan Dimes
The Adventure of the Invisible Weapon – Arthur Hall
The Backwater Affair – Paula Hammond
The Adventure of the Opening Eyes – Tracy J. Revels
The Man in the Rain with a Dog – Brenda Seabrooke
The Problem of the Grosvenor Square Moving Van – Tim Newton Anderson
The Dark Tavern – Robert Stapleton

## Part XLI: Further Untold Cases (1877-1892)
Foreword – Tom Mead
Foreword – Roger Johnson
Foreword Steve Emecz
Foreword – Emma West
Foreword – David Marcum
The Case of the Trepoff Murder – Stephen Herczeg
The Strange Case of the Disappearing Factor – Margaret Walsh
The Mystery of the Three Mendicants – Paul D. Gilbert
The Difficult Ordeal of the Paradol Chamber – Will Murray
The Amateur Mendicant Society – David MacGregor
The Amnesiac's Peril – Barry Clay
The Mystery of the Unstolen Document – Mike Chinn
The Adventure of the Infernal Philanthropist – Tim Newton Anderson
The Adventure of the Murdered Mistress – Ember Pepper
The Rouen Scandal – Martin Daley
The Adventure of the Cheerful Prisoner – Arthur Hall
The Adventure of the Tired Captain – Naching T. Kassa
A Dreadful Record of Sin – David Marcum
Mathews of Charing Cross – Ember Pepper
The Grey Lama – Adrian Middleton

## Part XLII: Further Untold Cases (1894-1922)
Foreword – Tom Mead
Foreword – Roger Johnson
Foreword Steve Emecz
Foreword – Emma West

*(Continued on the next page . . . .)*

Foreword – David Marcum
The Addleton Tragedy – Arthur Hall
The Book of Lucifer – Alan Dimes
The Adventure of the Curious Mother – Tracy J. Revels
The Mulberry Frock Coat Mystery – DJ Tyrer
The Tracking and Arrest of a Cold-Blooded Scoundrel – David Marcum
A Sudden Death at the Savoy – Dan Rowley
The Adventure of the Cardinal's Notebook – Deanna Baran
Death in the Workhouse – Thomas A. Burns, Jr
The Crimson Trail – Brenda Seabrooke
The Three Archers – Alan Dimes
The Three Maids – I.A. Watson
The Adventure of the African Prospector – Arthur Hall
The Unlikely Assassin – Tim Newton Anderson
The Two-Line Note – Chris Chan
The Stolen Brougham – Dan Rowley
The Theft at the Wallace Collection – Barry Clay
The St. Pancras Puzzle – Susan Knight
The Impossible Adventure of the Vanishing Murderer – Barry Clay
Mr. Phillimore's Umbrella – Paul Hiscock
Trouble at Emberly – Kevin P. Thornton

## Part XLIII: 2024 Annual (1874-1888)

Foreword – Daniel Stashower
Foreword – Roger Johnson
Foreword – Emma West
Foreword – Steve Emecz
Foreword – David Marcum
"Dr. Roylott, I Presume?" (A Poem) – by Kelvin I. Jones
Devil's Milk – Marcia Wilson
The Mystery of the Extraneous Cadaver – Mike Adamson
The Adventure of the Doubtful Conviction – Arthur Hall
The Case at the Turkish Bath – Brenda Seabrooke
The Silent Prisoner – Ember Pepper
The Predilections of a Pious Poisoner – Mike Adamson
The Devil's Snare – Paula Hammond
Umbrella Trouble – Robert Stapleton
The Adventure of the Siren's Tower – Tracy J. Revels
Lightning Strikes Once – Kevin P. Thornton
The Missing Calabash – P.C. Shumway
The Burning Heart – MJH Simmonds
The Curious Case of the Transmuting Tome – Daniel Lenois
The Adventure of the Restless Knight – Will Murray
The Six-Thirteen from Fairfield Junction – Denis O. Smith
The Most Terrible Murderer – Alan Dimes

*(Continued on the next page . . . .)*

Boxing Day, Brother Mine – Gretchen Altabef
The Case of Colonel Warburton's Madness – Jane Rubino
The Exploited Assassins – David Marcum
The Case of the Missing Docker – Jonathan Schneer

## Part XLIV: 2024 Annual (1889-1897)
Foreword – Daniel Stashower
Foreword – Roger Johnson
Foreword – Emma West
Foreword – Steve Emecz
Foreword – David Marcum
"Moriarty" (A Poem) – Kevin Patrick McCann
The Disputed Debutante – I.A. Watson
The Deaths on the Edge of Standish Woods – Stephen Herczeg
The Disappeared Doctor – Paula Hammond
The Adventure of Heirloom Necklace – Tracy J. Revels
The Case of the Ignoble Cuckold – Tom Turley
The Midsummer Murders – Paul A. Freeman
The Adventure of the Absentee Officer – Daniel Lenois
A Bucket's Worth of Help – David Marcum
Magic Squares – Marcia Wilson
The Adventure of the Moving Pictures – Shane Simmons
Death of a Mudlark – David MacGregor
The Adventure of the Serpent's Head – Arthur Hall
The Adventure of the Aged Actor – Tracy J. Revels
The Stratford Street Lodgers – Naching T. Kassa
The Other Woman – Susan Knight
The Adventure of the Surrey Revenant – Alan Dimes
A Generous Helping of Deceit – DJ Tyrer
Hollingbourne Grange – Mike Chinn
The Professor's Assistant – Chris Chan
The Mysterious Death of the Russian Anarchist – Jonathan Schneer
A Matter of ABC – Susan Knight
The Taverne Emerald – Alan Dimes

## Part XLV: 2024 Annual (1898-1917)
Foreword – Daniel Stashower
Foreword – Roger Johnson
Foreword – Emma West
Foreword – Steve Emecz
Foreword – David Marcum
"Heaven's Guise" (A Poem) – Alisha Shea
The Adventure of the Awakened Mummy – Tracy J. Revels
The Adventure of the Unknown Traitor – Arthur Hall
The Yorkshire Chieftain – Robert Stapleton

*(Continued on the next page . . . .)*

The Little White Lie – Jeffrey A. Lockwood
The Riddle of Parsons Lodge – Mark Mower
The Arthritic Beneficiary – Dan Rowley and Don Baxter
The Bell-Ringer's Requiem – Daniel Lenois
The Gemini Pearl Necklace – Roger Riccard
The Conk-Singleton Forgery – Alan Dimes
The Case of the Misbegotten Missives – Daniel D. Victor
The Missing Mathematical Timber – Ian Ableson
The Adventure of the Elfrincham Maze – Alan Dimes
The Bewildering Bicycle Business – Craig Stephen Copland
Death at the Diogenes Club – Tim Newton Anderson
Gruner's Diary – David Marcum
The Tsushima Legacy – Mike Adamson
The Problem of the Locked Room – Daniel D. Victor
The Beast of Birling Gap – Paul Hiscock
The Worker – Marcia Wilson
The Lambeth Twin – Martin Daley
"Now Comes the Mystery – Brett Fawcett

## Part XLVI: Occupants of the Canonical Realm (1861-1889)

Foreword – Dan Andriacco
Foreword – Roger Johnson
Foreword – Emma West
Foreword – Steve Emecz
Foreword – David Marcum
"Sherlock Holmes" (A Poem) – Joseph W. Svec III
The Adventure of the Two Brothers – Tracy J. Revels
The First Problem – Elbert Henry Smith
The X-Marked Boxes – David Marcum
The Neopolitan Conspiracy – Roger Riccard
The Boarding House Adventure – Brenda Seabrooke
The Wolf of Kensington – Mike Adamson
In the Flesh – Elbert Henry Smith
The Question of the Rival Criminalist – Will Murray
The Adventure of the Deadly Bird – Tracy J. Revels
The Adventure of the Scottish Coffins – David MacGregor
The Return of the Rival Criminalist – Will Murray
Lady Dragonfly – Robert V. Stapleton
The Adventure of the Willing Suspect – Gordon Linzner
The Notting Hill Murderer – Michael Mallory
The Last False Step – Tom Turley
Sophy Kratides in Peril – P.C. Shumway
The Romance of Reginald Musgrave – Jane Rubino
Such Profitable Treason – Mike Adamson
The Dockers' Tanner – Mike Adamson

*(Continued on the next page . . . .)*

## Part XLVII: Occupants of the Canonical Realm (1890-1898)

Foreword – Dan Andriacco
Foreword – Roger Johnson
Foreword – Emma West
Foreword – Steve Emecz
Foreword – David Marcum
"Mission (Some Sort of Sonnet)" (A Poem) – "Anon."
The Neckinger Mills Mystery – DJ Tyrer
The Debt to Jabez Wilson – David Marcum
Behind the Wells of Light – Marcia Wilson
The Voice in the Night – Arthur Hall
A Penny for the Guy – Brenda Seabrooke
Death of a Sails Man – Roger Riccard
Dinner at St. Lukes – Alan Dimes
An UnChristian Act – Paula Hammond
The Adventure of the Illustrious Author – Tracy J. Revels
The Georgian Dragon – Tim Newton Anderson
The Adventure of the Stradivarius – Steven Connelly
The Widow's Pique – Victoria Weisfeld
The Case of the Many Marshal Mendlers – Ian Albeson
The Lilac Flame – Marcia Wilson
The Adventure of the Unfortunate Cardinal – Alan Dimes
The Weird Adventure of the Particular Phantom – Will Murray
The Violated Grave – Paula Hammond
The Mystery of the Major's Music Box – Margaret Walsh
The Adventure of the Unexpected Corpse – Tracy J. Revels
The Case of the Benevolent Professor – Naching T. Kassa
Inspector Gregson at Bay – Susan Knight
The Case of the Spitalfields Man – Stephen Herczeg
The Unpaid Bills – Chris Chan

## Part XLVIII: Occupants of the Canonical Realm (1899-1924)

Foreword – Dan Andriacco
Foreword – Roger Johnson
Foreword – Emma West
Foreword – Steve Emecz
Foreword – David Marcum
"Last Words for Watson" (A Poem) – Christopher James
The Adventure of the Bishop's Gambit – Jeremy Branton Holstein
The Arc of Redemption – Gustavo Bondoni
The Case of the Circumspect Client – Dan Rowley and Don Baxter
The Adventure of the New Da Vinci – Arthur Hall
The Return of Agatha Davis – Ember Pepper
The Adventure of the Stolen Savant – Tracy J. Revels

*(Continued on the next page . . . .)*

The Adventure of the Deadly Threat – Arthur Hall
The Due Debentures – I.A. Watson
The Adventure of the Tall, Slim, Dark Woman – Craig Stephen Copland
The Perfect Spy – Martin Daley
The Swapped Names of the Saviour – David Marcum
The Ghost of Mycroft Holmes – Paul Hiscock
The Ebony Bastet – Roger Riccard
The Intrigue of the Torn Treaty – Shane Simmons
The Adventure of the Surprises – Dan Rowley
The Case of the Purloined Pistols – Mark Mower

## Part XLIX: The True Mr. Sherlock Holmes – England's Greatest Hero (1880-1888)

Foreword – Bonnie MacBird
Foreword – Roger Johnson
Foreword – Emma West
Foreword – Steve Emecz
Foreword – David Marcum
The Reader (A Poem) – Kevin Thornton
The Adventure of the Four Knaves – Deanna Baran
The Adventure of the Flagitious Sire – David Marcum
The Adventure of the Madman's Sister – Tom Turley
The Carpetbag Case – Brenda Seabrooke
The Adventure of the Prized Possession – Tracy J. Revels
The Single Shoe – Stuart Douglas
The Case of John Bull vs Brittania – Roger Riccard
The Widow – Marcia Wilson
The Arlington-Fisher Affair – Mark Mower
The Luxton Tragedy – Tracy J. Revels
The Mystery of the Missing Body – DJ Tyrer
The Problem at Arnsworth Castle – Jane Rubino
The Etherege Case – Hugh Ashton
The Youngest Client – Gordon Linzner
The Mystery of the Medical Misdiagnosis – Will Murray
The Adventure at the Art School – Stephen Herczeg
The Adventure of the Distracted Detective – Shane Simmons
The Adventure of the Headless Saint – Tracy J. Revels
The Case of the Australian Atlases – Paul Metcalfe

## Part L: The True Mr. Sherlock Holmes – England's Greatest Hero (1889-1996)

Foreword – Bonnie MacBird
Foreword – Roger Johnson
Foreword – Emma West

*(Continued on the next page . . . .)*

Foreword – Steve Emecz
Foreword – David Marcum
The Enigmatic Friendship (A Poem) – Jim Hawkins
The Adventure of the Twentieth Gun – Mike Adamson
Antoinette's Apparition – P.C. Shumway
The Adventure of the Intrepid Follower – Arthur Hall
Eyes of Wood, Judging – Marcia Wilson
The Sharpshooter's Revenge – P.C. Shumway
The Indiscriminate Paragraph – David Marcum
The Mystery of the Caroline Crown – Brett Fawcett
The Case of the Vanishing Adders – Ian Ableson
The Case of the Ghazi Genie – Paula Hammond
The Claws of Qift – John Linwood Grant
The Devil's Bridge – John Lawrence
The Second Strand – Tim Newton Anderson
The Adventure of the Twice-Murdered Man – Tracy J. Revels
The Murano Musician – Richard Gillman
A Yuletide Mystery – Alan Dimes
The Case of the Covent Garden Medium – Paula Hammond
The Adventure of the Tattooed Men – Arthur Hall
The Adventure of the Tallowed Cadavers – I.A. Watson
The Incident of the Poisoned Shipping Magnate – Sean M. Wright and
         DeForeest B. Wright, III
The Adventure of the Black Diamonds – Ashley Williford

**Part LI: The True Mr. Sherlock Holmes –
   England's Greatest Hero (1897-1901)**
Foreword – Bonnie MacBird
Foreword – Roger Johnson
Foreword – Emma West
Foreword – Steve Emecz
Foreword – David Marcum
Finding Holmes (A Poem) – Christopher James
The Case of the Three Cufflinks– Steve Lockley
Pease Poison Cold – Marcia Wilson
The Adventure of the Vanished Uncle – Arthur Hall
Murder in Grasmere – David MacGregor
The Case of the Bryniau Witch Tower – Paula Hammond
The Mystery of the Authentic Mystic – William Todd
Sherlock Holmes and the Female Detective – Susan Knight
The Case of the Puzzled Postman – Naching T. Kassa
The Uncle's Cryptic Clue – David Marcum
The Adventure of the Amnesiac – Dan Rowley and Don Baxter
The Adventure of the Murderous Clown – Tracy J. Revels
The Killing of Lady Grace Everley – Paul Nash

*(Continued on the next page . . . .)*

The Box – Robert Stapleton
A Puzzle in Porphyry – DJ Tyrer
The Adventure of the Fearful Printer – Arthur Hall
The Prophecies of the Brahan Seer – Paul D. Gilbert
The Clockmaker's Fate – Mike and Arianna Fox
The Wages of Loyalty – Mike Adamson
Death of an Uncommon Man – Geri Schear
The Adventure of the Long Arm – Alan Dimes

## Part LII: The True Mr. Sherlock Holmes –
## England's Greatest Hero (1902-1923)

Foreword – Bonnie MacBird
Foreword – Roger Johnson
Foreword – Emma West
Foreword – Steve Emecz
Foreword – David Marcum
The Adventure of the Disgraced Baron – Derrick Belanger
Sherlock Holmes: The End? (A Poem) – Joseph W. Svec III
Holmes the Hunter – Susan Knight
The Adventure of the Live Burial – Shane Simmons
Phantom of the Operetta – Tim Newton Anderson
The Ambassador's Dilemma – Peter Coe Verbica
The Adventure of the Dreaming Dragon – Josh Reynolds
The Disappearing Detective – J. Lawrence Matthews
The Adventure of the Unfinished Case – John McNabb
The Interrupted Retirements – Don Rowley
The Adventure of the Longest Case – I.A. Watson
The Clue of the Undamaged Stones – David Marcum
The Sound of the Grand's Piano – Paul Hiscock
The Adventure of the Fearless Postman – Andrew Salmon
The Adventure of the Cheapside Secret – Steven Philip Jones
The Adventure of the King's Code – Mike Chinn
His Longest Case – Martin Daley
The Bohemian Corporal– Orlando Pearson
The Riddle of the Sphinx – Liz Hedgecock
The Case of the One-Armed Crabbe – Roger Riccard
The Mystery of the Graveyard Angel – Adrian Middleton
The Adventure of the Wonderful Things – Craig Janacek
Epilogue: A Travel-Worn and Battered Tin Dispatch Box – David Marcum

*The following contributors appear*
*in the companion volumes:*
**The True Sherlock Mr. Holmes –**
**England's Greatest Hero**
**Part L – (1889-1896)**
**Part LI – (1897-1901)**
**Part LII – (1902-1923)**

# A Thousand Cunning Windings
## by David Marcum

"*. . . a thousand cunning windings . . . .*" So said Mr. Sherlock Holmes in "The Final Problem" to describe the path he traced when cornering Professor James Moriarty. But that phrase can also apply to over one-thousand brilliant Holmes adventures in *The MX Book of New Sherlock Holmes Stories*, now finishing at fifty-two massive volumes . . . .

Know this from *The Gospel* of The Church of the Traditional Canonical Sherlock Holmes:

> "*In the beginning was The Canon, and it was good.*
> *But it was not enough.*"
>
> – *The Book of Holmes*, (Chapter I, Verses 1-2)

And if that isn't clear enough, Verses 3 and 4 continue:

> "*Verily, verily, I say unto thee: There have*
> *NEVER been enough traditional and*
> *Canonical Holmes adventures.*
> *There NEVER will be.*"

And as Dickens wrote, "*This must be distinctly understood, or nothing wonderful can come of the story I am going to relate.*"

The initial original Canonical (and pitifully few) Sixty Tales were just the merest glimpse into the long lives of Sherlock Holmes and Dr. John H. Watson. Those Canonical adventures served as the main structural fibers of *The Great Holmes Tapestry*, but there were so many empty spaces in between that needed filling in order to reveal a full and vivid image. This is accomplished by way of post-Canonical adventures called *pastiches*.

The Canon relates sixty events across a period from 1874 ("The Gloria Scott") to 1914 ("His Last Bow") – from when Sherlock Holmes was twenty years old to when he was sixty. Forty years. But consider that most of those cases just take a day or so, or sometimes only a few hours. Forty years is approximately 14,600 days, and yet the total on-page narrative of most of the Canonical cases, when tallied, equals around six months – three days here, two here, and approximately one month for *The Hound*. (Even the off-stage events of The Great Hiatus, nearly three years in duration, is just a fraction of forty years.) There is so much more between 1874 and 1914 that is left undescribed – not to mention whatever happened in Holmes and Watson's lives before 1874 and after 1914.

And even though The Canon is the core of The Great Holmes Tapestry, the stories that make up this core were chosen by Watson as representative examples of Holmes's skills – they were not necessarily his greatest triumphs or "best" cases. Watson had thousands of recorded adventures from which to choose when selecting for publication, and he had reasons for what he picked . . . and for what he suppressed. *What about all of those other cases that weren't published in Watson's lifetime?*

That's where the Post-Canonical Chroniclers step in . . . .

*"Apart from what you have told me,*
*can you give me any further*
*information about the man?"*
– Sherlock Holmes
"The Illustrious Client"

In 2015, we knew less about Mr. Sherlock Holmes than we do now, for back then, there were over one-thousand fewer of his adventures that had been revealed to the curious public. Don't misunderstand – there were still quite a few post-Canonical Holmes narratives in 2015, but they were harder to find, *and there were not enough.*

*". . . we must hunt for this man's secrets."*
– Sherlock Holmes
"The Illustrious Client"

Growing up, I had the very-common experience of discovering and reading The Canon, and re-reading it, and then realizing with crushing disappointment that the ride was seemingly at an end. I was fortunate to discover Holmes in 1975, at age ten, just one year after Nicholas Meyer had ignited the current and still-burning Sherlockian Golden Age with his discovery of the lost manuscript for *The Seven-Per-Cent Solution* (1974). While it was flawed – the implications that Moriarty was not evil, and that the Great Hiatus did not occur, were obviously grafted onto Watson's original manuscript by some later Moriarty heir to posthumously rehabilitate the evil Professor's reputation – this book revealed the basic but staggering truth that Watson's stories *did not have to cross the First Literary Agent's desk to be both accepted and amazing.*

2

The hunt was on to locate Watson's other missing narratives, filling in all the gaps and spaces between what we know from The Canon. Meyer continued by finding an exponentially better second Watsonian manuscript, *The West End Horror* – and the dam holding back the release of these various historic documents was washed away forever.

> *"But that is not enough, Mr. Holmes."*
> – Lord Bellinger, Prime Minister
> "The Second Stain"

In the following years, I tracked down, collected, read, and chronologicized almost every existing traditional Canonical Holmes adventures – *but there were not enough.* And in the early 2000's, I noticed a disturbance in the Holmesian Force: Several media adaptations that incorrectly placed Holmes in Modern Times began popping up. One in particular gained a lot of traction, painting Holmes as a broken sociopathic murderer. That would be fine if it stopped there, for there have been a lot of insulting works over the years that similarly attacked Holmes – the worst up to that point being Michael Dibdin's *The Last Sherlock Holmes Story* (1978), in which Holmes was presented as a gleeful Jack the Ripper, whose death was arranged by Watson.

> *"We must not lose sight of our main inquiry."*
> – Sherlock Holmes
> "The Naval Treaty"

I was dismayed when aspects of this modernized sociopathic Holmes began creeping into what were supposed to be traditional Canonical adventures, as presented by people who should have known better: In these "traditional" adventures, supposedly Canonical Holmes now had a "mind palace". Watson's wound was psychosomatic. Mrs. Hudson was the widow of a drug dealer. Irene Adler was a dominatrix. Mary Watson was a secret agent assassin. And people were adapting to this – accepting this – as if maybe Holmes *had always been a sociopath*, or that Watson *really wasn't wounded*, if one just read The Canon a little more closely. Many said, "It's okay – as long as this attracts new people to Sherlock Holmes, who cares how they get there?" But they were all showing up with the expectation and looking for hints that Irene Adler really was a dominatrix, or that James Moriarty was . . . whatever that was supposed to be.

I became increasingly . . . shall we say *peeved*. And then I became motivated – a fiery motivation that has only increased every day since. And the proof is *The MX Book of New Sherlock Holmes Stories.*

*I little dreamed the strange shape*
*which that campaign was destined to take.*
– Dr. John H. Watson
"Charles Augustus Milverton"

One night in early 2015, I had a dream, and it abruptly awakened me. If I'd gone back to sleep, I might have forgotten it, but instead I went ahead and got up, as it was nearly time to arise anyway. And I kept thinking about that very-vivid vision.

I had dreamed that I'd edited a book of new Holmes stories, along the lines of *The Mammoth Book of Sherlock Holmes Stories* (1997), or the many volumes that Martin H. Greenberg co-edited with a number of other people over several decades – new Holmes stories, set in the correct time, indistinguishable from the Canonical tales that originally appeared in *The Strand.*

"*. . . we must take our own line of action.*"
– Sherlock Holmes
"The Disappearance of Lady Frances Carfax"

That morning before going to work, I looked around at my Holmes collection – now nearly 5,000 volumes, but somewhat less then – and saw a number of authors represented there that I'd love to invite. Later that morning, I emailed Publisher Extraordinaire Steve Emecz with the idea, and he was willing. (Steve has always been most supportive of various project ideas.) I had no idea that I'd started something that would be a huge part of my life for the next ten years:

That email is on the next page . . . .

David Marcum                                                    Jan 22, 2015, 9:40 AM   ☆  ☺  ↩  ⋮
to Steve ▾

Steve,

This is the idea I had for a future book. I was literally dreaming about it when I woke up this morning.

I would like to contact a specific list of authors (see below) – who I would pick because they write well and who write the kinds of Holmes stories that I would want to read – and have each one of them pen a Holmes short story.

The volume would be along the lines of all of those anthologies that have come before, such as *The Mammoth Book, Holmes for the Holidays, Murder in Baker Street,* etc. Like *The Mammoth Book,* I would arrange the stories by chronological date, and not by a perceived author importance.

I would be the editor, and I would format it. (As you know, I have strict standards.) I would ask that each story be 5,000-8,000 words in length, much like stories from the Canon. The stories would be traditional and Canonical Holmes only, as narrated by Watson. The characters would be in standard settings, and it would be like when authors were writing *Star Trek* novels, and they were told that they could use the characters, but essentially put them back as they found them when they were done. There would be no weird Alternate Universe or present-day stuff, no Holmes-is-the-Ripper, nothing where Watson is at Holmes's funeral or vice-versa. etc. Essentially nothing that shockingly contradicts what is in the Canon.

I would contact each author personally to explain the project and request a submission. That way other authors who didn't get to play wouldn't necessarily get their feelings hurt, since it would go on behind the scenes and the book would simply appear as a finished product.

Each author would retain the rights to his or her story, for use in a future collection of their own. To avoid the question of who gets what, royalties would go to Undershaw, or some other good cause of your choosing.

Also, it would generate some new Holmes stories that I would get to read, and that would be great!

If eight participated, it would be a pretty good nice book. If more played, so much the better. We could even consider doing two versions, the standard paperback, and possibly a collectible hardcover – that would be your call, of course.

So, what do you think? I think I could put this together fairly easily, once the stories arrived. It would be a lot of fun, and it would be something really cool for MX as well.

I await your thoughts....

David

. . . and if you can't easily read it, I wrote:

*January 22, 2015 9:40 a.m.*

*Steve,*

*This is the idea I had for a future book. I was literally dreaming about it when I woke up this morning.*

*I would like to contact a specific list of authors (see below) – who I would pick because they write well and who write the kinds of Holmes stories that I would want to read – and have each one of them pen a Holmes short story.*

*The volume would be along the lines of all of those anthologies that have come before, such as* The Mammoth Book, Holmes for the Holidays, Murder in Baker Street, *etc. Like* The Mammoth Book, *I would arrange the stories by chronological date, and not by a perceived author importance.*

*I would be the editor, and I would format it. (As you know, I have strict standards.) I would ask that each story be 5,000-8,000 words in length, much like stories from the Canon. The stories would be traditional and Canonical Holmes only, as narrated by Watson. The characters would be in standard settings, and it would be like when authors were writing Star Trek novels, and they were told that they could use the characters, but essentially put them back as they found them when they were done. There would be no weird Alternate Universe or present-day stuff, no Holmes-is-the-Ripper, nothing where Watson is at Holmes's funeral or vice-versa. etc. Essentially nothing that shockingly contradicts what is in the Canon.*

*I would contact each author personally to explain the project and request a submission. That way other authors who didn't get to play wouldn't necessarily get their feelings hurt, since it would go on behind the scenes and the book would simply appear as a finished product.*

*Each author would retain the rights to his or her story, for use in a future collection of their own. To avoid the question of who gets what, royalties would go to Undershaw, or some other good cause of your choosing.*

*Also, it would generate some new Holmes stories that I would get to read, and that would be great!*

*If eight participated, it would be a pretty good nice book. If more played, so much the better. We could even consider doing two versions, the standard paperback, and possibly a collectible hardcover – that would be your call, of course.*

*So, what do you think? I think I could put this together fairly easily, once the stories arrived. It would be a lot of fun, and it would be something really cool for MX as well.*

*I await your thoughts . . . .*

*David*

*"We must define the situation a little more clearly."*
– Sherlock Holmes
"The Red Circle"

When Steve approved, I also emailed a couple of Sherlockian friends, and their opinions were positive. So I started sending out invitations – and I was very clear: The books could have no actual supernatural solutions. There might be some element of *"What was that . . . ?"* at the end of the story – perhaps Watson looks back as they drive away and sees a mythical creature after all – but the crime could not have been caused by the creature. No real vampires or wolfmen or actual Jekyll-Hyde transformations. No aliens or Old Gods or intelligent brain-mutating parasites. Although one naysayer who is bored with The Canon and favors pure Holmes-versus-Actual Supernatural Creatures later sneered at these "Scooby Doo solutions", Holmes stated it exactly right: *"No ghosts need apply."*

Likewise, there could be no anachronistic elements. "Mind palaces" and other such incorrect modern references were forbidden. Technology had to agree with the year in which the story took place – with absolutely no Steampunk. The story itself had to fit into the Holmes and Watson chronology. For instance, close reading of The Canon shows that Watson only had a practice during those years when he was married. Watson's residences when living away from Baker Street – Paddington and Kensington and Queen Anne Street – had to be correct for the period in which the story occurred.

Finally, there could be no aspects of parody. People had been calling Our Heroes things like *Hairlock Combs* and *Fetlock Jones* since the late 1800's. It wasn't funny then, and it isn't funny now.

*"We must strike while the iron is hot."*
– Sherlock Holmes
"The Cardboard Box"

When I started sending invitations, I was afraid that no one would respond, so I kept widening the net. I went through my entire Holmes collection, looking for pasticheurs and finding ways to contact them. Then, to my amazement, I had the first positive reply – from Lyndsay Faye, who wrote back within a few hours of my initial email, stating: *"I'd be happy to – when do you need it by?"*

*Wow – this thing might happen after all.*

> *"Well, I think we must wait*
> *for a little more material."*
> – Sherlock Holmes
> "The Red Circle"

I'd been worried that there would be no interest, and I'd also thought that, at best, the final result might be a one-volume paperback of maybe twelve stories – if I was lucky. So I kept sending more invitations, and getting more replies from people saying that they were in. Then . . . the first story arrived, from Luke Benjamen Kuhns, and I first experienced that brand-new thrill – that *addiction* – of receiving new Holmes stories in my inbox.

> *"Our material is rapidly accumulating."*
> – Sherlock Holmes
> "The Dancing Men"

As 2015 progressed, word spread about this new project, and an increasing number of people wanted to join the party. I began receiving more emails and more stories, and pretty soon it became apparent that this was going to be a really big book. Maybe too big for just one book . . . .

> *"We will confine ourselves for the present*
> *with your permission to this very*
> *interesting document."*
> – Sherlock Holmes
> *The Hound of the Baskervilles*

Over several months, Steve Emecz and I worked out book lengths and sizes, and he was receptive when I shared that I thought it would become a two-volume set. And he was still receptive when that grew to three volumes. By late Summer 2015, the set had grown to 63 stories – more tales than in The Canon.

> *"We need certainly to muster all our resources."*
> – Sherlock Holmes
> "The Five Orange Pips"

From the beginning, the royalties from this project have gone to support the restoration of Undershaw, one of Sir Arthur Conan Doyle's former homes. For a number of years, the site had been in disrepair, and was more recently in danger of being torn down or cut up into private dwellings, disrespecting the historical significance of the place. A movement had helped to save Undershaw, and Steve Emecz and MX

Publishing had been part of that, having published several previous volumes whose royalties had also helped the site.

> *"Now, we must make the best use of our time . . . ."*
> – Sherlock Holmes
> "The Speckled Band"

Now the building was saved, having recently been purchased by the nearby Stepping Stones School for special needs children – and Steve suggested that the royalties from the new books go to the school. This only made the project more popular with the contributors.

The three volumes were published in Autumn 2015, and I was very fortunate to be able to travel to England – my second Holmes Pilgrimage – to attend a launch party high on a festive outdoor deck atop one of London's noted skyscrapers – at the location of Steve's then-employer. And then I returned home, and things settled down for a week or so . . . but it wasn't long before I started receiving emails about when to contribute to the *next book . . . .*

> *"Why should you go further in it?*
> *What have you to gain from it?"*
> – Sherlock Holmes
> "The Red Circle"

*Next book? Next book!* I'd had no plans for anything past the first three books. But receiving new Holmes stories by email *was* an addiction, and people wanted to contribute – both former and new pasticheurs – and others wanted to read further volumes with stories about the True Holmes, and most of all, *there are never enough traditional Canonical Holmes adventures. Never enough.*

> *"We must begin again."*
> – Sherlock Holmes
> "The Disappearance of Lady Frances Carfax"

So I wrote to Steve and explained, and we decided upon one more book – or maybe we decided on one new book per year. (I can't remember exactly.) In any case, I announced it, and more stories arrived, and Part IV, published in Spring 2016, had twenty-one stories. And then came the questions about the *next* volume . . . .

> *"We must begin from a different angle."*
> – Sherlock Holmes
> "The Illustrious Client"

It became apparent that there were so many contributors anxious to reach into Watson's Tin Dispatch Box, and also so many readers who were *starving* for more traditional Canonical adventures, that we could produce a lot more than one book per year – so it was decided to have a Spring *Annual*, and an Autumn themed volume. And 2016's themed Autumn volume was *Christmas Adventures* – 30 stories, (It's still one of the most popular of the series. We did another three-volume Christmas set in 2021.)

> *"We must hustle and put the thing through."*
> – Sherlock Holmes
> "The Three Garridebs"

By then, the pattern was set. I would announce a "Call for Submissions" about six months before publication of a particular set – the *Annuals* in Spring, and themed books in Autumn – such as Christmas, and Untold Cases, and seemingly-supernatural-but-not-really. More and more stories would arrive, necessitating that we eventually grew to six volumes per year – three for the *Annuals*, and three for the themed sets. I was usually reading new stories for the next set while also finishing final edits for the current set, and by the time the current set was published, fresh to the excited reading public, it was far in my rear-view mirror as I edited the new stories.

> *"We will raise as much as we can in money . . . ."*
> – John Ferrier
> *A Study in Scarlet*

In September 2016, the Stepping Stones School at Undershaw held their grand opening, and my deerstalker and I were invited as special guests (representing Holmes and Pasticheurs) because of the books' connection to the school. It was my own Holmes Pilgrimage No. 3. At that time – and since then as well – I was told that while the money raised for the school was substantial and useful – over $135,000 as I write this foreword – the more important aspect of the books' association was that they raised awareness of the school all over the world.

> *"We will have some indication as to*
> *where the document has gone."*
> – Sherlock Holmes
> "The Second Stain"

There were a number of milestones as the books progressed. A set of six volumes, taken from the early anthologies, were published in India by

Jaico. A single volume was translated and sold in Japan. Phil Growick, an initial contributor, had the brilliant idea of taking Holmes stories and assigning them to different artists – each of whom would produce a painting related to that tale, and all for charity. He published four different volumes of *The Art of Sherlock Holmes*, and almost all of the stories in those books were taken directly from *The MX Book of New Sherlock Holmes Stories*. He even had a gallery showing for one set of paintings, and more were planned before COVID shut things like that down. And contributor Sean Wright – who co-wrote (with Michael Hodel) *Enter the Lion* (1979), one of the best post-Canonical adventures way back in the late 1970's, not long after the current Sherlockian Golden Age commenced – suggested a volume of stories from this series that were contributed by members of the BSI – and thus *An Investee's Anthology* was published in 2022.

> *". . . he has done a considerable amount of writing lately . . ."*
> – Sherlock Holmes
> "The Red-Headed League"

During his lifetime, the late Philip K. Jones compiled an amazing database of post-Canonical stories – approximately 16,000 of them at the time of his passing, not long after the first MX anthology volumes were published. If one disregards the number of parodies and non-traditional non-Canonical stories that he included, then there are approximately 10,000 traditional and Canonical adventures listed – a fairly complete list up to that time. Since then, *The MX Book of New Sherlock Holmes Stories*, with these final four volumes, has 1,063 stories – or approximately ten percent (10%) of the other traditional and Canonical adventures ever written. Additionally, these books have had over 200 contributors world-wide. Some authors wrote a single story, while others have stepped up and contributed dozens – to my everlasting gratitude.

> *"We must each try our own way*
> *and see what comes of it."*
> – Sherlock Holmes
> "Wisteria Lodge"

I never cease to be amazed at the directions taken by the different contributors. From the common point of the traditional Canon, stories in these books may be comic or tragic. One might find a cozy murder or a strict police procedural murder investigation– or no murder at all. Holmes might investigate a stolen document or jewel – or something that ends up completely crime-free. The setting might be a British city or the countryside, or another country or continent. Holmes's client might be a businessman or a criminal, or a little old lady or Royalty. He might work for a private interest, or as an agent of the Government. The adventure might be a complicated swindle or a ghost story or a spy mission. The tale may be cerebral, or filled with breakneck action. Holmes might progress steadily from one witness to another, or he may be settled in to unlock a mysterious puzzle or code. Holmes might solve the crime from his armchair, or – as he says in *A Study in Scarlet* –"*Now and again a case turns up which is a little more complex. Then I have to bustle about and see things with my own eyes.*"

"*I should wish to go further into this matter.
It interests me.*"
– Professor Presbury
"The Creeping Man"

Another wonderful thing to me that occurred along the way was that these books gave some people their first opportunities to be published authors, and they went on to write more stories – about Holmes, and in other areas too. Some authors used these books as a "prompt" – reminders every six months to write more Holmes stories so that, as these accumulated, they would have enough to be collected into their own books. There have been quite a few volumes of these "children" of the MX anthologies.

"*. . . we will go out together and see what we can do.*"
– Sherlock Holmes
"The Norwood Builder"

One of the best stories of a "child" of these books was the creation and success of Derrick and Brian Belanger's *Belanger Books*. I first "met" Derrick when he reviewed one of my own books, and we became email friends. He was among the very first group of authors that I invited when I had the idea for the anthologies, and his contribution was his first written Holmes adventure. I "met" his brother, Brian, when he took over as MX's cover artist after the untimely passing of the previous artist. (I've since seen them several times on those occasions when I've attended the yearly Sherlock Holmes Birthday Weekend in New York.)

After Derrick had a taste of writing about Holmes, he and Brian had an idea: To form their own publishing company. I had an email from Derrick in August 2015 – a month or so before the first MX anthologies were published – asking me if I'd be involved in their publishing venture, and I've been thrilled to be associated with them ever since. I've edited over two-dozen books for them, and they've published both of my Solar Pons short story collections, with another on the way.

Belanger Books has published many Holmes anthologies since its inception, including several volumes in their anthology series *Sherlock Holmes: A Year of Mystery*. They have themed Holmes collections related to Poe and Lovecraft and H.G. Wells. There are sets devoted to The Early Years and The Denarian Years, and The Great Hiatus and World War I, and the Montague Street days Before Watson. There are Canonical sequels and team-ups with Solar Pons and other Great Detectives and Female Detectives, and stories centered around the Theatre.

I'm thrilled that Belanger Books came into being, and I believe that it was directly because of Derrick's initial involvement in *The MX Book of New Sherlock Holmes Stories*, and the joy he found when writing his first Holmes adventure. More important, I'm also thrilled that Belanger Books has gone on to be one of the two most-respected and important Sherlockian publishers ever – the other being MX Publishing. Both companies work together very closely to support each other's projects and charities, and spread the True Sherlockian Word far and wide. I'm very proud to be associated with both MX Publishing and Belanger Books.

> *"I cannot really see how we can get*
> *much further than our present position."*
> – Sherlock Holmes
> "Silver Blaze

In 2023, one of the MX contributors wrote, asking me what the future plans were for the series. He wanted to keep contributing for as long as the books continued, and he wanted to keep collecting every volume too, but he wondered how many stories that meant he'd need to write over the years, and how much extra bookshelf space he'd require. His email set me to thinking about an end game . . . .

> *"I think that we have gathered all that we can."*
> – Sherlock Holmes
> "The Priory School"

I'd joked before that the books should fittingly go to Part MX – Volume 1,010 for those who don't speak Roman Numeral – but sadly that wasn't realistic. When I started considering, we were then up to forty-two volumes, and I wondered if we could reach fifty – which seemed like a good number upon which to stop. If we had three Spring volumes in 2024, (Parts 43, 44, and 45), and three in the Autumn (Parts 46, 47, and 48), then we could reach fifty with just two volumes in Spring 2025. If the stories kept arriving at the usual rate, we would have over 1,000 of them upon reaching the Spring 2025 volumes. And personally, 2025 would be ten years since the books began in 2015 – a milestone – and personally I would turn sixty – my own milestone.

*"We must prepare for the worst."*
– Sherlock Holmes
"The Disappearance of Lady Frances Carfax"

The same person who had asked me about the books' future warned me that strictly limiting the final set to two volumes might be a mistake, as a lot of people would certainly want to participate at the end, but I was adamant: Fifty was a solid and pleasing number, and I would close the door. But that person – it was Kevin Thornton – was correct: Enthusiasm was high, and we were going to need extra volumes. I didn't want to increase to fifty-one – there's nothing pleasing about that number – but fifty-two felt good. There are fifty-two cards in a deck, and fifty-two weeks in a year – and an ambitious reader could read one volume of this series per week for an entire year. (I highly recommend this as a self-improvement activity, and would like to hear from whomever completes this Noble Quest.)

*"In over a thousand cases I am not aware that*
*I have ever used my powers upon the wrong side."*
– Sherlock Holmes, "The Final Problem"

As I write this foreword to the final volumes, I'm currently finishing the final editing process. As mentioned, I've been thrilled to receive new Holmes stories nearly every day for the last decade, and I'm going to miss that incredibly – although I will now have more free time to read other things, without my spare minutes and hours being devoted to printed-out stories on 8½ x 11-inch paper and with an editing pen in hand. I've also enjoyed being something of a Sherlockian influencer, able to nudge the Sherlockian ship in directions that I wanted it to go . . . .

*"Then we must take that as our working hypothesis."*
– Sherlock Holmes
"The Bruce-Partington Plans"

Not long after I first discovered Holmes in 1975 – before I'd even read all of The Canon – my parents gifted me with William S. Baring-Gould's incredible *Sherlock Holmes of Baker Street* (1962), the amazing biography of Holmes that establishes so many things – his birth date and background, his *other* older brother Sherrinford, his upbringing and schooling, his travels in America as an actor, his relationship with Irene Adler and his son, and the circumstances of his death. (That's right – as a historical figure, he wasn't immortal.) I don't agree with everything Baring-Gould posited, but I concur with much of it, and it was a great jumping off place when constructing my own 1,200-page (and ever-growing) Holmes Chronology.

> *"Well, we will take it as a working hypothesis*
> *for want of a better."*
> – Sherlock Holmes
> "The Man with the Twisted Lip"

As the editor of these fifty-two volumes – and a few dozen more as well for MX and Belanger Books, I've been able to nudge the ship in the direction I believe to be correct, encouraging certain ideas that I hope will become even more established in the reading consciousness as time goes on, in the same way that Baring-Gould's ideas have found popular footing. For instance, whenever the question came up, I encouraged contributors to reinforce the idea that Holmes lived at No. 24 Montague Street (as first discovered by Sherlockian Michael Harrison) before moving to Baker Street. I arranged the stories of each set in chronological order, and in the order to match what I believe is the correct chronology. I firmly aver that Holmes wore a deerstalker, and that he wore it in town and also the country. (Anyone who would shoot *V.R.* into his wall with a hair-trigger pistol would not be concerned by fashion dictates. He would dress as needed in useful clothing to go to work at a moment's notice.) Thus, he wears a deerstalker in these thousand-plus stories.

> *"We must look for consistency."*
> – Sherlock Holmes
> "The Problem of Thor Bridge"

These books helped to further establish that Holmes retired to Hodcombe Farm at Beachy Head on the Sussex Coast. Study of The Canon reveals that Watson had *three* wives – not two, not seven – and these books strengthen that conclusion. There is now much additional evidence, by way of these books, that Nero Wolfe was Holmes's son, and Solar Pons was his nephew. We know a great deal more about The Great Hiatus than what was revealed in "The Empty House", and we also know why Holmes "retired" in 1903, and more about what he was up to in those years leading to World War I and "His Last Bow".

*"Their cumulative effect is certainly considerable,*
*and yet each of them is quite possible in itself."*
– Dr. John H. Watson
"The Abbey Grange"

While these books are coming to a close, there are already plans for other similar volumes, although they will not be the size of the MX anthologies, and they will be one-time projects with much-less rigorous editing demands. But one thing will not change: The new books will absolutely stick to what made the original MX volumes so successful: *Firm adherence to the Canonical model.* Holmes will not be substituting for Van Helsing or Doctor Who. He will not be a sociopathic murderer with a "mind palace", and he will not be a joke, or realize halfway through and adventure that he's a character in someone's book, or be covered in tattoos while paying off a prostitute in the doorway of a modern-day Manhattan brownstone. These new books (when they arrive), as well as all fifty-two volumes (and over one-thousand stories) of *The MX Book of New Sherlock Holmes Stories,* hold to a basic premise: They were all generated by a desire for more traditional Canonical adventures – *and there are never enough traditional Canonical Holmes adventures.*

\* \* \* \* \*

*"Of course, I could only*
*stammer out my thanks."*
– The Unhappy John Hector McFarlane
"The Norwood Builder"

As always when one of these collections is finished, I want to thank with all my heart my incredible, patient, brilliant, kind, and beautiful wife of almost thirty-seven years, Rebecca – Every single day I'm more stunned at how lucky I am than the day before! – and our amazing, funny, creative, and wonderful son, and my friend, Dan (with whom I was able to share a multi-week Holmes Pilgrimage No. 4 around England and Scotland in Spring 2024). I love you both, and you are everything to me!

With each new set of the MX anthologies, some things got easier, and there were also new challenges. For several years, the stresses of real life have been much greater on all of us than when this series started. Through all of this, the amazing contributors have pulled truly amazing works from the Tin Dispatch Box. I'm more grateful than I can express to every contributor who has donated both time and royalties to this ongoing project. It's amazing what we've accomplished.

Finally, I cannot express how thankful I am to all of those who keep buying these books and making them the largest and most popular Sherlockian anthology ever.

I'm so glad to have gotten to know so many of you through this process. It's an undeniable fact that Sherlock Holmes authors are the *best* people!

I wish especially thank the following:

- ☐ *Steve Emecz* – From my first association with MX in 2013, I saw that MX (under Steve Emecz's leadership) was *the* fast-rising superstar of the Sherlockian publishing world. Connecting with MX and Steve Emecz was personally an amazing life-changing event for me, as it has been for countless other Sherlockian authors. It has led me to write many more stories, and then to edit books, along with unexpected additional Holmes Pilgrimages to England – none of which might have happened otherwise. By way of my first email with Steve, I've had the chance to make some incredible Sherlockian friends and play in the Holmesian Sandbox in ways that I would have never dreamed possible.

  Through it all, Steve has been one of the most positive and supportive people that I have ever known.

  From the beginning, Steve has let me explore various Sherlockian projects and open up my own personal possibilities in ways that otherwise would have never happened. Thank you, Steve, for every opportunity!

- ☐ *Roger Johnson* – From his immediate support at the time of the first volumes in this series to the present, I can't imagine Roger not being part of these books. His Sherlockian knowledge is exceptional, as is the work that he does to further the cause of The Master. But even more than that, both Roger and his wife, Jean Upton, are simply the finest and best of people, and I'm very lucky to know both of them – even though I don't get to see them nearly as often as I'd like. I look forward to getting back over to the Holmesland sooner rather than later and visiting with them again, but in the meantime, many thanks for being part of this.

- ☐ *Brian Belanger* –I initially became acquainted with Brian when he took over the duties of creating the covers for MX Books, and I found him to be a great collaborator, and wonderfully creative too. I've worked with him on many projects with MX and Belanger Books, which he co-founded with his brother Derrick Belanger, also a good friend. Along with MX Publishing, Derrick and Brian have absolutely locked up the Sherlockian publishing field with a vast amount of amazing material. The old dinosaurs must be trembling to see every new and worthy Sherlockian project, one after another after another, that these two companies create. Luckily MX and Belanger Books work closely with one another, and I'm thrilled to be associated with both of them. Many thanks to Brian for all he does for both publishers, and for all he's done for me personally.

☐ *Bonnie MacBird* – I first met Bonnie in 2013, during my Holmes Pilgrimage No. 1, when I was joining Roger Johnson and Jean Upton for lunch at The Sherlock Holmes Pub, and they brought Bonnie along. I didn't know she was famous then – just that she was a very nice lady. After lunch and an extensive exploration of the Holmes exhibit, Roger guided us on the route taken by Holmes and Watson, as described in "The Empty House", from Cavendish Square to Camden House in Baker Street. Later that evening, Bonnie attended my first book signing at the Sherlock Holmes Hotel in Baker Street. I saw her again in 2015 at the launch party of the MX anthologies, and then several times after that at Sherlockian gatherings in Indiana and New York. In the meantime, we've stayed in touch by email.

During our first meeting, along the way of the "Empty House" walk, she rather shyly stated that she was working on writing a pastiche. I hinted that I'd like to read it, but no such luck – until *Art in the Blood* was published in 2015 and I was able to read it as my book-of-choice while in London for Holmes Pilgrimage No. 2 – the first of her very successful Holmes series from HarperCollins. Bonnie has been an incredible supporter of these books from the very beginning, and I'm thrilled and thankful that she is a part of them for the final volumes.

And finally, last but certainly *not* least, thanks to **Sir Arthur Conan Doyle**: Author, doctor, adventurer, and the Founder of the Sherlockian Feast. Honored, and present in spirit.

As I always note when putting together an anthology of Holmes stories, the effort has been a labor of love. Looking back over ten years, this has never wavered. These adventures are just part of the many tiny threads woven into the ongoing Great Holmes Tapestry, continuing to grow and grow, for there can *never* be enough stories about the man whom Watson described as *"the best and wisest . . . whom I have ever known."*

David Marcum
*March 4th, 2025*
*The 144th Anniversary of*
*the monumental first day of the*
*Jefferson Hope Murder Investigation*

*Questions or comments*
*may be addressed to David Marcum at*
*thepapersofsherlockholmes@gmail.com.*

19

# Foreword
## by Bonnie MacBird

Well, here it is. Bringing it on Holmes, editor and Sherlockian scholar extraordinaire David Marcum presents the final volumes of his magnificent series for MX publishing, which has brought 52 volumes of over 1,000 stories by Holmesian writers from all over the planet – from the famous to the newly fledged, all writing from the heart and from the mind, reflecting our hero: Mr. Sherlock Holmes. This series has taken in more than $134,000 in support of the Undershaw school for special needs children.

You hold in your hands the last of these volumes, representing over ten years of David Marcum's creative life. He's diligently read, edited, championed, and also beautifully added to this astonishing collection of ongoing adventures of our heroes.

All of these works have been traditional, in emulation of that genius storyteller Sir Arthur Conan Doyle, whom we happily acknowledge here as the mastermind. He has enthralled thousands of readers for more than 130 years. His craft seems so effortless (until you try your hand at it), his prose both brisk and evocative, and even "cinematic", although most of it predates cinema. His wit is crisp, his insights subtle, his characters unforgettable.

How wise that he chose as the storytelling "voice" that of the pragmatic, energetic man of action, John Watson, who doesn't waste words on endless scenic detail or overweening innuendo but, by golly, gets cracking on with the story.

And how exquisitely drawn is Sherlock Holmes, with just enough mystery to the man himself to make us insatiably curious! He is acknowledged as the first superhero of popular fiction, but with no supernatural trappings. He seems to work miracles – but its sheer intelligence, knowledge, stamina, reasoning . . . and let's not forget . . . artistry that are his superpowers. He is a scientist, a logician, and an artist who sees what others do not. Of course, there's also a facility with baritsu, boxing, and single stick when needed.

Ah, the aspiration these stories awaken! Could we not be more like Holmes or Watson with practice, with learning? And wouldn't we be a better person if so?

But setting aside inspirational qualities of these stories, we must also acknowledge the absolute crazy fun they provide, and even more so, the comfort. In a world fraught with conflict and violence, with ignorance and prejudice, these stories amuse and entertain as they bring us close to characters who demonstrate what our world needs most – rational, fact-based critical thinking, courage, and friendship. Armed with those, these two men stand side by side to fight evil and win. Always win.

And at the end, we find ourselves fireside, once again at 221b. And so very glad to be there. Thank you, David and MX. And thank you, Sir Arthur.

Bonnie MacBird
Author, *The Sherlock Holmes Adventure Series*
*for HarperCollins*
February 2025

# "Let me recommend this book – one of the most remarkable ever penned."
## by Roger Johnson

That, you'll remember, was Sherlock Holmes's opinion of *The Martyrdom of Man* by William Winwood Reade (1838-1875), who was pithily defined by the *Dictionary of National Biography, 1885-1900* as "*traveller, novelist and controversialist*". The *DNB* noted of the book so remarkably endorsed by Holmes: "*in this work the author does not attempt to conceal his atheistical opinions*". S.C. Roberts, in the very first issue of *The Sherlock Holmes Journal*, observed that "*Holmes, with his social moodiness, his artistic temperament and his queer intellectual interests, had no doubt re-acted against the conventional beliefs of his squirearchical family and Winwood Reade's book was exactly the work that would catch him on the rebound.*"

Reade was an extraordinary man, who led an extraordinary life. The same could be said of Sherlock Holmes, of course, though his life was considerably longer. It was fairly early in their partnership that he urged John Watson to read *The Martyrdom of Man*. If the Good Doctor did so, he probably didn't accept Reade's statement that: "*The soul must be sacrificed; the hope in immortality must die.*" And if Holmes's own opinion at the time matched Reade's, we know that it did become more positive. Consider his discourse on the moss rose in the case of "The Naval Treaty":

> "*What a lovely thing a rose is!*"
> *He walked past the couch to the open window, and held up the drooping stalk of a moss-rose, looking down at the dainty blend of crimson and green. It was a new phase of his character to me, for I had never before seen him show any keen interest in natural objects.*
> "*There is nothing in which deduction is so necessary as in religion,*" *said he, leaning with his back against the shutters. "It can be built up as an exact science by the reasoner. Our highest assurance of the goodness of Providence seems to me to rest in the flowers. All other things, our powers our desires, our food, are all really necessary for*

*our existence in the first instance. But this rose is an extra. Its smell and its colour are an embellishment of life, not a condition of it. It is only goodness which gives extras, and so I say again that we have much to hope from the flowers."*

That has nothing to do with the case in hand – not directly, at any rate. The intention was probably to encourage his client Percy Phelps to a more optimistic attitude, but Holmes's observations are surely sincere, however unexpected. And no one, surely, can doubt the sincerity of his admonition to the tragic Eugenia Ronder:

> *We had risen to go, but there was something in the woman's voice which arrested Holmes's attention. He turned swiftly upon her.*
> *"Your life is not your own," he said. "Keep your hands off it."*
> *"What use is it to anyone?"*
> *"How can you tell? The example of patient suffering is in itself the most precious of all lessons to an impatient world."*

Detective stories didn't begin when Arthur Conan Doyle wrote *A Study in Scarlet*. Among the Baker Street sleuth's predecessors were the Chevalier C. Auguste Dupin, protagonist of three short stories by Edgar Allan Poe, Emile Gaboriau's Monsieur Lecoq of the French Sûreté, Inspector Bucket in *Bleak House* and Sergeant Cuff in *The Moonstone* – creations respectively of Charles Dickens and Wilkie Collins. Their exploits are still read and enjoyed more than a century-and-a-half later. But who now reads, for example, *The Boy Detective, or The Crimes of London* by Edward Ellis, the apparently endless exploits of Deadwood Dick by Edward L. Wheeler, or those of Jack Harkaway by Bracebridge Hemyng?

Even though he ranked the Holmes Saga low among his literary work, Conan Doyle achieved something remarkable: Fifty-six short stories and four novels, of genuine quality. At first, the detective appears to be essentially one-dimensional, but as we and Dr. Watson come to know him better, we realise that this is a character of real depth. It isn't merely the excitement of the crime and the solution that keep us reading and re-reading – there's also the fascination of his personality – and not only his but the admirable Doctor's as well. *

Even before the last remnants of copyright in the Canonical Holmes stories finally expired, there was a considerable output of parody and pastiche. Parody has different aims and different rules, but pastiche requires fidelity to the substance, the style and the spirit of the original, and that fidelity is too often missing – especially since the expiration of the Conan Doyle copyright – and the ability to post pretty much anything online. As they used to say, *"Never mind the quality, feel the width!"*

Fortunately, that does not apply to this book and its predecessors. David Marcum has worked tirelessly with his many authors to ensure that these new tales of Sherlock Holmes and John H. Watson are up to scratch.

And don't forget that none of the contributors will receive any financial reward, as the proceeds from the publication will go to the upkeep of Undershaw, the house that Arthur Conan Doyle had built for himself and his family near Hindhead in Surrey. Since 2016 it has been home to the Undershaw School, providing care and education for children aged eight to nineteen with Autistic Spectrum Disorder and associated learning needs.

Roger Johnson
BSI, ASH
February 2025

---

\*     Watson has so often and so unjustly been depicted as an idiot, especially on film! That will probably continue, but eventually, I hope, it will only be for comedic purposes.

# An Ongoing Legacy
# for Sherlock Holmes
## by Steve Emecz

Undershaw
Circa 1900

Fifty two is a wonderful number of volumes to complete the world's largest-ever Sherlock Holmes anthology. It's unlikely we will ever see another collection like this, with over twohundred Holmes authors participating. It has taken ten years and a mammoth amount of editing from David Marcum to gift the world more than one-thousand new, traditional stories.

As many have commented – the fifty-six short stories and four novellas that Sir Arthur penned was painfully few for the dedicated fan, and wading through the myriad of pastiches on offer is difficult for those yearning for more Conan Doyle. *The MX Book of New Sherlock Holmes Stories* is a haven for those wanting an extension to The Canon in a very similar voice to ACD.

Whilst the collection draws to a close, our work continues with multiple resulting projects coming from this huge set of stories. We come together on 17th May, 2025 at Undershaw to celebrate in person with David and many of the participating authors – and hopefully many of you online too. We'll raise a glass to Sir Arthur, who would no doubt be proud with what we all together have been able to achieve.

Steve Emecz
*February 2025*

The Doyle Room at Undershaw
*Partially funded through royalties from*
The MX Book of New Sherlock Holmes Stories

# A Word from Undershaw
## by Emma West

Undershaw
September 9, 2016
Grand Opening of the Stepping Stones School
(Now *Undershaw*)
*(Photograph courtesy of Roger Johnson)*

It is with immense gratitude that I write the final words from Undershaw for this last publication of *The MX Book of New Sherlock Holmes Stories*, a collection compiled in support of Undershaw's restoration.

These stories have not only entertained us, but have also played a vital role in transforming the lives of our students. Thanks to the generosity of MX Publishing, we have been able to maintain this historic building while developing an inspiring learning environment for 102 students with Special Educational Needs and Disabilities.

Our partnership with MX Publishing has enriched our school community, offering opportunities and experiences that may otherwise have been out of reach for many of our students. Undershaw stands as a beacon of creativity, learning, and success – fitting for a place so closely linked to the literary legacy of Sir Arthur Conan Doyle.

As we mark this milestone – 52 volumes in the series – we also look forward to celebrating with "A Soirée with Sherlock Holmes", a special event dedicated to the great detective and his creator. Led by MX

Publishing, the evening will include a wonderful auction, streamed around the globe, with proceeds directly benefiting our students. These funds will support the creation of a cutting-edge media lab, complete with state-of-the-art computers, cameras, editing software, and a green screen, allowing our budding writers to bring their stories to life in print and on the screen.

Undershaw is more than just a historic site – it is a place where storytelling, imagination, and creativity thrive. The legacy of Sherlock Holmes continues to inspire our students, equipping them with skills for the future while fostering a lifelong love of literature. We are incredibly fortunate to be part of this ongoing journey and deeply grateful for our enduring partnership with MX Publishing. Their unwavering support has helped change the lives of countless young people.

Though the final volumes of this incredible collection, the impact of these stories – and the generosity behind them – will live on. The pages may close on this chapter, but the spirit of Sherlock Holmes, and the difference this series has made, will remain. Thanks to the unwavering support of MX Publishing and their community of authors and readers, Undershaw will continue to inspire generations to come, ensuring that the Great Detective's legacy is not only preserved, but carried forward into the future.

With heartfelt thanks and appreciation,

Emma West
Headteacher
February 2025

"Undershaw" Hindhead Conan Doyle's House.

# Editor's *Caveats*

W hen these anthologies first began back in 2015, I noted that the authors were from all over the world – and thus, there would be British spelling and American spelling. As I explained then, I didn't want to take the responsibility of changing American spelling to British and vice-versa. I would undoubtedly miss something, leading to inconsistencies, or I'd change something incorrectly.

Some readers are bothered by this, made nervous and irate when encountering American spelling as written by Watson, and in stories set in England. However, here in America, the versions of The Canon that we read have long-ago has their spelling Americanized, so it isn't quite as shocking for us.

Additionally, I offer my apologies up front for any typographical errors that have slipped through. As a print-on-demand publisher, MX does not have squadrons of editors as some readers believe. The business consists of three part-time people who also have busy lives elsewhere – Steve Emecz, Sharon Emecz, and Timi Emecz – so the editing effort largely falls on the contributors. Some readers and consumers out there in the world are unhappy with this – apparently forgetting about all of those self-produced Holmes stories and volumes from decades ago (typed and Xeroxed) with awkward self-published formatting and loads of errors that are now prized as very expensive collector's items.

I'm personally mortified when errors slip through – ironically, there will probably be errors in these *caveats* – and I apologize now, but without a regiment of professional full-time editors looking over my shoulder, this is as good as it gets. Real life is more important than writing and editing – even in such a good cause as promoting the True and Traditional Canonical Holmes – and only so much time can be spent preparing these books before they're released into the wild. I hope that you can look past any errors, small or huge, and simply enjoy these stories, and appreciate the efforts of everyone involved, and the sincere desire to add to The Great Holmes Tapestry.

And in spite of any errors here, there are more Sherlock Holmes stories in the world than there were before, and that's a good thing.

David Marcum
Editor

**Sherlock Holmes** (1854-1957) was born in Yorkshire, England, on 6 January, 1854. In the mid-1870's, he moved to 24 Montague Street, London, where he established himself as the world's first Consulting Detective. After meeting Dr. John H. Watson in early 1881, he and Watson moved to rooms at 221b Baker Street, where his reputation as the world's greatest detective grew for several decades. He was presumed to have died battling noted criminal Professor James Moriarty on 4 May, 1891, but he returned to London on 5 April, 1894, resuming his consulting practice in Baker Street. Retiring to the Sussex coast near Beachy Head in October 1903, he continued to be associated in various private and government investigations while giving the impression of being a reclusive apiarist. He was very involved in the events encompassing World War I, and to a lesser degree those of World War II. He passed away peacefully upon the cliffs above his Sussex home on his 103rd birthday, 6 January, 1957.

**Dr. John Hamish Watson** (1852-1929) was born in Stranraer, Scotland on 7 August, 1852. In 1878, he took his Doctor of Medicine Degree from the University of London, and later joined the army as a surgeon. Wounded at the Battle of Maiwand in Afghanistan (27 July, 1880), he returned to London late that same year. On New Year's Day, 1881, he was introduced to Sherlock Holmes in the chemical laboratory at Barts. Agreeing to share rooms with Holmes in Baker Street, Watson became invaluable to Holmes's consulting detective practice. Watson was married and widowed three times, and from the late 1880's onward, in addition to his participation in Holmes's investigations and his medical practice, he chronicled Holmes's adventures, with the assistance of his literary agent, Sir Arthur Conan Doyle, in a series of popular narratives, most of which were first published in *The Strand* magazine. Watson's later years were spent preparing a vast number of his notes of Holmes's cases for future publication. Following a final important investigation with Holmes, Watson contracted pneumonia and passed away on 24 July, 1929.

*Photos of Sherlock Holmes and Dr. John H. Watson courtesy of Roger Johnson*

The
MX Book
of
New

# Sherlock
# Holmes
## Stories

Part XLIX
The True Sherlock Holmes:
England's Greatest Hero
(1880-1888)

# The Reader
## by Kevin Thornton

Through *A Study in Scarlet, The Sign of the Four,*
*The Hound of the Baskervilles, The Valley of Fear,*
I was entranced as a child by the great Conan Doyle –
By Holmes, and by Watson, his fine, steadfast foil.

Through the whole of The Canon, their short stories soared.
I read them again, but I still needed more.
From Holmes I found Poirot, Marple, and Pyne,
Tommy and Tuppence, Oliver, and Quin.

The Golden Years writers showed me the way –
Sayers and Marsh, Allingham, Tey,
Cox, Knox, and Heyer, Hammett and Chandler
Carr, Stout, and Simenon, Erle Stanley Gardner,
Nicholas Blake, Joseph Jefferson Farjeon –
until Chesterton led me back to the origin.

I've since re-read The Canon, every year.
Conan Doyle's on my pedestal, with William Shakespeare.
Both writers are timeless, their works resonate,
but "The Red-Headed League" outdoes *Henry VIII*.

"The Five Orange Pips" trounces drab *Cymbeline.*
"Speckled Band" is much better than "Sonnet XIV".
"The Priory School" beats Taming a Shrew,
and the entire Canon's better than *Henry Four (Part 2).*

You may call me Shakespearian, as many friends do,
But I'm a Sherlockian first . . . What about you?

# The Adventure of the
# Four Knaves
## by Deanna Baran

*A̶fter warning my wife that my evening's homecoming would be delayed and not to wait up for me, I visited the old lodgings in Baker Street to pay regards to my friend Holmes. I heard that during the course of his latest case, he'd had a lively encounter with some Camorrists, and I wished to reassure myself of his good health, and perhaps hear a tale or two that would be worth recording. Holmes's page admitted me to his rooms quite readily, for although between domestic life and the demands of my profession, I was unable to visit as frequently as I wished, I was not yet to be accounted a stranger.*

*The man himself was seated upon the floor, surrounded by relics of dozens of adventures past. Holmes had never been a tidy man, and indeed had been known to go a year or two as his papers accumulated into cluttered stacks piled high upon every conceivable surface. I wondered if his encounter with the Camorra had somehow inspired him to come down in a fit of system and organization, and rather thought that had I known, I would have encouraged him to take up a few more cases against the Mafia, and perhaps a few French or Russian gangs for good measure. There were many days when I had wearied of finding my chair and my dining place at the table both occupied by sheafs of documents, small boxes of obscure oddities, and disjointed notes scribbled upon scraps of paper which had surely had meaning when they were originally composed, but with time had become disjointed phrases bereft of any meaning whatsoever.*

*"You seem to be no worse the wear for your encounter," I noted. "I see the rumors of your injury seem to be most thankfully groundless."*

*"But a scratch," he assured me. "I have already rested for a few days, and am on to the next thing. I have been retained by the managers of a resort casino to discover the reason behind which they are losing more money than the odds would indicate to be proper. I will be departing by train first thing in the morning, so I thought I would use some of my spare time to set a few things straight. But as it turns out, I seem to be removing more things from my chest than depositing into it."*

*"That does seem to be the case," I said doubtfully, surveying the cascade of ephemera that encircled my friend. "If you had a thousand Watsons, you could never record all of your memoirs. Yet I suppose every single one of these items is its own story?"*

"Most certainly," said Holmes, tying up one packet with red tape and setting it atop another. "Here is the story of the blind beauty contestant. And here is the tale of the Dutch violinist. And here is Ullrich the dairyman. But of course, you didn't come here to hear of them – you came to hear of the Camorra, because you are a sensationalist at heart, and always have been."

It would have been useless to argue, for who could hide the truth from Holmes! So I merely responded with an amicable grumbling noise.

"However, many lives hinge upon the tale you wish to hear not being told. Although I trust your discretion, I fear that no amount of fictionalization can disguise this story, and it is imperative that certain critical elements remain shrouded in mystery for at least ten years more, if not longer. Perhaps someday. But when we are surrounded by such riches, how can we mourn for long over the absence of a single story?"

He flourished the envelope in his hand and a playing card fluttered to the floor. It was the Knave of Diamonds. "You speak of gambling and the resort casinos," I said, picking it up and returning it to him. "Do you deal with them often?"

"More than once or twice," agreed Holmes. "What are the greatest motivators of crime? Love, fear, and money – and anything else is most likely one of those three motives in a wig and grease paint. Gambling can be a pleasant pastime in moderation, but there are those who do not hesitate to exploit a perceived weakness in the system for their own personal gain.

In the case of this Knave of Diamonds, however, it isn't a memento of one man's ill-gotten gains, but rather, his attempt to claim that which was rightfully his. Under ordinary circumstances, perhaps, it would have been a very straightforward matter of inheritance, but their father was disappointed in each of them for various reasons, and was disinclined to make it easy for any of them to become his lawful heir.

One might even posit without fear of contradiction that he was downright disagreeable. It was possible, in theory, but unlikely in the extreme, that any of his children should have been successful in the task that he had set to them. However, one of them had the remarkable good sense of requesting my aid, and together, we managed. If I'm not mistaken, this card's three fellows are still here as well – " And he withdrew them from the envelope, displaying all four knaves in a fan.

"Do tell, Holmes," I said, settling down for his tale, which I now attempt to relay . . . .

It happened during that period shortly before our encounter at St. Bartholomew's, when Holmes was in the habit of visiting the poison cupboard during the course of his experiments, and thereby came on friendly terms with the staff of pharmacy assistants whose domain it was. Although Holmes was by no means a naturally gregarious individual, their common interest in chemistry was fertile ground for conversation, and conversations once begun along certain lines often devolve into entirely different territory. And thus it was that he learned of the identity of one pharmacy assistant, Robert Butler, who had been born on his father's plantation in the Barbados, along with an elder sister and two younger brothers.

"We were all disappointments to our father," admitted Butler. "My elder sister, Elizabeth, was the best at botany and chemistry of the four of us. I admired her very much, and was closest to her. She was like a mother to the three of us after we lost our mother, but at the same time, she was quite my best friend, even if it's an odd thing to say about one's sister. If we had remained on the island, I expect she would have inherited the management of the plantation over the three of us sons, and rightly so. Indeed, my father had set up a match for her with the son of a neighboring planter. In his eyes, it was a good and profitable match, especially given that the Harris Hills had even more land than what we possessed, and our holdings were not insignificant.

"Barbados has a most temperate climate, adequate rainfall, and fertile soil, giving ideal conditions for the growth of sugar cane. However, their son treated his employees very poorly, much to the disdain of my high-minded sister. She refused the match. She wanted nothing to do with him, whether matrimonially or professionally. She and my father had a beastly row about it, to the point where she fled to Trinidad, joined a convent, and taught Latin, botany, and chemistry at their school. My father was furious. Not only did he lose his daughter, but the plantation lost its most capable manager.

"I was a disappointment as well. There was a jeweler's assistant, a Frenchwoman from Martinique, who was employed at a shop in town. I greatly admired her to the point of proposing marriage. She accepted. My father, however, was furious, as he, like many Englishmen, had a prejudice against the French. He didn't wish a French daughter-in-law, and he did not wish for half-French grandchildren to befoul his family escutcheon. We married against his wishes, and he made himself so disagreeable to us that we left Barbados for Martinique. However, my wife developed difficulty with her sight, so that we left the Caribbean entirely to be closer to British oculists. I used my knowledge of chemistry and pharmacology to gain employment, and have been at Barts ever since.

"My other two brothers, Edward and Simon, were disappointments in more traditional ways, perhaps. Neither had any aptitude for sugar planting or interest in trade. Edward was an inveterate gambler. Simon was a drunk in frequent conflict with the Law. The entire island breathed a sigh of relief, I'm sure, when Edward joined a merchant ship that sailed between Europe and the Caribbean, and Simon enlisted in Her Majesty's Army. I suppose both of them craved more stimulation and excitement than agricultural cycles could provide, and even though they were unsuited for plantation life, both flourished under their new vocations.

"A few years after we left our father's roof, he sold his plantation in the Barbados during a period of unrest, and emigrated to England. He rented a tiny cottage in a small village where he quietly lived the rest of his days. When we heard of this, Suzanne and I wrote to him, offering to visit him and allow him to meet his grandchildren, but he rejected our proffered olive branch. Less than a month later, he passed away of pneumonia.

"I say all this to explain his state of mind when we received a letter from him, written on his deathbed. I say 'we', for he wrote the same letter to each of us – Elizabeth, Edward, Simon, and myself. He explained that he had a will that left everything to the Shipwrecked Fishermen and Mariners Benevolent Society. This had been deposited with his solicitor. There were also four newer copies of his will. Each of them was hidden in a different location, and each child was given a clue to find it. It didn't say specifically, but we assumed that whoever found theirs first would be able to execute this new will, which overrode the extant one in favor of the Shipwrecked Fishermen and Mariners' widows and orphans. Given the distances involved, as the four of us were scattered to the reaches of the Empire, he gave us a sporting chance of six months before his solicitor was instructed to open and execute the one will that disfavored all four of us equally."

This conversation, of course, did not happen all at once in a single monologue, but was confided in bits and pieces over the course of several months. By the time Butler mentioned the recent passing of his father, and the frustration of trying to interpret the single clue that had been left for him, Holmes's interest was piqued. He had little interest in the everyday affairs and problems of family life, or the disappointments parents feel towards their children when they take their own life paths, but he always had energy and interest for the challenge of a small puzzle, especially when the gauntlet has been thrown by a man as oppressive as Robert Butler, *père*. Robert Butler, *fils*, frankly expressed that he wished to claim the inheritance so he could share it properly with his siblings and thereby allow all of them to move on from beneath their father's shadow.

The letter from his father had a single enclosure: An ordinary playing card, the Knave of Diamonds. This, Butler gave over to Holmes. "It has no special meaning to me. Edward was no stranger to the gambling tables, so if he received a playing card, perhaps it would have been perceived as a cloaked sneer of derision. But to send a playing card to me? I cannot imagine what it references, unless it is a direction to converse with my younger brother?"

Holmes subjected the card to a multitude of tests for secret writing or hidden messages, applying heat, holding it up to the light, sprinkling it with water, and so on, but all to naught. In the end, the Knave of Diamonds was merely the Knave of Diamonds on a small rectangle of pasteboard.

Having exhausted the possibilities of it being a medium for a hidden message, there was now the question of whether it itself was a hidden message. A visit to one card reader advised that it was a message indicating hidden riches. A visit to another card reader suggested turmoil and opportunity cloaked as challenge. True enough, but entirely useless.

On a day off, Holmes and Butler journeyed to their father's little village in Dorset in the hopes of finding inspiration. However, his cottage was now let to a new tenant, and, when speaking to the agents, it seemed that the deceased Butler had left nothing of value behind.

"Which is extraordinary in and of itself," remarked Holmes. "One would think that a rich planter, who has sold his valuable sugar plantation, would have something to show for it. And yet he died with very little. No sentimental objects, no mementos of his family, no keepsakes of his former life in the Caribbean. Where is his money?"

"In the bank, I'm sure," said Butler gloomily. "My father had little affection for anything that didn't originate from the mint. But without authorization, I expect they will tell us very little."

And that was, indeed, the case. The bank was polite and apologetic, but firm. They didn't discuss such matters casually. Nor had the kindly vicar counted him a member of his flock. Nor could any friends of his be found at the local pubs.

"The Three Suns, The Running Footman, and The Blue Lion Inn," mused Holmes, surveying the High Street. "I rather wonder if there is somewhere in the area a place that is called The Knave of Diamonds. A country pub, or an inn, or a restaurant."

Further inquiry indicated that indeed, there was a Knave of Diamonds Inn in a nearby village a short journey away. It wasn't on the rail line, but a hired trap took them to the place they sought, and their interview with the innkeeper was profitable.

"Robert Butler? Why yes, I have an envelope that's been waiting for you," he said. "I received instructions to keep it for five years, and if he failed to return or no one else claimed it during that time, to destroy it unopened." He passed it into their hands, and they lost little time in examining its contents.

The envelope was oddly stiff. It enclosed a single sheet of paper as well as a key. The key was small, such as might fit a dispatch box, and the bow of the key was labeled with a paper tag bearing the emblem of a red diamond, such as might be found in the corner of any playing card of that suit.

"But this – !" said Butler, looking at the paper in dismay. For it had four lines of writing upon it, but the letters were merely a random jumble.

*rhydw cu je jxu*

*ij. cqjjxyqi*

*ydtkijhyqb*

*isxeeb veh reoi*

"'*rhydw cu je jxu ij. cqjjxyqi ydtkijhyqb isxeeb veh reoi*'," recited Holmes. "Obviously, a cipher. Was your father in the habit of using secret messages during the course of his business?"

"Frequently, when dealing with matters of trade and merchants, or minor secrets and matters of sensitivity," said Butler. "He employed a few different ciphers in different situations, when it was imperative that certain information not be easily accessible by the wrong eye. Not enough to defeat a spy, but enough to discourage the casual leakage of information he wished to protect."

"Which ones did he use?" inquired Holmes.

"Various sorts. Letters substituted for each other by a few places, or using numbers instead of letters, or things of that nature."

"Well, then. Give me a moment," said Holmes, and upon acquiring a piece of paper and a pencil, rapidly sketched out the alphabet twice vertically. With the judicious use of a penknife, he cut slits in one paper so that he had a sliding rule. "Let us do this the obvious way first," he said, and he began to shift the letters by one place—*rhydw* became *pkxcv* – by two places – *ojwbu* – by three places—*nivat* – by four places – *mhuzs* – until he reached sixteen places where *A* was *Q*, *B* was *R*, and *C* was *S*. Then *rhydw* made a sudden shift into intelligibility and emerged as the

50

word '*bring*'. From then, it was a very simple matter to obtain the entire message: "*Bring me to the St. Matthias Industrial School for Boys.*"

"We are fortunate that he was obnoxious," said Holmes, "but not as thoroughly obnoxious as he could have been with this. The matter is all but settled."

The St. Matthias Industrial School for Boys was a small institution on the outskirts of London that proved to be the charitable residence of a few hundred impoverished boys, teaching them skills such as tailoring, matmaking, cobbling, carpentry, and gardening. The grounds were neat and tidy. The boys they encountered were curious but polite, and they were swiftly ushered into the presence of the headmaster.

"Excuse me," said Robert Butler, for they had agreed it was best he do the speaking, "but I have been sent here with this key, and am told that you know something about what it fits." He produced the key with its diamond-marked tag.

"Why, yes," said the headmaster. "A gentleman gave us a gift of fifty pounds if I would hold a certain box, and instructions to hand it over to the one who brought the key that fits it. He described it to me, and said it would be marked with a pip just as yours is. Excuse me one moment while I retrieve it."

He absented himself for a short while, and returned with a wooden box that had a diamond-shaped cutout inlaid with brass. "Excuse me, but I had the further instructions that the box wasn't permitted to leave my office unless it was properly opened in front of me. A precaution against fraud, you see. The gentleman was very emphatic about that point."

"That sounds like my father," smiled Butler, feeling indulgent and ready to forgive his dearly departed father for his whimsy now that the goal was in sight. The key clicked easily in the lock. He lifted the lid, and saw the dispatch box contained a sheaf of legal documents. Retrieving it, his eyes danced along the pages – and his face fell – "This will favors Simon!" he exclaimed, his voice quavering somewhere between shock and outrage. "We did all this work – for Simon! Who knows what Simon would say about this if I told him!"

"Let us keep this," said Holmes, examining the box for a secret compartment or some other additional information. But the box was only a box, and had no further secrets to divulge. They left the St. Matthias Industrial School and returned to Barts much dejected over their success that had somehow turned to failure.

It was in the post a week or two later that that Butler received a communication postmarked from Barbados. "It is from Elizabeth!" he exclaimed the next time Holmes visited his poison cupboard. "She said she has no interest in playing father's games, but if it is helpful to me, she encloses her copy of father's letter, and also her clue. Her letter is nearly identical to mine, apart from the natural difference of the matter of address, but she received the Knave of Hearts. What do you think it means?"

"Let us find a place that does business under the name of The Knave of Hearts," said Holmes readily. "Although, being Elizabeth's clue, do you remember a place called The Knave of Hearts on Barbados?"

"No, and I expect it would have amused him to have sent her a useless clue she had no chance of chasing down," said Butler readily. "Still, it wouldn't hurt to investigate, just in case." They consulted a number of guidebooks as well as trade and local directories, covering both the colonies and England itself. The most logical place seemed to be a coaching inn of a type nearly extinct, which had done business for over a century under the name of The Hare and Hounds, but had been sold a few years previously to a new owner who had rechristened it as the Knave of Hearts.

This innkeeper also had an envelope for Miss Elizabeth Butler. He seemed to have no qualms about entrusting it to the pair of men who assured him they were Miss Elizabeth's agents acting on her behalf. Inside it were a key, labeled with a paper tag bearing a heart, and a sheet of paper.

BGOST ADRSO
RSRNM TTETA
TISNU TILCO
LOBYI EHMHI
SAHFO

"'*BGOST ADRSO RSRNM TTETA TISNU TILCO LOBYI EHMHI SAHFO*'," read Holmes. "It may be a simple substitution cipher as before, except this time, he has eliminated all the spaces between words, and placed them in blocks of five. Let me use my cipher rule to test this hypothesis – " but the message refused to yield its secrets to a straightforward letter-substitution cipher.

It took quite a few sheets of paper, and many tested and discarded hypotheses, before he identified it as a cipher that had been in common use by both sides during the American War Between the States a decade or so previously.

B G O S T A D R S O R S
R N M T T E T A T I S N U T I L C O L O B Y
I E H M H I S A H F O

BGOSTADRSORS
RNMTTETATISNUTILCOLOBY
IEHMHISAHFO

"The Industrial Home yet again!" said Butler fretfully. "He should have mentioned he had more than the one box."

"But you remember the instructions he was tasked to follow," reminded Holmes. "The box can only be surrendered to the possessor of the correct key. Unless you plan on burgling a charitable school, it may be easier to play his game. The ciphers are a minor annoyance, but he could have made them far more tedious to crack."

Another journey to the school, and another visit to the headmaster's office, and the presentation of the key with the heart label attached to it resulted in the headmaster bustling off to a secret location, and returning shortly thereafter with a similar wooden document box, this one bearing the emblem of a brass heart shape upon its lid.

"Not permitted to leave your office unless the box is opened properly in front of you? Now I see why your benefactor was so cautious about fraud," said Holmes with a wry smile. The key labeled with a diamond and the key labeled with a heart were very dissimilar to each other, despite the similarities of their boxes. There was little doubt that should additional boxes be necessary to discover, that their keys, too, couldn't be easily feigned.

"Here's hoping he was more indulgent in forgiving Elizabeth than he was with me," murmured Butler anxiously, as the lock's internal mechanism snapped open, and he raised the lid of the box to investigate the contents. His eyes raced across the pages within, looking for the pertinent information, and he gave a disgusted cry of, "Edward! Of course!" By way of explanation, he added, "He knew Elizabeth and I were close, and if any of us were going to work together, it would have been the two of us in collaboration with each other. So, from his point of view, you can guess that it was logical to not allow either of our successes to benefit the other."

The heart box was borne back to London, and they discussed the problem earnestly.

"Are Simon or Edward likely to cooperate with you by sharing their information?" inquired Holmes.

"Not likely. Even less likely, considering that I have a will in my possession that makes either of them the sole inheritor of everything," grumbled Butler. "I would prefer not to engage their assistance – especially at this point, where I have much to hide and much to lose."

"Well, then, perhaps we can make an educated guess. Based on the fact that your letter and your sister's letters were nearly identical, it would be a working hypothesis that there is nothing materially distinctive about Simon's or Edward's letters. Then the next leap of logic we might make is, out of all the cards to choose from, both you and your sister received Knaves. Might it have amused your father to have given all four Knaves to the four children who each disappointed him in a unique way?"

"None of us were deceitful, like one would think of a knave as being," objected Butler. "I rather object to being perceived as a knave, merely for marrying the woman I loved, regardless of her nationality. However, do you think that's a safe guess? What if there's an inn called the Seven of Clubs, or a pub called the Ace of Spades? I'm sure there are many businesses that have assumed the names of playing cards."

"But look at it as a matter of probability," pressed Holmes. "There are four out of fifty-two chances for a card drawn at random to be a knave. But the probability of two knaves to be drawn at random is the product of multiplying *4/52* by *3/51*. Without calculating it out, it's only a fraction of a percentage probability."

"Yes, but it isn't entirely random," argued Butler. "One is limited by the number of places of business that have adopted the name of a playing card to do business under, rather than the number of cards in a deck. I would say there are far more places that call themselves The Ace of Spades or The Queen of Hearts rather than places that call themselves The Three of Diamonds or The Nine of Clubs."

They continued to debate the issue, with Holmes reassuring Butler that he was perfectly welcome to investigate all the Aces of Spades and Queens of Hearts that he could find, but when he needed Holmes's help, he would be found in the chemical laboratory, conducting his work that had lain neglected while he traipsed about the kingdom. At this, Butler was anxious to soothe him, and assured him that surely his instincts were right, and let them investigate the existence of a Knave of Clubs and a Knave of Spades before worrying about Aces and Queens.

Matching cards were obtained of the Knave of Spades and the Knave of Clubs, should they be required. Two public houses meeting those requirements were duly discovered and visited, and each had their own envelope, with their own key and their own letters. By this point, Holmes and Butler were quite confident in the direction those ciphered messages pointed, and armed with that knowledge, it was agreeable exercise to determine how the messages had been hidden.

The cipher for Simon's Knave of Spades read:

*Bring Simon and me five guineas*
*to donate before the festival begins.*
*Saint Mark, Luke,*
*Matthias, and John.*
*Industrial -strength tonic.*
*School supplies appreciated for Robert's son.*
*Boys run fast.*

"I know what it's supposed to say, but I can't quite catch it," said Butler, frowning at it. "It was clearly addressed to Simon, because it is the message connected to his own unique Knave, and thereby couldn't have been acquired accidentally by anyone. Yet it appears to dictate to him to deliver guinea coins to himself, and also to a man who would be presumably deceased by the time the message was received. And what is the connection between evangelists and tonic and school supplies, and what does it have to do with a school that teaches trades to orphaned boys?"

"The information is there, but masked by the presence of extraneous information," explained Holmes. "It is a relatively simple technique to see beyond – " and with a few strokes of his pen, he marked up his transcription of the message and the pattern emerged.

*Bring Simon and me five guineas*
*to donate before the festival begins.*
*Saint Mark, Luke,*
*Matthias, and John.*
*Industrial -strength tonic.*
*School supplies appreciated for Robert's son.*
*Boys run fast.*

"I have seen better, but perhaps it is more an indicator that he didn't wish to tax Simon's ingenuity too far," was his most charitable comment.

Edward's Knave of Clubs message was also successfully acquired that same afternoon. The keepers of the envelopes didn't seem to have as strict instructions as the headmaster did with his boxes, and he surrendered it readily without any interest or concern in the envelope's contents. After extracting the expected key marked with a tag bearing the emblem of a black club, Butler examined the enclosed message.

2 18 9 14 7 13 5 20 15 20
8 5 19 20 13 1 20 20
8 9 1 19 9 14 4 21
19 20 18 9 1 12
19 3 8 15 15 12 6
15 18 2 15 25 19

"He could have made this far more difficult," said Holmes, with just a glance at the page over his friend's shoulder. "But he didn't. Again, perhaps he was showing his own form of mercy to your brother who was, by your account, not as much of a scholar as you and your sister were. *A* equals *1*, *B* equals *2*, *C* equals *3*. Most extremely straightforward. *2, 18, 9, 14, 7* is *B, R, I, N, G*. Yes, it checks out from beginning to end. Some people will shift the letters versus the numbers so that *A* equals *3*, or *10*, or *15*. Sometimes people will randomly shuffle the numbers so that *A* might be *5*, and *B* might be *1*. In those cases, a key and a prearranged system are helpful to know where to start, although with a long enough message, it may be deciphered through force.

"Sometimes as a precaution, people will use a variety of numbers to substitute for the most common letters, and thereby disguise the telltale presence of a double-*S* or a double-*L* or the frequency of an *A* or an *E*. Or sometimes people will combine *I* and *J* and *U* and *V* so that there isn't a full count of twenty-six. Sometimes a name or a place that is frequently referred to is referenced as its own number, rather than making the effort to spell it out letter-by-letter. Or any number of little minor modifications that must be worked through with some degree of effort, and sometimes may only be overcome with private knowledge and educated deduction.

But this is just sufficient disguise so that Edward needed to exert himself before having the same opportunity that the rest of you had. Minus Elizabeth, of course, for it is hardly playing fair to force a woman who lives in a convent on an island in the Caribbean to come visit a coaching inn in an obscure corner of England, far distant from the rail lines. That, perhaps, was hardly playing fair, but by the same token, it could be argued that it was thankfully unrealistic for your father to venture back to Barbados to lay his clues closer to her doorstep, even if he would be willing to abandon his theme."

"Let us go visit our friend the headmaster," said Butler. "I will look forward to this encounter."

The headmaster seemed agreeably surprised to see the pair return so soon with the two missing keys, and readily presented the boxes for opening. Simon's Knave of Spades key unlocked a box whose contents favored Elizabeth. Edward's Knave of Clubs key was inserted into the lock. There was some degree of uncertainty in the moments before the lock clicked and the lid lifted and the papers within examined! And then – a sigh of relief! No further obfuscations from the father, for Robert Butler the son was finally in possession of the papers which named him the sole heir!

*"And after that, there isn't much to say," concluded Holmes, who during the course of his narrative had raised himself from the floor and settled into a comfortable chair, his papers still strewn about and left where they lay. "Butler presented his copy of the will to his father's solicitor, and its validity was recognized and accepted. I presume he eventually burned the other wills, just as a precaution, after his own position as heir was secure and unchallenged. His father's fortune from the sale of his sugar plantation had been turned into the form of railway shares, both domestic and international. They were the predictably profitable kind, rather than the unpleasant experience that our fathers and grandfathers may have had with railway shares.*

*"He also had a certain amount invested in tea and cotton, as well as with various industries such as the mining of coal, and the making of bricks. Construction loans. Various things of that nature. It was quite sufficient that Butler was no longer obliged to put in his hours at the poison cupboard, and he ensured that his wife was under the care of the best oculists. I lost track of him for quite a while afterwards, as there was no further reason that our paths should cross. But he did justice towards his siblings and ensured that they received their portions out of his own generosity, rather than any dictate from beyond the grave. He also*

*acquired an interest in the work of the Industrial School, and became one of its patrons.*

*"I had my own share of reward, which was much appreciated during that lean period when I didn't have degree of reputation and the volume of business which I now enjoy. It wasn't enough to prevent me from having to share rooms, for which I am forever grateful, but it was quite enough to convey his gratitude. He did other things with his wealth, I have no doubt, for he was good-hearted and generous by nature, and even divided four ways, there was quite enough of it coming in. He kept the keys and the boxes for himself. I kept the playing cards and the ciphers as my own souvenir of this particular encounter.*

*"As I said frequently, the ciphers were quite superficial and easy to decrypt. It was only a casual attempt at obfuscation. The true challenge left by the deceased was making the initial logical leap that the playing card directed one to a place. Perhaps, if you're interested, I can show you my notes for my analysis of one-hundred-and-sixty separate ciphers, and some of the rather ingenious instruments I have assembled for the purposes of coding and de-coding – but it is rather late, and I wouldn't delay you any further from your own hearth. You must return another evening after I myself have returned from the resort casino."*

# The Adventure of the Flagitious Sire

## by David Marcum

### Chapter I

"Perhaps, Doctor, a walk would clear your mind."

"Hmm?" I asked, somewhat startled that the long comfortable silence had been broken. In truth, I had slipped into a waking doze, aware that quarter-hours were slipping past like boats on a steady current, but without the will to shake myself loose.

Sherlock Holmes shuffled some papers. "On several occasions over the last few months," he explained, sitting in his chair across from me alongside the fireplace, "when I have found myself in a fog over this or that case, you have reminded me that a constitutional through London would serve to provide a better outlook, a resetting of one's mental perspective, and I've found your advice to be sound." He turned and leaned over to place the stack of bank records he'd studied for most of the morning and early afternoon onto the floor near the foot of the curious octagonal table where his empty teacup rested. "I find that, after spending far too long following the thread of Colonel Waller's disastrous financial miscalculations, I could certainly stand from resetting my own perspective for an hour or so. And you . . . ." He smiled and stood. "You were moments from starting to snore."

I shook off my somnolence, glanced toward my desk and the labors I had abandoned before lunch, briefly considered the problem which had vexed me off-and-on for two days, and sighed. "Perhaps you're right," I said, making ready to rise as well. "A walk would be pleasant." Then, with a groan, I was upright.

In those days, not much more than a year-and-a-quarter after Maiwand, I had to move with more careful deliberation than that relatively carefree era before I'd received my wounds. Sitting before a warm fire for much of the day had only served to make me more settled. In truth, I should have pulled loose from my nest hours earlier. I'd long before discovered the value of getting up and moving around, both as a recuperative measure, and for the sheer joy and sense of well-being that comes from taking a long ramble.

Sherlock Holmes, of course, didn't have the burden of war wounds, and when he decided it was time to arise and go, he simply did so with complete ease. Of course that wasn't surprising due to his own energetic nature, and also because he was just twenty-seven years old at that time, and a young man of that age generally displays a natural vigor.

To Holmes's credit, he was rarely impatient when waiting for me to gather myself and then throw my often-sore form into motion. I say "rarely", for when he was impatient to rush out the door and follow up on some newly recognized thread of an investigation, he disregarded whether I was finding my footing or finishing my breakfast.

I could see through the windows looking upon Baker Street that the weather was still bright and clear, but the early afternoon was upon us and it would only be a couple of hours until the early October sun set. Though it had been a day of moderate and pleasant temperatures, the clear skies would rapidly allow the earth to cool as night approached. If our walk was typical of some others that Holmes and I had shared over the previous months, I knew to wrap up, as we might meander here and there, impulsively turning right when the quicker path home was to the left, ranging quite far before returning again to our warm hearth.

For a time we simply ambled, our route being where one or the other of us seemed drawn. There was unspoken agreement as we traveled, turning this way and that without thought in the way that a bird murmuration seems to know which way to go by consensus. Our murmuration of two drifted south, and then west through Soho, and back up into Bloomsbury. For the most part we progressed in silence. Despite his idea of looking for a better outlook, I knew that Holmes was likely thinking about Colonel Waller's unfortunate situation, in which the old soldier had been defrauded of what funds he still retained after his long and adventurous life. I know that I was still wrestling with my own problem – one of my own making, as I'd willingly taken on a task when I didn't need to, and now, in spite of the difficulty I'd encountered, I intended to see it through.

We turned south, along the side of Bloomsbury Square, and passing between where New Oxford Street became High Holborn, we entered Finsbury and that maze of lanes alongside Lincoln's Inn Fields. Holmes was in a more talkative mood by then, relating one of the cases from when he'd lived in Montague Street, which we'd not-long-before passed, when we traversed the narrow passage that opened at The Ship tavern. Finding that I had also spent time there before the war, Holmes suggested that we stop in for a few minutes, as he had developed a thirst. I agreed.

When we entered, Holmes stepped to the bar and ordered two pints. As he handed one to me, the door opened and a man walked in. He glanced at us and walked past, over to the bar. After a moment, he received a drink, paid, and turned our way, approaching in a heavy-booted scuff.

He was about fifty, somewhat less than six feet and heavyset, and settled in a way that made him seem shorter than he was. He was bald, and there were a few old dark scars across the top of his sun-browned dome, flat like small port-wine stains. Clearly he was one of those who chose not to wear a hat, even in the hottest sun or the coldest winter. He had a short grizzled beard that didn't do very much at all to hide his weak chin.

He was carrying a tall glass of whisky, held in short, stubby fingers that didn't look quite long or supple enough to adequately grip it, nor quite clean enough to ensure against some kind of inadvertent intestinal poisoning should one brush his dark lips. There was a squinty shiftiness to him, his eyes beady and close together, and his natural facial repose had a marked and unpleasant slyness. There was also the carried sense of suppressed violence, as when meeting a dog that has been beaten, and may go mad with rage with no prior warning or provocation. I didn't like him on sight – and that was entirely due to my own initial impression, without Holmes's influence or advice, although it was clear that he didn't like the man either, as reflected in his tone when he spoke.

"Watson, meet Foxy Huff." Holmes's tone was short, as he clearly resented the intrusion. He shifted to face the man, looking down at the intruder. "You've followed us for half-a-mile. Well, you've cornered us, Foxy. Is there something you want to say?"

The fellow's mouth pulled back in a vulpine grin, showing a number of stained teeth, but there was no humor or friendliness in his expression. He shuffled another step forward, offering his hand to me in greeting. I had no choice but to respond. His grip was dry and rough, and while there was implied strength, it wasn't too tight – as if his fingers couldn't close all the way to adequately wrap my hand. I suspected that, were he able, he would be the type who would try to win points in a contest that only he perceived by squeezing as hard as he could to assert his dominance. Little victories in a life without very many of them to list would be important to someone like Foxy Huff.

"I'm not ready for you just yet, Foxy," continued Holmes before Huff could reply to his question. "I still have one or two witnesses to line up before your arrest. My case will be complete in just a day or so. Stay or flee – it's no matter. I'll find you."

Then Holmes turned to me. "I first became aware of Foxy when he stole Marion Terry's diary from the Haymarket Theatre, four years ago. If he hadn't sold out his friends and traded information with the police on who lifted the plate from that jeweler who lived in Chitty Street – "

Huff threw up a hand, as if deflecting a blow. "Whoa, whoa, Mr. Holmes! Stop right there! That's water under the bridge! Old water! That diary was just a-laying there. I didn't know whose it was – just a book, it was. I just picked it up – thought it was lost. You understand – a fellow tries to do the right thing, and what does it bring him? Heartache! Heartache, I'll tell you! And that idea I squealed on my pals – you've got that wrong. I'm the most loyal fellow you'll meet . . . ."

His unpleasant voice had the victimized and mosquito-like whine one would expect, and he looked back and forth between us, his shifty expression trying to ascertain whether we believed him. "When I had a chance to read it later," he continued, "and to see who wrote it, I would've have returned it, but you just caught up to me too soon, before I was able. I explained it to you at the time. You remember?" His tone had started as a whining wheedle, but then he repeated, with darker shades, "You remember," as if there would be a hard lesson taught if the answer was negative.

Holmes was having none of it. "Remember what? That you promised to get even? And yet, here we are. Is that what you want now? To reiterate your threat?" When Huff didn't respond, Holmes started to turn away. "I thought not. Begone with you. I'll reach out my hand and find you in a few days for the plucking when the time is right."

Although none of this conversation was loud enough to be heard beyond the three of us, there was an apparent tension that had attracted stares from several nearby patrons, as if they sensed trouble rising. However, when Huff spoke next, he seemed to willfully reduce himself, working to diffuse the situation, and the nearby onlookers turned away.

"You have it wrong, Mr. Holmes. I heard you were asking around about me, trying to pin me to that stolen plate business in Green Street, but you're on the wrong trail. It isn't me that's involved . . . You see, it's actually my son."

In the months that I'd known Holmes, I'd rarely see him surprised, but it had happened. The time Cecily Davies lunged across the room and stabbed her father through his black heart with a pair of sewing scissors. The terrible discovery in Mrs. Wenceslas' oven. The tragic truth of young Nick Evans' bicycle ride in the village of Wenalt. Holmes had blamed himself after each event, feeling that he should have foreseen the possibilities of what might occur. Generally, he usually held most of the threads in his hand, or he was two steps in front of everyone, but sometimes events turned too quickly, or facts were revealed in ways that he didn't expect. Such situations could frustrate him, but mostly he enjoyed the added challenge. On several occasions over the previous months, he'd explained that if one such as himself had the details of a thousand cases in his head, then it wasn't so very difficult to figure out the thousand-and-first. But I could see that there was a disappointment at the sameness of the thousand-and-first, and he craved the unusual and the *outré*. The outlandish and the idiosyncratic. And Huff's statement that his son was mixed up in the Green Street affair, whatever that was, had intrigued and startled him.

"In what way?" Holmes asked, his eyes narrowing.

"He's gotten himself mixed up with Abel Farris. You'll have heard of him, I suppose, if you've made any progress on tracking the missing plate."

"I know of Farris, but not in relation to the stolen plate. What is your son's connection?

"He fell in with a bad crowd – Farris' gang. One thing led to another – the same old path to ruin you hear about – and before we knew it – that is, his mother and me – our Reuben was part of the crew. He was the lookout on the Green Street job. That's how they rope them in – things like being the lookout, and then a little more at a time, until the guilt won't wash off. Now he's been asked to go along when the delivery to the buyer is made tomorrow night."

"And how do you know all of this?"

"How does a father know anything? I listen, and I snoop. We've tried talking with him, and tried keeping him at home, but he's old enough now to ignore us."

"What do you get from this – from turning in your own son?"

"Why, I hope to put a stop to all of it. He needs a hard lesson, Reuben does – something to scare him away from that life, and nothing me or my wife say or do is going to reach him. Not anymore. He's had a taste of it – just a little taste – but he likes it. I'm hoping that you can do something – catch him and scare him. Nothing more than that," he added hurriedly. And then he fell silent, looking from one of us to the other with slow, metronomic blinks, as if he were a reptile staring into the sun.

Holmes gazed at the man a bit longer than one might expect – as if looking into a petri dish to watch the bacteria spread. It was enough to make Huff glance away nervously. Finally Holmes answered, "Where will this delivery be made?"

"Behind the St. Giles Workhouse – at midnight. Halfway along Betterton Street, between Drury Lane and Endell Street. I hear that Reuben will be there with some of the gang. If you're there too, Mr. Holmes – with your policemen friends, and this one here – " He glanced at me. " – and pick him up, it will do him the world of good . . . And if you'll put in a good word for him, and make sure that he isn't treated too roughly – Well, he just needs a good scare . . . ."

"I hadn't fancied you for a caring father, Foxy," said Holmes with a shake of his head. Then, "I'll look into it."

"That's all I ask. I'd heard you were asking questions about me, and I wanted to make sure that you understood you're on the wrong trail."

The man glanced at me, then back to Holmes, before abruptly turning without another word. He stepped to the bar, turned up his previously untouched whisky glass to quickly drink the contents – clearly that much whisky had no more affect than a tall glass of water. Then he set down the glass and departed without looking back.

When he'd gone, Holmes snorted in amusement or disgust – or both. At my querying expression, he shook his head.

"There's no doubt that Foxy Huff is deeply involved in the Green Street theft. All of the pieces of the Old Sheffield Plate were stolen last Thursday night while their owner, Sir Norman Devere was out of town. He returned the next morning, discovered it, and notified the police. I was consulted by Gregson. The staff saw nothing, and I'm inclined to think them innocent. Sir Norman is a widower, and his only son died in the Second China War, so it's a small household: Just an old butler, his wife the housekeeper, a feeble-minded lad of twelve or so to do the general labor, and two young maids. Whoever took the plate managed to enter without alerting the house – it wouldn't have taken much skill, as the servants sleep in another part of the building and the latches are old. They carried off a number of items, including the Threlkeld Platter, which the Crown would like to get back – and they would have decades ago, but for a long-standing and convoluted document related to some loan by the Deveres to a member of the Royal Family in Regency days. Sir Norman refuses to believe that the Crown might be behind this theft, to get the object back, but I'm starting to see signs to the contrary, and that Jimmy Farraday's crowd did the deed. There's a connection between Farraday and one of Queen's coachmen, and from there I can make a direct connection to Foxy Huff, one of Farraday's lesser lieutenants. There's no way a theft of this careful complexity was carried out by Abel Farris' gang. Farris is nothing more than a clumsy imitation Fagin, not even a score of years, and not much older than the lads he recruits. Nicking meat pies and breaking things for amusement is at the limit of their skills."

"Then clearly Huff thinks he's being clever to try and direct your attention elsewhere. But why implicate his own son?"

"Exactly. I hate to follow a trail laid out by Huff, but I'll make arrangements, just in case – if only see what kind of game Huff is playing." He turned his head. "You'll join me, of course?"

I considered that midnight in October in a most-insalubrious neighborhood might not be the wisest spot to place oneself. I was not yet fully healed, and the seeping cold that crept out of the cold air and the insidious fog and frozen pavement, standing still while hidden, watching and waiting for hours to observe something happening, could be quite unpleasant.

"Yes, of course." I answered promptly..

Holmes nodded. We finished our pints and resumed our walk.

## Chapter II

We worked our way west along Great Queen Street, and then turned north along Drury Lane. For a quarter-hour, we prowled several of the streets behind the workhouse, including Betterton Street where the rendezvous was supposed to occur. Holmes refreshed his knowledge of the area while I was – yet again – introduced to a region that, while looking like so many other parts of London, still had its own peculiarities.

Betterton Street was a row of shabby four-story brick buildings, none with any outstanding feature. Looking at it, I was reminded of a narrow canyon in Afghanistan where several of us had been pinched from both ends by the natives. We had escaped unscathed and had laughed about it later, thinking ourselves indestructible, fooled by the idiocy of youth.

"Nasty place for a trap if they bottle us up," I noted.

Holmes nodded but didn't comment. He remained silent as he looked in both directions, doing his best to anticipate where the meeting would occur, and the spot from which to best observe it. Then, apparently satisfied, he led me on toward the Endell Street side, and a route that was relatively more wholesome in comparison. He shook his head.

"This area is a self-perpetuating engine of crime," he said, gesturing vaguely southwest down a narrow lane we were passing. "Five-hundred feet along that passage is Seven Dials. It, together with St. Giles, form one of the worst of the Rookeries. I'd be hard pressed to put Petticoat Lane or the Ratcliffe Highway ahead of this one, although parts of Whitechapel and Spitalfields are festering sores, just waiting for a match to ignite – to mix my metaphors. Just over a hundred years ago, the Paving Commissioners pulled down the Sundial Pillar, just over that way, but it did no good – the riff-raff still gather there, even if there is no monument to draw them. They say the Shaftsbury Avenue improvements to clear some of the slums will help, but I doubt it. Thirty years ago, Dickens spent a dangerous night touring the area with a Scotland Yard inspector, and wrote about it, but what has changed?"

Endell Street had become Bow Street. Holmes had fallen silent, as he was sometimes wont to do when considering the scope of misery in the world, and how attempting to stand against it was like plowing the sea. As we passed the police station, Holmes suddenly stated, "Still, Dickens had the right idea. Writing about things is important." Then he glanced at me and asked, "Will you finish your manuscript?"

By that point in our gestating friendship – I'd known Holmes just a little over nine months – I'd mostly ceased to be amazed when he seemed to read my mind. Still, I wanted to confirm how he'd done so.

"I suppose you've seen me staring at my desk off and on for two days."

I didn't look his way, but I sensed that he nodded. "And you glanced that way again, first thing when you woke up this afternoon." After a pause of a few steps, he added, "You don't have to do it, you know," he said. "Finish it, I mean. If you feel as if you've promised it to me – an enthusiastic declaration made in the moment – please divest yourself of that notion. There is no obligation. I do not see it that way, but if you do, I release you from the burden."

I thought of the manuscript to which he referred, three-quarters complete, but now lying unfinished on my desk, laid open like a poor autopsy study. For some reason, something was missing, and I was having difficulty bringing it to life – an unusual occurrence for me. Writing had always come easy, even as a youth, and I had long kept detailed journals, as well as making the occasional attempts toward adventurous fictions that at best were poor imitations of Sir Walter Scott and, later, Robert Louis Stevenson. I'd learned that my efforts to fabricate such fantastical and adventurous literature left much to be desired, while detailing the true events encountered along my path were quite easily described. Since my injuries and discharge from the Army, I found that I wrote even more – during the days when I was too tired or sore to venture out into the streets, or at night, when I could not sleep. Time spent on these efforts had allowed me to accumulate a number of narratives relating my military adventures and, more recently as I'd accompanied Holmes on his investigations, I was beginning to amass a sizable stack of those sketches as well.

"Your merits should be publicly recognized, and if you won't do it, I will."

"You have other things to write about," Holmes countered. I started to bluster, but he interrupted me.

"You are a *writer*, Watson," he said. "You must write – or you will burst. I'll admit that, if the signs of your recent overseas adventures hadn't been so obvious when we first met, leading me to conclude you'd been wounded in Afghanistan, I would have been tempted to deduce that you were primarily an author – and not just because of the signs of drink that were upon you at our initial meeting. Thankfully that was not your typical character, or our association would have likely been brief.

"Knowing you all these months has only confirmed my initial conclusions that whatever other titles and skills you carry – Physician. Soldier. – you are a *writer*. You display all the signs, you know – the shape of your fingers altered to reflect how you hold the pen for such long periods. The ink stains upon your fingers that are more permanent and prominent than the nitrate of silver on your right forefinger that marks you as a physician. The smooth cuffs that might lead some with less experience to frame you as a clerk entering figures in a ledger during most of your waking hours are just as easily achieved by writing prose. You write whenever you get the chance – when the weather is too foul to go walking, or when I haven't called upon your time to consult upon an investigation. When you cannot sleep at night, due to insomnia . . . or due to your nightmares."

Some might have flared at this last intrusive statement – a cold-hearted comment on such personal aspects of one's life – but by then, I knew that Sherlock Holmes meant no offense, and he perceived no boundary that he had breached.

"I could only presume," he went on, "without having looked, that you've resumed work on that narrative concerning the Jefferson Hope affair last spring."

"I have."

Before I could elaborate, Holmes reiterated, "There's really no need, you know. Lestrade and Gregson already have the credit. Let them keep it. What difference does it to me?"

"It makes a great deal of difference," I replied with a sudden bit of heat, stopping on the pavement to face him. We were across from the pillars of the Lyceum. It was a discussion which we'd had before. "I know that you were bothered at the end of the Hope case when Lestrade and Gregson were credited with the solution, and when *The Echo* implied that you were simply some juvenile amateur who might someday learn a thing or two from the official Force– that in time, should you be so lucky, you might possibly achieve a fraction of their success."

"And you might also recall what you said to console me," countered Holmes. "Something like: 'The public hiss at me, but I cheer myself when in my own house I contemplate the coins in my strong-box.' What do I care if the newspapers give the police the credit, as long as the police keep seeking my advice and letting me pocket my fee?"

"But you also said – How did you put it? – 'I know well that I have it in me to make my name famous. No man lives or has ever lived who has brought the same amount of study and of natural talent to the detection of crime which I have done.'" Holmes glanced away, recalling the moment as well as I did. "I know you better now than then," I continued, "and I recognize that this was a true statement. You might allow the official force to take the credit, but you also seek acknowledgement for what you've accomplished. You *do* appreciate the praise. And making your name more well-known can only increase your reputation – and also increase the number of clients who seek your unique assistance.

"Clients? You know that I have many of those already."

"This is true, but I also see how you appreciate the interesting cases over those of little interest who seek your time during your routine daily consulting hours – to ask for guidance upon a lost pet or misplaced wedding ring. Those also give you a fee to pocket, but it's the interesting cases that stir your blood, the way a hound perks up when the horn sounds. Those cases when, as you put it, you have to 'bustle about and see things' with your own eyes are what pleases you most – and making the public more aware of your services can only open up more of those opportunities. And my promise to write about what happened during the Hope investigation, which I take quite seriously, can only help."

"But you've run into a difficulty," noted Holmes. "You were writing away, steadily and with purpose, and suddenly, yesterday morning, you stopped. You sat for the longest time making no forward progress whatsoever. Then you sighed, closed your journal, neatly replaced and set aside the pen, and took to your armchair, from whence you've regularly glared toward your desk ever since. What is the unexpected problem?"

"Jefferson Hope's narrative," I replied. "Relating his history, and his reasons for following those two men around the world, using up all the remaining decades of his life to achieve revenge . . . I have stumbled when it comes time to relate his aspect of the story – his background, and his motivations."

Holmes shrugged, his eyes looking ahead of us. "I don't understand the complication. Simply relate what he told us during our final interview, after his capture. It couldn't take more than a couple-of-hundred words. The Mormon leaders stole his intended bride, killed her father, and left Hope for dead. He dogged the two men most responsible, and eventually executed them. Or you can shorten it even more, if you're clever about it. I believe he stated something to the effect of, 'It don't much matter to you why I hated these men.' Surely that will suffice. Sometimes motivation is the key to understanding how to catch the criminal, but not always. In the end, it didn't matter why he was after those two men. He left enough clues that we were able to lure him into our trap."

I thought that it was generous of Holmes to refer to it as "our trap", as I hadn't understood what was happening whatsoever, even as it was occurring. "In this case," Holmes continued, "we were able to outthink Hope and he walked straight into our Baker Street web."

"It's considerate of you to state that '*we* were able to outthink him'," I said. "But I feel that the little we learned from him regarding his past – the story of the poor girl and her father, and Hope's great love for the young lady, and how Stangerson and Drebber and the others so ruined that part of Hope's life that he devoted the rest of it to destroying them – deserves more than a few hundred words."

Holmes turned a wary expression upon me. "Why," he said with a tilt to his head and a raised eyebrow, "do I have the sense that I should be uneasy about this narrative you're composing? It sounds as if you intend to fabricate some sprawling romantic fiction and graft it onto what should be a straightforward list of points outlining the bare investigatory facts."

I shook my head, suddenly chary as I carefully replied. "No, no. You misunderstand me. And in any event, I couldn't write anything of a fictional nature. I am no Scott or Dickens, able to generate such pretend events and conversations from my own mind. No, my journals – and now this slim volume – are simply my records of what I see and hear and understand. True narratives of true events."

He nodded, ready to take that as my final word . . . but there remained a whiff of suspicion and doubt. I didn't expand on my conclusion that the story *did* need more about Jefferson Hope – quite a bit more. The account required a substantial segment detailing the killer's past and his motivations, and what would drive a man to expend the rest of his days seeking vengeance. I'd reluctantly come to understand that to finish the story properly in the way that I felt it needed to be told, I'd have to find someone else – a literary partner – to write that segment. To flesh out the skeletal background that Hope had shared with us just before his death, and the tragic entwined destinies of those unusual people.

I'd written as much as I could from my own experience – a narrative explaining how I'd ended up in Baker Street and the beginnings of my friendship with Sherlock Holmes, and the events of the case, stretching from the day I was invited to get my hat and join Holmes when he examined the first dead body to the denouement when he and I had realized the Scotland Yarders were awarded the public credit for the solution. But I wasn't satisfied. There was the other aspect to be explored and expanded – Hope's narrative, which would almost feel like a separate book – grafted, as Holmes said, into my narrative. I would have to set the manuscript aside until such a time that I could find someone to help address my concern.

But now I had a new thought to worry me: When Sherlock Holmes finally read it, I greatly feared that he would object when discovering that it wasn't the dry and neatly scientific account that he envisioned.

Our walk continued for several more hours, working inevitably toward home. Upon reaching the Strand, we continued for a short time to the Embankment before Holmes plunged back into the quieter streets, leading gradually away from the river and toward home and hearth through a myriad of lanes, alleys, mews, passages, and paths, many without names, but all known to my friend. At one point we traversed Dean Street near Soho Square. Upon another, the long stretch of Titchfield Street to the east of Cavendish Square and the Langham. Our route led over to Devonshire Street, and thence to the workhouse near Baker Street Station, and so on, with the streets often – to me – appearing identical as the late afternoon grew more dark and cool.

Along the way, various spots suggested memories of Holmes's past cases. Once he pointed at a narrow building where Mansfield Street joins Queen Anne Street. "That was Sketch Rutledge's little temple. He wore a costume sewn from snake skins, and preached a unique interpretation of the Sixteenth Chapter of Mark, Verse Eighteen." And he then had a fit of that peculiar silent laughter of his which always boded ill for someone. He refused to elaborate, advising that neither the world nor his flatmate, despite my experiences on a number of continents, was ready for that story.

"And here," he provided a bit later, alongside the Castle Street marketplace, "was where Betsy Flynn tripped over a loose paving stone, unexpectedly revealing the Tavis-Gresham Hoard. You haven't heard of it, of course. The nasty machinations of three noble houses are still fighting for the rights, but I was able to squeeze enough Mammon out of all of them so that Betsy now owns her own house now in Chiswell Street, by the artillery ground, and also a little nearby tea shop."

The day was drawing to a close, and I was ready to return home. I knew that Holmes stayed aware of my condition, and if I'd shown indications of excessive weariness beyond what might be expected from such a traipse, he would have immediately insisted upon seeking a more populated street and a hansom cab – although funds for the latter were much more rare for both of us in those early days. At the same time, while I was somewhat sapped, I recognized the therapeutic benefit of pushing myself – even if I would pay for it on the morrow.

As we passed near Baker Street Station, Holmes looked around and, in short order, he spotted an unobtrusive lad of ten or so. He made a subtle and cabalistic gesture with the fingers of his left hand that sent the boy skittering off in the other direction with nary a change of expression, rather like a hare unexpectedly flushed from tall grass.

I laughed. "Did you cast some sort of spell upon him?"

Holmes smiled in return as we neared our door. "I signaled for him to have Wiggins drop by at his earliest convenience."

"All that from a one-second wiggling of your fingers."

"Those boys are sharp," Holmes countered. "You wouldn't be surprised to observe a shepherd direct his dog with such abstruse and miniscule signals."

"Not at all. I have seen such a thing many times, and it is endlessly fascinating and admirable. But surely you aren't comparing your Irregulars to canines – even the most intelligent of them?"

"Not at all. Rather to the contrary: If a smart dog can understand so much from so little, and with such focused intensity, then the Irregulars, who are intelligent but simply do not have the chance to make use of it, are exponentially wiser than the dogs. And now, we have returned. Shall it be tea or whisky?"

I opted for neither, asking Mrs. Hudson to bring up a pot of strong coffee. I suspected that I would sleep well that night, regardless of its stimulating effect so late in the day. Holmes indicated that she should prepare enough for the both of us, and within a few minutes, I was back in my armchair from whence I had departed several hours earlier – my haven from the trials of the world. Meanwhile, Holmes added coal to the fire, knocking back some of the chill that had worked into my bones.

Mrs. Hudson wasn't satisfied to simply bring a hot beverage, and soon after we were enjoying our dinner, consisting of roast beef and various vegetables cleverly prepared with sturdy and tasty herbs. My service in India had opened my appreciation for bolder flavors which Mrs. Hudson was not afraid to provide, and Holmes, indifferent to food, would eat whatever was placed before him – or not, depending upon the day and his mood. That evening, he had a less-than-middling appetite.

We weren't halfway through when the bell rang. There was some conversation down below, and Holmes and I could both imagine its nature: Wiggins had been summoned and wanted to go upstairs immediately, and Mrs. Hudson was leery of the idea. (These were still our first months of residency, but even then her heart was opening to the boys and girls that made up Holmes's unofficial Force. Over the past few months, her innate warmth and goodness had started her slipping them food, or worrying about rips in their tattered garments, holding one or the other back from immediate departure on one of Holmes's errands so that she could sew up some damage or defect. Oh, she would still be stern and gruff, but the

Irregulars saw through it, and understood they had more than one friend in that Baker Street house.

Holmes, never one to overeat, hadn't consumed but a portion of his meal, and when Wiggins entered, Holmes gestured him over to finish what was on the plate. I wondered if Mrs. Hudson would realize what had happened, or if she would think that this was one of those days when Holmes was truly hungry. The boy was grateful, and had finished the entirety of the serving before I'd loaded two more bites.

At that time, I'd only known Wiggins for seven or eight months, and in my mind he was more of a curiosity than anything – and I'm sure he thought the same of me. He'd met Holmes in the mid-1870's, when Holmes had first come up to London to pursue his unusual calling. This was still the *first* Wiggins, the original young fellow that was part of Holmes's initial recruits. Over time, he had earned the right of leadership over the Irregulars. There were many other Wiggins-es through the years, all of the same family and spread over several generations, who filled roles in that group. As I would learn many years later, * Holmes had rescued this particular Wiggins' mother from a charge of murder during the time he resided at No. 24 Montague Street, and the family in return seemed to have made some sort of oath or pledge of service to him. And this arrangement went both ways, as Holmes took it upon himself to see that the Irregulars were fed and clothed and educated, even when he could sometimes ill afford it, and when they reached an older age, past their usefulness as his agents, he found them jobs or apprenticeships or scholarships for further education, drawing upon favors owed to him by men and women up and down the social stratum.

This specific Wiggins, the first of his position, was still wary of me, possibly because of the unusual notion that Holmes might include someone else in his investigations. While living in Montague Street, Holmes had lived a rather solitary existence – monastic, as I pictured it – devoting his time to either investigatory work, or educating himself so that he would be better prepared for more investigatory work. He'd held to that pattern for several months after we began sharing lodgings in Baker Street, and it was only by merest chance that one morning in early March he'd unexpectedly and impulsively asked me to join him when summoned by the Yard to the murder investigation that I'd later attempted to chronicle.

When Wiggins has finished eating – the work of just a moment – he stepped back to the center of the room and presented himself for orders, standing at what he thought was attention. Holmes waved him to the basket chair, and I joined them before the comfortable fire, having finished my own satisfying repast. As I settled, Holmes asked the boy, "What do you know of Abel Farris?"

I'm not sure what question Wiggins expected, but this didn't seem to surprise him. He was rarely surprised, having seen so much already. "He's of no account," he replied promptly, twisting his head slightly sideways. I was reminded of the alert sheep dogs to which the Irregulars had been compared but an hour or so earlier. "Oh, he wants to be important, and he's gathered together six or eight little 'bunnies', as we call them – too harmless to make any difference one way or the other – to trail along after him. They try and bluster around the Dials, but it's only their good luck that they haven't gotten themselves cut up before now – but just because they haven't been worth the effort so far."

Holmes nodded. "That was my opinion as well, but I wanted to confirm that Farris hadn't elevated himself to the next level of mischief."

"No. There's a lot of others who are higher on that ladder, and they won't let anyone climb above them."

"What have you heard of the Green Street job?"

"The stolen plate over in Mayfair? Not very much. That kind of thing is rather above my head, you know. Is Abel mixed up in that?"

"We received information that he might be. What about Reuben Huff? Have you ever heard of him?"

Wiggins frowned, considering one after another of the myriad of Londoners that he'd internally indexed. "Possibly," he answered after a moment. "Fourteen or sixteen, maybe. One of the bunnies. If he's the one I think, he's run with Abel for a couple of months. Pretty boy – way too soft for whatever he's wading into."

I had trouble picturing a son of Foxy Huff as a "pretty boy", but life played many tricks. Perhaps Huff only thought Reuben was his son . . . .

"Yes, that's probably him," replied Holmes. He looked around for his pipe, where he'd left it on the side table. Beginning that complicated ritual pipe smokers will understand, he recounted our discussion with Foxy Huff, and the story told to us – the meeting on the following night to deliver some of the stolen plate, and the expected presence there of both Farris and Reuben Huff."

"I know Foxy," scoffed Wiggins. "If his mouth is moving, he's lying. What's his game, then?"

"That's what we intend to find out," Holmes answered. "I want you to learn more about Abel Farris and Reuben Huff. I'll poke into a few places myself and see what I can find. The usual rates."

Wiggins didn't need to receive a more finely drawn plan. He rarely did, which made him a most-effective lieutenant in charge of Holmes's roving eyes and ears. They arranged how to communicate the following day – where to meet or send messages, as Holmes expected to be out – and then the boy was gone, his feet pattering down the stairs. The front door, however, did not immediately slam, which led me to assume that Wiggins had paused to speak with Mrs. Hudson. Likely she had delayed him to provide some further left-overs of her own.

After Wiggins took his leave, Holmes settled deeper into his chair, the first of several pipes that night aiding in his cogitations. While still staring into the fire, he spoke.

"Sir Norman's stolen plate is just the latest in a number of similar thefts. Many of the stolen items used to belong to the Crown – art and coronets and objects and silver plate – that were shifted to various families over the years as collateral for loans, or as outright sales, to bridge some Royal over a financial chasm. Sometimes the Royal personage is able to redeem the pledge, or buy it back. On other occasions, in order to curry favor, the item is returned for free, and the loan forgivin and forgotten. But every once in a while, someone like Sir Norman Devere refuses to return the item for any reason. Sir Norman is of an age where he has no interest in currying Royal favor, and the high-handedness of the recent demands has rubbed him the wrong way.

"Which brings us to Jimmy Farraday. He's the illegitimate son of one of the Queen's coachmen, Cyrus Blair – a relationship that neither publicly claims. On the surface, the coachman is above reproach, although I've been assured by someone within the Government whose information is always reliable that there's a rotten spot in old Cyrus, although it's ignored by that peculiar freemasonry of his profession and position. In fact, he does very little to collect his pay, spending his time lounging about and holding court with his cronies. When certain dark and illicit tasks must be carried out to further the ends of Our Betters, Cyrus is the man they summon – and he in turn counts on his son Jimmy to complete the dirtier aspects of the job.

"Cyrus is able to function in this murky area between the law and the desire of some of the nobility who must have their wishes satisfied, and too many look the other way. Recently there has been a marked surge in the reclamation of items like the Sheffield Plate from people like Sir Norman. The unofficial and secret position within some of the noble lines seems to be that if these items cannot be retrieved legally, then other methods are authorized – for it is their right. All indications are that Cyrus and Jimmy Farraday are responsible for the actual thefts, working under the protection of some minor noble who has taken it upon himself to go after every object that the different houses want back. He's likely taken on this task as a way to win favor from those higher on the hill than him for his own purposes.

"It was my Government contact who arranged to have me called in last Friday following the theft of Sir Norman Devere's treasures."

I had heard Holmes mention this mysterious "contact" on several occasions, but it was obvious from his caginess when describing him that he had no plans to share this person's identity with me – and I could hardly blame him. Holmes obviously felt that information provided by the man was utterly reliable, and I already knew of at least a half-dozen cases where Holmes had been recruited to assist this individual on some discreet and urgent task – after which, he would comment that this person often provided him with some of his most interesting cases.

"In the past," Holmes continued, "Blair and Farraday have carried out several ambitious jobs, and quite a few more just recently, and they've never been caught – although their involvement is without question. The Peck-Memorial Methodist Chalice theft. The destruction of the Morningside *droit de seigneur*. The Lambert Farm deed, in which that cruel and corrupt family finally received their just deserts – showing that all of their thefts weren't necessarily bad, though still illegal. Cyrus has a crafty cunning – he's the planner, and the go-between to his noble clients – while Jimmy has a cruel and violent streak that he uses to control his myrmidons with absolute authority – even rough and broken pieces like Foxy Huff. They each have a specific function – acting as a single cog in the machine – and this division of labor has worked with notable success. Now, by way of my contact, I'm finally been given my own chance to have a crack at him. My contact – rather on his own initiative – feels that this has gone on too long.

"It didn't take me long to get a line on what had happened regarding the theft of Sir Norman's objects. Then, as events are moving toward their conclusion, we were unexpectedly intercepted by Foxy Huff. That's the part that makes no sense – and will need further thought."

He finally glanced away from the fire to where I sat. "I shall see you in the morning, Watson." And then he returned to his ruminations.

I could have remained there, sitting quietly and about my own business, but – in spite of the coffee – I was weary, and adjourned upstairs to my room, and soon to sleep.

Chapter IV

The next day, a cold rain had descended upon the city, giving my room a damp and unpleasant feeling. I dressed quickly and went downstairs to find that Holmes had already departed. Mrs. Hudson reported that he'd left soon after seven, "dressed up in that ostler getup he favors," she lamented as she set down my breakfast tray. "He did want me to make sure you saw his note."

In fact, I hadn't seen it, but only because I hadn't yet looked toward my armchair, where a folded sheet was propped.

> *Watson,*
>
> *If you wish to get out and move around, find out about Reuben Huff. The family resides at No. 4 Millman Street, south of the Great Ormond intersection, at the far end from the Foundling Hospital. Discretion is the watchword – perhaps you might present yourself as a doctor consulting at the hospital, and proceed from there . . . ?*
>
> *Wiggins has already given me a description of the family, and whatever else you provide will be additionally useful.*
>
> *Acres will collect you in Baker Street at nine p.m. for the conclusions.*
>
> *SH*

I wondered what else Holmes needed about the Huff family that Wiggins hadn't already reported. I didn't think that he would involve me in a pointless task simply to get me out and about, especially on such a rainy and unpleasant autumn day. The note was written as if to give me some choice in the matter – "*If you wish to get out and move around*" – but Holmes knew me well enough by then to understand that with such a specifically suggested task, of course I would go. The only question was how I would present myself. It must be recalled that this was early in our association, and was not nearly as experienced in carrying out certain aspects of investigations independently. I did, however, have the confidence of being a doctor – of walking into situations without any foreknowledge or preconceived notions, and with the presence of occasional danger as well, prepared to ask questions. Armed with my medical bag and service revolver, I departed an hour later, finding a hansom to take me to Bloomsbury.

I had read that Millman Street was named after a famed seventeenth-century landowner, but looking around at the conditions, I wondered what he would think, having his name and legacy tied to an area of this condition. It did not sink to the stink and squalor of many East End domains, but there was an uneasy feel to the place, even in daylight. I would not want to traverse the area at night if it could be avoided.

I began at the end of the street, knocking on the door of Number 1 and spinning a tale about being from the nearby Foundling Hospital and searching for whoever might have left a baby there with an anonymous note pinned to the blanket. This fictitious note was written on the back of a torn receipt showing *Millman Street*, but with the house number missing. Did the lady of the house have any knowledge of the wee abandoned child?

It was not the best story that I might have contrived, but it was quickly cobbled together and seemed to get better when I knocked at No. 2 – the lady at No. 1 being sympathetic but having no knowledge of who might help.

No. 2 was unable to assist me, and the same at No. 3. Then I was at No. 4, the home of Foxy Huff and family. I wasn't sure what Holmes wished for me to determine, but I certainly saw a show.

The front of the house was in good-enough condition, and there were flowerboxes beneath the windows, although they were empty at that time of year. Still, they were cleaned out, with no dead plants left to rot despondently through the coming winter months.

A knock at the door revealed a woman in her sixties, looking at me suspiciously. She was too old to be Foxy Huff's wife. Perhaps his mother? I introduced myself and quickly learned that she was the landlady. Three families, besides that of the landlady, were crammed into the building, similar in shape and design to 221 Baker Street, and the Huffs lived on the top floor. The lady was sympathetic to my tale, and while she had no useful information, she allowed that I might interview her tenants.

"But the Coolidges are out for the day, and the Arlingtons are away visiting family, but I believe that the Huffs are at home. Go on up – third floor." The she muttered, "Poor woman."

"What's that?" I asked, aware that it was probably spoken with the intent for me to respond.

"Oh, you'll see, Doctor. And if you might help her a bit . . . ."

I thanked her as she let me inside, trusting that I would soon understand. As I started up the stairs, I was suddenly icy inside, realizing that I hadn't thought this through very well at all. I had pictured knocking on the front door and Mrs. Huff answering, in the same way that women had answered at the first three houses I visited. Instead, I was moving upstairs, deeper into the house, to where I'd been told that "the Huffs are at home". I should have established whether Foxy was also there. Should I knock, hoping that Mrs. Huff alone would answer, without her husband being curious and coming to see who the visitor was? He would almost certainly recognize me from the day before, no matter now nondescript I pictured myself. I'd done nothing to disguise my appearance in the way that Holmes regularly did, and someone in Huff's line would make a point of recognizing people with whom he came in contact – and whom he considered a threat..

Should I wait a few moments in the upper reaches of the house before descending and departing, having done nothing to engage with the Huffs? I sensed that the landlady was listening below. Perhaps I should have a false two-sided conversation before leaving, one floor below the Huff apartment, to give the impression that I had called. But my steady climb had placed me at the Huff's front door without reaching a decision, and with a sigh, and with the hope that Foxy Huff was already away on his own daily business. I decided to complete my mission while also realizing that I might be causing unnecessary complications to Holmes's investigation, I knocked.

In a moment, the door was opened by a small brown-haired woman in her mid-forties, careworn, and with a suspicious manner about her. Behind her, the rooms were dark, and the woman held herself stiffly, as if she were cold. I took a deep breath, relieved that Foxy Huff hadn't opened the door, but realizing that he might be just inside. I began speaking softly, spinning my tale of the foundling child, while I tried to size up what little I could see of the woman. She had some native shrewdness in her expression, but life and its cares had worn her down. There were deep lines bracketing her thin lips, and her eyes were nested in dark puffy bags, themselves surrounded by radiating frown lines. Her hair was thinning and going white in streaks, and I saw the early stages of painful arthritis on the knuckles of her clenched hands.

I hadn't gone far in my story, my voice still low, when the lady's nostrils flared, and an angry spark flared in her eyes.

"You think that Reuben is the father!" she growled, stepping forward into the light of the window on the landing. I backed up a step. "That's why you're here – that little tramp named him as the father, because she knew he'd be too nice to deny it! Well, let me tell you, Caleb Deets is the father! My Reuben has had nothing to do with that girl, except try to be her friend! I told him not to, and look where it's put him! He has his life ahead of him!I won't let any of you tie him up with someone other boy's b-----d!"

She finished speaking, looking at me with antagonism, while my gaze was drawn from her angry expression to the side of her face, marked by a dark and substantial hematoma, fresh and angry, and the size of a man's hand.

"You're hurt," I said, and she flinched.

"No, no. It's nothing. I fell – against the wall. I was clumsy."

"I'm a doctor. Let me look at that – "

"No!" she shrieked, and I was again fearful that Foxy Huff was waiting inside, ready to charge to her defense – or, as I suspected, to deny that he had been the cause of her injury.

"You're here about that girl!" the lady reiterated. Then she cried, "Reuben! *Reuben!*"

She spun and raced back into the apartment, her body leaning forward as if she were a horse straining to gain speed for a jump. Without thinking I followed, fearful that the boy might also be the victim of violence – from his mother – for a reason that might or might not be true. In my haste, the thought that I might encounter Foxy Huff in his own den vanished from my mind.

But he wasn't there, thank Heavens. If he had been, there's no way he would have kept out of the *brouhaha* that followed.

I followed through the cramped front room, observing in passing a worn sofa and a couple of armchairs – one of them Foxy Huff's, no doubt. Then we passed through a narrow kitchen and dining area to the back of the floor, where there were two doors. The one on the right opened to a small dark bedroom. Mrs. Huff banged into the closed door on the left – not much more than a large closet. I could see the shape of someone still abed, and she stepped up to the figure and began to beat upon it with her closed fist, the way one would hammer dust from a rug.

"I told to stay away from that Yates slut!" she growled. "And now this man is here to pin you as the father! You're fourteen years old, Reuben – too young to throw your life away as I did!"

The young man under the covers howled and tried to force himself upright. Meanwhile, I was making every effort to end the chaos that I had inadvertently wrought.

"Mrs. Huff!" I said, trying to catch her flailing arm and pull her back before she did her son a permanent injury. "Mrs. Huff! You misunderstand – A babe was left at the hospital, and Millman Street was written on the note. We're simply asking if someone on the street might know in which house a child was expected."

Finally she seemed to calm down, looking at me and blinking while her breathing slowed. She really had worked herself into quite a state. Meanwhile, Reuben had extricated himself from the bedclothes and found his footing, standing beside us, but poised as if to flee through the doorway. Only then was I able to get a look at him.

Reuben was a slight fellow, with no muscles to him at all, and there was a cringiness about him too, as if he went much of the time fearing the types of beatings that his mother had just delivered – and from her bruises, received as well. I wondered if a medical examination would reveal bruising on his body – for there was none apparent on his face. There seemed to be a legacy of violence within this little family. He was quite a handsome lad with thick Byronic hair, and I could see that he would attract the attention of the young ladies.

The mother started to work herself up again, so I spoke over here. "Young man, are you aware of any women in the neighborhood who have been expecting? Who would have given birth in the last day or so?" As I spent more time subsumed in my role, the vision of this fictitious woman and baby were becoming more and more real in my mind.

Reuben Huff shook his head. "No," he said softly. "Ain't seen nothing like that." He looked at a pile of clothing on the floor, and then at his mother. "Can I get dressed?"

"You stay away from Amy Dillon!" she said with a growl. "She's a tramp, that one is. How many times . . . ?"

I extricated myself, and I don't think they knew I was leaving. I pulled the door shut and went quickly downstairs, where the landlady waited, an unspoken question upon her lips. I think she wanted to gossip, but I'd had enough, simply my head and passing by. Outside, I considered knocking on Number 5, in case anyone wondered why I didn't continue my quest down the street, but I was weary of it, and surely if the landlady saw that I didn't immediately go to the next house, she might think I needed time to find a pub and recover.

I walked for a bit until I found a hansom in Russell Square. I don't know what Holmes wanted me to see, but at least I had something to report, and I'd fortunately avoided getting caught by Foxy Huff.

## Chapter V

The rest of the day was spent in my chair. The rain outside stopped, but it was likely to return, and colder air had followed, with a wind that rattled the windows in their frames. I both dreaded going back out in it that night, and also I looked forward to participating in whatever was arranged to conclude Holmes's case.

*Nine o'clock*, Holmes's message had said. There were no other instructions, but I understood without being told that I should bring my service revolver. It was a lesson that was becoming more apparent whenever I joined an investigation.

At the appointed time, the cab arrived as planned. It was a driver with whom I was somewhat familiar – Creighton Acres – but I wasn't yet on the friendly terms with him that would be achieved in later years when Holmes and I rescued his sainted mother from a "Ladies Deposit" scheme of the sort popularized by Adele Spitzeder in Germany twenty years earlier – or so Holmes told me at the time, as his encyclopedic knowledge of crime had instantly shown him what we were facing when old Mrs. Acres' dilemma was described.

Holmes was waiting in the hansom, and he was now dressed as himself. Over the past several months, when learning about Holmes's unique profession, I'd heard about his various "hidey-holes", as he called them, squirreled throughout the city. He'd been to one of them to change his clothing.

As we rolled into motion, Holmes asked me about my day.

"I'm not sure what you expected me to find," I said in a few moments by way of concluding my narrative.

"I wanted your opinion of Reuben Huff. I thought that using the cover story, you might find a way to work him into conversation."

"I wouldn't have chosen that route," I responded. "Then I would have implied exactly what his mother quickly assumed: By mentioning him specifically in connection with an abandoned newborn, I would have been spreading the unfounded rumor that he was associated, and likely the fictitious child's father – and his mother's rage would have escalated ten-fold."

"What did you think of her?"

"Downtrodden. Hopeless. Surely her injuries were from a beating – almost certainly from her husband."

"Almost certainly, indeed. What you've told me confirms and augments Wiggins' report. Another of many dark spots on Foxy's low-dwelling character. And the boy? What is your opinion of him?"

"From the little I saw, he seemed to be rather timid and introverted – if one can assume that based on a couple of minutes where he was trying to defend himself against his mother's blows and accusations." I shook my head at the sad waste of it all. "She is a harridan."

"A fitting mate for Foxy," Holmes replied. "Many is the time, I've heard, that he's come home drunk and slept in the street because she refused to let him in. Clearly he exercises some vengeance upon her, when he has the chance. It sounds, at least, as if she's trying to raise her son to be decent, even if her methods are rough."

"And what is your interest in the boy?"

"To see if he's worth saving. It sounds as if might be."

At that point, I noticed that we seemed to be going in an unexpected direction. "This isn't the way to the St. Giles Workhouse."

"No, we have a different rendezvous to observe tonight."

I could see that he wasn't in the mood to share information, so I resolved – as was so often my lot – to wait until we arrived at our destination. At one point, we crossed the dark river, and the wind, which had been gusting throughout, rocked the hansom as we were suddenly exposed on the bridge, out of the protection of the various streets along our route. Finally noticing my interest in our route, Holmes explained, "Waterloo Bridge. We'll be observing a meeting in Howley Place, just on the other side."

And in a moment, Acres had stopped the horse in a dark stretch far from any gas lamps. Holmes and I slipped out, leaving the cab to wait for us while we melted into a side street, our eyes adjusting to the black night which denied us even the light of a star.

Holmes pulled my sleeve when I seemed to hesitate where to step, and in a moment we were in an areaway across from a humble dwelling. There was a sole light on the first floor, and I tried not to stare at it, preserving my night vision. A pair of dark shapes greeted us, one a constable, and the other speaking to reveal itself as Inspector Gregson.

"They're inside, as you advised us," he said. "We're cutting it close – we should conduct the raid now."

"Sorry I was late," replied Holmes. "I had to make sure my own agents were informed and in place, and then I'd arranged to swing by Baker Street and bring Watson."

I almost felt like apologizing – hoping that Holmes needn't feel obligated to include me if it meant some aspect of the operation might stumble and fail. But before I could speak, Gregson seemed to take Holmes's comment as agreement and gave a signal – putting a couple of fingers to his lips, he produced a soft but clear whistle which was apparently enough to spread the word to all quarters, for as we moved, I sensed other bodies doing the same to our right and left.

The front door was forced open, the building quickly secured to all sides, and in less than a minute we had gone from our coal-black place of concealment to an upstairs sitting room, where four men were taken without incident, fully shocked at our presence to the point of paralysis. Then one who I recognized began to curse – his tone flat and even and steady, never rising in apparent anger, but with his gaze fixed steadily upon Sherlock Holmes while using terms that I'd rarely heard, even from the roughest of men in the heat of bitter combat.

"I was warned of you," said Mr. Stephen Bedfield, a well-known Society figure who was quite visible about the capital and in the press. About forty and very well dressed, he was one of the more-wealthy minor nobles in the land. "They said you might be called in to investigate." He glanced at a much rougher man sitting across a small round table. "You did this, Farraday – you and your carelessness."

"Me?" was the angry response. "I didn't do anything wrong! Same as before – it's never gone wrong before."

"Perhaps," said the well-dressed fellow to Bedfield's right, "it might be best for no one to say anything."

Bedfield shook his head. "My attorney," he explained.

"Indeed," responded Holmes. "How nice of you to also fall into our net, Mr. Tennison. I had no hope that we'd pin you as well."

"Mr. Holmes," said Tennison, "you would be well advised to keep your slanderous comments to yourself – "

"What he's trying to say," interrupted Bedfield, "is that you've jumped in far over your head this time, Holmes. And you as well, Inspector – Gregson, isn't it? Make a note of that, Tennison. Neither of you have any idea of the support behind me. Some of the most important families want their artifacts returned, and they're tired of waiting through the tedious and fruitless process of offer and rejection, offer and rejection, or of placing their hopes in the courts. I have accumulated some powerful favors by taking care of things quickly and efficiently, and I can call in any one of them and make this incident go away – as will your professional standing, Inspector, and your freedom, Mr. Holmes. Even though my current agent has failed me – " He cast a contemptuous glance toward Farraday. " – you'll find that no charges will be placed against me – "

"Now hold on," growled Jimmy Farraday. "I did nothing wrong!" It seemed important that he made sure to establish that for which he could not be blamed. "I – "

"Ah, but you did," corrected Holmes. "You did do something wrong. You put your trust in a rotten link like Foxy Huff."

Up to that moment, Huff had been sitting quietly beside his master, the fourth member of the group, his face pale and sick as he contemplated the mire in which he was suddenly pitched up to his chin. But now, when things couldn't have seemed worse, he found that they were.

"What do you mean?" snarled Farraday, twisting suddenly to glare at Huff. Seeing how ill his companion suddenly looked shook his confidence. "What did you do, Foxy?"

"I . . . I . . . ." Words failed the shell of a villain.

"He took it upon himself to try and intervene," explained Holmes with a false friendliness to his tone. "Yesterday, he approached Dr. Watson and myself and tried to get us to believe that his son and some of his associates were responsible for the theft of the Sheffield Plate – and that right now, even as we have this interesting discussion, they would be involved in delivering it to a buyer. But as you can see, Foxy's poor efforts didn't distract us from the real delivery." He gestured toward the center of the table, where the silver objects rested. I was surprised that I hadn't noticed them before, but then I realized that when observing the human

83

drama around the table, the dead and dull collection was of little real interest.

"What?" asked Farraday. "What do you mean – tried to convince you that his son . . . ." He looked back at Foxy Huff, whose slack lips were working, but he produced no sound.

"That's right," said Holmes. "Huff is at a level of comtempt far beneath even a thief like you, Farraday – or you, Mr. Bedfield," added Holmes, glancing toward our inadvertent host. "To deflect suspicion from this meeting here tonight, Foxy came up with the notion to tell us a cock-and-bull story that his son would be behind the St. Giles Workhouse right now to get rid of the plate. He stupidly believed that he could sell me on that idea, and that we would be there now while you meet here in Lambeth. In fact, Inspector Lestrade is waiting in concealment there to pick up Reuben Huff and Abel Farris, and whomever else shows up. We'll determine later just how much they know."

A look of true disgust pulled down Farraday's features. "You cretinous little ---!" he snarled at Huff. "You threw over your own *son*?"

Huff again tried to speak, but just made some kind of soft whiny wheeze, like the passing away of an old and dying mosquito.

If it is not yet obvious, I thought very little indeed of Foxy Huff.

"I said that involving Huff was your mistake," said Holmes, continuing to speak to Farraday, "but that's not entirely accurate. Associating with a low type like Foxy is a mistake in any circumstance, but I was already onto you, and I'd known about this meeting here for a long time. Your sources really aren't that secure, and your father, Cyrus Blair, has become far too smug, complacent, and confident of his invulnerability. I've spent a bit of time with him in disguise over several days – including today – as he bragged about his various crimes, and provided details about tonight's meeting. He's under arrest now, too, even as we speak, and," he said, turning to Bedfield, "I can assure you that whatever power and influence you believe you've achieved has been washed away like the day's manure from the stalls where Cyrus Blair holds court. He's the sort that will throw you over for any promise of saving his own skin. You may have been working for some powerful friends, but you've also made a number of powerful enemies, and they were quite glad when I let them know that we had you, and that you are finally done."

The whole party was relocated across the river, less than a mile by road to Scotland Yard – with some of the group traveling in the back of a Black Maria. As soon as Gregson led Holmes and me to his office, we were joined by Lestrade, and both of them, whose rivalry served to sharpen one another as iron versus steel, began to tell of their respective adventures. We'd shared Gregson's night, but Lestrade's was news to us.

"They were all there, Mr. Holmes – Farris' entire little 'gang' – just as you said they'd be, shuffling around in the dark street behind the workhouse with a shabby goblet from the plate collection in their possession, waiting for someone to come and buy it from them. We approached, and they thought we were the men they were to meet. They waited for us just like those baby seals you hear tell of, not moving, and easy targets for the hunters to club."

"How many did you bag?"

"All six – Able Farris, and the Huff lad, and the others. Farris confirmed we have the whole lot."

"That's excellent. Perhaps this will put a rehabilitative scare into them before they get into worse trouble."

"One would hope so. Farris is a little older – he may be beyond salvage, but the others are younger, and only seem to be trailing after Farris because they have nothing better to do."

Holmes nodded. "I have some contacts, and I'm owed some favors. I'll see what I can do about that."

The next morning, we were back at Scotland Yard when the six members of Abel Farris gang were due to be released. Although they had been in possession of one small piece of the stolen plate collection, it was understood that they had been set up by Foxy Huff.

"I didn't know it was him," explained Farris, who was not much older than the boys he led. "I received a box with the cup, a five-pound note, and instructions about where to take it." He glanced at Reuben Huff, who would only stare at the floor. "If we could do this, we'd be trusted with something bigger. I didn't know that it was Reuben's dad that sent it to me . . . ."

Holmes nodded and then explained his idea – that he had positions lined up for all six of them, either in jobs that could grow to something better over time if they earned their employers' trust, or as apprentices in necessary crafts that would provide them a lifetime of gainful and respectable employment. All of the lads took advantage of the offer, even Farris, and, although the way wasn't always smooth, it was a happy ending for six lads whose stories might have ended in a much darker fashion – particularly if Foxy Huff's plan to sacrifice them had succeeded with no one to explain otherwise.

We were there when Mrs. Huff arrived to claim her wayward son. She recognized me, and wanted to rage in my direction – for she had a great deal of rage to express – before turning her attention upon her son.

But she was instrumental in keeping him on the straight and narrow path, and – with the removal of Foxy Huff from their life – her task was made easier.

When Foxy Huff was brought in – for Holmes wanted to orchestrate a reunion, if for no other reason than to see the performance of a human drama – I feared that Mrs. Huff might give away, forgiving him as she must have done so many other times, disappointment after disappointment after disappointment. After all, she had stayed with her husband through many years of such behaviors, and had allowed him to commit physical violence upon her, if my reasoning was correct. But when it was explained what Huff had done – how he had been willing to allow his own son to go to prison so that he could deflect interest away from Farraday's activities, her noted rage knew no limits. She flew at Huff, adding further scars to his scarred head, and no one made any move to pull her off him until she began to tire.

As that played out, it was rather heartbreaking to see Reuben Huff's face as he fully understood his father's treachery. He simply stared at the man who had sired him, expressionless.

"You understand," said Huff to his son, realizing that he'd now finally done something that was unforgiveable. "It was for all of us – to keep me in good with Mr. Farraday so that I could support the family. And I told Mr. Holmes about it beforehand – Didn't I, Mr. Holmes? – so that you would be picked up and given a light sentence. It was really to help *you*, Reuben! To *save* you! You see that, don't you? That's why I did it! You understand! Right? Right . . . ?"

Reuben Huff was able to escape his father's influence that much quicker when the man was shivved in a prison hallway not long after, to be remembered only by his former wife and son as an object lesson, and as a figure of derision in my notes.

The next morning, Holmes walked into the sitting room to see me in in my chair by the fire and staring toward my desk. After greeting me, he said, "So you've decided to let it lie."

"For now," I murmured, thinking of the effort expended so far into crafting my manuscript. Beyond my desk, I could see through the window where the rains from the day before had returned in excess, running in blurring and changing streaks down the panes.

Holmes nodded, poured a cup of coffee, and then chuckled and muttered for the next ten minutes while opening, sorting, and reading his mail.

He seemed satisfied with the idea that he'd deduced my abandonment of the manuscript, but he was wrong. More than ever, after seeing the drama that a malignant force such as Foxy Huff had brought upon his family, I was convinced that a narrative of Holmes's cases must relate the human element to lift them above some dry treatise – certainly informative for some student of crime, but desiccated when ignoring the underlying motivations. I would just need to wait until such time as the middle portion of the book – properly relating Jefferson Hope's incredible life and why he would spend it in pursuit of revenge – could be adequately told, cladding that skeleton with a different kind of meat.

Later that night when the rains ended, Holmes and I went for another long walk, and we returned to find a doctor from Brook Street, Percy Trevelyan by name, anxious to relate his own unusual story. After that matter was concluded, I was even more convinced that if I were ever to share more of Holmes's investigations with the public, the human aspect must not be ignored.

It would take years to confirm it, but my wary suspicions even then were correct: Holmes was not pleased.

**NOTE**

*    For more about how the Wiggins clan came into Holmes's service, and the saving of Mrs. Wiggins from a capital charge, see "The Gower Street Murder" in *Sherlock Holmes – Skeins* and *The Collected Papers of Sherlock Holmes – Volume II: Records*

# The Adventure of the
# Madman's Sister
## by Tom Turley

Despite his habitual disdain for politicians, as well as foreign potentates, Mr. Sherlock Holmes venerated our late Queen. He esteemed that Royal Lady not for any admirable qualities she personally possessed, but rather for her status as the embodiment and symbol of the British Empire. It was a source of satisfaction to him, therefore, that early in his career he was able to thwart one of the last attempts upon Her Majesty's life. It, like those that had preceded it, came at the hands of a deranged, pathetic individual who (as Holmes remarked) had sought to victimise Victoria for the manifold miseries of his own existence. Thanks to my friend's efforts, the would-be murderer was denied even the notoriety his predecessors had achieved, and his name never came before the public. Yet, Walter Jarrett's story was a tragic one, which I shall belatedly undertake to tell.

It began, for us, on a cold and rainy morning, the last day of December, 1881. I was installed before the fire, as dampish weather invariably made my wounded shoulder ache. Holmes was prowling restlessly about our sitting room, muttering at the lack of interest in the newsprint scattered on the floor. I began to fear a coming relapse to the cocaine-bottle, so my friend's excitement when we heard the bell was matched by my relief.

"A young lady to see you, Mr. Holmes," announced Mrs. Hudson, after a preliminary knock. "Shall I show her up?" Having by then a year's experience with her eccentric lodger, she had not done so at once, but entered instead to clear away the remnants of our breakfast. Holmes had dived into his bedroom. He now emerged, presentably attired, and joined our landlady in her tidying chore. I rose to do my part as well.

"Would you prefer for me to disappear?" I enquired of the detective, for in those early days my participation in his cases was not to be assumed.

"By no means, Doctor," my friend replied, his good humour quite restored. "I have long noted your interest in young ladies, and I have no wish to deprive you of the latest specimen. Mrs. Hudson," he concluded grandly, "you may show our visitor in."

The "specimen" who entered was perhaps four-and-twenty. Well-dressed, dark-haired, and slender, with classic features and eyes of sapphire blue, she seemed to tremble slightly when Holmes introduced me. I offered her my armchair beside the hearth, and Holmes took his favourite seat across from her. I dropped into the basket chair beside him. The lady's agitation was obviously not due to cold or shyness, for she immediately began to tell her story.

"My name, gentlemen, is Edwina Jarrett. I am presently serving as governess in the household of Sir Harold Caldwell." (I knew him to be prominent Harley Street physician.) "I have come to you, Mr. Holmes, in hope that you can find my brother."

"You are not a native Londoner," the detective observed, appearing to ignore his client's final words. "Your accent, while genteel, shows traces of the West Country – neither Cornwall nor Devonshire, I surmise, but – "

"Somerset." Miss Jarrett answered with more impatience than surprise. "Our family comes from Bristol. My late father, Christopher Jarrett, was well known as a manufacturer of furniture."

"It's a long-established firm," I offered. "Mrs. Hudson has a Jarrett sideboard in her dining room. She considers it the finest piece in her possession."

Holmes evinced no interest in our landlady's furniture. "Yet, as the daughter of this successful cabinet-maker, you have been forced to seek employment as a governess." He raised his eyebrows quizzically. "Why is that, Miss Jarrett?"

I was appalled at my friend's rudeness, but his client seemed to take it in her stride. "Father lost most of his money in a bank collapse," she told us. "Mother died many years ago, so my eldest brother, Charles, inherited the residue. Walter, who is two years my senior, and I have had to make our own way in the world."

"Walter is presumably the missing brother?"

"Yes." Miss Jarrett seemed relieved to speak of him at last. "I'm afraid, Mr. Holmes, that my brother's life has become exceedingly unfortunate. You see, five years ago, while he was still at Oxford, Walter was badly injured on the cricket pitch. His head was gashed, and he suffered a severe concussion. Sir Harold has informed me," she hesitantly added, "that it's likely there was hemorrhage of the brain."

"How terrible!" I murmured. "Such injuries often have long-term effects. Did this happen in your brother's case?"

"I fear so, Dr. Watson." Miss Jarrett gave me a wan smile. "Naturally, Walter left Oxford and came home to recover. He was under a doctor's care for months. His physical injuries healed in time, but mentally my poor brother was simply not the same. He suffered fearfully from headaches, and his personality began to change. He became despondent, and imagined that everyone he knew had turned against him."

"Surely," remarked Sherlock Holmes, "a degree of despondency could be expected in your brother's situation. His health was ruined, and his university career was gone."

"Yes, but there were also symptoms. Walter developed the delusion that his 'enemies' were keeping him from some 'God-appointed task' that he would not reveal. He accused our cook of poisoning his food. He had an odd obsession with the colour blue, saying that it 'belonged' to him. One day two years ago, he physically attacked our brother Charles because he dared to wear a blue cravat."

My friend's grimace was more amused than sympathetic. "And what was the result of this sibling enmity? Was Walter driven from the house?"

"No, but Charles insisted that he be examined by a psychiatric doctor, and he was admitted to Somerset Lunatic Asylum that very afternoon. Our father, who was already ailing, never recovered from the blow. He died before Walter was released."

"So, he *was* released," Holmes confirmed, "and did not escape from the asylum?"

"Oh, yes. Walter did so well there that after six months, he was discharged as cured."

"I'm afraid, Miss Jarrett," I said dubiously, "that a true cure would be unlikely, given the physical injury to your brother's brain."

"I know that *now*," our client replied, a little testily. "But Walter was never given a fair chance. Charles – who had inherited by then, of course – refused to have him in the house. He offered our brother a weekly allowance if he would agree to live elsewhere and not show his face at home again. By that time, as it happened, I had taken my position in London and was unaware of the arrangement until it had occurred."

"Was this allowance adequate for your brother to maintain himself?" asked Holmes.

"Not really, but in Charles's defence he did attempt to find employment for Walter. Sadly, there was very little he was fit to do. His headaches and inability to concentrate made clerical or accounting work impossible, and strenuous manual labour was beyond him. So Walter would drift from job to job. He soon left Bristol and began to wander all around the country, never staying in one place for long. It has been that way for eighteen months now."

"How do you remain in contact with him?" I enquired.

"Oh, he writes to us – to me more often than to Charles – and we send postal orders for his money every week to his last known address. But it seems that Walter often moves on before receiving them. I feel sure my poor brother has rapidly gone from bad to worse." Taking a kerchief from her reticule, our client wiped away the tears that had come into her eyes.

My friend shook his head reproachfully. "This situation is deplorable, Miss Jarrett. Whatever his mental state, the scion of a respectable family cannot be allowed to wander the byways of England as a common vagrant. If nothing else, he should be returned to an asylum, where he can receive at least a minimal amount of care."

The vagrant's sister humbly accepted her reproof. "I know that, Mr. Holmes, and I shall soon be taking steps to remedy the matter. In May, I shall be married to Mr. Ronald Peterson, a young solicitor in Bristol. Ronald has agreed that Walter may make his home with us, or – if that proves to be unworkable – that he shall return to the county asylum in Wells. It's only a few miles from Bristol. We can visit him and contribute to his comfort. Walter was reasonably happy when he was there before."

"And is your brother Charles to accept no responsibility?"

"No, Charles has decided that his own family must take precedence henceforth. He has written telling Walter to expect no further help from him."

"Unconscionable!" growled Holmes. "It seems, Miss Jarrett, that an acceptable solution to your brother's woes is at last on the horizon. After allowing a scandal to endure for eighteen months, what has prompted you to come to me?"

"Well, first she has to *find* her brother," I reminded Holmes.

"Indeed, Dr. Watson, but there is more to my anxiety than that."

Here our client removed from her reticule a letter, somewhat creased and dirty, and handed it to the detective. He briefly scrutinised the envelope. "Postmarked last Friday from Southsea, but there is no return address. Has your brother resided there for long?"

"Since early in the month, I think. Walter told me in a previous letter that he is staying in an inexpensive rooming house. I don't know where. Please read the letter, Mr. Holmes."

My friend did so, and as he progressed his face assumed a look of deep concern. "We must find him soon," he said quietly, and passed the note to me.

Walter Jarrett's letter, which I read aloud, went as follows:

*Dearest Eddie,*

*You will know by now that Charles has cut me off entirely, withholding even the insultingly small sum of 6s per week he has expected me to live on. If not for you, I don't know what I should have done. But it makes no difference now. My enemies are closing in on me again. They pretend to be friendly, only to annoy me publicly on every possible occasion. What chance have I to cope with the millions who are against me? If they don't cease wearing blue, I shall commit murder. I really think I cannot prevent myself having revenge upon the English people. If I cannot commit murder one way, I will another. All I can add is, if there is more difficulty, there may be more victims. By the time you read this, I may be in prison. I don't mind a bit if they hang me.*

*Your loving, but much-tried, brother,*

*Walt*

"We've always called each other 'Eddie' and 'Walt'," said Miss Jarrett, dabbing at her eyes again. Holmes affected not to notice.

"When did you receive this letter?"

"Not until yesterday morning. It must have been delayed."

"Have you consulted the police?"

"Yes, in the afternoon I called at Scotland Yard and spoke to an Inspector Jones."

"Athelney Jones?"

"I believe so, yes."

"*That* imbecile!" My friend's disgust stemmed from a recent case in which "the worst inspector on the force" (as Holmes referred to him) had shown more ineptitude than usual. [1] "Next time, you must ask for Gregson or Lestrade. What action did Jones propose to take?"

"Oh, he talked a great deal but said there was little he could do, as Walter had not yet committed any crime and might be anywhere in England. In the end, he suggested that I come to you."

"Ah," Holmes acknowledged, "that was sensible, at least. Very well, Miss Jarrett," he added, rising to indicate that the interview was over. "For the present, I shall keep this letter, if I may. It would also be useful to have your brother's photograph."

"I have one here." Rummaging once more in her reticule, our client produced Walter Jarrett's likeness. I joined Holmes as he examined it. The portrait showed a dark-haired youth in cricket whites, leaning on his bat and smiling at the camera. "This was taken at Oxford just before the accident," our client sighed, her voice again trembling with emotion.

"I daresay his appearance has altered considerably since then?"

"Oh, indeed. When I last saw Walter, he was much thinner and had grown a mustache. And it's been five years since I've seen that smile!" Here Miss Jarrett gave way to tears, collapsed on our settee, and sobbed into her handkerchief. At my friend's distracted gesture, I helped her to

92

rise and put my arm around her shoulder. She clung to me a moment while regaining her composure.

"You mustn't despair, Miss Jarrett. I'm quite sure Holmes will find poor Walter and restore him to you. Why, he's worth two of Scotland Yard!"

Our client coloured deeply and slipped from my embrace. "Thank you, Dr. Watson, and please forgive my weakness. I appreciate your assistance, Mr. Holmes. Should you require further information from me, please send a note to Sir Harold Caldwell's address. Now, if you will excuse me, I must return to my duties." Before the detective or I could venture a reply, she had fled across our sitting room and vanished through the door.

Holmes and I exchanged a look of mild bemusement.

"Worth *two* of Scotland Yard, Watson?" my friend quizzically enquired. "You might have placed the ratio somewhat higher."

"I wasn't thinking of mathematics," I admitted. "Your client flustered me. You must agree she's very beautiful."

"Very emotional, as well," he sniffed, watching through the window as Miss Jarrett emerged in Baker Street. "Alas, it is the curse of my vocation that I must view my clients as mere factors in a problem. Once I start taking them into my arms, I lose my objectivity." Yet, there was a certain wistfulness in his gaze out our bow window.

"No matter," Holmes concluded, turning to pull the *Bradshaw* from its shelf. "If you would be so kind, look up the trains to Bristol Temple Meads."

"Bristol?" I queried. "But Walter Jarrett's letter came from Southsea."

"Indeed, but although time is of the essence, I must have a better understanding of the man. What time is the next train?"

"There's an express leaving Paddington at half-past-twelve."

"Ah, then we must hurry! You had best pack a bag, Watson, for I intend us to be in Southsea by tomorrow. We're likely to be gone at least two days."

"Where are you off to?" I demanded, for Holmes, his hat in hand, was already heading out the door.

"Scotland Yard," he called up from the stairway, "to find an inspector more competent than Jones. I'll meet you at the station!"

"More competent than Jones?" I muttered. "That would apply to all of them!" With that unkind remark, I began climbing the stairs to my bedroom and my Gladstone bag.

Throughout most of our long detective partnership, Sherlock Holmes was extremely reluctant to reveal his plans. His reticence didn't apply, however, to this early case, one of the first in which I was entrusted with an independent role. My friend sought to employ my medical credentials to obtain more information concerning Walter Jarrett's madness. My assignment was to visit the asylum where Jarrett had been confined and, if permitted, to speak with the doctors who had treated him.

"Had our client not fallen victim to embarrassment," Holmes told me as our express rattled swiftly over the tracks of the Great Western Railway, "I should have asked her to provide a letter of introduction. As it is, you must do without one. I doubt that dissimilation comes easily to you, Watson, but perhaps you could pose as a medical friend of the family. That, in a sense, is true enough."

"What will you be doing in the meantime?"

"Imposing myself on Charles Jarrett. It is time that gentleman was called to account for his callous indifference to his brother's fate. Quite aside from family considerations, he is allowing a potentially dangerous lunatic to roam at large."

Before leaving London, the detective had called upon Lestrade in Scotland Yard. The inspector, whom Holmes considered, along with Gregson, "the best of the professionals", agreed to forward a copy of Walter Jarrett's photograph to the Portsmouth authorities and ask them to begin a search of rooming houses in the poorer quarters. "Any Yarder but Athelney Jones," Holmes grumbled, "would have done so yesterday. Nevertheless, with luck, the police may find Jarrett before we get there tomorrow."

Our train arrived at Bristol Temple Meads shortly after three o'clock. After wishing Holmes a successful interview with Charles Jarrett, I changed platforms to catch a local. Inconveniently, the branch line southward took a circuitous route, so the sun was low on the horizon when I reached the Bath and Somerset Lunatic Asylum outside Wells. Entering the spacious grounds, I found a number of large, two-storey buildings, all constructed of the same brown stone. The original facility had evidently exceeded its capacity, for a cottage ward had been erected near what appeared to be a farm, and a half-completed villa to the north would house perhaps another hundred inmates. There was also a chapel, a cemetery, and (to my surprise) a cricket pitch. The atmosphere, at least for a lunatic asylum, struck me as orderly and cheerful.

I headed for the central building, half-expecting to be turned away. Day was almost done, and the hospital's public hours likely to be over. Indeed, the receptionist was initially unwelcoming. However, upon emphasising my position as a doctor who had come all the way from

London, I was allowed to see the superintendent. This gentleman, while perfectly cordial, declared his inability to help.

"I am new here, Dr. Watson, and I expect the patient you mention – Jarrett, is it? – was discharged prior to my arrival. Let me summon Dr. Hitchins. He is the staff surgeon who interacts primarily with our younger men. Wait in my conference room," he added, nodding towards a door across the corridor, "and I shall send him in."

Dr. Hitchins proved to be a rotund, amiable person in his fifties. He well remembered "young Jarrett" and spoke of him regretfully. "A tragic case," the surgeon sighed. "I feel sure he was once a promising lad. When he came to us, Jarrett suffered from headaches and paranoid delusions. But he soon settled into our routine and improved considerably. Worked hard in the garden and particularly enjoyed cricket – even though, as I was told, his brain injury occurred while playing it. He was quite a skilful batsman."

"Did he have violent tendencies?' I asked, recalling Jarrett's disturbing letter.

"It angered him for anyone to wear the colour blue. I never understood the root of that obsession, but it was an easy trigger to avoid. Otherwise, Jarrett seldom gave us trouble, but he was frequently depressed." The surgeon paused thoughtfully a moment. "There was one other occasion on which he became incensed, if not physically violent. Oddly enough," he smiled, "it had to do with poetry."

"Poetry?"

"Oh, yes, the young man fancied himself a budding poet – although, if I am any judge, that bud should have withered on the vine. But while he was with us, Jarrett wrote an ode in praise of Queen Victoria."

"Indeed?" I laughed. "I don't suppose you remember it?"

"I do recall the ending. It went like this:

*'When history tells of your good reign,*
*They will think of you and say,*
*It's the Queen who made her people happy,*
*By affection and justice, that's how she ruled the sway. "*

"Oh, dear. I hope Her Majesty never had to read the rest of *that!"*

"I'm quite sure she never saw it, for the poem was returned with a curt note stating that Her Majesty never accepted literary offerings of any kind."

"And Jarrett took this rejection badly?"

"Yes, indeed! He roundly d----d the note's writer, as well as Queen Victoria and all her works! I'm afraid," sighed Dr. Hitchins, "that the incident somewhat set back Jarrett's recovery. It was several weeks before the poor fellow regained his previous level of composure."

"But he *did* eventually recover," I responded. "At least sufficiently, I understand, to be discharged some eighteen months ago."

My colleague peered at me uncertainly over his spectacles. "Just why is it, again, Dr. Watson, that you are here?"

I repeated my earlier assurance that I was acting on behalf of Walter Jarrett's sister. "She lives in London now and doesn't see her brother often. She wanted any information you're willing to provide about his time here."

"Oh, yes, the sister. I met her when her brother was admitted. Lovely girl!" Again, Dr. Hitchins briefly lost himself in thought. "Well, I can tell you, sir, that I was not altogether happy to release Jarrett. But we are very overcrowded here – I daresay you saw the new building under construction when you entered – and our new chief, Dr. Wade, is anxious to clear the wards of patients who may do well-enough at home. Most of our inmates come from the workhouse and are utterly without resources. But Jarrett has a wealthy brother, I believe, who should be able to provide for him."

"What degree of home care would he require?" I cautiously queried, hoping to avoid revealing Walter Jarrett's present situation.

"A full-time nurse, ideally. Obviously, good nutrition and pleasant surroundings are prerequisite. But he cannot live independently or without proper supervision."

"And suppose nursing care and your other prerequisites were lacking?"

"My dear Dr. Watson! The effect on the patient would be catastrophic! Why, he might not survive a month, and he would pose a danger to anyone with whom he came in contact. His paranoia and tendency to violence would increase tenfold. You don't mean to tell me the young man isn't being kept at home?"

Our interview ended shortly afterwards, with my assurance that every effort was being made to find Jarrett, and Dr. Hitchins' assurance that, once found, he would make every effort to have his former patient readmitted.

Darkness had fallen by the time I left. My leg, still weak from a wound at Maiwand, began to trouble me on the walk to the station, and I arrived barely in time for the last train to Bristol. Holmes was waiting on the platform at Temple Meads, having secured rooms for us at the nearby Grand Hotel. I was eager to recount my mission and to enquire as to his own success. To my surprise, however, the detective declined to discuss the case.

"It's been a long and trying day, Watson, and I feel the need to clear my mind. Happily, there is a concert at the hotel tonight. Brodsky's ensemble is playing a late Beethoven string quartet. A quiet dinner, I believe, followed by communion with the Master, will be the best remedy to restore my frazzled nerves."

And so, instead of rehearsing the morbid delusions of a madman, I spent that last December evening beside the only genius I had ever known, watching as he sat (eyes closed in blissful concentration) enjoying the last melodic musings of an even greater mind. It was evident that I still had much to learn about my enigmatic friend.

On an early train the Portsmouth the next morning, Holmes listened with interest to my report on Walter Jarrett's six months in the asylum. He was pleased to learn that Dr. Hitchins concurred with his own view that the patient would better have remained there. Moreover, my friend took the tale of Jarrett's rejected ode to Queen Victoria far more seriously than I had.

"Lunatics, so I am told, often fixate upon some prominent individual as the object of their adoration. Should their love fail to be reciprocated – as is inevitable, of course – that emotion may turn rapidly to hate. Like Jarrett's letter, it is a disturbing sign. Believe me, Watson, I shall feel much easier in my mind when that gentleman is back in custody."

"Is Charles Jarrett willing to assist us?

"My weariness last night was the outcome of that interview." The detective stared moodily out the window before turning back to me. "My enquiries revealed that the senior Jarrett lives in Clifton, one of Bristol's more affluent sections. His residence in Waterloo Street is a handsome Georgian townhouse, which he presumably inherited. Mentioning our client won me entrance there, but from the moment I spoke of Walter Jarrett, my welcome was rescinded, and I was quickly shown the door. Charles made it clear that he accepts no responsibility for his brother's actions or his welfare."

"Has he no sense of public duty?" I bristled. "Not to mention family feeling!"

"I fear," Holmes answered wryly, "that his attitude is much like that of his counterpart in the parable of the Prodigal Son. Charles, it seems, was required to stay home and help his father run the family business. Walter was indulged in childhood and sent to university. There was no love lost between the two before the accident, and now . . . ."

"The bounder should be horsewhipped!"

"Do not imagine, Watson, that Charles Jarrett has heard the last of me. Still, there is no point in fighting that battle until Brother Walter has been found. If we succeed in our endeavour, all may yet be well."

By now, having left behind one of Britain's great seaports, our express was entering an even greater one. We arrived in late morning at the terminal in Portsmouth and took a tram to the Southsea Police Station at the junction of Victoria and Albert Roads. My friend approached the stolid-looking desk sergeant and announced:

"I am Sherlock Holmes."

In future years, that name would ensure the instantaneous co-operation of any police officer within the British Isles. But at the time, few law enforcement agencies outside of Greater London had heard of Sherlock Holmes. The heavy features of the man before us showed no change in expression, though he did condescend to raise his eyes.

"Lucky you! I'm Sergeant Wilson. How may I help you gentlemen?"

Holmes retained his equanimity. "Yesterday, Inspector Lestrade of Scotland Yard sent your department the photograph of Walter Jarrett, a man we wish to trace. We believe he is living here in Southsea. Have you found him?"

"*You're* no Yarder, sir."

"I am a consulting detective, acting on behalf of Walter Jarrett's sister. This is my friend and colleague, Dr. Watson."

"A sister, eh?" The sergeant nodded wisely. "Well, there would be, wouldn't there, for two young fellows like you to get involved."

"Confound your impertinence!" snapped Holmes. A few years on, he and I wouldn't be subject to such chaffing, but on this first day of 1882 we were still in the latter years of youth. Sergeant Wilson's bland demeanour didn't alter, but a satirical gleam had come into his eye. Then he bellowed deafeningly, "*Allen!*"

A callow, eager-looking constable appeared. "Yes, Sergeant?"

"Gentlemen, this is Constable Allen. He and his mate Meadows were assigned to look for your missing man, Jarrett. Did you find him, Constable?"

"Well, Sarge, we did – and then we didn't!" Beside me, my friend stifled an impatient growl. The desk sergeant, for his part, couldn't repress a smirk.

"What do you mean, Allen? Explain yourself to these good gentlemen."

"Jarrett," the young constable responded, "had been staying at Mother Swanson's rooming house. But he left and set out for London a week ago tomorrow."

"On the twenty-sixth, you mean," said Holmes. "Did he go by train?"

"Oh, no, sir. He was walking it, so Mother Swanson said."

"He *walked* to London?" I couldn't help exclaiming. "Why, it must be eighty miles!"

"Seventy-four, to be precise," my friend corrected, his previous irritation overcome. "A man who walks the roads habitually could set out on a morning and arrive late the next afternoon. But he is evidently a very *poor* man, Doctor. Miss Jarrett's concern for her brother's well-being seems amply justified.

"Now, Constable," he asked our informant, "where can we find this Mother Swanson and her rooming house?"

"Straight down Victoria, sir," Constable Allen answered promptly, "until you come to Clarendon Road." He went on to chart a route that eventually led us to an obscure byway above the South Parade Pier. It looked vaguely familiar, for I had spent holidays in Southsea during my days at Wellington and Netley. As we observed the beach and lowering clouds before us, I pointed out several well-remembered sights to Holmes: The great fortress built by old King Henry, from which he watched the sinking of the *Mary Rose*, [2] the grand new pavilion on the pier, only half-completed the last time I saw it, and the shoreline of the Isle of Wight, looming dimly across two miles of sea. My friend's minimal responses indicated that scenery and history were two more subjects denied space in his "brain attic".

We came at last to Mother Swanson's, a small, two-storey terrace house, the last in its row. With clean white walls, large windows, and a fine view of the Solent, it must have been a pleasant refuge for the wandering Jarrett. The woman who greeted us was worthy of her appellation: Stout, middle-aged, and kindly-looking. From the fragrant odor wafting through the door, I was led to hope the mid-day meal was waiting.

"Good day and welcome, gentlemen! Come to spend a few days at the seaside? Well, you're just in luck. My only other lodger left this morning, so I've rooms prepared for both of you. Come in and join me for luncheon. A nice fish chowder's warming on the stove."

To my disappointment, Holmes declined this invitation. "Thank you, dear lady," he replied, with a suavity he employed for older members of the female sex. "Regrettably, we haven't come to stay. We wish to speak with you about another of your lodgers, a young man named Jarrett. I understand he left your house for London a week ago tomorrow?"

"If you know that, sir, why have you come to me?" Mother Swanson enquired less cordially. "I've no time for idle chit-chat. You aren't coppers, are you?" she added, with a suspicious look at me. I decided to be forthright.

99

"No, Mistress Swanson, I'm a doctor. My name is John Watson. This is my friend, the detective Sherlock Holmes. We're trying to find Walter Jarrett because – to be frank – we believe that he is mentally unbalanced, and possibly dangerous as well. His sister, Miss Edwina Jarrett, is most concerned about his welfare."

"A doctor, you say?" Mother Swanson weighed this revelation, then stepped back and showed us into her simple, sunlit parlour. "You'd best come in, gentlemen. Take that divan before the hearth. I'm sorry I haven't lit the fire, but this room's had the sun all morning. Let me fetch us all a mug of beer. The chowder isn't quite ready." Holmes and I had hardly exchanged surprised glances before our hostess returned with a tray. After distributing the beer, she took the rocking chair across from us.

"It's sad to think young Walter might be dangerous. He seemed a nice lad in his way, though I could tell there were loose tiles on the roof!"

Holmes, restored to his element, began the questioning. "How long was he here?"

"Oh, just under a fortnight. He was short the cost of the lodging, but he told me he was employed as a writer for *The West Sussex Gazette*. I didn't believe a word of it. He was too shabby for *that* kind of job. But he paid the rest before the week was out – said he'd had the money from his sister."

"How did Walter occupy his time?" I enquired curiously.

"At first, he'd wander the town looking for work, but there's none to be had, it being out of season. Later, he said he spent most days walking on the beach, or looking at the Isle across the Solent. That I could believe, for he'd be half-frozen when he'd come in at night. It's main cold and windy here in December, and he hadn't any kind of proper coat."

"You say he spent time gazing at the Isle of Wight," the detective noted. "Did he tell you the reason for his interest?"

"Why, Osborne House!" Mother Swanson laughed, referring to her Isle of Wight residence. "Walter boasted that he was the Queen's most loyal subject. It thrilled him to think that she was just over the water. He asked if Her Majesty ever came to Southsea – if he might meet her one day strolling on the beach! Poor boy: That's when I realised he'd gone soft in the head."

"Yes," I began. "We learned he even wrote – "

Holmes lifted a forestalling hand. "Did Jarrett ever attempt to go to Osborne?"

"No, but he walked to Gosport when he heard the Queen was to take the train from there to London. They turned him away at the dockyard. It was the first time," our hostess sighed, "that I'd seen Walter angry."

Noting my friend's severe countenance, she added pleadingly, "You mustn't get the wrong idea about him, Mr. Holmes. Much of the time, unless his head was hurting him, Walter was as pleasant a young man as you could wish to meet. He had a little concertina that he'd bought in Brighton, and he'd play for me and Hooker – he was another of my lodgers – on our evenings 'round the fire. There were brains in his head, too, for all that they were addled. Why, Walter used to lecture us on 'political economy' (Whatever *that* may be!) unless I made him hush."

"But something about Jarrett worried you," Holmes insisted. "As Shakespeare says, '*The lady doth protest too much.*'"

"Aye," admitted Mother Swanson mournfully. "The morning Walter left, he bought a pistol. Must have used the few shillings I paid him for his concertina. I didn't know it 'til I met Jem Fields, who's got the pawnshop 'round the corner, that same afternoon.

"'Your lodger bought hisself that old Belgian six-shooter I had,' Jem told me. 'Likely he'll blow off his own head.'

"'Why'd he want a pistol, Jem?' I asked him.

"'That was the barmy part,' says Jem. 'Said he had a "God-appointed mission" to fulfill. *God-appointed mission!* A beefsteak woulda done that lad more good than any pistol.'

"'You tellin' me I don't feed my lodgers, Jem?' I says to him. 'Well, you know – '"

But Holmes sprang to his feet, cutting off this anecdote. "Watson, we must take the first train back to London!" He moved for the door, then, recollecting, turned back to our hostess and produced a smile. "Many thanks for your co-operation, Mistress Swanson. You may have performed an invaluable service to The Crown. Please allow me to . . . ." He began groping in his waistcoat pocket.

"A gold sovereign!" Mother Swanson marvelled, when my friend achieved the object of his search. "Well, put it back in your pocket, Mr. Holmes, for all I require is a few more minutes of your time. The next train to Waterloo don't leave for another hour. Now, come into my kitchen and have a bowl of chowder. Then I'd like a word with Dr. Watson."

So, while the detective fumed impatiently in her front room, I held a consultation with Mother Swanson on a matter I shall not record. [3] Happily, I was able to lay her fears to rest, and we parted company with the assurance that Sherlock Holmes and I would always have a place to stay when we returned to Southsea.

Before we left Portsmouth, Holmes telegraphed Lestrade to begin a city-wide search for Walter Jarrett. He reported that the wandering lunatic was armed, and intimated that "a certain august person" was conceivably at risk. Our train pulled into Waterloo by early evening, and we returned immediately to Baker Street. Inside our sitting room, we found a cold collation laid out for our supper.

My friend also sent a note to our fair client, asking her to call on us as quickly as she could. "Finding one vagrant in a city of four millions [7] is virtually impossible," said Holmes. "Jarrett's sister may have some idea where he would go. Perhaps he will attempt to visit her. Were our quarry thinking rationally, he would seek to lose himself in the anonymity of Stepney or Whitechapel. However, given the nature of his mania, Jarrett will likely lurk around the royal palaces, where Her Majesty will eventually appear."

There was, the detective reluctantly admitted, nothing we could do before tomorrow. I was weary from our travels, so after supper I climbed the stairs to my bedroom. It was, alas, quite some time before I slept. Late into the night, I could hear my friend sawing out improvisations on his violin, as he often did to soothe his nerves. On this occasion, I forbore to complain that his renditions failed to soothe my own.

Early the next morning (the second of January), I came downstairs to find Holmes already dressed as a common labourer, with tousled hair, ragged clothing, and a pasted-on mustache. It wasn't my first experience with his disguises, and I had seen him convincingly descend below his class. Even so, I wondered what was in the offing.

"Do you intend to plumb the drains?" I asked facetiously.

My friend acknowledged the quip with a sarcastic smile. "No, I'm off to Westminster. According to *The Times*, the Queen will hold a drawing room today at Buckingham Palace, where she has been since Saturday, before returning in late afternoon to Windsor. There are always crowds about the palace. Lacking any other idea of his whereabouts, it's as good a place as any to start looking for Jarrett."

"I regret to say, Holmes, that your attire won't pass muster at a drawing room."

"This is no time for pawky humour, Doctor! My intention is to mingle with the crowd outside, identify Jarrett if he is there, and alert a policeman to his presence. In this guise, I can approach him far more easily than as myself. I'll ask Lestrade to put extra constables on duty to assist me."

Whatever the merits of this plan, the detective wasn't destined to pursue it. We heard the bell just at that moment. A familiar voice spoke briefly to our landlady, and there came a clatter of footsteps on the stairs.

"Lestrade," I said to Holmes.

"And a young woman, judging by her step. No doubt it's Miss Jarrett answering my summons." He opened the door to find his judgement verified.

"Mr. Holmes?" Our client's lovely face expressed surprise. "I hardly recognised you."

"Oh, it's him, all right," laughed the little inspector. "I've failed to know him more than once in his outlandish get-ups. What's the occasion this time, Mr. Holmes?"

"An idea now superseded by your timely arrival," my friend replied with satisfaction. 'Good morning, Miss Jarrett. Please take that chair while I restore myself to a respectable appearance. Watson, perhaps you could stoke the fire."

After extending greetings to our visitors, I performed the necessary service. Holmes returned, properly dressed, in a remarkably short time and took his usual chair.

"Now, what new development has brought you here this morning?" His expectant gaze alternated between his client and the Yarder.

"Mr. Holmes," quavered Miss Jarrett, as though again suppressing her emotions, "I have had another letter from my brother. It arrived in the early mail and, as you instructed, I went straight to Inspector Lestrade at Scotland Yard."

"And I brought her straight to you," the inspector said complacently.

In his eagerness, Holmes almost snatched the letter from his client's hand. He read its postmark with a cry of glee. "Ha! Posted last night from Windsor. We've got him, Watson! We've got him!" Without removing the letter from its envelope, he passed it to me. Rather dumbfounded, I returned it to its addressee.

"What do you mean?" enquired Lestrade. "I don't follow, Mr. Holmes. Windsor's a smaller place than London, obviously, so our search is greatly narrowed. But we still have to find Jarrett."

"There's no need to, now, Inspector." Smiling at our puzzled frowns, the detective added patiently, "I'll explain in a moment. In the meantime, Miss Jarrett, please read us what your brother had to say."

"I fear," our client sighed, "that this letter is even more disturbing than his last one." Her hands trembled as she took the folded page from the envelope and, with an apologetic smile, handed them to me. "If you would, please, Dr. Watson. I really cannot bring myself to say the words aloud."

I read aloud the following note. It was post-dated and began without a salutation:

*I should not have done this crime had my brother Charles Jarrett, as he should have done, paid me the 10s per week he promised instead of offering me the insultingly small sum of 6s per week, and expecting me to live on it. So you perceive the great good a little money would have done, had I not been treated as a fool, which set me more than ever against those bloated aristocrats, led by that old lady Mrs. Vic., who is an accursed robber in all senses.*

*Walter Edward Jarrett*
*2 January, 1882*

"My God!" exclaimed Lestrade. "He's going to kill the Queen! He's going to kill the Queen *today!* We've got to find him, Mr. Holmes – but how?"

"Had you not seen this letter?" Holmes enquired.

"I wouldn't show it to him," Miss Jarrett admitted softly. "I was afraid his constables would shoot Walter down on sight."

"You might have had more faith in British justice!" the inspector snapped. "Besides, Miss Jarrett, our constables don't go armed. But the question remains, Mr. Holmes: How do we stop this man in time?"

"It is simplicity itself, Lestrade. As Watson and I learned in Southsea, Jarrett has been stalking Her Majesty throughout the month. He was thwarted from accosting her at Gosport, and he evidently missed her on Saturday when she left Windsor for Buckingham Palace. It follows, therefore, that he'll be at Windsor Station when the Queen returns this afternoon. We have only to ensure that we arrive before him and are ready to prevent this putative assassin from doing any harm."

"Oh, Mr. Holmes," cried the assassin's sister. "I can't imagine that Walter truly wants to harm Her Majesty. It's simply that he's desperate, because he believes Charles and I have deserted him."

"As regards your elder brother," the detective noted acidly, "that is indeed the case."

"Yes, but can't we *help* poor Walter?" She turned hopefully to the Scotland Yarder. "Inspector, if we can stop him before he commits a criminal offense, surely you can return my brother to his family."

"That's as may be, Miss Jarrett," Lestrade replied imperturbably. "I can promise you only that we'll take any and all measures needed to protect the Queen." Turning to Holmes, he continued, "I know George Hayes, Chief Superintendent of the Windsor Borough Police. He's an excellent officer, and I expect he'll give us full co-operation. When Jarrett shows up at Windsor Station, he'll find himself surrounded by our men in blue!"

"Oh, no!" began our client, but Holmes smoothly intervened.

"Visible police presence would present a problem in this case, Lestrade. However, if the Doctor and Miss Jarrett are willing, I have an idea as to how it can be circumvented. Give me a moment and let me explain to you my plan . . . ."

He was interrupted by a firm knock upon the door, and Mrs. Hudson entered with a determined air. "I know you didn't want an early breakfast, Mr. Holmes," she said, "but it is now approaching ten o'clock. I've plenty on hand to feed the four of you, but my savoury eggs and crumpets will be inedible unless they're taken fresh and hot. Gentlemen, I do have other things to do today! May I bring up your breakfast?"

There was a momentary pause, while Miss Jarrett looked sympathetic, Lestrade and I looked hungry, and Holmes was caught between annoyance and appetite. Unusually, the latter won the day.

"Why not?" he said magnanimously. "We've time enough to make our preparations, and I can think of no better start to an eventful day than one of Mrs. Hudson's fortifying breakfasts. My dear lady, we are at your command."

"Hear, hear!" the inspector and I echoed.

At half-past-five o'clock on that gloomy, rainy afternoon, I found myself in the first-class waiting room of Windsor Station, watching Sherlock Holmes pace nervously as he awaited the advent of the Queen. Her train, precisely on schedule, had arrived five minutes earlier, but the Royal Party hadn't as yet appeared. All our preparations for Her Majesty's protection – and Jarrett's apprehension – were in place. Standing with me were his sister, Inspector Lestrade, and Chief Superintendent Hayes of the Borough Police. Among the crowd congregated on the platform were constables in mufti, strategically placed to shield Victoria and her retinue as they passed from her saloon car into her private waiting room. Other plain-clothed constables from Windsor and Westminster had secured the road and now patrolled the station-yard, where two closed carriages stood waiting to transport the Royal Party from the station to the Castle. The only missing element was Walter Jarrett.

He had, perhaps, been seen. An hour before, while the resplendent waiting room was briefly empty, Smythe, the station-master, had found "a dirty, ill-dressed ragamuffin" seated at one of the mahogany writing desks beneath a gilded mirror, evidently trying to compose a note. Despite his protests about the bitter cold, this vagabond had been summarily evicted and, according to Smythe hadn't been seen again. To confirm his

105

supposition, Miss Jarrett and I walked among the public gathered on the platform without finding brother Walter. Holmes was both relieved and mortified that our quarry was so easily discouraged, for his meticulously laid trap seemed likely to remain unsprung.

Just at that moment, the doors of the saloon car opened, and its august passengers started to descend. Naturally, I recognised Her Majesty and her youngest daughter, Princess Beatrice, and I saw General Ponsonby (whom Holmes and I would serve a few years later) [4] amid the entourage. The Queen and most of her retainers studiously ignored the cheering populace, but the Princess had to repress a fleeting smile. Within moments, they were lost to view inside their waiting room, and the exciting spectacle was over. However, Her Majesty's subjects weren't yet satisfied. They abandoned the platform and rushed into the public rooms, crowding the exits to the station yard where their sovereign would soon appear anew. Among them I saw several boys from nearby Eton College.

"Well, Mr. Holmes," the Chief Superintendent remarked glumly as we trailed the congregation out the door, "it looks as if your bird has flown. I'll grant it was a worthwhile exercise in case an assassin *should* appear, but I'm not sorry to see you proven wrong."

"Hush!" my friend said tactlessly. His eyes were fixed upon the farthest corner of the station ground, where a dark figure had emerged from a small coppice beside the road to Windsor Castle. It momentarily disappeared as spectators arrived and swarmed around it. Then we saw it had retained its place along the route by which Her Majesty's carriage would inevitably travel.

"That's Jarrett," said Sherlock Holmes. "We must implement the plan that I laid out this morning. Does everyone remember what we are to do?"

"How can you be sure it's him?" Lestrade enquired, peering short-sightedly through the misting rain. "In this weather, I wouldn't recognise my mother at that distance."

"No doubt," snapped Holmes. "But no one on the platform was wearing those hideous plaid trousers. What do you think, Miss Jarrett?"

"It *could* be Walter," our client said uncertainly. "The height and colouring are right, but the man's face is turned away from me."

"Then let us act upon that supposition. You and Watson approach him from the edge of the yard beside the wood. Allow the crowd to screen you for as long as possible. Lestrade and I shall come in from the other side, along the road. Chief Superintendent, can I depend on your constables to cut off Jarrett's routes of escape, either to the town or to the Castle?"

"The road has been already blocked in both directions," Mr. Hayes replied, "but I'll alert the men myself." He slipped away as the rest of us prepared to move into position.

"Got your pistol, Doctor?" asked Lestrade.

"Yes, but I don't expect to use it." The Yarder had insisted that we all go armed, even after our client angrily enquired if he planned to shoot her brother dead in front of her. I now gave Miss Jarrett a reassuring smile, and we moved quietly towards the woodland, masking ourselves behind the milling crowd. Our quarry, I could see between the gaps, had begun to watch the station house. So far, there was no sign of the Royal Party.

My fair companion, having taken my arm, clutched it suddenly in agitation. "That *is* Walter!" she whispered urgently. "Dr. Watson, we *must* reach him before the others do." We quickened our pace, and as Jarrett returned his attention to the road, his sister and I came up behind him.

"Hello, dear Walt," she called softly, and I could only admire her steadiness of tone.

Aside from certain patients I had treated in Whitechapel, the man who turned to greet us was the most wretched-looking individual I had ever met. His youthful, vapid face was gaunt, blackened with grime and stubble. The bowler hat he wore was dented, his trousers torn, and his overcoat too threadbare to keep out cold and rain. I couldn't credit that the shoes he wore had made the trek from Southsea. Jarrett swayed and shivered as he stood before us, whether from amazement, fear, or simple hunger and exhaustion I could hardly say. His right hand, I noticed, remained in his coat pocket.

"Oh, Eddie," he quavered, "is it really you?"

"Yes, my dear. I've come to rescue you." Ignoring his squalor, Miss Jarrett embraced her brother and kissed his filthy cheek. Her tears came then, but he smiled and gently patted her shoulder. Then he turned his eyes to me.

"Eddie, is this the man you're going to marry?"

"Oh, no!" his sister blushed. "This gentleman is Dr. Watson. He and his friend, Mr. Holmes, have helped me find you."

"Dr. . . . Watson?" Jarrett shook his head in puzzlement. "I don't remember you."

"No, we haven't met," I assured him. "But I bring greetings from Dr. Hitchins, whom you knew in Wells. He's been very concerned about you, and hopes to see you soon."

"Yes, at the asylum." Surprisingly, this memory seemed to bring the madman comfort. "You know, Eddie, I was rather happy there. They let me play cricket!"

"I know," said Miss Jarrett. "But now, Walt," she added, "you must come away with us and these two gentlemen." She gestured uneasily towards Holmes and Lestrade, who had come up from the road and now stood behind her brother. To my dismay, the inspector seemed about to draw his pistol. I raised a hand to urge him to refrain.

"I can't leave now," Jarrett replied. "I have a mission to fulfill. Look, Eddie, look!" he cried excitedly. "Her Majesty is coming!" Across the yard at Windsor Station, the Royal Party was at last preparing to depart. I saw the Queen and Princess Beatrice, accompanied by an older lady, enter the first carriage, while the remaining courtiers climbed into the second. In a matter of seconds, they would be upon us.

It was my friend who took prompt action. "Mr. Jarrett," he said with quiet urgency, "my name is Sherlock Holmes. I know about your mission, and please believe that we are here to help you. But, as you must surely know, you will not be allowed to harm the Queen."

"Dear Walt," coaxed Miss Jarrett, placing a soothing hand upon her brother's arm, "I can't believe you *truly* want to hurt Her Majesty."

"Sometimes I do," Jarrett acknowledged, "but only when my head is bad. When I'm myself – as I am now – I don't wish the old lady any harm. But I'm *starving*, Eddie!" He groaned and massaged his temples briefly, trying to retain a modicum of self-control. "You see, Mr. Holmes, my plan is that by shooting *at* Her Majesty – not really hitting her, of course – I can alarm the country and draw its attention to my pecuniary woes. Public opinion will *force* Charles to give me back the money he has promised, and I can go on.

"That's all I want, you know," the madman told his sister. "Just to go on."

"Oh, my dear," sobbed Miss Jarrett. She moved to take her brother in her arms, but Holmes forestalled her. He turned upon Walter Jarrett the full force of his personality.

"Then you must give me your pistol, Mr. Jarrett, and you must do it now. A sham assassination will not achieve your object." He glanced at Windsor Station, where the Royal carriages were under way and ready to turn onto the high road. "There isn't a moment to he lost."

"*Very* well," Jarrett sighed petulantly. He handed the detective what looked to be a cheap and poorly manufactured revolver.

"Thank God!" muttered Lestrade. There was more relief in those two words than I had ever heard him use in dealing with a miscreant.

"Am I to be arrested?"

"It may be, lad," said the inspector, "that you're guilty of high treason, but whether to charge you is a decision for wiser heads than mine. For now, I think you'd better remain within our custody. Let's get you away from here."

"May I not stay long enough to see the Queen go by?" Jarrett enquired eagerly, "I've followed Her Majesty halfway 'round the country this past month, but I've yet to set eyes upon her countenance. Oh, *please*, Mr. Holmes!"

There was no time to answer him, for the royal vehicles were thundering down the road to Windsor Castle. The Queen's, pulled by a handsome pair of greys, drew level with us, and the madman waved his battered bowler.

"God save Your Majesty!" shouted Walter Jarrett.

No one had the heart to tell him that the lady he had glimpsed was Princess Beatrice. Her mother was seated on the other side.

In the end, the madman wasn't charged with treason. A hearing was held in Windsor the next afternoon, at which it was established that Jarrett (his appearance improved by a wash, a shave, proper clothing, and hot meals) hadn't committed any overt act against the Queen. Prosecution by the Crown must therefore rest upon the defendant's possession of a weapon and his last letter to his sister, which ostensibly violated the Treason Act of 1351 by "*compassing or imagining*" his sovereign's death. However, the note's language was so ambiguous that a conviction seemed at best uncertain. Moreover, it was quickly obvious to anyone who met Jarrett that executing him would be a travesty. For two more days, representatives from various authorities (including, I learned years later, Mycroft Holmes) debated the matter, while the happy prisoner remained in comfort. Then Walter Jarrett was released into his family's care, with the stipulation that he live the rest of his life under constant supervision.

Holmes and I accompanied the siblings on their journey back to Somerset, where Dr. Hitchins readmitted his patient to the Bath and Somerset Lunatic Asylum. Our next stop was Bristol. When it was revealed to Charles Jarrett how close he had come to infamy as the brother of a regicide, that gentleman opened his purse. Walter Jarrett would lack for nothing during his future years in the asylum. He never recovered, but he lived there fairly happily, making periodic visits to his sister's family on seaside holidays in Weston-super-Mare. To the best of my knowledge, the poor man still survives.

As for Edwina Peterson, *née* Jarrett, we rather soon lost touch with her. Naturally, she was more than grateful for our help, and browbeat brother Charles into paying Holmes a handsome fee. Upon meeting her fiancé, we were promised an invitation to their wedding, but it didn't arrive. Letters regarding Walter's progress quickly ceased, so my subsequent information came from Dr. Hitchins. Quite irrationally, I was aggrieved by this neglect, even as I recognised that my attraction to the betrothed beauty had been bootless from the start. One autumn evening as we sat by the fire, I asked Holmes whether he had experienced a similar

109

result with other female clients. My friend favoured me with an ironic smile.

"You might better ask if I have *not*, but of course I neither wanted nor expected any other outcome. Nor has a client's gender affected the equation. My clients – well, perhaps by this time I ought to say *our* clients – " (My readers can imagine the pleasure I took in this remark.) " – are, as I have said before, only factors in the problem. They come to me, often in desperation, and while I work to solve their case I am the most important person in their lives. Once that case is over and their situation eased – or at least resolved – they go their way, and their lives return to 'normal', whether old or new. They may remember me with gratitude, or I may become an unwelcome reminder of their painful past. No, I can count upon one hand the times I have remained long in contact with a former client, and none were female. Mrs. Peterson was more diligent than most. If I may presume to advise you, Watson, there is no future in becoming too involved."

I appreciated the eminent good sense of this discourse, which aided my recovery from a foolhardy infatuation with the madman's sister. Indeed, it remained helpful whenever a pretty client crossed our threshold, and over the next two years we encountered a good many. (I am reminded especially of Miss Helen Stoner.) Of course – like most excellent advice – Sherlock Holmes's was finally disproven. It happened six years after his delivery of those remarks, when a fateful card upon a salver announced the advent of Miss Mary Morstan into my life.

# NOTES

1.	See "A Yuletide Tragedy" in Part XXVIII of The *MX Book of New Sherlock Holmes Stories* (London: MX Publishing, 2021), pp. 69-85. The story is also contained in my collection *Watson's Wives and Other Tales of Sherlock Holmes* (London: MX Publishing, 2023), pp. 1-18.
2.	Henry VIII built Southsea Castle in 1544 as a bulwark against French invasion. Having recently been modernized, it was still on duty during Holmes and Watson's visit. At the Battle of the Solent in 1545, the great carrack *Mary Rose* capsized and sank while fighting French galleys. A distraught King Henry was watching from the shore.
3.	Mother Swanson would shortly have access to another doctor. In June 1882, after completing his initial medical studies and serving as ship's surgeon on a voyage to West Africa, Arthur Conan Doyle arrived in Southsea with less than ten pounds in his pocket. He established a practice at 1 Bush Villas in the Elm Grove neighborhood, but he was ultimately unsuccessful. It was during this period that Watson's future literary agent began writing fiction. *https://en.wikipedia.org/wiki/Arthur_Conan_Doyle*
4.	General Sir Henry Ponsonby was Her Majesty's private secretary from 1870 until 1895. The service to which Watson refers is recorded in "The Case of the Dying Emperor," the first of four historical pastiches found in *Sherlock Holmes and the Crowned Heads of Europe* (London: MX Publishing, 2021), pp. 1-96.

## Historical Note

As Dr. Watson mentions early in the story, Walter Jarrett's attempt on the life of Queen Victoria was not quite the last one. Only two months later (March 2, 1882) a remarkably similar attempt was made by another impoverished madman, Roderick Maclean, who fired a pistol at Her Majesty's carriage as it was leaving Windsor Station. Although Holmes and Watson were not present, the assassin's aim was thwarted by the intervention of two Eton boys. Unlike Jarrett, Maclean was captured and tried for treason, only to be acquitted due to his obvious insanity. The Queen, "surprised and shocked" by this verdict, browbeat Prime Minister Gladstone into sponsoring a bill to change the verdict in such cases to "*Guilty, but insane*". The Trial of Lunatics Act was duly passed in 1883, and applied to other felonies as well as treason. Roderick Maclean spent the rest of his life in Broadmoor, where he died in 1921. The sources below provide more information on Maclean's attempt.

## Bibliography

McCabe, Sophie. "The Life of Roderick Maclean, the Man Who Tried to Kill Queen Victoria." *Express*, March 2. 2023.
*https://www.express.co.uk/news/royal/1741412/queen-victoria-assassination-attempt-roderick-maclean-spt*

Mendip Hospital Cemetery. "Roderick Charles Maclean (1854-1921): An enthusiastic cricketer with murder on his mind. Facebook post, April 26, 2019.
*https://www.facebook.com/mendiphospitalcemetery/posts/roderick-charles-maclean-1854-1921-an-enthusiastic-cricketer-with-murder-on-his-/2058335087798719/*

Murphy, Paul Thomas. *Shooting Victoria: Madness, Mayhem, and the Rebirth of the British Monarchy.* New York: Pegasus Books, 2013. [pp. 420-520 are relevant to this story.]

# The Carpetbag Case
## by Brenda Seabrooke

"I hope this beastly weather today isn't a template for the entire winter," I remarked one morning in early December. Betty, the maid, had just cleared away the breakfast things when sleet pelted the front windows, reminding me of distant fire on a subcontinent battlefield.

"Winter is on its way, Watson, and as you know, there's no stopping it, however much you may want to. No sense in dreading it. Be prepared and meet it head on." Holmes took up a newspaper from one of the piles by his chair. The fire murmured agreeably, and I felt a nap coming on when the bell sounded downstairs.

Betty answered and two sets of footsteps ascended the stairs. "Someone to see you, Mr. Holmes. A Mr. Biggers. He's a dustman." This last was spoken in a whisper.

"Ah, my friend, Biggers. Send him in please." Holmes let the paper slide down to join the others on the floor.

"Mr. Biggers, do come in and take a seat." I pulled the basket chair closer to the fire and moved to the drinks cabinet. "I know it's early, but would you care for a wee dram to take the edge off the cold morning?" I was already pouring whisky into a glass. Dustman he might be, but he did valuable work and deserved to be treated accordingly. Holmes had helped him not long before, and in return he helped Holmes with a case.

"Don't mind if oi do." As he advanced into the room, I noted his dress which, while not exactly natty, was vastly improved since he had last visited. His clothes more nearly matched and had been neatly mended in places. The amount of dust, considerable in the past, was of little concern. He sank into the chair, accepted the glass, and laid a large parcel on the floor.

"How's the world been treating you?" I asked as I regained my chair.

"Can't complain, oi can't." Biggers sipped the whisky with a sigh of satisfaction.

"Married life seems to agree with you," Holmes observed the sartorial changes.

"Hit do. Does."

"What brings you to Baker Street?" I asked.

Biggers finished the whisky, bent over, and picked up his large bulky parcel. "Hit were this." He removed the brown paper wrappings to reveal a very large carpetbag. "Oi found this not two hours ago. Oi were finishing me morning rounds when I lifted aside some papers and found this bag. Oi looked inside and come straight 'ere. Oi didn't know what else to do."

He opened the bag to reveal a confection of a bridal gown embroidered with silver thread and pearls. Even I could see that multitudes of hours had gone into the making of this garment. Why would it have been put in a dustbin?

"Oi were 'oping for a reward, but oi wanted you to 'andle hit, Mr. 'Olmes. Didn't want no one to say oi stole that dress."

Holmes removed the gown from the bag and unrolled it for us to contemplate. It was even more beautiful when seen in full, with the drapings, the embroidery, the tiny pearls gleaming in the firelight.

"There's more." Holmes lifted a veil from the bag, and then another bridal gown and veil.

"Two o' them!" Biggers said. "Oi didn't know."

The gowns – lace and satin, ruffles and flounces – filled the room like a frothing sea.

"They appear to be identical," Holmes said.

"My word – were they meant for twins?"

"That is one possibility."

"Perhaps one husband-to-be backed out because he couldn't bear to be around a copy of his bride," I theorized. "Then the other groom confessed to the same thoughts. The gowns were packed up to be taken somewhere and were lost in the haste of the sisters rushing to escape opprobrium from being jilted almost at the altar."

"Watson, I order you to stop writing down my cases in your journals and move on to concocting stories for those yellow books you like to read so much."

"How do you know that I don't already?"

He almost smiled. "You surprise me. That doesn't happen often." He rubbed his hands together briskly. "Now to the business at hand."

With the gowns and veils spread on the sofa, he looked over the large carpetbag. "The design of it is Indian, wouldn't you say, Watson?"

"I would. Darker than the usual, but that could've come with usage, or contact with an element that darkened the dyes used. It's possibly the largest one of its kind I've seen.

"No matter. It has been well-used. No doubt it was chosen over other types of bags for its size and ubiquity." He ran his finger over the nameplate. "'*Carstairs*'. That could be the original owner's name, should the bag have been stolen."

"Why would the bag be stolen?"

"Why is anything stolen?"

"For money, of course."

114

"There's no way of telling how many times this carpetbag has changed hands." Holmes ran his fingers over the interior and emerged with a sewing pin. "Ah."

Biggers waited for an explanation, but none was forthcoming.

Holmes sniffed the bag. "Camphor, wouldn't you say?"

I confirmed that the bag did indeed have that odor.

"Which is used on long sea voyages. Do you also detect a tinge of the briny?"

That I wasn't as sure of, but I nodded because camphor is used to ease seasickness.

"Biggers?"

The dustman sniffed. "Oi don't know about no briny, but it do smell of camphor. Oi' had occasions to smell hit on me rounds."

"This bag has been on a sea voyage. Camphor was packed in it in the event of rough weather and consequential *mal-de-mer*. That could be from the original or a subsequent owner, but without a doubt this carpetbag has been on one or more sea voyages."

He turned his attention to the two gowns. He picked one up by the shoulders. The long embroidered sleeves swung loosely as he turned it around. The back was equally sumptuous. He exchanged it for the second gown. Both were somewhat crushed from being crammed into the bag, but the bottom one more so. As Holmes turned it, a white card fell out of the folds.

"Here. What's this?" Holmes let the gown glide with a silken whisper down beside its twin and picked up the card. "'*Gowns by Mrs. Charlotte Diamond – Charlotte Street*'," he read. "There you have it, Biggers. You could've found the card for yourself."

Biggers shook his head. "Not me, Mr. 'Olmes. Oi never woulda found that card. I didden dare take them dresses outa that bag. Oi didden know what trouble this might lead to."

"Shall we pay a visit to Mrs. Diamond?" Holmes asked us.

"Beggin yer pardon, Mr. 'Olmes. Oi needs to finish me rounds. Oi'm alreddy late coming 'ere."

Holmes nodded as if he weren't surprised. "I'll see to the reward. Check back in a day or two."

"Will do."

Biggers was downstairs before we had repacked the bag. "He doesn't want to miss any future treasures," Holmes said.

"He could've sold the dresses for a goodly sum and the bag as well."

"True, but as he pointed out, he might have run into difficulties – perhaps accusations – if he'd tried to sell such obviously expensive garments. These gowns are fit for a duchess or a queen."

115

We wrestled the dresses and their veils back into the carpetbag, replaced the brown paper, and wrapped ourselves up against the weather. The sleet mercifully tapered off by the time we reached the kerb, but enough ice pellets remained in the street for the wheels of the hansom to crunch as we drove over them to Charlotte Street. The noise put me in mind of passing over bones, an unsettling and disagreeable sound.

The dressmaking establishment of Mrs. Diamond was housed in a narrow building that had been a house at one time. The brick was a dark shade of red, though not yet blackened like most of London.

"Here you are, gents," the cabman said. I paid him and followed Holmes and the carpetbag to the balustraded steps. Before I started up, I noticed a young woman flimsily dressed for this weather ducking underneath the steps, not quite out of sight.

I walked around to find out if she were ill. Her face was tear-stained. She wore a maroon-colored dress with a dark blue pinafore over it, and a skimpy pale blue shawl barely covering her shoulders.

"Here now, what's the matter? Are you ill? I'm a doctor."

"No sir. I'm not ill. I've been sacked."

"Has your work not been satisfactory?"

"Yes – no sir. I'm an excellent seamstress. And I'm the chief designer for Mrs. Diamond."

And then she quickly told me a most extraordinary tale.

"Watson, are you coming?"

"Just a minute, Holmes. You need to hear this."

When he joined us under the steps, I nodded at the seamstress. "Tell him what you told me, Ella."

"We made a bridal gown for a rich lady and it were stolen. It had a lot of work on it, but we made another one in two weeks. Charley delivers our gowns. He just came back and said he'd been robbed again. Mrs. Diamond decided that I gave the information about the delivery of the dress to the thief and she sacked me. I don't know what I'll do." She shivered in the icy wind.

"Did she sack Charley?" I asked.

"No, He had a lump on his head, just like last time."

Holmes pushed aside the brown paper and opened the carpetbag, revealing the silken froth within. "Does this look like the dress?"

"Oh sir, it is! How did you get it?"

"Come inside with us."

She shrank back against the balustrade. "Oh sir, I cain't go back in there! She'll have the bill on me! I had to run out in a hurry without my things."

116

"You'll be safe with us," I assured her, but the footman who answered the door didn't think so.

"Ella, you need to get far away. She's in an angry fit. You aren't safe here."

Holmes handed him a card. "Take this to her, and tell her Sherlock Holmes is here to help. Don't mention Ella."

He was gone only minutes, but it seemed longer with Ella twisting the ends of her shawl. I stared at the black-and-white tiles, the delicate French sofa, the crystals in the chandelier. Mrs. Diamond did well for herself.

The footman appeared on the stairs and beckoned us to come up to the next floor. "She'll see you, but Ella needs to get away fast."

"Don't worry," Holmes said. Then the girl accompanied us upstairs.

Mrs. Diamond was somewhat past forty and no doubt fond of sweets. Sharp black eyes darted out at us from underneath a lace cap atop her graying hair. She wore a gray wool dress with wide lace cuffs and a high collar, pearl necklace, and ear-drops. She was shorter than Ella and started toward us with a smile.

"Welcome, Mr. Holmes – " Her welcoming smile turned to rage, and I was afraid she would box Ella's ears. "What is that thief doing back here? Vernon, get the police!"

"That will not be necessary, Mrs. Diamond. I have something here that may interest you."

Holmes removed the brown paper from the parcel. He opened the carpetbag and allowed some of the silk to escape.

Mrs. Diamond dropped her fists. "Oh my! Where did you get it?"

"A dustman I have dealings with brought it to me. Is this the stolen gown?"

She fingered the embroidery. "Yes. This is mine, the second one made for a bride. The first one was also stolen. Why would a dustman have it?"

"If you will be so good as to give me the address the gown was going to, I shall deliver it myself to ensure it's a safe arrival."

"'Twas for Miss Anna Palmer," and she rattled off the address.

"No doubt the thief accomplished his purpose with the thefts," Holmes said, "and with no further use for the two gowns, he rid himself of them as quickly and efficiently as he saw fit."

"Both stolen gowns are in that carpetbag?" Mrs. Diamond lifted a carefully shaped eyebrow. "Have they been harmed?"

Holmes nodded at me. "Watson?"

I pulled the second gown out of the bag and unrolled it over a chair, as Holmes did with the first gown. Ella, another apprentice seamstress, and

Vernon crowded around as Mrs. Diamond examined the first gown for harm. "Well, don't just stand there," she said to Ella and the apprentice, "Look for damage."

They looked over the second gown, one checking in front and the other the back. "They seem to be in perfect condition," Ella reported, "except for wrinkles."

"We shall deliver them ourselves to ensure its safe arrival," Holmes stated.

Mrs. Diamond nodded. "Ella, wrap them up for delivery."

"I am no longer employed here, Mrs. Diamond," Ella said.

"Nonsense. You're my top seamstress."

"In that case, perhaps a raise in salary is in order," I said.

Mrs. Diamond paused. "Very well. I'll raise your salary a tuppence a month."

"A month?" Holmes repeated.

"A week."

"Only a tuppence?" Holmes said.

"A shilling a week," replied the owner with a sour expression, "and not a penny more."

"Excellent. Ella, if you will wrap the gowns, we'll be on our way."

The young man who had been attacked twice while delivering the gowns wandered in from a back room. "Want me to deliver them again, Mrs. Diamond?"

"No, Charley. Mr. Holmes will be doing that."

Charley opened his mouth, unhappy at losing the delivery job, but Holmes held up his hand. "Something for Charley for being attacked twice in your employ?"

"Come with me, Charley." Mrs. Diamond went to her desk and gave Charley two shillings for being attacked twice. He looked as though he would gladly be robbed again for a shilling a throw.

"Don't even think about it . . ." Holmes said to him when Mrs. Diamond's attention was elsewhere.

"And you," he said *sotto voce* to the other seamstress, "don't even think about tipping off anyone about delivery times."

She scowled at him and turned away as Ella brought in the gowns wrapped in two parcels in brown paper tied with string. I took one and Holmes took the other and picked up the carpetbag. "I rather think this belongs to the dustman when all is said and done."

Miss Anna Palmer lived in an imposing house in Mayfair. I saw a cartouche of a palm tree embedded in the bricks over the front door as I used the brass palm tree knocker on the shiny black door. Holmes nodded at it. "The Palmers made their money importing palm oil."

"A lot of it, I daresay."

"Old Mr. Palmer was a grocer before going into the more lucrative commodities trade."

"I wouldn't think enough palm oil would be used in cooking to pay for this." I nodded at the perfectly kept house.

"Nor I, but palm oil has far more uses than for cuisine. Besides candles and soap-making, it's used as a lubricant for machinery in manufacturing plants."

"How convenient to carry the name *Palmer*."

"Old Mr. Palmer chose that convenience. The original name was 'Cratcher'."

The door opened and a supercilious butler said, "Deliveries at the rear," and made to close the door.

Holmes stuck his foot in the door and handed the butler a card he had at the ready.

"Kindly inform Miss Palmer that Sherlock Holmes and Dr. Watson are here with something she'll be interested in seeing."

The butler accepted the card and closed the door with a solid thud that brought a peppering of old snow down on us.

While we waited, it occurred to me to ask, "You believe that Charley and the other girl helped to steal the gowns?"

"I do – but it would do no good to pursue that line, as whomever paid them to do so would have taken care to avoid leaving a trail."

After a few cold minutes, the door opened again. "Miss Palmer will see you briefly. This way."

He didn't take our hats or overcoats. We left them on until we were in Miss Palmer's presence.

"Sherlock Holmes and a Dr. Watson – Miss Palmer."

"Thank you, Seldon."

When we removed our hats, a few bits of still-frozen sleet rolled onto the Aubusson rug. Holmes didn't apologize. The butler, realizing what he hadn't done, shook out a snowy white handkerchief and scooped up the offending moisture.

"Well, Mr. Holmes, what do you have for me today?" Miss Palmer was an attractive young lady in her mid-twenties. She had a clear complexion and sky-blue eyes, crowned by fair hair in a loose knot. She was dressed in a morning gown of fine merino in a violet shade.

"First, tell me who is trying to sabotage your upcoming wedding?"

She blinked and sat back on the yellow velvet sofa. "I don't see that my wedding is any concern of yours."

"You will." He loosened the paper and string wrapping the parcel he held to reveal the first wedding gown, while I did the same with the second one. We laid them over chairs, the veils on other chairs.

Miss Palmer leaned forward, shocked. "Where did you get these? Did you steal them?"

"Certainly not," I said. "Mr. Holmes is a noted consulting detective. He aids Scotland Yard in their criminal investigations."

Holmes deigned to smile. "Thank you, Watson. Now as to the business at hand, I ask you: Who doesn't want you to marry?"

"I don't know anyone trying to stop my wedding."

"Do you think it's a coincidence that two wedding gowns were stolen?"

"I did, but now I don't know. Where did you find them?"

Holmes explained about Josiah Biggers. "He didn't want to be accused of stealing them. He asked that I intercede for him. Now explain to me about your wedding."

"It was originally set for late November in Christ Church, here in Mayfair. When my gown was stolen, the date was changed to mid-December, but just this morning we learned the second gown was stolen. I'm afraid my great-uncle immediately canceled that date as well. Now I have both dresses, but nowhere to hold a wedding. There are no dates free until January. My fiancé is furious. His heart was set on starting the New Year as man and wife."

"Couldn't you have worn some other dress?" I asked.

"My uncle brought the materials for the gown from Paris, and he insisted that I wear a gown made from them, based on something a fortune teller or some seer from the East told him: His descendants should be wed in the finest of fabrics in order to assure a blessed life. My fiancé said he didn't believe in that, and he would marry me if I wore black bombazine. But my uncle . . . ."

A tear slid down her left cheek as she smiled.

"Commendable," Holmes said.

A noise in the front of the house caught her attention. She half-rose when a handsome man burst into the drawing room. He took in the girl's tear, the two dresses, and snatched down a sword hanging over the mantel shelf. With fire in his eyes, he advanced on me. "Who are you, you thieving blaggard?"

"I am John Watson, late of Her Majesty's service in India and Maiwand, and I'm aiming my service revolver straight at your midsection." I spoke calmly, but my finger curved around the trigger of the Adams in my pocket.

He lowered his gaze and dropped the sword point as he saw my right hand withdrawn and the gun pointing at him. "Sorry, old chap. Rum business, Maiwand."

"William, please return Papa's sword to its rightful place. This is Sherlock Holmes and Dr. Watson. These two gentlemen have returned both of my stolen gowns. Gentlemen, this is my fiancé, William Marwell – the Earl."

As she spoke, Marwell replaced the sword. He was a fine figure of a swordsman and a man. His clothing fit him like a glove – elegant fawn, blue, and tasteful grey, and boots like mirrors. He was perhaps a year or two younger than Miss Palmer, but what matter when there's a title involved?

An older rather portly gentleman followed him into the room, a stout matronly woman at his heels. Family members?

"That's excellent news," the older man said. "Now the wedding can go forward." He turned to Holmes. "Thank you for their return. Where did you find them?"

Holmes explained, showed him the carpetbag, and offered his card.

"A consulting detective? I haven't heard of such. A dustman procured your services?"

"The dustman found the gowns and asked Mr. Holmes for help," explained Miss Palmer. She introduced the newcomers as her maternal uncle, Gerald Fithian, and his sister, Miss Violet Fithian. "They have lived with me since my parents died. I don't know what I would have done without them."

Holmes and I uttered polite responses. Fithian nodded at us as his sister seated herself beside her charge. Fithian remained standing, as did William.

"I'm afraid I'm the bearer of bad news." Fithian showed his teeth with a smile. "The church date was relinquished this morning. If only you had come sooner."

He made it sound as if Holmes, by withholding the gowns, had stopped the ceremony.

"There's no other date we can use for the wedding?" the potential groom asked, a scowl darkening his features.

"Afraid not," Fithian said. "The wedding can be scheduled for sometime in January. I'll see to the invitations."

"Hold up there, Fithian. I am determined Miss Palmer will be my bride as we enter the New Year."

"And how will you accomplish this feat without a church for the wedding?" Fithian asked.

"Easily. We shall all remove to Beddingham Hall. The chapel there will suffice. It's a family tradition for the Earl to be married there. The local vicar will be glad to officiate. I initially accommodated my fiancée who wanted a wedding in London attended by friends. Now, we shall have the wedding in the chapel with family in attendance. Later, we shall invite friends for a celebration in London. I'll start preparations immediately. Miss Fithian, please see to the packing. Mr. Holmes, I trust that you and Dr. Watson will take charge of the gowns. Don't let them out of your sight."

Before anybody could object, he had left the room.

Miss Fithian rose in a flurry of muttered reminders, " – my lavender velvet, the diamonds, a hamper – must send to Fortnum – " She retired from the room, leaving phrases in her wake.

"Mr. Holmes," Miss Palmer asked, "you will you take charge of the two gowns and accompany us to Kent? We'll leave on the afternoon train."

"Indeed we will. Watson, if you'll kindly see to our necessaries." He glanced at my coat where my Adams was again pocketed.

"Take this." He handed me the carpetbag.

"I'll pack our bags and return within the hour," I responded.

Right on time, the entire wedding party, consisting of the bride, her aunt and uncle, and the two of us departed by train for Kent – the groom having already gone ahead to prepare. Holmes and I each carried a gown done up in brown paper parcels. Two maids and the supercilious butler were in charge of the baggage. Holmes and I had a compartment to ourselves with our oversized baggage.

"This is an interesting turn of events, I must say," I observed, "conveying a pair of wedding gowns to an ancient seat."

"There's more to this wedding than the theft of a pair of gowns."

"Indeed." I waited for more, but he settled himself with a book he'd picked up at the station.

I contented myself with the passing sights until we reached our destination.

A coach stood waiting for the bride and her aunt and uncle. Holmes and I were relegated to a farm cart crowded with our baggage, the gowns, the maid Nellie, valet Francis, and the butler, Seldon. It was driven by an ancient retainer from the Hall. "Used to be John Coach, I were," he said in a growl.

Holmes sat beside him while I was amongst the staff. They were insulted by the transportation and vocal about it. "Never have we ridden in an *animal* cart," Nellie sniffed. Seldon simply sulked, while Francis grumbled he might have grippe or quinsy, if not catarrh from exposure to the biting cold. I couldn't disagree with him. Perhaps the Earl forgot that night fell early in winter.

Beddingham Hall loomed through the falling snow as we drove through the park. Through the dark December evening, we could see an impressive grey stone edifice old enough to bear crenellations atop walls and towers for archers to shoot arrows down on invaders.

Holmes and I each carried a parcel through the massive entry and into a courtyard. The Earl met us there and welcomed us to the Hall. We adjourned to a small anteroom where a great fire warmed the walls. Trays of drinks and bowls of hot soup soon warmed us.

The Earl apologized for the cart ride, explaining that his assistant coachman was ill and his old retainer was no longer fit to drive a coach. "He really is out to pasture now, but helps out any way he can."

"Indeed," Holmes said. "Well, we are here now. When is the wedding scheduled?"

"Eleven in the morning," the Earl said. "That is, if the vicar is able to get here. We weren't expecting snow."

We were shown to our rooms where cold collations awaited us. Holmes and I had discussed keeping the gowns separate and how to protect them. I locked the door to my room and put the key in my pocket.

Before eating, I deposited the gown parcel under the bed and pushed furniture on two sides to block the way. On the other side, I leaned my valise and stacked books to prevent easy access. Any wedding gown thieves would need to remove objects to get at the gown and I would awaken. I laid my Adams on the candle stand by the bed and sat in front of a small fire to enjoy bread, cheese, sliced meats, and a selection of sweets with a bottle of wine. I had thought to talk to Holmes, but the food made me sleepy. I changed into my night clothes and then lay down to rest and . . . .

"Watson! Watson!"

When I was able to open my eyes, I saw Holmes standing by my bed. "You're already dressed for the wedding."

"Brilliant observation."

"How did you get in? I locked the door."

"It wasn't locked just now when I stepped through it."

I sat up and rubbed my eyes in confusion. Then I remembered. "The gown! Is it under the bed?"

"No. Whoever opened the door removed it. No doubt something you ate or drank last night laid you out."

"I feel fuzzy and tired."

"Drugged." He handed me a substantial mug. "We've no time to waste. I've brought up a cup of strong coffee to wake you up."

I took a big gulp. I could feel its rejuvenating properties down to my toes.

Holmes walked to the window and stood looking out while I dressed.

"Where's the other gown? It wasn't stolen too, was it?

"No. I refused the repast. I heard someone try my door, but when I chased him or her – I know not who – he or she got away. I then looked in on you and found that you were drugged, and they had visited your room first. The gown you'd hidden was gone – but at least we saved one of them. This morning, I took the one in my possession to Miss Fithian, who is overseeing its session with a smoothing iron. Our task is done. We can now enjoy the ceremony without concern for the wedding gowns."

"I don't know how I slept through the theft. I must've been really tired."

"Watson, I told you – someone drugged the wine."

"Oh yes, you did. Are you sure? Did you test it?"

"No need. It's done. We need to find out why, and then we'll know who."

"Surely the 'why' was to steal the gowns. Do you have a suspect in mind?"

"I do, but as I said, I'm not yet sure of the reason. Let's go down. You need breakfast – and more coffee."

"And you don't?" But he was already outside the door. We found our way down to the breakfast room by following the aromas. Everyone but Miss Palmer and her aunt was already at table.

I filled my plate at the sideboard with kippers, eggs, and scones, and sat down with another cup of coffee. The eggs were a trifle runny, but I managed. Conversation was desultory, but I didn't feel like talking anyway. Halfway through, the Earl made an announcement.

"It is now half-nine. The ceremony will begin at eleven sharp, to be followed by the wedding luncheon. The chapel opens off the entry courtyard. Please be on time."

"You seem awfully eager," old Mr. Fithian said.

The Earl narrowed his eyes. "The wedding has been postponed twice. Fate and thievery have been working hand-in-hand to prevent this marriage."

"It's certainly a beastly time of year for a wedding," said Mr. Fithian. "Any more snow, and we'll all be marooned here."

"Last night's snow was unusual, and not likely to be repeated," the Earl said in a clipped tone, as if daring the weather to defy him.

After breakfast, Holmes wanted to tour the hall and I, feeling myself again and with nothing to occupy my time, elected to join him for an hour.

Holmes didn't say much, and at half-ten we returned to our rooms to don the morning dress I'd brought from Baker Street for the wedding.

My room was as cold as a morgue, causing me to hurry. As I finished tying my tie, Holmes knocked on the door. "We have a few minutes. Tell me your impression of the hall from what we saw this morning."

I closed my eyes and remembered what I'd seen. "The main rooms are warm and well-kept, but the others are closed off and shrouded in dust sheets, with the furnishings seemed to be rather sparse. There were bare spots where a chair or table might have stood. I noticed several pale spots where pictures might have once hung for several centuries. Some rooms lacked rugs, and the conservatory plants appeared dead in their pots. I may have even seen an icicle or two hanging here and there."

"Any conclusions?"

"I'd say the Earl has recently had some big debts."

"Quite right. His grandfather spent lavishly, especially on the horses and other gambling venues. He died five years ago, necessitating the payment of death duties. The Earl's father died barely three years later, necessitating – "

"More death taxes," I said.

"Indeed. The present Earl faces poverty. This marriage is intended to refurbish the coffers. He wouldn't do anything to delay the ceremony. Who else seeks to gain or lose from this marriage?"

Downstairs a gong rang mournfully through the Hall.

"That must be our cue to assemble."


The chapel was tiny in comparison to the rest of the hall. Indeed, it seemed to have been tucked into a corner of the courtyard. We entered from an anteroom, designed so worshippers wouldn't be exposed to the weather by going outside. A fine, albeit small, petaled window allowed light to enter above the altar. The plain wooden pews would hold perhaps ten on each side of a center aisle.

The Earl stood alone at the altar. Several retainers sat at the back of the chapel. Holmes and I went to speak to the groom. Up close he was quite stressed. His hair was rumpled and his tie was askew. I straightened the latter and suggested he smooth his hair. He raked his fingers through it, rumpling it more.

"The vicar hasn't yet arrived," Holmes surmised.

"The vicar was unavailable, but a reverend has arrived – or so I'm told. A Methodist marriage is as legal as a Church of England one, is it not?"

"Most certainly," I said.

Footsteps sounded behind us. We turned, hoping to see a man of the cloth, but instead observed Mr. and Miss Fithian. The lady smiled at us as they took their seats in the front pew on the right side of the aisle. She was fashionable in plum with a violet shawl against the chapel's chill and a lacy bit of a bonnet on her greying curls. Beside her, Mr. Fithian's face was red from the cold – or perhaps morning wine.

We stayed with the groom. I wondered what we could do if the minister wasn't actually there. "Perhaps we could all take a train to Scotland," I suggested. "Gretna Green shouldn't be snowbound yet."

The Earl lifted his anguished eyes as Miss Palmer appeared at the end of the chapel's center aisle. He groaned under his breath. She was a vision of loveliness in the rescued gown. She carried a white bouquet.

"Wherever did you find white tulips?" I asked the Earl, partly to distract him. He murmured some vague reply as quick footsteps approached.

"This must be the minister," Holmes said.

The man that pushed past the bride and hurried up the aisle wore a dark suit and clerical collar. He was medium height, somewhat stocky, with pale brown hair under his hat and brown eyes in a face also red with the cold. His suit seemed rumpled, but he'd had a long drive on an icy day.

"Reverend Taylor?" the Earl said.

"That's right. The vicar was ill and sent me. Sorry that I was late, m'boy. Ran into a bit of ice, don't you know, but I'm here now." He swept the hat off his head. "Let's get started. Where's the bride?"

Holmes and I took our seats in the front pew on the left side of the aisle as Miss Palmer began her slow procession to the altar. She walked in silence as the chapel lacked an organ, though it may have once had one.

The Earl smiled at her while Reverend Taylor waited, Bible in hand, to join this man and this woman in Holy Matrimony. Candle flames flickered with the breath from his voice and then he faltered. He reached for the leather string that marked his place to check the words in the Bible.

"No!" Holmes thundered, arcing toward the altar, taking the bride down with him as the Earl leaped in front of her. A shot reverberated in the small chapel sounding like a cannon shot. The reverend scowled as he regained his balance and then ran down the aisle.

I was on my feet to lay chase, but Holmes gathered himself and raced after him, saying, "Look to them, Watson!"

I helped Miss Palmer up and noticed the Earl hadn't risen from the floor. His eyes were closed and the shirt under his coat bloomed red.

I knelt and pulled out my handkerchief as well as his. I opened his shirt to find a bullet hole, blood pumping out with every breath. I placed the folded handkerchief over the wound and pressed down on it. "Run to my room and bring me the small black leather bag!" I ordered one of the maids, watching to one side.

Beside me, Miss Palmer gasped, "Is he dying?"

"No." *Not yet*, I thought to myself, *but he easily might if I can't stop the bleeding.*

With the help of staff, we laid him on a pew. Miss Fithian folded and tucked her shawl under the Earl's head, and I sent her to the kitchen for hot water. When the maid returned, she had brought my bag and also a blanket. Miss Palmer unfolded the blanket around him.

I asked maid to open my bag and hold it so that I could retrieve my bullet forceps. Miss Palmer touched my arm. "Can you get it out?"

"I've had a lot of practice. I was a military surgeon in India." I looked at the maid, who appeared to have drafted as my nurse. "Can you bring the candles over? I need more light."

I wanted to do what needed to be done while the Earl was unconscious. Miss Fithian returned with hot water from the kitchen. I washed my hands with carbolic soap and had Miss Palmer pour water over them in the bowl. The boiling water still smoked, but cooled quickly in the frigid chapel.

I sprayed the bullet hole and the forceps with carbolic acid and began probing. The Earl groaned, but Miss Palmer held his shoulders and soothed him with her voice. She was explaining to him what I was doing.

The wound wasn't deep and I found the bullet immediately. I dropped it on the floor and sprayed the wound again with the acid. Its surgical uses were discovered almost twenty years earlier by Dr. Lister, * but the medical profession had ridiculed him – until they began to notice his success rate in surgeries.

I sutured the wound and sprayed the bandage.

"Will he recover?" Miss Palmer asked, worry darkening her blue eyes.

"He should." I sat back on the pew. Surgery was exhilarating, but also exhausting.

"That bullet was meant for me," she said. "He jumped in front of me just as Mr. Holmes knocked me down."

"You know he is marrying you for your wealth."

"I know. That's what they all want from me."

"His grandfather – "

"I know. Double death duties. I also know that he's a kind man and risked his life for me."

"What will you do?"

"I don't know. Shouldn't we move him to his room?"

Miss Palmer took charge of my patient.

127

By the time I had cleaned up, Holmes had returned. The murderous minister had fled on horseback after cutting the hitching to the dog cart. Holmes had quickly bridled a horse and ridden after him.

"I'll inform Scotland Yard, but I suspect he's already on a boat in the Channel. That's where I'd be if I'd done what he did. We found the vicar, Reverend Jones, in a disused barn. The miscreant had asked him for a ride going this way and the kindly minister said yes. Soon after, he knocked him unconscious and his clothes were taken. He locked the unconscious man in the barn and came straight here. He left the reverend in his underclothes. Fortunately, he was able to wrap himself in an old horse blanket. We found him shivering – and enraged."

When the Earl was awake and sipping the soup that Miss Palmer spooned for him, the wedding party and the real minister, dressed in some of the Earl's clothing, met in his room.

"This was a strange case from the beginning," Holmes began. "A dustman brought a carpetbag to me containing what he thought was a wedding gown. When we removed the gown, we discovered another one identical to it. *Why two gowns alike?* we wondered. We soon learned from the maker of the gowns that the bride had to be exquisitely gowned, and the wedding had to be held before the first of January."

"Why the first of January?" The reverend asked.

"That is when the Marriage Act takes effect," Holmes said.

"The act that gives a married woman complete control over her property," Miss Palmer said crisply.

The Earl looked away in shame.

"Yes, William. I know all about that. I've talked with my lawyers. But after what you did for me today, I will still marry you – here and now, as I am."

We all looked at her, still dressed in her wedding finery, her gown splotched with red from the Earl's blood.

"No, indeed," the Earl said in a faint voice. "We can marry anytime after the first of January, if you'll still have me."

"No, I don't want to marry you in January. I will marry you here. Today. *Now.* We have the reverend – the real reverend – and witnesses. Even the flowers!"

"Ooh!" Daisy and Miss Fithian sounded like they were swooning.

"I'll get the tulips," Miss Fithian said.

Someone had put the tulips in water and placed them in the sickroom. White tulips are lovely for a bride, but for a sickroom pink or apricot would be a cheerier color.

128

The ring was procured, the reverend rounded up. Despite my protests, the Earl was determined to stand for their vows. After the shortened version of the marriage ceremony, he took to his bed again, but in a sitting position while his bride plumped and arranged his pillows.

The snow held off, allowing us to get the afternoon train to London.
"I think they'll do very well," I said on the train back to London.
"Indeed."
"What about the murderous minister?"
"The Yard is looking for him."
"Why did he do it?"
"He was hired."
"By whom?"
"By Uncle Fithian. It was clear to me that he had the greatest motive for delay, and a couple of telephone calls while you retrieved our clothes from Baker Street confirmed my suspicions. He's been handling Miss Palmer's business for years, and taking her money for his own uses. I suspect he has stolen a great deal of it. I explained this to the Earl and his new bride. He acts the jovial uncle, but he is a vicious man. He tried to have Miss Palmer killed before she could marry so he would inherit and retain control. No one would know of his thievery, and he would be rich at last and not have to depend on relatives. I doubt he ever tried working."
"What about his sister?"
"She wasn't involved. She wanted the wedding to go forward. She was only trying to hold the family up in the eyes of society. The Palmers were trade. She didn't want to give anyone a reason to speak ill of Miss Palmer. On the other hand, Mr. Fithian tried every way he could to prevent the wedding. He paid Miss Diamond's staff to steal both wedding gowns, and he arranged for the real reverend to be waylaid so his cohort could kill the bride with that gun hidden in the Bible. I suspect the fake preacher and the dress thief are one and the same."
"Wait – the Bible held the gun? How is that possible?"
"The pages are glued together around the edges. They are cut out of the center to form a hollow box. The gun is attached with the cord or leather string dangling as if it's marking a passage, but when it's pulled, the gun shoots a bullet wherever the Bible is aimed."
"It becomes a deadly Bible," I said. "Malevolent."
"Murder is malevolent," Holmes said.
"How did you know about the trick Bible?"
"I'd read about such an instrument. Francesco Morozini, the Doge of Venice in the late Seventeenth Century, had one. When I saw the fake reverend's hand go for the string, the Doge's deadly Bible flashed in my

mind and I moved to stop it, but the Earl took the bullet. He was lucky the killer's aim was off."

"Who would ever suspect a man of the cloth?"

"I did. A minister wouldn't need to read the marriage service. He would have officiated at so many weddings, he could probably recite the service backward."

"It was excessively complicated," I stated. "Her uncle could have just had her shot at any time."

"It was too obvious. His type always wants to dress things up to spread confusion." And don't forget that there were two plots taking place – "

I thought about this for a meoment. "The Earl wanted to marry before the Marriage Act took effect," I said, looking out at the stark white landscape scrolling past my window.

"Yes. He thought he needed control over Anna's money."

"But he changed his mind after he was shot."

"Yes. Suddenly in a life-or-death situation, people understand what really matters. The Earl suddenly realized as Anna took care of him that he did truly her and wanted to marry her, and the money didn't matter. Anna is an astute young woman. She knew why he was initially marrying her, but saw that it didn't matter when he risked his life to save her, and that's why she insisted the wedding take place."

"Romantic."

"Isn't it?"

"What will the police do about her uncle? He set up the attempt on her life."

"I explained it to the Earl. He's sharp – for nobility. He didn't want to press charges, and his new bride agreed. But I suspect the uncle will be confronted about what he's done, and then sent away for a rest cure in a private asylum. They don't want to be the subject of gossip any more than they already are."

A week after our return, Mr. Biggers called around. He was quite happy to receive a substantial reward for his honesty, as arranged by Holmes by way of the grateful newlyweds. Holmes gave him the carpetbag for his troubles, and also a bottle of champagne from the Earl. He also sent one to Holmes and me as a thank you for our services. The Earl may have been selling furniture and paintings, but he'd left his grandfather's cellar contents alone. This had been a good year for weddings and wine. We opened one on Christmas and toasted the New Year with the other. It seemed that 1883 was off to an excellent start.

# NOTE

\* For more about Holmes and Watson's meeting with Dr. Lister, see "The Odour of Neroli" by Brenda Seabrooke in *The MX Book of New Sherlock Holmes Stories – Part XIII: 2019 Annual (1881-1890)*

# The Adventure of the
# Prized Possession
## by Tracy J. Revels

"I suppose, Mr. Holmes, if the Shakespeare room was untouched, I should not be here, seeking your assistance. Of course, if so, she would not be considering her cruel act. I can understand the need to raise funds, and quickly, but – Father valued those items so much it seems, well – I fear I may be wasting your time, and I certainly would not wish to do so – you are a very busy gentleman, I am sure – Yet I cannot unsee what I have seen, or unhear her words and so – "

"Mr. Fernsby," my friend said with some impatience, "I can only judge the merits of your conundrum if you state it plainly and concisely."

The young man's pale face flushed red with embarrassment. He was perhaps twenty years of age, rather overdressed, with pale blond hair and the look of a scholar or clerk due to his hunched shoulders, delicate hands, and perpetual squint. He adjusted his small spectacles nervously.

"Forgive me, sir."

"I generally find those who are called 'Yankees' to be most direct in their speech. However, it may be your decidedly British roots which are tangling your tongue."

Mr. Fernsby started as if prodded with a hot poker. Holmes gestured languidly.

"Your distinct accent and your clothing mark you as American. Indeed, sir, you shall never pass as the pure British article in those boots, but your English surname is rare and quaint, as is that antique signet ring upon your finger." Holmes tilted his head. "For whom are you in mourning?"

The gentleman again looked startled. I pointed to the hat that he had placed on the divan beside him, with its distinctive black band.

"Oh. My mother, sir. She died a month ago."

"My condolences on your loss. Now, if you will be so kind . . . ."

"Of course," he began, with a harsh clearing of this throat. "I fear I must tell you some family history, or my problem will make very little sense. My parents were a sadly mis-matched pair. My father, Uriah Fernsby, was an aspiring playwright and a noted collector of Shakespearean artefacts. My mother was the former Judith Howell of Boston, who came to London in 1861, with her father, who was a secretary to the American Union ambassador, Charles Francis Adams. Mother was a strikingly beautiful woman of twenty years and Father – who was almost thirty when they met – was considered a handsome fellow. Unfortunately, my grandfather wished my mother to accept a proposal from Lord Jameston."

Holmes shuddered. "A famously disease-ridden old reprobate. One sympathizes with the maiden."

"Yes. I believe she married Father merely to escape the pressure of the unwanted match. I wish, Mr. Holmes, that this was the end of the tale, and true love had conquered all. But I fear it was just the opposite.

"Mother soon came to regret her decision. First, there was the presence of another child. Father was a widower with an infant daughter named Brenda, whose existence he did not even reveal to Mother until after the honeymoon. The second issue was Father's passion for collecting. Whenever he acquired any extra funds from his writing – another shocking discovery was that his regular income came from a very small stipend from a maiden aunt – he feverishly spent his money on building his collection of items related to the Bard.

"Mother's unhappy state only deepened with my birth. When I was a year old, and my stepsister had just turned three, Mother fled London, taking me with her while Father and Brenda were abroad, visiting Father's aunt. Mother returned to Boston, to her father, who agreed to support her, provided she live separate from her husband. There was a protest, as you might imagine, but Grandfather stifled it with a significant cash settlement. Throughout my early childhood, I saw Mother read and then discard letters from Father. When I was about seven or so, I began rescuing these letters from the fire or the trash bin. They spoke of matters my young mind was not ready to comprehend, but each ended with the same sentence, always underlined: '*Return FF to me and you shall be freed to remarry.*'"

"Your initials," Holmes said.

"Indeed, sir. I am Frederick Fernsby, and of course I am Father's heir. He had every right to demand my return. Mother caught me reading one of the notes and afterward was more careful in destroying them. She refused to speak of Father, no matter how often I asked childish questions about my origins. When I was ten, she gave me his old signet ring – the one now on my finger, one which she had worn as a love token in their courtship – but still demurred answering any questions about him.

"When I was twelve, a letter arrived for me. It was a miracle I received it at all, for Mother was fierce in censoring the mail, but she was out on a visit that day, and I happened to collect the correspondence. My name was written in a beautiful feminine script, and immediately I focused upon the foreign stamp. The letter was from Brenda, saying that she wished to know me better. At last, I might receive answers to my questions!

"I replied immediately, and gave her the name of a classmate, asking her to send future correspondence to him, knowing he could smuggle the letters to me. Brenda shared with me the truth about my parents' sad marriage. Brenda described Father's mania for collecting and told me how the 'Shakespeare Room' was a veritable museum. Father had paintings and lithographs of famous thespians, playbills and souvenirs from many theaters, and personal scripts with annotations made by distinguished directors. There were costumes and props associated with the most illustrious British players – a comb belonging to Catherine Clive, a cloak worn by David Garrick in the role of Richard III, the dressing gown once used by Edmund Kean. There was even a pair of slippers said to have been worn by Fanny Kemble as Juliet.

"Brenda informed me that the little museum was so spectacular that Lord Renwood, perhaps Britian's most noted collector of Shakespearean materials, had offered to purchase it, for twice its value, but Father refused. As I was quite fond of the theater myself, I looked forward to the day when I would view this special chamber."

"And you also developed a sense of your sister's personality while exchanging letters?" Holmes asked.

"I did. She was warm and kind, very witty, and a keen observer of people and places. I sent Brenda my photograph and begged for hers in return, but she would never forward one, saying that she feared her looks would cause a camera to shatter.'

"Sadly, just six weeks ago, Mother was diagnosed with an advanced cancer, and her doctors told her she should make her peace with God. She quickly fell into a decline, and I called in nurses to sit with her. But on the morning of the day she died, she sent them away and spoke to me alone. She told me she had a secret that she did not wish to take to her grave.

"'I committed a terrible offense against your father,' she said. 'I did it out of sheer spite. I stole what he loved more than life.'

"I promised her I would go to Father, as soon as she was at rest. Then, Mr. Holmes – Forgive me for laughing, but it is so absurd! – she glared at me and told me not to be a fool, that she was not referring to me. She snapped that I had meant nothing to Father.

"'But what of that line in the letters, where he demanded the return of *FF*? Surely, he meant – '

"'His *First Folio*! It was a copy once owned by John Milton. I took it because I could, and because it would hurt him, and because should he ever make any move against me, the threat to burn it would stop him. It is there – in that bookcase. Do what you will with it. I am certain it would fetch a pretty penny.'

"I rose and went to the spot, taking the book from the shelf. Mr. Holmes, it is indeed that most rare and precious of tomes, and on the flyleaf the immortal poet's autograph! I turned to ask more questions, only to find that in the interval of crossing the room, Mother had perished."

The young man sighed. We could sense how difficult it had been for him to tell his story. Holmes coughed and gently guided him back to his tale.

"You wrote to your father of your mother's demise?"

"I sent a cable that afternoon. A reply came within hours, asking me to come to London immediately and – these words are verbatim – '*bring* FF *with you*'. It saddened me that Mother should be proved correct, and Father had more interest in the book than in me, but I replied that I would be in London shortly. I kept Father abreast of my plans, and every reply was curt to the point of cruelty. More than once I considered cancelling the journey, but then I thought of how much I wished to meet Brenda.

"And so, Mr. Holmes, at eleven a.m. yesterday morning – after a very late arrival and taking a room at the Northumberland Hotel – I presented myself at Father's door. A butler in rather antique livery, complete with silk stockings, met me and took my hat, and then ushered me into the Shakespeare Room. I walked around it almost in a dream, recalling the vivid way Brenda depicted it in her missives. But now, strangely, the room was almost empty. Several bare dress-fitting forms were shoved into a corner, suggesting costumes had once been displayed, and a few glasses cases contained pictures and a book of autographs. But it was hardly the museum Brenda had described.

"The door opened, and my half-sister entered the room. Gentlemen, imagine my feelings. I felt I knew her very soul from her letters, yet her adult person was an enigma. I stood for a moment, simply mesmerized by her. How could she have ever claimed she was 'too hideous to photograph'? I tell you she was a vision of loveliness, with long auburn hair, bright green eyes, and flawless skin. She was dressed simply and modestly, with a great blue cameo upon her throat.

"'Brenda! Sister!'

"'Oh, Frederick.'

"I confess, Mr. Holmes, I was somewhat surprised, for since the beginning of our correspondence, she had always called me 'Freddy'. I chided her for being so formal.

"'Well, this is a solemn occasion, is it not?' she asked. 'Perhaps I should honor the event accordingly. I am so glad you have come. Where is the Folio?"

"'Take me to Father first,' I insisted.

"She shook her head and motioned for me to sit in a chair. She settled with a deep sigh.

"'I did not wish to tell you this via a cable, Freddy. In the very same week your mother died, Father fell extremely ill." Brenda twisted her hands and clutched at her throat. "I have been spending every shilling we possess on doctors, specialists, and medicines. I have sold furniture and pictures, hoping to keep bill-collectors at bay. It is why you find this room almost bare. But come . . . I will show Father to you.'"

"She led me upstairs, and I saw, as we moved along the passage, that the house was indeed being stripped of its furnishings, that there were marks upon the walls where paintings had once hung, and scars where rugs had previously been tacked down. A rather fleshy maid curtseyed to us outside the bedroom door and said our father was sleeping. Still, Brenda led me inside so that I might see him.

"The chamber reeked of the sickroom. Father was sunken into the deep mattress, the covers pulled nearly to his chin. Sir, I have only seen a photograph of my father, made when he was a much younger man, and while I would say the sharp nose and jutting chin were familiar, the blackened teeth and the nightcap pulled low over pale wisps of hair made him seem strange and alien to me. Brenda gently tried to rouse him, but he continued to loudly snore and wheeze, a most distressing sound, all too familiar from my recent experience with Mother. I indicated I did not wish to stay, and we returned to the room below.

"We lingered there for an hour. The maid and butler brought in a luncheon for us, a pitiful meal of bread, cheese, and stew. Brenda asked me questions about my journey, and how I was finding London, but it seemed a forced and awkward conversation. I could tell that her reduced circumstances shamed her.

"Just as we were finishing our meal, I heard something – a thin, screeching cry like a beast caught in a snare. Just as suddenly as it came, it was muffled. I over-turned my teacup on my plate."

"'Good Heavens, what was that?'

"'Pay it no attention,' Brenda said. 'I believe it is a ghost, for I hear that cry from time to time, and can think of no other explanation.'

"I was stunned. 'You never mentioned a specter in your letters.'

"'What good would it have done me to have told you of it?'

"'But Brenda, you have always been fond of gothic stories! You were so quick to ask me about the ghostly tales of Boston, and if there was truly a headless horseman in Sleepy Hollow, and to tell me how you saw the spirit of Anne Boleyn when Father took you to visit the Tower! I would think you would have relished a phantom in your house.'

"She frowned and shook her head. 'I said a great many silly things as a child. I hope I have outgrown them.' Brenda then ran a bell, and the maid waddled away with the dishes. 'Brother,' she said, very seriously, 'did you bring the Folio with you?'"

"Mr. Holmes – the way she spoke – as if she were a dealer at a store, impatient to get to business – rattled my nerves."

"'I did – but I placed in the hotel safe.'

Her pretty face twisted in frustration. "'Why? Did you think I would steal it? Don't you realize how precious it would be to Father, to see it again?'

"'I wished to know more of Father's circumstances before – "

"And then, Mr. Holmes, what should have been a warm reunion came to a strange, unsettling end, because Brenda burst into tears and angrily ordered me out of the house. I returned to my hotel and spent the afternoon in anguished thought. Something seemed so amiss to me – and Brenda was nothing like she had portrayed herself in her letters. Had father's illness and her sudden poverty unhinged her mind? I took my lonely dinner at the hotel and was about to undress and prepare for bed when, much to my surprise, there was a knock at the door. A porter had shown Brenda to my room."

Holmes nodded, as if he had expected just that development in the tale.

"I was shocked at her arrival, so late in the evening, and I feared the worst. She sat down in the chair and removed her hat and veil. To my horror, I saw that her left eye was swollen, and her cheek was bruised.

"'Brenda, what – ?'

"'Father did this,' she whispered. 'I know it was not his intention, to swing at me so wildly, and yet – You see what you see. Freddy, I must be plain with you now that we are alone with no servants to overhear our conversation: I have lived in Hell for twenty years.'

"I know I must have babbled something in protest. She shook her head. Tears coursed down her cheek."

"'What could I have told you in my letters, when I knew they might be intercepted by Father, or by your mother? We both were prisoners of our wicked parents, and I knew that even if I revealed the truth to you, there was nothing you could do for me. No, Freddy, everything I wrote to you was a fiction, made to keep up my spirits, allowing me to pretend my life was a happy one. But I can bear it no longer. Father must die.'

"'Murder!' I cried. She begged me to lower my voice.

"'I will do the deed – I absolve you from all blame. A few drops of poison, and he is gone. As ill as he is, and in so much pain, death will be

137

a mercy. All I ask of you is to help me flee the scene and give me enough money to book passage on a ship.'

"Brenda, the police will find you.'

She grabbed my hand and spoke with barely controlled passion.

"'No, Freddy, for I have planned this ever since Father fell ill. Here is what I will do: I will send the servants away tomorrow evening. There are only two of them. You shall arrive afterward, with the Folio, and show it to Father. As cruel as he has been to me, I would give him one last moment of happiness before he dies. Once he is dead, I will overturn a candle beside his bed. You and I will flee before the alarm is raised.' She tossed her hair proudly. 'I do not care a whit what you do with the Folio. Only help me escape this torment I have endured for so long!'

"Mr. Holmes, you cannot imagine my state of shock and horror. But at last, I found myself talking to her as if discussing the premise of a bad play, or a cheap novel.

"'Brenda, even if the house burns to the ground, the police will seek you for questioning. You will become a wanted person.'

"'They will assume I am dead.'

"'Why?'

"'Because they will find a woman's charred body beside Father's. You recall the scream you heard in the house? A year ago, Father and I grew curious as to the source of that haunting cry. Father knew our home was once the site of a gaol. We dug about and found an old cell. There, still in chains, was a withered corpse, a mummified body of a woman! Father left it wrapped up, hidden in the cellar, for he did not wish to have the police involved and cause a scandal in the neighborhood. I will place one of my dresses on this deceased woman and lay her beside the bed. When she is found, they will assume it is me! Freddy, I need only your help to flee this country.'

"We talked for an hour. Mr. Holmes, Brenda told me so many horrible, unspeakable things – crimes against nature, sins committed by our father – I finally begged her to cease speaking. I told her I would think it through and promised I would not betray her intentions. She instructed me to come at seven tonight. As she rose to leave, I took her in my arms and whispered in her ear words I felt certain would offer reassurance – *Apres la pluie, le beau temps*. But this did not comfort her. Instead, she pulled away from me with a look of great confusion and was gone before I could blink."

"And you slept upon this information?"

"I would hardly call it sleep, sir. No, I have not shut my eyes all night. I will not help her commit patricide, of that much I am certain. But I cannot go to the police, I gave her my word. What should I do? I can hardly sit passively while she executes Father, even if he truly deserves to be killed!"

Holmes rose and moved to the window, looking down into the street.

"Mr. Fernsby, I want you to think very deeply. Close your eyes and imagine you are an artist, about to paint a picture. How do you envision the butler at your father's home?"

The young man was startled by this request. He looked to me in confusion, and I encouraged him to answer Holmes as best he could.

"I . . . I recall very little except . . . He was tall, and broad-shouldered. His coat seemed much too small for him, and I wondered why he wore such an old-fashioned livery, almost like a servant to nobility, which Father is certainly not! The man's hair was dark and combed back with pomade."

"No scars or moles upon his face?"

"None, sir."

"His age?"

Our guest frowned. "Young, I would think. Perhaps not even thirty. I recall thinking to myself that Grandfather's butler was far older."

Holmes began to smile.

"And the maid? Can you describe her?"

"A large, slovenly woman – not tall, and with grizzled hair drawn back in a mob cap. I would say she was somewhere in her sixties. When she opened her hideous mouth, a front tooth was missing."

Holmes rubbed his chin. "By any chance, Mr. Fernsby, did Miss Brenda discuss these rather interesting family servants in her missives?"

"Not that I can recall. To be quite honest, I had the impression Father had no staff beyond faithful old Mrs. Eleanor Harrison, the housekeeper."

"But this isn't the same female you met in the home?"

"Indeed not. When Brenda spoke to her maid, she called her Lynn."

"Did your sister ever write to you of entertaining friends?"

Mr. Fernsby frowned and rubbed his fingers on his forehead, as if he could draw out forgotten memories, drag them from his brain by force.

"She rarely mentioned friends, beyond some she made while at school in Paris, and all of them remain in France. Perhaps . . . Yes, once or twice she wrote that there was a girl named Pamela, whose family were actors, and that the two of them commiserated together over their fathers being obsessed with the theater. But that is all I can remember."

"No recollection of the lady's last name?"

The client winced. "Who can keep such female chatter straight? It was something with a *D* and a *worth* – Dogworth, Dollworth . . . ."

"Dartworth?" Holmes asked sharply. The young man snapped his fingers.

139

"Yes – By golly, that it the name! How did you – ? But Mr. Holmes," our guest said, as my friend handed him his coat and stick, clearly indicating it was time for him to depart. "What do you advise me to do?"

"Leave me the address of your father's home, but under no circumstances return to it," Holmes said. "Instead, go back to your hotel, lock your door, stay in your room, and await further instructions. Is that clear?"

The young man's face went white. "Sir, you make it sound as if . . . as if I am in danger."

"I fear you may have found yourself unwittingly placed in very strange circumstances," Holmes replied. "But if you do as I ask, you should have nothing to fear."

"Time is of the essence," Holmes said, as soon as our client departed. He took down his commonplace book and began scribbling names and addresses from it. "Watson, I believe it is essential that we divide to conquer."

"What do you mean?"

"I am entrusting you with an aspect of this investigation. I may be condemning you to a frustrating afternoon, but I fear it cannot be helped."

"I am grateful to be of service."

"You will be essential." Holmes handed me a paper with a list of employment agencies on it. "These are placement services for domestics. All of them cater to better, but not elite, households in the city. You are in search of Mrs. Eleanor Harrison, formerly the housekeeper at the Fernsby home. Feel free to make up a reward of at least ten pounds for the person who successfully finds her for you. Hint at an unexpected inheritance, if you feel the need."

"And if I succeed in locating her?"

"Bring her back to Baker Street, if possible. If not, inquire pointedly as to the circumstances of why she is no longer employed by Mr. Fernsby."

Good fortune was mine that day. I had just begun to grow a little footsore when the proprietor of the fifth establishment I visited said Mrs. Harrison had been by only that morning. A half-hour later, I met the lady at her lodgings, and she was more than willing to return to Baker Street with me, as she had a great deal to say about the circumstances of her dismissal.

"I have been badly treated. The very nerve of them, to dismiss me so abruptly after all these years! Though, if anyone, I blame Mr. Fernsby, not Miss Brenda. He was always so absent-minded. Nothing interested him except his collection and . . . Oh, if I had never gone to Bath, to help my Aunt Harriet!"

"And this was – "

"It was a week ago, when I received a telegram saying that my Aunt Harriet – She is my maiden aunt, who raised me when my parents died, and is more mother than aunt to me, if you will. The message said she had fallen and broken her hip and was in the hospital. Of course, I asked for leave to go to her, as she has no other family, and Mr. Fernsby granted it and even gave me funds to make sure I was comfortable in my travels. But then – Thank you for the tea! – and these cakes are delicious, I must ask your landlady where she buys them! – Oh, how my thoughts run away. Where was I?"

"There was something amiss in Bath?" I coached.

"Oh yes! Dear me! When I reached Bath, they said there was no such lady in the hospital. I thought perhaps the sender of the message had erred in the location, so I visited every hospital and rest home in the town, and no one had any record. I was so distraught – But at last, very late that evening, I simply went to my aunt's house, and you will never believe what I found!"

"She was well and had never sent the message?"

"Sir, you must be a detective! We found we had been the victims of some foolish prank. Naturally, I was on the train back to London the next morning. Yet when I returned . . . Well, it hurt me quite badly, what transpired. I was met at the door by a large, slatternly woman who rudely tossed a carpetbag at my feet. She told me it contained my clothes and that my other possessions had been boxed up and shipped off to my aunt's residence! 'What kind of nonsense is this?' I demanded. Then another woman came to the door – and this one I recognized!"

"Who was she?"

"Miss Pamela Dartworth – a friend of Miss Brenda's. I had seen her about the house on several occasions, though paid her little mind. Now she acted as if she was the mistress of the place. She told me the Fernsbys had suddenly gone off to France to have a play produced, that they were intending to sell their house in London, and had decided my services were no longer required. She gave me an envelope with a week's wages in it and told me I was not to trouble the family any further. I had served Mr. Fernsby for twenty years, and to be dismissed in such a way! It grates, Doctor . . . It grates upon my soul."

"Did you tell anyone of this strange development?"

The lady's broad face slowly turned pink. "No . . . for when I protested, the girl made a threat which I took to heart. She said I had better not make a fuss, or the police would wish to speak to me about some items that had gone missing from the home. Of course, that was rubbish to imagine I had stolen from my employer! But Doctor . . . I confess I was less than an angel in my youth . . . I even served six months in a house of corrections . . . and the thought of having any of my personal business sniffed over by constables unnerved me. I called the woman an ugly name, grabbed up my bag, and stomped away."

I remembered a detail from the young gentleman's story. "Did you ever hear strange noises in the home? Perhaps the kind that a child might blame on a ghost?"

The housekeeper shook her head. "No, but the home was built on the foundations of an old gaol. We found an empty cell hidden in the cellar a few months ago, when some renovations were done, but I cannot say that we ever felt haunted."

Holmes returned at just that moment. He seemed to sense Mrs. Harrison was a loquacious individual, and asked if he might call upon her in the morning, as his investigation had taken an unexpected truth. She was puzzled but amenable, and within minutes of her departure we were in a carriage, racing toward the Northumberland Hotel. I quickly told Holmes what I had learned from the lady.

"Ah, my suspicions are doubly confirmed. This will be valuable information to assist Mr. Fernsby in going to Scotland Yard and asking for official assistance. A warrant will be required, but I have no doubt as to its necessity now."

"What do you mean?"

"Watson, it was clear from the start that our client was being deceived. The young woman he met at his family home isn't his half-sister. Nor is the elderly gentleman upstairs his father."

"But how are you so certain?'

"Why a maid and a butler in antique livery – More likely a costume! – in a home where the residents are reduced to selling pictures from the wall, and breaking up a beloved collection just to pay for medicine? Recall also that the lady didn't use her favorite pet name for her stepbrother, and her answer when confronted with this fact was clearly a dodge. The father with blackened teeth, lying in an invalid's bed, was also an easy trick."

Holmes shook his head, leaned through the window, and shouted at the driver to pick up the pace. He dropped back on the seat with a scowl. "But it was the interview last night that confirmed the imposture beyond all doubt. The behavior was uncharacteristic. Clearly her stories were disturbing falsehoods. And consider her brother's parting words, the French phrase, her confusion. No young woman who attended school in Paris would have been unfamiliar with the expression. An English woman unexperienced with Continental travel, however, might be confused as to its meaning." Holmes shook his head. "These are people with knowledge of the family and its quirks. The imposters were aware that Mr. Fernsby had never seen a photograph of his half-sister, so he would accept any woman of the correct age as this individual. The villains also knew the housekeeper could be lured away for a day and then silenced with a threat touching upon her unfortunate past. All this implies a certain level of intimacy with the Fernsbys."

"But what would be the point of such an elaborate charade?"

"The point is simple: The Dartworths are after the First Folio."

"Who are these Dartworths?"

"A family of failed thespians. I knew some of their story from the police courts. The rest I learned in the past hours by speaking with my friends in the theatrical world. Jack, Lynn, Pamela, and William Dartworth – father, mother, daughter, and son – were booed from every stage in the city before turning to various confidence games and petty crimes."

"And the Fernsbys have fallen into their clutches."

"That is the way I read it. William is the youthful butler, Jack is portraying the aged father, Lynn has taken on the role of the maid, and Pamela is pretending to be Miss Brenda. I am hopeful that one or both of the Fernsbys are being held prisoner, and not murdered already."

"The cry from the basement! Do you think – ?"

We had arrived at the hotel, and before I could complete my question, Holmes sprang from the vehicle. I paid the driver and hurried to the front desk. As I approached, I saw something was amiss. Holmes was leaning forward, his face pale, his teeth bared.

"I don't know who they were," the clerk said. "Only that Mr. Fernsby departed between them half an hour ago. There was a lady in a veil on one side, and a rather tall gentleman on the other. I feared Mr. Fernsby might be ill, as he was pale and unsteady on his feet, but he asked for the package he had placed in our safe, and I gave it to him. Just then, Lady Heatherway appeared with both her poodles and – "

Holmes whirled with a curse. Outside the hotel, he spotted one of his young urchins lounging before a store window. Holmes called him over and scribbled out a note.

"Take this to Scotland Yard and give it to Inspector Lestrade. Invoke my name if anyone in a uniform should attempt to stop you. Do you understand?"

The dirty, barefoot little lad snapped a salute that would have made a major general proud, then scurried away to do my friend's bidding. Holmes whirled and gestured down the street.

"With this traffic, we will be faster on foot. Let us hope our prey will be slowed by it."

143

"Holmes, what has happened?"

"The worst, I fear. Our client was followed to Baker Street. They know he consulted me. Now they must hurry through with their plan."

"Which is?"

"Theft of the First Folio – and cold-blooded murder! Run, Watson!"

It wasn't far to the Fernsby home, yet by the time we reached it, my lungs were burning and my old wound aching. Holmes had gained on me, being faster and more talented at dodging, ducking, or hurdling every obstruction in his path. As I came up the street, I heard Holmes raise the alarm, and saw what he had feared – a coil of gray smoke rising from a first story window. I took up the shout, and some men hurried off to seek help. Holmes ran to the door, only to find it locked.

"To the rear, quickly."

Behind the house was a narrow yard with an open gate. We charged into the house through the kitchen, where thick smoke was already filling the narrow confines of the ground floor. I followed Holmes's lead in wrapping a handkerchief around my face.

"Upstairs!" he ordered. I shook my head.

"If they are imprisoned in the cellar – "

Holmes had no patience for argument. He drew me up the narrow stairs to a long hallway, quickly locating the room that would correspond to the window where the smoke was first sighted. He slammed his shoulder against the stubborn doorway until it broke free. Inside, we found a horrifying scene: An elderly man in bedclothes, plus Frederick Fernsby and a young woman both lying in a faint beside the bed. Holmes threw the youth over his shoulder while I scooped the girl into my arms. One quick glance told me there was no need for further heroics: The elder gentleman was dead and had been that way for quite some time. The flames licking at the rug abruptly leapt to the tattered bed curtains, and we hurried out with our burdens, only to meet a phalanx of burly firemen breaking down the front door. It was too late, however, for there were clearly accelerants splashed about the building, and the fire seemed to be racing in every direction, curling and twisting like the tenacles of a hellish octopus, rapidly devouring all that remained of the home.

"I have always held that there is nothing new in the annals of crime," Holmes told our guests, four days later, when they paid a call at Baker Street. "However, your tragic situation bears some unique characteristics. I would be interested to learn how well the reality of your ordeal matched my theories."

"Well, sir," Mr. Frederick Fernsby said, "if it was a theory that saved us, I am grateful. And I know dear Brenda feels the same way."

The young woman smiled. It was true she wasn't a beauty, but there was a purity and gentleness in her face, with its great brown eyes, that would have put any woman of paint, powder, and fashion to shame. She spoke softly and sweetly.

"I am indeed in your debt, sir. You may ask me anything, Mr. Holmes, and I shall do my best to answer."

"When did your father make the acquaintance of the Dartworths?"

"We saw them in play two years ago. Afterward, Father treated the family to dinner. I didn't enjoy myself. I found Mr. Dartworth overbearing, while his wife quickly became embarrassingly intoxicated. William, their son, made unwholesome remarks. But their daughter Pamela was my age, a witty and clever girl who quickly sensed that I was lonely. She played me like a fiddle, sir, and won my sympathy by claiming that she wished to be free of her family's noxious influences. She visited often and became intensely interested in Father's collections of theatrical memorabilia. She heard from Father's own lips the story of the stolen First Folio. In fact, it is safe to say she became obsessed with it, often asking me if Freddy might be induced to come to England and show it to her and her family! These requests became so frequent and aggressive I had begun to think it would be necessary to end my association with her."

"You should have told me in your letters!" young Fernsby chided. She squeezed his hand fondly.

"It seemed a silly thing to mention. But Pamela was with me on the day the cable arrived from America, informing us of Mrs. Fernsby's death. Father dictated the reply, which was warm and loving. Pamela offered to carry it to the telegraph office, as Father was quite unwell at the time, and I needed to stay at home with him."

"It was she who ordered your brother to bring the Folio," I said. Miss Brenda nodded.

"I believe so. She made a pest of herself in the intervening weeks, always eager to know the contents of any telegrams from Freddy and taking any replies we sent. Now I see how she must have altered them to fit her plans."

"She timed the distraction that lured your housekeeper away," Holmes said. "It was then that you and your father were taken hostage."

"Exactly, sir. Mrs. Harrison had barely been gone an hour when the Dartworths arrived at our door. Father welcomed them in – His kind and loving nature couldn't imagine they would do him any harm. – and within moments of entering our dwelling, they easily overpowered us. I was taken below and confined in the old cell. I lost track of time in the darkness, but

145

then Pamela came to me, bringing me scraps of food. She coldly told me that Father was dead, and she was only allowing me to stay alive for her own purposes.

"'I might need you yet,' she said. 'For details of your correspondence with Frederick.'

"'I will tell you nothing.'

"'We shall see.'

"I existed in darkness and dread. More than once I worked up the courage to scream at the top of my lungs, in hopes that some passerby might hear me, but one of the Dartworths was always stationed outside my prison. I was beaten so harshly for my shouts that I dared not repeat them very often. At last, Mr. Dartworth himself appeared at my cage and said, 'We are done with you.' He seized me and pressed a foul-smelling rag to my face, and I knew no more until I awakened in the hospital."

"And you, Mr. Fernsby?" I asked.

"I followed Mr. Holmes's instructions and returned to the hotel. Later that afternoon, I heard a knock at the door, and a gruff voice saying it was you, Mr. Holmes. I rather foolishly threw open the portal and there stood that woman and her butler, both pointing pistols at me. They forced me back into the room, telling me it would be worth my life to scream. They demanded to know where the Folio was, and I told them it was still in the hotel safe. As soon as I confessed it, I felt a needle press into my arm. My will was suddenly not my own. I did as they commanded, retrieved the book, and was guided out into a carriage. The last thing I remember was the door of Father's bedroom being opened by that awful fat woman, and a terrible stench assailing my nostrils. Thank God you both arrived in time, or we would have been cremated, along with poor Father's corpse!"

"The Dartworths murdered your father because he was a liability to their scheme," Holmes said. "I felt certain, when I saw the smoke that you had both been placed in your father's room, to give the scene the look of a horrific accident. I trust Scotland Yard will bring the Dartworths to heel soon. Perhaps the items that were stolen will be recovered."

The Fernsbys shook their heads. "It appears that Father's obsession brought nothing but misery – an unhappy marriage, murder, and attempted murder," Miss Brenda whispered. "I am content to start my life anew, free of any attachments."

"Except to me, I hope," Mr. Fernsby said. "We are both orphans now. Come to America, Brenda. You will always have a home in Boston."

The Fernsby siblings departed arm in arm, but Holmes remained restless, checking his watch and looking out the window. At last, I heard him give an exclamation of delight. Moments later, Inspector Lestrade appeared at our door. I was astonished by our old friend's appearance: He was clad in a tattered coat, with a dirty shirt, a greasy pork-pie hat, and filthy boots. His face was rubbed with soot in places, and he sported a bristling black wig.

"Inspector," Holmes said, "welcome. I am surprised Mrs. Hudson admitted you."

"I had to pull off the false hair before she would," he snapped. "Do I look the part? You said I should resemble a disreputable character."

Holmes shook his head as he once more glanced through the curtains. "You may have overcommitted yourself to the role. But there is no time for a new costume! I see that the final member of our ensemble has just arrived in his carriage. You have your pistol I presume?"

"I'm wearing my trousers, aren't I?"

Holmes smiled. "Fortunately, yes. Watson, if I could trouble you to pocket your army revolver – Swiftly, now! And please allow me to do the talking."

I had just managed to conceal my firearm when Mrs. Hudson opened the door and announced our visitor. Tall, spare, and elegantly clad in a long cape, Lord Henry Renwood swept into the room. He glanced at each of us with a cold eye before placing a leather case upon the table.

"I am not sure that our business requires so many witnesses," he growled.

"You don't have a choice in the matter," Holmes said dryly. "Unless, of course, you are content to retain a replica of the First Folio, instead of acquiring the actual one."

The nobleman scowled. "You are certain that it is genuine?"

Holmes languidly gestured toward Lestrade. "This gentleman was kind enough to – *Ahem!* – acquire it discreetly from the buyer the duplicitous Dartworths sold it to. But I am curious: How much money did the family defraud you of?"

Lord Renwood sneered. "I will say only that when Brenda Dartworth alerted me to her familiarity with the Fernsbys, and her ability to seize the Folio upon its return to England, I gave her *carte blanche* to steal it and the rest of Uriah Fernsby's collection." One thin eyebrow rose on his lean face. "And you truly hold the original, as your man said?"

"I do. Let us toast to achieving our desired ends. You will not drink?" Holmes shrugged and put aside his decanter. "Very well. My fellow told me it was quite the clever switch the Dartworths pulled. He also says the family has run away to India."

"It seems your man has been deceived. They have fled to South Africa."

147

"Ah, a slip of the tongue on my part. But I guarantee there is no confusion about the Folio. You are fortunate that my light-fingered friend here is willing to sell it to you."

"While you make a tidy profit, no doubt, as an accessory to his crime," Lord Renwood snorted. "I never believed those tales claiming the brilliant Sherlock Holmes was a servant of righteousness. Consulting detectives, private agents, whatever you call yourselves – You all crawl about in the same cesspool of filth and deceit, associating with criminals and the lower orders."

"Present company excepted, I presume?" Holmes asked. "But enough of this chit-chat. My friend has the original First Folio, and you do not. He has appointed me as his broker. Shall we make the exchange?"

"Only if you explain the reason why you insisted that I bring the false copy, rather than throwing it into the fire, where it belongs."

"Lord Renwood," Holmes laughed, "a replica fine enough to fool you, England's most noted Shakespearean expert, will easily trick a less-discerning collector. Such a splendid fraud will fatten my coffers."

"You confirm my low opinion of you."

"I am gratified to do so."

"Very well. The book is in that valise. But I shall not give you the money until I am assured you possess the original."

"A reasonable compromise. You may inspect the article."

Holmes motioned toward his favorite chair, where he had placed an item covered with a silk cloth. Renwood lunged forward, turning his back to us in his eagerness to claim his prize. He ripped away the covering, staring at the book's cover.

"What the devil – ?"

He spun to the sound of three pistols being cocked. For a moment, he simply stared at us in disbelief. Then he threw up his hands and the cheap copy of *In Praise of Folly* fell to the floor.

"How kind of you to return the First Folio, tell us where the rest of the collection went, provide a lead to the location of the Dartworths, and confess to conspiracy before multiple witnesses – including an inspector of Scotland Yard," Holmes said languidly. "The Dartworths were petty thieves. There had to be a greater criminal deploying them. Who better than the man rebuffed from buying Fernsby's collection years ago? Covetousness leads inevitably to crime. Do take him away, Lestrade."

Moments later, Lord Renwood was ensconced in a police carriage. Holmes and I perused the First Folio, admiring the annotations scribbled in the hand of the author of *Paradise Lost*.

"One final question," I said, as Holmes sat down to draft a message to the Fernsbys. "Who was the underworld figure skillful enough to convince Lord Renwood the real copy was a fake one?"

Holmes smiled. "One man in his time plays many parts, my dear Watson! You are looking at him."

# The Single Shoe
## by Stuart Douglas

"There is something unnerving about a man removing a shoe in public."

The speaker was my friend Sherlock Holmes, and I must admit his words brought a smile to my lips. He had complained of late of a degree of boredom, and the idea that something so commonplace might have piqued his curiosity was both humorous and pleasing.

We were standing in the bay window of a shop on the corner of Baker Street and Marylebone Road. Until quite recently a rather good tobacconist had stood there, but sadly for the pipe smokers of the borough, the elderly owner had recently announced his intention to close his business and move to the country to live with his sister. Holmes had arranged to meet the man at his premises to buy the remainder of his stock of strong Turkish shag.

"What's that, Mr. Holmes?" that worthy, though hard of hearing, gentlemen asked, but Holmes simply shook his head.

"Oh, nothing to trouble you, Mr. Mackenzie," he assured the shopkeeper, though barely looking in his direction. "But if you would be so kind as to send the tobacco 'round to Baker Street, I would be much obliged."

Apparently keen to be gone, he gestured I should precede him out of the door. I hesitated on the lintel as the skies – which had glowered above us all day in menacingly heavy black clouds – chose that moment to open and drench the streets in a deluge reminiscent of the onset of an Indian monsoon. With an irritated grunt, Holmes pushed past me and I found myself hurrying to keep up with him as he dodged between passing carriages and made his way across the wide thoroughfare.

The road was a busy one at that time of day, and by the time we reached other side, having been forced to pause by the passage of a long, horse-drawn omnibus in front of us, whoever had initially caught Holmes's eye had gone. In his place – whoever he might have been – lay a single shoe, a well-shone brown brogue. It sat in the middle of the pavement, apparently abandoned. Of its owner there was no sign, though Holmes quickly looked down a nearby alleyway and over the low wall which lined the main road.

Then, oblivious to the curious stares of the few passers-by who had not taken shelter from the downpour, he knelt down on the dirty pavement

150

and peered at the shoe from all angles, even going so far as to prod it with a pencil. Only then, satisfied in some way I couldn't fathom, did he pick them up and, with a cry to follow him called to me over his shoulder, set off at a brisk pace across the road and along Baker Street to the rooms we shared.

"Really, Holmes," I complained when finally I slumped, soaking wet, into an armchair and caught my breath. "I wonder at times if you actually go out of your way to appear eccentric to our neighbours." I gestured towards the object he held in his hand. "I fail to see what can possibly be so interesting about a shoe that you should feel the need to sprint along Baker Street like that."

"A shoe?" Holmes seemed confused for a second, his brow creased and his eyes strangely clouded, and then he looked down at his hands as though seeing them for the first time. "Oh, you mean *this*," he said distractedly, holding the brogue up. "I hardly think that need concern us just now." Without looking where he aimed, or even taking a moment to check where it landed, he tossed the shoe over his shoulder, where it bounced once and thumped against a tottering pile of scientific journals, which slid down to cover it in an avalanche of paper.

"*This*, however . . ." he said, unfolding his hand to reveal a slip of sodden white paper, ". . . this is an entirely different matter."

"Well, what is it?" I asked, exasperated already by my friend's love of both the dramatic and the opaque. "Is it a letter of some kind?"

"I have no idea at present," he said, "but it should be easy enough to find out." He smiled and laid the paper down on an occasional table which sat by his chair. Carefully, using the tip of a penknife, he teased the folded sheet apart and let it fall open.

"Now that is unfortunate," he muttered to himself.

I leaned forward and examined the paper, still unsure as to Holmes's interest in it. Having done so, I was none the wiser, for the rainwater had evidently contrived to get inside the shoe, even in the presumably short time it had been exposed to the elements, and whatever had been written there had been smudged beyond identification, save for two words: "*With Ale*". All I could think of was that it was something to do with beer, but I failed to see how that might interest Holmes, and I hesitated to mention it.

"I had hoped that all would be made clear, but as I feared, the unexpectedly inclement weather has put paid to that." Holmes reached for his magnifying glass and peered down at the offending paper, murmuring under his breath as he did so. Several minutes passed in this manner before he spoke to me again.

"In the absence of the message itself, we must consider how it came into our possession," he said, looking across at me.

"Happily," I said. "If only you would be so kind as to explain just how it did so."

"I have had recourse before, Watson, to comment on your singular inability to take note of even the most obvious events occurring around you, but I must admit I hadn't thought it possible you could have failed to notice the disturbance across the road from Mackenzie's shop not five minutes ago."

I was still feeling a slight pain in my chest from the unexpected sprint back from the tobacconists, and so was a little more sardonic than usual in my reply. "I can only apologise for letting you down so badly. I fear that my experience of lost shoes is perhaps not as great as your own, nor my knowledge of old boxes."

"It's quite all right, my dear fellow," Holmes replied in all seriousness. "The fault lies almost certainly with the school teachers of your youth. No doubt, in their cold Presbyterian way, they thought only to ensure you know your catechism and such dull scientific subjects as would suit you to a life on the frontiers of the Empire."

I might have bridled at the observation were it not so accurate, so instead I busied myself filling my pipe and waited for him to proceed, as I knew he would in due course.

"But if you failed to observe the events across the road from Mackenzie's shop, then I suppose it falls to me to describe the facts to you, and then perhaps you might tell me what you glean from them?"

I nodded, but said nothing. I had played this game with Holmes before and had yet to emerge the victor.

"While you were eyeing up the Chacom briar pipes with Mr. Mackenzie, I happened to glance out of the window and caught the eye of a gentleman standing immediately opposite. He was taller than average and painfully thin, but otherwise unremarkable and I would have turned away, had he not very quickly, without taking his eyes from mine, removed his left shoe and placed it on the ground directly in a line between us. That done, he gave a tiny nod in my direction and, I believe, curled one finger towards me." Holmes shrugged. "As you know, at that point I attempted to cross the road towards him, but that confounded omnibus passed between us and by the time it had gone on its way, he had used the cover it provided to abscond, and all that remained was the shoe." He stared at the wet scrap of paper again and shook his head. "Now tell me, what do you deduce from that?"

I took a moment to consider what he had said. I had little confidence that I would be able to suggest anything which hadn't already occurred to my friend, but not for the first time, I found his attitude needlessly condescending, and I was determined to give the matter my best attention.

"You said this mysterious man was a gentleman," I began. "On what do you base this description?"

"An excellent first thought, Watson. Never blindly accept the word of a witness. Always question every aspect of his tale. Both because he or she may – inadvertently or not – have misspoken, and because interrogation itself often brings new information to light." He gestured behind himself, to the pile of fallen papers, beneath which the toe of the shoe peeped out. "That is an expensive calf-leather brogue. It appears to be brand new – If you examine it, you will note the relative lack of scuffing on the sole. Though the heel has become partially detached, it would be easily mendable, and is hardly the sort of item to be discarded by anyone not of substantial means. Observe too the paper on which the lost note was written. It is of good quality, heavy and expensive, and here . . ." He indicated the top right of the page. ". . . it is clear that the page has been cut – very carefully, but obvious enough when magnified – presumably to remove the address printed which was printed there.

"Additionally – though here you will have to take my word for it – the fellow I saw was smartly dressed and carried himself with what I would call a military bearing." He held up a hand to forestall my next question. "I don't say that he was a military man necessarily, but he held himself stiffly upright in a manner which suggested to me an army background. Finally, though I admit this is less tangible evidence, his actions themselves spoke of someone used to authority, with a mind capable of complex planning. I hardly think that implies a chimney sweep or a bank clerk."

He leaned forward. "So much for the gentleman himself. Now what of his note?" He held the object out to me, but I wasn't yet ready for it, and shook my head.

"I'm not sure I've exhausted this shoe yet," I protested mildly. "Why have you dismissed it so quickly? What makes it of less importance? At the very least, it is an unusual receptable for correspondence?"

I was rather proud of this observation and was pleased when Holmes grinned in response. "Perhaps not quite so good a second thought as your first," he said, however, dashing my feeling of satisfaction. "Can you not answer that for yourself though?"

I took a full minute or more, walking across and picking up the shoe, which was just as he had described, but could think of nothing of note to say about it. I grumbled as much to Holmes and he laughed and clapped his hands together.

"Exactly! There is nothing *to say* about it. That is the very nub of the thing. In itself, it is unremarkable, but by removing it in so public a place and positioning it so precisely, its former owner was able to catch my attention and hold my interest. As I said before, his actions spoke of a mind used to planning and strategising."

"The shoe was merely a lure, then?" I said, grasping his point now.

"Certainly. Even its condition – almost good as new, with nothing about it to identify its owner – indicates its role as bait, disposable once its purpose has been served."

Suddenly, he jumped to his feet and strode to the door of our rooms. "Mrs. Hudson!" he shouted downstairs. A moment later I heard our landlady confirm her presence with rather less force.

"Has anyone been to see me in the last few days whom you have turned away for whatever reason?" Holmes shouted again. I couldn't make out Mrs. Hudson's reply, but when Holmes walked back towards his chair, I could see from his face that she had answered in the negative.

"No one has called on me and been denied entry," he said. "The most obvious reason for this little performance isn't, therefore, the correct one." His voice trailed off as he slumped into his chair and stared into the distance, everything forgotten bar the problem whirling and tumbling in his prodigious brain. "Of course," he said after only a few seconds. "He hasn't been to see me here because he fears being seen *with* me. He is being watched – or we are."

Once more he jumped to his feet. He stalked across to the rain-streaked window and looked down into the street below. He gave a small grunt. "There is nobody outside who shouldn't be there," he said over his shoulder. "This downpour has all but cleared the streets, thankfully. That doesn't rule out someone observing from one of the other houses, of course, but none at the moment are available for rental, nor have any been sold recently. I think we can assume for now that it is our new friend who is being watched, and not you and me."

"So what do you we do? Simply wait for him to get in touch again?" It seemed to me that with only an illegible note and a discarded shoe as clues, we had no way of progressing the case – if case it was. Part of me wondered by what bizarre means he would contact us, and I smiled to myself at the thought.

Holmes, however, was suddenly a blizzard of activity. "I think we can do better than that," he exclaimed, reaching for his hat and coat. "I fear our friend had played me for something of a fool. In my haste to retrieve his shoe, I allowed myself to be distracted from the man himself."

"How so?" I asked. "You said yourself that he was obscured by the omnibus and was thus able to make good his escape down a nearby lane."

"Exactly! Think, Watson. He cannot afford to be seen with me, so he concocts this peculiar ruse to catch my attention. Yet having done so, still he cannot afford to be seen with me, and so he must ensure that I have taken the bait, and then immediately vacate the scene."

I shrugged, confused by the point he was making. "Is that not what I just said?"

"Not quite. Ask yourself this: How did he decide when to make himself known to me? Mackenzie's wasn't the first establishment we entered this morning, nor was it intended to be the last. So why that shop in particular?"

"He must have been following us. He saw you looking out the window in Mackenzie's and took his opportunity."

"Agreed – but consider the coincidence that he was able to catch my eye just as an omnibus crossed between us. As you say, he must have been following us, but the reason he removed his shoe at that precise moment is because he knew that omnibus was due to pass by." My face must have continued to register my confusion, for Holmes tutted impatiently. "He didn't disappear down a nearby lane, as you suggested. He jumped on board the omnibus as it passed, thereby both making his escape and avoiding drawing attention to himself by making his way through London while wearing a single shoe."

"You don't think a man wearing only one shoe would be remarked upon on an omnibus? I admit I have little experience of them, but I fancy that would be unusual in any circumstance."

By now, Holmes had fastened his coat and handed me my own. "You may be right," he admitted, striding towards the door in the certain knowledge that I would follow. "Which is why we need to visit the offices of The London General Omnibus Company."

The London General Omnibus Company was obviously a successful one. Its offices in the City were rather grander than I would have expected for a business which charged a penny a ticket. Even so, it took the young man we spoke to only a few minutes to identify the exact omnibus which would have passed by as we left Mackenzie's shops, as well – with a little more reluctance – directions to the warehouse in which the omnibuses were kept when not on the road. Luckily, the one we sought would have completed its morning journeys and could be found there within the next hour, at least.

We proceeded there in a hansom cab, Holmes chuckling as we bounced along at my anxious concern that the omnibus drivers might take this as an insult.

Fortunately, the horses which drew the omnibuses were stabled elsewhere, and so the smell inside the carriage warehouse was of polish and axle grease rather than anything more pungent, and we were quickly directed to the bus in question by a helpful lad at the door.

The vehicle was painted a dashing yellow colour all over, even down to the wheels and the halter which would, during working hours, be yoked around a pair of horses. A brown sign advertising the daily route in yellow paint stretched the length of the bottom deck, above which I could see two benches for passengers inside, facing one another. A curved staircase at the rear gave access to the upper floor seating, open to the elements, but given some protection at waist height by another sign, this time advertising something called *Oakey's Knife Polish*. I admit that I was quite taken by the sprightly nature of the décor, and decided to make use of just such an omnibus when the opportunity next arose. I was just about to remark on this to Holmes when a figure appeared from the other side of the vehicle, wiping his oily hands on a dirty rag, and asked in a smoke-roughened voice how he could help us.

"Good afternoon," Holmes said politely, though without offering his hand, I noticed. "You are the driver of this omnibus, I take it?"

"Conductor," the other man replied carefully. "Driver's away." He squinted from Holmes to myself, evidently wary of us and wondering what business we had with him. "If this is about that lamp-post . . ." he began to say in the unmistakable tone of the British workman explaining that some problem or other wasn't his fault, but Holmes held up a hand to stop him before he could get any further.

"It is nothing to do with any lamp-post, I assure you, Mister – ?"

"Flitcroft," the man said, wariness now replaced by uncertainty. "Jonathan Flitcroft. I'm the conductor on this bus," he repeated. "I take the fares. Petey Ransom's the driver, if it's him you want. He'll be back in half-an-hour, I reckon."

Holmes's smile was as wide as it was genuine. "Not at all, Mr. Flitcroft," he beamed. "You are precisely the man we wish to speak to. We are looking for information about a passenger on your vehicle earlier today. He would, I hope, have stuck in your memory as he was wearing only a single shoe."

Flitctoft shook his head slowly. "Nobody came on with no shoe – not that I saw, anyway."

"This would have been at the junction of Baker Street and Marylebone Road, some two hours or so ago?"

Again, he shook his head. "No, nobody like that." He frowned and scratched at his chin. "I did find a shoe upstairs, though, stuffed under the knifeboard." He pointed to the upper deck, where the seats backed onto

156

one another, forming a central peak somewhat like the blade of a knife. "I said to Petey, I said, 'Where do you think that come from?' but he had no more idea than me. It was the strangest thing," he concluded thoughtfully, shaking his head one final time, presumably at the inexplicable behaviour of his fellow man.

Holmes, however, had no time for such philosophical considerations. "Do you still have the shoe?" he asked impatiently, leaning towards the conductor in his eagerness.

Flitcroft nodded and reached into the rear of the carriage. "Here it is," he said, holding out the twin of the brown brogue Holmes had collected across the street from the tobacconist. "I was just about to hand it into the office, but if you want it, you can have it, I suppose. I don't reckon anyone's going to turn up looking for just the one shoe, even if it is a nice one like that." He looked at us quizzically, but Holmes was already twisting the shoe around in his hands, examining it minutely, and so it was left to me to thank the man and slip him half-a-crown in reward for his efforts. He briefly touched his hand to his forehead and, with the slightest of shrugs in Holmes's direction, headed off towards the wide, open doors of the warehouse.

"You were right," I said, indicating the retreating conductor. "Even if Mr. Flitcroft cannot remember our man, the presence of his other shoe confirms that he was on this bus."

"More than that, Watson," Holmes replied, holding the shoe out to me and pointing to a stamp inside. "The manufacturers have left their mark here. *Loakes of London*, it says. These are expensive shoes. I would very surprised if they didn't keep a record of who they were sold to."

The assistant manning the counter at Loakes' shop in town was called Block, and his name suggested, he was considerably less obliging than the fellow at the Omnibus company.

From the beginning, he appeared to view us as suspicious characters, bent on some type of eccentric footwear-related mischief, and consequently treated us with a good deal of undisguised scepticism.

"So, let me see if I have this straight. You've got this pair of shoes with a broken heel, and you want them fixed, on account of you just purchased them. But you can't give me your name or tell me when you bought them from us, nor can you give me even so much as an address so that I can check our records? Is that about right?"

It was on the tip of my tongue to berate him for his impudent manner – and I would have done so, were the situation not exactly as he had described – but Holmes was utterly sanguine.

"I would say that just about covers everything, yes," he agreed with a ready smile. "An admirable summary, in fact, and one which I would like to replicate, if you have no objection?"

The assistant said nothing, only stared glassily at my friend as though awaiting a new trick.

"So," Holmes went on, "let me see if I have *this* straight. You have been working at Loakes for some time, and have been given a good deal of responsibility. You are engaged to be married, with a fiancée keen to set a date, and until recently didn't have enough money saved up to allow you to marry. This has left your fiancée concerningly aggravated, which in turn has been causing you a great deal of worry and concern, and has led, sadly, to your embezzling certain small amounts from your employer. You now regret that you were ever so foolish, of course, but should your employer discover your dishonesty, the best you can hope for is dismissal without a reference, which would be a disaster for a young man on the verge of setting up home with his new wife. Is *that* about right?"

I had no idea where Holmes had plucked these suppositions from, but their effect on the shop assistant was immediate. His face blanched pure white and sweat began to trickle from his hairline down towards his eyes as he glanced nervously around the otherwise empty shop. "How do you know?" he stammered. "How *could* you know?"

"It isn't difficult," Holmes explained calmly. "You have worked for Loakes for long enough that you are trusted to deal with customers on your own, hence there are many times, as now, when you are alone in the shop except for a lone paying customer. There is a slight indentation on your finger, such as might be caused by a gentleman's engagement ring, worn for some time, but now removed to be melted down and the gold included in your wedding ring, which I believe is a fashionable custom at the moment. That interest in fashionable living contrasts with the slight fraying of your left-hand shirt cuff and the rather careworn collar you are wearing, suggesting that your income and your ambitions don't match – or didn't until very recently. The fact that you have finally given your fiancée your engagement ring indicates that you now believe you can afford to marry. The cuticles of every one of your fingers are red and inflamed, caused, I would warrant, by your habit of biting them when worried or nervous – a habit I noticed you indulge in as soon as I suggested you had been stealing from your employer, when an honest man would surely have protested his innocence at once."

"And his regret at being so foolish?" I interjected on the young man's behalf, for he seemed to have been stricken dumb by Holmes's words.

My friend smiled, but there was no warmth in it. "Would you not regret your actions if a complete stranger walked into your shop and laid them out before you in the way I have just done?" he asked.

"What . . . what are you going to do?" Block stuttered, his eyes flicking from Holmes to me and back again. "I do wish I'd never done it, I swear, but Alice was so insistent that I name the day, and that swine Alfie Bessetter's been hanging round, making cow eyes at her . . . ."

I thought for a moment he would burst into tears, but at the last moment he seemed to collect himself. "It was only a few pounds, I promise. Please, tell me what I can do to make it right."

Holmes took a second to consider, then tapped one long finger on the counter. "Fortunately for you, I believe you when you say you haven't taken much money yet, though I doubt it would have remained so small an amount had I not come into this shop today. What you need to do is repay the money you stole – anonymously, of course – and then hand in your notice. I will return here in one month to check you have done so, and if you have, no more need be said about the matter."

The red-faced assistant began to stammer his thanks, but again Holmes cut him off. "More immediately, you can search your records for recent purchases of shoes such as this, and give me a list of the name and address of each purchaser."

The assistant nodded, not taking his eyes away from Holmes. "I don't need to check," he said, licking his lips. "We've only sold one pair of them in the past month. Mr. McMurty it was who ordered them."

"Mr. McMurty?" Holmes prompted quietly.

"He lives in a big house down the road. He's Irish, I think. He does himself well – buys a lot of shoes, boots, and the like."

"Is he a tall, slim man, with a military bearing?" I asked quickly.

"Mr. McMurty?" Block began to laugh, then clearly remembered the predicament he found himself in and choked it off. "No, he's nothing like that. He's about eighty, if he's a day, short with a big round face and a stomach to match. He had factories back in Ireland, I heard. Sold them all and spent the last twenty years collecting china, or paintings, or teaspoons or something." He shrugged nervously, obviously more interested in whether Holmes was really going to let him off than the activities of McMurtry.

"You do have his address, though? You can manage that?" I spoke sternly – unlike Holmes, I didn't view theft from one's employer as a minor matter.

He nodded and scribbled a note on a piece of scrap paper before pushing it across the counter. Holmes glanced down at it then slipped in his pocket.

"I will be back one month from today," he said as he turned to go. "I don't expect to find you here."

As we looked up and down the street outside for a cab, I considered challenging Holmes on what I saw as his rather high-handed decision to take the law into his own hands – but past experience had taught me that the effort would be wasted. Instead, I asked him what exactly we were doing, for it occurred to me that, for all our morning had been spent on the trail of an unknown man, we didn't actually have a crime of any sort to investigate.

"Is this some kind of intellectual exercise?" I asked. "Have you grown so bored with your cases recently that – again – you have taken on one of your own devising?"

"Intellectual exercise?" Holmes considered my words for a moment. "Yes, I suppose in one sense that is exactly what this is. But in another, I believe that the actions of our shoeless friend point to a greater malaise than the mere loss of a shoe. There is intelligence behind his actions, and real purpose. Why should we not be interested in that intelligence and purpose, merely because there appears to be no obvious criminal activity attached to it?"

I could think of several answers to that question, but thinking better of each of them, I simply nodded my agreement and asked what Holmes intended to do at McMurtry's house.

As a growler pulled up alongside us, he held open the door and, as we settled in our seats, he explained his plan.

"Good morning, Miss," Holmes murmured deferentially to the maid who answered his knock on the kitchen door. "I wonder if your master might be interested in contributing to our fund for indigent veterans of war?"

He held up the sheet of paper he had collected from Baker Street, which was indeed headed *Association of Veterans of War*, under which he had typed details of a fictitious appeal for funds. I would need to ask him later just why he has such notepaper to hand, but for the moment, I merely tugged at the too-tight collar of the workman's shirt he had insisted I put on, and wished I was wearing one of my own suits and not the one he had forced on me, which smelled of mothballs and cheap tobacco. The fact that Holmes was similarly dressed as an archetypal middle-class committee man was of little consolation.

"Oh, I don't know about that," the maid said with a shake of her head. "Mr. McMurtry don't like visitors." She made to close the door, but Holmes slipped his foot in the way and winked at the girl, with a smooth smile which I thought verged on the obscene but which she seemed to appreciate.

"Then, if not your master, is there perhaps any member of the household staff who is himself a former soldier and might be willing to speak to us? We've got lads who bravely served Queen and Country sleeping in the streets tonight, and every little helps get them back on their feet. Without it, some of them won't survive this winter, and some of them with wives and kids too."

"Oh, the poor things," she exclaimed, putting her hand to her mouth. "I don't like to think of that, really I don't." She hesitated, her hand still on the door, but the pressure on Holmes's foot gradually easing. "There's Alf, who does the garden. He's always going on about doing twenty years with the army in Aldershot. Or there's Mr. Beckwith, I suppose. He's the master's valet, but I heard him telling cook more than once about how he was out in India and I don't know where else, fighting natives and such."

Holmes clapped his hands together enthusiastically. "Capital! It sounds as though Mr. Beckwith is *exactly* the man we're looking for." He leaned forward slightly and allowed his long fingers to rest briefly on hers where she held the door. "Could you be a dear and fetch him for us? We'll only take a minute of his time."

The little maid coloured and pulled her hand away, but quite slowly, I noticed. She bobbed her head and murmured, "Wait here then, and I'll see if I can find him," and disappeared back into the house, leaving the door ajar and Holmes still smiling.

As soon as she was out of sight, I rounded on my friend, though I was unsure whether to berate him for manipulating the girl so blatantly or to laugh at the idea of Holmes the Lothario. In the end, I had no time to do either – evidently Mr. Beckwith had been nearby, for before I could speak, the door opened again and a tall figure stood in front of us.

For a moment, nobody spoke and then, at the same time, the new man said, "Sherlock Holmes, I presume?" just as Holmes opened the bag he wore over his shoulder, and indicated the brown brogues inside, saying, "Yours, I assume?" as he did so.

Beckwith nodded and quickly pressed the bag closed again. He glanced back into the kitchen and stepped towards us, closing the door behind himself. "Perhaps it'd be best if we took a turn round the garden while we speak, gents," he said overly loudly. "Cook's got dinner to get ready, and she won't want us old soldiers getting in her way." He held out a hand towards a pebbled path that wended its way through a gap in the nearby hedge and, presumably, into the rest of the garden. McMurtry's home was a large and imposing one with, it seemed, grounds to match. We followed Beckwith, I at least no wiser as to what was going on.

"You found my note then?" Beckwith said quietly, as soon as we were a reasonable distance from the house. "I admit, I couldn't be sure you'd seen me at all, but I thought you had, and I was running out of time. I'd been following you all morning, waiting for the right moment to slip my note into your hand, but I saw the omnibus coming and realised I could use it to make my escape. If you were looking at me, I reckoned, and if everything I've heard about you was true, well, you'd not let a man doing something as odd as taking off his shoe and leaving it in the street pass without investigating."

He stopped, as though unsure how to proceed, and I took the opportunity to have a good look at him. He was tall and slim, clean-shaven with close-cropped grey hair, which was receding badly, giving him rather a high forehead. He held himself ramrod straight, and I could see why Holmes had recognised him as a military man.

"In fact, your note was ruined by the rain," Holmes said, filling the silence as he fished the illegible message from his bag. "As you can see, all that remains is the end of your name, and the middle portion of your occupation."

Beckwith tutted to himself. "Perhaps my plan wasn't as solid as I thought. But I only had a moment, and since I made sure to break the heel as I took the shoe off, I thought I would at least have an excuse for abandoning it, should certain other people find it."

Holmes smiled reassuringly. "I think you may be getting a little ahead of yourself, Mr. Beckwith," he said, indicating a long wooden bench at the side of the path. "Perhaps if we take a seat and you tell us exactly why you wished to speak to me, then we night resolve whether we can be of assistance?"

To my surprise, Beckwith looked around nervously before sitting down. "We don't have long, Mr. Holmes," he said as we took seats on either side of him. "I don't know when I'm being watched."

Holmes nodded and slid a thin folder from his bag. He opened it and laid it on his knee, pointing to the top of the sheet of paper inside. So far as I could see, the words typed there were sheer gibberish, a collection of nonsense words and random letters which were more like a spy's encrypted code than legible English. Before I could ask, he explained "I had assumed that something of that nature was the case – or else, you would surely have simply knocked on the door of our rooms in Baker Street – and so let us pretend for now that we are showing you important documentation related to our fund-raising. Now," he went on, still tapping at various points on the page, "obviously you think yourself under surveillance, both here and in London in general. Perhaps you can begin by explaining why this is the case?"

Beckwith coloured red but said nothing, and I had the strongest sensation that he was ashamed of what he was about to say. "I have made the most terrible mess of things, Mr. Holmes," he said eventually, just as I was beginning to think that any onlooker would be sure to wonder why we were sitting in silence. "I have betrayed my employer, who has never been anything but good to me, and I have put my son in danger, who should be able to look to his father for protection."

Holmes nodded and pulled a pen from his pocket. "Quite so," he said loudly, scrawling nothing intelligible on the sheet of paper on his knee then, equally briskly but more quietly, "How so? In as much detail as you can manage, if you please. Only with all of the information will I know if I can help you."

"I have worked for Mr. McMurtry for almost ten years, ever since I left the army. He isn't a military man himself, but he was looking for a valet when I needed a job, and having served as a batman in my time, I was fortunate enough to land the position you find me in now, and able to raise my son Edward here, too, his mother having died just before I handed in my papers. He was always a child with a weak temperament and, as he reached adulthood, he proved to have little will of his own. When he turned eighteen, with no mother to guide him and myself always busy with work, he fell in with a bad crowd. Thugs and criminals to a man, as I was later to discover, but at first they seemed pleasant enough, charming when they wanted to be, if a little rough around the edges.

"Edward even convinced me to obtain two of them positions here with Mr. McMurtry, one in the kitchen and another helping old Alf with the garden." He rubbed his knuckles into his eyes tiredly. "What a fool I was! Within a month, a sum of money was found to have gone missing from Mr. McMurtry's room, and Edward admitted that it was he who had stolen it. Worse, he kept quiet until the last moment, after the police had been called in to investigate, and as a consequence was sentenced to two years in prison." He turned to us each in turn, his eyes red and his brow furrowed with worry and loss. "You may imagine how crushed I was. I offered my resignation to Mr. McMurtry immediately, of course, but he would have none of it, and insisted that I shouldn't pay the price of my son's foolish mistake."

A silence fell over Beckwith. He stared down at his shoes, rubbing first one then the other against the back of his trouser leg, until Holmes gently prodded him with an elbow. "But that isn't the reason you wished to speak to me," he said quietly. "Even I can do nothing about a crime already committed and a sentence already passed down."

"No," Beckwith agreed, so quietly that I could barely hear him. "Though the problem I have relates to what happened to my son. You see,

Edward didn't steal the missing money." He held up a hand before Holmes or I could say anything. "I know what you both must be thinking. A father choosing to believe his son incapable of wrong doing is the oldest story there is, but I assure you that even though Edward admitted to the crime, and said nothing in his defence in court, he is innocent. In fact, the person who did steal the money came to see me on the afternoon of Edward's sentencing and told me all about it." He shifted on the bench, sitting up more straightly and squaring his shoulders, as though remembering his previous life as a soldier. "You will no doubt have guessed the culprit, Mr. Holmes? Edward's so-called friend Steven Allcock, who I had found a job in these very kitchens, in cahoots with the gardener's assistant Peter Fairley, had stolen the money and threatened Edward into taking the blame. And, adding insult to injury, when I grabbed the swine by the throat, intending to drag him to the police station, he informed me that he had many friends in the same prison as my son. If I didn't do exactly as he said, he could make Edward's life an even greater misery than it already was."

"And?" Holmes prompted, though it seemed to me that the poor man's story was complete. "There plainly must be more to your tale than that."

"That was eighteen months ago," Beckwith admitted, "and since then, they've been holding that over me."

"Holding it over you in what way? What have they forced you to do?"

Beckwith groaned and allowed his head to fall forward. He rubbed his palms across his face as if to revive himself. "Mr. McMurtry has a famous collection of time pieces, a collection he's built up over the past twenty years. But he isn't as young as he once was, and he rarely looks at them now. Those two felons made it clear that if I didn't take individual watches and clocks and hand them over to them, then my boy would suffer."

Now I understood his initial reluctance to speak. He was evidently a proud man, with a strong moral sense, like all soldiers, and to admit to theft (and perhaps more painfully, to a betrayal of trust) must have caused him great shame. As though to confirm my thoughts, Beckwith groaned again. "Allcock said that he, or one of their colleagues, would be keeping an eye on me at all times, in case I should feel the urge to speak to the police. I feared even to speak to you, Mr. Holmes – hence my indirect approach today." I saw him clench his hands tightly together, so that his fingers blanched white with the pressure. "Mr. McMurtry has never been anything but good to me, and to Edward. He gave us a roof over our heads and gave me a position when there's plenty of old soldiers without one. He's provided the means to clothe and feed me and my boy for all those years, and this is how I repay him!" He thumped his fist down so angrily on the arm of the bench that Holmes had to caution him in an undertone to look less like an aggrieved father and more like a Christian soul considering making a donation to a good cause. "Easy for you to say, Mr. Holmes," Beckwith growled, "but when I think of the position in which I find myself – Why, even the shoe I left for you was a gift from Mr. McMurtry, not a month since."

"About that?" Holmes said, his attention, as sometimes happened, briefly caught by what seemed to be an unimportant detail. "I assume you stuffed the other shoe under the omnibus seat because a man hobbling on one shoe is more noticeable than a man with no shoes at all?"

Beckwith nodded miserably, the fight going out of him as quickly as it had flared up as he considered Holmes's question. I wondered if that had been my old friend's intention. "I did, for that exact reason. Though, in fact, I gave a tramp two shillings for his broken-down boots as soon as I got off the omnibus and wore them home."

Holmes nodded, apparently satisfied. "One more thing," he said, folding up the sheet of paper in his hand and returning it to his bag. "My assumption is that something has changed in the household which means you fear exposure in the very near future. Otherwise, you could simply wait another six months until your son is released from prison and leave this place behind."

Beckwith rose to his feet and looked down at Holmes. "Mr. McMurtry has decided that, since he is no longer able to enjoy his collection, it is time it was broken up and sold. A representative of an auction house arrives tomorrow to make a catalogue. The missing items are bound to come to light then. Only you can help me!"

"Quite so," Holmes replied. "You understand that I am not a miracle worker, however? You say this auction house fellow arrives tomorrow?" His brow furrowed in thought. "I think that you must speak to Allcock and his friend Fairley and suggest one last theft. A big one this time, as big as you can convince them of. Explain, if they don't already know, about the auctioneer and the certainty of discovery, and impress on them that this is their – your – last chance to make any money from your master's collection. Tonight, I think. At midnight. Say you will stay with them at all times, Beckwith – that should alleviate any suspicions they might have." He stood too, and held out his hand to Beckwith. "Thank you very much for your very generous contribution," he said loudly then, more quietly. "And leave everything else to me. Whatever else might happen, I guarantee your son will not suffer for it."

As we turned to go, I saw a pale faced man standing at the back door, staring at us. Holmes obviously saw him too, for he prodded me in the

165

back and nodded towards him. "Perhaps it would be best if you took this – " He handed me the folder from his bag. " – and see if you can get him to contribute to our veteran's fund. Mr. Beckwith and myself will be there shortly."

I did as he asked, even though I was unsure if my acting abilities were up to the task. Fortunately, the man – who grudgingly introduced himself as Steven Allcock – exhibited no inclination to charity and made his excuses as soon as I mentioned the word "donation". Holmes soon appeared from the garden, and after once more shaking Beckwith's hand and thanking him for his contribution, we made our way back onto the main road and into a cab.

I tried to speak to Holmes, but he was even more withdrawn than usual, and eventually I gave up the attempt.

Not entirely to my surprise, Holmes had the cab stop at Scotland Yard on the way back to Baker Street.

"There's no need to wait." he said as he jumped down to the pavement and gestured for the cabman to continue on his way, but though he smiled as he spoke, I couldn't help but feel he was worried about something. The scowl which replaced his smile as he turned away from me and thought himself unobserved did nothing to change that opinion. For a second, I considered telling the driver to stop so that I might follow him into the Yard, but long experience told me that Holmes would tell me his plan in his own time and not before.

Still, I was surprised when he arrived back at Baker Street an hour later and, with the sun setting outside, settled himself in front of the fire with his pipe and made no attempt at conversation. I wondered what he had said to Beckwith while I was speaking to Allcock and what he had been up to at Scotland Yard, but though I brought the matter up several times, on each occasion he simply grunted and returned to his pipe, refusing to be drawn.

As the evening wore on and it grew closer to midnight, I glanced up from my book at increasingly frequent intervals, but Holmes showed no sign of movement. Finally, my patience at an end, and feeling myself rather poorly treated, I laid the book down and confronted him directly.

"What on Earth do you intend to do to help Beckwith?" I asked, my impatience, I think, plain in my voice. "It is now half-past-eleven, and you did tell him to arrange his mock robbery for midnight."

"Indeed," Holmes replied laconically, puffing at his pipe and sending smoke rings towards the ceiling. "But I must admit, Watson, I am at a loss as to what you think we should be doing?"

He could be the most infuriating of men. "Well, presumably whatever it was you were doing at the Yard, it had something to do with it?"

Again, he admitted the truth of my observation. "It did, but once I had set the wheels in motion, as it were, there was nothing more for me to do. There *is* nothing more for me to do, in fact." He sighed and tapped the bowl of his pipe against the fender of the fire. Suddenly, he looked terribly tired. "What would you have me do, Watson?" he asked. "You heard what I said to Beckwith. I am not a miracle worker."

I shook my head, unsure what he meant.

"His son is in prison, and he has stolen a great deal of valuable watches from his employer. I cannot make either fact cease to be true. I can, however, do something about his son's acquaintances and the pernicious hold they have over him, though the price he will pay must, unfortunately, be a steep one."

Something in Holmes's eyes, the way they flicked to one side as he spoke, as though unable to meet my own gaze, suddenly brought home to me what he meant. "You don't mean to help Beckwith escape, do you? You've arranged with Scotland Yard to catch the entire gang, including poor Beckwith, in the act!"

Still not looking at me, he nodded slowly. "Beckwith knows what it about to happen. I explained all of this to him while you were speaking to Allcock, and he accepted that the price is a fair one. Lestrade and his men are waiting in the darkness around Mr. McMurtry's house as we speak. They will apprehend Beckwith and the others as they leave and take them into police custody."

I could make no sense of this. Holmes must have realised my confusion, for he went on quickly, before I had time to speak.

"It was all I could do, Watson. Like Beckwith, I had no choice. Should I have arranged for just Allcock and Fairley to be arrested, and let Beckwith go free? How would that seem to those two rogues and their compatriots? Edward Beckwith would have paid dearly for his father's freedom, and his role in the earlier robbery would still have become public knowledge, once Allcock had the opportunity to make his statement. Or should I have let them escape with their stolen watches? I allowed that pathetic shop clerk to avoid the police earlier today and I could see the disapproval on your face as plain as day. And even if I had, do you imagine that Beckwith could have stayed on where he was? No, he would have to flee with the others, and spend his life forever waiting for a policeman's hand on his shoulder."

"But . . . ." I said the word, but could think of nothing with which to follow it up. I believe Holmes didn't even notice that I had spoken.

"No, Watson," he said, "I did the only thing I could do. I explained to Beckwith that I would ensure his sentence was served in the same prison as his son, so that he could watch over him for the few months until the boy's time was served. And I spoke to Lestrade and made him aware of *all* of the circumstances, so that – while there will be no suspicion amongst Allcock and his gang that Beckwith had betrayed them – whatever can be done to lessen his sentence and ease his time in prison will be done." He shrugged, weariness evident on his face. "So I ask again, what else would you have had me do?"

I had no answer and joined him in staring into the fire as the clock ticked towards midnight and the rain began to patter softly against the window.

# The Case of
# John Bull vs Brittania
## by Roger Riccard

### Chapter I

It was mid-June 1883, shortly after we had completed the adventure I have recorded elsewhere as "How Green the Valet". It was mid-morning, and Holmes was examining the daily papers in search of a new case. I was organising my notes on our latest investigation when the doorbell rang. The tread on the stairs indicated our landlady, Mrs. Hudson, was showing a guest up to our rooms. She knocked and, when invited to come in, she was accompanied by a rather astonishing sight.

"A gentleman to see you, Mr. Holmes," she announced in her pleasant Scottish accent, at which point the fellow behind her stepped up to her side. He was short and stout of late middle age by the looks of him. The remarkable aspect of him was his attire.

He wore a dark blue tailcoat, white breeches, black boots, a low topper hat, and a waistcoat patterned as the Union Jack. In other words, he was the spitting image [1] of John Bull, every political cartoonist's representation of Great Britain.

He pointed at my companion and cried, "Sherlock Holmes – I need you!"

Holmes gazed up from behind *The Daily News* and said, "Yes, I imagine you do, Mr. Robert John Bullbank. Do sit down. Thank you, Mrs. Hudson."

Our visitor seemed a bit taken aback at this pronouncement and entered the room slowly now, instead of at the energetic pace he had previously displayed. He removed his hat and sat in the chair indicated, while Holmes folded his paper and set it aside.

"Where did you get my full name?" he asked. "I haven't used it in years."

"It is my business to know things.," Holmes replied. "In your case, I had a client in the past with a shop near yours, and during my investigation, I looked into the backgrounds of all the neighbouring establishments. That is how I discovered that, for business purposes, you shortened your real name to 'John Bull'."

Turning to me, he said, "Watson, please be good enough to offer Mr. Bull a cigar, for I see he has forgotten his snuff box, and he is a bit jumpy from a lack of nicotine."

I held out our cigar box to him, and he gratefully took one of the Piedras and lit it. Then he asked, "How did you know I had forgotten my snuff box?"

Holmes waved his hand as if it were a foolish question, but deigned to answer it all the same. "Your waistcoat is part of your daily costume. Therefore, it has taken on not only the shape of your physique, but also become creased by the objects you habitually keep in your pockets. Your pocket watch is in your right-hand pocket, as its circular shape has left its impression there. Therefore, when I see the rectangular outline on your left pocket lying loose from emptiness, I conclude the missing snuff box. This arrangement also tells me you are right-handed, as you take out your snuff box with your left hand and gather a pinch of the powder with your right.

"But that is of small consequence compared to the reason for your visit. What can you tell me of the substitution that has not already appeared in the press?"

I was at a loss as to what Holmes was talking about until he held up the paper he had been reading, and I realised it was one of the morning editions I hadn't seen yet. From where I sat, all I could make out was a picture of a statue of Britannia.

"Well, for one thing, I can tell you the police are baffled, which is why I've come to you."

Holmes smirked and then asked, "For the sake of Dr. Watson, who hasn't had a chance to read of your mishap, please tell us all that has occurred."

I pulled out a pencil and paper as Bull sat up straight and waved his cigar in our direction. "It was night before last that it happened. Sometime between close of business Saturday and Sunday morning, when I was passing by my shop on the way to church, Someone stole the statue of John Bull that sits outside my shop and substituted a statue of Britannia. You can see the picture, there in the paper."

Holmes handed it to me, but kept his eyes on our client, bidding him to continue.

"My statue, rather the *John Bull* statue, as the face doesn't resemble me, is carved from solid mahogany, and has a weighted base to keep it from being knocked over. Altogether, it weighs about fifteen stone. [2]

"This new statue is so bulky that three constables couldn't budge it. It appears to be made of bronze with a heavy wooden base."

"Is it larger than your John Bull statue?" Holmes asked.

"Oh, yes. Not so much the statue itself, but the base it sits on is quite a bit bigger. It nearly takes up the whole pavement between my shop front and the street."

"Is it in the same spot as your old statue?"

"Well, as I said, Mr. Holmes, the base is bigger, but yes, it completely covers the spot where my statue stood."

"And you've received no note of explanation. No ransom demand for your old statue or anything of the sort?"

"Not a word."

"Have you noticed anyone paying particular attention to it lately or taking measurements?"

"No, no one like that."

"As I recall, yours is a curio shop, selling novelties, antiques, and the like, especially patriotic items. Have any of your customers complained lately?"

Bull puffed himself up with pride. "I only sell quality items, not cheap junk like some others. No one has ever complained about my merchandise."

Holmes sat back and tapped his pipe stem to his lips. Finally, he said, "I shall be happy to look into the matter for you. Who is the inspector on the case?"

## Chapter II

Holmes was pleased to hear that Inspector Lestrade was assigned to the investigation. He immediately suggested that we return to our client's shop, The Bullpen and examine the scene. Afterwards, we would continue on to Scotland Yard to consult with the inspector.

During our cab ride, Holmes assured our client, "Lestrade is one of Scotland Yard's best men, Mr. Bull. We have worked with him before. He is tenacious as a bulldog, and won't quit until he gets his man. I'm sure that, between the doctor, myself, and him, we shall have your statue back in place quickly."

He then turned away from our client and gave me a wink. Lestrade was tenacious, as my companion had said. But he was also lacking in imagination, and often found himself at sixes-and-sevens in the middle of a case, which was usually when he called on Holmes.

We arrived at Bull's shop on Nottinghill Gate Road, just west of Kensington Gardens, where passersby were admiring the Britannia statue. It was really a beautiful monument, and the bronze reflected the brilliant sunlight on this bright summer day. Whoever the artist was, he or she showed a clear talent for bronze work. I wondered if that fact would be useful in Holmes's investigation.

The wooden base seemed to be walnut with a beautiful grain pattern, which complemented the bronze of the sculpture. Holmes took several measurements and examined the base closely with his magnifying lens. Stepping up on the base, he also made close scrutiny of the bronze work. He knocked on the metal in several places and made notes. Then he stepped down and turned his gaze toward the street, looking up and down. I couldn't tell what he was searching for and asked, "Are you thinking the artist is nearby, admiring his work?"

He smiled at something – or someone – that he saw, but I couldn't discern who, as a small group of pedestrians were walking away on the other side of the street. "Possibly. But I was primarily admiring the location the artist chose."

I looked around. There were several shops up and down the street. None of them stood out to me in any peculiar way, and I said as much. "You're putting limitations on yourself, Doctor," the detective replied. "Expand your vision, and let your imagination see why Britannia is appropriate to this particular location."

I frowned and he shook his head. "Well, think on it, while we take a ride to visit friend Lestrade at the Yard."

Inspector Lestrade was a gentleman I knew from my early days living with Holmes in Baker Street before I was aware of his occupation. The weasel-faced fellow was a frequent visitor seeking advice. I got to know him better during the case I would later publish as *A Study in Scarlet*. His office at Scotland Yard seemed to be an organisation of piles of paper. It wasn't quite as untidy as my companion kept our sitting room, but it was far from prim and proper.

We found the fellow seated at his desk reading through a file. When he looked up and saw us he frowned. "Hello, Mr. Holmes. Doctor Watson. No offence, but I hope you aren't here to bring me some new crime. As you can see, I'm quite busy."

"On the contrary, Lestrade!" Holmes boomed out with enthusiasm. "We are here to assist on the John Bull case."

"Ah, well that's different. You're more than welcome to give me any information or advice on that one. Seems like a silly prank to me, but a theft is a theft."

"May I enquire as to what steps you've taken?" asked Holmes.

"We've narrowed down the time of the incident, due to the schedule of the constable rounds in that neighbourhood, and determined it occurred between three and four in the morning. I'm also looking into trucking companies with crane equipment. As I see it, the culprits arrived in two vehicles. One, a large wagon with the Britannia statue. The other, a portable crane wagon to lift away the John Bull statue and replace it with Britannia. Then they drove away with the John Bull."

Holmes cocked his head, blinked an eye and replied, "You believe that they drove into position, moved the John Bull statue aside, then changed the harness to the Britannia statue and placed it precisely in the position where John Bull was, then moved the harness again to the John Bull statue so they could raise it onto the empty space on the wagon vacated by the Britannia statue, then drove off – all in the space of one hour?"

173

The inspector shook his head. "I know it sounds difficult, Mr. Holmes, and it must have taken a very efficient crew, but I can think of no other explanation."

Holmes shook his head and mumbled, "No, likely not." Louder he stated, "This portable crane wagon must be extremely rare."

"Well, I've never actually seen one," Lestrade admitted, "but what other explanation is there?"

The detective looked at me, then up at the ceiling, as if trying to make a decision. Finally. he informed Lestrade of his deductions.

The inspector gazed upon him in astonishment. "Are you sure, Mr. Holmes?"

"It's elementary, Inspector. Any other explanation is much too cumbersome."

"You've solved it then?"

"Only half of it," answered my friend. "We know *how* the statues were exchanged, but we need to find out *who* and *why*."

## Chapter III

I spoke up. "How do we do that, Holmes? Why would anyone wish to substitute Britannia for John Bull?"

"That is the question," replied the detective. "When we answer why, then we will be dull indeed if we cannot determine *who*."

He stopped a bit, then turned to the inspector. "Lestrade, I suggest you look for a moving van large enough to transport the Britannia sculpture. Keep me informed of your progress. I shall be at Baker Street."

Off we went. Holmes was silent during the cab ride, and I didn't interrupt him. But once back in our sitting room, I questioned his purpose for returning here.

"I need to think, Watson," he replied. "This is at least a two- and possibly a three-pipe problem. I also need to be around my reference books and newspapers should an idea present itself. I beg you not to speak to me for at least the next hour. In fact, why don't you step out and purchase the afternoon newspapers?"

He reached for the Persian slipper hanging on the mantel and filled it with tobacco as he pulled out his old briar pipe. As he did so, I stepped out the door, satisfied in knowing that Holmes had determined where the John Bull statue was, even if we didn't know why it was switched.

I took some time gathering up the afternoon editions, and I decided to stop at a nearby pub for a glass of ale before returning to the aura of cognitive manipulation which I knew would permeate the atmosphere of

174

our rooms – not to mention the choking clouds of smoke from Holmes's pipe.

Imagine my surprise, then, to find the room free of tobacco smoke, and Holmes missing from his favourite chair. I called down to our landlady. "Mrs. Hudson?"

She stepped out of her kitchen to the bottom of our staircase. "Oh, Dr. Watson, you're back. I am sorry I didn't hear you come in. Mr. Holmes said to tell you that 'The game is afoot', and then he left in his vicar disguise and said he wouldn't be home until dinner. You are to skim the newspapers for anything related to women's groups."

I thoughtfully tilted my head and replied, "Thank you. Could I please have a pot of tea?"

She nodded and returned to the kitchen while I sat in my usual chair, lit a cigar, and settled in with the afternoon editions. The only relevant item I noted was a small notice of a meeting of *S.O.W.E.R.* – *The Society of Women's Equal Rights*. It was to be held the next afternoon at Burnfield Hall in Holland Park Avenue near Norland Square.

Most historical women's clubs served social and charitable purposes. These have included voluntary civic service purposes such as:

☐ Opening lending libraries and seeking funding to create permanent public libraries;
☐ Pursuing historic preservation;
☐ Aadvocating for women's suffrage and other rights for women;
☐ Serving as professional women's clubs, comparable to historic men's clubs of London;
☐ Serving as athletic clubs, or otherwise supporting sports and physical activity;
☐ Addressing sanitation and health issues;
☐ Hosting social activities, including card games;
☐ Hosting lectures and otherwise engaging in education; and
☐ Addressing employment and labour conditions.

The passage of the Married Women's Property Act of 1882, which became effective on 1 January, 1883, resulted in a flurry of such groups arising to keep pushing the women's movement for equal rights forward. I set the notice aside for Holmes's review upon his return.

I found no other stories or notices of the type Holmes had me seeking, but did locate a few articles of interest to me. These kept me occupied the rest of the afternoon, and well into the evening. Holmes returned just after seven-thirty, when the sun was low in the summer sky. I had only turned up the lamps in the sitting room when he strode in, removed his moustache, spectacles, clerical collar, and priest's hat, poured himself a whisky, and dropped into his chair with an air of satisfaction.

"You must have had an epiphany shortly after I left you," I stated. "Was this particular disguise essential, or did you merely assume the easiest at hand?"

"Ah, Watson, there are times when I even surprise myself," he replied. "I seem to have developed an instinct which takes over my mind without a second thought. If you had asked me what disguise would have worked for the task today, I could have given you a list of half-a-dozen. But choosing this particular one hid my features and allowed me access to our suspect as a trusted soul."

"You have a suspect?"

"Indeed."

I handed him the S.O.W.E.R. meeting notice and asked, "Does he or she have anything to do with these people?"

My companion read the notice and chuckled. "Watson, you have hit upon the very group wherein my focus lies."

"How did you discover them?" I asked.

"You asked me this morning, as I was gazing across the street, if I was seeking out the perpetrator of our crime. As I recall, I advised you I had determined a possible reason for the location chosen, in addition to searching the crowd for an admiring foe. Have you thought any more along those lines, my friend?"

I shook my head, as I wasn't sure my answer would meet his satisfaction. "All I could come up with was that John Bull's shop is known for its patriotic goods, and that someone seeking publicity for their artistry in creating the Britannia bronze would wish to appeal to that type of crowd."

To my surprise, he applauded. "Excellent, Watson! You have indeed hit upon a very important aspect of the crime – if we can indeed call it such. The other side of that coin is the substitution of a female representation of Great Britain for a male depiction."

I had stood and was pouring myself a brandy as a precursor to dinner when I replied, "Hence your interest in the S.O.W.E.R. group. You believe they intend to take advantage of this substitution to publicise their cause."

"Not just take advantage," responded Holmes. "They are the ones who perpetrated the act, precisely so they could call attention to themselves and their cause."

"What will you do now?"

"I have sent an invitation for ten o'clock tomorrow morning to the head of S.O.W.E.R., Mrs. Evangeline Hammersmith, and her husband. I have also asked Mr. Bull to drop by at ten-thirty. If all goes well, I suspect

176

we can relieve Inspector Lestrade of any further police involvement in this case.

## Chapter IV

At precisely ten the next morning, Mrs. Hudson showed up a remarkable couple. Mr. Albert Hammersmith was a barrel-chested fellow, nearly as tall as Holmes, but weighing considerably more at about sixteen stone.[3] I guessed his age to be in his early thirties, as his hair was a thick, rich, chestnut brown, with a moustache to match. His wife was equally exceptional in that she was broad-shouldered and tall, perhaps five-foot-nine, as her amber eyes were barely lower than mine when we exchanged greetings. Her hair was light brown, long and straight as it hung down her back nearly to her waist. The hand that shook mine was big and strong, and the nails were short. I would have put her slightly younger than her husband, perhaps twenty-eight or so.

They declined refreshment as the husband got right to business. "What was the meaning of your invitation, Mr. Holmes? Who are you, and what do you think you know?"

Holmes stood while I sat and took notes. "In the interest of time, let me answer your questions and tell you what I know without interruption, for Mr. John Bull will be arriving at ten-thirty."

The couple looked at each other, unable to hide their surprise or fear at this revelation. Holmes took a few seconds to let them digest that statement, then started in.

"I am a private detective, hired by Mr. Bull. First, I will tell you what I know. Then I will give you my speculations, and you may confirm or deny them. I know that in the early morning hours of Sunday last, you, Mr. Hammersmith, backed your moving van up to the front of John Bull's shop and, using the boom-and-pulley system inside, lowered the hollow, bronze Britannia statue *over* the top of the John Bull statue. You then bolted the nameplate onto the Britannia statue using long-enough woodscrews to attach it to the base of the John Bull statue so that it would appear heavier than it actually was."

Before the husband could interrupt, Holmes turned to the lady. "You, Mrs. Hammersmith, are the sculptor of that fine bronze piece. Your hands betray your work with the plaster castings, and your hair retains the indentations where you frequently tie it back to keep it out of your way.

"You chose John Bull's shop for three reasons. One, which Dr. Watson discerned, was that you wished to draw publicity to your work among patrons who favoured patriotic works. Two: You wished to call attention to the fact that women can represent Great Britain as well as men, and thus should have equal rights. And three: His shop lies on the road to

177

Kensington Palace, where many Ryal family members and politicians are likely to behold it."

Now Holmes stopped. "Are you sure you will not take some refreshment? Mrs. Hudson's tea is excellent and hot." They each shook their heads, and the detective continued his narrative.

"I met with each of you yesterday, where you inadvertently took me into your confidence. As the Reverend Homer Cousins, I came to you, Mrs. Hammersmith, at Burnfield Hall, where I had followed you, after seeing you admiring your work from across the street from John Bull's shop. As you recall, I watched you rehearsing the speech you're planning to give today. Your intentions were clear in that you believed your group should use Britannia as their symbol of strong women. Comparing her with America's Columbia, France's Marianne, Lady Justice, and Queens Elizabeth and Victoria was quite inspiring. When you finished, I questioned you about your stance versus the traditional Bible roles so often quoted by the clergy. Again, you eloquently reminded me of the stories of Ruth, Deborah, Esther, and Mary, as well as the proverb of the smart businesswoman who inspects a field, buys it, and makes it profitable. All during that discussion, I was observing your hands, hair, and other physical characteristics that identified you as a sculptor."

Turning to her husband, Holmes continued. "As to you, sir, no doubt you recall my coming by your business after learning of your trade from your wife, who likes to promote your agreement to her beliefs, despite being in a manly trade like moving and storage. I asked you about transporting a statue we had ordered from Italy from the docks to our parish, and you showed me your moving van with the boom-and-pulley system, which would ensure safe transport and delivery."

Holmes stopped to let them digest what he had revealed. Finally, the husband asked, "What now, Mr. Holmes? Are you going to the police?"

Holmes rubbed his hands together and replied, "Mr. Bull will be here soon. If you wish, you may leave, and I will merely tell him that his statue is still in place underneath Britannia, and all he has to do is unbolt the nameplate and hire someone, perhaps Hammersmith Transfer and Storage, to lift it off and haul it away. With his statue back in prominence, the perpetrator will not really be that important to him, and I believe he will not pursue it. He may even decide to leave the Britannia statue out front of his shop as well. One on either side of his door should make a nice display, and certainly, the perpetrator will not seek its return for fear of being charged.

"On the other hand," continued the detective, "we may all meet with him together and explain your motives. I believe we can convince him to not only refuse charges, but to embrace the Britannia as a fixture for his business. While I was observing you from inside his shop yesterday, Mrs. Hammersmith, I noticed he has a great many female clientele purchasing decorations, toys, and gifts. If he can be convinced of the benefits of supporting at least some aspects of your movement, it would work out well for all concerned. I also believe, should you wish it so, that I can keep both your names out of it."

The lady spoke up. "How will you explain our presence here then?"

"If you will trust me, I can explain the situation easily enough in a way that, should he be disagreeable, you can leave with him none the wiser."

The husband and wife discussed it briefly and decided to take Holmes up on his offer. They also took tea while we awaited John Bull's arrival.

The shop owner was there exactly on time, and began to question Holmes before he noticed there were others in the room. "Have you found it, Mr. Holmes? I . . . Oh, I beg your pardon! I didn't realise you had visitors."

Holmes responded in his smoothest and most affable manner. "Quite all right, Mr. Bull. Allow me to introduce Mr. and Mrs. Hammersmith. They have offered to assist with your case."

"Assist?" asked the shopkeeper as he removed his hat, bowed to our guests and sat down. "How?"

"First, let me explain that your John Bull statue isn't missing at all. The Britannia statue is hollow and was lowered over it, then fastened to it by the bolts in the nameplate so it couldn't be moved."

"What?" sputtered the shopkeeper. "It's been there the whole time?"

"It was really the only logical explanation," replied Holmes smoothly. "Switching the statues for each other would have been far too cumbersome and time-consuming."

Bull nodded his assent and asked, "But then, how can these people help?"

Holmes, in his most persuasive tone, said, "They have offered to assist with the removal of Britannia. Mr. Hammersmith owns a transfer and storage company, and can safely lift off Britannia without damaging your John Bull statue underneath. Mrs. Hammersmith is the head of a women's organisation that would like to use the Britannia bronze as a symbol of their movement.

Bull nodded. "That would be fine with me, as long as I get my statue back out front. It is the symbol of my store, after all."

At a signal from Holmes, I handed Bull a cup of tea. In addition to providing a relaxed atmosphere, it would also prod him to stay for Holmes's next proposition. "We were all just discussing that very thing," said Holmes. "I noticed that in your shop yesterday, the majority of the customers were women."

"That's true enough," replied the merchant.

Holmes continued. "Mrs. Hammersmith suggested that perhaps you would wish to keep the Britannia statue, and have each of them flanking your front door, to attract buyers of both genders. In return, she would be happy to promote your shop among members of her society. All she would ask is that they could occasionally have a photograph taken for publicity purposes – publicity, that would also reflect favourably upon your shop."

The living image of England sipped his tea, then set down the cup and said, "Mrs. Bull would certainly be in favour of that. She's always off marching for this and that cause for women's rights. I have to admit I was in favour of the Married Women's Property Act. If anything happened to me, I would certainly want my Abigail to inherit it all, rather than that no-good brother of mine."

He took another moment and finally replied, "All right, on one condition."

"Yes?" replied Evangeline Hammersmith.

"You can publicise any cause you like with those photographs, as long as they don't show the name of my shop in anything that promotes women's suffrage. I'll not have my name connected with supporting votes for women."

Holmes and I turned to the lady in apprehension. I saw her stiffen and her fingers curled into fists, but her husband gently laid a hand upon her forearm and said, "Considering all the other women's causes there are, that seems reasonable. Doesn't it, my dear?"

I could see his fingers tighten ever so slightly as he endeavoured to calm his wife. She took a breath and forced a smile. "I believe that would be acceptable, Mr. Bull."

I saw her mouth form another syllable, but no more sound came forth.

"Well, then." Bull slapped his hands upon his knees and stood. "When can you lift Britannia and arrange the statues, Mr. Hammersmith?"

"I'll have a crew come by at noon tomorrow," answered the mover.

"Well, fine." Then turning to my friend he said, "If you find out who did this, Holmes, you can just tell him I'm keeping the statue, and he can't have it back. That'll teach him for disturbing private property."

"I will do that, Mr. Bull," answered Holmes. "I will also inform Inspector Lestrade that you won't be pressing charges, and he can cease his investigation."

"Fine, fine," waved the stout merchant who then bowed to our guests, plopped his hat back upon his head, and strode out the door as if he were England off to inspect the Empire.

Once he was safely out of earshot, Mrs. Hammersmith started to spew a host of invectives directed at our client. Her husband, however, let out a sigh of relief. "Thank you, Mr. Holmes."

My friend, ever the diplomatist, turned his attention upon the lady. "Mrs. Hammersmith, let me point out one prominent fact you are forgetting."

"What's that?" she seethed.

"Bull said the name of his shop couldn't be in any photos used to promote women's suffrage. I do believe your husband could place the statue of Britannia in such a way that you will be able to gather members of your group around it, and have an angle that will not include the name of the shop in the background."

He looked to the mover and Hammersmith nodded. "Yes, I think I know just how to place it. Problem solved! You get everything you wished for, darling!"

With that realization, Evangeline lifted her teacup to my flat-mate, smiled, and said, "Thank you, Mr. Holmes. And you can tell *Reverend Cousins* he is welcome to our meetings anytime."

After the couple left us, I turned to Holmes and said, "You have made your opinion of women quite clear in the past, Holmes. What made you take the lady's side in this matter?"

Holmes sat down and lit his churchwarden pipe. Pointing the long stem at me, he replied, "I have come to realise that denying benefits to deserving women because of the actions of some foolish females isn't just. The more I see of mankind, the more I'm aware that there are also men who are worthless to actually cast an intelligent vote, or receive rights and privileges denied to the fair sex, simply because of their gender. In my discussion with Mrs. Hammersmith yesterday as *Reverend Cousins*, I found her arguments compelling. Thus, at least for this instance, I have chosen to amend my former opinion. But Watson . . . ."

"Yes, Holmes?"

"Do not hold me to it in every case."

181

## NOTES

1. The concept and phrase "spitting image" were in circulation by 1689, when George Farquhar used it in his play *Love and a Bottle*: "*Poor child! He's as like his own dada as if he were spit out of his mouth.*"
2. 210 pounds.
3. 224 pounds.

# The Widow
## by Marcia Wilson

London sat, a shadow-manufactory. Her roof-stacks, a forest of gnomons, cast smoking talons and spread down into the alleys and mews and streets, the oldest of which were no more than arm-long, cramped spaces lurking betwixt the walls and forgotten smears on antique maps. These pale shades plunged from the birds' realm, mixing into darkening tempuras as they touched sill and stair, until finally into icy glooms where ash and coal-soot settled without an atom-wide glimpse of the sun's rays.

Here the cold lingered long after winter's pass. Dank chill trickled, and the deepest shadows flicked snaky tails, running over rubbish-heaps ahead of the weary collectors. Someone always coughed in these lightless gin-mazes, weak in the roots of the city.

Fingers of yellow fog greased the muddy streets, thickening the air. Feet clapped the uneven cobbles, splashed the ribbon-thin pools. These wanderers broke through the misty firmament, trailing broken tentacles of the choking yellow mist, and then vanished by inches as they walked into the next poisonous cloud. One heard one's neighbors long before one saw them.

A new set of foot-falls tattooed through the darkness. A tiny yellow light swayed back and forth a yard off the imagined ground, an old bulls'-eye lantern clasped in a firm left hand. *Clip-clip-clip* went its bearer's heels – *Hurry-hurry-hurry.*

*Clip-clip-clip.*

A woman emerged from the clammy darkness, regal as a singer stepping away from her stage curtains. She was tall for this malnourished East Side, three inches over five-foot, and sturdily built with proper blue skirts over proper blue trousers. A tight-lipped jacket of the same wool made armour of her breast-bone and battering-rams of her arms. The light burned forward through the fog, illuminating her straightforward steps.

Closer now, she bore up the weight of a canvas pack on her shoulders, and her lampless hand held a long, limber pole that jumped and wiggled for every heel upon the cobbles. The veil off her slate-blue hat fluttered, making room for a tiny pipe and hiding deepset green eyes over a no-nonsense mouth. Beneath the veil laced a dark snood, barely chaining a fine collection of greying chestnut hair.

*Clip-clip-clip.*

She vanished into the fog.

*The Lancahsire Rose, a small Cooking School not far from Paddington Station:*

Clea Cheatham was already tired when her brothers drove her to The Rose – and with true brotherly impatience deserted for business on the cuts. They didn't even try to cadge a cup of tea in the farewells.

*At least they paid for my cab,* the tiny woman thought in rueful amusement. Outside of her cynicism, she knew they had looked the shop over quick-and-hard for any tell-tale signs of scandal-mongers hoping to find their baby sister alone.

One would think scandal be just another form of food for a Cheatham out of Lun's Pool, but the family wanted to better themselves now that the sale of their cotton mill rendered them temporarily rich. Back home, they wouldn't have been *new money*, but London was different. It was amazing how many of their neighbors of house and chapel were waiting to see if they rose or fell. The results would determine if they were worth the bother of knowing.

Clea's "Overnight Girls" had slept on floor-pallets in the warmth of the kitchen and risen hours ago to light the ovens and start the dough. Yeasty steam soothed Clea as she hung her hat and coat.

*You can do this,* she told herself. *You know you can. Put in your day's work.* Was this any different than her late mother walking among the toughest, drink-mazed alleys of the impoverished mill-workers as she dispensed soup and succor? If anything, she was very fortunate. Her fiancé was a policeman. Geoffrey would escort her home and provide one last breath's escape between work and house. She could already see him in her mind, stepping neatly around the muddle of tables and diners, one hand to the side for the truncheon sewn inside his coat, and his clipped southernish accent: *"Mr. Lestrade for Miss Cheatham."*

"Good morning, Miss," Lizzy cheeped. For a big girl, her voice was tiny. "Bread's hot for the oven."

"Good. You'll show Regina how to load them proper."

Miss Cheatham needed a bit of time by herself with tea as she worked through the week's items. Running a shop-that-was-a-cooking-school was exhausting, demanding cleverness, no waste, and a never-ending vigil against scandal. *And you'll be married soon – Mrs. Lestrade!* She sighed as she prepared for a precious scrap of uninterrupted time with her papers.

"Miss! Miss Cheatham!"

Clea blinked at a worried Aggie half-in and half-out of the doorway. The girl was clenching her remaining teeth together and trying to twist her hair around her fingers, despite its cap. This might have been comical if she wasn't so clearly out of sorts.

"Well, Aggie?"

"We've got a visitor. I mean a customer. I mean, widow, I mean, *The Widow*. I mean . . . c-could you come out?"

"*What* dust tha mean?" Clea always forgot her school-talk when confused.

Aggie gnawed her lip with her one front tooth, but Viola's dark head popped up from behind her bony shoulders.

"We've got an important customer coming," she whispered. Then to Aggie, "*Now stop fretting. You knew it'd only be a matter of time before she showed herself!*"

"Who?"

"It's *t'Widow*, Miss! Parky saw 'er comin' down the street. She's headed *here*. She's got 'er collectin' bag. He came runnin' as soon as he caught on."

Clea took a deep breath. "Who is 'The Widow', if you please?"

Surprisingly, Aggie found her spine. "She comes to the shops, Miss. She buys up what tea and coffee and tobacco bits nobody wants. She renders 'em down clean and sells 'em again."

"It's almost good luck if she comes to your place, too," Viola confided.

"'Almost'?"

"She'll drive out the rabble. You watch!" Viola clapped her hand over her mouth. "Please, Miss! Don't mind my manners! When she comes, she 'spects to be treated like reg'lar."

"Well of course, but why is she just called a 'Widow'?"

"*The Widow*, Miss." Aggie gulped hard. "She's a copper's widow. No nonsense in her a'tall. She can smell a lie!" Her voice dropped just in case the subject in question could hear her from the streets. "Their fault her 'usband died. She don't forget! They mind her!"

"An' I don't blame 'em!" Viola exclaimed. She was so excited she was dancing on her toes. "Please, Miss! You'll see! It'll be a good thing if she starts comin' by! She'll get rid of – " And now Viola's voice went down. " – that lot sittin' in the corner like mourners."

Aggie nodded wildly. "Nice people will come here if she becomes a customer."

"Are you saying I don't have nice customers *now*?"

The girls paled. "No, Miss! Just . . . if you just meet her for yourself, ye'd understand!"

"It looks like I'll have to do," Clea muttered as the bell over the door rang. The girls' heads shot to the side, then raced back to facing-forward.

185

"That's not her, but we see her! Oh, Hurry, Miss!"

By now Clea was inclined to roar with laughter. This was more a low drama from the music halls than intelligence! She stood and the girls vanished to tend to the customers.

In the brief time it took to get herself into the dining room, she saw nothing extra-ordinary. The tables were half-populated with various men and women, familiar faces like old Mr. Peavensey there in the back, nibbling on his bread and tea over yesterday's newspaper. A few women gathered in the darkest corner, hard-bit but clean. They always ordered tea and bread with last night's drippings. She knew one was stone-deaf from the way she moved her head. Another had the sloped face of too much lead in the blood.

Aggie was waiting on a fresh customer: A plump youth in country tweeds off the train anxious for a pasty. He paused as he left to bow and hold the door for a woman dressed in slate.

*It is like watching a very slow train come straight at you,* Miss Cheatham marvelled. The lantern moved through the fog as a single glaring sun, closer one step at a time with the darker outline of a small woman inside large skirts behind it. A face-warmer pipe puffed jets of smoke straight up like a train's chimney. Over the glum shades of folk flitting back and forth between lamp-pools, she was one of the objects they moved around, like the fog and the posts.

"Ah, thank you, lad." She paused and turned sideways to make room for herself and break down her long pole like a fishing-rod. In a single twist, it was thrust against the corner and her lantern closed, the pipe snuffed. "Finally, a place that knows how to keep warm."

Clea wondered if she was talking to herself or passing judgment.

The Widow settled without taking off her coat. Her hat was set carefully to the side along with its hat-pin, which could have understudied for Hamlet's dagger. Clea had seen some startling things since moving out of Lancaster's tough mills and into crafty London, but that pin was easily the most dangerous object to walk into her shop. Shaped like a child's toy sword, the top half was a ridiculously overcarved hilt with lilies and roses. Its other half was shaped like a very thin broadsword, also deeply grooved with flowers.

*The jeweller's gone mad . . .* Clea thought in wonder.

"What tay is 'er, Miss?"

Clea could see from the side of her eye that every one of her girls had melted like morning dew. A glance at the butler's ball in the ceiling confirmed a suspicion. They were cowering behind the half-doors leading to the kitchen, watching and waiting.

186

Clea lifted her chin. "Good black tea. Assam. Green we have, but isn't cheap to buy that without the poisons."

"I'll have your non-poisonous green tea if there's no mint in it. If I want mint, I can get it for free."

What form of English was she speaking? It was brief to the point of elegancy – an efficiency that one admired for its inability to flower into poetry.

Clea tipped her head. "Lucy, water. Mind our customers." She went to her office, returning with her tin of Gunpowder. It was a monstrous inconvenience of Taiwan's confused idea of what Westerners used for storage, but it did the job . . . and the girls were convinced it was a foreign propellant. Only she dared to touch it.

Lucy tiptoed up with the tray, set it before the woman, and ducked her head before running. Clea pulled up her own chair, not asking. Not in her own shop would she ask, thank you. The newcomer doffed her gloves. Her green eyes glittered as the leaf balls measured into cups and covered in water off the boil.

The Widow picked up the tin to glare inside it and gave a strange little nod of satisfaction at what she saw before setting the tin back. Clea honestly did not know if she should be insulted or not.

"Zhejiang?"

"It *is* gunpowder."

The combatants stared at each other over the table.

"You don't have a buyer for your old leaf."

"Used leaf is the right of the cook."

"I listen. I've got eyes. You don't sell the customers that mouldy dross. No sloe, no country leaf. Just tea. There's a market for leaves like yours. No worry about small brains and no sense – " (Here Clea was absolutely convinced her guest glanced straight at the corner of bread-and-tea women because behind her all conversation froze.) " – putting poisons in the cup. I can always use a good black, but green's hard to find."

"What do you do with old leaf?"

"Lots of things. My business. I don't ask you where you get potatoes, do I?"

"You ought, if you thought I was buying from a bad greengrocer."

"Ha. I like you. Direct is the only way to speak." Another look in the corner. "I pay for leaves, grounds, and tobacco."

"I don't carry coffee, and what grounds I have goes in its own bin. I'm starting a garden next year. The spinach wants it."

"What about tobacco?"

"Goes to the boy who sweeps my floor."

"He sells them to the Hard-ups, and you're missing your rightful cut."

"I'm not interested enough in the weed to make money off it, and the boy does a better job if I let him pay himself. If he doesn't do good, he shan't sweep my floors anymore."

Now her guest was smiling. She looked down. The loosened tea-balls floated in a buttery gold liquor. "You brew soft water."

"Yes."

"You're the only girl-Cheatham. You've got that brother in wrestling arter your da, and other brothers rising in business. Noticed you held your own with Mr. Quimper. Ugly man, he. Has his fingers in a lot of nasty pies around here. Or he did before his arrest." She paused and added, in contemptible tones, "Brewed his tea with pump water."

Clearly, this was the worst judgment possible upon mortal man. Clea wished she had the wit to really fathom it. "Thank you," Clea said tightly, "But I do possess some gratitude to him. After all, his arrest most courteously allowed a graceful way of getting out of an unwanted engagement." [1]

"And to a better'n." Now the stout little woman was grinning. "That Mr. Lestrade. I buy his landlady's leaf. Drinks his weight in Willowherb."

Clea cleared her throat even as she made note of this uncomfortable tit-bit of news.

"You teach these girls how to work," continued her guest.

"I teach them the kitchen." Clea's temper was close, but curiosity was closer. Outside of her sex, it was the greatest gap between herself and her impulsive brothers.

"Clean and ship-tight," the woman continued as if Clea hadn't said a single thing. "I'll buy at one-eighth the price of what you paid for it freshly used leaf, dry weight. Show me the receipts and I'll write my own."

"My ovens are large, but my kitchen is small. If I must keep the leaves while I'm waiting for you to pick them up – "

"Nothing like tea for keeping the flying pests out of your flour-bins. I'll not charge you for making use of them in the nonce. Pickup's every Tuesday. I've got responsibilities. Got to be dry leaves. Keep the green from the black. White tea, I give half-price from first purchase, but I examine it first."

Another shot of those green eyes over Clea's shoulders was enough. The table behind Clea deserted *en masse*, still chewing or stuffing unclaimed bread into their pockets and one last gulp of tea before handing the cup to the girl at the door. The deaf woman poured her cup into a flask that, as she passed, did not smell at all like tea. "You're a Christian girl, letting in all sorts."

"Christ said nothing against the poor. These pay, they don't shed fleas nor lice, and they mind their manners."

"I 'magine they would."

Clea gave up. "If we're doing business, you may call me more than Miss Cheatham, should it please you."

"Well, I'm Mrs. Walsh. Ask anyone on the street for t'Widow. Word gets to me." She swirled her tea, watching the pattern of the floating leaf. "My trade's leftovers and news. I sell at my own price and my own terms." She leaned back and pulled out a small wooden box, painted with (of all things) a blue daffodil. A *pop* of the lid revealed clean, sweet-smelling black curls that must have once been a lovely pekoe. "I'll be by this time next week for your leaves." She handed the dumbstruck Clea a knobbly fist of white linen drawstring bags. "Put it in these, and pin 'em up over the stove or someplace dry and warm. They'll be fine for pickup in no time at all." And she added clothespins for the bags.

"You aren't asking me for leaves now?"

"We just started the deal, Miss Cheatham. I know my manners better'n that."

Clea was still staring as the woman clipped away and back into the fog that birthed her. The girls crept up to her side.

"Drove 'em out, she did!" Aggie breathed.

"Who?" Clea snapped.

"Them harpies in the back." Aggie's mouth was an angry clamshell. Clea didn't think for one minute Aggie knew what a harpy even was, but she was a bright girl and knew to pick up words from the dictionary on the lips of London. "Didn't want to say it, Miss. They ain't proper. Their men do drags. They sell what news they find."

"That deaf one knows what you're sayin' if she can see your lips move," Lizzy chirped.

"Spies?" Clea twisted to her feet to look at her students, heart lurching. "And you haven't said anything?"

The girls looked ashamed. "We thought you wanted to give 'em a fair chance, like you did us. If you felt differn't, you'd have told us, ai?"

"Besides, we make sure Aggie's the one who serves their table. She don't have enuf in 'er gob to make it easy to read." Violet cheerfully elbowed a giggling Aggie.

"I hope she don't mind Mr. Lestrade," Lizzie added. She promptly blushed. "Do forgive me, Miss. She might overlook him, seein' as how he'll be your husband."

"She might treat him better because of *me*?"

"It's . . . possible?"

189

Clea's only solution was to laugh into the bottom of her cup, but no wisdom was found in the leaf's abstract patterns.

Inspector G. (Geoffrey) Lestrade didn't know his ears were burning. He was too busy trying to breathe.

The little professional had many consultants, but there was one who stood out – to begin with, he didn't seem to need oxygen.

"Counterfeiters, Mr. Holmes, are a special monster. I don't know why you want this . . . ." He placed the packet on the table, feeling his cheeks warm in the embarrassment of this topic. He sounded like a scold to his own ears, and no man wanted that title. Part of it, he could admit to himself, was the strangeness of sharing the Met's names of informants and spies with a civilian. Skilled though Sherlock Holmes may be, and much as he worked with the police, he still wasn't *of* the police. Lestrade couldn't help but feel like he was committing bigamy.

". . . but I'm only letting you have this list because I know you'll be discreet."

This was a shallow and complimentary threat, but some things needed to be said for their respective records. Lestrade reminded Holmes of his duties to the Law, and Holmes in turn exposed the flaws in the legal process with every opportunity.

Sherlock Holmes smiled as he took his prize. "Excellent, Lestrade. I trust it wasn't difficult."

"Oh, no. We have a few specialists here and there in the Yard. They keep their eyes out for this sort." Lestrade clasped his hands behind his back and rocked back and forth on the balls of his feet. "I simply don't understand. You've got your own sources, same as I do. You probably have a copy of this in your desk drawer!"

Lestrade's small tirade ended in a hasty cough, for just then and behind Holmes, Dr. Watson, normally a paragon of optimism, had been re-organising the papyrus horrors that was their pigeonhole shelving. He had looked up and given the visitor a molten glare of weary wonder. *If he did have a copy, do you think it could be found in this disaster?* was the message.

Lestrade coughed too and then looked elsewhere: At the piles of loose papers, a pyramid of odd-sized books, an atlas holding up a broken table-leg, a chemist's carboy full of . . . something . . . and the knife harpooning the considerable white whale of Holmes's correspondence to the mantel.

"Ah, Lestrade, but just as we both can hardly confide all of our work to each other . . . ." Holmes paused to light a fresh pipe.

It was at this point that Dr. Watson descended from his step-stool. With a martyred nod to the policeman, the man silently opened the window in defiance of the chill.

"Be that as it may be, Mr. Holmes, this is an odd way to settle our debt – "

*Tap-tap-tap.*

Two sets of eyes went to Watson, who was frowning out the window into a choking yellow fog. Before his nose wobbled the tip of a collapsible rod, the sort found amongst anglers.

*Tap-tap-tap.*

The stick against the sill was the source of the sound.

"Holmes, did you call for a knocker-up?"

Lestrade snorted. "Ha. Mr. Holmes would have to sleep to need one."

"The compliment rings true, Lestrade." Pipe firmly in teeth, Holmes joined Watson to peer down to the street below. "Good Heavens, Lestrade, I believe this one is yours."

"Eh?"

*"Wake up!"*

Watson winced. "If I wasn't I would be now."

*"I heard that, you! Got a call, I come! And I've got a list, sir! You're not the only one on it! Assure me this is the correct client so I can go on!"*

"Oh, dear." Lestrade hurried to the window, pushing aside Holmes and Watson (who promptly moved back for a better vantage because they knew a free show when it came calling). "Here, now, Madam! There were no calls for your service at this address!"

*"Oh, I'm a 'madam' now, am I?"*

The poor constable guarding Lestrade's cab was trying to be invisible against the wall of 221 Baker Street. Watson put his finger in the ear closest to the window. "How long can she bellow like that?" he whispered to Holmes.

"Hours," Holmes whispered back.

*"This is on the list, and I'm going down my list! You'll have to take this up with whoever in your building paid me!"*

"Must I charge you with disturbing the peace?" Lestrade was half-hanging out the window by now. Watson saw the veins over his collar. He braced himself to grab the little man by the tails, should his fervor override his relationship with gravity.

*"I'm only doing what I's paid to do!"*

"Then I'll pay you to cry off!"

Holmes and Watson watched, impressed as Lestrade pushed himself back into the pipe-perfumed indoors, grabbed up his hat, and flew down

191

the stairs. Watson didn't think he heard the little man's feet hit the steps twice.

"Does she . . . happen often, Holmes?"

Lestrade barreled out as the knocker-up broke down her rod. In an ill show, he counted a handful of coins and dispensed them into the tormenter's gloved palm. "There you are!" (*Said in undertone: "What's the news?"*)

"Always obliged to do business with a gentleman!" (*Answered in the same: "She's bein' watched by the Peahens. Daphne Post an' Yarra Bliss."*)

Out loud: "Thank you, Mrs. Walsh!"

Out loud: "No need for that. Just 'The Widow' will do. *As you'll recall.*"

Lestrade wasted no time running back upstairs.

The Widow spared the cowed constable a single look from behind her pipe and continued down the street.

*Clip-clip-clip.*

"What was that *fol-de-rol*?" Watson asked, fully suspicious once Lestrade's business had concluded and they were alone. Holmes credited him with patience.

The detective shrugged as he pulled out one pipe after another for inspection. "The most fearsome knocker-up west of Aldgate, Watson. Her title is 'The Widow'. Her husband was a constable with Lestrade, but through a combination of bad luck and worse incompetence, he was killed in the line of duty. She now fends for herself. Her bread and cheese are tea, coffee, tobacco, and gossip, when she isn't walking the rounds to ensure her clients wake at their proper hour."

"I've never seen her before, and I should think I would remember such a person."

"She does prefer to be seen. I believe her philosophy is to allow her enemies time to escape." Holmes sniffed a tarry specimen before putting it back. "She rarely stops here. Her regular clientele is unable to hear the Bells well enough to wake."

"Does she dislike Lestrade? They do not appear friendly."

"She calls no policeman 'friend' after their betrayal. She will do business with them if they mind her. Lestrade is one of her clients . . . or perhaps she is his. They trade information a great deal." Watson was almost reconciled to Holmes's use of dirty little children as his informers. He was surprised Lestrade made use of a woman for the same purpose, and he said this.

192

"My impression is she needs to communicate with him over some business, and this is how they may arrange a later, clandestine palaver."

"Clandestine?"

"It would never do for them to be seen together in camaraderie, Watson. No, not at all if they are both each other's clients in intelligence." Holmes chuckled softly over his smoke. "Watson, policemen cannot openly petition their informants. It would endanger their privacy and reputation. Thus, it must be in disguise or a trade-off that they meet."

"By what do you mean, a 'trade-off?'"

"Only outsider policemen will publicly question the informants under a case, so they usually bring in an unknown man from another district or employ a new transfer. On rare occasions I have conducted the service for them, but it is under strident oaths and much swearing of conduct. The Widow will only speak with a few policemen, so they, like Lestrade, go through some efforts to do it without being recognised.

"Lestrade most likely hired her to keep an eye on his fiancée, Miss Cheatham, in his absence. He usually pays her to watch out for women in need."

Holmes expected Watson to speak after this, but in the following silence he looked from his pipes to his friend. The doctor was sitting at his desk and looking thoughtful.

"I beg of you, Watson, don't write of her! She'll demand a tithe!"

Inspector Lestrade yanked his bowler tight over his head and hopped out of the cab with a hot wish that his half-coach was not at the hatter's. It was fancier, but it gained him more respect when he was walking the crowds – and in these crowds he needed every advantage. Poor PC Alain followed, tired from keeping up with the little man.

The address had seen better days, yet might become better again with the proper application of fool's luck, financial stability, and a miracle. The steps, that first demonstration of pride, were crumbling and scrubbed. Tiny windows dressed in faded check curtains reeked of boiled white vinegar. Someone with a Biblical level of faith in better things had bravely planted lettuces and spring onions in the window-box. A chipped milk-bottle vase bearing a peahen's tiny crest-feathers perched on the sill. The little professional frowned at it, but his stern face softened to see it had been painted with flowers by a child's hand. Over the front door hung a carefully hand-painted placard (with useful illustrations), pronouncing:

*Buttons, Cufflinks, and Whalebones*
*Inquire Within*

Lestrade didn't know if he should shake his head in pity or whistle in admiration for the proprietress' defiant spirit. From rag-catching to gewgaws, she was determined to survive.

He doffed his hat, took the step, and knocked on the door.

The woman who opened it was as faded as her curtains, but in the kindly shadows she was still beautiful. Clea would have recognised her.

"I thought that might be ye," was the weary greeting. "Knew it was only a matter of time onc't that Widow showed 'er face."

"How are you on wares?" Lestrade asked drily, just loud enough for any nosy neighbors to hear nothing more than a gruff business transaction. "We've complaints about a man coming around with a forged license. Sold some trinkets on the sly and scarpered off."

"Ye better come'n look, then."

He entered, hanging his hat on the wall-hook. (It had once been the broken-off head of a cane, now given new life and purpose with the cleverness he had come to associate with the hostess.) The first room was for business. In the back with the sleeping-pallets lolled a puppy's pile of three shaved children curled by a gasping three-legged box stove at least thirty years old. Their tiny hands almost touched the metal in hopes of warmth. Everyone wore overlarge night-gowns of the same striped ticking that had once wrapped someone's mattress – going by the amount of clothing, it had been the bed of a very large man.

*Gowns instead of day-clothes. Their clothes are back in the pawnshop.* Lestrade made note of the faces. He didn't see the eldest, a son. Likely out working the streets (doing God knew what) in the only clothes they could spare from pawning. A moggie stalked from wall to wall, fur bristled as she pawed the hidey-hole of a foolish mouse. It was blocked up with newspaper too old to burn for warmth. In all the years Lestrade knew business with this woman, she had always kept the same huge cats: Grey and black-striped single-minded killers of vermin. Even rats avoided the pedigree of Yarra Bliss, and suffering families paid well for this furry dragon's rare progeny. The shop walls were decorated with odd-sized standing cases of whalebone and buttons, clasps, and pins. Without a word he settled in one of the three chairs. She brought a lap-case of men's cufflinks and tiepins. Should anyone peep in the windows, they would see a frowning policeman picking through quite a lot of blotched and cheap jewellry as she waited on an offer.

"Why are you watching Miss Cheatham?" he asked without lifting his head.

"They don't tell us, y'know. Just tell us what to do." The spy frowned. "It isn't her we s'pposed to watch, though. I'll tell you that."

"Oh?"

194

"We're s'pposed to keep an eye on the people coming in."

"Such as?"

Mrs. Bliss sighed. "Just see who comes in from the trains. Who talks. No more, no less. Shilling a day, and cuppa tea and bread. Good money!"

*Good money? Havers*, Lestrade thought, for she was *starved*. He knew Clea's bread. It was that pitiable bit the children were passing around, one bite at a time. "Well, Mrs. Bliss, no matter who you weren't supposed to be watching, you tell Jolly it will have to stop."

"I been seen," she agreed wryly. "Held out longer than I thought. Wan't a bad disguise, neither. That Widow saw right through it, but wimmin are better at seein' other wimmin." She sighed for the end of the tea and bread. "They give me a dress an'shoes to wear for the job. Jolly said I might keep 'em."

Was he over-reacting? Lestrade wondered if he should relax a bit. *Clea's shop is close enough to the trains that it would make sense for the gangs to watch who came and went. The gangs might just be looking for a show of strength. Well, we shall see if it lasts.* More and more police were coming to The Rose for meals. It would be a brave scoundrel to make it his balliwick! But Jolly, though . . . Jolly was more than a scoundrel. She was crafty, tough, and fearless. She inspired loyalty. Women left the Peahens, but many returned because Jolly's protection was a sounder bet than one's own menfolk.

Lestrade held up a pair of carnelians in gold. "This isn't your usual lot off the mourners."

"Only nice thing in the bag. Died of consumption and everyone feared to touch it!" Mrs. Bliss snorted. "The rest's all mother-of-pearl! Giant things, too big to be practical. I mean, big as gleanie eggs, truth! Foolish! Nobody's wantin' that unless they's the Costers, and them's got standards."

"We're still looking for those 'missing' sapphires."

"Woman's stone," Yarra scoffed. "Won't be on a man's things."

"You never know. Shall we do business, Mrs. Bliss?"

"Depends. What're you offering?"

"A trade. I'll not pursue you if you stop going to The Rose. Tell Jolly her ladies have the same offer, but it starts now."

Mrs. Bliss nodded tiredly. "I'll tell her, but I'll not speak for her."

"I've never known anyone alive who could speak for that woman," Lestrade assured her. "But . . . Jolly must have offered you more than a bob for you to go back to your old ways."

"Mebbe I was curious. I can be curious. People talk. Miss Cheatham's got celebr'ties in her family."

195

Lestrade gave his hostess the courtesy of pretending to believe her. "Yes, prime Lanky wrestlers with a reputation for more temper than brain, and their baby sister – my fiancée." Lestrade kept his voice quiet. "Try again."

Mrs. Bliss stared into her lap.

"Is *he* back?"

The wild guess struck ore. Lestrade was stunned to see her eyes fill with tears.

"Had to go under the house," she sniffed. "Poor little cat got stuck. I heard her crying." Lestrade couldn't help but notice the "poor little cat" was heartily eating a rat the size of a Thames seagull. It stopped long enough to glare at him. "What did you find?"

She just shook her head at his gentle question, and her eyes slipped to the side, aiming at the kitchen. The children had stopped hovering around the stove and were holding each other, the yellow youngest sneezing between them in their bony arms. They all looked like their sire. It was not a compliment. Lestrade counted to ten. He got up and opened the door to his constable.

"Sit here with Mrs. Bliss, Alain. There's a bag of brown coal in the cab – get up the stove for them."

"Where will you be going, sir?"

"Down."

The little policeman hung up his coat with a sad familiarity to his chore and walked through the clot of children to a ring set in the floor. He bent, pulled up, and to the bobby's consternation, vanished.

PC Alain tapped his helmet to the worn woman, went to the cab, and retrieved the fifty-pound sack of lignite. Getting the old stove to respond to the offering was an art in itself. It had burnt too low on sorry fuel. The children were fascinated at how a lump could catch fire. They touched the clods with shy fingers, and pressed his leather belt, metal buckle, and the felt-topped cork helmet about his head.

"What's the matter, Love?" He asked the oldest girl. "Ain't you nair seen a Bobby?"

She shook her head. "They don't come *here,* thir," she whispered.

The heat caught, quick and hard. They crept over. A tin cup of water on the top steamed. Excited, they found three more cups from a bucket. They lined them up on top of the iron platform and hovered. There was no food on the open shelves, but they kept looking at a painted wooden box. *Cocoa* was scratched into the grain.

The constable's long mustaches drew down. He pulled out his bottle and put a handsome splash into each glimmering cup. They thought his tea (boiled down to gluey sweet syrup and declared an inedible poison by even Inspector Gregson) was brandy and looked at the offering in happy awe.

"Don't drink it 'til s'warm all the way through, Loves," he admonished, and the bald heads bobbed in agreement. He did not know it was at this point the children were mentally brokering the marriage between their mother and this paragon of providence.

A gloved hand emerged from the depths of the floor, followed by a dusty head and shoulders. Lestrade's neatly oiled hair was wild and loam-powdered. He looked like a hellfire judge mummified by cobwebs. Tertiary clay painted his furiously-jutted chin. He hopped up, soles clicking on the uneven floor. "How long d'you think that's been there?" he demanded in a dangerous voice.

A head-shake was his only answer. Mrs. Bliss didn't know.

"Right." Lestrade took a deep breath for composure, sneezed, and tapped his fingers on his arm. His eyes blazed like the lignite in the stove and thank the Lord, this strange rage had nothing to do with Alain or the woman and children. The constable felt lonely. The expressions between the Inspector and the Lady of the House were creating lectures' worth of conversation, and he did not know the language.

Holmes's breakfast of plugs and dottles had passed and he was contemplating elevenses with Cavendish in Briar. On a day with such fog, there was little hope for clients, and his productivity was lowered to another perusal of the newspapers. The rooms were perfumed with smoke and paper-paste.

Watson was on the verge of asking Holmes a question just to break the monotony, but the fog broke upon the window, and he glanced out. "Is that Lestrade again?"

Holmes looked. "How odd."

Together they waited for the familiar sounds of bell, voice, and trod upon their steps. Their friend was harried and attempts to wipe dust off his face and clothing had met with poor success. "I've got a little puzzle for you, Mr. Holmes, if you have the time."

As Holmes's boredom could be measured in the replacement of breathable gases for burning carbon, this was a splendid display of manners. Watson could have cheered for the stout good health of British stoicism.

Holmes chuckled. "A puzzle should not be a drain upon my time. Present it, my good man."

Lestrade nodded and put down a small purse upon the mantelpiece. Holmes's fee for police consultations. He had taken to heart the amateur's scorn for finances and always ensured the payment never sat between them. That allowed Holmes the gentleman's freedom to reject the case if he chose. "I need proof that John Bliss, also known as Rakosi, is alive."

"The garrotter? That would be bold, even for him! As I recall, his standing had fallen so low in society that the Courts declared him sufficiently dead, and they did not expect him to be so rude as to show his face upon this plane again."

"I know, Mr. Holmes." Lestrade twisted his hat in his hands, placing the brim in jeopardy. "But there are rumours, and I do not like them. His wife . . . 'widow' . . . is as terrified as her children. She's returned to her old ways! The Peahens promised her protection if she goes back to spying for them."

Holmes had been exhaling smoke. He inhaled it back. "It would take such a threat to bring that woman low again!"

"You know how it is on the other side of Lambeth. She's alone. The youngest's two-years now, though it looks half its age."

"Have you a report?"

Lestrade pulled out a thick envelope, sealed hastily with candle-wax and stamped with a thumb-print.

"I shall see to it. Call if there are any new developments." Holmes took the paper. "Who is the victim of her subterfuge, Lestrade?"

"It was Miss Cheatham." Lestrade coloured a bit, but held the ice-grey gaze with ice of his own. "Not watching her, so much, I'm told . . . as who patronises her cooking."

"Ah. A shifting in the gangs. Jackals are seeking the next lions to follow."

"I'm afraid so. Well, a few more police stopping by for a plate will solve that problem, and we'll only have to worry about the spies in our own ranks." Wilted with relief, Lestrade drew up. In a sudden crisp movement, he placed his hat upon his head, tapped the brim with his two extended first fingers, spun about, and left.

Three minutes later, Holmes muttered language picked up on his routes in disguise. Lestrade had wrapped a button in his letter. On it strutted a crude rooster with a proud fan and crowned comb. Watson marvelled at its oddness.

"A low beast has returned to his old grounds, Watson. He goes by more names than we have fingers, but Rakosi – "the Crab". 'The Garrotter' he is called by the Tinkers, for he scuttles as a crab hunting its prey."

"Garrotter? You mean he is a man of violence."

"Oh, that and much more. An assassin when he works for pay, a common murderer without it. He is an abhorrent member of The Roosters, an assassin's fraternity. Their trademark is murder in the dark.

"Each member wears these buttons loosely sewn inside their clothing, for when their work is concluded they rip it off and place it at the location of the crime. Or regrettably, discard it before it can be used as evidence in an arrest. Luckily for us they are also easily lost, just as Rakosi apparently left this in a hole beneath his wife's rooms. Only someone as stubborn as Lestrade would crawl into the grave of a prospective victim for clues! Rakosi intends to murder that poor woman – his very own wife. It is his signature to dig a hole under the victim's own lodgings and, work done, bury them in it. She cannot afford light more than anyone else on her impoverished street. Each night she must lie awake in darkness, waiting for him to come to her one last time."

Watson blanched. "This is atrocious! Has she no allies?"

"Mrs. Bliss' strongest ally is her foster-sister, a ranking officer in the women's gang called the Peahens. They collect gossip for pay and favours, which are quite lucrative and impossible to trace. Their connections to unknown and powerful criminals will stall Rakosi, but ultimately they cannot stop him."

"But why would he kill his own wife and mother of his children!"

"That is the question. Mrs. Bliss' only wealth is her children, whom she loves devotedly. Find the connection, and we find Lestrade's proof."

"Holmes! Why is Lestrade asking for proof that this man has returned from the grave? That is a strange request."

"Because the Inquiry declared him dead! It is true there was '*a*' body found in the wrackline of the Thames, but there was not enough distinguishing characteristics outside of the clothing. Clothing, Watson! Imitation detection, or most likely corruption and bribes, for the police, limited as they are in their brains, have minimal standards of competency. The man who closed the case died soon after."

Watson stared. "This was not declared suspicious?"

"I was not at the Inquiry, but I heard that the effects of drink and gravity were deemed very un-suspicious indeed."

Watson made a gargling sound of disgust.

"The case is closed. Re-opening it is a betrayal of the Brotherhood of Policemen, so Lestrade must ask for my help." Holmes tutted. "He is foolish with fire, Watson, and he will get burned."

"He does not appear foolish to me."

"He is personally involved. Mrs. Bliss is a spy in his fiancée's establishment."

Clea Cheatham was keying the shop door for the night when someone cleared his throat. She turned to smile up at a small (she was smaller), dapper man. He hoisted his stick in the air and half-bowed. She half-curtseyed his whimsy back to him and the couple laughed together.

"Now that we've made a spectacle for your Annie," Lestrade nodded at the merry girl on the other side of the barred window, "shall I see you home?"

"That you may. T'would reassure my family you are punctual."

"Part of the duty of being a policeman, Miss Cheatham – and a policeman is never off duty. You look tired?"

They fell into step, she pulling the dust-veil about her face and wishing (not for the first time) the impossible wish of clean air. "I suppose I am. It was an interesting morning." She related the events with the tea and the missing patrons, and he listened without a word until she finished.

"I don't wish any woman to feel like they aren't welcome in my shop." Cheathams were infamously strangers to thought, but Clea bit her lip in rare indecision. "Even those who . . . consort with men they shouldn't. It is dreadfully hard for a woman to have a safe place to eat and drink!"

"The Widow's well known," he said at last. "Word will get out, and it will be a foolish trouble-maker who stays. The rest will honor the peace of your roof."

"Is it really that simple?"

"So long as no one gives her cause to pull out that hatpin!"

"That . . . thing is really a hatpin?"

"Er, she uses it as such. She'll keep the nonsense away from your shop."

"I've got six brothers and a father, and they all know how to fight – some do it for a living! How would nonsense make its way to my shop? I've a cooking school!"

"Yes, but . . . Well, they're *men*, Clea. Men look to men for trouble. The Widow is looking for trouble amongst the women."

"What a sad world. My girls say she is a policeman's widow?"

"Davvy Walsh. A good 'un – best you'd ever meet. He died in the line of duty, and it was hastily closed up. She holds a grudge."

"What happened?"

"The Roosters are a secret club of hired assassins. They . . . kill in the dark. One of them had . . . finished a paid job – *Ahem!* – and Walsh was walking his patrol. He came running when he heard the murder."

"What happened?" Clea breathed, though she already knew.

"He was killed too," Lestrade said simply. "I'm sorry, there is no nice way to say it. The uproar made it bad for all Roosters and they broke up. Some left the country. Others went to ground. Either way, the gang's been nothing but wraiths and wisps of its former strength."

200

"Was the killer never found?"

"There's no telling who he is. They're a secret Society. We just know they're . . . 'hurting for finances' . . . now that they've been broken."

"I feel cold to think of that."

"I am sorry."

"No, don't. But . . . it is so wrong, Geoffrey." Clea Cheatham wrapped her arms deep into her coat. "Everyone jokes that all of London is available for a price. But murder too? That is too much!"

"Of course it is. That is why we have policemen."

Night dropped, stacking black atoms of soot before the eyes. Lestrade was dressed for war in this hostile land. A muffler about his face wound tight, and his stick waved first one way, then another, testing the parts of streets and alleyways just outside of human eye. A heavy straw rope of purple and pink garlics depended over one shoulder and bobbed down his back. Even though he knew every step of his journey, he was still almost blind to his destination until he was on top of it.

"*Mat ar jeu?*" He knocked on the door.

"Is it morning?" asked the voice on the other side, and he grinned under his shield of wool.

The Widow creaked open the door and shook her head at him. "You took your time."

"I am zorry." This was said in a dreadful accent.

"Well, let's see it. I asked for a manouille this time."

The rope was passed to the little inspectress, two-handed. She pulled it up and down in the air, testing its weight. She tugged. She pulled in smoke from her face-warmer and exhaled over the button bulbs. When nothing small and entomological flew away she nodded. "You've got two different garlics in here. I know the pink one. That's Latrec. Are you trying to sneak me Southern bulbs outside the tax?"

"They were grown in Roscoff!"

"These purple ones too?"

"Both long-season, both hard-necked. Good scapes if you plant in the spring."

"Wouldn't know what to do with scapes."

"Cook them like chives!"

"Don't know chives."

He clutched his head. "I will show you!"

"Maybe. I'll see if there's anything left in my purse."

"*Mat-mat.*" Lestrade stepped in and put his back to the door. A last puff of fog gasped out and died in the heat of the fire.

The Widow demanded a clean, ship-tight shop. The grate glowed cherry red as it burnt up paper logwood, and cotton cords hung from the web-free ceiling, clutching little paper bags of tea and tobacco. Lestrade ducked under them all and dropped into a half-barrel chair, sweating in the warmth. "How can you tell the tea from the tobacco?" he asked in his normal, so'west-studded English.

"It ain't always easy." The Widow pulled her iron kettle off the stove and poured two-handed into stout cups. "Coffee for us. I've been handling tea all day. Reckon you're not much of a tea drinker this hour."

"I like tea when there's a good cup!"

"And how often d'you get *that*?"

The two sat and sipped in companionable silence for almost a minute. Good manners sternly dictated they do this, even if Lestrade was too restless to knuckle down for a "pleasant chat about nothing", and The Widow loathed anything that wasn't straight to the point. It was one of the many glues that held their odd friendship together.

"I took this to Sherlock Holmes." Lestrade opened the floor. "I know I paid you to watch Miss Cheatham, but this is bigger than I thought."

The Widow stopped to puff on her pipe. "That Mr. Holmes . . . He's not one of you."

"No. He'll find answers where we can't. No oaths binding that one, save his work."

She sipped her coffee. "Is he as smart as people say?"

"I've never met anyone as smart. Or annoying."

"Smart ones get under the skin," she agreed. "I buy from his landlady. She's decent, but those lodgers of hers . . . I've picked up better tobacco-bits from Newgate!"

Lestrade cleared his throat, signalling a darker turn of conversation on the road. "I saw Mrs. Bliss. *He's back.*"

The woman's hand, surprisingly large for her sex, tightened around the tiny pipe. "Wondered what it would take for her to lose her spine."

"He left more than his calling card." Lestrade held her eye. "He's digging a hole under the building. Not much, but enough to put a small woman in it."

"Rot his soul. She can't leave, can she."

"Not with all those childer. The younger ones're coughing badly. This fog's going to last a Welsh fortnight."

"Love to get my hands on him," The Widow muttered. "Well, any one of 'em will do, but he's asking for it special."

Lestrade sighed. "The question is why would he kill her? The courts called him dead. He should be living free as a lark!" Anger ground his fist into his leg. "Money's their only reason for doing anything."

"He's working for himself now?"

"Maybe. If that's to scare his wife, well done. He's the only thing she fears." Lestrade gulped his hot drink in the chill of this ice-blooded talk. "I barely recognised her today. Her starch is gone. The children are far too thin. They're terrified. Usually, they swarm around me like ants up a hill – but they wouldn't speak above a wisp's whisper."

"Strange way for children to act."

"Not strange at all, Mrs. Walsh. They're *listening*. They're listening for *him*."

In two days with Sherlock Holmes, Watson learned more of the art of killing for personal gain than he had in the entirety of Afghanistan. The doctor's senses were battered under the constant flow of motion as he followed Holmes through London's rabbit-warrens, the detective explaining the Roosters Gang when they had a rare moment alone.

This was the latest of such moments, following Holmes's collection of baffling conversations with the shrunken, shifty-eyed starvelings of the East London shores. After, he led Watson to the first available street open to cabs and whistled until one swam out of the fog. Holmes promised the driver extra wages to take them to an address recommended by an unkempt rag-woman. The doctor did not know why Holmes had chosen this roundabout way of interviewing when they could have simply taken a cab to Mrs. Bliss' from Baker Street.

"The Roosters began as a confederation of soldiers fresh from the Nine Years' War. They had a proclivity for killing and it was peacetime. Their founder's name is lost, but he did give them their unusual name."

"Roosters bluster and crow. I can't imagine a more unlikely emblem for killers in stealth!"

"We may guess the founder was educated. As Socrates drank his hemlock, he joked of the need to sacrifice a rooster to Aesculapius, the God of Healing, for death was about to be the cure for his life."

Watson clapped his brow in the obvious-ness of the explanation. "I doubt Socrates would approve of the tribute."

"Agreed, but the Society – which Lestrade insists on calling a 'low gang' to their fury – has existed ever since. They rise and fall in fortunes. War fuels their coffers, but the era in which one may tastefully purchase assassination has passed. The Society was already dying when the murder of PC Walsh sounded its death knell."

"This is fascinating and gruesome in equal proportion, Holmes, but why are we visiting Mrs. Bliss? You have led me to believe there is no love lost between man and wife."

"He intends to kill her, and that has my curiosity."

"A murderer does not actually need a reason to murder. I have unfortunately seen how men may be addicted to the act of killing, just as a man gripped by strong drink."

"True, but I dislike presuming an emotional motive without data, Watson. At any rate, here we are." The door opened upon Holmes's rap.

A woman looked at them both, her lean face wary.

"May I help you, gentlemen?"

A half-hour later, Holmes had finished an exhaustive search of the meagre tenancy – he had started under the floor but spent less time there than Lestrade. A quick word and quicker coin happily created his passport into the rest of the building, and Watson simply could not keep up with his aching leg. He and the children sat by the decaying stove and listened to the noise of Holmes's search drift further and further away.

"I think he'th on the top floor," a little boy whispered.

"I think you're right," Watson said. Boredom led him to pass time by checking over the health of the children – his teachers would not approve of *pro bono* charity, but Watson reasoned there should be some proper return for this invasion of privacy. Anyway, it felt good to use his doctor's bag – Holmes had insisted he take all fifteen pounds of the satchel with him because "fewer people look at two gentlemen in this neighborhood when one is a physician." Holmes had been proven right (as usual), but Watson still had no idea why a man with tools and drugs would be given shrift in a borough that would pickpocket a man's gun out of his pocket and thriftily use it to rob him.

A giant pot simmered a mighty sulphur onion inside its jacket over the tiny stove. When Watson squinted, he could see the extraordinary expense of three bobbing peppercorns, a weak splinter of nutmeg, and what might possibly be a pluck of Sweet Nancy, the peasant's mace.

"Would you like to thtay for thupper?" the oldest girl asked politely. She was giving the toddler a lump of coal to chew.

"Oh, but I couldn't impose." Watson tried not to look horrified at the baby with the coal. He glanced away and found himself eye-to-eye with a monstrous cat in the corner. It glared at him and went back to playing ball with a rat's skull.

"Ith all right. We can thare."

Watson flinched. He thought of places he'd seen even poorer than this. He rummaged in his bag and pulled out a packet marked *Clean Lard* for wound-salving and passed it to the child. "Put that in for some flavour."

She obeyed to the letter.

Watson opened his mouth and then gave up. The wrapping was only paper, and would probably dissolve . . . and the ink was made of purple grapeskin, so it would hardly poison them . . . The children sniffed happily, watching the disks of fat rise and dance on the top of the softly-simmering water.

"Well! This was all very interesting, my good woman." Holmes was bouncing back, hopefully without breaking any of the steps on his way down. "I can assure you the building is secure. Now, what are your wares?"

"These are interesting." Holmes held up a pair of carnelian cufflinks. Watson could see a carved teardrop bending in a half-circle with a single dot in the center of the base. "Have you more?"

"No, nothing like. Mr. Lestrade noticed them too."

"They would complete a set I have. Are you certain?"

"They's the only cufflinks in a bag of death-clothes. Nothing else had metal – it was all fancy mother-of-pearl buttons, too big to sell."

"Really! I collect mother-of-pearl buttons!"

"They big as Gleanie eggs," she warned. "Not useful. Must've chafed awful."

"What were the clothes like?"

"Just . . . clothes?"

"Are you certain the clothes and cufflinks belong to the same gentleman?"

"Well, who can say for certain of anything?" She produced a sewing basket groaning with its trophy of buttons in unimaginable variety and quality. "They ten in all – 'is buttons have the same mark as the cufflinks, so I'm guessing yes, but you'd have to ask him for sure, wouldn't ye? An' he's dead of the lungs, so they just bundled up his things in the sheets and tied em up. I bought the whole thing off the maid for a penny out the laundry door. Made profit on the bedsheets alone, onc't I washed em off!" She nodded proudly at her children. "Ticking and canopies I put to good use. Should last 'em at least three years if they're careful. Ain't that right, Blissfuls?" The tots proudly patted their new striped cladding.

Watson didn't know it was possible to feel so guilty and relieved about ending a visit in his life. His head buzzed and his legs throbbed from matching Holmes's longer stride. The poverty of that little hovel was somehow magnified by the mad level of determination and defiance on part of its Mistress. She would keep her house and children clean. She would make do.

Their cab rattled and shook for almost an hour, the horse tip-toeing through the murk and avoiding straighter paths for better-lit ones. Several times the driver apologised for the greater intellect of his horse, but Holmes merely laughed and assured him they would always have time to arrive safely at their destination.

The detective made notes with his pocket-lamp, but Watson was drawn within his own thoughts, which often took dismal turns in the sad atmosphere of London in smoke.

The doctor knew this weakness within himself and could only soldier on, waiting for the return of softer weather and new leaves. For now, he accepted the dark paths within his mind that circled like their horse – eventually getting there, but not in anything resembling a straight route.

"Why did we not see Mrs. Bliss at the first?" he asked when Holmes paused notetaking to shake his fingers free of cramp.

"I wanted to see the other Peahens. What affects one, affects all. They communicated to me various degrees of concern for Mrs. Bliss."

Watson paused too, thinking of the peculiar honour among thieves, and women at that. "Why did Lestrade want you to see her wares?"

"He did not. On occasion a piece of interest will wind up in the collection of such a vendor. I thought the cufflinks interesting."

"Interesting enough to buy." Watson shook his head. They were too gaudy for gentlemen, and he couldn't imagine Holmes wearing them unless he was in disguise as a languid fop.

"Lestrade should have realised the importance of those buttons, but as usual he does not see the obvious." Holmes did not volunteer more information or clues as to what was happening, but he hummed to himself and, when he ran out of paper, used his cuffs as a writing-desk. He knew better than to ask Watson for his own notebook. That would have been trespassing.

They lurched. The horse had seen better than the driver and repairs blocked the way. "Only two streets short!" Holmes hopped like a grasshopper into the atmospheric soup. Blind as the world seemed, the driver saw well enough to catch all three coins Holmes tossed up. Holmes cheered and launched his long legs forward. Watson followed slowly. His leg ached.

It took ten minutes' foraging before they found their goal. A gasp of air brushed the fog away long enough for a badly weathered sign over their heads:

*Balm of Gilead*
*Retirement House*
*Vacancies*

A dour doorman in an equally dour black uniform held the door with his right hand, his left tucked like Napoleon's into the front of his coat. On both wrists one could glimpse a swallow tattooed upon pallid pale flesh: The man had sailed many thousands of miles in his life.

206

He doffed his hat with what Watson thought was a strong expression. Something about the fellow and his shrunken blue eyes inside a coarse-grained face made him look hard, but the man pretended to find something interesting in another direction. The rivalry between British Navy and British Army was the stuff of legends. In the brief trade of glances, the two men sized each other up, found the other wanting, and silently threatened his rival to behave with composure.

*Rudeness*, Watson thought. *Probably memorising all the faces in case a thug comes in.* He tried to be less sensitive about it, but when he wore his Campaigner's Pin, he saw more of this derisive attention. His jaw set in resolve to wear it proudly, every day, just for men like this doorkeeper.

Inside, the Gilead was refreshingly clean. Pungent cleaning chemicals [2] hovered about the low-lit atmosphere, and Holmes led the way to the desk, where a plump woman crowned by her matronly bun and spectacles maintained a tottering stack of papers.

"Good afternoon, Madam. We are here to see a friend and colleague you may know as 'Cap'. Perhaps you know him? He has Chinese tattoos about his wrists."

"Oh, that is bad news for you, sir! Poor Captain Ogburn passed away just on the third! From consumption, it was."

"I am most sorry to hear that! Did he leave any debts? Perhaps I could help – "

"Why, no, sir. Not at all." She drew herself up like a hen guarding its nest, lowering her glasses to her nose for a closer look at the guests. "Our residents have ordered their affairs to the last inch! I can even give you the address of his plot if you wish to pay respects."

"I would indeed. It is never too late for courtesy! And, if I may: Cap and I shared a passion for our collections. I had mailed him a piece to examine last month. Might I pick it up? It was in a very distinct walnut case, of precisely twelve by twelve inches."

"Dear me! It grieves me to tell you that our policy disposes of a consumptive's belongings! For the health, you see. It may be in his rooms still, for we fumigate twice before we let to the next resident. You are welcome to look and take it if you see it! Mind the doves."

Holmes collected the room-key with a grave mien that meant he was fighting to keep from laughing out loud – he often had that look when a ruse went particularly well.

"What is it?" Watson finally whispered when they found the late captain's door in a dim cul-de-sac of a hall.

"Oh, if I am correct . . . we shall see. What do you think of this day so far?"

"First, I have never heard of an entire family lisping before. It is peculiar. Second . . . you appear to know more than you have told me!"

"First, the sibilant '*S*' is the easiest to hear. They do not wish to give themselves away or dull their own ear to the sound of their lamented father's stealthy approach into their house."

"Good God!" Watson breathed.

"And second, I have not told you everything, so of course I know more." With a look of pure mischief, Holmes pressed open the door and stepped inside. "As the good woman said, mind the doves."

"I cannot believe in our enlightened age of science people still believe doves purify air," Watson growled under his breath. But now that his offense was aired, he relaxed and followed his friend. It was a tiny room but well-kept and tightly swept and polished, the bed and wardrobe stripped down to skeletons. A cage of white birds cooed curiously at the men and watched them for lack of anything better to do.

Holmes paid the furniture a bare courtesy. He was more interested in looking behind the pieces, the tiny mirror, and under the bed. With Watson's help they examined the mattress – bright and new – and the small cracks in the walls. A zymotic cleaner had scoured everything. Its chemical haze made their noses wrinkle.

"Nothing, but I expected as much. The real prize is gone."

"What prize?"

"Oh, about a thousand pounds' worth, if I am correct."

Watson managed to close his mouth as Holmes returned to the desk.

"I apologise for your time, my good woman. It is clear my case was misplaced, perhaps when he was feeling ill and not thinking clearly? It was not valuable but held some sentimental worth. Mayn't I leave my address? I am hoping he sent it to one of our clubbing companions in error."

"Oh, sir, these things happen! I would be pleased to have your address. If one of your collector friends sends it back here, then straight to you it shall go!"


"Holmes, you do not seem very upset for a man who has lost a collection – of whatever it is."

"Well, it was only sentimental value, and I am not a sentimental man."

"The lady did not seem worried at your loss."

"Because I described something that did not exist. Her glasses were for myopia. She would have remembered something like that, so she has already decided her late tenant did something with the case before he died. Even in death, she protects his privacy!"

208

Watson scratched his chin. "And you looked in a room where you expected to find nothing."

"Of course. And nothing is what I found."

"Holmes . . . are you trying to drive me mad?"

"You, my good fellow? Never." Holmes opened his watch and peered at the numbers. "We have time for a dish of curry."

"And then what?"

"Fishing. For which we must pick up the proper net."

"What net?"

"The Widow's net."


At Scotland Yard, Inspector Lestrade was finishing up his latest obligation of reports. It was unpleasant, but he was as determined to succeed with it as he was with everything else in his world. That it let him avoid a new invitation by his fiancée's family sweetened the deal.

"Just go and get it over with," Mr. Bradstreet advised. He was no lazy inspector and had read the sign on the desk as soon as he'd come in with the tea: A growing stack of forms versus a lonely letter with the Cheatham's Lancaster Rose on the red wax.

Lestrade grunted. "I'm starting to not mind them, Roger. They're not so . . . overbearing once you get to know 'em. Just . . . too confident by half. Men on the rise make the best gulls."

"Ain't that so. Too trusting because they're used to settling things honest with their fists. Or clogs. In their case . . . both." Bradstreet chuckled. "So – agree to whatever they're invitin' ye to."

"Not until I've cleared up some matters first."

"What matters?"

"The Peahens are watching Miss Cheatham's cooking school. The Rose would be a perfect spyhole . . . nice, clean, respectable . . . close to the trains . . . ."

"Peahens? That would be Jolly's business." Bradstreet crushed his face up in thought. "Someone's payin' her a bright coin to do it. She knows to keep her lasses away from a policeman's fiancée!"

The two men traded conspiratorial looks. In the privacy of Lestrade's office they could freely discuss unpopular opinions, such as the terrifying competency of women who chose crime as a profession. Jolly had avoided absorption into the larger gangs by insisting she only provided the service of information and 'small favours'. A similar policy of 'courtesy' kept the worst of the law off her affairs.

"By themselves, I wouldn't be worried. They usually just sell gossip to the highest bidder, like Langdale Pike or that bloated art dealer,

209

whatever-his-name-is. Oh. Thank you." Lestrade had noticed his teacup and began his ritual of saucer-and-blow.

"Could it be they're only spying for gossip? London gets thousands of newcomers every day, and that means fugitives. It would be something fresh and new for those ragged newspapers – Geoffrey, when was the last time you slept?"

"Hmm? I get plenty of sleep." This was said into the man's palm, which was propping up his head.

Bradstreet took a long, long drink of tea. "Geoffrey, let's pause a bit." The Runner perched his huge frame with ridiculous delicacy on Lestrade's guest chair. "It seems to me there has been a renewed interest in establishments within convenience of the railways."

Lestrade glared fireballs at his best friend, but knew there was a point to this. "That new train act." [3]

"That would make sense." Bradstreet nodded. "I heard the Rail Police are bucklin' down for the cheaper fares about to happen. We'll see more people on the rails than ever before."

"More people equals more crime. That's a Law of Nature. Pickpockets, kidnappers, prostitutes . . . as soon as they leave the railway, they'll be our problem. Good Lord, Roger – my future in-laws need to learn to stand on their own so they don't become a mark for every trickster about to swarm their way." Lestrade set his empty cup down, *clunk*. "News runs London more than coal! At least it *is* Jolly's ladies – they have stiff rules and cloggers to enforce their territory. Could be worse – could be the Forty Elephants!"

Bradstreet sipped daintily around his mustaches. "We don't mention devils by name."

Lestrade tried to smile, but the topic was too serious. "They've got Yarra Bliss back. That has me worried."

Bradstreet spilled his tea. "She worked like the devil to get out! What sent her back to her old ways?"

"The only thing that *could* scare that Amazon."

Bradstreet paled. "Geoffrey, you don't think . . . ."

"I don't just *think*. Rakosi's alive. She's gone to the Peahens for protection – such as it is. But . . . even Jolly can't stand against a Rooster for long."

"Heavens, Geoffrey! What are you going to do?"

"I've already done it." Lestrade's smile was not nice. "I paid Sherlock Holmes to bring me proof that Rakosi is back."

"You do know that a lot of guilty parties wind up dead around Mr. Holmes, don't you?"

"Hope was already dead – he just hadn't laid down yet – and Roylott was playing with fire. Those are the provable cases. The rest is just exaggeration."

"Gregson's making a list."

"Of course he is. He's idle by nature."

"You know what Mr. Holmes constitutes as 'proof', don't you?"

"Yes. Iron-clad."

Bradstreet held up his hand-cuffs. "Best have yours."

"You've caught me out the door."

Grown men had quailed before The Widow's voice. Sherlock Holmes tipped his hat. "It is urgent enough that I could not delay."

"Then you won't need much time to talk."

Holmes placed Ogburn's carnelians on The Widow's fruit-crate desk. Behind him, Watson held blue hands over the stove and stamped numb feet. "Do you recognise this symbol?"

"Chinese cut thing."

"Is it called the *Yang*. It is a Taoist symbol for the *rooster.*"

"I'm listening. Keep talking."

"Intelligence has never riddled out the funding for the Roosters. I believe I now have that answer. These cufflinks were in a bundle of possessions of ship's captain – John D. Drake."

"I know that name." The Widow pulled out her pipe and struck fire into it with chill intensity. Her green eyes never blinked over the flame and smoke. "He was a Rooster."

"One of the first to vanish when your husband met his death." Holmes produced a mother-of-pearl disc. It was large, a *Yang* carved in the center. "Have you seen this before?"

"Not that, no. I seen the like." She picked it up. "That looks Chinese."

"Correct. This is a Chinese gambling token. Each den has its own currency with each assigned a different value depending on its size, shape, and carving. There is a repulsive little dive in East London where its emblem is the *Yang*. Opium and gold flow there in equal amounts. With the two, assassinations are sure to follow.

"Hiring the Roosters was simply hidden in plain sight: The client played a rigged game, and his loss, the payment, was pre-calculated. If for some reason the contract failed, the client simply returned to the Den and collected his refund in the form of these redeemable tokens."

"A lot of work, Mr. Holmes, but impossible to track if all you saw was a game. What's the name of this Den?"

"I would rather not tell you until I have more information."

"You're afraid I'll go there."

211

"Yes."

"How much is this thing worth?"

"One-hundred pounds. Drake absconded with a thousand pounds' worth of their own tokens. The already weakened Society could not accommodate its loss. He changed his name to Abraham Ogburn the Second and sewed the tokens on his bedclothes in what appeared to be a derisively amusing but harmless display of an old man's vanity, but he did not go into hiding alone. He had a compatriot – an accessory to the theft."

"Rakosi?" Watson murmured.

"Yes. For years Drake lived quietly as an elderly pensioner. I imagine his tokens were insurance for a harder future that never came. But Rakosi was still in the gang, even if he was living a double life pretending to be dead from the public so he could operate for his masters."

Watson winced. "The Roosters must have helped him falsify his death so he could work in secret for them, looking for Drake."

"Exactly." Holmes clapped.

"Only he was being paid by both sides! He guarded Drake, and told the other Roosters he had seen not hide nor hair of him! But where was he?"

"Why, he was the very doorman who let us in the Gilead! He had lost much of his seafaring browning, and shaving has exposed the ills covered by the beard he once wore, but he could not hide his remarkably small pupils, nor his missing left thumb. How he must have chafed at the administrators who would not let their precious staff touch the possessions of a consumptive – but they would sell it to the ragwoman! No doubt he believed the tokens were his rightful inheritance.

"It really was a clever scheme, if you want to live in hiding for the rest of your life. Drake stayed in his comfortable rooms, content. Upon his death, his possessions were bagged up with his clothing. By misfortune, there was a woman so poor she came to the back of the Gilead's door, not the front where the doorman served. She bought up Drake's effects in hopes of selling the salvage to feed her children."

"Yarra Bliss. Oh, dear."

"Yes. One may hope to avoid crime, but old patterns can never be escaped. Her wretched husband had schemed to secure this wealth for himself. How he must have raged when it was collected by the very wife he abandoned! He plans to kill her and take the treasure she does not know she possesses. He accidentally left his mark of office under the floor as he quietly dug the start of her grave, and were it not for the accident of the cat, she never would have known his intentions.

"A mother is a she-bear in the defense of her children. She wasted no time in running to her old gang, who re-extended their protection in trade

212

for her skills in spying, and that in turn led to a paid job in spying on the little shop run by Mr. Lestrade's fiancée."

"Someone should have warned her about running an establishment so close to the trains." Mrs. Walsh somehow conveyed that all of London had failed in their duty.


Sunset was passing and the darkness would soon be true, not this pretend fog-night. Mrs. Bliss and her children ate their soup, soaking it with lumps of the rock-hard bread her son had collected on his rounds. He had little to brag about: A tuppence for each errand or delivery run. The fog took more than peoples' lives. It also took livelihoods.

"I'll be in the back, Blissfuls. Mind when Jolly knocks."

They nodded, and everyone wrapped their arms around each other for a good night. The woman wearily sank upon the pallet uncurled from the back and closed her eyes, the youngest asleep inside her thin arms.

It was too soon when she was shaken awake. "Jolly'th here."

Her foster-sister was already in the rooms, rubbing cold hands. Her sallow face was pink with a high emotion Mrs. Bliss could not read. By the door huddled two tall women, their sharp eyes peering back into the dark streets with the alert cynicism of raptors.

"Yarra!" Jolly hissed. "I said I'd sit up with you, but I think you might be safe tonight."

"I ain't safe 'til there's his funeral," Mrs. Bliss snapped.

"You just might get one," Jolly grinned. She pulled off her peahen's-crest hat and waved it in ferocious glee.

"What are you saying, woman?"

"Look to your door. No, Yarra! Look to your door *outside!*"

"Ye're cracked!"

But Mrs. Bliss bundled up and shuffled to the door.

Someone had carefully taken off her business placard and neatly placed it under the window where it would be safe from the elements. Then they had just as neatly hung their own sign in its place.

Mrs. Bliss stared, her mouth hanging open at the emblem of a daffodil painted in policeman's blue above ten chalked circles with a *Yang* teardrop. Just in case the point had failed to translate, a chalked skull was arrowed to the earth: *Stay Back.*

She put her hand to her lips. "Oh, my Lord Above."

Jolly cackled. "I knew this would happen someday."

Yarra Bliss gulped hard. "Think she knows what she's doing?" she whispered.

"What else would make her do this?"

*"He'll kill her! He'll go straight to her house!"*

213

"She knows, Yarra."

Yarra began to shake. It was just the cold, she told herself. She tried to remember a time when she had been that brave, but all she could think about was her children.

"Come," Jolly murmured and patted her on the back. "Let's get your little ones over to Josie's place. It ain't much of a risk if we wrap 'em up and move quick."

"But – but . . . my cat!"

"Oh, bring that witch if you please. She can earn all your keeps by cleaning out the vermin!" Jolly shuddered. "We must *go*, darling. We can do it – I'll wrap the little ones. You . . . you take care of that thing you call a cat."

Holmes's arrangements with The Widow had been fruitful, and they were now staying in the room above her shop. At base rate, the doctor recalled, his annoyance mixed with respect at her negotiations.

*After all*, she informed them, *should I be asked to let my rooms, I can hardly say yes, can I?* And those snapping green eyes went dark. *There'll be questions of my payment at the end, you know. Oh, yes. There will be payment. I need to show something respectable.*

Watson was not so far from Maiwand that he could forget how boredom sank its venom into the brains of hapless men on watch. The bolt-hole Holmes had contrived was far from the hospitals of Kandahar . . . but there was something mentally insidious about the confining four walls, dull of ornament, and infested with peculiar *minutia* of the building's owner. He was beginning to fear he would suffer the scars of monotony for the rest of his life.

The men lived quietly, taking turns at watch through the night while the other idled and napped. They subsided on soup, sandwiches, and coffee, or the occasional pot of tea (part of their rent). Her brews were palatable, mysterious, and strong as firebrick. The accommodations were warm enough from the radiant heat coming off the shop's stove, but the limited view soon had Watson gauging his own boredom against his own impatience for justice.

The first night passed quietly, but Holmes woke the soldier up with a low utterance, a "*Harrumph!*" of quiet rage.

Watson sat upright, left hand already closing upon the Adams he kept at ready, but the streetlight filtrating in through the cloudy curtains gave the sharp outline of his friend mashing his fist into his hip with frustration.

"Did you see him?" he whispered.

"I saw a rat," Holmes answered just as softly without taking his gaze from the window. "A shadow, lingering too long in the alley-way across

214

from her steps. This area is known, and the neighborhood is full of gossips. But yes, I am sure it was our little fish."

"Can you tell if it is only a shadow?" Watson put aside his Adams and put together the makings of a cigarette. The actions kept thoughts level, for one could not devote too much time to fretting when fingers had to be steady.

"The shadow was waiting too long, Watson. He is hoping for signs of life. That in turn will offer him a pattern. When he sees nothing, he will determine she is the only resident." Holmes could speak easily now. Dawn would arrive soon and the sounds of the city were rising. "What are you thinking for such an expression?"

"Her comment about payment. And respectable. I thought I sensed another meaning in her words, but I cannot fathom them."

Holmes chuckled approvingly. "Her payment will be the end of a vile man. That is really why she is helping us." Below their feet, a muffled thump and a clang and curse underscored their hostess' attempts to wake up her little cookstove.

The first twenty-four hours bled to the next. It was Watson's turn on the following night, and he studied the streets hard, thinking of bolt-holes and his ignorance of the terrain. The shadow appeared again on the edge of light from the street-lamp. It barely moved, but it did not belong and stayed perhaps a quarter-hour before retreating into the darkness, fluttering up again after an hour or two. Watson was a cautious man himself, but he was also a man who decided matters quickly, and he found he had a growing contempt for a coward who went through such painstaking lengths to murder. It was not, he felt, a wise expenditure of one's brains, nor his nerve – but their quarry was deficient in morality and that made up for anything resembling such virtues.

They were watching the only possible way in and out. Anyone seeking honest business or evil intention had to briefly cross the pool of light to get to her narrow shop door. Holmes had even scoured the stout little cellar before moving in, ruling out secret passages or tunnels. The two ground-floor windows had been nailed tight for winter, and their first-floor rooms were packed with storage.

"He could come in through the roof," Watson suggested, for devil's advocacy was a talent newly uncovered with his association of Sherlock Holmes.

"Unlikely for the view," Holmes shrugged. "There is too much open space up-top. Mr. Walsh bought the building with all the cynicism of a proper policeman. Should someone burglarise the residence, he felt they ought to invest a little effort."

"Ah."

It was not for the first time that the Good Doctor paused to contemplate the strange relationship criminals had with the men who hunted them.

The third night lumbered on. The attic room dwindled from tiny to smothering. Watson wondered if he was numb to everything in the endless cycle of watching, dozing, and sandwiches. Holmes was oblivious. Being on watch sang to his hunter's instincts. That was just as well. The fog was getting worse. Earlier they could at least see the faint outlines of the other shops and tenants' windows, leaking chips of lamplight through cracks and holes in the shutters. Now, even the streetlamps were choked into useless dots of dirty light the color of raw amber.

Holmes barely twitched. He stared below the window into the tiny pool of murk that marked the door of The Widow's little shop. In his concentration, he pulled on a long-dead pipe – but it was possible, Watson thought unkindly, that he was subsiding on the sips of London fog slithering through the cracks in the walls.

Holmes muttered. "The fog will finally be our ally."

"Finally" was too long in coming, as Watson calculated. He had stopped checking his gun days ago. "You mean as the fog is hiding us?"

"Rakosi. He only hunts in darkness. We *need* him to be hidden. He will have more confidence to lurk about under such conditions."

"Holmes . . . ." Watson lowered his voice. "You still have not explained why Rakosi will come here."

"He has no choice. He believes The Widow has the tokens."

"That is madness! If he accosts her, the police will surely hunt him down!"

"The Widow is no friend of the police. She has made this known daily since her loss." Holmes tilted his head as faint bells sang over the rooftops. "She will not beg their help. Her challenge to him is personal. She has long expressed her desire for revenge against the Roosters."

"She is a single woman, Holmes. She should not be alone."

"We are here, are we not?"

"Did you tell Lestrade? This is his case!"

"It is *my* case and I decide how they go. Lestrade hired me to prove Rakosi alive. I prefer my proof to stand in court."

"Does she truly have the tokens?"

"Lestrade is keeping them. If you peep through the front door of the shop, you will see something that might resemble one of the tokens propped on her desk."

Watson thought about it. He could not stop thinking any more than he could stop breathing. "Holmes, a question . . . ."

"Yes?"

216

"You are prepared for this vigil."

Holmes did not respond at first. Long, measured pneumatics off his empty briar was the answer for many long minutes.

"My dear fellow," began the low voice from the corner. "I treasure your discretion, and that is ironically why I speak so little of my work."

The young veteran sat up, propping his aching back to the wall of the storage room. He could ignore the gnawing teeth in his leg for the moment. "Do go on. I wish only to be trusted with your confidence."

"I pay my informants in money. You've seen me do it. There is another payment they demand of me, and that is to *listen*. I may go where they cannot. They have complaints, grievances, and grudges that could never be taken to court. From these complaints, I glean impressions of greater things. Think of them as bellwethers, or birds whose behaviors predict the coming storms."

Holmes sighed. An invisible motion betrayed only by the sound of the small, hot room above the stove downstairs.

*Creak.*

*Thump.*

An unladylike curse floated up – *Thump!* An angry heel ricocheted off something wooden, and a loud huff of exasperation finished the unseen drama.

"This is one of the times where you pay in that coin."

"Yes. The coin may not be silver, but it is sterling."

A new crash from downstairs rattled the floor-boards as gravity won against a wooden crate. Despite the grim situation, the men smiled. They knew the ritual now. Below their feet the door pitched open. Holmes set his back to the edge of the windowsill, his long fingers signalling. Watson held his breath and slipped to the opposite side to look down.

The Widow dragged a heavy sack of rubbish out of the shop, her back to the street. She puffed for air, her fairy-pipe shooting blue into the yellow of the fog. She stopped for breath, bent down, and pulled again. At long last she dragged it against the side of the opposite wall where the rest of the street's rubbish collected for the day.

The Widow took a deep breath and straightened her back. Her pipe had gone out. She exclaimed and fixed her hat about her head, for nothing would stop her from being properly covered. Grumbling and muttering to herself, she clipped her feet back to her shop.

Watson watched as she stopped at the doorway and packed fresh tobacco from a pouch. She rested her back against the iron rail guarding her door and fought to gain a fresh vesta into the clay bowl. The doctor was still smiling at the performance when, with a sharp crash of glass, the nearest street-lamp went black. A child hooted rudely and ran, the beat-bobby racing after him with an angry roar. Neither could be seen in the sudden plunge of night.

"Oh, no," Watson breathed, for the world had transformed into a terrible realization. Holmes had already jumped to his feet. The darkness spun into two long arms behind The Widow – faster than it seemed possible and from the wrong direction.

The Widow's pipe shot up in her teeth. Smoke clapped her face and her hand clutched at her hat as her body was flung backwards into the gloom. The hat fluttered down upon the cobblestones like a sad bird and a sudden shriek split the fog.

"He dug under the floor!" Watson bellowed, his nerves afire. His nerves ached with fury as he leaped for the door – Holmes yanking it off the hinge and plunging down the steps, half-a-flight at a time. They ought to have known! The doctor excoriated himself. Hadn't Rakosi done this very thing under his own wife's roof? Holmes was long gone. Somewhere in the glum streets, policemen were shouting.

Watson caught up with Holmes at The Widow's side, just around the corner from her shop. She had her back to the bricks, feet spread apart for balance as she struck a fresh light into her trembling pipe. Holmes nodded at Watson, his pale face a sliver in the lamplight.

"I am a fool," Holmes said quietly. "And I very much doubt the police will find the boy Rakosi paid to kill the light."

"Far smaller a fool than he," The Widow corrected bluntly. "'E went for my hat-pin."

Watson saw something dark on the concrete. "Blood," he said quietly.

"I should hope so."

Holmes had picked up the hat-pin. "This is a venerable pin for hats, my good woman, but I see no blood on it."

She laughed coldly. "I didn't say I got him with that, did I? Ever'body knows about my hat-pin. I'd be silly to use it in a fight, hmm?" She lifted her arm, where the tiny slit of a hidden sleeve emerged. "He won't be going far."

"No. You're right about that, Mrs. Walsh."

Lestrade's angry face reflected the white-gas of the lanterns as he emerged from the fog. He led the way. Two constables dragged a limp form. It groaned weakly between their gloves, even as it tried to run. A terrible blade rested in the little detective's gloved hand. It was a primitive brute, the sort a Traveller would fashion if he had a bit of flat metal and horn. The tip was chiseled into a fish-hook and gleamed with blood. "You may have spared the new hangman."

"Allow me to be the judge of that," Watson retorted and answered the call of his duty.

"Pity," The Widow mourned. "Got to watch them ethical doctors. Can't bribe 'em to do the right thing."

Lestrade privately agreed, but gave her a stern look for the sake of his conscience. "He tried his best to kill you. I'm glad you were too fast."

"Fast?" The Widow grinned around her pipe-stem and pulled back her coat. A miniature version of a policeman's leather collar stared back at the men. "Had Mr. Walsh's collar tooled down to size."

Lestrade whistled. "If only they let women on the Force!"

"I get better pay here."

Holmes laughed. Lestrade flushed, but forced himself to see the joke and smiled weakly. Watson returned to the group, and his sun-swarthy skin was almost as pale as Lestrade's. "He just died," he said curtly, and his gaze upon the little woman was of soldierly respect. His heels clicked and he bowed.

"Thought he would," she muttered. Her hands were still trembling. "I expect you'll need me to go in n' make a statement."

"Later," Lestrade admonished. "For now, it would be best if you stayed in the shop until we've taken care of this."

"Good enough."

The men watched her go.

"Does she always have to have the last word?" Watson asked.

"She doesn't even know she's doing it," Lestrade grumbled. "I think it's her version of manners – she wants you to know she's heard you, so she speaks back."

Holmes was smiling wryly to himself, but he said nothing until Watson asked him his thoughts. "I was merely wondering at the smallness of London, Watson."

"London? Small? I do not understand you."

"This city of millions is still finite. Rakosi is . . . or was, I should say . . . a member of the same gang as the man who killed her husband. Maybe he *was* the man. She has waited with the patience of a stone for some sort of revenge."

Lestrade grumbled. "I knew something like this day would come." He played with his hat, head down, and they saw the soot of sleeplessness beneath his eyes.

"I know her look," the small man continued at last. "I know why her hands were shaking. She isn't scared, upon my word. *She got one*. She's tasted blood. Now I'll always wonder . . . whenever we find a Rooster dead . . . will she be the cause?"

"Will she be safe?" Watson murmured. He had already coined to Lestrade's mixture of emotions. The woman had been married to his friend, after all.

"You don't know them, Doctor, more the blessing to you! He'd stolen their money. She saved them the trouble."

"Will they leave Mrs. Bliss alone too?"

"Oh, I daresay," Holmes sniffed. "She is now twice a widow. Widows are pariahs." Only Watson saw how the colour winked out of Lestrade's face at that comment. He struggled to recover, but his hands were suddenly pushed into his pockets to steady himself. Watson contemplated the things passing over the little policeman, and dread for his future wife loomed the largest. Slowly, Lestrade took a breath out, dispersing his demons.

"Perhaps." The inspector had found his cigarette-tin in the pockets and was guiding the constables into splitting up: One to guard the body, the other to send for the cart. "I'll talk to Miss Cheatham on the morrow. Mrs. Bliss is about to come into more money than she's ever thought of in her entire life." The little professional offered his lit cigarette to a grateful Watson. "I shall see that she gets Rakosi's 'estate'. She can use a bit of it to pay off her debt to the Peahens. After that, she'll be free to find a safer place to live with those young ones. And a better job – a much better job, honest enough that the wrong sort won't come by."

"You can hardly create a job for her, Lestrade."

"Actually, I think I can," the little detective snapped. He drew himself up to his height and set his jaw. "Miss Cheatham is very strict against nonsense. I'm thinking a reformed spy in her school might be just the thing she needs."

Watson's cigarette had caught. He was offering the share the service to Holmes. The detective bent and, in a single puff, pulled a coal into his own smoke.

"Sentimentality is not my field, but you offer a neat solution."

"It isn't sentimental if you're thinking of your own neck, Mr. Holmes. What would Miss Cheatham say to me if she knew we used Mrs. Bliss and then threw her back to the wolves? She comes from a family of wrestlers, and they do not overthink!" Lestrade shook his head and, for the first time in days, they saw him smile. "Ah, well. You did prove Rakosi alive, Mr. Holmes. At least briefly."

Holmes laughed. "That will not affect my rates. It was a small problem."

As one, the men regarded the corpse in the alleyway.

"Perhaps not a pretty problem," Holmes admitted, "but a satisfying one all the same."

# NOTES

1. More about the encounters with Mr. Qumiper, and Miss Clea Cheatham's tempestuous courtship and engagement to Inspector Lestrrade, can be found in the novels *Test of the Professionals: The Adventure of the Flying Blue Pidgeon*, *Test of the Professionals: The Peaceful Night Poisonings*, and *Test of the Professionals: Leap Year*, all by Marcia Wilson

2. For cleaning carpets and polishing floors, and also deodorizers, insecticides, fungicides, medicinals – and the list goes on.

3. The Cheap Train Act of 1883. This made train travel more affordable than it ever had been – and of course some people were against it.

*About Working Widows (and One in Particular):*

Mrs. Walsh is the summary of several years' work. A short story is the smaller outer shell wrapped around a much larger mountain of paper called "research" and "background development".

We can pat ourselves on the back and be glad our times are easier than they were "back then", as if loneliness and poverty doesn't influence our life's decisions in any way. Yes, it was a much harsher and colder deal for women surviving marriage, but the fears and obstacles are the same. The scarlet thread, as Sherlock Holmes describes, is everywhere. It tangles with motives to be comfortable and without want.

Mrs. Walsh is a representation of a hardscrabble form of Victorian life: A working-class widow under circumstances where it is easier to descend than to rise. She was already an independent woman when she met and married Davvy Walsh. She had to be, this stubborn grand-daughter of the Black Country. When there are no men to do the work, the women must do. She cultivated a reputation simple and pragmatic, knowing that streamlining her life was not always appreciated or respected. It would be impossible to accurately analyze the existing data to answer the modern question of gender and identity, but many widows, once their duty was done with marriage, chose not to return to a conventional marriage for a variety of reasons. I believe she was one of those women who, upon the death of her partner, decided there was no more of that and lived how and however she chose.

Most of the time, women were not "allowed" to run a shop at all unless they were widowed. There were more ladylike matters, perhaps, such as milliners, glove-makers, and seamstresses. They were the place to see women in business where their lower intellect would not bother the public. (A policeman's wife is not allowed to also be a shopkeeper of any sort. Miss Cheatham bypasses this by turning her shop into a charity school). Mrs. Walsh gave it up willingly if not completely, but returned to it the day after her husband's funeral. She kept up with her old business contacts and managed a little "work" here and there, but instead of working for set wages, she saw the value of working for information. Policemen and private investigators, not to mention scandalmongers, newspaper-writers, and politicians are always willing to pay good coin, often out of their own pockets, to know what someone else is doing. Thus, Mrs. Walsh carefully created a level of trust among her clients and kept her nose clean. If her news was harmful, she refused to sully herself by selling it. Should someone suggest she have that in common with Langdale Pike, they would have seen the wrong end of her hat-pin in short order.

When Officer Walsh died, she *could* have remarried, but she had no pressing need. There were no children to support and she was firm in health. She had no interest in taking on another man's name. His had been enough. Her little house was soon fitted out to her old tea, coffee, and tobacco business once again, and the contacts she'd kept up as a Policeman's Wife kept her good when she re-entered her work as "*The Widow*". In 1883, the Met opened employment as Matron for female prisoners, and policemen's wives and widows were considered ideal for the work, but that would take away her time from her (dare we say) better income in tea and news. Lonely as she was, being in control of her life was the heavier advantage on the scale. Besides, this Matron's position was a new idea and might not last.

She keeps up with her relatives by kith and kin. On occasion she takes in an outlying young relative on the cusp of homelessness: A girl to help with the corsets and tend the fires, or a lad to run messages. Hard but fair, they all leave her doorstep for bigger and better things and well-equipped for the shocks of life. If affection can be measured by physicality, surely the pile of gifts that appear upon holidays and her birthday is a mark of her success. Some, I regretfully say, found the undertow of criminal means stronger, but their eye to her continued health and wellbeing remains as strong as the rest.

If you take the time to read through The Canon of Sherlock Holmes (and I recommend it as time well spent, not to mention an aesthetically pleasing addition to your shelves), you will soon notice the use of family betrayal and how it affects women. We see a homicidal and violent man determined to murder his step-daughters to keep his claws in a rotting estate. There are larcenous fathers forcing daughters to sign over their property. Another step-father pretends to woo his wife's own daughter (with his wife's permission!) for her share of the estate, even as she already gives them everything she owns. Poor Lady Frances, scammed and buried alive. Mary Morstan. The vicious Oldacre with his grudge against rejection. Brenda Tregennis, murdered for her share of the family property. Timid Effie with her secret child . . . the list goes on and on. Mrs. Walsh is far luckier than many. She is still relatively young, mature, and has the pluck and nerve to carve her way through the world with her work. She honours her late husband's legacy and pride of policemanship by discreetly providing his old mates useful information – for a fee of course. She is not a gossip. They reveal news for free.

In the world of news-taking, Mrs. Walsh keeps one ear for business, and the other for events. Her sellers are the women who take the used tea-leaf back when the lord and the lady of the house are finished with their tea-tray. Used leaves have a hundred uses among the household staff, and are traditionally the right of the highest-ranking female servant. What isn't kept by these women are sold to people such as Mrs. Walsh, who – being a good customer for their wares – will nod sympathetically in all the right places and listen to their tales of woe with new guests, fractious visitors, and the Mister's troubles with his bank.

This leads to the other leg of her business, which she employs as she makes her rounds: The knocker-up, or the human alarm clock paid to make sure you get out of bed. The tradition was still going strong in some parts of England, especially where time cannot be marked (or heard). These people could be rather clever in how they could get you out of bed without going into your house: Normally a long pole, capable of tapping on your bedroom window, was sufficient, but one woman was photographed with a dried-peashooter, and we are certain it was aimed with unerring accuracy against the glass.

Mrs. Walsh is the creation of an interesting contract, a fan who asked me to write a new story about Lestrade. The work had three conditions, and two of them were normal enough but the third was interesting: I had to promise to punch this person's ex in the face if ever seen in my home state. This fan was quite pleased with this result, and more than happy to imagine the former spouse as the man who so rashly went up against Mrs. Walsh, and so soundly lost.

# The Arlington-Fisher Affair
## by Mark Mower

It was a damp and chilly evening in the spring of 1884. Holmes and I had just eaten one of Mrs. Hudson's delicious pigeon pies, which we had washed down with a choice bottle of Beaune given to us a week before by one of Holmes's grateful clients. Having anticipated a quiet evening in and the prospect of reading a historical novel in front of the fire, I was a little annoyed to find that the "*Rat-a-tat-tat*" on the downstairs door knocker had signalled the arrival of a police officer intent on engaging the great detective's services that very night.

Police Constable Jenner entered the upstairs sitting room at the direction of an equally disgruntled Mrs. Hudson. It was clear that she had not welcomed the disruption to her planned evening of dressmaking.

"Please excuse me, gentlemen, but I come here at the direction of William Poyntz, the Chief Constable of Essex," announced the fresh-faced, blonde-haired, officer, as he was beckoned towards the armchair closest to the hearth.

My colleague responded with evident enthusiasm. "Indeed, a fine fellow! I had the pleasure of collaborating with him briefly while he was serving with the Nottingham force. A case which hinged upon the discovery of a paperweight in a bed of roses. This is my colleague, Dr. John Watson. Please tell us how we can assist."

Jenner smiled and nodded in acknowledgement. "Certainly, Mr. Holmes, for time is of the essence. In short, there has been a theft at the home of Charles Arlington-Fisher, a wealthy investment banker who has a large property on Ardleigh Green Road in Romford. As I understand it, the theft took place this afternoon during the celebrations to mark the fortieth birthday of the gentleman's wife, Mrs. Celia Arlington-Fisher. The item in question is a diamond bracelet – a birthday gift given to Mrs. Arlington-Fisher by her husband earlier in the day. Despite their efforts, my colleagues have been unable to ascertain the whereabouts of the missing jewellery, which seems to have vanished into thin air. As such, Mr. Poyntz believes this to be a case in which your unusual skills could prove to be invaluable."

"I see," replied Holmes, smiling at the reference to his *unusual skills*. "I take it that you haven't been to the property yourself, Constable?"

"No. I'm currently on attachment to the Metropolitan Force and received a telegram from the Chief Constable only an hour ago. Knowing that I work near Baker Street, Mr. Poyntz asked me to deliver this request to you personally to ensure that you understood both the urgency and gravity of the situation in which he finds himself. He is already at the house in Romford, and has detained several people present at the birthday party. The celebrations were taking place in the property's large library. As no one left the room, the Chief Constable knows that the bracelet must either be hidden, or in the possession of one of the people present. And yet, despite their searches, the officers present cannot find it."

I was a little bemused to learn that the William Poyntz was taking such a direct interest in the theft, given his status. And when I quizzed Jenner on that particular point, he explained that his superior was off-duty and had been invited to the party as an acquaintance of the Arlington-Fishers. That being the case, he was keen to keep the theft out of the public gaze for fear that it might reflect badly on his reputation and that of the Force. He hoped Holmes would be able to resolve the matter that evening to avoid any press scandal.

Having enlisted my support, Holmes said that we would accept the challenge. Jenner then explained that he had arranged for a cab to carry us immediately to Liverpool Street Station, where we could catch the 8:40 Great Eastern train to Romford, which was due to arrive at 9:15 p.m. Holmes then suggested that as a precaution we should pack an overnight bag in case we needed to stop overnight at a local inn. Asked if he would be joining us, Jenner admitted that his own duties at Scotland Yard prevented him from accompanying us, but he did agree to despatch a telegram to the Chief Constable to say that we were on our way.

The short excursion to Romford passed off uneventfully and, having reached the station as planned, we were pleased to be able to book a trap for the onward journey to the property on Ardleigh Green Road, situated just over two miles away.

Arriving at the door of Trenton House a little after 9:30 p.m., we were greeted immediately by Chief Constable Poyntz, who wasted no time in shepherding us into the entrance lobby of the large eighteenth-century house, and from there into a small side room which looked to be Charles Arlington-Fisher's study. He was a tall man, with dark, greying hair, and a distinct military bearing, tempered somewhat by his boyish blue eyes and soft Dublin accent.

"Gentlemen, I cannot thank you enough for agreeing to assist me. This is a most peculiar state of affairs. I see that you have overnight bags. Please rest assured, if there is a need for you to stay over, the Arlington-Fishers have already indicated that you are more than welcome to stay here in the house. Now, to the case itself. I have two of my officers in the library to ensure that no one leaves the room until you've had the chance to look around and question those present. Did Constable Jenner explain the nature of the conundrum?"

"He did, but we would be grateful if you could run through all the pertinent facts as you see them before I visit the library. Perhaps you could start by telling us more about the Arlington-Fishers and how you come to know them?"

"Certainly, but I must ask you to be discreet, for the couple are well-connected and very influential in the area." He pointed to some chairs in the study and invited us to sit before he began his deposition. "I have known Charles and Celia for about three years. I was introduced to them when I first became Chief Constable in November 1881. Charles is a member of the Essex Watch Committee, which oversaw my appointment. Since that time, we have become firm friends. I often play golf with him, and we regularly dine together."

"So," Holmes ventured, "a man you would trust implicitly?"

There was a degree of hesitation in Poyntz's reply, which the man sought to explain a little later. For the moment, he continued. "Let me come back to that if I may, for I know that you like to be appraised of all relevant information, however trivial or seemingly unrelated. Let me first outline some of the events which unfolded this afternoon.

"Charles wanted to ensure that Celia had a fitting birthday celebration. A couple of months back, he asked her what she would like as a present, and how she might like to mark the occasion. Celia is an extremely attractive woman, some ten years younger than Charles, and I don't think it is unfair of me to say that she enjoys all the trappings of her middle-class lifestyle. As well as an extensive wardrobe of the finest frocks and gowns, she is known to have expensive tastes in jewellery. Her suggestion of a diamond bracelet didn't come as a surprise to Charles. In terms of the celebration itself, she agreed to organise an afternoon party for close friends and family, expecting only that Charles would fund the cost of the festivities.

"I was a little surprised to receive an invitation myself. I would describe my relationship with Charles as close, but business-like. We tend to talk about policing and business affairs, but rarely talk about his home life. In fact, until today, I had only visited this house once, and have socialised with Celia on just a handful of occasions, so I can't claim to know her well at all.

"The party was due to begin at three p.m. today, with a champagne reception and canapes. Charles had asked me to arrive a little earlier, as he said he had some business to discuss. While I am off-duty, I arranged for

226

my driver to transport me to the house and wait until the festivities had ended.

"When I did pull up in the drive, there appeared to be some commotion outside the house. It seems that one of the young housemaids, Alice Colden, had received an unwelcome visit from Richard Templeton, a local brickmaker and rogue. Celia explained to me later that the young girl had been seen walking out with the fellow, who had apparently hinted at marriage. However, that afternoon he had arrived at the house in a drunken state to call off their engagement. Amid all the party preparations, this was a drama which the hostess didn't welcome, and Templeton was told plainly to make himself scarce. At the point I arrived, Alice was clutching her handkerchief, her head buried in Templeton's shoulder, crying loudly, and beseeching her former lover to reconsider. Seeing that Celia was berating the man and shouting for him to get off her property, I intervened, and frog-marched Templeton down the drive to the gate. I warned him that if he returned, I would have him arrested."

"You described Templeton as a 'rogue'," Holmes interjected. "Was that based on Mrs. Arlington-Fisher's assessment, or your own observations?"

"My knowledge. Templeton is a petty thief, well known to my officers."

"Then if the diamond bracelet has indeed been stolen," I ventured. "Templeton could be a suspect."

Poyntz smiled. "A fair line of enquiry. In fact, that very thought occurred to me the moment we realised that the bracelet was missing and couldn't be found in the library. I later tasked one of my officers to locate Templeton and find out what he did after he left Trenton House. But he has a solid alibi for the whole of the afternoon. Half-a-dozen locals at The Spencer Arms, only a short distance from here, confirmed that he had been seated outside the pub drinking, in the company of his father. He didn't leave until six p.m., well after the time the bracelet had vanished."

"I see," said Holmes. "And after the incident with Templeton, did the party proceed as expected?"

"Yes. Celia was relieved and thanked me for my intervention before heading off to supervise the preparations in the library. But I was first ushered into the hallway of the house by Mr. Spall, the butler, and then greeted by Charles, who invited me to step into this study. What followed next was as unexpected as the disturbance outside the house. Put simply, Charles explained that several of his main investment funds had gone sour, and his firm faces financial ruin. He wanted to tell me because he believed that I would hear it in any case. He went on to say that he would have to sell his home and move to more modest accommodations, none of which would sit well with Celia, who had yet to be told. He wanted the party to pass off successfully before he enlightened her the following day. And it seems that the diamond bracelet was something of an annoyance, for he explained that it cost a hefty sum of money which he had expended before learning of his business losses."

It was a sensitive question, but I felt compelled to interpose. "Is it possible that Charles Arlington-Fisher arranged for the bracelet to go missing so that he could recoup some of the money?"

Poyntz didn't seem troubled by the enquiry. "Call it a copper's instinct, but that same idea crossed my mind. I'm getting ahead of myself, but when we had later searched the library and some of the staff and guests without success, there seemed to be but one possibility – for the only people we didn't insist on searching were Charles and Celia. So, you see my dilemma, and one of the reasons I was keen to get you involved, Mr. Holmes. If I am to retain my friendship with the couple, I need to have some evidence before assuming that one or both have sought to mislead me. I should also point out that when I specifically asked Charles an hour or so ago whether the bracelet had been insured, he replied, "Oh yes, for a very large sum.'"

"That is most compelling," said Holmes, "but let us not get fixated on one theory at this stage. We still have information to gather. Now, please tell me how the party unfolded."

Poyntz returned to his narrative. "The guests began to arrive a few minutes before three o'clock. Some who lived locally walked to the house, while carriages dropped off those from further afield. By three-fifteen, the doors of the house were closed by Mr. Spall, who was the last to enter the library, having supervised the collection of the guest's coats, hats, and scarves. In total, there were twenty-four people in the room at that stage, and one other attendee – the Arlington-Fisher's pet basset hound. Alongside the hosts, there were four staff in attendance: Alice Colden, Mr. Spall, and two of the kitchen staff, who were stood behind trestle tables serving the food and glasses of champagne. In addition to myself, sixteen guests had been invited to the party. You will see the layout of the room when you enter the library, but seats had been arranged, theatre-style, towards the back of the room for the entertainment which was to come. You see, Celia had booked a magician to provide some fun.

"After a period of mingling, drinking, and eating, Charles invited all but one of the guests to take a seat and then gave a short speech, before inviting us to raise a glass in celebration of his wife's birthday. Celia added a few words to thank everyone for being there, before revealing the diamond bracelet to the delight of those assembled and thanking Charles for his wonderful gift. She then introduced Vernon Saunders, the magician, otherwise known as 'The Illusionist', who had remained standing at the front during the speeches. He then performed for about three-quarters of an hour."

Holmes interrupted to focus in on a point of detail. "At the time of the performance, was the magician the only person who remained standing at the front of the room?"

"No," came the reply. "The two kitchen staff had remained at their station, standing behind the trestle tables. The maid, Alice Colden, and the butler, Mr. Spall, were positioned behind Saunders close to the door to the library. Everyone else, including the Arlington-Fishers, had taken seats."

"Did anyone get up from their seats during the performance?"

"No, with the exception of Celia, who was asked at one point to stand and assist the magician with a couple of card tricks."

"I see. And what happened after that?"

"She was asked to return to her seat. Saunders then performed the most remarkable part of his act, which culminated in the appearance of a live rabbit from inside his top hat."

I expressed some confusion. "How did that work?"

"Saunders removed his hat and revealed the inside of it to us. It was clear that it contained nothing. He then placed a large handkerchief over the upturned end, before walking over to Alice Colden and asking her to remove it. She gasped as she did so, for it soon became clear that the hat now contained a white rabbit.

"The delight of the audience was short-lived, for all Hell broke loose with the appearance of the rabbit. The basset hound, which had, until that time, been sprawled out beneath Charles's chair, jumped up suddenly, barked loudly, and ran across to attack the poor animal. It was all the magician could do to keep the rabbit from the canine's jaws. Alice Colden stepped forward to restrain the hound, grabbing it by the collar and dragging it towards the door of the library. She looked across at her mistress, who nodded for her to remove the animal from the room."

Holmes frowned as he heard this. "Alice Colden left the library with the dog? Constable Jenner stated earlier that no one had left the room."

"Yes, but she was gone for only a few seconds. She pulled the dog across the hallway, opened the front door, and released the animal onto the drive."

Holmes wanted to be clear. "Did you see all of this happen?"

"The door to the hallway remained open, so I could see her heading in the direction of the entrance. I didn't see her reach the door, but I heard it open and then close. My driver later confirmed that she had merely opened the door and released the dog. It ran off down the drive."

"Did the performance continue after that?" I asked.

"No. Alice Colden had only just returned to the library when Charles uttered a loud exclamation. I looked across at him. He was clutching his wife's wrist and announced with some anger that the bracelet was missing. Celia began to sob uncontrollably. Before pandemonium could set in, I stood up and shouted for everyone to stay calm and to remain where they were standing or sitting. I then moved towards the hosts and looked beneath their chairs to see if the jewellery had slipped to the floor. Clearly, it hadn't."

Holmes mused on the events described. "Interesting. This is all very instructive. How did you proceed after that?"

"I reiterated the need for everyone to remain exactly where they were, and then left the house for a few moments to instruct my driver to make the journey into Romford to collect four constables to assist with the investigation. He returned with the men half-an-hour later, at which point we began to search in earnest.

"I sent one constable off to find the whereabouts of Richard Templeton as I explained earlier. The other officers undertook a full search of the library and the small reading room which adjoins it. Finding nothing, I was then faced with a difficult decision. It was clear to me that the bracelet must be in the possession of someone in the room. But I also speculated that the majority of those present hadn't had any opportunity to steal the piece. We had all seen the bracelet when Celia showed it off prior to the start of the magician's act. From that point on, none of the seated guests had risen from their seats. I therefore worked on the basis that only seven people were in any sort of position to steal or conceal the jewellery. Two of these – the kitchen maids – I discounted immediately. They hadn't moved from behind the trestle tables and were some distance from the seated guests and Vernon Saunders. This left only the butler, the maid, the magician, and the Arlington-Fishers themselves."

"A perfect summary!" exclaimed Holmes. "I take it that you allowed all but the five to leave at that point?"

"Yes, it was best to do so. There were some very wealthy and important people in the room, and tempers were beginning to be frayed. My next difficulty was in conducting the personal searches. One of the constables conducted a search of Mr. Spall and Vernon Saunders in the privacy of the small reading room. I was convinced that the magician was guilty, as he'd had the only real contact with Celia that I'd observed. But as you know, we found nothing. Then came the difficulty of searching Miss Colden. In the interests of propriety, I couldn't allow the constable to search the maid, but the girl's mistress came to the rescue. Celia agreed to conduct the search, which, again, revealed no bracelet. At that stage, I was left with the dawning realisation that any guilt in this affair might indeed lie with the Arlington-Fishers, given their financial position. It was then that I despatched my driver to deliver the telegram to Constable Jenner, explaining the situation and asking him to contact you."

For some reason, my thoughts turned to the removal of the basset hound. "Did you conduct a search of the hallway by any chance? And what happened to the dog?"

William Poyntz nodded. "Yes, I extended the search to the hallway when we had finished in the library. As for the dog, it returned of its own accord just before you arrived. My driver let it back into the house."

"I see. Well, that being the case, we should now venture into the library," said Holmes. "Have you kept all of the suspects shut in since the searches?"

"Pretty much," came the reply. "I was prepared to allow the Arlington-Fishers to go about their business, but they seemed content to await your arrival when I told them of my plan. As for the other three, I have ensured that they had refreshments. In the case of Vernon Saunders, the Arlington-Fishers have agreed to pay him extra for his time and can accommodate him this evening, if that is required."

"Splendid," said Holmes, standing and striding off towards the door of the study.

Having made our introductions, it was agreed that Holmes and I would interview the five people in the library individually, taking advantage of the small reading room. We began with Charles Arlington-Fisher. He was a man of some bearing – tall, muscular, and direct in speech. His height and manner gave him a certain *gravitas*, but I could also detect in his eyes some trepidation.

Holmes sought to set him at ease. "Thank you for agreeing to talk to us, sir. Chief Constable Poyntz has appraised us of all the events which occurred earlier this afternoon, so I don't think we will need to detain you for long. I have but a few questions."

The preamble had the desired effect. "Certainly, Mr. Holmes. Fire away."

"Perhaps you could tell us how you first met your wife."

The question was certainly unexpected, but the banker responded positively. "Yes, I'm happy to. I have always enjoyed going to the theatre, and met Celia some twenty years ago in the West End. At that time, she was an aspiring actress, performing musical sketches and comedy skits under the stage name 'Nellie Fontana'. I was introduced to her one summer evening at the Theatre Royal in Drury Lane. When I was in town, I would frequently attend all her performances and, over time, a romance developed between us. She agreed to be my wife a year after we had first met."

"That is most illuminating," replied Holmes, enigmatically. "And how would you characterise your marriage?"

I was beginning to get a little concerned at my colleague's line of questioning, but Arlington-Fisher didn't seem perturbed. "We have a strong marriage, I would say. Rarely a cross word. Celia has been fiercely loyal and supportive of me and my career. I, in turn, afford her the best life that I can."

"I'm sure you do. But how do you think she is likely to react to the news of your firm's financial losses?"

This was a low blow by anyone's standards, and I saw the gentleman's hackles begin to rise. "My personal and professional business is of no concern to you, Mr. Holmes. I thought you were here to help us find the jewellery. I fail to understand how these questions will assist you in that regard."

Holmes ignored the challenge. "The police have been unable to locate the whereabouts of your wife's diamond bracelet. As they conducted an extensive search, it seems likely that someone has stolen or concealed the wristlet. If we were to discount the theory that you or your wife played some part in its disappearance, it would suggest that one or more of the three other people detained in the library are guilty. Do you have any views on that, given that two of the three are your own household staff?"

The question clearly rankled with him, for I saw his jaw set hard. "I can assure you that neither I, nor my wife, are likely to have taken part in such a diabolical act. Look how upset Celia was when she discovered the bracelet to be missing. And as for my staff, they are both loyal and trustworthy. Mr. Spall has been with me for over twenty years, while Miss Colden has been a companion to my wife since the days before our marriage. It seems obvious to me that you need to be questioning the magician fellow!"

Holmes assured him that we would indeed be undertaking a rigorous interview with Vernon Saunders. For the moment, he returned to the thorny issue of the banker's finances. "I appreciate that this may be a delicate issue, but when did you first learn that your business had run into difficulties?"

I believed that the man would explode in a fit of rage at this point, but Arlington-Fisher maintained his composure. "If you must know, three weeks ago. Our finance director, Leonard Coulson, came out to the house on a Sunday afternoon. I knew it must be unwelcome news, for he wouldn't normally deal with work matters on a weekend."

"I see. Well, that concludes my questions. In the light of your earlier comments, I will now speak to Vernon Saunders. I feel certain that the magician's evidence will help us to get to the bottom of this affair."

"I dearly hope so," was all that our host added, before leaving the room.

I cast a glance at my friend before Saunders entered. He gave me a wry grin as he whispered, "All will become clearer in due course, Watson!"

Vernon Saunders was a short man with wiry, greying hair and a large black moustache. He was still wearing his professional attire: A sparkling blue waistcoat, black-striped trousers, a tall top hat, and a vibrant red cape. He smiled inanely as he sat before us, which I imagined to be another part of his act. "How can I assist you, gentleman?"

"Mr. Saunders, we're sorry we kept you waiting. I just have a couple of questions."

"Take as long as you wish, Mr. Holmes," he retorted, with a further flash of his false façade." I'm being paid by the hour."

"Very well. When were you booked to perform at the birthday party?"

"Two weeks ago."

"And who made the booking?"

"It was Mrs. Arlington-Fisher herself. She visited me at one of the theatres where I regularly perform."

"Two weeks is very short notice. Did that not compromise your other scheduled performances?"

He answered confidently. "No, Tuesdays are usually my day off. It's all extra money to me."

"Had you met Celia Arlington-Fisher previously?"

Saunders eyed Holmes keenly. "No, why do you ask?"

"No particular reason. It just seems strange that a lady would visit you in person, rather than asking her maid or butler to sort out the arrangements. When we spoke to Mr. Arlington-Fisher a few minutes ago, he mentioned that his wife had herself once performed in several London theatres. It occurred to me that the two of you might already be acquainted. She used to be known as 'Nellie Fontana'."

This time there was no smile. "No, sir. To my knowledge, we've never met."

"Just before it was discovered that the diamond bracelet was missing, I understand you performed a number of card tricks and invited the lady of the house to assist you?"

"That's correct. It adds a personal touch."

"Can you recollect seeing the bracelet on her wrist at that point?"

"No. I was too focused on my own performance to notice much else."

Holmes moved on. "At the conclusion of your act, you made a live rabbit appear from your top hat. I believe you needed further assistance with that trick?"

"Yes, but not from Celia. Alice, the maid, did the honours."

"What colour was the handkerchief she removed to reveal the animal?"

Saunders snickered at the specificity of the question. "Blue tartan, Mr. Holmes."

"Excellent. That is all I need to know. Now, I would be grateful if you could ask Mr. Spall to join us."

The butler looked to be in his early sixties, with an oval-shaped face, emerald-green eyes, and a kindly disposition.

Holmes welcomed him into the room before asking, "How long have you worked for the family?"

"A little over twenty-five years, sir. I was previously under-butler to Lord and Lady Smy, who had a large house in Gidea Park. It was there that I first met Mr. Arlington-Fisher. He would often come to the house to discuss the Smy's financial portfolio. When he explained one day that he was looking for a full-time butler of his own, I was thrilled to accept his offer. I have never regretted the decision."

"Thank you, Mr. Spall. Were you aware that your employer had purchased the diamond bracelet for Mrs. Arlington-Fisher?"

"Only this morning. The mistress was busy explaining the arrangements for the party, and said that just before the magician was to perform, she wanted to show the guests her birthday present. In doing so, she showed me the bracelet for the first time."

"I see. Now, I believe you were positioned close to Alice Colden when she revealed the rabbit in the hat?"

Spall nodded in confirmation.

"Could you tell me the colour of the handkerchief covering the hat?"

The butler thought for a couple of seconds. "Blue, sir. It was patterned, but blue in colour."

"Excellent. And once Alice had removed it to reveal the rabbit, did you see her return the handkerchief to the magician?"

"No, she didn't. I distinctly remember Mr. Saunders taking the hat from her. I don't recall seeing the handkerchief after that."

"Thank you. And, finally, could you describe what happened when the dog saw the rabbit."

His recollection of the incident was close to the description given by Chief Constable Poyntz. However, there was one point of detail which we hadn't heard before: In describing the struggles which Alice Colden had in pulling the dog from the room, he mentioned that, "She needed both hands to grasp the thick leather of the dog's new collar, but eventually managed to manoeuvre him through the door of the library."

Holmes had no further questions and thanked Spall for his time. It was now Alice Colden's turn.

The maid was tall and slim, with a fringe of auburn hair showing beneath the bonnet of her domestic uniform. She had strong, dark eyebrows which framed her light blue eyes and generally elegant features. I guessed her to be in her early forties. When she was seated comfortably, Holmes began.

"Miss Colden, perhaps you could explain how you first came to work for the Arlington-Fishers?"

She nodded courteously. "I've been a maid to them for something over twenty years. They've been very good to me."

I interjected. "Mr. Arlington-Fisher said that you were already working for his wife prior to their wedding. In what capacity?"

"We were friends. I was something of a companion to her."

Holmes was evidently annoyed by her evasiveness. "In what specific capacity were you employed?"

"I was working at the same theatre as her. Occasionally, I was called upon to play minor acting parts, but most often I assisted backstage with costumes and make-up. As Celia was beginning to forge a name for herself, I became her personal assistant. When she decided to give up her career and marry Mr. Arlington-Fisher, she asked me to be her maid."

"That's much clearer, thank you. Now, when Watson and I first arrived here this evening, the Chief Constable told us that during the afternoon, before the party started, you received a visit from a local man named Richard Templeton. Could you tell us what that concerned?"

"It's a personal matter, sir. I'd prefer not to say."

"We understood that Templeton had called to break off his engagement to you. Is that correct?"

"If you say so."

"No, I'm asking you to confirm whether that is correct or not."

She continued to be slippery. "Something of the sort. Wouldn't be the first time a man has let me down."

"I see. And were you aware that Templeton is known to the police as a thief?"

"That's the first I've heard of it. Are you suggesting he stole the bracelet? He was drinking at the pub all afternoon."

"Do you know who did steal the jewellery?"

She answered confidently. "No, sir."

"I have just one final question for you: Have you given any thought to what you'll do when the Arlington-Fishers move from here into a smaller property?"

The maid responded conceitedly. "Celia has said that she will never see me out of work."

We concluded our interview at that juncture. Yet rather than call Celia Arlington-Fisher in for questioning, Holmes announced that he had all the information he needed, and that chat with the hostess wasn't required. He had only to gather three more pieces of information, and the case would be solved. Not for the first time in our association, I found myself at a loss for words, and completely in the dark about any solution to the case.

Back in the library, Holmes announced to the group that we had concluded our business for the evening, and everyone was free to go. His only stipulation was that no one was to leave the house. In the morning, at breakfast, he would reveal what had happened to the missing diamond bracelet.

All the suspects began to leave the room. As they did so, I saw Holmes squatting down on the floor to pat the head of the Arlington-Fisher's basset hound. He seemed to be in a playful mood, and it was clear that the dog was enjoying the attention. Some moments later, he fell into a deep conversation with the Chief Constable and one of the other officers.

I was unsure what to do, so walked out into the hallway and stood for some time talking with Mr. Spall, who explained where Holmes and I would be accommodated that night. In due course, Holmes joined us, but rather than follow the butler up the stairs, explained that he was arranging for one of the constables to head back into Romford to send a telegram for him. After that, he was to accompany Poyntz and the remaining constables on "some unfinished business", the nature of which he wouldn't disclose until the morning. Feeling drowsy after the long evening I had endured, I was content to let him go off on his merry mission and wished him the best of luck.

I was awakened the following morning by the butler, who announced that Holmes and the Chief Constable had arranged for everyone to meet in the library at nine a.m.. I had sufficient time to wash, dress, and have a cooked breakfast before joining the others. The only other person I saw during the meal was Vernon Saunders, who was distinctly unsociable.

I made my way to the library ten minutes before the planned meeting. Holmes greeted me with a smile and a nod, which suggested that all his plans the previous evening had gone well. Chief Constable Poyntz was dressed in his full police uniform, indicating that today he was on duty, and this was no social occasion. In the brief chat I had with him, he explained that he had made his way home at the end of the previous evening, rather than stay over.

By nine o'clock, everyone had assembled in the library. Alongside Holmes and Poyntz, there were three uniformed constables at the front of the room. Poyntz said a few words of introduction and acknowledged that he was grateful to both Holmes and me for getting to the bottom of the mystery surrounding the disappearance of the diamond bracelet. He finished by saying that he would allow my friend to explain all.

Holmes addressed the room in a loud and confident tone. "Thank you for once again making yourselves available. While this has been a straightforward case, the difficulties were in identifying all the players involved in this particular charade. I should tell you that last night we arrested Richard Templeton, who lodges at The Spencer Arms. In his room, we discovered the missing bracelet."

There were a few gasps. "His testimony enabled me to complete my understanding of how this affair unfolded. His role was simply that of receiver. When the jewellery reached him, he was to 'fence' the bracelet – selling it on to a silversmith in Hatton Garden who was prepared to pay a tidy sum for it. As a petty thief, the bricklayer had done this on earlier occasions. He hadn't acted quickly this time, as he was concerned about the police activity at Trenton House. And there was no romance between him and the maid, Alice Colden. This was a myth perpetuated to explain why the couple were spending so much time walking together."

Everyone turned to look at the maid, who blushed and then began to sob quietly into her handkerchief. Holmes responded by keeping the attention on Colden. "Have regard to the handkerchief which our errant maid is now holding, for it played a part in our drama as we will shortly discover. Some of you will be wondering how Templeton managed to get his hands on the bracelet when he spent all the afternoon drinking outside a pub. We know that the item was removed in this very room, and yet no one left the house. How then did the bracelet reach him? The answer was blatantly straightforward. It was carried to him by the basset hound.

"Last night, before you all departed for bed, I examined the dog's collar. In talking to us, Mr. Spall had indicated that it was indeed a 'new collar'. Templeton had it made specifically by a leather worker in Romford. It has a small pocket, sufficient to secrete a small bracelet. When released by the maid, the basset hound was content to run off from the house in pursuit of Templeton, for it was a game that it had played in the three weeks leading up to the party. Alice Colden was responsible for walking the dog twice a day around fields on the outskirts of Romford. Having recruited Templeton as part of the overall plan, the pair began to walk together on the pretence that they were lovers. In fact, the dog was being trained to follow a scent which was routinely sprayed onto Colden's handkerchief. Templeton would also wear the unusual scent, which the dog would then follow to where he sat outside the pub.

"Prior to the party, Templeton had ventured up to the house to double check that the plan was still going ahead. Colden intended to spray some of the scent on to his jacket as they had done previously, but had no opportunity, as Chief Constable Poyntz arrived at the party earlier than the other guests. The maid is no stranger to acting, so had to improvise. Pretending that she and Templeton were in the midst of a lover's tiff, she pressed the handkerchief against his shoulder to transfer the scent onto him. With her head also buried in his shoulder, she gave every impression of being upset."

"And very convincing you were too, Miss Colden!" said Poyntz, addressing the maid directly. He then turned to Holmes. "You mentioned in passing that she was 'no stranger to acting'. What did you mean by that?"

"Miss Colden told us last night that she had once worked in a theatre and occasionally played minor acting roles. In fact, prior to meeting her future employer, she had a much more colourful career." He withdrew a small piece of paper from his inside pocket and held it aloft. "Late last night, I sent a telegram to a colleague in London. He is a theatre critic for *The Daily Telegraph*, and has an encyclopaedic knowledge of past performers. In the information I requested, I asked him if he could recollect an actress by the name of 'Alice Colden'. Not only did he remember her, but stated that she had previously entertained audiences in a different capacity – specifically, as a magician's assistant!"

Further gasps echoed around the library. This time it was Vernon Saunders who fell under the spotlight as Holmes continued. "Yes, Miss Colden once worked with 'The Illusionist'. I imagine she was responsible for suggesting that Mr. Saunders be brought into the plan. You see, they needed to find a way of removing the bracelet from Mrs. Arlington-Fisher's wrist without being seen. What better than a magician? There was little risk as far as Saunders was concerned. If he managed to take the bracelet as planned, the jewellery wouldn't be discovered on him. If someone saw him take it, he could always claim that it was part of the act.

"He removed the bracelet and hid it within a blue tartan handkerchief. This was then used to cover the top hat in which he had already placed the live rabbit. The bracelet was slipped in beside the animal. As the magician's assistant, Colden had only to remove the bracelet from the hat, along with the handkerchief. There was plenty of activity to disguise what she was doing. She knew the dog would react to the appearance of the rabbit. She and Templeton had encouraged the basset hound to chase wild rabbits on their numerous field walks. This gave her the opportunity to hide the bracelet in the collar before removing the dog from the library and releasing it down the drive."

Charles Arlington-Fisher had a look of incredulity as he now addressed the detective. "I am grateful to you, Mr. Holmes, and your colleague, Dr. Watson, for recovering my wife's bracelet and putting this matter to rest. Mr. Poyntz is a good friend, and he deserves credit too for involving you in this matter and calling in his officers to assist. These revelations concern me a great deal, given the trust I have placed in our maid."

Holmes responded with candour. "There are some facets of this case which I still need to reveal to you, sir. They may give you further cause for concern." He looked directly at the lady of the house. "Mrs. Arlington-Fisher, do you wish me to continue, or would you prefer to explain everything to your husband?"

The woman looked stunned. "How did you know, Mr. Holmes?"

"When Mr. Poyntz explained all the events which occurred at the party yesterday, it was clear to me that the dog must have been used to remove the bracelet. It was the only explanation which fitted the facts. All of which implicated Templeton, Miss Colden, and Vernon Saunders. But I also recollected that you had been present when the maid pretended to be overcome with emotion as the Chief Constable had arrived for the party. I began to wonder if you might be implicated in the affair.

"The interviews we conducted last night gave me a much clearer insight into the relationship you have had with Alice Colden. The two of you have been firm friends for many years, having first met while working at the theatre. I speculated that the plan to 'steal' the bracelet could have been perpetrated by both of you, for the same end."

"Which was?" asked Mr. Arlington-Fisher with a degree of scepticism.

"To recoup the money you spent on the birthday present and claim the additional insurance money for the stolen bracelet. When Leonard Coulson visited you three weeks ago to tell you of your firm's financial losses, you said you knew it must be unwelcome news. I believe that your wife felt the same way. It is my contention that she asked Miss Colden to listen at the door of your study. Last night when I questioned her, it was clear that the maid knew of your financial difficulties, as she was already aware of the need to move to a smaller residence. And it was your wife who approached Mr. Saunders. The magician was hired just a few days later as part of the plan."

At this point, Celia Arlington-Fisher spoke up. "What Mr. Holmes has said is all true, Charles. I was desperate to find a way of getting back the money for the bracelet without alerting you to the fact that I knew of your losses. It seemed an innocent enough plan, as no one would get hurt. Alice suggested getting Vernon involved. I also knew him from our theatre days, as I'm sure Mr. Holmes found out from his theatre critic friend."

Holmes nodded. "Yes, and when questioned, Mr. Saunders also referred to you on one occasion as 'Celia', which suggested an acquaintance."

"Then you have laid bare our little scheme, sir. How do you now propose to proceed? What charges are we likely to receive?"

It was the Chief Constable who responded. "I am not at all pleased to have been embroiled in this unholy affair, Celia. If it was within my powers, I would, at the very least, charge you all with wasting police time. But I am inclined to let the matter rest there, given the damage this could do to both Charles's reputation – as a serving member of the Essex Watch Committee – and that of my force. I don't know how you feel about that, Mr. Holmes?"

My colleague didn't feel inclined to roll over quite so easily. "This is, of course, a decision for you professionally, Mr. Poyntz. But I will say that this doesn't sit well with me. Money and status shouldn't buy influence where the law is concerned. I feel certain that if Richard Templeton had been the sole architect of this plan, you wouldn't have been so lenient with him."

It was a sour note on which to end, but I couldn't help but agree with Holmes. We left Trenton House a few minutes later to catch a train back to London. In the aftermath, no charges were brought against any of those involved in the affair. I did read some weeks later that Charles Arlington-Fisher had resigned from his position on the Essex Watch Committee. And three years later, William Henry Poyntz retired from police service. Needless to say, Holmes and I did not receive an invitation to his retirement party.

# The Luxton Tragedy
## by Tracy J. Revels

"She did not run away, sir – of this I am certain. Laura Harvey was not a foolish girl, and while she may have been unhappy, she would never have done something so senseless. More than once I have heard her mention how cautious she was whenever she crossed the railroad tracks, especially at night! Sir, I am a poor girl, and the money in this purse reflects all that I have of my own, but I promise you, if you take my case, I will come to London and be your servant for however long is required to discharge my debt."

I studied my friend, Mr. Sherlock Holmes, with deep interest. Only an hour before, he had been complaining about the number of investigations he was engaged in, both for private clients and the official forces. It had been a summer of hard work and little rest, and his features were all the sharper as a result. His fingers tapped nervously upon the arm of his chair as our visitor – Miss Aubrey Alston, a charming young country woman of some twenty years with striking blonde hair and a sensible if slightly worn and patched walking dress – told him the purpose of her visit. Now, I wondered what words he would choose to gently send her on her way.

Miss Alston had quickly made it clear that she had come on behalf of her late friend, Miss Laura Harvey. The lass, who was just a month shy of her eighteenth birthday when she died, had been a resident of a farm near the village of Luxton. Five days previously, she disappeared from her family's fireside, and a desperate search throughout the night failed to find her. At daybreak, the girl's badly mangled corpse was discovered along the railway, and the Coroner's Jury had concluded, after hearing testimony from the train engineer, her family, the searchers, and the youth who discovered her body, that Miss Harvey had been a runaway girl, and was killed accidentally by a passing locomotive. It appeared, at least to my casual reading, a sad yet completely sound conclusion.

Holmes rose and plucked up the little purse from his desk, where our guest had deposited it. He pressed it back into her hands.

"My work is my own reward, Miss Alston, and I confess that there are certain elements in the story of your friend's demise that I have found unsatisfactory. Watson," he added, with a quick glance in my direction as he resumed his seat, "I haven't mentioned it to you, but I have been pondering the matter. Now that I am called, I shall answer. Justice for a girl is more pressing than the other items before me."

"Thank you, sir," our guest said. "I will tell you what I know as quickly as I can. The details which have been written up in the newspapers are mostly correct in the essentials of the case – but there are hidden truths which I tried to bring forward, yet no one was willing to listen to me. My mistress would be furious to learn I am consulting you. She has warned me to be silent and simply forget that I ever knew Laura. But that I cannot do.

"I met Laura Harvey a year ago, when her family rented the little farm a quarter-mile from our own. They were Americans, originally from the city of St. Louis: Along with Laura, a father, a mother, and an older son named Jeffrey made up the household. Neither Mr. Harvey nor his wife seemed very sociable. Jeffrey, who was about twenty, soon developed a reputation as a bully. Laura was put to work in the house and tending to the animals on their farm.

"Laura and I were but a few years apart in age, and naturally I was happy for another girl to live so close to me. We quickly became friends, and every Thursday at six she would meet me in the lane and walk with me into the village, to hear the 'Ladies' Lectures', improving talks on subjects of feminine interests. She eventually confessed to me that her life wasn't a happy one. She was not the daughter of her parents. Rather, she had been adopted from an unfortunate woman when she was a baby. The Harveys forced her to work harder than any servant. The Harveys were often harsh with her – I saw more than one bruise that she was quick to cover with a sleeve or scarf. She told me when she turned eighteen, she would leave the family and begin her life anew. 'Even if I must scrub floors and mend clothes for a living,' she would say, 'I will do it for people who will pay me, and not strike me when I make an error.' But even so, Mr. Holmes, she was never impolite or intemperate in her speech toward the Harveys."

"The newspapers portrayed her as unhappy and disobedient," Holmes said.

"A vile lie, sir! She was a good girl."

Holmes nodded for Miss Alston to continue.

"It was about three months ago when I saw Laura hanging out laundry, and I came through the gate of her yard, eager to share news about a lad who wished to spark her. When she turned, I saw terrible marks upon her face, as if she had been seized and slammed against a wall. Her left eye was swollen shut. I gave a cry of alarm, but before she could tell me what had happened, Mrs. Harvey shot out of the house like a bolt of lightning and ordered me to depart. 'Tis none of your business!' she shouted, and warned me that if she caught me conversing with her daughter again, she would set their dog upon me! You can imagine my horror. I threatened to go to the constable, but Laura gave a quick shake of her head, and in her one open eye I read a plea for me to hold my tongue, that any action on my part would only lead to more mistreatment. But oh, sir, how I wish I hadn't kept silent!

"Through the village gossips, I learned the Harveys were telling people that their daughter was an incorrigible girl, whom they hoped to discipline. Laura no longer attended the lectures, or church, or came to the village on market day. Then, five days ago, she vanished completely. As you read in the papers, the Harveys claimed they travelled to a neighboring parish for a family picnic, returned to their farm at about four, and then missed Laura at supper. Mr. Harvey and Jeffrey rode out in search of her, just after nightfall. I happened to see them as they rode by, in a wagon piled high with cabbages and other vegetables. They questioned every family along the road to the village, and then alerted the constable. People looked high and low for her, but they didn't find her until the next morning, almost three miles from the village, at . . . ."

Miss Alston began to weep. Holmes assured her that she need not recite the details. The girl daubed a handkerchief to her eyes.

"Thank you, sir. I don't wish to think on it. My master was summoned to be on the Coroner's Jury, and he said that Mr. and Mrs. Harvey both swore their daughter had been 'unmanageable' all day, disobedient and disagreeable, even as they tried to enjoy their little family holiday. They returned home in the afternoon and heard the rear door open and close as the clock struck five. They assumed Laura had gone outside to settle her nerves and hoped that a long walk would put her in a better humor. When she didn't return by seven, they grew concerned, and at eight Mr. Harvey retrieved his wagon to ride in search of her. The place where she was found very early the next morning is lonely, and quite covered in trees and bushes. The railway curves there, in a kind of gully, and it would be difficult to quickly scramble up the other side if a train suddenly flew around the bend."

Holmes nodded. "I recall from the papers that the engineer said he was unaware his locomotive had struck anything."

"That is true, sir. And yet . . . you must believe me, she didn't run away, nor would she have thrown herself in front of the train!"

"You admit she was unhappy. A dissatisfied – or abused – young person might well have fled from a cruel home, or been driven to a rash act."

"Sir . . . there is more. Some things that I would have shared, had anyone permitted me to speak."

Holmes nodded for her to continue. The girl had removed her gloves and began to nervously twist them in her hands.

"The morning of the day that Laura went missing, I was sent by my mistress to the apothecary's. I saw awful Mr. Harvey there. Forgive me my bluntness, sir, but I dislike the man. He has a bristling black beard, and small, rat-like eyes. He grows his hair long and leaves it unkempt, probably to hide the fact that his left ear is jagged and torn, as if some beast had dined on half of it. This cruel man didn't hesitate to beat Laura with a strap for the crimes of spilling cream or burning bread. He was standing at the counter, talking with the clerk. I turned my back to him, mulling over a display of fancy soaps, but I heard their conversation clearly.

"'I am sorry sir, but I cannot sell you that item.'

"'I had no trouble acquiring it in America!'

"'Be that as it may, sir, I am not allowed to sell it to you here. My master is very strict and wouldn't hesitate to sack me.'

The nasty Mr. Harvey muttered some oaths, then seemed to realize there was a lady present. He turned and departed with barely a nod in my direction. Naturally, I was curious about what I had just witnessed, and by good fortune the clerk – Eddie – is rather fond of me. I promised to pony up with a kiss on his check if he would tell me what Mr. Harvey wanted.

"'He tried to buy an entire bottle of prussic acid! He said he needed it to clean a sealskin cape. Have you ever heard of such? And think how odd he would look, walking about in that outfit, like some kind of sailor on an Arctic cruise. Oh well. Americans are a strange lot.'

"I thought no more about it, Mr. Holmes, until I saw Laura again, and at the very hour the Harveys claim she was 'out for a stroll'. I was walking along the road at about five-thirty in the afternoon and I saw her in her garden. She waved to me and ran over to the fence, looking pale and wane. Mr. Holmes, she whispered the most wonderous thing – 'He has come for me!' she said. 'An angel, all in white, to free me. I saw him talking with Father, and he said he would have me soon, but then Father said the papers must be clear, and he went away. But he will come again, he said, and I will be his!'"

"What on earth did she mean?" I asked.

"I wish I knew. Laura looked so sickly, her eyes were wide, and her face was gray. There was a shout from inside the house. Someone had called her name. She motioned me away and hurried back to her door. I never saw her again."

"Perhaps she was truly ill," I suggested gently. "A physical ailment can provoke a mental disease and induce hallucinations that seem very real to the sufferer."

"But, sir," Miss Alston said, her voice trembling as she spoke, "I have seen the angel of whom Laura spoke."

Holmes's brows rose.

"You must believe me. It was the day after Laura was buried. I went to the little cemetery, bearing some flowers, and I saw a man standing over her grave. He was . . . all in white, just as she said. His coat, trousers, boots, even his hat were like snow. His skin was likewise so very pale, and his iron-gray hair was long to his shoulders. He was such a shocking figure to behold that I confess I gave a cry of alarm, dropped my offering, and ran away. But I saw him again that afternoon, standing at the corner of the field near Laura's home, simply staring at the house. I dared not approach him, for I wasn't sure if he was a real man or a ghost."

"Or an angel," Holmes corrected, with a quirk of his lips. "I presume you saw no wings?"

The girl blushed. "I did not. As I watched, I saw Jeffrey emerge from his house. But then he too caught sight of the man and whirled about, running back into his dwelling and slamming the door as if the Devil himself was after him!" The girl sighed. "By the time I looked around, the man in white was gone. And at that point, I resolved myself to find a way to come to London to speak with you."

Holmes frowned. He pulled out his pocket watch and consulted it.

"What time did you intend to return to Luxton, Miss Alston?"

"There is a train at three."

"And it is but eleven-ten now." Holmes rose and rang our bell. "I'm certain you must be famished after your journey. Mrs. Hudson is no doubt preparing our own repast at this moment, and I would ask that you go down and have her fix you a bit of luncheon. I must consult with the doctor on a few matters, and in an hour, I may have some answers. I presume this is acceptable?"

Hope caused the young lady's eyes to glisten. "It is. Thank you."

The door opened to our good landlady, who quite naturally drew our young client to her side with the promise of a piping hot shepherd's pie. Holmes began to snatch newspapers from the clutter about our room, laying them out in order on his desk.

"You look startled that I took her case, Watson."

"You are very much engaged at the moment."

"Indeed, but – I wasn't dissembling when I said the matter had been troubling me. I had hoped that Lestrade or some other member of the official forces might call me in. Look here: The first article tells the initial tale succinctly. The Harveys are Americans. There is an older son, and they reside on a rather lonely farm. In fact, they lack neighbors for two miles in either direction along the lane."

"Did not the lady say – ?"

"She did indeed, Watson. She made a claim of residing only a quarter-mile distant. But let us brush it aside for a moment." Holmes made a wry smile. "The reporter also notes that the family claimed the girl suffered from melancholy and often refused to do her chores, but they in no way judged her to be suicidal. No doubt the jury agreed with the parents that moodiness and disobedience are known symptoms of the disease called *adolescence*. On the night she went missing, her father and brother drove a wagon filled with produce into the village, and banged on many doors, inquiring if the girl had been seen. Does that not strike you as odd?"

"I see nothing unusual in searching for a missing child."

My friend's eyes climbed skyward. "The wagon, Watson! If you were in a panic over a missing lass, would it not make more sense for you to saddle a horse and gallop into town? Or to at least send your grown lad in one direction, while you hurried away in another? Instead, both men came into the village in a single wagon. And why was the vehicle filled with vegetables?"

"Perhaps they had already loaded it, in preparation for a market day."

Holmes tapped the paper. "The article states that market day had been held three days previously. There was no reason for the cart to be so burdened."

"You think – ?"

Holmes rapidly shuffled the papers. "Look here – the testimony of the witnesses. The train's engineer heard and saw nothing – no screams or cries. The body was found close to the tracks, with its lower half utterly mangled. Yet the face and shoulders were unharmed, making identification instant. Sad experience has taught us that when a person stands upon railroad tracks or leaps into the path of a moving locomotive, that person's body is inevitably knocked off to one side, thrown quite a great distance by the violence of the impact. So clearly the young woman didn't hurl herself in front of the train."

I shuddered. The image my imagination cast up was a gruesome one. "Could she have laid upon the tracks and waited?"

"Possible, but highly improbable. It would take nerves of steel to commit to such a deed – and I have never, in my career, encountered such."

"You think she might have been restrained?"

"Now you are drawing closer to my thoughts. A young woman tethered to the tracks couldn't have escaped a horrible fate. Yet these articles make it clear that no signs of ropes or chains were found, nor was there any evidence that the young woman was gagged. I find it impossible to imagine a villain who would have left his victim screaming at the top of her lungs, even in a lonely place, for fear she might be rescued and could identify him."

"Then she was unconscious."

"A much better deduction, though even that raises problems for our culprit. If he deposited her on the tracks in a swoon, the vibrations of the oncoming train might have jolted her into awareness. Again, there is the possibility of escape. No, Watson – look here at this final detail. In it, we have our answer."

I leaned down and read the line he indicated.

"No blood!"

"Indeed, and Luxton has fools for its coroner and constables, to ignore the implications of such evidence. No significant amount of blood was found on the tracks or on the train. The body wasn't dragged any distance – we know this from the relatively slight damage to the head and arms. Yet despite the horrible event, there was no great splashing of life's precious fluid, as one would expect to find. The conclusion seems inevitable: The girl was dead when she was placed there. The body was likely exsanguinated at some other place." Holmes moved away from the table, his arms folded and his chin upon his chest. "I would very much like to have a look at that cart, beneath those cabbages."

What Holmes was suggesting left me cold and filled with revulsion. "You think she was murdered by her family, her body transported in the cart, and laid upon the tracks for the train to destroy?"

"I am certain of it." My friend took down his pipe and lit it. "Let us consider another strange factor of this case: Why was Miss Laura left with her head and shoulders *off* the tracks? In general, it is in a murderer's interest to make a body *harder* to identify, if it cannot be disposed of completely. Yet in this case, our killer made it easy to place a name upon the child, while making the choice to have the lower half of her body utterly ground to pieces. Why?"

"I cannot imagine."

Holmes scowled at me. "An obvious theory presents itself."

At first, I didn't take his meaning. Then I considered how the girl had been removed from public view for months and forbidden to associate with her friend.

"Oh Holmes – surely not!"

Holmes nodded. "Perhaps this poor girl was to be a mother."

I shook my head. Could anyone really be so cruel? Holmes's gaze remained firm.

"Yet one clue argues against this thesis."

"And that is?" I asked.

"The request for prussic acid. There can be no question about the intent when poison is sought. If she was *enceinte* and the family wished the babe destroyed, there are many pills for 'ladies' complaints' that may be used for that purpose, along with 'old wives' potions of pennyroyal, tansy, and juniper that might be tried. But no, Mr. Harvey attempted to buy prussic acid, indicating the Harveys didn't merely wish the girl to lose her infant, if indeed she was expecting. Rather, they wanted her dead. But why?" Holmes frowned, then suddenly began to dig about in his untidy pile of papers. Next, he flipped through his commonplace books. A great stream of unintelligible murmurings followed. Meanwhile, I sank into my chair.

"What do you make of this 'angel'?" I asked.

"I would dismiss it as a fantasy, were it not for a single report in a more sensational paper – Ah, here it is! '*Strange figure at inquest – gentleman in white, a curious character unknown to any in the village – sat on the front row during the testimony – Harvey and son seem unnerved by his presence.*'" Holmes gave a short laugh. "Our intrepid reporter has done us a favor by tracking the odd fellow to The Leaping Hart Inn. He even claims to have bribed the proprietor to let him see the guest book. He says the gentleman is a Mr. Ange, from New Orleans, America."

"French for *angel*!" I cried. "What do you plan to do?"

Holmes kicked the now even-more untidy pile of newsprint to one side.

"In a few moments, I propose to ask Miss Alston up, and inquire why she told us so many lies."

I confess I sat for a moment, slack jawed. At last, I recovered my power of speech.

"How do you know that – ?"

"First, the error in distance. Even the most unobservant female would know a quarter-mile from two. Next, it is clear Miss Alston isn't an English girl, despite a capable mastery of the accent. It is the idioms that gave her away – '*sparking*' for courtship, to '*pony up*' to pay off a debt. There are also the boots, and the narrower skirt, clearly American in style. I see that the young lady has had the misfortune to drop her glove. Give it to me, if you please." Holmes plucked up his glass and examined the accessory. "Well-worn, but there is a slight mark here upon the inner leather. This glove was made in New York. I would also note that Miss Alston's hands were far too soft, and the nails too well-trimmed, to belong to a country maid employed on a farm. Plus, why the wig? Surely, Watson, you recognized the false hair, which no girl as healthy as she should require. She has clearly misrepresented herself."

248

"But who is she? Why would she craft such outrageous falsehoods?" I scowled. "Is the whole business a pack of lies?"

"There is a dead girl in Luxton – that we know to be a fact. But now we must apply some pressure to sort further truth from fiction. I confess I find myself intrigued. Is there *some* veracity to her tale or – Hello, Mrs. Hudson. We were just about to come down to fetch your guest."

Our landlady looked between us. Her gentle face grew quite perplexed. "But Mr. Holmes, the girl said she was coming back up here. She told me she dropped her glove and was afraid she would forget it if she didn't retrieve it immediately. That was some ten minutes ago, and she never returned to the kitchen. Her pie is getting cold!"

Rarely have I seen Holmes more outraged with himself. For two hours he paced about, smoked three pipes, sent and received a pair of telegrams, and cursed himself as a fool for ever letting the "clever little vixen" out of his sight. Finally, he turned to his other cases, and became engrossed in a chemical experiment he felt certain would, if successful, save a man from the gallows. I amused myself with a yellow-backed novel and had almost slumped into a late-afternoon doze when our door was thrown open with a bang.

"Mr. Holmes!' Inspector Lestrade shouted. "You must come with me immediately! There's been a bad business in Luxton, and from the messages I've received from the locals, I think it would be best to have you there from the start."

Holmes put aside the test tube he had been delicately manipulating over a burner. "Luxton. That village has been much in the papers of late."

"Yes. A sad business with a girl run down by a train. But it was an accident, and this is cold-blooded murder, barely an hour old."

Holmes shot me a glance, which I interpreted as a request for silence. I wasn't to reveal anything about our morning visitor.

"Tell me of it," Holmes said.

"I can give you the details on the train."

"I would much prefer you to inform me now."

Lestrade crinkled his face. "Very well. It is the same family that lost the daughter. All were seen about their property early this morning, but just after four a neighbor called upon the mother and, getting no answer, she went into the house through the open doorway. There she found the three Harveys, hanging from the beams in their kitchen."

"A triple suicide?" I asked.

Lestrade's expression was grim. "A triple murder. Though all were hanged, the chairs they stood in were neatly pushed beneath the table, five feet away. No, this is a cruel, cold-blooded execution."

Holmes rubbed a hand against his chin. Lestrade began to sputter.

"Well – will you help me or not?"

"Unfortunately, Inspector, a man's life hangs upon the result of this experiment, so I cannot in good conscience abandon it at this moment. However, if you will do one slight favor for me today, I will be completely at your disposal tomorrow."

Lestrade looked resigned and unhappy. "What favor is that?"

Holmes rose, snagged a page from my notebook, and jotted down a sentence. Lestrade scowled at the writing.

"Reply by telegram immediately?" he asked.

"It is most urgent."

"But does it relate to the murdered family?"

"I feel certain that it does. I shall have more for you in the morning."


Holmes continued to tinker with his chemistry experiments until nine, when a message arrived for him. He gave a cry of satisfaction upon reading it, snatched up the newspaper, and then turned to me.

"What would you say to an evening stroll about the docks, Watson?"

"I can think of far more pleasant environments for a constitutional."

"Yes, but tonight we aren't merely amusing ourselves with a ramble. The game is afoot, and we must go hunting! Into your coat and hat. We haven't a minute to lose."

I struggled to engage Holmes in conversation as we travelled to the less-savory side of London, inquiring as to why he didn't want to follow Lestrade to Luxton.

"I know you lied to the inspector," I chided. "You completed the essential experiment an hour earlier and were merely dabbling in some new compounds."

"Perhaps I was corrupted by our young visitor," Holmes chuckled. "But the reason I felt it best to remain in London is because I believe we can catch the murderers of the Harvey family here, not in the village. I gave Lestrade the instruction to inquire at The Leaping Hart as to when Mr. Ange had departed and where his luggage was sent. The reply was much as I had expected. Ange removed himself from his room this morning, and his luggage was tagged for the offices of the American Comet liners. A quick check of the newspaper revealed exactly what I had suspected – their vessel *Cajun Queen* is departing at midnight, bound for the port of New Orleans."

"And the killer will be aboard her?"

"*Killers*, Watson." Holmes thudded his cane on the roof of the carriage, signaling to the driver to halt. We walked the final streets, and I noted how bright Holmes's gaze was, how his eyes darted everywhere. We were almost to the gangplank of the sizeable vessel when he stopped and asked me to step into The Blue Mermaid tavern and procure an isolated table for, as he called it, a "most enlightening interview". Then he was off amid the slow-rolling fog. I quickly stepped inside, and the mention of my friend's name resulted in the possession of a large booth, discreetly tucked into a corner. Not a minute later, Holmes appeared, accompanied by two striking individuals – a middle-aged, gray-haired gentleman who was clad completely in white, and the charming young woman who had so shamelessly spouted falsehoods in our suite.

"Dr. Watson, allow me to introduce our guests. Miss Aubrey Alston you have met. And this is Mr. Lucien Isador Ange, late of the great city of New Orleans."

The young woman had undergone a metamorphous. In Baker Street, she had been crowned with blonde hair, but now her curly locks were cut short, almost like a boy's, and shone deep russet in the candlelight. The walking dress had been replaced by a stylish mauve ensemble, complete with fine gloves and a smart leather reticule.

"If I may be so bold," Holmes said, sliding onto the bench to face the pair, "I would compliment you on your coiffure, Miss Alston. It is a far better fit for your adventurous nature than the wig you wore this morning."

"Thank you, sir. Tell me – Do you know my real name?"

"I fear I do not."

She offered a coquettish smile. "Then I have achieved a true feather in my cap. Mr. Sherlock Holmes did not know Miss Vivian Fletcher."

Her moniker meant nothing to me, but an electrical pulse seemed to run through Holmes.

"My compliments, Madam. Does your mother still work for the Pinkertons?"

"Long-since retired and looking after my sister's babies. I took her place to be trained, before going into the private inquiry business." She glanced over at the sad-faced gentleman. "Mr. Ange is my first client. But considering I have not kept faith with you, and therefore you may not trust me, perhaps the story should come from his lips."

"Indeed," Ange rumbled. "And if there is to be punishment, then let it fall on me. I was the one who tied the nooses and kicked the chairs away."

Holmes shook his head. "But Miss Fletcher held the guns on your victims."

Neither denied the accusation. A barmaid brought glasses of ale. Miss Fletcher drank eagerly, but her client merely slid his aside.

"I shall tell you the truth. Almost two decades ago, I was a wild and foolish young man. I met a beautiful woman named Annette, and we loved passionately, but not wisely. We quarreled – she left me – and almost seventeen years passed before I saw her again."

The gentleman hesitated, clearly in the grip of strong emotion. Anger and deep sadness were both etched upon his aristocratic features.

"One day I looked up, and there was Annette, standing at my office door. Before I could embrace her, she dropped to the floor and slipped into a faint. Of course I summoned a physician, and soon learned that my lost love had come to me *in extremis.* She was dying of consumption and wished to make a final peace with me. She rallied enough to tell me that she had settled in St. Louis, where she delivered our daughter, whom she named Laura. Alone and rejected by her kin, she gave her infant to a family named Harvey, with the understanding that she could reclaim the child when her situation improved.

"They seemed comfortable, she said. They had money, and nice clothes, and fancy china on the table. She thought how lucky her girl was, to be fostered by such people. But one day, when Laura was just a toddler, Annette went to the Harvey house for a visit and found it empty. Their landlord was furious, for they had fled in the night, and were in arrears on their rent. Annette tried for years to find them, and only recently had received a clue that they had gone to England, where it was said the wife had people. This was all she knew, and with her dying breath she begged me to find our girl.

"I spared no expense, but the search took time. At last, three months ago, the Harveys and my daughter were found, living in the tiny village of Luxton."

"Why did you not reclaim Laura then?" Holmes asked.

"As much as I wanted her back, I suspected she had been raised in ignorance of her origins. If she had been brought up as the beloved child of this family, she would have no reason to believe my tale. I could not simply walk into her life and cause her grief. I needed to know more, to decide how to best approach her. Miss Fletcher came to England on my behalf, secretly, to assess the situation and advise me."

The female agent leaned forward. "I quickly learned the gossip from Luxton's maids and daughters – how the Harvey family had taken a lonely farm, and how the village girls who had befriended Laura had come to suspect mistreatment, as Laura had been forbidden to leave her family's abode for weeks. They also spoke of how Jeffrey Harvey was cruel and had even attempted an assault on one girl's virtue.

"I was determined to find the truth by seeing Laura for myself. I called on the family in the guise of a timid church missionary. Laura opened the door for me, and I was able to look her over before Mrs. Harvey intervened and ordered me away. Laura's swollen face, her deathly pallor

252

– it all hinted at terrible abuse – perhaps even the worst abuse of all, since they would not allow her in public. Mr. Ange was in New Orleans, awaiting my reports. I told him he should come at once to rescue her."

"And so I did," the gentleman rumbled. "I arranged to meet the vile Harvey in a private place. I told him who I was and what I wanted. I offered Harvey vast sums of money to give Laura to me. I promised I wouldn't make any trouble with the law for him. I assured him I would take Laura far away, and he would hear no more from us. However, if he balked at my offer, I would take my knowledge of his unkind treatment of Laura to the authorities." Mr. Ange groaned and raked his hand through his snowy hair. "I should have gone to the police first, but I read Harvey as a greedy, mean man, perhaps a former petty thief who would respond readily to cash. Miss Fletcher had warned me there was the possibility my daughter was expecting a child and, if so, I hoped to spare Laura the humiliation of a public scene. Harvey claimed he would give her to me without a fuss provided I produced certain documents from America. I told him it would take me two weeks to acquire them. We shook hands and I went back to London. But the very next day . . . ."

"He ended her life," I said.

Holmes looked to the lady agent. "Was your story of the apothecary a truthful one, Miss Fletcher?"

"Yes, except for the business of kissing the clerk. I heard Harvey ask for prussic acid and be denied. I alerted Mr. Ange immediately, and he returned from London on the next train."

"But we couldn't find anyone about the farm that afternoon," Ange said, hissing his words through clenched teeth. "They claimed they spent the day picnicking, yet no one saw them. Somewhere, hidden from view, they murdered my child and kept her body concealed beneath those cabbages until cover of darkness, when they could place her upon the tracks so the train would mutilate her body! And then they claimed to have been seeking her the whole time."

The man's fist came down on the table.

"I wanted to kill the Harveys at the inquest. I had a pistol in my pocket. But Miss Fetcher persuaded me to wait."

"The testimony at the inquest proved they had staged the accident," the lady said. "They must have been confident that by portraying Laura as a runaway, killed by misfortune, Mr. Ange could make no case against them for abusing his daughter, and whatever they were hiding would stay hidden." The young woman looked to Holmes. "Have you learned what their motive was for slaying her? Surely it was something beyond covering the cruel way they had treated her."

Holmes nodded. He pulled a telegram from his pocket.

"I grew curious about the reference to St. Louis as the former home of the Harveys. I reasoned that if your assessment of his personality – and your depiction of his ravaged ear – were both true, then perhaps my friends in that city's police might have made his acquaintance. I gave them the name and the description. The lawmen of St. Louis were very forthcoming, for they immediately recognized this individual. It seems that Mr. Harvey was far more than minor criminal who ran off without paying his rent – he was known to them not as 'Harvey', but as 'Hurley', the 'Midnight Blade', an assassin for a dangerous gang. He was wanted for the murder, some three years ago, of four boys and two women, the innocent family of a rival gangster. I believe Laura witnessed one or more of the killings. Harvey worried that once free of his clutches, Laura would, as you say in America, 'rat him out'. Quite frankly, I doubt the Harvey family would ever have allowed Laura to leave their household alive."

"My God!" Ange whispered. He slumped in his chair. Holmes addressed his words to Ange's companion.

"But why did you come to me and tell such an embellished tale? What was its purpose?"

The young woman had been gently patting her employer's hand. She lifted her head proudly.

"I sought you out because what I had seen and what was reported in the inquest led me to believe Laura was murdered to keep a deadly secret. However, as this is my first case, I wished to hear confirmation of my suspicions from the most brilliant man in England. Therefore, I concocted lies around the central truth of the matter, and added the bit about the angel because I knew of your love of the bizarre. After our interview, I evaded your housekeeper and tiptoed back to your door. I heard you work through the evidence just as I had and be puzzled by the same part of the matter that had confounded me: What secret was she keeping? And then, when it became clear you knew I was an American, I fled. We had already engaged an express to whisk us back to Luxton, to deliver justice." The young woman picked up the telegram. "I should have thought of this. I must cultivate friends in the official forces, who might aid me in my investigations. I have learned a valuable lesson."

"How was the murder of the family done?" I asked. Mr. Ange answered wearily.

"Miss Fetcher gained admittance to the house in the guise of a lad seeking work. I followed on her heels, and both of us were armed. The old man and woman begged for mercy, but the boy sneered and, with filthy language, bragged of the wrongs he had done to my innocent girl. I fixed the nooses while Miss Fetcher held the pistols. I kicked away the chairs, then replaced them." Mr. Ange shook his head. "I wanted the world to know they were criminals who died as criminals. Otherwise, they might have been pitied."

Holmes leaned back, his eyes slowly closing. I found myself wondering if our companions remained armed and wouldn't hesitate to shoot us to make their escape. Holmes exhaled gently and opened his eyes.

"You have committed murder on British soil. Whatever your reasons – and I can understand your desire to avenge your daughter – I cannot endorse your actions."

"You are arresting us?" the man asked.

"I have no legal power to do so at this moment," Holmes said. "However, it is my duty as a citizen to be truthful with the police, should they inquire about you." He opened his watch. "I see that the *Cajun Queen* will depart within the hour. I have promised Inspector Lestrade that I will assist him in the morning, in Luxton. Make of that what you will. Watson, a good night's rest will be beneficial. Mr. Ange, Miss Fletcher, I bid you *bon voyage.*"

My friend was true to his word. The next morning, we journeyed to Luxton, only to find that Inspector Lestrade had arrested the apothecary, the blacksmith, and the local vicar, having spun a bizarre fantasy about how all three of them had been paying court to Miss Laura Harvey, and had murdered her family in revenge for her untimely accident. Holmes unraveled this absurdly tangled knot and set Lestrade upon the proper path. Lestrade quickly telegraphed his counterparts in New Orleans, to have the vessel met and Ange and Fletcher arrested.

However – and much to Holmes's amusement – when the New Orleans police stormed the stateroom assigned to the pair, they found two rather intoxicated specimens of London criminality, a husband and wife, who claimed they had been 'gifted' the trip by a mysterious couple they met on the docks, just an hour before the ship departed. They were so generously supplied with money that they had spent the entire Atlantic crossing in a blissful alcoholic haze and were clearly not the individuals Lestrade was seeking.

We heard no more of Mr. Ange and Miss Fletcher, though for some years afterward, on the anniversary of Miss Laura Harvey's death, a single, pristine white rose would be delivered to Baker Street.

# The Mystery of the Missing Body
## by DJ Tyrer

When we arrived at our destination, a house in Belgravia, Inspector Lestrade of Scotland Yard was waiting at the door for us. He had a disgruntled look upon his face and greeted Holmes and me in the most-perfunctory manner, his tone aggrieved.

"Your message said there had been a murder," said Holmes, striding past the inspector and into the entrance hall. I followed after them and was surprised at just how shabby and empty the hallway appeared, an impression reinforced as I glanced into the reception room.

"Yes, last night," said Lestrade. "We assume there has been a murder."

I looked at him in surprise.

"'*Assume*'?" said I, wonderingly. "Whatever do you mean?"

"No body, Doctor. No body – just blood and suspicion."

Holmes turned and flashed Lestrade a smile. "'*Blood and suspicion*'? A murder with no corpse? Now, this sounds as if it might be a case worthy of my attention."

The inspector grimaced as if my friend had just fed him a lemon. "I thought it would interest you. Come. Upstairs is where . . . Well, where it happened – *if* it did."

It was unusual to see the inspector quite that uncertain and perturbed.

"Lead on," said Holmes, and we followed Lestrade up the stairs to a dressing room.

There could be no doubt that the room had been the site of some act of violence, for there was blood splashed across the top of the dressing table and over its mirror, as well as further splashes on the chair and a wide pool of it upon the floor. A turtleshell hairbrush lay discarded beside the chair.

Lestrade gave a curt nod towards the scene, but said nothing.

"I think you're right," said I, looking down at all the gore. "If that blood all came from one person, and from its spread, that seems a certainty, it's highly likely that he or she is dead. Even with prompt medical attention, for which we have no evidence, the odds of survival wouldn't be good."

"I concur with your assessment," said Holmes, absently as he took in the entirety of the room. I noted that the inspector seemed a little happier to see that his assumption about the crime was correct.

"No weapon?" Holmes asked Lestrade.

"None."

"And the jewellery box . . . it was missing when you arrived?"

"Correct. Just like the body."

Holmes directed my attention to an area upon the dressing table where the varnish was a slightly darker and of a deeper hue. There were also four faint indentations where the box had rested. Had he not shown it to me, I'm not sure I would've managed to recognise the signs.

"It seems we have a possible motive. But – " He steepled his fingers and looked to the ceiling for a moment before continuing. " – why remove the body without attempting to clean up the blood? A thief might kill for what he desires, but what does this gain him? The blood tells there was a victim, so the act of murder is not concealed. Or was the killing the reason, and the theft a superfluous red herring? But again, what does removing the body gain the killer?"

Holmes turned to Lestrade. "I presume you know who the victim was. You mentioned suspicion."

Hiding the victim's identity, of course, was the obvious reason why someone might wish a body to disappear.

"I do, and I'll come to that in a moment."

"There is more, Inspector?"

"Besides what you see here – or don't see – we discovered a partially-burnt bedsheet in a fireplace downstairs. It was heavily stained with blood. My assumption from this was that the sheet had been used to move the body downstairs, but had to be abandoned because it was too gory to risk anyone seeing. This, of course, seemed to confirm that a murder had indeed taken place, as so much blood had already been lost up here."

"You will show me the fireplace," said Holmes. Although his tone was somewhat imperious, the inspector had learned to accept that my friend was merely stating a necessity when he issued such commands and took little umbrage from being ordered about, merely saying, "Yes, yes," before continuing.

"Although I set my men to searching the house, in case the body had been left hidden somewhere within, it seemed most likely that it was removed from the building, and so I made my second assumption: That a clean sheet had been used to transport it on the next leg of its journey. This was confirmed by the maid, who reported that four sheets in total are missing. I suspect the body was multiply wrapped to prevent the blood staining through and becoming obvious."

"Your suppositions would seem to make sense," said Holmes.

"Leaving a couple of constables here to keep an eye on the place and finish searching, and a couple more checking the street outside, I led the rest of my men into Hyde Park, where we carried out as thorough a search as possible in the darkness, my reasoning being that if the body has been taken to a private property, we have no idea where that might be, but if it was being disposed of with speed, that was the nearest open space where it could be taken."

Holmes nodded. "Yes – a shallow burial, concealment in dense growth or, perhaps, depositing it in the waters of the Serpentine."

"It was there, caught on a bush, near the lake, that we found a bloodied handkerchief. It was subsequently shown to the maid who identified it as one belonging to her mistress."

Lestrade's identification of the victim's sex caused us no surprise. The fact that she had apparently been killed while seated at the dressing table, using the feminine hairbrush, had told us the likelihood a woman had been slain, despite the inspector's coyness.

"So," said I, "it seems your guess paid out and her body was disposed of in the park."

"I have my men continuing their search by daylight and dragging the lake."

"You'll surely have your body soon and its absence will be moot," I said, "although I can see why its vanishing might concern you. Even when there is overwhelming evidence that a murder has taken place, can a man be convicted of it without the body?"

"Actually," said Holmes, who was busy striding about the room, taking in every corner and crevice of our surroundings, "I think you will find that a body isn't actually required in law when prosecuting a murder charge. Of course, that assumes the police will bring a charge at all – " He looked at the inspector. " – given that they might have their doubts, and it must be considered that bringing a case to court precipitously might see the killer acquitted, only for the body and better evidence to be discovered subsequently. But even if the police were bold enough to pursue the case, it would be a rare jury that would convict, unless a watertight case were to be argued."

"Which is why you're here," said the inspector. "If anyone can produce an indisputable argument for a corpse-less killing, it's you, Mr. Holmes."

"I thank you for the compliment, Inspector, but should I fail, it seems to me that the absence of the jewels will not be an impediment to a charge of theft."

"A-ha. That's where you may well be wrong."

"Really. Pray tell why?"

"That is one of the facts I was saving until I had explained what we had achieved so far, before summoning you."

"Then," said Holmes, "why don't we descend to examine the fireplace and you can explain on the way."

"This way."

We followed Lestrade downstairs to the drawing room and he went over the remaining details of the case.

The victim was a Mrs. Jermyn – Olivia Jermyn *née* Richfield – the wife of Mr. Fitzgerald Jermyn, the owner of the house. Her husband, according to the inspector, was a gentleman of weak character, licentious and a gambler, who was deep in debt to his creditors. The only other inhabitant of the house, the singular member of staff, all others having been laid off over the past couple of years to meet his reduced income, was the maid, whom it seemed had been expected to fulfil every household position, despite a wage that had been reduced to nigh-slavery levels.

"It is my opinion," said Lestrade, "that she remained solely out of concern for her mistress."

Jermyn's debts explained the denuded and dilapidated nature of the house – all non-essential possessions had been sold off to meet them, and the money that should have gone on maintenance and repairs likewise.

As if all that wouldn't have been sufficient to sow discord in the Jermyns' marriage, the inspector further reported that both the maid and their neighbours had heard more than one loud argument due to Jermyn's demand for his wife's dresses and jewels to pay off his further debts, which she had objected to most strongly. He had shown no concern for her sensibilities and had, indeed, sold most of her dresses and all those jewels that he had bought for her ornament, those remaining his property despite having been given to her. The only jewels that hadn't been disposed of were those that resided, so the maid had affirmed to the inspector, in the missing jewellery box.

These last jewels had been bequeathed to Mrs. Jermyn by her mother, and thus were legally hers and not his, so couldn't be sold against her will. They were the last items of any real value in the house, and her husband had demanded that she allow him to sell them in order to finance his gambling – something which she had steadfastly and ever-more-loudly refused.

"But," Lestrade concluded "if Mrs. Jermyn were to die – "

" – the jewels would doubtless pass to her husband," I surmised.

"Exactly. He is our primary suspect."

I understood, now, what Lestrade had meant about Holmes being wrong about a charge of theft: If Jermyn had taken his wife's jewels following her death, no theft had occurred. Had he hidden her body expecting the police to be unable to prove he'd killed her, clearing the way for him to sell the jewels?

We were now at the fireplace in the drawing room and Holmes was crouched beside it, examining both the ashes within it and the partially-burnt sheet that one of Lestrade's men had left neatly folded beside it. Holmes frowned and I suspect he would've like to have seen the sheet *in situ*, though what it might have told him, I had no idea.

"There would seem to be a paucity of suspects," said Holmes, standing. "Indeed, only two likely culprits, the husband and the maid, with the possibility of a creditor's involvement – unless we assume burglars took the jewels. But in such a case, even more strongly than the others, why make Mrs. Jermyn disappear?"

He looked at me and I felt as if I must answer. I told him about my conjecture.

"Yes, that would make sense, but without a body, he might be unable to convince the courts to declare her dead, leaving him unable to legally sell the jewels until seven years had passed."

I frowned. He was right: The same reason why he might wish to dispose of her body was also an argument against his concealing it.

"He might not have considered that," said Lestrade.

"Possibly," said Holmes.

"Can we be certain it wasn't a kidnapping gone wrong?" I asked.

Lestrade snorted. "By your own observation, Doctor, the woman was mortally wounded, either killed outright or rapidly dying. What would kidnappers want with a corpse?"

"Indeed," said Holmes. "If they wanted to hold her for ransom, why not take the jewels instead? After all, they were likely what would have paid for her release."

He shook his head. "Murder is easily explainable in this case, but moving the body isn't. Surely if the husband killed her, he would want her body found so that he could inherit the jewels. If the maid killed her mistress for the jewels, there is no motive I can see for her to move the body."

"A task for which she is ill-suited," interjected Lestrade. "She's a dainty little thing."

"Indeed. Besides, she would surely have plenty of opportunities to take the jewels unobserved, so why kill? No, it makes sense for it to be her.

"Now, burglars might kill if disturbed or otherwise obstructed in their theft, but they would have no desire to cart off a corpse. If a creditor had her killed as a threat to her husband – and surely stealing the jewels would be more productive – the absence of a body dilutes the threat. An act of rage, unpremeditated? Perhaps – but again, the same mystery."

"Could it be something about the body would give away the killer's identity?" I said.

"Not impossible, but unlikely."

"Maybe the killer moved the body in order to buy time."

"Buy time?" said Lestrade. "Whatever do you mean?"

"You're wasting your men and your time on trying to locate the body, rather than hunting down the killer." I saw the sour expression on the inspector's face and sought to mollify him. "By waste, I make no moral judgement, nor even express a personal opinion. I only mean the words from the point of view of the killer."

"Yes, I believe you have the closest of it," said Holmes. "Buying time . . . It is the only motivation that makes sense of what little we know."

Then, he turned back to the inspector.

"Now, Lestrade," he said, "you mentioned loud arguments. I trust that it is too much to ask for an eyewitness to the events that transpired here last night, yet I can see from your face that you have more to tell."

"Not an eye witness, I'm afraid, but we do have something almost as good – something that, in my mind, serves to confirm that the husband as the guilty party."

"Really?"

"Yes. Yesterday morning, the husband and wife had a particularly loud and violent fit over breakfast – a bowl was thrown and smashed, a chair overturned in anger. During this argument, which was clearly overheard by the maid and the butcher's boy, both of whom were in the kitchen at the time, the husband declared that he wished his wife were dead so that she might be of some use to him."

"The jewels," I murmured and Lestrade nodded.

"Yes. He wished her dead and, that night, it seems she was."

"Convenient," I said.

"Nobody heard her cry out when she was killed?" countered Holmes. "Who discovered the body?"

"That's just it . . . According to the maid, she believes she did hear her mistress cry out when she was killed. But, she says, when she rose to check on her, she met her master on the landing and he told her that his wife didn't want to be disturbed, and she went back to bed until later when he woke her up."

"Well," Holmes replied, "that does all sound rather damning."

"Oh, of course, he denies saying any such thing. Mr. Jermyn claims he was asleep through much of the afternoon and evening – drunk, going by the smell of him when we arrived – and that when he woke to find his wife hadn't come to bed and the hour late, went to look for her and found the bloody mess in the dressing room, after which he roused the maid. Together they searched the house. Then he sent her to a neighbour to telephone for our assistance."

"And what did he say when you first arrived?"

"He told the first constables to reach the house that his wife must have been kidnapped by a man to whom he owed money. Indeed, he was acting more as a man inconvenienced than one worried for his wife's life when I arrived to take charge. He's a cold, uncaring man, and I have no doubt he's capable of murder.

"But," he added, "can we prove it?"

Holmes gave an odd little sigh, then suggested that it was time for us to speak to the husband and maid. Though he questioned them carefully, we learned nothing new that the inspector hadn't already gleaned. I took a dislike to Mr. Jermyn, who showed an utter lack of concern for whether his wife was alive or not, and whose agitation made me think of a zoo lion padding back and forth in its cage, ever seeking an escape.

The maid, Holmes told us, was holding something back.

Lestrade chuckled. "Probably nothing more than that butcher's boy."

"You may be right," Holmes said, but he remained thoughtful.

"Could the two of them be working together?" I said. "Mr. Jermyn and the maid, I mean."

"It seems unlikely," said Holmes. "I detected no positive feeling between the two, and the maid was quite critical of her employer's treatment of his wife, and certain he must be the killer, as well as having provided evidence to that effect. If they are confederates, it is a most-peculiar game they're playing."

"So," asked the inspector, "what do you think? Can we make a case against Mr. Jermyn? Could we prove to a jury that the man's a vicious killer, even without a body."

Holmes was silent for a moment, marshalling his thoughts. Then he said, "I think you could, but it is by no means a certainty. Of course, if this were a civil case, it would be easy to achieve, as the balance of probabilities positively screams that he did it. But in a criminal court, a man is assumed to be innocent until proven guilty, and reasonable doubt will be his shield. His wife isn't dead. Another person killed her. Those will be his arguments, and ours will be hard pressed to meet them. With his threat and what the maid has to say about him directing her not to check on her mistress, I suspect a jury would find his guilt reasonable."

The inspector smiled. "I must admit that you've quite raised my spirits, Mr. Holmes. Of course, I'm still hoping my men will locate the body, which would definitely strengthen our case against the dastard, but

I feel that, with a little more effort to tie it all together, we should have a solid case to present."

"Perhaps," said Holmes, "but I would rein your certainty for now, Inspector. There are still a couple of avenues I wish to explore first. Oh, don't grouse, Lestrade. If the man is guilty, a little more time will hardly make him innocent, but will allow us to close off an avenue or two that might lead him to a *Not Guilty* verdict."

In spite of his words, I was certain there was something he was holding back, but I didn't have a chance to think more on it because Holmes had a question for me.

"Now," he said, "did you make a note of the name of Jermyn's main creditor?"

I had. It was a Mr. Harridge. His address was about a mile away.

"Good. I want you to go and speak to him. You know what to do . . . beat the under-brush and see what emerges. Are there any indications he is involved – any thing to suggest his guilt."

"Very well," said I.

"And you, Mr. Holmes?" asked Lestrade.

"I shall take a further look at the evidence, if I may. We shall reconvene at Baker Street for afternoon tea, if you will join us, Inspector."

Lestrade gave a grudging nod, then said his farewell to me as I exited the house and sought a cab.

The home of Mr. Harridge wasn't too dissimilar from that of his debtor, yet it looked far grander, for it was well-appointed and in a cared-for condition. One could imagine that the money that should have provided the upkeep of Jermyn's house had doubtless done its duty here instead. From what Jermyn had said and Holmes had dredged up from some corner of his spectacular memory, Harridge was barely one step up from a backstreet thug, a man as unsavoury in his own particular manner as Jermyn was in his. Yet he was living well.

I rang the doorbell and the door opened to reveal a butler of imperious mien who asked me my business with a tone that implied I was dismissed before even I had spoken.

"My name is Doctor John Watson, and I am here on behalf of Mr. Sherlock Holmes with the intention of speaking to your employer." Although my friend made no effort to publicise his successes and frequently allowed others to take credit for the cases he had solved, tales of his unique investigative style and insight into the criminal mind had nonetheless spread throughout London, and his name was recognised more often than not.

"I shall tell Mr. Harridge that you are here," the butler said, leaving me standing on the doorstep for a minute or two before he returned and allowed me inside the entrance hall, where his employer was waiting.

"You wanted to speak to me?" Harridge asked. Where his butler had a refined voice and an aloof manner, Harridge's accent was still strongly that of a Cockney, and he had a bluffness to his character seldom seen in this quarter of the city. I almost wondered if the two men had swapped places in some kind of jape, then realised that the butler reflected what the man, risen thanks to his unsavoury business dealings, wished for himself – the same things every Englishman secretly wishes: Acceptance and class.

"Yes. You will be unaware, but the wife of Mr. Fitzgerald Jermyn was murdered last night."

There was no flicker of an emotion across his physiognomy, and I couldn't be certain if he were supremely controlled, or if he failed to see why such news should concern him.

"The man owes you a considerable sum of money," I pressed on.

"He does."

I decided it was probably best to be blunt with the man and sound him out.

"Were you in anyway involved in the lady's murder?"

Harridge laughed. "No! Look to Jermyn if you want a villain: The man's a blackguard, a liar, and a cheat, though I should think him too much a coward to kill anyone. Now, if you will excuse me, I am a busy man."

"Too busy to speak to Inspector Lestrade, should he have more questions?"

"If he does, they shall have to wait, for I am at this moment packing to leave for France, where I have business. Tell your inspector that I'm sorry to inconvenience him. Good day."

And with that, his butler stepped forth and practically shoved me out through the door. I stood at the bottom of the steps for a few minutes, looking up at the house and pondering the fact that the man clearly didn't want me there.

The questions in my mind as I headed back to Baker Street were whether the man had other reasons for wishing rid of me, or whether Jermyn was the killer, and I had no answer.

When I entered his rooms, I was surprised to find Holmes busy at work at some chemistry experiment.

Seeing me, he gave a satisfied look and said, "Nearly done."

Then, he glanced at the clock and added, "And well timed, too – us both – for it is very nearly the hour when the inspector is grace us with his presence. Kindly remind Mrs. Hudson that we are expecting a guest and shall shortly require afternoon tea."

I conveyed the message and returned to find that Holmes was done.

"Have you heard of the current research in the field of blood-work?" he asked out of nowhere.

"I believe I've read something about it in a medical journal," said I, somewhat nonplussed.

"I have been corresponding with some of the researchers for a while," said Holmes. "Blood, of course, is of particular fascination and relevance to me."

"Of course," I replied, not knowing where this was leading.

"They have proposed a fascinating and most-useful theory: Blood of different species is characterised by different proteins. Thus, if one knew which proteins to test for, it would be possible to tell from which species of animal blood has come from."

I told him I didn't follow.

"Including the *human* species. Early forms of the test might allow us to tell if blood – say that found at the site of an apparent murder – is human blood or animal blood. Indications are that the blood at the Jermyn house is *not* human blood."

"Wait, you mean –?"

"Yes, I do. Mrs. Olivia Jermyn hasn't been murdered. Or, at least, she wasn't murdered in her dressing room and her body carried away in a sheet."

"But . . . Goodness!"

"Goodness has nothing to do with it. Our murder scene was staged and the copious amounts of blood splashed about was that of an animal and not a human being. A-ha! And here comes the inspector. I hear the door and his familiar tread upon the stair, and now it falls to us to deliver the bad news."

To say that Lestrade was shocked by my friend's revelation would be an understatement, and it took more than a cup of Mrs. Hudson's tea to restore his spirits to their full faculty. The poor man had allowed his doubts about the existence of the crime to be wiped away, only for Holmes to reveal that he had been right to have them.

It was left to me to ask Holmes why he had even thought to test the blood.

"I mean," said I, a little shamefaced, "it seemed so obvious that someone had been attacked there."

"Oh, one must admit it was a cunning ploy and almost perfect in its execution, such that few would notice aught amiss."

"You did . . . How?"

"What first caused me to feel a pang of suspicion was the blood upon the chair. Had the person been seated, as the scene appeared to imply, there either would be no blood upon it, or else it would be smeared by them, but the blood was well-defined, copious, and appeared to have been – indeed, as we now know, must have been – *poured*.

"Then, there was the turtleshell hairbrush on the floor. There wasn't so much as a drop of blood upon it. Yes, I grant, not an impossibility, but after the chair, it gave me pause. Further, there were no splashes of blood – droplets – as would be expected from a savage attack, save those surrounding the large splotches, and the blood was oddly confined to the immediate vicinity of the chair. Again, not an impossibility, but when the unusual begins to collect, one must wonder at one's assumptions.

"Then, of course, there was the lack of even a single droplet of blood on the stairs or any floor outside of the dressing room."

I struck my brow at that.

"Of course! Given how soaked the sheet was, there ought to have been some."

"Then, there was the fact that the sheet was only half-burned. Too convenient! And the kerchief? Somehow, our killer could move a body through a house without leaving a single drop of blood, yet was leaving convenient clues to reinforce a story of murder? Nonsense!"

"Why didn't you say anything?" Lestrade almost shouted the question. "Why the charade of questioning Jermyn and the maid, and discussing how the murder might have been carried out?"

"I said nothing, my dear Lestrade, because I was still unsure. What was I missing? Questioning them, I hoped to learn something that would clarify my doubts, but all I could conclude was that Watson was right when he said someone was buying time. But who? That remained a mystery, and until I was certain about the blood, I could say no more."

"So then what? She was kidnapped? For what ends, if the jewels were stolen?"

"The jewels weren't stolen."

"You're saying they're still in the house."

"Let us return there and I think I shall be able to make everything clear."

Jermyn was just as bemused as we had been when Holmes announced the news to him and his maid that his wife was still alive. The maid, on the other hand, appeared extremely nervous, and I recalled that Holmes had earlier detected that she was concealing something.

"So," said Jermyn, "what happened to my wife?"

"She faked her death so that she could disappear," explained Holmes, "and on that score, I cannot reproach her. You truly are an obnoxious man, Mr. Jermyn."

He spluttered, but a stern look from my friend silenced him.

"There can be no doubt once every element of the case is considered. Her jewels are missing – jewels that she refused to hand over to you. Only if she went willingly and took them, her inheritance, does the situation make sense. The only reason to kidnap her would be obviated by the fact the kidnappers could take the jewels instead, and the jewels are gone. The only reason for both her and the jewels to be missing is if she chose to go and took them with her.

"Then, we consider the presence of the blood. The scene was too-clearly intended to make us think she was dead. Why would kidnappers waste time doing this?

"Where does a gentlewoman get large amounts of blood? Buckets of blood aren't something one associates with women of breeding – not even those whose husbands have fallen into penury.

"Someone else had to provide it, and where would be the best place to obtain it? Doubtless, a slaughterhouse or butcher's."

"The butcher's boy!" I exclaimed, and Holmes concurred.

"Conveniently, a witness to the most-damning words attributed to Mr. Jermyn when he argued with his wife – words I suspect were never uttered.

"How would such a lad be roped into the scheme? Hardly someone a refined woman is likely to come into contact with, let alone form a bond of sufficient trust to foment such a plot. No . . . But she might very well confide her plans to her maid, someone who sees the lad on a regular basis, perhaps developing a close attachment, allowing her to inveigle him into the conspiracy."

With a cry, the maid buried her face in her hands and began to sob, muffled words of confession escaping every so often.

Lestrade sent a constable to detain the butcher's boy for questioning and possible charges, although as he told Holmes, "I'm not entirely sure what laws apply here."

With a little gentle coaxing, Holmes managed to calm the young woman and convince her to reveal what her mistress had planned.

"She couldn't take his – " The girl gestured at her employer. " – bad behaviour any more. Then, one day, the man he owed money to came to the house. The master was out, so he insisted on talking to the mistress. Maybe he intended to scare her, or maybe he hoped to appeal to her, I don't know. What I do know is that the mistress told me how kind and pleasant he was, and she began to meet him in secret and . . . they fell in love.

"She didn't want to be married to this one any longer, so she began to think of how she might escape. Then, he began to demand her jewellery and it all fell into place. She knew I was in love with Billy and that he'd do anything what I asked him to, so she had me ask him for the blood. Then, after that last argument, she told me and Billy to lie about what he said – that he'd said he wanted her dead. She also asked me to lie about him stopping me from coming to her. She wanted him to look guilty."

"But why?" I asked. "Surely, if her plan was to give herself time to get away, just making it look like she'd been killed was enough?"

The maid gave a bitter laugh. "He treated her proper cruel, he did, and she wanted revenge. If nothing more, she wanted to damage his reputation, such as it is, even if he escaped the hangman's noose. And if he didn't . . . It's no more than he deserved."

"Where is she now?" asked Lestrade.

"France," I said, with a sudden realisation. "At least, she is if Harridge was honest about where he was headed."

No wonder the man had seemed unconcerned when I announced her death and had been so keen to have me leave. There was every possibility I'd been mere feet from her as I stood in his hallway.

The maid gave a defiant look and I knew I was right. Mrs. Jermyn was doubtless already *en route* to her new life on the Continent.

Lestrade sent constables to Harridge's house, but it was empty, the man and his staff already having departed, and Mrs. Jermyn doubtless with them. He cabled Dover, but the last ferry for the day had already left. Kent Constabulary promised that guest-houses would be checked and visitors to the county questioned, but we had no real doubts that they were already on the far side of the Channel.

When the last telephone call had been made and the final telegrams sent and received, Lestrade said, "They're beyond our reach, and there's no point in trying to get them back to England. Jermyn has no desire to have his embarrassment publicised, and there are questions of whether she or they committed a crime, and, if so, one worth pursuing."

I asked him where that left the maid and her beau.

Lestrade snorted. "I gave the pair of fools a telling-off and let them go. Easier than wasting my time trying to find something to charge them with."

Holmes smiled. "While I cannot say I approve of what she did, neither can I claim to be too disappointed to see her get away. I hope her future with Harridge is brighter than her marriage with Jermyn was. As for your pair of fools, Lestrade, I think you did right."

"All I'm certain of," said the inspector, bitterly, "is that the whole thing was an utter waste of time."

Holmes shook his head. "On the contrary. Had we not solved the mystery, there was a real, if remote, chance that an innocent man – an odious one, yes, but an innocent one – would have hanged. That miscarriage of justice was prevented. We can take satisfaction, I think, in a life saved."

# The Problem at
# Arnsworth Castle
## by Jane Rubino

"*But you will concede, Watson,*" *said Holmes as he took up his cherry-wood pipe, "that in your records of our little adventures, you have occasionally, whether by carelessness or design, referred to certain cases in such a way as to lead the public into error – particularly that segment of the public who come late to your tales, and so have no recollection or first-hand knowledge of the matter.*"

"*You will forgive me,*" *I said, with some asperity, "if, in my carelessness and guile, I have ever given you less than your due.*"

"*My dear fellow!*" *he cried. "I fare well enough in those accounts you have been so good as to publish. Rather, I refer to allusions dropped in those you have chosen not to publish. What effect do you suppose the mention of red leeches and giant rats has upon the public's imagination? Or when you cite the Arnsworth Castle business? I daresay your readers imagined us scaling battlements and crawling through dungeons.*"

"*I quoted your own words.*"

*Holmes shrugged his shoulders.*

"*Perhaps I will publish the account of it, then,*" *I grumbled, "if you do not think the public will be disappointed by the absence of battlements and dungeons.*"

"*My dear Watson, I have every confidence that, if you ever should record the case, you will not fail to do it justice . . . .*"

The matter to which Holmes referred began early on a Monday morning in February. While I waited, somewhat impatiently, for breakfast to be laid, I wandered to the window, looking from the dull sky to the barren pavement. For the past few days, the temperature had dropped and then risen, turning snowfall to an icy rain, and then overnight, the temperature had dropped once more, leaving the streets in too-treacherous a state for all but those who had a matter of some urgency to venture from hearth and home. And yet, as I looked down upon the street, I spied a lone figure, a woman in a heavy black overcoat, a shawl thrown over her head, slipping and tottering along the pavement in a distracted fashion. "What a curious figure!" I cried. "I believe she is lost. I have a mind to go down and see if I might be of some help."

Holmes rose from his armchair and came up to look over my shoulder. "There is no need to go down – I think she will soon be shown up. Surely by now, you recognize the symptoms. Note the manner that is both anxious and purposeful. See how she stops at each door – she is looking for an address, and I wouldn't be surprised if the address that she seeks is ours. Ha!" he cried triumphantly, as we heard a sharp peel of the bell.

A few moments later, Mrs. Hudson was at our threshold, but the lady from the street hurried past her and looked from one of us to the other and then cried, "Mr. Sherlock Holmes!" as, with her keen woman's instinct, she fixed upon my friend.

"Thank you Mrs., Hudson," said Holmes, and when our landlady withdrew, he closed the door and introduced me, and then said, "It is a very cold morning, Madam. Pray, take that seat near the fire."

The woman threw off her shawl as she sank into the chair, and I saw her countenance more clearly. She appeared to be a woman in early middle age, with delicate – even noble – features that might have been handsome, had her complexion not been so unnaturally pale, and her expression so agitated and drawn.

Sherlock Holmes sat beside the woman. "Clearly, it isn't ill-use by your employer that troubles you, Miss – ?"

"Bennett. Anne Bennett."

"I see that your mistress is both generous and kind."

The lady gave a start. "Do you know Lady Frances?"

"I know that you wear a coat and frock of excellent material, though some years out of date and with signs that they have been altered for your figure – the previous wearer was a somewhat shorter woman. It isn't uncommon for a lady to pass down items of her wardrobe to her personal maid. Boots," he added, with a nod to the lady's footwear, "will not fit as readily as a frock, however. Those you wear are new and of the best quality, and far more costly than a lady's maid salary will allow. A mistress who makes such a gift must be a kind one."

"Yes, her Ladyship is very kind."

"Lady Frances."

"Yes – Lady Frances Arnsworth. Her father was the Earl of Rosemont, and her husband was the late Philip Arnsworth."

"She is a widow, then."

"Yes. She had been widowed the year before I came into the household. The late Mr. Arnsworth had been a very successful businessman – coal and shipping, for the most part – and he left his wife a considerable fortune."

"How long have you been in her Ladyship's service?"

"Nearly twenty years." Her faint smile seemed to anticipate what Holmes was too diplomatic to ask. "I was just twenty-one when I was offered the post. I am forty now. Ill health compelled her previous maid to give up the post rather suddenly, and though I had very little in the way of references or experience, I had the advantage of being a very distant and very poor relation. Lady Frances agreed to give me the post, and I have been with her ever since."

"You have a mistress who is both generous and kind, an excellent situation, and a pleasant one, if you have remained with it for nearly twenty years. And yet something quite unpleasant – and quite pressing, I presume – must have occurred to bring you out on such a morning."

"I don't know whether it is pressing or trivial! That is the worst of it! It may be that there is no real cause for alarm. If there were anyone I might turn to – but I have neither family nor friends to advise me as to what I ought to do."

"My dear Miss Bennett – what you ought to do is to tell me what alarms you, and I will do my best to furnish the advice. I assume that it is a domestic matter, in which case," he said as he leaned back in his chair and stretched his long legs toward the fire, "you might do well to begin by telling me something of the household."

"As I said," began the lady, "the late Mr. Arnsworth was a wealthy man, yet while he and Lady Frances were generous toward their staff and a number of public charities, they preferred to live in a modest style. Not long after their marriage, they came upon a villa at Hampstead. It was far more humble than the country manors and town mansions of their acquaintance, but it struck their fancy, and so they purchased it and, on a whim – or perhaps as a jest directed toward those mansions and manors – decided to call it Arnsworth Castle. It is no castle, not by any means, but the rooms have the advantage of both comfort and taste, and the grounds are lovely. In fact, the gardens were laid out by Lady Frances herself. She is a fellow of the Royal Horticultural Society, and even won a prize for a hybrid that she crossed, the Rosemont Gold.

"As for the staff, it isn't a large one – there is the cook and manservant, who are a married couple, and two maids. All have been with the household for many years. As for her Ladyship, she is now seventy-three, but still quite active. She is often asked to give an address to the Horticultural Society and continues to be involved in several charities. When the weather allows, she will do most of the gardening herself. Of course, she isn't without her eccentricities – I imagine that most wealthy people have the means to indulge their fads and fancies, and that they aren't uncommon to those of her age. But on the whole, I couldn't wish for a better mistress."

"And what are her eccentricities?"

"Her meals, for example. Lady Frances prefers to dine at midday, and her evening meal is no more than a full tea. She continues to wear only black, though it has been more than twenty years since she was widowed. Yet while her dress is very modest, it is always adorned with an item of rather costly jewelry. It had been the late Mr. Arnsworth's custom to present his wife with jewels on their wedding anniversary, and she now has a quite valuable collection, and wears one of the pieces every day. She will not entrust them to her banker, but keeps them in a jewel case that is laid on her dressing table every morning, so that she may choose which she will wear, and then every night, before she retires, she will make certain each piece is accounted for, and then lock the case away in a small safe at night."

"Where is this safe?" Holmes asked.

"In her bedchamber."

"Pray, continue."

"Other than her jewels and her flower gardens, she had one other object of devotion, and that was Teddy, who passed a few months ago."

"I think that it must be more painful to lose a child than a spouse," I said.

"Oh, no – Lady Frances and her husband had no children. Teddy was her dog. Many years ago, her Ladyship had been returning from an appointment when she spied the little beast shivering in the gutter and brought him home." A faint smile passed over the woman's face. "I think there may be children who aren't loved as much as Lady Frances loved that dog, and I don't think any parent wept over the loss of a child more than she wept over Teddy when he died. Teddy was one reason that she felt her jewels were secure. Her chamber and sitting room are on the ground floor, and the long windows open upon a small veranda and gardens. Teddy slept in her room, and it took little more than a gust of wind to wake him. If anyone set foot upon the veranda, much less tried the windows or doors, I daresay his bark would 'rouse every living soul for a mile around."

"Other than the loss of Teddy, your portrait is of a very tranquil household, Miss Bennett, and yet, you are twisting your wrap into knots."

The lady looked down at her hands which indeed had been wringing at the shawl upon her lap. "Until quite recently," she sighed, "it had been very peaceful."

"And what has occurred to disrupt that peace, and how recently?"

"As I have said, Lady Frances and her husband had no children, but Mr. Arnsworth had a younger sister, who married a poor Frenchman named Gorot. Both died a year or so before Mr. Arnsworth, leaving behind a son – Richard – who was perhaps three or four years of age. There was only a pittance left for the boy's maintenance, and so Mr. Arnsworth made arrangements for his nephew's care. He brought the boy to England and had him placed in a school, supported him at university, and set aside an allowance that he might claim after he left university, so long as he met with certain conditions. Unhappily, Mr. Arnsworth died the following year, but to her credit, Lady Frances has faithfully carried out her husband's wishes regarding the boy, providing for his education, and even bringing him to Arnsworth Castle on his school holidays."

"Has he left university?"

"Yes, nearly three years ago. He then took rooms in town, though he has had a standing invitation to come to Arnsworth Castle on week-ends."

"I think very few young men will prefer week-ends in a quiet Hampstead villa with an elderly aunt over the diversions of London," Holmes observed. "Unless that allowance you spoke of will not support them. You said it was dependent upon certain conditions. What were they?"

"Her Ladyship once told me that her husband believed amusement and indulgence to be the ruin of too many young men. Mr. Arnsworth had come from nothing, began as a clerk in a shipping company, and by way of hard work, had made his way upward. It was his desire that his nephew should do the same. He decided that Richard, after he left university, ought to be given just enough to find lodgings and that once he found employment, he would receive an allowance, paid to him quarterly, in the amount equal to his salary."

"Certainly that would be an incentive for the young man to apply himself."

"It ought to have been," she replied. "And yet, I know from her Ladyship that Richard was an unexceptional student. I imagine that he got on by employing the same coaxing manners that he employs to get around his aunt."

"The aunt who controls his allowance."

"Yes. When Richard left university, he found – or, rather, was given – a post as clerk at a firm that had been his uncle's, and which was now managed by the sons of his uncle's former partner. He began at fifty pounds-a-year, which is very little for a young man to live on in London, but the clever ones will advance very quickly and their salary will rise as well."

"And those unexceptional ones who hope to get by on coaxing manners will not. Of course, his allowance gives him an additional fifty pounds, and he might find ways to practice economy – sharing lodgings, for example," Holmes added with a smile.

"He might if he had a turn for economy, but few young men do, I think. I know that once or twice, over the past months, Richard spoke to his aunt privately, and afterward she confided to me that he was distressed for money and asked if his allowance might be increased. He told her that that fellows who began with him at the firm are now earning three times as much, but that his employers deliberately hold him back so as to avoid any charge of favoritism toward Mr. Arnsworth's nephew. He said that if he is to mix with those who might help him advance, he must dress the part, and go about now and again, and that this couldn't be done on a hundred pounds-a-year."

"And was her Ladyship persuaded to be more liberal?"

"I think it pained her – she wished to honor her late husband's wishes, and at the same time, help the young man toward independence. Once or twice, I believe he was able to coax her out of a small gift of money, and his display of condolence and commiseration when poor Teddy died got him a hundred pounds. Then, there was an incident, little more than a month ago, that might have undone all of his fawning. He came to Arnsworth Castle for his weekend visit – or rather, he was *brought* there, and somewhat the worse for drink."

"Brought by whom?"

"A gentleman named Talbot – Sir George Talbot – who had put up Richard's name at his own club. It seems that Richard had been spending much of his time there, among, I suspect, a very fast set, where there was a great deal of . . . ."

"Amusement and indulgence?" said Holmes.

"So I imagine. Sir George took full blame for urging Richard to drink more than he ought, and he apologized so persuasively, and smoothed over the matter in such a winning fashion, that Lady Frances forgave all and invited Sir George to tea. I take my meals with her Ladyship and so I was able to observe that, whatever charms her nephew might possess, they were nothing to those displayed by Sir George Talbot. He is a remarkably handsome gentleman, his manners were faultless, and there seemed to be no subject that he couldn't address with intelligence and wit.

"He happened to admire the diamond-and-sapphire bracelet that Lady Frances wore – it is her favorite piece, and most valuable, I believe – and with some authority, proceeded to remark upon the gemstones' clarity and absence of inclusion, terms which meant nothing to me, but Lady Frances was flattered. She took the gentleman's praise as a tribute to her late husband's taste. She even removed the bracelet so that he might examine it more closely. He studied it carefully, and then with a show of gallantry, fastened it back upon her wrist. He left not long after. Lady Frances invited him to call again. Richard saw him out, and returned as the maids were clearing the table, and it was then that Lady Frances noticed that her bracelet was missing."

"Indeed!"

"Oh, it was found after a brief search. Richard spied it beneath her chair, and said that perhaps his friend hadn't fastened it properly. Her relief seemed to put them back on good terms – Richard' drunkenness was forgotten, and to further ingratiate himself, he arrived on the following Saturday with a gift – a replacement for Teddy – the most ungainly, unruly canine creature you ever beheld. From the first, the little beast caused such turmoil that if Richard had chosen to deliberately plague the household, he couldn't have done better. Scamp – for that is his name – immediately made himself at home. In those first days, he dragged the coal scuttle across the carpet, tore three cushions to shreds, yanked the cloth and everything upon it from the breakfast table so that he might gobble up a plate of rashers.

"He has claimed the chair nearest the fire as his own, and there he lies, working the marrow out of one of the great soup bones that Richard brings for him. When the marrow is gone, and the bone has been reduced to a hollow cylinder, Scamp will carry it to the window and paw and whine until he is let out upon the grounds, so that he might bury it, and then return to demand another – but not before he has dug holes on the lawn, uprooted the bulbs, and gnawed at the shrubbery. It is a mercy that he hasn't yet exhumed Teddy, who was laid under Lady Frances' favorite rose bush."

I saw Holmes's mouth twitch for a second and struggled to repress my own laughter.

"It was with these events, some weeks ago – Richard' episode of drunkenness and the arrival of Scamp – that the problem became evident, though there may have been some earlier signs that simply went unnoticed."

"What problem?"

"Lady Frances has become rather absent-minded. I know Richard' hints and pleas for money have unsettled her, and certainly Scamp's mischief would drive the most rational person to distraction. Of course," she conceded, "it is possible that her forgetfulness may be a symptom of advancing age."

"And how does this forgetfulness manifest itself?"

"Lady Frances has begun to misplace things – a brooch, a jeweled hairpin, an earring. She insists that she laid the item on her dressing table, but when she goes to return it to her jewel case, it is gone, only to turn up afterward in a drawer or under a napkin or beneath a cushion. Not long ago, a pearl ring was lost for two days and was discovered in a letter tray under her correspondence."

276

"Has it always been an item of jewelry?" Holmes asked.

"Well, once a silver butter knife was found on her Ladyship's secretary desk, and an amber comb in the coal scuttle, but yes, for the most part, it has been one of her jewels."

"Has Lady Frances been examined by a doctor?" I asked. "Unhappily, these may be the early symptoms of senility."

"I would think so, too, if her Ladyship's inattentiveness applied to other matters – if she neglected the household accounts, or forgot what day of the week it was, or addressed one of the staff by another's name – but the problem seems confined to the mislaying of a small personal item."

"And you must acknowledge that to mislay a choice memento need not be a symptom of mental decline," I said to Holmes. "I believe that you once found the remains of the last cigar smoked by Palmer the poisoner in our butter dish."

"I wish that her Ladyship's bracelet *would* turn up in the butter dish," Miss Bennett said earnestly.

"What – the diamond and sapphire bracelet you spoke of? Has it been lost?"

"Yes, and we have all but turned Arnsworth Castle upside down looking for it."

Holmes leaned forward in his chair, and rubbed his hands together. "Tell me everything that occurred yesterday to the point where the loss was discovered – and pray, omit nothing."

"On Sunday, the entire household attends services at the parish church. The staff will lay out breakfast, go off to the nine o'clock service, and return at eleven. Then Lady Frances, Richard, and I leave to attend the eleven-thirty service."

"And her jewel case had been taken from the safe and laid on her dressing table?"

"Yes."

"Did her Ladyship wear the bracelet?"

"No – I believe she thinks it is too extravagant for church. She wore a pearl necklace. The bracelet remained in her jewel case. I saw it myself."

"And the jewel case remained on her dressing table all day?"

"Yes. The staff returned and Scamp, seeing that her Ladyship was preparing to go out, began to howl. He is as attached to Lady Frances as she is to him, and he doesn't like for her to go off and leave him behind. He snatched her Ladyship's shawl and led us all on a merry chase, finally retreating under her bed. At last, Richard lured him out with a good, stout marrow bone and the little beast was persuaded to exchange the shawl for the bone. He was settled on his favorite chair with his prize, and so we closed the sitting room doors to prevent him from getting into mischief and made our escape. At one o'clock, we returned, and Lady Frances went straight to the dining room where there was a good fire, and asked me to put away her overcoat and bonnet and bring Scamp to her. When I passed through the sitting room, I came upon Richard standing at the French windows, looking out upon the grounds."

"'Where is Scamp?' I asked.

"I saw that I had startled him, and turning from the window, he said, 'He was scratching at the glass, so I thought it best to open the window and let him out. He snatched up his bone and made straight for the grounds,' he added with a laugh. 'You needn't wait – he will settle on the perfect burial plot and then hurry out of the cold and I will bring him to my aunt.'

"I looked out upon the grounds, which were sodden and marked with patches of crusted slush. 'No, you go to your aunt, Richard. I'll ring for Sarah and have her bring a basin and towels to clean Scamp so that he doesn't track mud through the house.'

"He protested that he had let the dog out into the dirt and ought to be the one to clean him up, but I had already rung for the maid and so he went off to dine. The remainder of our Sunday passed in the usual fashion. After tea, Richard prepared for his return to town, and offered to exercise Scamp before he left. 'It will spare the staff the trouble,' he said. 'I must go out in this vile weather anyway.'

"'Very kind, Richard, but Radley will see to him. I believe Scamp has fallen asleep.' She then took a candlestick from the sideboard, lit the candle, and pushed open the door to her chamber to reveal Scamp, curled up and snoring loudly, upon her bed. As she turned away, her gaze fell upon the jewel case, and she gave a start and declared that it had been moved. She then raised the candle in one hand, she threw back the jewel case lid with the other, and spilled its contents onto her dressing table.

"'My bracelet!' she cried. 'It's gone!'

"'Now, Aunt, be calm,' Richard urged. "'I'm certain you have just laid it down somewhere and forgotten about it. You have misplaced other pieces, and they have all turned up.'

"'It was right here the morning. I have *not* misplaced it!' she insisted, and her hand began to tremble so badly that the candle tumbled from it's holder and dropped to the carpet, setting the dressing table's skirt afire.

"Great Heavens!" I cried.

"Her Ladyship, by instinct, reached for her jewels, but I pushed her away and screamed, 'Fire!' and then took up the water jug to douse the flames."

"And young Gorot? He got her Ladyship to safety, no doubt."

Miss Bennett shook her head. "No, he ran to the bed and seized Scamp – "

"His impulse was to save the dog and not his aunt!" I ejaculated.

"Yes, I thought it strange at the time," said Miss Bennett. "*Very* strange when I reflect upon it – but in an emergency, we do not always think clearly."

"Well, you did, Madam," replied Holmes. "Pray, continue."

"Richard hurried toward the door, Scamp in his arms, but the dog leapt free and ran back to Lady Frances, seized the hem of her skirt in his jaws, and attempted to drag her toward the door. I had doused the flames – they weren't very great – and smothered them with the bedspread for good measure, and by then, the servants had rushed to the scene. Lady Frances was helped to an armchair in the sitting room, and sat cradling Scamp on her lap while the servants tore away the dressing table skirt and ensured that the flames had been thoroughly snuffed out.

"When that commotion settled, Lady Frances ordered her jewel case brought to her, and going through it piece by piece, she saw that each item was accounted for, except for the bracelet."

"The most valuable piece, you said. What was its value, pray?"

"I believe it was last appraised at nearly twenty-thousand pounds."

Holmes let out a low whistle. "What did you do next?"

"Richard continued to insist that the bracelet had only been misplaced, and to soothe his aunt's distress, he asked the servants look around, paying particular attention to any place that the other lost items had turned up. When it wasn't found, he said, 'I must not miss my train back to town, but you must have Bennett wire me daily with any news. I depend upon it, Aunt, though I am confident that your bracelet will turn up well before my return on Friday.'"

"He was certainly very cool about it," said Holmes.

"I thought so, too, Mr. Holmes, though he was correct to say that all of her Ladyship's other misplaced items had been found. I decided that the best course was to lock away the jewel case and then have one of the spare rooms made up for Lady Frances until her own chamber could be aired and cleaned.

"When Richard left, I urged Lady Frances to take a sleeping draught and settled her in a spare bedroom. Then I made another search of the house, probed every drawer and corner and cranny but with no success, and then let Scamp out the sitting room window for a nature call before I retired. As he waddled onto the lawn, the clouds happened to part and in the moonlight I saw – I believe that I saw – "

The lady began to twist at the shawl upon her lap once more.

"What did you see, Miss Bennett?"

279

"A man – no more than a shadow – creeping across the lawns. I cried out, 'Here now! I have a police-whistle!' and then Scamp began to bark furiously and the shadow retreated toward the hedgerow that surrounds the property."

"You are quite certain that it was a man's shadow?"

"Well, it was not Scamp, but it may have been a trick of the moonlight."

"Would the dog have barked at a trick of moonlight?"

The woman's sigh conceded to Holmes's point.

"What did you do next?"

"I was too shaken to sleep, so when Scamp came back inside, I secured the window and put him in the spare room with her Ladyship. I then returned to the sitting room, lit a lamp, and took up a book, though I scarcely read a word. As soon as it was light, I dressed and summoned one of the maids. I told her than I had an urgent errand in town, and she was to see to Lady Frances until I returned. I came straight to you, Mr. Holmes – I have read you in the newspapers, and so I thought perhaps you might hear me out and tell me what I should do."

Holmes was silent for several minutes, and then he asked a peculiar question: "The dog – young Gorot gave it to his aunt in lieu of the one that died. You said that he couldn't have chosen a more troublesome animal. Why did he choose it? Did it resemble the dog his aunt had lost? Or it a favorite breed of the lady?"

The lady shook her head. "He looks nothing like Teddy. He is an ungainly lump of a mongrel. I believe Richard said that a friend or colleague had told him of a tradesman in Lambeth who takes in stray dogs and – "

Holmes sat bolt upright. "Lambeth? Did Gorot mention this benevolent gentleman's name?"

"He didn't say. I imagine that Richard chose the creature because the fellow wanted to get rid of him and would let him go cheap."

"Hmm! And the dog keeps to the house, for the most part?"

"He is allowed to come and go out as he likes. The lawns and gardens are a graveyard of his buried bones."

"But he sleeps inside the house."

"Yes, with her Ladyship."

"And the grounds are surrounded by a hedgerow, you say?"

"Yes. There is a gate at the front path, though both the gate and the hedge are no more than four feet high."

"Not enough to keep out an active man, then?"

"Or woman, I think," she replied, with a faint smile.

Holmes sat for some minutes with his elbow propped upon the arm of his chair, his chin resting on his fist as he stared into the fire.

"Where does young Gorot work?"

"Talbot and Sons – it's in the vicinity of Fenchurch Street."

"And how late does he work?"

"Until six or six-thirty, I think. Somewhat earlier on Friday, because he usually is at Arnsworth Castle for tea."

"At this time of year, it would be past sunset," Holmes muttered. "And what is his club?"

"Crockford's. I believe that is what Sir George said."

"Ah. Well, Miss Bennett, there are one or two enquiries I should like to make this morning, before I decide how to proceed."

"You do not think the matter is trivial then?" she said, in some relief.

"A bracelet worth twenty-thousand pounds has been lost, Madam. No, I do not think it is trivial. In the meantime, I would suggest that you return to Arnsworth Castle and do what you can to reassure your mistress. Within a day's time – less, perhaps – you will hear from me again."

Holmes saw the lady to the door, and then turned to me. "The weather aggravates your old wound, I daresay."

"I'm still soldier enough, if you need me," was my reply.

"I may need you for an evening's vigil, but it may be a long and cold one."

"Then I am your man."

With that, Holmes retreated to his room and emerged dressed in a modest tweed suit, carrying an overcoat and hat that had seen some wear, a spot of color brightening his cheeks. With his remarkable powers of disguise, he had transformed himself from the astute thinker and scientist to an earnest young clerk down on his luck. Without a word, he departed in this costume and didn't return until it dusk, whereupon he threw off his camouflage and rang for a plate of sandwiches and a pot of tea. "You will want a dark overcoat and hat," he said to me. "Fortunately in this weather, you may cover your face with your muffler and it will not be taken amiss."

Clearly, his investigations of the afternoon had directed him toward a course of action that had us hurrying through our simple meal and then bundling ourselves against the bitter cold for a journey to Hampstead.

Arnsworth Castle was a large property at the end of a row of villas, a handsome brick-and-stone residence, surrounded by grounds and set well back from the road. There was no sweep, only a narrow path that led from the gate to the front door, and the gate was set into a thick hedgerow that enclosed the house and grounds.

Holmes unfastened the gate and we slipped onto the property, keeping to the shadows as we made our way around toward the gardens.

A faint light from the curtained sitting room windows gave some illumination to the veranda and grounds and we were able to make out the landscape. Upon the stretch of lawn were silhouettes of a half-dozen dogwood trees, and spheres of burlap sacking that, I imagine, covered up rose bushes. The lawn itself was a broad stretch that would have been even but for what appeared to be a scattering of mole hills. "Scamp's burial grounds," Holmes chuckled.

In the far corner was a veteran oak that may have pre-dated the villa itself, it's broad trunk at least three feet in diameter, its thick limbs groaning and shuddering in the wind. "That must be our screen," Holmes said, and he led me across the far boundary of the garden to the great tree.

We wedged ourselves into a narrow recess between the tree and the hedge, a hiding-place that gave us some shelter from the strong winds. To this point Holmes had said nothing, but as we settled in for our vigil, he laid aside the lantern he had brought, drew a flask from his pocket, and handed it to me. "What do you make of the garden?" he asked in a low voice. "It is well laid, eh? One doesn't always see such a happy marriage of artistry and common sense."

"It must be quite pleasant in spring and summer."

"Not the work of a woman whose mind is weakening."

"The loss of mental powers may come on slowly or quite suddenly."

"Or a woman may be persuaded that her wits are failing, so that when a valuable piece of jewelry is stolen, she may believe – or be made to believe – that she has simply mislaid it."

"A vile trick to play on an elderly woman, if that is the case. But, of course, you haven't met the woman herself."

"I have not, but today I did meet some interesting young men. In the character of a fellow looking for a berth, I lunched at a public house on Fenchurch Street, one patronized by clerks from the nearby offices – Talbot and Sons, among them. I struck up a conversation with a few of them and found that Miss Bennett's assessment of Gorot was universal: His manners are charming, but his performance is slipshod. Everybody likes him, but no one wants to work with him. There are whispers that he would have been sacked if old Talbot hadn't been a close friend of Arnsworth.

"I slipped Talbot's name into the conversation and learned that several weeks ago, Sir George had come to the office on a matter of business. This was, quite likely, the occasion when he and Gorot met. I daresay Gorot saw Talbot as a man of the world and his entrée into the sort of society that can't be managed on a hundred pounds-a-year, while Talbot, whose gambling losses have burdened him with number of debts of honor, saw a young fellow who was the sole relation, and presumably the sole heir, of an elderly – and very wealthy – woman. He befriends the young man, arranges to meet his aunt, admires the valuable bracelet she wears, learns that it is one of a collection of jewels – and so a scheme is set in motion to make off with them."

"'Them'?"

"I daresay the bracelet was meant only to be the first."

"And this scheme was Talbot's?"

"I don't think that an unremarkable student and slipshod employee would have the imagination for it. He was a willing accomplice, but no more."

Holmes paused abruptly and held up his hand for silence. After a moment, I detected what Holmes's keen hearing had already picked up: A rustling of shrubbery and a cautious footfall padding across the lawns.

Holmes put his lips to my ear, and whispered, "He's come!"

"Talbot?"

"Gorot. We must wait until he has it in his possession."

"Has what?"

"The bracelet!" he hissed.

"I thought you said he'd stolen it."

Holmes shook his head, vigorously. "I said he'd made off with it."

I sighed. "Perhaps instead of attempting to understand, I ought to just have you tell me what you want me to do."

Holmes slowly rose to a standing position. "I'll go for him as soon as he's got it. On my order, light the lantern."

Holmes stepped around the oak's broad trunk and, peering into the dark, he crept forward a few paces. "Now, Watson, now!" he hissed, and I illuminated the lantern and threw its beam toward the lawns.

The light picked up a man's figure springing up from the grass. I caught a muffled face and pair of startled eyes, and then Holmes sprang at the fellow and the two figures tumbled, wrestling, into the shadows. Holmes's cry and the scuffle set off a frantic barking from the sitting room, and I saw the curtain drawn back and the window opened to release a stout, barking canine upon the grounds. The intruder managed to free himself from Holmes's grasp and, with the dog at his heels, he bolted across the lawns, scrambled over the hedge, and vanished.

"Holmes!" I cried as I dashed toward my friend. "Are you all right?"

"Scarcely the worse for wear, but at least I have it," he replied. He held up what appeared to be a dirty wooden cylinder and then, pocketing the object, he called out, "Good boy, Scamp!"

At the sound of his name, the creature turned away from the hedgerow and ceased barking, then trotted up to us, his bulk wriggling in excitement. "Good boy!" Holmes said again, and gathering the dog under one arm, he walked toward the veranda where the silhouettes of two ladies stood at the window.

"Miss Bennett!" Holmes called out.

"Is it . . . Mr. Holmes?"

"And Doctor Watson – and Scamp as well."

The two ladies stood back and allowed us to enter a handsomely furnished sitting-room. Holmes set the dog down and looked from Miss Bennet to her elderly companion, a delicate, black-garbed lady who surveyed us with the keen – if somewhat puzzled – expression of a woman whose wits were in good order.

"I hope you will forgive the dirt," said Holmes, with a gesture toward his soiled coat and trousers. "I was compelled, with Scamp's able assistance, to discourage an intruder."

"Lady Frances, may I present Mr. Sherlock Holmes and Doctor Watson. This morning, I consulted with them about your bracelet – I am sorry if I transgressed, but I made up my mind that it was them or the police."

"At least," said the lady with a grave smile, "you did not consult with an alienist."

"There is no need for that, my Lady," said Holmes. And then, drawing the object from his pocket, I saw that it wasn't a cylinder of wood, but a stout, hollowed-out bone.

Scamp began to bark and bound at the sight of his prize. "If I may, Madam," he said, taking out his handkerchief and wiping the bone clean of its dirt. "I will return this to Scamp – but first," he added, poking a finger into the center of the object, "I must return what is yours." And with that, he drew out a glittering blue-and-crystalline object.

"My bracelet!"

Holmes dropped the bracelet into the lady's outstretched hand and presented the bone to the dog.

She clasped the object to her bosom. "Do you say that the bracelet was inside one of Scamp's buried bones?" she cried. "You must be a very clever dog indeed!" she said to the canine, who wriggled against her skirts, delighted with what he took for praise.

"Clever enough," said Holmes. "But I think blame for the theft of the bracelet must be laid elsewhere. Pray sit, Madam, and I will tell you what I know, and what conclusions I have drawn from what I know. How you proceed from there is entirely up to you."

Miss Bennett helped her mistress into a chair and then sat beside her, while Scamp settled at her feet, the bone between his paws.

"You may sit as well," said Lady Frances to Holmes. "You needn't worry about dirt on the cushions – Scamp has done worse, I assure you."

Holmes and I sat, and Holmes said, "I must warn your Ladyship that in explaining what has occurred, I must say what you may not wish to hear."

"If it is the truth, I am not afraid to hear it."

"This morning, Miss Bennett came to ask for my help in finding your bracelet. She said that lately you had misplaced certain items, an occurrence which might suggest that the bracelet, too, had been simply mislaid and would turn up. Now there were certain points in Miss Bennett's account that were quite suggestive, the most significant among them was the fact that these episodes all occurred within the past few weeks. If your seeming forgetfulness had been a chronic and long-standing trait, or if it had been accompanied by some other recent medical issue, I would be inclined to think that consulting a doctor rather than a detective would have been the better choice. But as a detective, I look not only to the incident itself, but to any relevant occurrences that may have preceded it. Any recent incident that might have been out of the ordinary."

"Nothing extraordinary has recently occurred at Arnsworth Castle – except, of course, for Teddy."

"Your dog who died."

"Yes."

"Well, let us begin there, then. The loss of your dog distressed you, but it was not the only cause for distress – you were troubled by your nephew's continual pleas for money."

Lady Frances looked toward her maid, whose face flushed. Still, Miss Bennett defended the disclosures. "I did not think it right to withhold anything from Mr. Holmes," she said.

"Quite right!" Holmes declared. "Neither a doctor nor a detective can decide upon the treatment if the symptoms have been withheld. Your young nephew's arguments for his allowance to be increased became more pressing when he was introduced to Sir George Talbot."

Lady Frances seemed to consider the truth of the statement and then nodded.

"Talbot brings young Richard to his club, introduces him to a circle far above what his hundred-pounds-a-year might procure. They become on terms intimate enough for confidences to be exchanged, whereupon Sir George learns that his young friend is the sole relation of a very wealthy woman. Now, whether it was Richard who told Sir George of your jewels, or whether the subject came up when that gentleman was invited to tea, it was clear that you kept jewelry worth tens of thousands here at Arnsworth Castle. To a gentleman in debt – and I have learned that Sir George is quite heavily in debt – the prospect of making off with such a prize would have been irresistible. But there were obstacles to getting at the jewels in your home. Burgling a home is a precarious undertaking for all but the most skilled cracksman. So the scheme wasn't to get into the home, but to get the jewels out of it. Difficult, but not impossible – provided one has a pair of willing accomplices."

"Richard," the lady murmured. "But who was the other?"

"The other, Madam, is lying at your feet."

"What – Scamp?"

At the sound of his name, the dog looked up and cocked his head.

"Your nephew told Miss Bennett that Scamp had been acquired from a purveyor in Lambeth, a man who collected dogs from the streets and sold them when he could. She didn't have to give me the fellow's name. I have some peculiar associates who have been of use to me in the past, and I suspected that one of them was the fellow who sold the dog – not to your nephew, but to a handsome, aristocratic fellow, some years older than Gorot."

"Sir George Talbot," said Miss Bennett.

Holmes nodded. "The gentleman knew precisely what sort of dog he sought – one that has a tendency to *cache*."

"To . . . *what*?"

"Caching is a behavior exhibited by certain dogs, often those who have been abandoned and have to fend for themselves. They will compulsively bury objects – food, bones, toys – and apparently Scamp had a boundless propensity for this behavior, as you yourself observed. There are nearly three-dozen mounds scattered around your lawns where Scamp has laid his depleted bones to rest.

"Talbot had your nephew give you the dog – as a replacement for the one you lost presumably. Now, as to your jewels: During the day, they are left on your dressing table. You saw no harm in it – no visitor would enter your bedchamber, and your household are all long-time, trusted servants. But when you and your servants are in another part of the house, it would be nothing for someone to enter and take an item – not to steal it, but merely to lay it elsewhere so that you, Lady Frances, would be persuaded that you had simply misplaced it. As for the bracelet: You stated, Miss Bennett, that yesterday, when you returned from church, Lady Frances went to the dining room, and when you were sent to fetch Scamp, you found young Gorot in the sitting room, watching at the window as the dog buried another of his bones – bones generously supplied by the young man himself. I have no doubt that while you went into the dining room, Gorot came up, took the bracelet, worked it into Scamp's hollowed bone, and set him loose upon the grounds. An ingenious hiding place – once the dog consumed all of the marrow from the bone, a bracelet, a ring, a brooch would fit very nicely into the cavity. Scamp would bury it, and sometime after the household had retired for the night, Gorot would retrieve it. When the loss of your bracelet was discovered, the young man immediately tried to persuade you, Lady Frances, that you had merely misplaced it and that it would soon be found, as the other items had been. But then, there was a very curious incident: You, Lady Frances, were so shaken that you dropped the candle and set your dressing table afire."

"Under the circumstances," protested the lady, "I don't think it was curious that I should be shaken."

"Nor do I. But I have had the advantage of past observation, you see, and have noted that in a fire, a person will seize what is most treasured. A mother will reach for her child, a childless woman will reach for her jewels, and I, were I your nephew, Madam, would have immediately carried *you* out of the room. And true to form, young Gorot went for what he most treasured – the accomplice essential to the scheme to rob you of your jewels."

Lady Frances brushed back a tear and leaned down to stroke the dog's broad head.

"Then it was Richard that I saw last night!" said Miss Bennett.

"Yes. Your cries frightened him off, and then remained in the sitting room all night, with the lamps lit, which would discourage him from a second attempt. But when I heard your account, Miss Bennet, I had no doubt that he – or his wicked ally – would not hesitate to make a second attempt as soon as possible. And as that is the case," Holmes added, addressing Lady Frances. "I might suggest that if you treasure those gifts from your husband, you would do well to entrust them to the safety of a bank vault without delay. As for how to proceed with Master Richard, I leave that to you. Perhaps tonight's adventure will have frightened him into remorse and reform. As for this wayward accomplice," said Holmes as he rose and reached down to pet the dog. "I think remorse is foreign to his character, and reform is not possible, so you must settle for a respited sentence with a recommendation of mercy."

*"When a woman thinks that her house is on fire, her instinct is at once to rush to the thing which she values most. It is a perfectly overpowering impulse, and I have more than once taken advantage of it. In the case of the Darlington substitution scandal it was of use to me, and also in the Arnsworth Castle business. A married woman grabs at her baby; an unmarried one reaches for her jewel-box."*

– Sherlock Holmes
"A Scandal in Bohemia"

# NOTES

1.  Crockford's: A gentleman's club noted for gambling, long defunct.
2.  Palmer the poisoner: William Palmer, a.k.a. The Prince of Poisoners, is cited in "The Speckled Band" as an example of a doctor whose nerve and knowledge make him "*the first of criminals*" when he goes wrong.
3.  A tradesman at Lambeth who takes in stray dogs: Very likely old Sherman, who provides Toby in *The Sign of Four*.
4.  Caching behavior: An innate survival behavior, not limited to dogs. The animal will hide or bury food or other objects to be retrieved later.

# The Etherege Case
## by Hugh Ashton

*"I heard from you from Mrs. Etherege, whose husband you found so easy when the police and everyone had given him up for dead."*
— Mary Sutherland
"A Case of Identity"

There are those who would have it that Mr. Sherlock Holmes, the celebrated detective, was a man devoid of human feeling or emotion. In that number, one might be tempted to include Holmes himself, who would at times refer to himself as a machine or engine, needing action to continue its useful existence.

However, as one who was proud to be called "friend" by Holmes, I was privileged to observe this unique individual at close quarters for extended periods. In truth, I believe I was the best placed in the whole world to be able to pass judgement on him, and I can categorically state that Sherlock Holmes, whatever face he cared to present to the world, was in private far from being the inhuman reasoning machine that formed his public image.

I do not mean to state that he was sentimental or given to deep displays of emotion, but, quite apart from whatever marks of friendship and, dare I say it, love, that existed between him and me, he was deeply attached to our long-suffering landlady, Mrs. Hudson, in small ways which demonstrated themselves on an almost imperceptible, but near daily, basis.

For young Wiggins, the chief, if he may so be termed, of The Baker Street Irregulars, the group of street urchins that served as Holmes's eyes and ears in the metropolis, he had a particular affection. Recognising Wiggins's natural abilities, Holmes recommended him to the police officers with whom he enjoyed friendly relations, and when Wiggins entered the force as a constable, remained zealous for his advancement, at last having the satisfaction of seeing his protégé promoted to the rank of Inspector.

The mask of inscrutability which Holmes wore when investigating a case did, upon occasion, slip, and it was evident that a man who experienced the same passions and emotions as did the rest of humanity was there.

One affair where this was particularly apparent was the strange case of Mr. Josiah Etherege, whose conclusion, I confess, brought tears to my eyes, as it did to those of Holmes, much as he might care to deny such a thing.

As with so many of Holmes's cases, it started with a letter, enclosed in an envelope simply addressed to "*Sir Sherlock Homes* [sic]*, Consulting Detective, London*".

I smiled as I passed the letter to my friend as we sat at breakfast.

"I must congratulate you, it seems, on your elevation," I chuckled.

"Tut, tut," he answered but he was also smiling. "If knighthoods are to come our family's way, there is one much more deserving than me." At that time, I had no idea of the existence of his brother Mycroft Holmes, who it transpired played such an important role in the government of our nation, but I forbore from further enquiry.

He scanned the letter, and then passed it to me, together with the envelope. "Tell me, what can you make of it?"

I examined the envelope, with the aim of demonstrating to Holmes that I had profited from his teaching. "Posted yesterday evening from Barnet, possibly the last post. The address, although incomplete and inaccurate, appears to be in a practised and educated feminine hand. The envelope seems to be of an unusual size, and there is a slight smell of an unidentifiable nature emanating from it."

"The perfume is hardly unidentifiable," Holmes laughed. "Even I, with my limited experience of the female sex and the various concoctions with which the members of the sex anoint themselves, am able to identify it as lily-of-the-valley. As to the shape of the envelope, I'm surprised that you failed to recognise the distinctive proportions of the standard French envelope. Now for the letter. Please read it aloud to me."

I took up the letter, whose paper matched that of the envelope, and commenced reading.

*17 March*

*Mr. Homes,*

*I am writing to you on an affair of extreme urgency. It is concerning the matter of my husband who disappeared earlier today under circumstances which I believe to be impossible. It is of the utmost importance that this is to be solved at the earliest possible time. Accordingly I will be visiting you.*

*Cordially yours,*
*Mrs. Francine Etherege.*

"Given your identification of the envelope as being of French origin, I would hazard that the origin of the writer of this epistle is also France. The crossed seven in the date would add support to this notion."

Holmes said nothing, but nodded in seeming agreement.

I continued, holding the paper to the light from the window. "At least a part of the watermark is there, but I do not recognise it. The paper is of good quality."

"Excellent quality, in fact, and I believe the watermark to be one from a factory near Limoges, though I'm not positive on that point. Indubitably French, though. But what of the content?"

"Her husband has left her, but I cannot conceive of any circumstances surrounding such an action that might be described as '*impossible*'."

"She uses the word '*disappeared*' – even given the fact that English isn't Mrs. Etherege's native tongue, there is a piquancy to this that is of interest."

"And the urgency?"

Holmes shrugged. "We will see. The fact that she folded the letter before the ink was dry would seem to underline the importance she attaches to the subject." He leaned back in his chair, and lit a cigarette. "I anticipate an early arrival of Mrs. Etherege."

Indeed, scarcely had he spoken when the rattle of wheels outside our window, followed by the sound of the front door being opened, and the noise of footsteps on the stairs leading to our rooms, informed us that we had a visitor.

"Mr. Holmes has a young lady to see him," Mrs. Hudson informed me when I had opened the door in answer to her knock.

I ushered in our visitor, attempting to deduce what I could from my observation of her, following the rules I had learned from Holmes. I saw a young woman dressed in mourning, with a veil that failed to hide completely an attractive face, albeit one lined with the signs of grief. Her shoes, though polished, had splashes of mud on them, as did the hem of her skirt. In her hand, she carried a small bag.

I invited her to the chair facing Holmes in which his clients typically sat, and she settled timidly, almost bird-like, and she introduced herself as Mrs. Francine Etherege, who had written the letter which we had just examined.

For his part, Holmes sat quietly, observing her through half-closed eyes.

She broke the silence, which had lasted for a minute or more. "Excuse me, sir," she begin, in a voice that betrayed more than a trace of an accent. "Before I ask for your help, I must warn you that I am not possessed of the means that would allow you to receive the fees that you would expect from some of your other clients."

Holmes opened his eyes and raised a hand which he waved negligently. "Mrs. Etherege, you must believe me when I tell you that if I decide to take up your case, you will have no worries about money."

At these words, our fair visitor's face fell. "But sir," she said, a piteous tone in her voice, "do you not take the part of all who come to you? You must help me. If you do not . . . ." The accent was more pronounced, and as her voice trailed off, I feared that our visitor was about to start weeping.

"I take those cases that interest me," Holmes replied. "I do not concern myself with missing dogs, or errant husbands, or routine matters of that kind. If your husband has left you, then that isn't an affair in which I care to involve myself."

At these words, which to my ears sounded more than a little harsh, Mrs. Etherege burst into almost hysterical tears. I hastened to fetch her a glass of water and, as I did so, shot Holmes a glance to express my extreme displeasure at how he had addressed this woman.

I confess that it was to my surprise that he replied with a few muttered words of apology, after which he and I held our peace.

Our silence and the water did their work, and at length Mrs. Etherege found it possible to speak again.

"If it were only as simple as that, sir," she said. "My husband is dead."

"You mean that he is now missing, and you believe him to be dead?" I asked. It had occurred to me that there might be some problem connected with our visitor's relative unfamiliarity with the English language.

"*Non!* No, no!" she protested. "He is dead. I saw his body. The doctor signed the paper. He is dead. See here." From her bag she produced a piece of paper which she handed to Holmes, who studied it and passed it to me. It proved to be the death certificate of a Mr. Josiah Etherege, of Barnet, dated the previous day. The cause of death was given as "*weakness of the lungs caused by consumption*".

"And yet he is missing?" Holmes asked gently.

"Yes, yes. He is gone. My poor Jo." She fell to weeping once more. Eventually she composed herself and continued. Her speech was far from appearing fully rational, in an order that was scarcely coherent, and delivered in English that was far from fluent, and frequently interspersed with French words.

Rather than subject the reader to a verbatim account of her story, I will summarise here what Mrs. Etherege told us.

Mr. Josiah Etherege was a widower of middle age. Some years before, his previous wife had died in childbirth, and the child hadn't survived. There was no other issue from the marriage.

On taking a trip to Le Touquet, Etherege had met our fair visitor, who at that time was working in the hotel where he was staying. They became friendly, and he informed her that should she ever come to England, he would be happy to welcome her and to act as her guide to our country, should she so desire.

This came to pass, and following a week's tour of the West Country, during which, we were blushingly informed, Etherege behaved "as an English gentleman should", he proposed marriage to her. She accepted, and without even returning to France to inform her parents of her impending nuptials, she married him a month later.

By her account, her marriage had been a happy one. Etherege worked as a senior clerk in the City, taking the train every morning. She hadn't enquired too closely into the nature of his employment, but believed the name of the firm to be "Butterworth and Flint", and the nature of the business to be that of importing agricultural machinery from the United States. Though not wealthy, it seemed that the household was far from being poverty-stricken, though recently it seemed that money wasn't as readily available as it had been in the past.

However, despite the happiness of their life together, it appeared that Etherege's health wasn't robust, and he had succumbed to consumption relatively recently. Only three days before, he had fallen into a coma, and was pronounced dead the two days later by the doctor who had signed the certificate we had seen earlier.

"He lay on our bed, so cold and still," she said. Not trusting her command of English to manage the business of securing the services of an undertaker and arranging a funeral for her husband, she left the house to speak to a neighbour, a Miss Sutherland, with whom she had formed a friendship, to beg her assistance.

Miss Sutherland promised to assist Mrs. Etherege with the funeral arrangements, and expressed a wish to pay her respects to her husband. However, on returning to the Etherege house and entering the room within which Mrs. Etherege had left the body of her husband lying on the bed, there was no sign of the corpse. In answer to Holmes's questioning, Mrs. Etherege answered that the bed showed traces of having held her husband's body on it, and that nothing else seemed to have been disturbed.

"And had you locked the door when you went to visit your neighbour?" Holmes asked.

"I had. I distinctly remember unlocking the door when I returned with Miss Sutherland."

"And is there a back door to your house?"

"There is, but it was always kept locked. It had occurred to me at the time that someone might have entered, and when I checked, it was locked, and the key hung on the hook."

"And the windows of the house?"

"All closed."

"May I ask what your husband was wearing when you last saw him?" I asked.

The question seemed to bring on a fit of weeping, and I inwardly cursed myself for my insensitivity.

"He was wearing his nightgown," she told us, "as he was when he passed away."

"You have informed the police of this disappearance?" asked Holmes.

"I did. They told me that since my husband was deceased, there would be little point in their employing their usual methods. Quite frankly, sir, I believe that they suspect me of having murdered my poor Jo, and having somehow disposed of his body elsewhere. I do not think that they believe me. But I assure you, sir, that everything I have told you is true."

"I see," said Holmes after a pause. "This does seem to be something of an unusual case. It is almost the first time that I have been asked to discover the whereabouts of a man who is deceased. There was the case of young Lord Galway," he mused, "but the circumstances were very different."

"There is more," Mrs. Etherege informed us. "As I was about to leave the house this morning, my attention was caught by a scrap of paper which appeared to have been pushed under the front door of the house. Here." She reached in her bag once more and handed to Holmes a small piece of paper, on which some words had been written, seemingly in pencil.

"Thank you. '*My dear Francine, Do not worry. All will become clear soon. Your J.*' 'J' for Josiah? You believe this to be from your husband?"

"I do."

"And you recognise this as his handwriting?"

"I thought you might ask me that very question, and to that end I have brought some examples so that you might make a comparison."

"Excellent," Holmes told her, taking the papers she now offered him. "Yes, there are definitely enough points of similarity for me to accept that this morning's note was written by the same hand that wrote these letters you have given me. Do you recognise the paper? It appears to have been torn from a notebook of some sort." He held the paper to the light. "No obvious watermark, but of a very common type of paper."

294

"I cannot be sure, but I think that it may have come from my husband's memorandum book that he always carried with him."

"And do you have that book now?"

"I do not, I fear. I searched for it in the bedroom where he died, as I had a memory of having seen it not two days previously, but was unable to locate it."

"Most singular. Is anything else missing, to your knowledge?" She shook her head. "Very well. I take it you will not take it amiss if Dr. Watson and I visit you later? Your address?"

After ascertaining this, and the details of the doctor who had signed the death certificate, as well as those of the police officer with whom she had spoken, she took her leave of us.

"Well, then, what do you make of that, my dear fellow?" he asked me, lighting his pipe.

"I confess myself baffled."

"I confess that there are aspects of this case that I find a little unclear," Holmes confessed. "Much depends on what we will find at *Chez* Etherege. But before we call there, let us pay a visit to Inspector Barnes, who was consulted by Mrs. Etherege, and then to Dr. Geoffrey Woodhead, who signed the certificate."

Inspector Barnes received us courteously enough when we presented ourselves at the police station.

"I've heard of you, Mr. Holmes," he told us. "I confess that I never thought that I could be of assistance to you, though. How can I help you?"

Holmes explained the situation.

"Yes, of course I remember. A pleasant enough little woman. She came into the station at about two in the afternoon, I suppose. When she told us that her husband was missing, I assumed the obvious. And then she told us that her husband was in no condition to chase after other women, being dead, I am afraid I believed it to be a prank of some kind. In my experience, Mr. Holmes, dead men do not vanish from locked houses."

"So you ascertained that the doors had been locked?"

The police agent had the grace to look a little shamefaced. "To be honest, Mr. Holmes, we did not visit the house. The whole story seemed so unlikely that we didn't feel it to be necessary to do so. To be frank, Mr. Holmes, I'm surprised at your bothering with a story that is so preposterous."

"It is precisely because it is so unlikely and preposterous that I am undertaking this investigation. What did you tell Mrs. Etherege?"

"We told her that if her husband had been pronounced dead by a doctor, he was certainly unlikely to leave the house, and that if he wasn't in the house, then there was no hope of his being traced." He shook his head. "Trust me, Mr. Holmes, I have better things to do than to send my men on a wild goose chase."

"Even when the dead man sends his wife a message after disappearing?"

Inspector Barnes expressed surprise. "This certainly changes the aspect of things. Are you satisfied that the note is genuine?"

"I am reasonably certain, yes."

"In which case I hope that you will let us know if there proves to be any wrongdoing. The case is more complex than I had previously imagined, but I'm happy for you to investigate it."

As we left the police station, Holmes observed that the police lacked imagination. "Tell me, Watson, if you had been in the position of the good inspector whose acquaintance we have just had the pleasure of making, wouldn't simple curiosity drive you to visit the scene of the incident?"

I agreed that this was so. After walking for a few minutes, we found ourselves at the address of Dr. Woodhead. On ringing the bell, we were admitted by a maid who took our cards, after first ascertaining that we weren't seeking "the master's" medical attention, explaining to us that he had finished his practice for the day. We were ushered into a well-appointed room, and our host entered.

He was a small, ill-favoured man of about my age, whose eyes darted to-and-fro like those of a frightened rodent. His voice was somewhat thin and reedy.

"Mr. Sherlock Holmes himself. And Doctor Watson, too. To what do I owe this honour? Sit, sit," indicating two chairs and taking another himself.

Holmes explained our errand, concluding with "And since you signed his death certificate, I was hoping that you could shed a little light on the subject."

"Well, bless my soul," Woodhead exclaimed. "A body simply disappearing is outside my experience."

"Did you know Josiah Etherege before you signed the certificate?" Holmes asked.

"I did. He was my patient. Sadly, all the medicines and advice I gave him were unable to save him, poor man."

"So it was consumption, in your opinion?" I asked.

He almost glared at me with those small rodent-like eyes. "I'm not accustomed to having my diagnoses questioned," he protested.

"I apologise," I said. "My question was merely to ascertain that Mrs. Etherege had understood her husband's condition."

"I understand," he said. "But I am failing in my duties as a host. A brandy-and-soda for you gentlemen? I generally partake at this time of day."

We both refused, but Woodhead rang the bell and ordered a drink for himself, which arrived in the form of a bottle of brandy and a soda syphon, and three large tumblers. After once more offering us a drink, which we refused, he poured a generous amount of brandy into the bottom of one of the tumblers and added a splash of soda.

"What sort of man was Josiah Etherege?" Holmes asked.

"I hardly knew him," Woodhead answered, "other than as a patient." He took a long drink. "He paid his bills to me promptly and in full, though I do not think he was in any sense a wealthy man. For example, I don't think he could ever have afforded to go to the spas I would otherwise have recommended."

"Would you be kind enough to describe for us the circumstances under which you came to sign the certificate?" Holmes asked.

"I received a message from Mrs. Etherege asking me to visit their house. I had previously been attending Josiah – that is to say, Mr. Etherege – for a few weeks previously. He has – or rather had – a weak chest, and I feared that he was developing consumption. He weakened, and eventually slipped into a coma. On his last day, my worst fears were sadly realised when I reached the house. He was very weak by then, and was unconscious of his surroundings. He drew his last breath while I was there. His wife was downstairs at that point, and I saw no advantage to bringing her to witness what would have been a most painful scene for her." He refreshed his glass, which by this point was empty.

"So, you were satisfied that Mr. Etherege had in fact departed this life?"

Woodhead's face flushed with anger. "How dare you, sir? Are you casting doubt on my abilities as a medical practitioner?"

Holmes's reply was mild. "Not at all, my dear sir. A matter of form only, such as a coroner might pose at an inquest."

The effect of these words was remarkable. The doctor's face, which had been a fiery red, drained of colour to an almost deathly pale. "There will not be – I mean, why on earth would there be an inquest?"

"I feel it is extremely unlikely given the circumstances," said Holmes. "You need not fear a coroner's cross-examination, I feel."

"That eases my mind," answered the other, and expressed his relief by swallowing the last of his drink.

"I'm glad to hear it," said Holmes. "Come, Watson, let us leave on this happy note. Thank you for your time, sir. No, pray do not rise. We will see ourselves out."

Once on the street, Holmes began to laugh silently. "I do believe we now have most pieces of the puzzle in our hands."

"What do you mean?"

"As a fellow practitioner of medicine, how would you rate your colleague whom we have just left?

"A little too fond of the bottle, I would say."

"Clearly so."

"And not too prosperous – I would say his practice has fallen on hard times. His brass plate was none too clean, and the hat we saw hanging in the hall was hardly new. Of course, that might merely mean that he pays little or no attention to fashion."

"Bravo. You are coming on very nicely. Yes, I think I smelt a distinct shortage of money just now. And perhaps a certain lack of professional ethics."

"That is quite possible," I admitted.

The Etherege house was but ten minutes' walk from that of Dr. Woodhead. Holmes's conversation en route was not, as one might have expected, of the case on which we were engaged, but on the merits of an Austrian violinist who was apparently taking the musical world by storm.

Eventually we reached the house and knocked at the door. Mrs. Etherege opened it to us.

"Oh, sirs," she said. "Another one," and without further ado, she handed a sheet of paper to Holmes.

"Thank you. '*It will be soon*'," he read. "'*Do not fear. Your loving J.*' The same handwriting as before. And how was this delivered?"

"Pushed under the door as before. I'm sorry to keep you standing like this. Please enter."

We followed her into a meanly furnished front parlour, and she invited us to take tea, which we refused.

"I'm afraid I will have to ask you some questions that may bring back painful memories," Holmes told her.

"I am ready," she replied.

"May I ask who laid out your husband for burial?"

"Why, no one." Seeing our surprise, she added, "I did not feel I was equal to the task of doing this on my own, so I went to call on Miss Sutherland to ask her assistance."

"I see. So you didn't close his eyes?"

She shuddered. "I have a horror of such things, sir. No, Dr. Woodhead performed that service on my behalf."

"But you did see your husband after he died?"

"Certainly."

"And you were sure that he was, in fact, deceased?"

"The doctor had already examined him and pronounced him to be so. I had no reason to think otherwise."

"Quite so, quite so," Holmes murmured. "Perhaps we could examine the room where you last saw him?"

She led us upstairs to a small room at the back of the house, dimly lit by a small window, to which Holmes first directed his enquiry, examining the sill and the catches before peering out towards the small back garden.

He then turned his attention to the bed and its immediate surroundings, at one point dropping to his knees and closely examining the thick rug that lay beside the bed. Rising from there, he then asked to examine Mr. Etherege's garments. These proved to be few in number, and of good quality, though well-worn.

"Thank you," he said at length. "I believe I have seen enough here. Perhaps I might examine your back door?"

We were led through the kitchen to the back door, which was fastened with a lock of solid appearance. Mrs. Etherege took the key from a hook and unlocked the door.

"One moment," said Holmes. "Was this key in the lock when you returned with Miss Sutherland?"

"It was not, sir. It always hangs on this hook."

"And it is the only key to this door?"

"It is."

"Very good," said Holmes, and stepped outside. There was a small shed in the garden by the back fence, on the other side of which was some sparse woodland.

"What is in there?" he asked, pointing to the shed.

"Gardening tools and the like. Jo used to be so proud of his vegetables. Look." And she pointed to a row of minute green shoots emerging from the earth. "They'll be cabbages and onions and carrots in a few months." The sight of the vegetables seemed to affect her, and she seemed close to tears.

"May I enter?" Holmes asked, indicating the shed.

"Of course, though I have no idea if you will find anything of interest in there. Jo was the only person to go inside, and only for gardening. It will be unlocked. He never locked it."

Holmes and I made our way to the shed. As we had been told, it was unlocked, and stooping slightly to pass through the low doorway, we entered.

"I take it," Holmes remarked to me, "that when we were examining the effects of Josiah Etherege, you noticed the state of his boots."

I racked my brains, but couldn't remember having noticed them, and said as much to Holmes.

"You wouldn't have noticed them," he said to me. "They were not there. There were no signs of any outdoor footwear. What does that indicate to you?"

"That someone removed them? Mrs. Etherege?"

"Possible, but unlikely, I feel."

"Then who?"

"Think, man, think!"

I racked my brains, but was unable to come up with an answer to my question. We continued searching the shed.

"Ha!" exclaimed Holmes, pointing to an object on a shelf. "Do you recognise this?"

"It is a key."

"Not just a key," he corrected me. "If I'm not mistaken, it is a key to the back door of the house. It appears to be identical to the one we saw just now."

"But we were told there was only the one key, were we not?"

"We were."

"Which means that either Mrs. Etherege is being less than truthful with us, or that Mr. Etherege, the only person whom we know to have entered this place, was in possession of a duplicate key, without his wife's being aware of it."

"For what purpose? To enter the house without anyone's being aware of his doing so?"

"It is more likely that he wished to leave the house without others being aware."

"But . . . How does a dead man *leave* the house, even with a key in his possession?"

Holmes laughed. "My dear fellow, you have met the doctor who signed the death certificate. Would you entrust your health to such a one?"

I shook my head. "Surely no doctor, no matter how attached he was to the bottle, would be mistaken as to whether a patient had departed this life or no?"

"I'm sure he wasn't mistaken. I am reasonably certain that Etherege persuaded him, with the aid of a financial inducement, to sign the death certificate."

"To what end?"

"In the usual way of such matters, I would say *cherchez la femme*, but in this case, since Mrs. Etherege has been receiving notes from the supposed deceased, we must seek another answer. I believe we may find the solution here in this shed."

I drew Holmes's attention to a slip of paper which seemed to have fallen from the shelf on which we had found the key.

"A-ha! This is most significant. This is an itemised list of clothing ordered from J. Thigsby and Company, Drapers of Liverpool Street. Where did Mrs. Etherege say that her husband worked?"

"Some firm importing agricultural machinery from the United States, was it not?"

"Of course. Your memory serves you well. Butterworth and Flint? Does that jog your memory?"

"I believe that was the name, yes."

"They have an office near Liverpool Street, if I'm not mistaken. Now, examine this note. The items ordered consist of a complete gentleman's outfit, except for boots – and we have already noted the absence of these. It is noticeable that when a man wishes to disguise himself, the last items that he will change are his boots. Women, on the other hand, seem to be reluctant to change their gloves. Strange, eh? What else can we discover here?"

However, a few minutes' searching revealed nothing further of interest, and we returned to the house.

"Mrs. Etherege," Holmes addressed her. "I am certain your husband is alive."

"Oh!" She pressed her hands to her breast with an expression of unfeigned joy on her face. "Thank you, sir!" She paused, and added, "Where is he?"

"I do not know," Holmes confessed, "but I'm certain that I will find him very soon. I promise you this."

For my part, I had no idea as to how my friend could achieve this, but I held my peace until we were seated in the carriage of the Great Northern Railway train which would take us back to London.

"How will you find Josiah Etherege?" I asked him.

"I think he will come to us, possibly tonight."

"What? He will come to Baker Street?"

"No, no. He will come to Tudor Close in Barnet and meet us there."

"The house that we have just left?"

"Precisely."

"But you didn't tell Mrs. Etherege that we would be returning."

"I thought it better not to do so."

We returned to Baker Street, and Holmes spent the time consulting his "Index", by which title he named his scrapbook of those items of news he found interesting – that is to say, items relating to criminal activity.

"There is nothing under '*Etherege*'," he complained, "but then I scarcely suspected there would be. No matter. I'm sure that we will find the answer to this riddle tonight."

I had some previous experience of nocturnal adventures in Holmes's company, and accordingly I prepared the dark lanterns that formed a usual accompaniment to such proceedings.

"Excellent," Holmes remarked when he saw what I was doing. "I'm sure they will be useful."

"Do you wish me to bring my revolver?" I asked.

"No, no. Tonight's adventure will hardly warrant such a thing."

Suitably dressed, we took the train to Barnet, but to my surprise, we didn't go directly to Tudor Close, but to the area of rough woodland close by.

"We are going to wait in the shed," Holmes whispered to me. "Follow me."

I followed him along the narrow track that led through the wood, and we came to a wooden fence.

"I noticed two loose boards earlier today," Holmes said. "These will form our quarry's point of entry. Ours as well, I feel." A little searching along the fence, and Holmes pronounced himself satisfied that we were in the right place.

Making our way through the gap left by the removal of the boards, which we replaced as we had found them, we entered the shed where we had previously discovered the key and the note from the clothiers.

"And now we wait," said Holmes.

"You are sure he will come tonight?" I asked.

"I shall be very surprised if he does not," was his reply.

It was a warm night, but even so I was glad of the shelter provided by the shed. After a period of time that I estimated as being about two hours, Holmes tugged at my sleeve.

"He is here!" he whispered. "Can you hear?"

I strained my ears and could make out the sounds of the loose boards in the fence being removed. Next came the sound of the door of the shed being opened, and it was at that moment that Holmes opened the slide of his dark lantern, illuminating the startled face of a man dressed in a tweed jacket and twill trousers, as had been itemised on the clothiers' list.

"Mr. Josiah Etherege?" Holmes enquired pleasantly, extending a hand.

"My God!" exclaimed the other. "If you have come to kill me, do it now, but for God's sake, do not harm my little Francine."

Holmes laughed. "My dear Mr. Etherege, nothing is further from my mind, or that of Watson here. We have no wish to harm you or your charming wife, but we would very much appreciate your telling us the reason for your disappearance from your deathbed – a feat, I may say, that is almost unique in my experience."

302

"You don't know how it was accomplished, then?" His expression was almost one of delight at being asked to tell his story.

"I believe I do, but if it will give you pleasure to confirm my suspicions, pray do so. A cigarette?" He offered his case to Etherege, who waved it away. "By the way, I should introduce myself. My name is Sherlock Holmes, and this is my friend and colleague, Dr. John Watson."

"Sherlock Holmes, eh? I suppose my wife sent for you, clever little thing that she is. No wonder you found me so easily. Very well, I will tell you the why's and the wherefore's of this little escapade."

He took a deep breath and started. "I met my wife in France. She believed I was there on holiday, but in fact, I had been sent there by my employers at the time to negotiate a piece of business for them. In the course of the negotiations, a considerable sum of money went missing. I knew that it was one of my French colleagues, but he swore, with all the Gallic oaths that you may imagine, that it wasn't he who was responsible.

"Worse than that, he claimed he could produce evidence that I had stolen and hidden the money. On my return to England, I was able to make up the loss from my own savings, and my employers were none the wiser. However, this wasn't the end of the affair. My marriage was a happy one. I cannot conceive of a more harmonious and blessed relationship.

"About six months ago, I received a letter from France. The writer, whose name I recognised as one of those who had threatened me, now proceeded to threaten me again, telling me that if I didn't pay a certain amount of money to him, he would present proof of my larceny to my wife, in such a form that she would have no choice but to leave me. I paid the money, though I could ill afford to do so, and hoped that was the end of the business.

"Alas, it was not to be. I received two more such letters, each time demanding larger sums, and I was forced to find a way to escape this tyranny. Eventually I hit upon the idea of disappearing, and what better way of disappearing than to die?" He smiled at us, and Holmes returned the smile.

"What better way, indeed?" replied Holmes.

"However, I had no intention of actually making away with myself. I had previously encountered Dr. Woodhead, and knew him to be a less-than-reputable physician. I took him into my confidence and arranged that he would diagnose me as suffering from consumption, and when the time came, to pronounce me dead and sign my death certificate. His price for all this was a mere half-dozen of brandy."

"A bargain," Holmes laughed.

"So it seemed to me. I reasoned that once I had been officially pronounced dead, my tormentor would cease his attempts to extract money from me, even if my corpse was nowhere to be found. A death certificate would surely guarantee that I was no longer on this earth. I had previously purchased a suit of clothes, the one that you see me wearing now, and I kept it here in this shed. I had also caused a duplicate key to the back door to be made. My idea was to reassure Francine by leaving messages – "

"She showed them to us," I told him.

"Good. I hope she believed them."

We gave him this assurance, and he continued. "I have been making arrangements to leave the country and go to America. Today I purchased the steamship tickets for Francine and myself, though I am sorry for her that we will have to travel steerage. I sold some of my shareholdings, but I believe we will still have enough cash to start anew in the New World.

"All that remains now is for me to explain all to Francine and take her with me. The ship sails tomorrow night from Southampton. You will not try to stop me, I hope?"

"I see no reason to do so," Holmes told him gravely. "Maybe you have broken some law or another in the matter of your supposed death, but I cannot for the life of me think what it might be. Watson?"

"Nor I," I replied. "It is possible that Dr. Woodhead has committed some offence, and should probably be struck off the register, but I cannot see that he has caused anyone any lasting harm."

"In that case, please wait while I bring Francine here. The key from the shelf there, if you please."

Holmes handed it to him, and he slipped out of the shed. We strained our ears, and after a short time, we could hear a cry, seemingly of joy, that had presumably emanated from the throat of Mrs. Etherege. A few minutes later, it was possible to make out two figures coming over the grass towards us.

The light of our lanterns showed us two faces, and I didn't think it possible that mortals could experience such joy in this life. Their faces were radiant, and it was clear that we were in the presence of such a union as one seldom finds on this earth.

I confess that I felt a surge of emotion welling up inside me, and to my surprise, I could see that Holmes was similarly affected.

"Thank you, sir," said Mrs. Etherege to Holmes. "I see that you are a true magician."

"Hardly that," he replied gruffly.

"We must go, *Chérie*," said Etherege to his wife. "We must buy you some clothes for the journey."

We watched them leave, and soon we heard the sound of the fence planks being removed and replaced.

After a few minutes we set off. Holmes led us back along the path we had previously taken to reach the house. We had missed the last train to town, but started walking, and reached Baker Street just before sunrise.

As a postscript, a month later Holmes received a letter postmarked from Albany, New York.

*My dear Mr. Magician Holmes,* [it read]

*I cannot begin to thank you enough for your assistance –* ("Pah! I did nothing!" Holmes exclaimed.) *– and support. Jo has a post with the American company with whom he previously did business, and we are both settling down well, though many of the customs here are strange to me, and I sometimes find it hard to understand American speech. I have taken the liberty of informing my friend Miss Sutherland of the recent events, while binding her to secrecy.*

*Cordially yours,*
*Francine Etherege (Mrs.)*

There was a postscript in handwriting we recognised as that of Josiah Etherege.

*I must add thanks from one who is officially deceased for your understanding and assistance. I will never forget what you did for my wife.*

"Well," I said to Holmes as he laid the letter on the table, "maybe you are a magician after all – restoring a lost husband to a loving wife."

He didn't deign to answer, but took up his violin and started to scrape away – but it was noticeable that his music seemed to contain a little more emotion than usual.

# The Youngest Client
## by Gordon Linzner

It was a cool yet invigorating, rather than unpleasant, breeze which greeted Sherlock Holmes and me as we left the pub that evening towards the end of November in 1887, and my friend had just that morning wrapped up what he described as a particularly convoluted case. In contrast, I myself had recently published my first public account of one of his cases in that year's *Beeton's Christmas Annual*. As a reward, he decided to spend that late afternoon in my company, attending a concert by one of his favorite violinists, Pablo de Sarasate.

Afterwards, while heading back to Baker Street, we'd stopped at a local pub for a light dinner and some burgundy. My friend, being in one of his unusually good moods, couldn't resist from time to time humming a few bars of one or another of those violin tunes we had heard, waving his hands slightly in rhythm. This action amused several of our fellow customers as well as myself, although I couldn't help noticing that it did visibly irritate a few other patrons.

"We aren't all that far from Baker Street," Holmes noted when we finally left the establishment to take in the refreshing autumn air. "Ten, perhaps fifteen minutes, on foot. Are you up for a stroll?"

We had already started walking and were halfway down the darkening street. "I've no problem with that."

"I thought not." Holmes's lips curled in a faint grin. "It looked to me as if you could definitely use the exercise. Stimulate those brain cells of yours, and so on."

I paused to meet his steady grey eyes.

"It isn't as though I don't enjoy a good walk," I countered, "with or without your company, but is there any particular reason you believe I need one at this time?"

"You grew steadily quieter in the hour or so during which we dined," he replied. "Your responses to my conversation grew more terse. You picked idly at your roast duck. It appeared to me as if our day's activities had begun to take their toll."

I snorted as we started walking again. "This reaction," I replied, waving my hand, "from a man whom I've often seen spend half his day and more in bed when not working on a case."

306

Holmes shrugged. "I've confessed to you more than once how much I dislike wasting my energy."

"And if I confess instead to spending more time at my meal this evening simply because my roast duck seemed to be a tad underdone, would you consider that an alternate explanation for my eating slower than usual?"

Holmes rubbed his chin. "And the reason for your growing silence in the establishment?"

"At one point, I felt tempted to snap at those two young men at the end of the bar who were giving us harsh looks. My better sense prevailed. Instead, I decided to ignore that annoyance with silence."

Holmes offered a rare chuckle. "Indeed. I have admitted to you more than once that, however my observations might seem the likeliest explanations in most circumstances, they still might not be wholly correct. This, despite the way that you describe them when writing up our cases – at least, those cases which you have allowed me to read."

"The last thing I would ever wish to do," I replied with a sigh, "is publicly present you in a bad light."

"Except when I admit to a mistake?"

I shrugged, pulling my collar closer as a sudden chill breeze whipped by us. "Occasionally I do acknowledge as much, yes. But only to demonstrate how your mind works to correct itself."

Our conversation then moved on to more interesting topics as we grew nearer to the Baker Street rooms, until I abruptly paused again. A small figure lurked in the shadows near the entrance of 221b. On noticing our approach, the stranger shifted forward, stepping into the glow of the streetlamp, providing us with a clear view of a small child. Save for an elderly man with a cane who was crossing the street further down, the pavement was empty.

"Could that little girl be wandering about this neighborhood on her own?" I inquired. "At this hour?"

"It isn't all that late," Holmes corrected. "Midnight remains a few hours away."

"May I assume, then, that she is one of your Irregulars? Could her presence here mean you might have another job tonight, after all?"

"Not in the least. That child appears much too young to be one of them. She is six or seven years of age, at most. And remember, right now my Irregulars are all male. Ignore her, Watson. There's a good probability her mother is entertaining a client nearby, and she didn't have time to drop her child at home, or in some other safe spot. No doubt she'll soon return here to retrieve her daughter. This is hardly the first time I've seen this sort of thing, though rarely so close."

"We can't just leave a child that young out here on her own!" I protested. "The night is growing colder, and that coat she's wearing looks much too thin."

I stepped in front of Holmes before he could protest further. As I did so, the girl raced toward me.

She looked straight up until her eyes met mine. "Herr Holmes?" she asked. Her voice was high-pitched, with a faint lisp. "Excuse me. I mean, *Mister* Holmes?"

"No," I replied. "My name is John Watson,"

Her lips turned down in a pout. I then added, pointing behind me, "My friend, here, is Mr. Sherlock Holmes."

I didn't need to meet Holmes's gaze to sense his annoyance. Nonetheless, he managed, for the moment, to keep that sullen mood out of his tone.

"And a good evening to you," he addressed the girl, lowering himself to one knee in order to make better eye contact. "Miss – ?"

"I'm Hannah." She clutched her thin jacket more tightly about her shoulders as another chill breeze shot up the street. "Hannah Weisskopf."

"And what, if I may ask, Miss Weisskopf, brings a young lady such as yourself to call on me, an older gentleman and a stranger, at this hour? I trust – I hope – that your parents are nearby?"

"My mother . . ." the girl began. Suddenly, she choked back a sob and rushed into my friend's arms.

Again, Holmes's steady grey eyes fixed me with a sharp, accusatory look, even as he tried to console the trembling child with an uncharacteristic hug.

"You're quite right," he replied over her shoulder. "We cannot leave young Hannah here, out on this street, alone, unprotected, as the night grows increasingly cold. Let us go inside. I'll leave you to post a note on the door so that, if her mother does come looking for her . . . ."

"'If'?" I repeated. The girl let out another sob.

"*When*, if you prefer."

"She . . ." the girl began, then buried her head in Holmes's shoulder.

Holmes finished her sentence. ". . . will know where to find you, as well as being assured of your safety."

Following Holmes's request as he led the child inside, I tore a page from my pocket notebook, scrawled a brief note, and wedged it tightly up against the door knocker so that the wind wouldn't sweep it away.

Holmes had meanwhile brought our young guest halfway up the stairs by the time I stepped inside. He paused to look back down at me.

"Do us one more favor, would you, Watson? Ask Mrs. Hudson to bring up a cup of hot chocolate. Perhaps a slice of her delicious sponge cake as well, if she has any left."

I glanced at the hall clock. The hour was, as Holmes had previously affirmed, not terribly late. Mrs. Hudson would still be awake, most likely reading her recently purchased copy of Anna Katherine Green's *The Leavenworth Case*.

Mrs. Hudson did indeed quickly answer my knock, then paused in the open doorway to her own rooms. She offered a curious glance at my odd request, but no more than that. Over the past few years, she had grown used to unusual activity, having Holmes as her tenant. Nor did I wish to spend much time explaining his reasons for our request, let alone describing our guest. We would be sharing those details with her soon enough.

What I first noticed, upon stepping through the door and into the sitting room, was the sobbing child curled up on the armchair usually reserved for clients. The girl glanced up, blinking at the sound of my entrance. Her quivering lips tightened in acknowledgment.

"You really do need to calm down, Miss Weisskopf," Holmes ordered, sitting across from her. The edge in his voice, more strident than usual, demonstrated he was starting to lose any sense of adopting that mood himself. "Allow me to address you less formally, Hannah. I can be of little help until you provide me with some idea of your present problem. Let us start with a bit of background. I assume this problem involves your mother. Tell us about her. What is her name? Where might she be at present? Why would she have sent you to call upon me, at this hour, leaving you unprotected on the streets of London? I trust she didn't simply abandon you on our doorstep, for reasons yet to be determined."

The girl trembled again, her tiny fingers tightening on the arm of her chair. Her eyes darted from Holmes to me, then back to him. Perhaps the child was considered that she might have made a mistake calling in Baker Street after all.

I was about to offer her my own reassurance when we were interrupted by Mrs. Hudson pushing open the flat's door with her left hand. In her right, she balanced a tray which bore slices of cake and a cup of hot chocolate.

Her eyes softened at the sight of the frightened child. I pulled a table up alongside Hannah's chair to accommodate the tray.

"You're sounding more strict than usual this evening, Mr. Holmes," Mrs. Hudson chided. "I couldn't help but overhearing your instructions as I climbed the stairs."

Holmes turned to face her. "I am trying to determine how I might best help the child, Mrs. Hudson – if, indeed, my help is the reason that she was abandoned at our doorstep this evening. If it wasn't the case at the time, it certainly is now."

"Soften your tone," she advised my detective friend, "or I will be forced to lead this poor child downstairs to my own chambers to calm her."

Hannah straightened up on her chair, gripping one arm tightly. She violently shook her head. "No! I stay here! I need to stay . . . ." Her words again broke off with a sob.

Holmes gave Mrs. Hudson an exasperated look, sighing. "You realize that I cannot – " he began, then paused. He stretched out his right hand and continued in a softer voice, "You are correct, Mrs. Hudson." He nodded toward the girl. "Hannah is far too young to be one of my Irregulars, and I shouldn't address her as sharply as I would some of them. Watson – "

I stepped forward. "What is it now?"

"You've surely examined children this age in your career, have you not?"

"I have," I admitted. "I gained initial experience while studying at Barts."

"If you will allow me," intervened Mrs. Hudson, "I may be able to help you. In a motherly fashion, of course."

"You're not my mother!" the child abruptly screeched, pressing her face against the cushioned back of her chair, sobbing.

"I did not say so." Mrs. Hudson knelt alongside the chair, addressing the child face-to-face in a soothing tone before either Holmes or I could intervene. "Nor would I claim to be, Hannah. May I call you Hannah? Still, I remember how well my mother tended to me. I have also, a time or three, house-sat for the neighbors' children."

Hannah turned her head to look up at Mrs. Hudson again. Her expression grew slightly softer. "I am here – " the girl started. "I mean, my mother sent me here. She wanted me to get help. From Herr Holmes." She pointed at my friend.

"I have never met your mother," Holmes replied.

"Nonetheless," I advised, "your reputation does precede you. I have heard people on the street mention you from time to time, and in the last week you received some attention from the story I wrote – "

" – Which few people have read."

"Few, but some. That woman may have sent young Hannah here because she saw you as the person who was best able to help her. Help the mother, I mean. Well, both of them. That she was unable to be here herself, instead of allowing her daughter, a child too young to be wandering

London's streets at night, would indicate that Mrs. Weisskopf herself felt she was in much more danger."

"I might also add," Mrs. Hudson commented, "that, like any decent mother aware of your reputation, Mrs. Weisskopf would want you, in particular, to help her distraught child. Nonetheless, Mr. Holmes, you should deal with Hannah in a more tactful manner than what is required by your older clients."

"And with a bit more understanding," I put in, as if our landlady hadn't been clear enough.

Holmes glanced at me and Mrs. Hudson, then to young Hannah, and finally back to Mrs. Hudson. He shrugged.

"You are quite right. Would you mind staying with us a few more minutes, to ensure that I will be offering the proper mood and advice?"

"Of course. Assuming Hannah herself doesn't mind my presence." She peered sympathetically at the child.

Hannah stared back for a long moment. Mrs. Hudson gently pushed the cake a little closer to her.

The child nodded, grasped the cake with both hands, and took a huge bite.

"Excellent!" said Mrs. Hudson.

Holmes leaned forward. "Then I must first ask you – Yes, by all means, enjoy your cake, take more bites, you need not answer me until you're ready. – exactly why it is that you have come to visit this humble abode, alone, at so late an hour?"

"My mother . . . ." Hannah's voice cracked again, after she swallowed her mouthful of cake.

"Your mother, yes," Mrs. Hudson repeated, in an encouraging tone. "She was the one who sent you here, did she not?"

"Yes. No." Hannah stared at Holmes again, then continued in a slightly calmer voice. "My mother had just read of your adventure in that Christmas magazine. She likes mysteries. Sometimes she reads one to me at bedtime, instead of fairy tales. She was 'specially excited because you're real. Heard about you from friends."

Now that Miss Weisskopf was further relaxed, and had gotten over most of her sobbing, she opened up more.

"There is nothing inherently wrong with fantasies," Holmes murmured. "They are not to my taste, but I understand their appeal to the younger set."

"Oh, I like them, too! Goblins, and giants, and fairies! But mysteries – those are Mother's favorites!"

311

"I quite understand the appeal of those, although they, too, can often go far afield." Holmes's quick glance in my direction almost made me regret the times I'd allowed him to look at my journal.

"What about those mysteries, Hannah?" asked Mrs. Hudson. "How do you feel about those kinds of stories?"

Hannah nodded briskly, having now warmed to our landlady. "I like them too. Yes. But I wish there were some elves and princesses in them."

*So might we all,* I mused, covering my grin with my left hand as I looked back at Holmes.

"And where exactly might your mother be at the moment?" asked Holmes, taking on his formal role.

Hannah's mood sank again. "*Ich weiss nicht.* I don't know."

Mrs. Hudson gently rested one hand on the girl's shoulder. "Then that is the mystery that Mr. Holmes needs to resolve before anything else. Am I right?"

"You are, indeed, Mrs. Hudson." Holmes stepped away from the female pair to retrieve one of his pipes before settling down in his usual chair, legs crossed. He didn't light the pipe. His long fingers merely toyed with it, no doubt to provide a distraction for the child, so she might relax further.

"Please continue, Hannah," he said, softening his tone once more. "Take your time. It is essential that I hear every possible detail that might have led to your mother's disappearance. . . . ."

"Zechariah Potts!"

Holmes growled, rising to his feet and moving away quickly so as not to frighten the young girl with his obvious displeasure.

"Do you know him?" I asked. It had taken a few minutes for Hannah to recall the name of the man who'd been harassing her mother over the past couple of days. Even then, she had mispronounced it.

That didn't prevent Holmes from identifying the man. Quite the contrary.

"I've run across him. A petty, insecure, unstable fellow. Only once did he directly interfere in one of my cases."

"Until now?" Mrs. Hudson asked.

"Until now," he confirmed. "The closest I've come to dealing with this fool was when I prevented him attacking an older gentleman who, at the time, was being led off to Scotland Yard for fraud."

"Was that the Mark Stephens case?" I asked.

"Yes, Watson. A man I later proved innocent. Over the ensuing months, I have heard rumors of similar incidents involving Potts. I even kept a file of my own on him. But there have been no other such incidents directly in my path."

"Until now," repeated Mrs. Hudson.

"Precisely. On the positive side, this Potts isn't a very bright or imaginative fellow. From the little research I was able to do on him at the time, I am aware of at least three likely places where he might be holding Mrs. Weisskopf."

Holmes snatched a sheet of paper from his desk, quickly scrawled some notes, and handed it to me. "I need you to go to the Yard, Watson. I believe Inspector MacDonald is on duty tonight. We could do far worse than use his help."

"Why don't we go see the inspector together?" I asked, folding the sheet to place it in my pocket.

"Because I believe it essential for me to locate Mrs. Weisskopf as soon as possible. There is no telling how much danger she might be in. If I find Potts in time, I'll be able to stall him until the official police arrive. Assuming Hannah's mother is still alive and unharmed – "

Mrs. Hudson placed her hands over Hannah's ears, although not quickly enough.

Seeing the girl's eyes start to swell with tears again, Holmes quickly added, " – which of course she will be. We can more-than-likely get her safely home by midnight, if not before."

"No," Mrs. Hudson interrupted.

Holmes and I turned as one to stare at our landlady, standing with arms folded.

"Mr. Holmes," she continued, "from what little I've been able to gather here, I believe you still need all the help you can get. Allow *me* to call on Inspector MacDonald myself. I shall bring Hannah with me for her well-being, as well as to assure her of her mother's safety. Whereas you, Mr. Holmes, shall certainly require the Good Doctor's assistance."

I bowed in her direction, flattered.

"Of course, I need his company," Holmes replied. "I was merely going over my possibilities aloud. Thank you for your kind offer, Mrs. Hudson." He turned to the girl. "Hannah, Mrs. Hudson will take excellent care of you. You're in good hands."

I also nodded to the wide-eyed child in reassurance.

Holmes was already at the door, coat in hand. "Watson! Bring your revolver! The game is afoot!"

The first of the three locations Holmes had planned to investigate was an abandoned warehouse in a run-down waterfront area of London. An outside streetlamp provided a mix of dull light and deep shadows within, visible through the shattered windows. Its door was unlocked, and even hung slightly ajar. Holmes carefully pushed it open.

At his signal, we paused upon entering, letting our eyes adjust to the dim interior.

Suddenly, Holmes grasped my elbow and silently pointed to the far wall. There, I could just make out the thin figure of a light-haired woman, who lay curled atop a rough wooden bench.

"Could that be Helga Weisskopf?" I asked Holmes. The answer was obvious. We had found our location on the first try.

"Hush!" Holmes whispered harshly.

The woman obviously heard our words. She shifted awkwardly onto her left side, to turn toward us. Even in the poor lighting, and being several yards distant, I was able to see her eyes widen in . . . Surprise? Fear?

She couldn't call out to us. A thick cloth was bound tight across her lips. Her arms, too, were tied behind her, hindering her movements. Her shoulders shivered, likely from more than the cool November air.

Holmes softened his tone further, so that I could barely make out his words. "We must approach her with due caution."

"Better you do not approach at all!"

That sudden shrill voice echoed through the near-empty warehouse space. The speaker rushed from the shadows to stand between us and his captive. A long, dark gray coat covered the man from shoulder to knee, while the light from outside glinted off his near-bald skull. His scraggly moustache curled above a disturbing grin.

What attracted my attention most, naturally, was the revolver that he pointed in our direction.

Holmes gave the weapon a brief, indifferent glance, while making no immediate move to address the threat, or even raise his hands in surrender. "Zechariah Potts."

The man snorted. I took this response as a yes.

Holmes continued. "I wonder, might you introduce us to your guest? We haven't formally met, but I'm told that she – "

"That woman?" Potts spat. "You want me to introduce you to this worthless piece of trash?"

He nodded toward the tied woman, who now managed to sit up awkwardly behind him. The wide-eyed victim wasn't attached to the bench itself. I assumed this was so Potts could drag her with him, serving as a human shield, should he feel the need to flee.

"That seems rather a harsh thing to say," my friend replied.

"That rat-bag wants nothing less but to destroy my life!" Potts barked. "She deserves whatever punishment happens to her tonight!"

"On the contrary," Holmes replied, an edge creeping into his voice, "from what little I know of you, you are quite capable of accomplishing any misfortune on your own, Mister Potts."

The abductor spat again. "You are one to talk, Mister Sherlock Holmes! Oh, I remember you, right enough. And that fool standing beside you? Is he the one who wrote up that case in the recent *Beeton's*? Of course he is! How he twisted the way the London public should perceive you!"

Potts continued waving his gun between Holmes and me as he ranted. I considered shifting further aside, in order to make his targeting more difficult. Unfortunately, the man's deep, animalistic growl discouraged that.

"And you would know that latter fact how, exactly?" Holmes questioned.

"That story was too unrealistic to pass as accurate detective work. Stand still, Doctor Watson!"

My only move had been to shift from one leg to the other, but it attracted his attention, as I'd intended. In the shadows behind our assailant, I could still make out his captive, arms bound to her sides, struggling to her feet. If Mrs. Weisskopf could safely slip outside while her captor concentrated on Holmes and myself, our task here would be more than half done.

"Now," the mustached man continued, "I order both of you to remove your guns and lay them on the floor. Don't pretend you aren't armed! Do it!"

I started to reach into my pocket, but then, seeing Holmes make no such move, paused.

"I might be more concerned, Mister Potts," my friend stated calmly, "if I thought the weapon you are holding was actually loaded."

"Eh?" Potts' eyes narrowed. "You speak nonsense! I put the bullets in the chambers myself, not two days ago."

Holmes shrugged. "So you say. Given the ease with which you wave that weapon about, however, it definitely appears to lack that additional weight."

Potts shook his head again in denial, but he couldn't resist raising the revolver in front of his eyes for a quick look.

That action was all the opportunity Holmes needed. He leapt forward and, with a quick swipe at the man's wrist, sent our opponent's gun flying. It struck the floor within a few feet of myself.

Unexpectedly, at that same moment, the bound woman lunged forward, shouldering Potts from behind. Pinned between his two assailants, Potts crashed to the floor with a groan. The woman, too, toppled, but landing on his body softened her impact.

While Holmes bent to slip a pair of handcuffs from his coat pocket onto Potts' wrists, I knelt down to retrieve the man's weapon.

"What the devil . . . ?" Potts groaned. The woman rolled off him, then spun around to kick him, once in the stomach, and again lower down.

Potts rolled onto his side, glaring silently at the three of us in turn.

"Yes, do be quiet!" Holmes snapped. He gently pulled the woman aside and helped her to her feet. "We've heard enough nonsense from you."

"Holmes?" I addressed him with a frown.

"What is it?" he asked, as he undid Mrs. Weisskopf's bindings.

I raised Potts' weapon into my friend's line of sight, careful to keep my own fingers away from the trigger, then spun open the chamber. "I don't wish to cause you any additional distress, but the gun is, indeed, loaded. Fully."

"I thought it might be," he replied.

"But you just told him that it wasn't . . . ."

"I implied that it likely wasn't. A small exaggeration on my part. I expect that you, Watson, given your military experience, would be aware that the small extra weight of a handful of bullets can be barely noticeable. Given Mister Potts' mental state, I felt certain he would feel compelled by my remark, if only for a moment, to doubt his own memory of when and how he loaded the gun."

"And suppose he'd decided to check that little detail by firing the gun at you, rather than simply looking at the chambers?"

"It was a calculated risk." Finally, Holmes removed the cloth that had dug so tightly between the woman's lips.

She coughed, took a deep breath, and spat twice to clear her throat.

"Take your time, Mrs. Weisskopf," Holmes advised, offering his hand. "We have ample opportunity to talk. You are Mrs. Weisskopf, are you not? Hannah's mother?"

She nodded, reaching out with one arm to support herself against a nearby empty crate. "*Ich bin Helga, ja*. I mean 'Yes'. Herr Holmes, I must know: Where is my daughter?" Her eyes nervously circled the room.

"She is in good hands, Mrs. Weisskopf, of that I can assure you. We expect to reunite the two of you shortly."

"*Gott in Himmel!* Ever since that *wahnsinnig*, that maniac, began following me, I worried about my child! He claimed his actions had to do with how I was bringing her up, and the stories I told her!"

"I understand your pain," Holmes agreed. He then turned towards a rustling sound that came from the main door. "Ah! I believe we have company."

"*Mein Gott!* Potts has friends?"

316

Holmes shook his head, smiling thinly. "That seems most unlikely, Mrs. Weisskopf." He turned to face a trio of figures as they entered the open space.

"Good evening, Inspector," Holmes greeted. "Better late than never."

Inspector Alec MacDonald's tall, bony frame slowly approached us, accompanied by two constables. His dark eyes focused on Holmes, Mrs. Weisskopf, and myself as we stood to casually meet them. Zechariah Potts, who lay tightly bound on the rough wooden floor before us, merely grumbled, being less pleased by the new visitors.

"I'd expected to run into you a little sooner, Inspector," Holmes greeted. "This abandoned warehouse was the first place on my list."

"Indeed, it was," MacDonald replied. "Based on the way in which you sometimes work, however, Mr. Holmes, I expected that list had been compiled by you in reverse order, therefore allowing more time for you to resolve the case on your own."

"My apologies. We both miscalculated, then. I shall bear that in mind in the future. This evening, however, the situation has worked itself out quite well."

"*Mein* daughter!" the woman suddenly cried out to the detective. "Have you seen her?"

MacDonald gave her a reassuring nod. "Have no fear, Mrs. Weisskopf. Hannah is being looked after at the station. A cute little child she is, too." He turned to his accompanying officers, then pointed to the seething Zechariah Potts. "It appears we will have some additional company there this evening."

The rest of the night could hardly have gone better.

That next morning, while I sat in my usual armchair in the sitting room, sorting through some papers, I heard an all-too-familiar sigh. Holmes stood in the doorway of his bed chamber, tying his dressing gown. As expected, when he wasn't actively working on a case, or doing research elsewhere, the hour was close to noon.

"It appears to me," he observed, before I could utter a single word, "that you have already begun working on your notes in regards to our little adventure last night."

I shrugged, lowering the papers I'd been perusing onto my lap.

My friend stroked his chin. Then he said, "I hope, for my sake, that, should you plan to publish more of our escapades, this tale will not be one of them. I fear I accomplished very little in the way of actual deductive work this time."

I couldn't help raising an eyebrow. "I might agree with you on that point."

317

"Mind you, I understand you might feel it necessary to write up every case we share, but not all of them would be of interest to the general public."

"I absolutely concur," I replied. "Many of these stories will be best left in my dispatch box, since there is nothing to learn from them."

"Excellent. I'm glad we share that idea."

"Considering the lukewarm response to the one I did finally have published, I may prefer to simply write up your cases for my own amusement."

"I might not go that far . . . ."

"But what I have here on my lap at the moment has nothing to do with last night's case."

Holmes leaned forward, eyebrows raised, to stare more closely at the documents. "Indeed it does! The handwriting is obviously not your own." He rubbed his thumb and forefinger across the top page. "Furthermore, this is not even your usual stock of paper."

I offered a thin smile. "Mrs. Weisskopf had these pages delivered to me this morning, *via* Mrs. Hudson. She, at least, was impressed with my published interpretation of one of your cases, and therefore wished for my opinion of her own work. English is her first language, so much of her style comes off as rather stiff. Nonetheless, from what I have so far read, I feel certain that the editor at *Beeton's* might be interested in publishing her work."

Holmes clapped his hands together. "Capital!"

I pulled out one particular sheet and handed it to him. "The girl, Hannah, also included this sketch of your pipe, since you seemed to like playing with it while the two of you talked."

He gave a sharp laugh, reaching out eagerly. "My best compensation in some time! I'll hang it in my room. Now, if you'll excuse me, I have a few notes to go over myself. I plan to call on Inspector MacDonald later this afternoon, concerning Mr. Potts. You are, naturally, more than welcome to join me."

I raised my papers again, rattling them. "Let us see how much further I can get through this manuscript by the time you're ready to leave."

With a brief nod, Holmes slipped back into his bedroom to change.

He knew, of course, that I'd be only too glad to join him.

# The Mystery of the
# Medical Misdiagnosis
## by Will Murray

During my career as a medical practitioner in London, I have treated a considerable number of patients from all walks of life. I consider myself to be a more-than-competent physician, and in my association with Mr. Sherlock Holmes, London's only consulting detective, I have been privileged to offer such medical insights into his cases as were needed. I note with pleasure that my knowledge has on more than one occasion assisted my friend in resolving a difficult investigation.

As Holmes's friend and flat-mate, it was inevitable that he would turn to me at those rare times whenever his health faltered. I must assert that despite Holmes's leisurely and often indolent habits, his health was of the steady sort. Only rarely did he ever become seriously sick. Now and again, the odd cold came and went, but left no lasting mark. So it was that one rainy winter evening in the year 1888 that I returned home from my medical duties to discover Holmes seated by the hearth, his pipe resting cold and empty upon the mantel, looking altogether miserable.

Doffing my waterproof, I asked, "Are you ill, my dear fellow?"

Nodding, Holmes said, "I fear that something unpleasant is coming on."

Taking my customary chair, I observed him for a few moments and began to suspect a commonplace cold.

"What are your symptoms?" I asked.

"They vary. My nose is stuffy. I have a bothersome headache, and now and again a chill passes through my frame."

"That sounds as if you have caught a cold."

"This doesn't feel like a cold, or any other respiratory problem of my previous experience, although some of the unpleasant sensations I'm currently suffering support your preliminary diagnosis."

"Perhaps you should take to your bed."

"I would prefer not to, for I have a problem to solve."

"It must be quite interesting for you to forsake the comfort of bedrest, for you know it's the perfect tonic, and can be counted on to speed along your recuperation."

Holmes frowned disagreeably. "I'm of a mind to think that I'm not traveling in the direction toward recuperation, but rather that I'm slipping further into inconvenient illness."

319

"All the more reason to seek your bed," I encouraged. "I find that when illness overcomes a man or a woman, sleeping for prolonged lengths of time greatly assists a patient in passing through the various stages of his malady."

"There will be time enough to rest in a few hours," returned Holmes stubbornly.

I then abandoned this tack, for I knew it would do no good.

"Tell me of your latest problem," I requested.

"For the moment," said Holmes, "I'll have to beg your indulgence, if not your forgiveness. I have the mental strength to apply my brain to this particular problem, but not to share it. Perhaps later."

"Very good," I responded. "Would you like me to have Mrs. Hudson brew you a strong pot of tea?"

Here, Holmes wavered. He appeared to my practiced eye to have some difficulty concentrating. At length, he responded by saying, "It will do no harm to do so. And I thank you for suggesting it, for my mouth is unaccountably parched."

Going downstairs, I went to speak with Mrs. Hudson, and before long she brought up a tray of strong-brewed tea, along with cream and sugar.

"Mr. Holmes!" exclaimed Mrs. Hudson when she set eyes on him, shivering in his chair. "Forgive me for saying that you look positively frightful."

"Thank you, Mrs. Hudson," said Holmes in reference to the tea. "I feel negatively unwell. There is nothing positive about my condition."

Mrs. Hudson didn't seem to know how to take Holmes's remark, so she simply withdrew.

I took the liberty of pouring two cups of tea and handed one to Holmes. He took his in both hands, and I noticed the acute paleness of his fingers and of his countenance. This bothered me.

As we sat drinking our tea in silence, I studied Holmes further.

As a doctor, I was trying to observe symptoms in an effort to render an intelligent diagnosis. One of the problems of my field is that so many symptoms point to entirely different diseases. One must never jump to conclusions prematurely, lest one misdiagnose a patient.

The significant part of the art of diagnosis is drawing out the patient in terms of his salient symptoms, as well as recent experiences that may illuminate the problem. Here, I was somewhat stymied by Holmes's reluctance to talk, so I was left to study him in silence. My observations tended towards the onset of an incipient cold or influenza. However, Holmes's chance remark that this felt like no respiratory illness he had previously experienced stayed me from concluding a concrete diagnosis.

Over the course of the next hour, we drank the teapot dry, and I noticed that despite the blazing fire in the hearth, Holmes continued shivering.

I waited in vain for him to speak, but he simply sat thinking, and the fact that he didn't once avail himself of his black clay pipe was so unusual as to be disturbing. I didn't know what to make of that. Listening carefully, I heard no wheezing suggestive of lung trouble, but that didn't mean it wasn't coming on.

Sherlock Holmes is a man of odd habits. One of his most peculiar customs was that he often stayed up late and arose early. It was rare when he did the opposite.

However, on this particular evening, he retired at nine o'clock. This rather staggered me, and made my concern only the more acute, but I knew that it was for the best, so I forbore to remark on the alteration of his nightly habit.

"Good night, Holmes," said I.

"Good night," he replied dully.

And so the door to his bedroom closed shut, and I was left to contemplate the unhappy prospect that my good friend's health was in decline.

During the next day, I ministered to Sherlock Holmes to the best of my ability.

Regrettably the best of my ability fell far short of my own professional standards, for Holmes's condition worsened with a slow steadiness that unnerved me. I had observed many patients over the course of my medical career and was alert to any symptoms that would aid me in understanding Holmes's particular ailment. During this time, I considered and rejected many sound possibilities. The poor man didn't have a fever. Instead, he suffered from the onset of chills, but these were intermittent.

I inquired as to his recent meals, but the only item that alarmed me was that he had consumed some mutton stew that might have spoiled. However, I had partaken of the same stew, and I felt perfectly well.

"Are you certain that you've eaten nothing that might have led to your present condition?" I asked at one point.

"Absolutely nothing," he groaned.

Having satisfied myself on that point, I considered other maladies and their causes. The symptoms that presented themselves didn't assist me in that endeavor. They were perplexing and problematic. I found myself balked in a way to which I wasn't accustomed.

Examining my familiar patient for insect bites, I discovered nothing of the sort. Nor were there any wounds that might have contributed to an infection or poisoning. This wasn't tetanus. Nor was it an infection of the skin.

Momentarily, I wished that medical science would produce a machine that would allow a physician to peer into the human body and discover processes that were hidden from view. Alas, if there was anything untoward transpiring within Holmes's physique, I had no access to it.

Nor could I imagine what the problem was. I confess that it was entirely baffling.

By the morning of the following day, Holmes was sinking. I had no choice but to summon the ambulance brigade to convey him to my old *alma mater*, St. Bartholomew's Hospital.

By this time, Holmes was deathly pale and his skin clammy. I began to fear the worst outcome possible. Fixing my expression into a professional mask so that my grave concerns didn't reveal themselves, I conferred with several hospital doctors, all of whom were equally puzzled. Numerous theories were offered and discarded as a poor fit.

On the morning of the next day, I visited Holmes, who complained that he couldn't eat his breakfast. Furthermore, he couldn't force himself to consume any solid food. Only water, which he drank for his dry mouth.

His features were now sunken, and he shivered from time to time, as if afflicted with palsy.

I began to suspect poison. In that era, unfortunate Londoners were prone to coming into contact with dangerous substances, which led to accidental poisonings. Arsenic was the chief culprit, but there were many others.

"Tell me," I asked in an even tone that concealed my worries, "have you been engaged in any interesting cases of late?"

"Nothing extraordinary," he replied. "I have recently been around to Scotland Yard, where I gave Inspector Lestrade the benefit of my insights on matters that were cluttering his desk. None of those cases were mine, and none struck me as compelling."

I took Holmes at his word and once more struggled to understand what was happening within his constitution. Although not a robust man, being spare of frame, I knew Holmes to be almost preternaturally strong, in spite of his lean physique. Seeing him lying prostate and increasingly unable to muster up his strength, I commenced to despair inwardly.

That afternoon, Holmes turned his head on the pillow, looked at me in a kind of controlled agony, and groaned, "Watson, you must help me! I'm sinking rapidly, and I fear that I shall die. Consult all medical experts. Find the solution to this insufferable ailment."

"Don't despair," I reassured him. "You reside in the best hospital in all of London, and the most competent doctors are at your disposal."

"I'm aware of that. Just as I'm keenly aware that my condition worsens by the hour. I'm fast losing hope."

With that, he turned his drawn face away from me, and I stood up, shaken to the core of my very being.

Sherlock Holmes appeared to be dying. It seemed so impossible that I struggled to accept the idea, but once I did, a firm resolve welled up within me.

I wouldn't allow it. I simply wouldn't permit this great and wonderful man to pass from this earth. Not without a vigorous fight.

I consulted one of the resident physicians, Doctor Winters, whom I knew quite well. He was ten years my senior and a physician of unparalleled skill and experience.

"I begin to suspect poison," I told him.

"If Mr. Holmes has been poisoned, I cannot imagine by what agent. He displays none of the traits of a man laid low by nightshade or cyanide or any of the other common poisons."

"Nevertheless," I returned, "I have eliminated all other possible causes. He isn't suffering from any recognizable malady. Therefore, poison is what remains, even if the poison is an unknown one."

Dr. Winters couldn't convince me otherwise, and I believe he began to suspect the truth of my supposition. But what was the truth?

I was reminded of what Paracelsus famously observed: *"What is there that isn't a poison? All things are poison, and nothing is without poison. Solely the dose determines that a thing is not a poison."*

Returning to Holmes's private room, I plied him with questions.

"Is there a case," I began, "in which you are engaged that you have left hanging?"

For a minute, Holmes didn't stir himself. Finally, he found the strength to reply. "I had been assisting a Mrs. Carbon on a certain matter, but the trail had gone cold, and I had recently informed her that I was at an impasse."

"Would you like me to convey to Mrs. Carbon your regrets that you are at the moment indisposed?"

"If you think it important. She lives in Earl's Court. The address is 13 Suffering Mews."

"If I have the opportunity, I may drop by and reassure the woman that you haven't forgotten her."

Holmes didn't reply to that. I gathered that he had expended his available strength in answering my questions and was sinking back into his oppressive lethargy.

At that point I quietly took my leave.

Departing from the hospital, I found a hansom cab and engaged it. The driver straightaway took me to 13 Suffering Mews, where I knocked on the plain door.

A woman answered my knock. She was bundled up in a shawl, and although she looked somewhat aged, her visible hair was quite black, even though shot with grey. She was a small creature who stood leaning upon a wooden walking stick. She looked up at me with dark suspicious eyes in an oval face that tended toward swarthiness. The touch of olive in her complexion made me suspect Greek or Italian parentage.

"Are you Mrs. Carbon?" I inquired.

"Yes, I am. What can I do for you, good sir?"

"My name is Dr. Watson. I'm a friend of Mr. Sherlock Holmes. He asked me to come round and reassure you that he hasn't forgotten you."

"Ah. I have been wondering. It's been several days since I saw him. Is he well?"

"On the contrary, Mr. Holmes is presently at Barts."

A sparkle of interest came into the old woman's eyes. "Is that correct?" she asked without a trace of surprise. "And what is his condition?"

I thought the question slightly impertinent, but didn't say so. After all, it was no business of this woman.

"Mr. Holmes has taken to his sick bed," I informed her, "but I have every confidence that he will arise from it quite recovered."

The interest in the old woman's eyes seemed to subside.

"I imagine good Mr. Holmes will make himself known before too long," she said. "I thank you, Dr. Watson, for bringing me this news."

"You are entirely welcome, Madame. Good day."

From Suffering Mews, I returned to Baker Street.

The homey sitting room I shared with Holmes felt strangely empty and forlorn when first I stepped into it. I was accustomed to him being absent for days and weeks at a time when on an investigation, so the silence was a familiar one.

Knowing that there was a risk that Holmes might never return from the hospital, the atmosphere stuck me as positively funereal. No doubt some of this was my imagination, but I couldn't shake off the unpleasant possibilities that stretched out ahead in the unimaginable future.

Taking my customary chair before the blazing hearth, I sat and smoked cigarettes in silence. There, I racked my brains for solutions to the problem.

Again, I reviewed everything that Holmes had said he had eaten, where he had gone, and with whom he had had contact. Nothing suggested a misadventure culminating in a life-threatening illness.

As the fire took away the winter chill, I fancied that I could hear my friend lecturing me in his urgent way: *"Think, Watson, think!"*

Alas, my mental processes proved fruitless. I hadn't Holmes's superlative mind. That was his, and his alone.

I slept fitfully that night. My brain wouldn't succumb to rest. The many possibilities went 'round and 'round in my head. Regrettably, they arrived at no logical or conclusive destination.

I kept thinking of Holmes's famous dictum that once all possibilities were eliminated, whatever remained must be the truth, no matter how improbable.

This brought me to a single inescapable, if improbable, conclusion.

The following morning, I found Holmes to be in a distressing condition. Nevertheless, I addressed him in regard to my singular suspicion.

"I paid Mrs. Carbon a visit yesterday," I told him. "She expressed concern about your condition."

Holmes nodded wordlessly.

"I was rather surprised, once I told her that you were indisposed, how quickly she jumped to the conclusion that you had been ill for some time."

"It is a reasonable conclusion to jump to," he replied weakly.

"Perhaps," I returned. "But I thought there was something off or even untoward about it."

"I don't know you to be an imaginative man," Holmes remarked in a tired voice.

"I don't consider myself to be particularly subject to flights of fancy," I agreed. "However, I've been applying your dictum about eliminating all conceivable possibilities to this distressing matter."

At that, Holmes perked up.

"Have you arrived at any conclusion?"

"Only a tentative one," I rejoined. "It has crossed my mind that I have never seen Mrs. Carbon in our consulting room. Tell me, why is that?"

"She is quite frail and cannot make the journey. In response to her letter of inquiry, I visited her dwelling in order to confer on her case."

"I gathered that," I replied. "And how often have you called upon her?"

"Only twice."

"Tell me, did she serve you refreshments?"

"Only tea."

"I see. Black tea?"

"Yes."

"And did it taste in anyway dubious?"

325

"Not in the least," said Holmes.

"So one could rule out poison in the tea?"

Holmes sat up with great difficulty and turned his head in my direction. His eyes were feverish and noticeably dilated.

"I would rule it out entirely," he said firmly. "What leads you to suspect such a thing?"

"Because all other possibilities of which I'm aware have been excluded. You have no other clients at this time. You didn't seem to have come into contact with very many people, and certainly not any who would wish harm on you."

"While that is sound reasoning," he declared, "for the tea to be poisonous, it would have to be a rare and untraceable concoction, for it tasted perfectly ordinary."

I reminded him of Paracelsus' observations regarding poison and added, "Until recent years, accidental arsenicosis of women and children wearing clothing dyed with Scheele's green was an English scandal. It took many tragic deaths before the dye's lethal nature was suspected. By that reckoning, perhaps you have encountered some other substance not yet known to have a deleterious effect on the human system."

"I can think of no unfamiliar substance," murmured Holmes.

He sank back onto his pillow and stared up at the ceiling. His profile, which was normally as sharply-etched as an American Indian, seemed somehow less defined, as if dissolution were setting in.

His silence told me that he was thinking.

This process of cogitation went on for a considerable period of time. I knew my friend well, and long enough that I didn't interject myself into the flow of his innermost thoughts. They were like a river seeking an appropriate level. I didn't want to be the accidental dam that inhibited the all-important process.

After some minutes, Holmes turned to me and said sincerely, "I believe you have hit upon it."

"You do?"

"Mrs. Carbon had engaged me to find her long-missing husband. She has been writing letters to distant towns and receiving answers. Both times I came around her place, she would serve me tea and tell me the latest information about her husband's presumed whereabouts. However, my own investigations went nowhere. Absolutely nowhere."

"Do you think she was leading you on?"

"No," returned Holmes, shaking his head slowly. "I now believe she was leading me in circles. I find myself questioning whether in fact there ever was a missing Mr. Carbon. Perhaps the purpose of these meetings was to gull me into drinking her tea."

Holmes fixed me with a bleary eye. "Do you think you can pay Mrs. Carbon another visit?"

"I am certain that I can."

"See if you might inveigle her into inviting you in. Tell her that I have made some progress in the quest for her husband. No, that will not do, for he may not exist. Better still, inform her that my health is failing and I'm unable to complete the investigation. That may do the trick."

"It well may, but what else do you want me to do?"

"If she's willing to serve you a cup of tea, and I suspect that she will, pretend to drink it and see if you can't steal away with the teacup."

"I fear that, though a simple task, it would also be rather challenging."

"If you cannot, see if you can't surreptitiously pour some of the tea into a flask. In either event, bring back whatever you can. Whatever you do, Watson, do not permit the contents of the cup to touch your lips. And please do not fail. Your efforts may go far in saving my life."

"You have my word that I'll do my utmost," I said, laying a reassuring hand upon his wrist. It felt cold and clammy. Involuntarily, my fingers recoiled from the touch.

Going back out into the London morning, I wasted no time in finding a cab and instructing the driver to take me to Suffering Mews.

Arriving at the woman's home, I knocked on the door, which duly fell open. Leaning upon her cane, Mrs. Carbon looked rather startled to see me.

Recovering her composure, she asked, "Have you fresh news of Mr. Holmes?"

"I'm afraid that I have unfortunate news. May I come in?"

Again that unusual gleam came into her eyes. It was almost eager. Certainly, she suspected what I was about to convey. Her face twitched into a concerned look, and I couldn't tell whether or not it was genuine.

I followed into her modest kitchen, where she invited me to sit, and then asked, "Would you like a spot of tea?"

"I would welcome one," I returned.

She put the kettle on the stove, prepared the teapot, and sat down while we waited for the water to boil.

"What news have you?"

"As I mentioned, I am a medical doctor. I fear that he is sinking, and may not survive the week."

"That is terrible news," replied the woman in a flat tone of voice. Was there a trace of disappointment in her expression. It seemed so to me.

"Mr. Holmes asked me to convey his apologies and regrets to you. He doesn't think he can complete his investigation on your behalf."

327

"That is very kind for a dying man, but I quite understand."

The woman's dark eyes took on an inward look. And she seemed to be thinking very deeply.

I studied her. Her true feelings were difficult to read, yet I was taken aback by her lack of emotion. Women are often more sympathetic to tragedies than men, who attempt to temper their true feelings.

The kettle was soon hissing steam. I watched carefully as she prepared afternoon tea, first setting out two porcelain cups she took from her cupboard. Hot water was carefully poured into a waiting teapot, and allowed to steep. Finally, she poured the dark brew into the empty cups. There was no sign of introducing any extraneous substance into the mixture. Indeed, had she done so, I would have observed it clearly.

Carrying the steaming teacups to the table, she set one before me and took her seat. I noticed that our cups were decorated by images of two different Catholic saints, neither of whom I recognized.

I let mine cool for a bit, and then pretended to take a sip. She watched me with more than casual interest. Fortunately, my mustache aided my subterfuge.

Mrs. Carbon drank from her own teacup freely.

Raising my cup to my lips and tilting it backward, I made a pretense of taking another sip. Replacing the cup on its saucer, I nodded as if I had found the beverage agreeable to my taste.

"As a doctor, have you diagnosed Mr. Holmes's ailment?" she asked me.

"No, it is entirely baffling."

She nodded to herself, yet didn't reply. Then, catching herself, she added, "How unfortunate."

I noticed that Mrs. Carbon didn't pursue the question any further. She appeared devoid of curiosity.

I took another feigned sip of tea and wiped my lips carefully with a table napkin.

I remarked, "There are doctors at Barts who are wondering if Holmes hasn't been poisoned."

Mrs. Carbon took that in and, once again, I noticed her lack of curiosity. Neither did she comment.

"However," I continued, "I myself have ruled out poison. The known poisons are specifically symptomatic. None of Mr. Holmes's symptoms point to a known poison."

"Perhaps, Dr. Watson, there is an unknown potion that you and your doctor friends don't know about."

I forced a short laugh. "I doubt very much if there are poisons of which London doctors are ignorant."

"Oh, you would be surprised," she said with a peculiar little laugh.

I pressed the point. "Have you ever heard of a poison that is unknown to the medical profession?"

"If I had heard of it, kind sir, it wouldn't be unknown, now would it?"

"No, I imagine that it would not."

Mrs. Carbon's slow smile was quite thin. After a reflective pause, she commented, "Mr. Holmes must have a remarkable constitution."

"What makes you say that, Madam?"

"Because he has been sick for so long, yet hasn't yet succumbed to his ailment."

Here, I had to steady myself, for I shook with the shock of recognition.

I hadn't told Mrs. Carbon how long Holmes had been ill, but she seemed to assume it had been much longer than my suggestion of the previous visit.

"This tea is quite delicious," said I. "Mr. Holmes remarked upon it more than once."

"I'm glad that he enjoyed it, although it is nothing special – merely common black tea mixed with a modest dose of Keemun."

"Well, it is quite good."

"I noticed that you haven't finished your cup."

"I am savoring it."

"Very good. You may take your time. I'll brew another, if you will take it."

"I think this will be satisfactory," I returned.

"Well, I think I'll have another, since you are so slow to drink yours."

Standing up and turning her back on me, she fixed another cup from the teapot reposing on the sideboard.

During this interval, I removed a small glass flask colored cobalt blue from my coat pocket and poured the tea into it, capping it hurriedly and replacing it in my pocket.

When she returned with a fresh cup, Mrs. Carbon had no inkling that I had emptied the cup without drinking any of its contents.

Upon her return to the table, I engaged the woman in innocuous conversation, then announced that I had to be on my way.

"I imagine that I'll read about Mr. Sherlock Holmes's fate in the newspapers," said she, reaching for her cane.

"I fear that you will," I replied in a melancholy tone.

With the help of her cane, Mrs. Carbon rose to let me out. I had the cup in my hand, and slipped it into my coat pocket without her seeing me do so.

After I bid her farewell, I walked the wintry streets until I found a cab rank and ordered the hansom driver back to Barts.

When I saw Holmes lying in his bed, for a moment I thought he had succumbed to his ailment. He looked deathly pale. His eyes were closed, and the rhythmic rising and falling of his chest was almost undetectable.

"My dear Holmes!" I began.

Alas, my friend didn't respond.

Placing a hand on his chest, I could feel his heart beating, although rather faintly. Feeling for his pulse, I found it thready and weak.

But Holmes was breathing regularly. So there was that.

"I have succeeded in getting a sample of the suspect brew," I advised.

My words seemed to penetrate his lethargy, and he opened his eyes. Turning his head to me, he said, "Very good, Watson. Have it analyzed for poison."

I did so. Several toxicologic tests were conducted by a chemist in the hospital's chemical laboratory, including the Marsh Test for arsenic. The results were disappointing. I conveyed them to Holmes.

"I'm afraid that little noteworthy was discovered, no doubt owing to combination of hot water and tea, which would mask foreign solutions. A small amount of grit was detected. Arsenic trioxide, dissolved in hot water, reveals itself as a precipitate when the water had cooled completely. However, this meagre quantity of white arsenic appears to be an insufficient amount to accomplish any murderous result. And your host of symptoms points in so many directions that arsenic alone cannot explain them."

"In that case," said Holmes, "there remains only one explanation."

"What is that?"

"One that should have occurred to me, I must confess, but I have been so ill and my brain so lethargic, the truth had escaped me until your timely intervention. For that, I sincerely thank you."

Holmes forced himself to sit up.

"There exists an obscure poisonous mixture known as *Aqua Tofana*. A professional poisoner named Giulia Tofana first formulated the concoction. It is all but undetectable, being tasteless, colorless, and without telltale odor. *Aqua Tofana* is of Italian origin, and its ingredients aren't known to this day. However, it is thought that white arsenic is among them. Its use was common during the tumultuous period in Italy corresponding to the middle 1600's. *Aqua Tofana* has the property of inducing illness with the first dose, which might or might not pass medical scrutiny. However, the women who employed it to do away with their husbands in that era would feed them individual drops slowly over time, leading to a progressive deterioration, ending in certain death."

"My word! I have never heard of the mixture."

"It is virtually unknown in England. Our domestic poisoners have no access to it. Hence, it baffled you and your medical colleagues."

"I observed the woman closely, and it didn't seem possible that she introduced any foreign solution into my tea. We drank from the same pot."

Holmes considered this information.

"I'm inclined in the belief that the brew itself wasn't poisoned, but the interior of the cup was coated with the insidious solution."

"That is entirely possible, I suppose, assuming that she would have had a contaminated cup prepared in advance."

"*Aqua Tofana* is cunningly mixed so that small dosages of the elixir are administered over time, producing the appearance of a progressive illness rather than a poisoning, thus reducing suspicion in the victim and his medical attendants."

"Is there an antidote?"

"Alas, not a certain one. A solution of vinegar and lemon juice has proven efficacious. However, it isn't yet clear that I have ingested sufficient quantities of the poison to end my life." Steel entered Holmes's tone. "Watson, I must persevere in order to bring this wicked woman to justice."

"What could be her motive in poisoning you?"

"That, my dear fellow, is a question that must await another day. The entirety of my attention must be directed toward recovery."

I said nothing in response to that brave declaration. By this point, Holmes was rather far gone. I was dubious as to his eventual recovery. I could not help but reflect that I had first encountered my dear friend in the chemical laboratory of this very hospital. Now I feared that we would be parted by death on these same grounds.

However, I shared his information with the other doctors. Together, we strove mightily to change the course of the frightful condition. We mixed a drink consisting of vinegar and lemon juice, which Holmes drank with difficulty. By forcing himself, he managed to consume three glasses each day. They didn't agree with him, but within one day, I detected a slight improvement in his color.

I discussed this with Dr. Winters. He was of the opinion that inasmuch as the ingredients of the mysterious solution known as *Aqua Tofana* were unknown, it was conceivable that other of its ingredients were calculated to obscure the lethal effect of the arsenic, or possibly to delay its pernicious effects.

"Some of Mr. Holmes's symptoms might be laid to mild arsenic poisoning," he observed, "but the totality of his condition suggests a larger cause."

"Perhaps the concoction included other noxious substances in order to confuse the issue, and so inhibit proper treatment."

"I suspect that any recovery is up to the will of the patient," Dr. Winters observed.

I could only concur.

Another day passed. Holmes neither recovered nor deteriorated. However, there was about him an entirely new aura. It was as if this revelatory information had enabled him to place his entire attention on recovery. No longer limited by the uncertainty of the root cause of his decline, he threw his entire will into battling back to good health.

I was not entirely surprised when, by the fourth day of the ordeal, Holmes had thrown himself out of his sick bed. To my surprise and delight, I found him walking around the hospital corridors, albeit unsteadily. During these determined perambulations, he relied heavily upon a hospital cane.

Holmes ate prodigiously and took up his black clay pipe once more. The latter more than anything else seemed to revive his spirits – that and the unanswered question of Mrs. Carbon's motives.

We discussed this question on the first day of his return to Baker Street, for within days, he was well enough to be discharged. This occurred on the morning of the sixth day of his convalescence.

"She might simply be a madwoman," I advised.

"She might, but I rather doubt it. I think she harbors some fell personal motive. I further imagine that the search for the missing Mr. Carbon was a red herring. There may not be such a person."

"Surely she could have no animus against you."

Holmes considered that statement at length. He smoked furiously. The question clearly consumed him.

After a time, he took down a book from a nearby shelf and consulted it at length. I recognized the volume. It contained newspaper cuttings pertinent to his career.

At last, he found something of interest. "Listen to this: Four years ago, there was a poisoner by the name of Carlo Carbonara, a laborer from Sicily. He acquired the detestable habit of taking out life insurance policies on his relatives, who had the convenient habit of passing on while young – convenient to Mr. Carbonara. Not so much to his victims. When the insurance company became suspicious of these deaths, the man fled, whereupon I fell upon his trail, and as a result, he was caught and sentenced to be hanged, a sentence that was duly carried out. Hmm. I wonder if Mrs. Carbon might not be the Widow Carbonara, hiding from the scandal of having the disgraced surname of a convicted poisoner?"

"That would certainly give her a personal motive to do away with you. But where will you find proof?"

"If I cannot find it, then I may concoct it."

"I beg your pardon?"

"You understand my meaning," Holmes returned gravely. "Even if you cannot imagine how I might go about this."

"I know that I cannot imagine it."

"At the moment, neither can I," said Holmes slowly. With that cryptic statement, he lapsed into a prolong silence.

The problem of Mrs. Carbon stood unaddressed for several days.

One afternoon, I returned to Baker Street and found Holmes smoking his cherrywood pipe. This was something he did only when in a certain mood. I could tell by the fixed expression on his lean features that this determined yet foul mood had entirely overtaken him.

"Ah, Watson," he said by way of greeting. "There you are. I have been waiting for you."

"You sound like your old self again," I remarked.

"I should like to think so. If you would, kindly keep your coat on. I have something for you to do."

"And what is that?"

"I would like you to pay another visit to Mrs. Carbonara – if I may be so presumptuous as to refer to her by that tainted name."

"Truly? For what purpose?"

"I would like you to inform her of my untimely demise."

"I take it you wish for me to report her response or reaction."

"That is part of it. I would also like you to remark upon the deliciousness of her tea in the hope that she will invite you in for another cup."

"I do not care for that opportunity, I must admit."

"You need not drink it. And of course, you will not, but as much as she has already attempted to poison you once, I think she may try again. The fact that you are a friend of mine would be sufficient motivation for a criminal poisoner. But by now she must have noticed the absence of the deadly teacup."

"And what is the purpose of this new visit?"

"That, my dear Watson, I will, for the moment, keep to myself. But I would like to accompany you on the ride."

"Keeping out of sight, I imagine."

"Keeping well out of sight," returned Holmes.

My mission imperfectly understood, I accompanied Holmes to the street below, where we availed ourselves of a waiting hansom cab.

Off to Earl's Court we went. Seated beside me, Holmes was unusually silent. When he did finally speak, it was to divest himself of an opinion pertinent to the matter at hand.

"Of all the types of murderers I have encountered in my career," he began, "the poisoner is the lowest of the breed. A man with a knife must be intent upon mayhem and perforce possess the steel with which to inflict his will to kill. A man with a pistol may shoot at close range or from a distance. Either way, he is correctly branded an assassin. A low type. But a person who would introduce lethal substances into an unsuspecting person's food or drink, I submit to you, lies at the bottom of a very dirty barrel."

"I cannot disagree with you," I conceded.

"An intended victim may fight back or flee a knife attack, and even do so successfully. A gunshot isn't always fatal. But it is rare when the poisoner's dirty work goes unaccomplished."

"Why do you suppose you survived this particular attack?" I asked.

"I suspect because I fell seriously ill prematurely. As you know, individuals possess unique characteristics and constitutions. A tincture of *Aqua Tofana* mixed to fell a grown man over successive doses might conceivably require three, four, or five doses. I fell ill after the second cup of tainted tea. Therefore, I didn't imbibe a third cup. This may be what initially saved me. Beyond that, the good offices of yourself and the physicians at Barts no doubt also played a significant role in my recovery. A solution of vinegar and lemon juice may taste abominably, but for the man who can stand it, it is a proven life saver."

"I would think your own constitution to have been a signal part of it."

"I won't disagree. In any event, I was given two doses, when three or four were necessary to dispose of me. But for that fact, I would probably now be lying in my grave."

"I shudder at the thought," said I.

"The fact that revenge was a motive doesn't absolve or excuse the poisoner from being branded the lowest of the low. I had no opportunity to defend myself. I was gulled into an unfounded sense of security by the old woman's gentle manner and expressed plight. Although I didn't suspect it on the two occasions I visited her, I was entirely at her mercy. And she had none. My destruction was her sole goal. This is unforgivable."

Hearing the manner in which Holmes delivered this last remark, I asked, "Does the desire for revenge drive this errand?"

Holmes frowned. "I'll not deny that my feelings toward this woman are cold and remorseless, but I won't sink to her putrid level. I'm a man of scruples. No, I merely wish for you to convey to her a false impression of the success of her despicable actions, and to carefully observe her reactions, which will be predictable."

"I'll do my best to accomplish this. And I'm pleased to hear that I'm not going to be an accomplice to murder, even if some might consider it justified."

"Murder is rarely justified," Holmes remarked. "And if justified, it cannot rightly be called murder."

That plain statement entirely allayed my vague fears, which were of course groundless. I knew Sherlock Holmes all too well. But rarely had I seen him so consumed with righteous anger.

Turning into Earl's Court, Holmes asked the driver to let him off prematurely, which he did. As the cab continued on, I saw him hurry along, and then conceal himself in an alley. After the hack drew into Suffering Mews, I alighted and stepped up to the door of Mrs. Carbon's flat. I knocked several times and at length I could hear the tapping of her cane as she approached the door.

After it fell open, her expression upon beholding me was a peculiar one. It seemed as if she was quite pleased to see me.

"Good day to you, Mrs. Carbon," I greeted.

"Hello, Dr. Watson. What brings you here? Further news of poor Mr. Holmes?"

"Alas, yes. But I think the tidings I bring must be tendered in private."

At that, she visibly brightened. "In that case, please step in. I'll put on some tea."

I followed her into the kitchen, where I took a chair at her small table.

As she busied herself preparing a pot of tea, Mrs. Carbon spoke softly.

"Am I to assume that the reason for your visit is that Mr. Holmes has at last succumbed to his illness?"

I nodded solemnly. "I thought I should inform you in person."

"That is good of you."

I watched as she took down two porcelain tea cups from the cupboard. I noticed for the first time that she selected one cup from a dim corner, where it reposed in isolation. The other cup came from a group sitting at the other side of the cupboard.

I suspected the isolated cup to be the lethal one.

Once the water had boiled, she poured it into a pot and let it steep.

Finally, she filled one teacup and then the other. Bringing both to the table, she carefully served me the isolated cup. I saw that my cup was

335

adorned by the image of the same Catholic saint that had graced the cup from which I had been previously imbibed. This realization gave me a slight chill of apprehension.

I sat there, observing the woman, and I must confess I was seeing her through entirely new eyes. She struck me now as quite cunning and practiced in the subtle yet fatal art that she apparently practiced.

I let the tea cool. Mrs. Carbonara was quite quiet. It was as if the thoughts in her head so dominated her brain that she couldn't rouse herself to make conversation.

"I imagine you will have to find another consulting detective," I observed.

The woman looked up. "Mr. Holmes was helping me search for my missing husband, for I miss him terribly. Unfortunately, he wasn't making progress. Perhaps my husband will never be found. I imagine I must make peace with that sad fact."

Her eyes took on that inward reflective look that I had seen before. Even though she was addressing me, it was as if I wasn't in the room with her. Her thoughts were no doubt far away.

With the knowledge I now possessed, her attitude convinced me of her guilt – not that I had had any doubt previously. I experienced a momentary chill thinking that before me sat the steaming cup of slow, remorseless death.

Coming out of her reverie, Mrs. Carbon looked up and observed, "You have barely touched your tea."

"It is too hot still. I must let it cool."

She lifted her own cup in hand and took a long sip.

"Mine is perfectly fine. It isn't too hot to the taste."

"I fear to burn my tongue," I returned.

Absorbing my remark, she looked at me rather quizzically, as if trying to divine my thoughts. I detected a tremor of suspicion on her wrinkled expression. She understood as well as I that the tea wasn't too hot to imbibe.

"Do you happen to know where Mr. Holmes will be buried?" she asked abruptly.

"I understand that it will probably be in Highgate Cemetery."

"I should like to attend the funeral and pay my respects."

"That is very good of you. Mr. Holmes held a firm opinion of you."

Mrs. Carbon didn't seem to pick up on the word firm. Or if she did, she let it pass.

"I believe the tea should be ready to drink now," she prompted.

Having no other choice, I lifted the cup to my lips and made the usual pretense. I wiped away any residue with a table napkin.

In that moment, I belatedly realized that Holmes had failed to give me sufficient instructions to carry me through this interview. I began to wonder what was the point of it all.

Then came a sharp rapping from the front door.

"You appear to have a visitor," I remarked.

"I rarely have visitors. Two in one day is noteworthy."

Reaching for her cane, she took it up and walked to the entrance foyer. I took that opportunity to pour half of my cup into the sink. I would have ridden myself of the entire contents, but I thought that would look suspicious.

As events developed, it was good that I did so.

From the entrance, I heard a sharp cry of exclamation. It was Mrs. Carbon, evidently startled to the point of panic.

Rushing from my chair, I made my way to the front door.

And there, standing in the doorway beyond the woman, loomed no less than Sherlock Holmes himself.

Turning at the sound of my approach, Mrs. Carbon fixed me with her dark eyes, crying out, "You told me that he was dead! And here he stands – alive yet!"

I said nothing. What was there to say? My gaze went to Holmes.

And so I failed to see the old woman swing her cane about and hurl it in my direction.

"Liar!" she cried. "You tricked me! Liar!"

I caught the cane in one hand. It landed with such force that I thought my wrist might be sprained, but it was only bone shock.

"That will be enough of that," exclaimed Holmes firmly. "You played a wicked game, Mrs. Carbonara, but it is over now."

At the sound of her true name, the woman turned back to Holmes and fell on him with a series of wild shrieks and hands like ripping bird claws.

Taking hold of her frail wrists in his strong fists, Holmes overmastered her quickly.

"What is the meaning of this?" she demanded.

"The meaning is that you are under suspicion of attempted murder by means of *Aqua Tofana*. Watson, do you still have your cup?"

"Yes, I do."

"Seize it as evidence."

From the woman's thin lips came a stream of unintelligible invective. I believe the language was Italian, but I didn't recognize any of the words.

"Mrs. Carbonara," declared Holmes with great gravity, "I must ask that you accompany us to Scotland Yard. There, you will be placed under arrest and charged with two counts of attempted murder. One against myself, and the other against Dr. Watson."

337

Holmes produced a pair of handcuffs. Rather forcefully, he snapped each ring around her thin wrists, locking them securely.

Thus restrained, the woman shrieked in protest, "You aren't a policeman! You cannot arrest me!"

"And you cannot prevent me from conveying you to Scotland Yard," returned Holmes firmly.

To me, Holmes said, "Be good enough to hire a suitable carriage, and don't forget to bring the incriminating cup."

I did this as quickly as possible while Holmes kept the woman under firm control.

I found a carriage, directed it to the door of 13 Suffering Mews, and Holmes forced the protesting woman into it. I had explained to the driver who I was and identified Sherlock Holmes. He expressed some hesitation about conveying two men who appeared to be kidnapping an older woman, but when we mentioned that our destination was Scotland Yard, this mollified him.

The ride to the Yard was an unpleasant one. Mrs. Carbonara shrieked and cursed vociferously. There seemed to be no end to it.

In due course, we arrived at Scotland Yard's gate. We took the woman inside, where we duly presented her to Inspector Lestrade, who was holding forth in his office.

To my mild surprise, Lestrade appeared to be expecting us.

"Is this the woman in question?" he asked as we entered.

"Is there any doubt?" returned Holmes.

"I imagine not," said Lestrade dryly.

It was then clear to me that Holmes had previously apprised the inspector of the trap he had laid for the wicked poisoner.

Mrs. Carbonara was made to sit down. By this point, she had expended her fury and showed every sign that the grim reality of her predicament was sinking in. The iron handcuffs clamping her wrists no doubt impressed the gravity of her position firmly upon her agitated mind.

Tendering to the inspector the teacup I had carried away, I said, "This is the cup that contained the potion this evil woman served me. It is proof of her guilt, for it is infused with *Aqua Tofana*."

Carefully, Lestrade took the cup and laid it aside.

The inspector attempted to interrogate the woman at length, but she refused all cooperation. Ultimately, he summoned one of his constables to convey the guilty woman to Old Bailey for arraignment.

Before she was escorted from Lestrade's office, Mrs. Carbonara made a request that chilled me to my marrow.

"I should like a proper cup of tea, if you please."

On the face of it, this was an innocuous request. But when uttering it, Mrs. Carbonara indicated the cup of evidence beside Lestrade.

"Madame," said Holmes, "you know that there is insufficient *Aqua Tofana* in that cup for the purpose of suicide."

"I'm willing to take my chances," she said dully.

"That is evidence in the case," snapped Lestrade. "Out with her," he told the waiting constable.

The woman was lifted to her feet. Turning to her erstwhile victim, Mrs. Carbonara all but sneered. Her voice dripping with venom, she said, "Such a small dose of tea, Mr. Holmes, but you would shrink from its taste as you would cower in the presence of a viper, would you not? You have tasted my bile, and found it too strong for your liking, didn't you? If my husband was here, he would – "

I don't know what kind of a reaction the woman expected from Holmes, but he simply regarded her without comment or emotional expression. This appeared to deflate her.

Inspector Lestrade regarded the woman with accusing eyes. "I believe that you will be following the same dark path that your late husband blazed before you."

Hearing these words, the finality of her situation evidently sank in, for Mrs. Carbonara's sharp tongue failed her. The constable took her away.

This denouement was rather anticlimactic from my point of view. But what led up to it was excessively histrionic. I was glad that it was over.

I listened quietly as Holmes and Inspector Lestrade went over the facts of the case.

"I would have preferred to have dispatched a policeman to arrest the woman," the inspector remarked.

"I quite understand," allowed Holmes, "but I wanted the satisfaction of seeing the look in her eyes when Mrs. Carbonara saw that I was still holding forth above the soil."

"I imagine that the sight of you was quite shocking to her."

"The woman put up a fight, but she was no match for me."

"Attempted poisoning is a grave crime, even if the victim didn't succumb. I imagine it will go rather hard on her."

"I think it should," returned Holmes. "If for no better reason than to dissuade future poisoners from plying their despicable trade."

"Very good," said Lestrade. "Well, I presume that you gentlemen will be perfectly willing to testify against her in court."

"I look forward to it," declared Holmes. "I would like, however, a modest favor. Permission to search her house for the bottle of *Aqua Tofana*. As you know, I have written a monograph on exotic poisons, and I had to gloss over this one due to an absence of verifiable facts. I would like to subject her solution to certain chemical tests in the hope of unraveling its secrets."

"I'll not object to that, but insist that you share your findings with Scotland Yard."

"Of course. I shall be delighted to do so."

That detail settled, we stood up and made our goodbyes. As we took the long way back to Baker Street, where Holmes searched the flat at Suffering Mews until he found several bottles labelled *Manna of St. Nicholas,* which Holmes explained was the name of an old cure-all elixir traditionally used to conceal its true poisonous contents.

I recognized with a cold chill that Nicholas was the name of the saint whose image was branded on the tea cup which Mrs. Carbonara had twice placed before me.

While Holmes collected the bottles, I examined the cane that had fallen to the floor after I had fended it off.

"Intriguing," I remarked.

Holmes took notice. He eyed the walking stick sharply. "I fail to see anything noteworthy about it."

I explained, "This cane is made from the branch of a hemlock tree."

"Which, as you know, is unrelated to the poisonous hemlock plant," Holmes pointed out.

"It is an interesting coincidence," said I.

"If it is a coincidence," Holmes stated without hesitation. "Beyond her fixation for revenge, the woman is clearly mad. Otherwise, why would she twice attempt to poison you, who had done her no harm in this world?"

"I would imagine that her hatred for you spilled over onto anyone associated with you," I pointed out. "The fact that I was unlikely to visit her often enough to succumb to her machinations was beside the point. In her reason-blinded rage, she only wished to stab you in the heart, as it were, in any way she could."

"That, Watson, is so irrational an explanation that I fear I must accept it without further consideration."

I'm pleased to report that in short order, Holmes had determined most of the chemical constituents of *Aqua Tofana,* but he admitted to me that others eluded him. Lead and belladonna were present. Arsenic trioxide was among them, although in small quantities.

"I have no doubt that some of the deeper secrets of this solution lie in the Italian province of Sicily to this day," he told me. "Perhaps one day, I'll fully unravel the riddle this diabolical brew."

As for Francesca Carbonara, to give her full name, she was convicted and sentenced to live out the remainder of her life in Holloway Prison.

Holmes and I were present in the courtroom when the judge's verdict was announced. After she received the final summation of her fate, Mrs. Carbonara turned and glared at Holmes. From her lips came a vicious torrent of words, none of which were comprehensible to me. But I didn't require a translation. The unleashed hatred in her voice communicated more than any words could ever do.

The widow Carbonara ultimately served out the entirety of her sentence – that is to say, she lived another dozen years and now lies buried in a pauper's grave. While she made several attempts to do away with herself by ingesting various lethal substances, none of these extreme attempts to escape her lawful sentence succeeded. I believe that, in the end, her heart gave out.

As for Holmes, his final comment on the entire sordid matter was typical of him.

"Although I didn't relish my ordeal," he mused one day, "some good came out of it."

"If it did," I admitted, "I fail to perceive what it might be."

"Although I paid a price for the opportunity, I was quite pleased to acquire a bottle of *Aqua Tofana* so that I might uncover some of its subtle yet sinister secrets."

Speaking strictly for myself, I thought this a sacrifice for science where the sacrifice was far greater than the reward received. But I offered no contradictory comment. It was typical of Holmes to look upon so distressing an experience as this with an analytical equanimity that brought into question his human side. Sometimes, he stuck me as more machine than man. Whatever his deficiencies might be, he was yet a man through and through.

# The Adventure at the
# Art School
## by Stephen Herczeg

"Oh, that's Stour House," said Mrs. Vandermeulen, in answer to my question. "It's rather striking, isn't it? That colour brick is unlike any other manor house in the area." She nodded towards the large, deep-red brick building, with its tall central spire. The building sat resplendent amongst acres of greenery, with ornate gardens encircling the house itself.

I had been told to call her Maryam, but even though we'd known each other for years, and she was the widow of a former commanding officer of mine, Colonel William Vandermeulen, I couldn't bring myself to simply use her first name when directly addressing her, and chose to refer to her as Maryam only when keeping my thoughts to myself. Something to which she had accepted, if not with a little derision.

Maryam had played host to Holmes and me for the last two days after I had received a telegram announcing that Colonel Vandermeulen had passed away two weeks previously. A small funeral had been held a week before, attended by a small coterie of family and closer friends. My invitation was to a memorial service in honour of the Colonel. I had asked Holmes to accompany me, to which he had accepted, much to my relief. The prospect of attending such a solemn occasion was not the most agreeable circumstance, but also the possibility that I would be alone amongst virtual strangers left me wanting as well.

Upon arriving in Colchester, we found transport and journeyed to the Colonel's estate on the outskirts of the town. Maryam had been an enthusiastic host and welcomed both of us with open arms. She took a particular shine to Holmes, and was well versed in some of his more spectacular exploits.

The service the next day was anything but a morose affair – more a celebration of the life of the Colonel. It was almost an enjoyable experience, if not for that twinge in the back of one's mind that kept a constant reminder that you were actually commemorating the passing of a well-respected friend. I met several military men that had served with or under the Colonel, and reacquainted myself with some others that I had known during my years as well. Throughout, Maryam kept Holmes within reach, introducing him to all and sundry and espousing tales of his deeds. It was almost as if she used him as a crutch to ward off any reminders of her husband's demise.

Holmes showed no signs of weariness, which was a credit to him, as I could only imagine how much being the centre of attention for so long would be dragging against his resolve.

Finally, as the sun dipped below the horizon, the guests slipped away, leaving Holmes, Maryam, and me alone in that huge house. A light supper was served in one of the many drawing rooms, and the three of us virtually slumped into our chairs, in an awake stupor amidst a pleasant silence.

After we had mechanically eaten, the butler removed the dishes and presented each of us with a pleasing glass of brandy. Even Maryam appeared to brighten as the alcohol eased through her system.

"That was a lovely day, but incredibly tiring," she said, draining the last of her drink before standing. "I can only thank the two of you for your generosity in being so attentive today – especially you Mr. Holmes. Your presence gave me cause to avoid all those annoying conversations that occur at funerals. My greatest wish is to grieve in solitude, and if I had to answer any more questions regarding my presence of mind or mood, then I would have needed to scream."

I smiled at this. It seemed I had been right.

"It was my pleasure, Mrs. Vandermeulen," said Holmes, standing with me as Maryam made her exit. "Should I be in your situation, I myself would much prefer to express my emotions in private, and fully understand."

"Now, if you will excuse me," she said, "I will retire for the night." She held up a finger. "But tomorrow is another day, and we have plans."

With that, she left, plunging us into another silence that was full of unanswered questions.

"I had hoped we could journey back to London tomorrow," I said.

"Me too, but it seems we are still needed here," answered Holmes. "I think we can afford Mrs. Vandermeulen one more day, don't you?"

Nodding I added. "Yes. I think she would welcome the company. There is something simmering in her mind that hasn't been allowed to come forth. I don't wish to be nursemaid to her emotions, but I think a time will come soon where she needs a strong shoulder."

"Quite so."

"Good morning, gentlemen, I do hope you slept well," said Maryam, entering the dining room where a breakfast banquet had been laid out by the servants. Holmes and I had risen much earlier and were just finishing a second cup of coffee when our hostess arrived. "Now, just on lunch-time today, I have quite a special event for us to attend."

343

Intrigued, I asked what it was, but was a little disappointed by the response. I saw no change of emotion on Holmes's face, but could only gather that he shared my dread.

"Oh, the local Dedham Art School is holding an exhibition. I am a patron, so couldn't imagine missing it. The works on show have been executed by the best and brightest students, and there will be quite a few dealers up from London to look over the exhibits. We have such hopes that they will be purchased, and in some cases that invitations to the London schools may be forthcoming for some of the students."

"I do know of the colleges in London," I answered, "but am afraid that I'm not familiar with this local school."

"Oh, it is quite the place. It was set up by the grandson of John Constable in honour of his career."

"Ah, yes, Constable," murmured Holmes. "Born and bred in this area. If I recall correctly, many of his landscapes depict scenes of the countryside of Essex and the surrounds."

"Yes, that is he. A marvellous painter, and very well respected and honoured in this region. The school teaches his techniques, but also more contemporary styles as well. It also houses a small collection of his original paintings."

"Well, we shall be honoured to accompany you." I was intrigued, but part of me believed that the afternoon would be a tawdry affair requiring another heavy dose of light banter and good will.

Later, as we passed on from the red-brick splendour of Stour House and the conversation dropped to silence, I noticed a slight tinge of sadness cross Maryam's face. I took it that the building had triggered some memory of her late husband, or she had simply recalled him in the void left by the hush.

As I opened my mouth to say something, I noticed Holmes. He locked eyes with me, flicked his glance towards Maryam, then back and slightly shook his head. I remained quiet and turned my attention to the wonderful landscape of rolling fields and tiny farmhouses.

Our host brightened once we reached Dedham, and was much more herself as we drew up before a set of four terraced houses built in the Tudor style. Although they had been recently painted and looked fresh, the bent timbers of their frames couldn't hide their true age.

As I helped Maryam alight from the carriage, she gave me a small smile, and then looked at the building. "Oh, this old place is wonderful. It's where Constable lived for many years, painting his lovely landscapes."

"I can only assume this is where the Art School has found a home," I said.

"Yes. The estate bequeathed the home to the township, and they in turn decided to use the property as a school and gallery dedicated to his memory. It's small, but it is fitting."

She was very correct. The main doors led into a small entrance foyer. I had to duck my head, but poor Holmes was forced to stoop several times until we entered a larger room with higher ceilings that was where the exhibition was being held.

Inside we all separated, and I looked around at the exhibit. The students' paintings adorning the four walls were admirable in their attempt, but even with my non-artistic eye, I could tell that they weren't great art, merely examples of a dalliance that involved no great skills. The two canvases presented on their own easels to the front of the larger room were the exception. Both were extraordinary in comparison, and very reminiscent of the style that I remembered from John Constable's own works.

"Exquisite, aren't they?" a voice asked from behind me. I turned to find a grey-haired man with a slight stoop. Before I could answer, he thrust out a hand and introduced himself. "I am Gerald Leady, the curator and teacher for this school. I haven't had the pleasure of your acquaintance, I feel."

"No, no, you haven't," I answered, taking his hand and shaking it. He had a soft grip, and I felt a mote of tension as I returned a firm shake. I realised, almost immediately, that as an artist he was possibly very protective of his hands. "It is a pleasure to meet you, Mr. Leady. I'm Doctor John Watson, from London, here to visit Mrs. Vandermeulen."

"Oh, that poor woman. The Colonel wasn't much for art, but he did accompany his wife and support her interests, though of late his health became so poor that I rarely saw him."

"Yes. He was one of my superior officers when I served in Afghanistan. I hadn't heard from him in many years. The telegram I received shocked me to the core, and I felt I had to attend the memorial service at least. Mrs. Vandermeulen invited me and my colleague to stay with her at the estate."

"A lovely place. She has many of my students' paintings. I do hope she decides to take one of these with her." He indicated the two canvases. "But I wouldn't be surprised if her feelings are elsewhere at the moment."

"Indeed." Nodding at the paintings, I inquired, "These are quite exceptional. This one in particular." I pointed to the one on the right. "Very reminiscent of Constable's work."

Mr. Leady nodded. "Yes. One of my finest students, young Archie Jordan." Turning, he added, "In fact, I was sure he was around here not long ago." He scanned the room, before indicating a young, dark-haired man standing amongst a gaggle of white-haired ladies. "Ah, yes, poor Archie is the favour of many of the local widowers."

"Oh?"

"Nothing like that. They're simply attracted to his talent as an artist. He has all the hallmarks of one who will become famous before too long. Excuse me for a moment." The curator waltzed away, insinuating himself into the middle of the young man's uninvited harem before taking his arm and extracting him from the group and leading him towards me. The young artist looked none-too-impressed by the crowd, or possibly with the attention thrust upon him.

"Now, Archie," said Leady, almost thrusting the boy towards me, "this is Doctor Watson from London. A friend of Mrs. Vandermeulen." The last sentence was given considerable emphasis, and almost shouted out. I took it to mean that Maryam was an important contributor to the school, and her friends should be afforded extra attention. I was slightly flattered, especially knowing that I had no real sway with the lady in question. "Doctor Watson was just telling me how much he liked your paintings."

The young man brightened a little and took a sideways glance at the works. He shrugged and mumbled, "Not my best work."

"Really?" I said, surprised at the admission. "But these are wonderful. I don't know a lot about art, but I do know what I like and what good style looks like." The painting to the right was a fine example of a still life, almost as if it were a school exercise. There were other similar versions around the room, but none executed with such flair. Behind the painted bowl of fruit and vase of flowers, Jordan had added a wide rolling landscape, likely drawn from the neighbouring area, and painted very much in the Constable style.

"Archie is very modest," piped up Leady. Sweeping an arm around the room, he added, "But as you can see, he far surpasses the other students in ability. In fact, I would say he is the best student I've ever had."

Watching the young artist's face, I could tell that the fawning of his teacher simply annoyed him rather than building his ego. Luckily, as I was about to say something, an older lady motioned towards Leady from across the room. He made his apologies and scampered across to her, leaving Archie Jordan and me alone. I could only assume that she was be a patron or potential buyer, and smiled at the inner business mind that Leady appeared to possess.

"Well, apart from all the flattery from your teacher, you are quite accomplished. Well done." This received a simple nod of thanks, and shift of the young man's feet, as he seemed uncomfortable with any attention, no matter how well-intentioned. "What aspirations do you have for the future?"

"Just like to paint, really," came the stilted reply.

Gazing around the room, I said, "You could do worse than to find yourself a sponsor. Take up the art full time without any interruptions." Looking back at the paintings, I added, "With a bit more practice and application, you could be the next Constable."

Turning back to face Jordan, the look I received chilled me to the bone. The young man's face grew red, and his expression was full of rage. A guttural sound came from his throat. "I am better than Constable." Without another word, he stormed past me and fled through a nearby door, leaving me slightly gobsmacked.

Recovering and shaking my head in surprise, I simply whispered to myself, "Artists. Such delicate sensibilities."

It was as I turned back towards the paintings that I spied Holmes out of the corner of my eye. Maryam had his arm in an almost vise-like grip, talking very animatedly to a pair of women of a similar age. Normally, Holmes is very astute at maintaining a stoic countenance, but I could see that his façade was threatening to slip. I started to make my way across the room to relieve him when I was stopped by an older couple. The man I recognised from the previous day's service for the Colonel. They engaged me in a long-drawn-out conversation about my time in Afghanistan, and when I looked back towards Holmes, he had disappeared. He filled me in on events when we met up later.

Seeking a break from the overcrowded gallery area, Holmes had taken the opportunity to step away when Maryam finally released his arm to pursue a guest, possibly with the intent of showing Holmes off once more to another of her coterie.

Sidling up to a nearby doorway, Holmes's luck was in when he found it unlocked. Opening it carefully and stepping through, he was pleased to find himself alone in the main Constable gallery: A room of slightly smaller size to the main gallery, but lined with landscape paintings in that very familiar style.

Similar to the main gallery, the smaller Constable room had a single painting on an easel set up towards one end of the space. Holmes slowly made his way around the room, admiring the paintings, but viewing them with his trademark studious gaze. He remarked later that the works were exceptionally well executed, the subject matter useful from a historic sense as they depicted the landscapes as seen through the eyes of a man from earlier in the century, but when pressed as to whether they were fine creations, he shrugged and seemed indifferent.

It was while standing before the final painting set upon its own easel that a voice from behind drew Holmes's attention.

"You have an eye for excellence in art, Mr. Holmes," said the voice.

Holmes turned to find the curator, Mr. Leady, standing just inside the entry door. "Oh, I do apologise," said Holmes. "I sought out a haven from the noise in the main gallery and found this room. I can only assume it is normally open, but has been closed off to focus the guests' attention on the students' artworks."

Nodding, Mr. Leady strode forward and joined Holmes before the easel. "Yes, you are completely correct. As you may have surmised, this room holds some of Constable's priceless works. It is normally available by appointment, but today, we have closed it off. I'm surprised that Constable Coppin didn't stop you from entering. The fool should have been on duty near the doorway."

"I did notice him being led away by one of the other guests. Please don't hold him to task."

Leady's sudden dour expression quickly became a smile as he changed the subject. He held out a hand to the painting before them. "So, what do you think of our latest find?"

"Latest find?" asked Holmes, genuinely surprised.

"Yes. It is a rare event indeed that a newly discovered John Constable painting comes to light. This one was found in the attic of a nearby farmhouse, where Constable appears to have resided for a time before his fame. The owners were incredulous when they showed this to me, and I verified its creator."

Studying the painting in a new light, Holmes discovered several locations that we had passed by during the morning's carriage ride. The artwork depicted a common subject to those familiar with Constable's work, the Dedham vale landscape. (Upon later seeing the painting myself, I realised that it was from the edge of the township looking out over the valley.)

"I recognise some of the features of the painting," said Holmes. He pointed at several places on the image. "Constable seems to have sat on the edge of Dedham looking southwest across the fields." Singling out one particularly familiar building, which was tiny on the painting, but still held its uniqueness with the deep-red bricks and central spire, he added, "That looks like Stour House. We passed it on the way into Dedham this morning."

Leady leaned into the painting. "My word, you have a good eye," he said. (When I viewed the painting later, I realised that Stour House would be virtually unrecognisable except to someone that had examined the building and taken in the details. It appeared tiny on the painting, and I took my hat off to Holmes for recognising it.)

At that point, the curator stepped back from the painting and engaged Holmes in some light banter. From what my colleague told me, it appeared that even though Holmes had been introduced to Leady with reference to his occupation, the art teacher had taken in none of the details, and was more interested in extolling his own virtues. It was at the point that Holmes was deciding on how to extricate himself that I arrived on the scene.

"Ah, there you are," I said, peeking in through the side door and being struck in amazement at the contents of the room.

"Watson," Holmes replied, then indicated his companion, "I think you met Mr. Leady earlier, did you not?"

I entered the gallery, but only had eyes for the paintings on display, slowly walking past each in what must have seemed a very disrespectful display. Finally, my eyes were drawn to the artwork on the easel. Leady appeared more effusive about the painting than making my acquaintance again. "Our newest piece," he said.

"Mr. Leady was telling me that they found this Constable in a nearby farmhouse – one once occupied by the painter himself. No one even knew of its existence until now."

"Awe inspiring," I mumbled. I must admit I was taken aback, not just by the number of Constable paintings in the room, but by the fact that a formerly unknown artwork was standing right before me.

"Yes, we are very proud of this find. In fact, there is a lot of interest from several London Art Galleries, and other prospective buyers."

"You're thinking of selling it?" I asked, dumbfounded. "Such a treasure should be kept on display for posterity, surely."

"Ah, but it isn't my choice, sadly. The farm owner who discovered it has already decided."

"A shame," I said, turning back to the painting.

At that point, Mr. Leady gave his apologies. "I am sorry, but I must be getting back to the throng. The curse of running this place, I suppose. Please stay here if you like. Enjoy the peace. I will find that layabout policeman and put him back on guard." Without another word, he left us alone amongst the wonderful landscapes.

"Now, this is interesting," Holmes said, pointing to the small red blob on the painting before us.

"What is that?"

"Given the colour, and the intended layout of the paint on the canvas, I would say it depicts Stour House, the red brick building we passed on that way here."

"How did you surmise that?" I leaned in closer and could finally detect the central spire and more squat surroundings of the building before nodding in agreement.

"That isn't the interesting thing though." Holmes stepped away and indicated each of the other paintings. "That canvas is the only one that depicts the Dedham valley in the way presented. Supposedly on the southwestern edge of the village, looking further southwest. It is also the only painting to include that red-brick building."

"Surely there are others of a similar nature. This is only a small part of Constable's complete works."

Holmes nodded slightly. "Yes, that's true. It was simply an interesting conclusion drawn from this collection."

"There is a large collection of his paintings in London. It may be an enjoyable excursion to see them when we return."

"Hmm. It may well be. We shall see if time permits once we return."

To that I nodded, and we made our way back into the main gallery.

The next morning, I awoke with a pounding headache and a slight fog across my vision. I put it down to the ongoing cacophony of voices echoing around the gallery the day before. I resisted the urge to delve into my bag and extract a dose of headache powder, which I carried for professional use, but I disliked taking it regularly, should I find myself becoming dependent on it.

Downstairs, I found Holmes looking extremely chipper and partaking of some breakfast while reading the local paper.

"Watson, you look positively dreadful."

"Yes. For some reason, I feel like I expected to find you. How do you look so alive after yesterday's continuous assault on the senses?"

"Oh, one learns to wipe such things from one's mind. A roomful of little old ladies shouldn't present too much of a problem to someone that understands the application of mindful presence to clear one's thoughts."

I smiled. "There are still so many things I need to learn from you."

Sitting, I poured myself a strong cup of coffee and dropped two slices of toast onto a plate ready to apply butter and jam. Sipping the strong brew, I pleaded for the caffeine to hit my senses and help clear them as easily as Holmes's mindful presence had his.

Just as I finished my second cup of coffee, I was relieved to find my headache subsiding. I began to ask Holmes whether he had seen Maryam when the door opened and our hostess breezed in, looking remarkably well-presented, as if about to leave for a social engagement.

"Hello, gentlemen," she said. "I'm afraid I have to some tawdry business to attend to in respect to the Colonel's affairs. I will be in

Colchester for the morning, but hope we can catch up for luncheon before you make your way back to London."

We both stood and before I could answer, she had strolled through the room and exited. A carriage crunched across the driveway from behind the manor, and we watched as Maryam stepped into the cabin and was whisked away.

"Hmm," I said, "I had hoped we could get away this morning, but looks like our plans are a little on hold."

"Yes," said Holmes, his face showing a slight air of bemusement.

As I poured another coffee, the sound of carriage wheels crunching on the gravel outside crashed through the silence, followed closely by a loud rapping at the front door.

"My word, it's like King's Cross Station here this morning," I remarked.

Within moments, the butler ushered a slightly dishevelled policeman into the dining room. I recognised him immediately as Constable Coppin who had floated about the gallery the previous afternoon. His held his helmet in his hands, turning it with nervousness. His eyes flashed towards me, and then to Holmes.

"Ah, sorry to disturb you gentlemen, especially during your breakfast, but – " He stopped, trying to form the words, or at least utter them.

"This is no disturbance, Constable. What seems to be the problem?" asked Holmes, trying to calm the policeman down.

"Ah, sir, there's been a murder."

"I saw this fellow only yesterday," I remarked, slightly aghast at seeing the cooling corpse before me.

Coppin had ushered Holmes and me into his carriage and whisked us away back towards Dedham. He told us that the Senior Sergeant was away visiting his sick mother, and everything had been left up to him. He didn't want to send word to Colchester until he had at least dealt with the corpse.

The now-familiar sight of the red brick Stour House flashed by at a much higher speed than on the previous day, and we pulled up outside a slightly dingy little cottage on the outskirts of the village.

As we rushed towards the building, Holmes slowed us down and began to meticulously examine the front pathway and steps that led to the door, and the entrance-way itself, before convincing himself that there was either nothing to see, or it had been disturbed beyond usefulness. "Hmm. Nothing unusual here. I assume that the dead man is inside."

"Yes," replied Coppin. "It's horrible."

The constable hadn't been very talkative on the way over, which led me to believe that this may have been his first murder investigation, and the poor lad was probably torn between the horror of the event and his own confusion as to what to do next.

Once inside, I recognised the unfortunate victim straightaway. Our brief conversation flashed through my mind, and the last lingering memory was of his apparent disdain for Constable's work, as if it was no match for his talent. The impression that remained was that of the epitome of a prodigious talent that was still to be heralded to the level of his own expectations. Archie Jordan, the school's prize student, lay before us. It was his paintings that had inspired awe in everyone in the room. Now, sadly, that talent would be expressed no more.

Upon seeing the dead man again, Coppin let out a small cry of shock, before Holmes tried to make him focus.

"Constable, how did you learn about him?"

"One of the neighbours, a young lass who I think had feelings for Archie, dropped by to bring him some fresh bread she'd baked. She told me that the door was unlocked, and when she called out and there was no answer, she let herself in, so that she could leave the loaf on his kitchen table. The poor thing, she's ever so distraught. Her father sent for me, and we both came over and found the poor fellow like this."

I waited for Holmes to finish his examinations and simply stared at the dead artist. The cause of death was plainly obvious. He lay on the ground before his latest painting, an unfinished landscape that would remain so. A pallet knife protruded from his left eye. It had been driven in as far as the handle flange, but I could tell what it was by the other similar shaped items on the table next to his easel.

"Such a horrible way to die," said Coppin.

"And quick," added Holmes, standing up from studying the floor around the corpse. "There's hardly any blood, and no other wounds. Whoever did it struck quickly and ended the poor chap's life almost immediately. He fell backwards, and that's where he stayed."

I decided to add my own observations. "Left eye, so can only presume the killer was right-handed – which includes most of England. The knife handle is pointed up, so the strike came from above, the assailant striking downwards. It could mean they were of similar height, or the killer was slightly shorter. But it gives the impression that the act wasn't premeditated, but perhaps acted out on a moment of anger."

"Yes," said Holmes pointing next to the easel. "The pallet knife came from that table. Given the number of them lying there, it wasn't a carefully chosen weapon. It just happened to within be in arm's reach when opportunity presented itself."

"Spur of the moment then? Not planned?"

"Yes, but look there." Holmes indicated the area beneath the table. Several paint brushes and other pallet knives were scattered across the floor. "There was a slight scuffle." Holmes moved towards the corpse and turned to face the small table. "Jordan stood here and possibly pushed his assailant, who then knocked against that table, disturbing the paraphernalia on top. He then reached for the nearest thing at hand. The weapon isn't one that would normally be associated with a pre-meditated murder – more a chance encounter or spurious action." He stepped back and viewed the scene from a little distance. "This has all the hallmarks of a sudden flight into rage, not of any planning or deliberation on behalf of the perpetrator. Possibly an argument that quickly went out of hand."

"Yes. Jordan seemed to have a temper. He was most upset when I compared his work to John Constable's."

Holmes stood for a moment, his head on his hand, one finger raised to his cheek. "Constable Coppin, did this fellow have any enemies that you know of? Any other young girls that have found his fancy, but may already have suitors?"

"I . . . I didn't really know him that well. I've seen him about town, and at the art school, of course, but he seemed to be a likeable chap, if not a bit of a loner."

"I see."

The loner label, given to him by the policeman, seemed to fit. The cottage, though small, had every wall and available space occupied with paintings. Almost every surface was overflowing with drawings, scribbles, and smaller paintings which appeared to be tests for his larger works. I wondered where the man's money had come from.

"Was this fellow well off, do you know?" I asked.

"I dunno. Why?"

"Well, he lived in this little cottage all alone. He had lots of artist supplies, which are in themselves not cheap. He also attended the art school, which I cannot believe would charge a reasonable tuition fee."

"Good point, Watson. I am also wondering where Mr. Jordan's income came from. He is quite adept at the craft, but enough to afford him a decent living? That is a question to be asked."

"I don't know much about the bloke, but he didn't have another job, as far as I know. Swanned around the town a bit, but mostly kept pretty much to the school, and here at his home."

"I would suggest that you fetch a doctor or whatever passes for a coroner in these parts. Watson and I will continue to investigate until you return, but I can't see us finding much else from the body as such."

353

"Right you are," said Coppin before stepping from the room. Within moments, the crack of reins and crunch of carriage wheels rang from outside and we were left alone.

"Thoughts?" I asked.

"Oh, the usual. An act of a lover betrayed, perhaps? A young, strapping lad who possibly become too familiar with the wrong lady."

"That would be disappointing for you."

"Yes. I do so despair at violent acts of the heart. So much loss for such little gain."

With that, Holmes pottered around the room once more, examining details, dropping to all fours at times and pulling out his glass to check some miniscule piece of possible evidence. "Ah, this is interesting." Standing, he held up another small-bladed palette knife. "There's blood on the tip. I believe our artist may have grabbed his own weapon and extracted a wound before being felled."

"So our assailant will have an injury or sorts."

"Yes," Holmes replied, placing the evidence on a nearby table and dropping back to the floor.

Nodding, I left the room to search for something to place over the artist's body. I felt that I should endeavour to give him as much dignity as I could, and having him simply lying uncovered on the floor did nothing for him.

Finding a spare bedsheet in a cupboard, I carefully slid it over him, wincing when I saw the elevated point where the pallet knife protruded from his eye – but I knew that I should leave it for the coroner or local doctor to examine.

By then, Holmes had stopped his examinations and was studying the dead man's artwork. Joining him, I said, "It is sad. The boy was quite gifted."

Nodding, Holmes murmured, "Perhaps too gifted – and might I say, a little troubled."

"How so?" It was then I turned and studied the paintings hanging on the nearby walls. At first, I had simply seen them as more landscapes in the familiar Constable style, but upon looking closer, these were far more disturbing. Stepping closer I realised that the artist had depicted a simple rendering of the nearby countryside, or chosen a building as the central image, but then modified the work with monstrous details. A simple cottage, beautifully detailed down to the individual stones used to build it, was besieged by all manner of monstrosities. In one, a huge tentacled monster hovered in the dark sky above the building, its appendages winding down possibly to destroy the building. In others, demons danced around a bonfire erected in a field. And in the largest of all, the art school

354

was depicted in beautiful detail, only to be under attack from the same tentacled beast. The long sucker-covered arms grew from blackened windows, winding around and taking the building in their grasp in an attempt to crush it in the creature's horrendous grip.

"I don't know much about the fine arts," Holmes said, "but I can see that these paintings began life as simple studies in the style of Constable, with these monstrous details added in later." Sweeping a hand towards the sheet-covered corpse, he added, "Young Jordan picked up much of the same artistic expression that his fellow local artist Constable had. The choice of subject is similar. He focused on depicting the nearby countryside. His colour palette was reflective of that used by Constable, but that could be down to the fact that the colours of the local landscapes are of a similar hue. And the brush strokes and style are very reflective of the way Constable painted as well."

"That could simply be credited to the art school. Leady mentioned that he does teach a similar style to Constable, partly as an homage and partly to preserve the artist's style. This fellow would definitely have picked up on that."

"Hmm. Yes, that could be it. I can only assume that these paintings started life as art school projects, but then Jordan brought them home and added his own depictions from his tortured mind." Holmes wandered off through a nearby doorway, leaving me to stare at Archie Jordan's last painting.

"This is interesting," came Holmes's voice. I followed him through the doorway and found him in another large room which stored more of Jordan's finished works. They were piled up, leaning against the walls. Flipping through them, I found that many were standard landscapes, buildings, and still-lifes. The others were filled with more works in line with the tentacled monster and its brethren. The contrasts were enormous, and showed the workings of a very disturbed young man torn between a need to produce fine art and a desire to delve into the darkest recesses of his imagination and throw that imagery upon the canvas.

Holmes pulled a large canvas from one of the piles and leaned it against the wall. It was remarkably different to many of the others – not a landscape, or one of the nightmare images, but a faithful portrait of one particularly striking building.

"It's quite remarkable," I said.

"Yes, he has captured that vivid red brick colouring quite well, and given it a subtle hue all of its own in the dying light of the day – and this one has survived his alternative vision."

"I wonder if he did any others like it."

355

"I'm sure we could drop by Stour House and ask the owners. If I was to see such a fine depiction of my house, I would be more than happy to procure it. The view is also one we weren't afforded yesterday. It must be from the other side of the building. Did you notice the detail on the front door lintel, showing the date?"

"I assume that's when Stour House was built."

"Me too. Which means the house is only twenty years old."

"Which would account for its rather fine condition."

"True, and it's in much better condition than John Constable himself was at the time of its completion."

I contemplated on the life of Constable and smiled. "Well, yes, he had been dead for thirty years by then."

"Which is a very interesting thing, don't you think?"

"Why?" And then it hit me. "Oh, my, I see what you mean. How can Stour House be depicted in a John Constable painting, when it didn't yet exist?"

"Quite so, and I believe our answer lies dead in the other room."

When Coppin returned, with the local doctor in tow, we apprised him of our investigation.

"What do you mean there's a building in a painting that didn't exist when the painting was done?" he asked, truly perplexed by the idea.

"I'm of the mind that the building is there because it existed when the artwork was actually painted," said Holmes, using a slow, languid voice, the sort one uses to address a small child.

Coppin chuckled at this. "So you're trying to tell me that Constable is still alive and painting?"

A smile grew on my face, even the doctor looked up from his examination, his face a mask of dismay at the policeman's inability to comprehend Holmes's story.

"Or, perhaps, someone else undertook the work in the style of Constable."

Realisation dawned on Coppin's face. "Now that would make more sense, wouldn't it?" We simply nodded and allowed him to consider the information. "Perhaps it's one of the students at the art school. They learn all about Constable."

"One may even posture that the student in question was, in fact, poor Mr. Jordan here."

Coppin turned and stared at the body, then his eyes rose and took in the painting on the easel. His eyes opened wide. "Yes. That's it, isn't it? This fellow was forging Constable paintings. I reckon a potential buyer found out and done him in. We need to tell Mr. Leady before he sells it off. He might be in danger himself."

Holmes replied, calming Coppin down and suggesting that they wait for the doctor to finish his examination, before they loaded the poor artist into the rear of the police cart for transport to the hospital mortuary. "I'm sure that Mr. Leady is quite safe, but I do believe we should engage with him. For a start, we don't know how many paintings that Jordan has produced, so we need to see Mr. Leady to understand if he has been involved in selling any other possible forgeries."

"Yes. That's fair. We'll wait then." Turning to the poor doctor, Coppin added, "Are you finished yet?"

The doctor gave him a withering look in return. I found I had to stifle a chuckle.

It was an interminable journey all the way to Colchester in the police wagon. As he drove, Coppin was agitated, muttering under his breath the entire way. We could hear him from the other side of the thin wall where he sat driving the carriage. Holmes, the doctor (whose name we finally discovered was Lester Brown), me, and the body of Archie Jordan were all jammed together inside.

Doctor Brown had served as the local Dedham physician for nearly forty years. He was an affable fellow, but couldn't recall the last case of a murder in the town. We discussed what should happen next, and I was slightly relieved to hear him state that he would stay with Jordan's body until the local coroner could attend and verify both his and my assumptions regarding the artist's demise. I say relieved, as I could only imagine that as soon as Doctor Brown returned to Dedham, the news of Jordan's death would spread like wildfire, if it hadn't already. Knowing Holmes, I assumed he would much prefer silence on that matter until the culprit was caught.

Finally we arrived at the small country hospital and stood watching as two orderlies removed Jordan's body and placed it on a stretcher to carry it into the morgue. Constable Coppin and the coroner discussed matters for a few minutes, before the policeman returned to the driver's seat, and we left the dead artist, along with Doctor Brown, and hurried onward towards Dedham.

Arriving at the art school, Coppin almost leapt from the carriage and raced inside. Holmes and I followed, and I noticed a slight smile on my colleague's face, I assumed it was amusement at Coppin's eagerness.

As we entered, we found a surprised woman standing in the foyer with an armload of books. She nodded her head to the left and said, "The policeman went into the Constable gallery, over there. Strange fellow. Mr. Leady's also in there with another gentleman."

Entering the outer gallery, we noticed that the doors to the room were thrown wide open. Murmuring voices echoed from within.

Stepping into the gallery that both Holmes and I had previously had privilege to enter, we found Coppin explaining events to Mr. Leady, while a confused older man stood before the recently found Constable painting – which we now knew was most certainly a forgery.

"Dead. Someone killed him. Knife to the eye. Horrible. Had to get here to make sure you were safe."

Leady stood with a hand over his mouth to hide his open-mouthed expression. He tried to interject, but Coppin was far too excited.

Finally, Coppin stopped and took a breath, absorbing the fact there another man was present. Immediately, his suspicions were raised. His tone dropped and was filled with hints of mistrust. "Who's this?" he asked, eyeing the other man with a questioning gaze.

It was then that Leady noticed Holmes and me and nodded towards us. "Please calm yourself, Constable Coppin. I'm as devastated as you are. Poor Archie! Who would do such a thing?"

"Who indeed?" asked Holmes. Turning towards the stranger and holding out his hand, he added, "Sorry to involve you in this, sir. I am Sherlock Holmes, and this is my colleague, Doctor Watson. You will have identified Constable Coppin by his presence and uniform. And you would be – ?"

"Professor Michael Stuckey, curator of the National Gallery in London," the man said, his face still a mask of confusion and annoyance. "What in the blazes is going on?"

"Ah, there has been an unfortunate incident. A young student, of this very school, was found murdered in his house – possibly the first such death in this area in a generation. Constable Coppin here was in fear that the same culprit might target Mr. Leady."

"Oh, the poor fellow! I'm sure the miscreant will be found quickly." Stuckey turned towards Leady. "But why would Leady be involved?"

"We aren't really sure at this stage."

Coppin, his expression changing to confusion, spoke up. "But, Mr. Holmes, you said – "

"Now, now, Constable. These gentlemen don't need to know all the sordid details. I'm sure they're far too interested in the painting that we see before us."

"Yes," said Leady, "Professor Stuckey is here on behalf of the National Gallery to purchase this newly found Constable painting." I noticed the emphasis that Leady put on the artist's name.

"That is precisely why I'm here." Addressing Leady, Stuckey added, "Now, I'm more-than-convinced of the authenticity of this work. The style, the brush strokes, the depiction of the local area – all hallmarks of the great man. I will arrange payment forthwith, and you can organise delivery to the Gallery." He shook Leady's hand to seal the deal, before adding, "It's remarkable that you are still finding Constable's works hidden about the area. He was prolific, and every new find is simply another irreplaceable treasure in the eyes of the Gallery."

"I thank you, but I've had my students scouring the countryside, and it was remarkable that we were able to find this one – but I do believe it is the last."

"Shame, that. As I said, treasures."

It was then Holmes piped up. "It is strange that you would mention, almost as fact, that no more paintings will be found. And this one is such an intriguing work, Mr. Leady. Unique, if I was to characterise it against all other paintings by John Constable."

"How so?" asked the Professor, a lone eyebrow raised in question.

"Well, if you look at the lower right corner of the painting – " All eyes turned towards the spot. " – you'll notice the slight detail of a strikingly red building."

"Ah, yes, intriguing. Not a normal colour for Constable to use."

"Quite so, and even more intriguing is the object of attention. It is called Stour House."

"Stour House? Never heard of it."

"A rather spectacular manor house, just southwest of this little village. Built in eighteen-sixty-eight, don't you know."

The last remark took a moment to connect in the Professor's mind. "Eighteen-sixty-eight – What? But that's thirty years after Constable's death – How?" He looked at the curator and a look of rage came to his face. "What are you trying to pull here, Leady?" Leaning in closer to the painting, Stuckey studied it long and hard before turning back to the curator. "Who painted this? It's good – brilliant if you like – but that detail means it isn't a Constable." He stopped, waited for a reply, his breathing suggesting he seethed with indignation inside.

Leady simply looked stunned, his mouth opening and closing like a fish out of water slowly suffocating to death.

"If I may, Mr. Leady," said Holmes, "perhaps this wasn't painted by John Constable, but was in fact painted by your now ex-student, Archie Jordan."

At the mention of Jordan's name, Leady's face snapped towards Holmes, his eyes growing wide in fear. It was then I noticed a slightly bloodied bandage affixed to Leady's left ear.

"Well, Leady?" growled Stuckey. "Answer the man. Did this Jordan fellow, rest his soul it seems, paint this picture?"

The curator's eyes dropped at the accusation. He visibly shrank and stepped away, reaching behind him until he felt the back rest of a nearby chair. He dropped heavily onto the seat and took several deep breaths before glancing up once more. Nodding slowly, he said, "Yes. Archie Jordan was an enormous prodigy. His talent was as good, if not better, than Constable's. I convinced him to emulate the great master. He did it effortlessly. Even an eye such as yours, Professor, couldn't tell the difference."

"But he had a darker side, didn't he?" asked Holmes.

Leady let out a deep sigh and gazed at Holmes with another nod before speaking with a slight shake of his head. "Yes. He was a typical artist. Sullen, introspective, angry at the world for no apparent reason. He revelled in the monstrous. If you've been to his cottage, you've seen his works: Blasphemous depictions of demons from the imagination. His addition of monstrous beings attacking the local landscape was his rebellious nature. I pleaded with him to channel his energies into images of beauty, but he wanted to use his talents in that way."

"How many Constable homages did he paint?"

"Oh, possibly a dozen."

"The four I've bought off you previously?" asked Stuckey.

Leady nodded. "Yes. There were never any newly discovered paintings. They were all Jordan's work. I brokered the sale. The money I used to keep this place going, and to keep Jordan supplied with a house, food, and painting to his heart's content."

"But he grew tired of it, didn't he?" asked Holmes. "As you said, he had other subjects in mind. He wanted to end his emulation of Constable at your bequest."

"Yes. When Doctor Watson pointed out the red-brick addition to this painting, I knew I needed to confront him. He laughed in my face, admitting brazenly that he added the building with full knowledge of its construction date. He wanted it all to finish."

"And you attacked him over it?"

A tired shake of the head. "No. We argued. I tried to get him to fix the painting before the Professor arrived, but he refused. He flew into a rage, picked up a palette knife, and slashed at me with it." His hand went to the wound in his ear. "I fell backwards. Knocked into a small table. Things fell. I heard them. I reached back to steady myself. My hand closed around something, and my anger boiled over. In that sudden moment, I hated Archie with a blind fury. All that I had done for him – All that I had sacrificed to bring out his prodigious talent – I lashed out, not realising what I held, and then . . . ." He dropped his head into his hands.

"What then?"

"He went down. The horrible thing sticking out of his eye. I knew he was dead. I fled. Hoped that it would be seen as a robbery. I know I should have reported it, but I was to blame. I'm ashamed of what I did, but I had too much to lose." He looked around the room. "This place – without me, it will all be gone."

"Well, to be honest, you won't have to worry about that. Constable Coppin, I think you should take Mr. Leady here into custody."

My eyes fell on the young policeman's face. He was more shocked than any of us, and I'm fairly certain he wasn't quite sure how to proceed. His hand absent mindedly dropped to the pocket of his jacket and he withdrew a pair of rarely used handcuffs before stepping up behind Leady, asking him to stand, and placing the cuffs on.

As Coppin lead the distraught curator away, the Professor spoke. "This is awful. That blighter has swindled the gallery out of hundreds of pounds. I'll be a laughing-stock. I'll need to have those paintings removed."

"I have an idea," said Holmes, "Without Leady, it is more-than-likely that this art school will close or continue as more of a community arrangement."

"Yes, go on."

Sweeping a hand around the gallery, he added, "There are at least a dozen authentic John Constable paintings here. I'm sure that you will be able to make a deal with the town council for them to save their reputation, as well as your own. And the offending forged paintings can probably be returned and displayed under the correct artist's name."

"Hmm. Yes. You might be onto something there. I'll see to it right away." He strode from the room, still mumbling under his breath, but agreeable to the idea.

"Nasty business," I stated.

"Yes, Watson. A tawdry tale all up. A prodigious talent coerced into using his skills for crime, and then a fit of rage ends that career before it has even started."

"Do you mean to tell me that nice Mr. Leady was a criminal?" asked Maryam, pouring herself a coffee.

We had travelled back to the manor house to collect our things and say our goodbyes before returning to London.

"Yes, I'm afraid so," said Holmes. "It seems that even the generosity of the local community, yourself included, wasn't enough to pay the bills.

When Archie Jordan's talent began to show itself, Mr. Leady jumped at the chance to use his student's skills to deceive the local community and the artworld itself."

"Oh, how terrible. And it all ended in such a horrible calamity."

"Yes. Anger sometimes knows no bounds."

"What will happen now?"

"I can only assume that the town council will need to make that determination. They still have Constable's reputation in their favour, but whether they will have the appetite to bring in a new teacher to keep the art school going is a question only they can answer."

"Hmm. That is very upsetting. I dearly loved our art school. Some of the students had talent, and others not so much, but at least they tried."

"It may be worth your while to sit in on the meetings, if you have a mind, to foster support amongst your friends," I added.

Maryam thought for a moment before sipping her coffee and adding, "Yes, I think I will. The Colonel left a good deal of money when he passed, so it's only fair that I put it to good use."

"Delightful," said Holmes, sipping his coffee. "I look forward to seeing the results."

# The Adventure of the
# Distracted Detective
## by Shane Simmons

The thing about reporting for duty at Baker Street is that you never quite knew what you'd be walking in on. Often it was just breakfast. Other times, it was an experiment involving chemicals that could rot through the floor, or firearms that might blow a hole through the wall. Sometimes it was clients seeking help, or subjects of investigations seeking satisfaction or outright revenge. Today, it was only Dr. Watson, who had been absent of late, pending his nuptials.

I had walked in on a quarrel. One of many lately, inspired by the doctor's concern for his friend, who would soon be living alone for the first time in years. No more flatmate and no new cases didn't sit well with the detective.

"You've been dosing yourself morning, noon, and night for weeks," protested Dr. Watson. "How many injections has it been?"

"If we are to assume thrice a day," said Mr. Holmes, "then the sum relies on the number of days, of which I have not been keeping a count. Have you?"

"I've lost track!"

"Then we are both the better for it," said the detective, sinking deeper into his armchair.

"This must end, Holmes."

"It will end when a suitable case presents itself."

"Given the abuse you have subjected yourself to, I have no great confidence you are in any condition to judge the merit of the next case to walk through that door."

The doctor threw his arm wide, gesturing towards the very door, and only found me standing there.

"Wiggins," he said, "tell me you're here with news of some pressing mystery."

"The only mystery I know is the one about why I've been called here at all," I answered.

By my reckoning, Mr. Holmes's seven-per-cent solution weren't no solution to anything. Most men get their sauce out of a bottle, but his pick of poison was in a hypodermic. A nip of spirits could take the edge off, but Sherlock Holmes liked to stay sharp. His formula to keep boredom at bay didn't take the edge off so much as put him right on it. He wasn't the same man when he was leaning on the cocaine crutch, and I understood Dr. Watson's concern.

"The most intriguing case of your entire career could be on its way up the steps now, and you might miss out on it, given the state you're in!"

Mr. Holmes raised a hand to his ear and leaned towards the entry to his rooms.

"I hear no footsteps and am expecting no one other than Wiggins."

"Nevertheless . . . ."

"Not once have my diversions stood in the way of accepting a worthy challenge."

"What about the string of murders in Whitechapel? Scotland Yard practically begged you to look into it, but you were too . . ." Dr. Watson tapered off, selecting his next words carefully. ". . . distracted by your chemistry research."

"A mindless slaughter by a depraved animal," Mr. Holmes sneered, waving his hand like he was shooing away an annoying gnat.

"The papers seemed to think there was more to it."

"Sales and subscriptions were what they saw in it. Cast enough blood upon the page, and it will move a mountain of pulp."

Ladies of the evening turning up dead in the east end or floating in the Thames weren't much of a novelty, and most of the time it was a pimp whodunit. Still, there were a few wrinkles with Mr. Leather Apron sending love letters to police and leaving strange clues about. I wasn't much of a reader back then, but I heard what the papers had to say about it, and thought Mr. Holmes might have at least given the murders a glance.

"Wiggins," he said, breaking off from his words with the doctor, "there is a package awaiting delivery and you are to deliver it. Here, to me, within the hour."

"Is it bigger than a bucket or heavier than a brick?" I asked after the burden to come.

"You will find it quite portable. Merely some more chemicals for my experiments."

"It is yourself you experiment on, Holmes," said Dr. Watson. "And it is no experiment if you well know the results these chemicals provide."

"Therein lies the science of it!" said the detective, making no move to relocate himself from the chair he was rooted to. "Predictable results against a persistent problem."

I had never disobeyed Mr. Holmes's direct orders before, but what he needed most didn't come out of the end of a needle. Rather than go to the address he gave me, to talk to a man not spoken of in polite society, to procure an item everyone would rather not mention, I went straight to

Scotland Yard. Not to report any nefarious activities, of course. It weren't none of their business. What I hoped, instead, was that they had some business to dole out.

Popping by The Yard was getting less and less simple as time went on. You had to know where you were going. Scotland Yard had been expanding since the early days of the peelers. When one building wasn't enough, they took up two. Then three. Lately they'd been constructing a whole new headquarters down by the Thames, and already the bobbies were talking amongst themselves, speculating if that would be enough to house all our city's police and the crimes they were looking into.

It was one policeman in particular I was after. He, at least, was still stuffed in the same spot since I'd first made his acquaintance in the early days of my working for Mr. Holmes. Inspector Lestrade looked cramped in his little office, with barely enough room to squeeze in between his desk and all his files. He must have looked forward to stretching his legs in the new diggings, if only they'd hurry up and finish laying the bricks.

"Wiggins, is it?" he asked, when he spotted me sticking my nose in. "Who let you in?"

"Let?" I wondered. I hadn't been let in so much as not seen as I slipped past doors left ajar, around darkened corners, and up flights of stairs when no one was about.

"Never mind," said the inspector, knowing well enough who I worked for. "What is it?"

"It's Mr. Holmes, sir. He's in a bad way."

Lestrade looked genuinely concerned. He'd be in a right mess if the consulting detective he was always consulting wound up dead or injured on the job.

"One of his enemies hasn't gotten to him, I trust! Not an assassin or a hired hatchet man? Someone looking to cover their crime by removing the man most likely to expose it?"

"He's in one of his moods," I said.

The inspector sat back in his chair again, relieved. Lestrade nodded, like he knew all about Mr. Holmes and his dark days. I dared not say more on the subject. I didn't know if he understood the root cause or suspected.

"Sherlock Holmes is lost without work," he said, "and particular about what work he'll take."

"I was hoping you might have something for him."

"What I have is too much paperwork," Lestrade said, swinging an arm at the files in his office. More like shrugged at them. There wasn't room enough for a proper swing. "All of it mundane busywork. Not the sort of thing that will interest Mr. Holmes, unless he's developed a sudden passion for petty robberies with a list of obvious suspects composed of repeat offenders."

There was a knock at the door as a low-ranked officer of the law arrived with a delivery.

"Telegram, sir."

Lestrade took the report and read through it in moments.

"Is this accurate?" was all he wanted to know.

"Just came in," said the officer. "They're about to send a man out to have a look."

"Wire them back at once," instructed the inspector. "Tell them no one is to approach the body under any circumstances."

The man left to do his duty at once as ordered.

"A body?" I asked, perking up.

"A dead one," Lestrade specified.

"An interesting one?" I hoped.

"Very. It seems the Grim Reaper himself has taken pity on your Mr. Holmes and has gifted him a baffling crime no one can make head or tail of. He'll want to know about this right away."

I was back at Baker Street in no time at all. The police aren't so stingy when it comes to dropping a coin on the convenience of a hansom cab, and it saved me another hoof on foot. I'd been given an hour to run my errand and still had half the time left if this attempt to get Mr. Holmes out of his chair didn't succeed.

"Wiggins, did you bring my medicine?" he asked when I appeared in the door.

"Of a sort," I said. "What I brung you ought to make you right as rain, I figure."

"Lestrade," said Mr. Holmes, seeing who I had in tow.

Dr. Watson perked up at the arrival of the familiar face.

"Tell me this call is official rather than social," he said.

"I'll get straight to the point, Mr. Holmes. There is a man lying dead in an open field in Nounsley. The local constabulary is clueless. Largely because there aren't any."

"Constables?"

"Clues."

"There are always clues, Lestrade."

"Not this time," said the inspector. "The body is fresh and wasn't there yesterday. The field it lies in is mud, still moist from rain. Yet there are no tracks to or from the body. Not even those of the dead man."

It was the first details I had heard. Inspector Lestrade hadn't been forthcoming during the cab ride over. I was, after all, only the hired help.

366

Hearing it now, I was relieved that the case sounded genuinely mysterious. It was only a matter of Mr. Holmes agreeing. But he didn't sound so impressed.

"I suppose the same clueless local constabulary have been busy rectifying that, trodding all over the scene and moving the body about."

A spoiled scene was just the sort of thing that might swing Mr. Holmes towards more unhealthy solitude instead of getting him out and about.

"That's just it, Mr. Holmes," Lestrade said. "They haven't. I've seen to it. The dead man was spotted at a good distance, and the case crossed my desk shortly after it had been reported. I got word out in time that a wide perimeter was to be cordoned off, and no one was to approach the body until I arrived."

"A completely unblemished site," Mr. Holmes mused. "How very rare."

Lestrade approached the detective in his chair, bending down and lowering his voice. The inspector had him on the hook and only had to reel him in.

"So unblemished," he practically whispered, "there exists no hint how the dead man died or came to rest where he lays. Not one jot."

"Intriguing," was all Mr. Holmes would say aloud, but I could tell his mind was already turning over the many possibilities in quick succession.

"I thought it might strike your fancy," said Lestrade. "As did your lad when I mentioned it to him."

"And how was it Wiggins found himself in your office when he was sent on an errand elsewhere?" inquired Mr. Holmes.

"I thought I'd stop by and say hello on the way," I said.

"On the way to the opposite end of town?"

I thought I might catch a harsh word, if not an outright dismissal for disobedience, but Lestrade changed the subject and covered for me.

"When I told the Nounsley constabulary I was coming, I said I would be bringing a consultant who specialised in strange cases. Did I make them a false promise?"

Before he could answer, Dr. Watson was at his friend's side, presenting him with his deerstalker. Suitable fashion for a trip to the countryside.

"Nounsley is hardly your usual jurisdiction, Lestrade," noted Mr. Holmes, once we were all comfortably seated in a cabin of the first train steaming east.

"It's close enough to London they'll ask Scotland Yard for assistance if there's a crime more nefarious than a horse borrowed without permission, or a fox-related chicken slaying."

"You've been out there for police business before?" asked Dr. Watson.

"In my junior years," said Lestrade. "I'm well-known locally for solving 'The Adventure of the Bloviating Bovine', as it came to be known."

"Lend an ear Watson," said Mr. Holmes. "You may wish to take notes. Such a case history may be worthy of chronicling for future generations of criminologists."

"Ah, well," said Lestrade, put on the spot for more details. "Foul play was suspected when a cow kept waking up half the hamlet in the middle of the night with inconsolable mooing. Always between two and three in the morning. Burglars skulking around in the wee hours was believed to be the cause of the fuss, and the whole village was on edge. The nocturnal activities failed to alert any of the other livestock, but the lone Hereford was most insistent. I spent three wet and miserable nights staking out the area, downwind of a slurry pit, waiting for the thieves to make themselves known."

"Sounds like a job for a veterinarian, not a police inspector," said Dr. Watson.

"Well done, Watson," said Mr. Holmes, slapping his friend on the knee and smiling for the first time in many days. "You beat me to the punch."

"Your medical diagnosis might have saved me several nights of sleep," said Lestrade to the doctor. "A bowel blockage was the true culprit. A painful gaseous buildup, worsening in the cool night air, inspired the plaintive bellowing. Thankfully I was called back to London, and was not further engaged for the procedure to clear the obstruction."

"Few in our line of work are graced with celebrated success at the start," said Mr. Holmes. "Rest assured, many of my earliest cases were equally inglorious. I, at least, have always had the luxury of choice. I think I would go mad if I were a police inspector with no say as to my assignments."

When it came to crime, Sherlock Holmes was a man of discerning taste. Inspector Lestrade was a man a duty, even when that duty was thankless. Not that he was above accepting the thanks due Mr. Holmes, but he only did that with the consulting detective's blessing.

When we got off at Hatfield Peverel, we were met at the station by a constable named Rutherford. He'd brought a carriage to bring us down to the tiny hamlet of Nounsley, a short ride away, where the body was waiting for us in the middle of a fallow field. The field was just off a bend in a road that was too narrow to be a proper road, so they called it a lane instead.

"He's just over there," Rutherford said, pointing as we pulled up.

Ten yards removed from the lane, I saw stakes set in the ground at regular intervals, with a line of twine tied around each until a wide octagon had been fenced off, making it clear to anybody passing by or coming to gawk that the area inside the perimeter was not to be disturbed. Dozens of farmers and other locals had come to see what the fuss was once word spread, and a second constable had remained on site to make sure none of them trespassed beyond the border set out on the orders of Inspector Lestrade.

"Quite the local attraction," said Mr. Holmes of the gathering.

Enough people were milling about to block the view of said attraction, but given the amount of attention it was getting, I could guess where the body must be lying.

"One might think those stakes were marking the spot where a travelled fair was pitching a tent," Dr. Watson commented.

"A fair is a more common sight than a stranger lying dead on the outskirts," said Rutherford.

"Well done keeping the mob at bay," said Mr. Holmes. "Who first spotted the body this morning?"

"It was the driver of a delivery cart passing along the lane at first light. He stopped long enough to call out to the dead man, concerned he might be passed out in the field after a night of drink. But as the rising sun fell across the body, the driver could see no movement, and noticed a deathly pallor and rigor that suggested the man had been dead for hours."

"He didn't approach at all?" asked Dr. Watson.

"No," said Rutherford. "He stayed with his cart and pressed on. I will say that he appeared quite shaken when he arrived at the station to report what he had discovered."

"Shaken, you say?" asked Lestrade. "Has he been detained as a suspect?"

"Don't let your time in the police force dull you to a normal human reaction upon discovering a cadaver, Lestrade," said Mr. Holmes. "What is commonplace to us in our line of work may well be shocking to the uninitiated."

Young as I was, I was glad to be amongst the initiated. I figured it's better knowing what awful things go on in the world than to have it take you by surprise when you least expect it – or don't expect it at all.

"You don't consider this delivery driver to be a suspect?" said the inspector, ever the suspicious policeman.

"I barely consider him a witness," replied Mr. Holmes. "We shall soon have a better look at the body than he ever did. Only then will we know if some crime has been committed that would warrant a suspect at all."

Rutherford and the other constable busied themselves getting the crowd to stand back as we approached the line and got our first good look at the scene. The field of dirt was flat and even, unmarked except for the man in the middle. He lay on his back, his wide eyes staring up at the sun, fixed and unblinking. The nearest footprints were a good thirty paces away from the body and we couldn't help but add to them as we approached, the soil was so soft. Warm sunlight was slowly baking any marks into a solid crust that would remain until the next stretch of wet weather.

Stopping at the edge of the recent disturbances, we slowly made our way around the perimeter, observing the site from all angles. Sure enough, there wasn't a hint of how the dead man could have ended up situated as he was without cutting a trail through the mud. Not that it was a perfectly smooth surface. A jagged uneven circle surrounded the body. At first I thought someone must have tried to highlight the spot, but the pattern hadn't been drawn with a stick. Rather, it had a natural texture to it, and was more raised than indented. The mud had had hours to settle, and a circle that might have once been distinct had become subtle. I wondered if the mud had been liquid-enough overnight to seep into any previous footprints. But even if it had, the earth wasn't nearly soggy enough to so perfectly wipe away all record of indentations.

Once he was satisfied he had seen all there was to see at a distance, Sherlock Holmes swung his long legs over the twine and approached the body, setting down the first set of footprints on the otherwise pristine site that was so pristine, no one could even say if there had been a crime at all.

"I think we have him, Doctor," I heard Lestrade mutter.

"Fingers crossed this will keep him occupied all week," said Dr. Watson. "Perhaps longer."

We watched as the detective crouched over the body and peered at it with his piercing eyes, searching every feature and article of clothing as thoroughly as a microscope might. Once he had collected all relevant information in sight, he proceeded to probe the dead man's pockets for additional data, but found them empty.

"You may approach," he announced, standing up straight again, satisfied there was nothing the rest of us could spoil with our clumsy footsteps. Even so, we joined him with caution, ever concerned there might be some case-breaking clue buried in the mud we were trodding through.

"What do you make of it, Holmes?" Dr. Watson asked of his friend. "I see no conceivable solution, nor any way to seek one out."

"It does appear quite impossible, does it not?" replied Mr. Holmes.

The doctor did his best to hide his pleasure at these words, but he could not stop himself from swapping a sly smile with Inspector Lestrade. Our excursion promised to have the desired effect of keeping Sherlock Holmes on the job for the foreseeable future.

"Therefore," continued the detective, "I have eliminated the impossible. What remains is the only possible truth."

All smiles, sly or otherwise, were wiped from our faces in an instant.

"You can't have solved it already," said Dr. Watson, his dismay obvious. "There's no evidence!"

"Evidence is redundant if there is only one explanation," said Mr. Holmes.

"What is it then?"

"A balloon," declared the detective, offering his solution.

"A what?" we all said, in near unison.

"A hot air balloon," specified Mr. Holmes. "The poor man fell out."

We couldn't help but cast our eyes to the clouds at the suggestion.

"Where?" asked Lestrade.

"Not above us, obviously," said Mr. Holmes. "It will have sailed away without its pilot. Given the prevailing winds, it should come down somewhere in the German Sea. I expect we'll hear a report of a fishing vessel happening upon it in the coming days. The fabric will prove buoyant and quite colourful. Impossible to miss for long."

"It's a bit of a leap isn't it?" said Dr. Watson.

"Certainly," agreed his friend. "Especially for the dead man."

"I mean to assume he fell from a balloon."

"I have made no assumption. Merely a deduction."

The blank looks told Mr. Holmes that none of us could see what he had. Three extra pairs of eyes on the dead man brought us to no conclusion, and the detective would have to explain what we were looking at.

"The body lies low in the mud," he said. "Although the soil was wet enough to settle back around him, you can still see a distinct splash pattern all around. The corpse didn't simply come to rest here. This was a point of impact. And the impact was the cause of death."

"Surely there was some foul play at work," said Lestrade, still sounding anxious to arrest someone.

"There is no sign of violence beyond what was inflicted by the fall," said Mr. Holmes. "He wasn't pushed by a companion, nor is it likely to have been an accident. The sides of balloon baskets are quite high to prevent anyone tipping out. More likely this man was despondent, and chose to part ways with his craft and his life. A few simple inquires will determine where the balloon came from and who took it up."

Mr. Holmes retraced his steps back to the line and informed the pair of attending constables that the body could be removed and the perimeter disassembled. Dr. Watson and Inspector Lestrade were so deflated they looked like they wanted to have a lie-down in the mud next to the dead man.

"Come along then," Mr. Holmes said. "If we hurry, we can be back in London for teatime. A cup and a bite to eat, and I look forward to resuming my chemical experiments. As soon as Wiggins fulfills his delivery duties, of course."

The look Mr. Holmes gave me suggested no more delays or side trips would be tolerated if I wanted to remain on the payroll.

Constable Rutherford brought us back to the station and thanked us for our time, which hadn't amounted to very much time at all. Mr. Holmes had solved the whole mystery so quick, the train we'd arrived on was only now pulling away down the track, still in sight. The next train back to London was waiting in the station, and I was given enough money to buy us all tickets. With such good rail connections, we'd barely managed to distract the detective for more than a couple of hours.

By the time I was done with the ticket queue, the inspector, the detective, and the doctor were letting themselves into a compartment for the trip home. I joined them at the first blast of the steam whistle and was barely seated when I saw Constable Rutherford running across the platform. He must have spun around and returned to the train station within moments of him reporting back for duty.

"Inspector Lestrade! Inspector Lestrade!" he cried out as the train began rolling down the track. We were still going slow enough for him to keep pace.

"I'm glad I caught you!" he said. "There's a telegram from The Yard, marked urgent."

He was able to pass Lestrade the message through the window before the train pulled ahead and left the constable puffing at the end of the platform. The inspector was quick to read through the vital message that had very nearly missed us.

"Impossible!" he declared.

"I thought we just had an afternoon of eliminating the impossible, Lestrade," commented Mr. Holmes.

The look on the inspector's face was one of incredulity as he reported, "They've discovered a human torso in the cellar of Scotland Yard's new headquarters! No public statement has been made yet, but one of my men thinks it's a match for an arm found off the shore in Pimlico last month."

"Last month?" Dr. Watson practically shouted before catching himself. "You might have consulted Holmes about it. He could have used the diversion."

"We thought it was a medical student prank. Now this!"

"On the bright side," said Mr. Holmes, "you may have the whole body before the end of the year if the culprit continues to deliver parts to your doorstep."

Lestrade's dismay was such that he couldn't help himself from spreading it.

"The building isn't even finished yet," he lamented, as he handed the confidential telegram to Mr. Holmes, "and now it's the location of a crime."

"A most embarrassing christening for the Yard's new abode," said Mr. Holmes, as he read through the scant details that had come across the wire.

"Do have a look, won't you Mr. Holmes?" Lestrade practically pleaded.

The detective fell silent, tapping his lip with a finger as he stared out the window at the passing countryside. We were all at the edge of our seats, waiting for his decision, but knew better than to say anything and interrupt his process.

"The cellar, you say?" he wondered aloud. "At least we are safe to assume this corpse didn't fall from the sky."

I could hear Dr. Watson's sigh of relief over the chugging engine and grinding wheels. Lestrade pointed a finger at the detective's monumental brow and practically laughed.

"I can see the gears are already turning!" he said.

"I suppose my experiments can wait for another day since this one has become so busy," came the final verdict.

"That's the spirit, Mr. Holmes! As soon as we're back in London, I'll have you neck deep in all the grisly details and stomach-churning horror. You should feel right at home."

"I trust you still have the disembodied arm on ice," Mr. Holmes said.

"Of course, of course!" Lestrade assured him. "Nothing but the finest in evidence for Scotland Yard's favourite consultant."

Sherlock Holmes may have missed out on the notorious Whitechapel Murders, but thankfully he was in the right frame of mind to look into the Whitehall Mystery, which the press was quick to suggest was more of the same, only worse. I ain't at liberty to confirm or deny such speculation, but I can say that Mr. Holmes had it sorted out before the new Scotland Yard building opened its doors for business.

People still call the Whitehall Torso an unsolved case. All I can say is there are some cases what get solved and tried, and others that never make it to court for various reasons. Reasons that are such a scandal, you dare not even write them down, let alone put them in print.

But maybe one day.

# The Adventure of the
# Headless Saint
## by Tracy J. Revels

"Go on, Clark. Mr. Holmes has often been of service to Scotland Yard – there's no shame in asking for his assistance. He may be an amateur, but he is a supremely talented one."

My friend smiled languidly and held out his cigarette case. "Do indulge, Inspector Clark. I can see that a smoke would help settle your nerves."

The man grimaced, but accepted the offer and the light. Our guest was perhaps thirty-five years of age, with the air of a world-weary policeman. His long, pale mustache was much-stained, and several small burns on his jacket and sleeves – which Holmes drew my attention to with a quick nod – confirmed that the man was both addicted to tobacco and rather absent-minded.

"Do you miss being able to play rugby?" Holmes asked.

"What?" our guest sputtered, turning on his companion. "Tobias, you are correct – this man *is* the devil!"

Gregson's face turned pink, but Holmes merely laughed. He was in a fine mood that evening, as several cases had been satisfactorily concluded. He stretched out his legs and placed his palms together.

"It is no great deduction, Inspector. You have the build of an athlete, but you entered these rooms with a limp, and your frame is now developing the usual weight carried by a previously fit body denied regular training. Still, you bear the look of a determined mid-fielder."

"And when Holmes mentioned that you were coming up with Gregson," I said, unable to resist a bit of fun, "I recalled a chap named Reginald Clark who played for Hampstead. I wondered if it might be you."

Holmes chuckled. "Watson is the conjurer's assistant who gives away the tricks! But enough of this foolishness – I can see that you come to us in sincere distress. Is it the matter of the Storley village murders?"

The newcomer shot a hard glimpse at Gregson. "You told him."

"The inspector did no such thing," Holmes said. "But one can hardly escape the sensational press. Desecration, murder, three bold robberies, all in less than a month, not to mention a specter named Black Ben rising from an unhallowed grave. I find myself intrigued, Inspector."

Clark shifted uncomfortably on the divan. "I wish I could say the same, Mr. Holmes. But I'll be damned if I can make any sense of it all."

"It began, I believe, with petty vandalism," Holmes coached. The inspector leaned back, his cigarette smoldering between his fingers.

"Perhaps. At least, that was the first I learned of it. It was the sixth day of November when Father Miller informed that me the head of the statue of St. Agnes, which stands just inside the churchyard, had been stolen. He was quite incensed, but as the previous evening was Guy Fawkes night, a time when mischief runs amuck, there was little I could do about it."

"This statue is, I understand, a landmark in your community?"

"Yes – the saint was carved by Matteo Bruni, formerly of Naples, who has made quite the name for himself in the village as a sculptor of monuments."

"And there was damage done to this same sculpture a year earlier?" Holmes asked. "I am merely curious as to how accurately things have been reported," he added, when Clark made a sour face.

"Indeed. About a year ago, St. Agnes was found with her head knocked off. Luckily, Matteo was able to make repairs within days and fit it once again to the body. The priest offered to pay him for the restoration, but he refused, saying it was an act of devotion. Now, may I continue?"

Holmes's smile was thin. "Please do."

"I assured Father Miller there was no anti-Catholic prejudice afoot. Storley is a small village, and there are almost as many Papists as Anglicans among us. However, I promised to investigate the desecration."

"'I do wish you would, and quickly,' the priest said as he took his leave. 'Matteo is quite upset – he came to me this morning in such a state I feared for his sanity.'

"The morning after Father Miller spoke to me, Matteo was found dead in his workshop. It was an obvious murder, for he had been shot three times in the chest. The bullets were small caliber, and the poor man must have been in agony for hours. He had tried to write a word on the floor, in his own blood, but we could make nothing of it. Here, as best we could interpret, are the letters."

He passed a paper to Holmes. Written on it was *Leidiav*.

"How long had Matteo been dead when he was discovered?" my friend asked.

"His apprentice came upon the scene when he arrived for work at six. The youth ran immediately to my door. When I reached the workshop, I found Matteo's blood was dry, his body completely stiff. The apprentice confirmed that Matteo was wearing his previous day's clothing."

"Implying that the killing occurred in the evening hours, or the very early morning." Holmes nodded. "What happened next?"

Inspector Clark grimaced. "Two days after Matteo's death, the schoolmaster opened his doors to find his classroom ransacked. Books were knocked from shelves, inkwells overturned, some *graffiti* scrawled on the chalkboard. He was certain one of the boys had broken in, and when he could not induce the perpetrator to confess, all the lads were given a sharp whipping and sent home for the day. He called me over afterward. He was surprised that the lads' tuition money, which he had collected the day before and was keeping in a box on his desk, hadn't been pilfered. He also pointed out a beautiful ivory bust of the Queen which survived the assault. Clearly, the vandalism was nothing but a schoolboy prank, and I advised him to forget it, for the only item he could find missing from his schoolroom was the ledger in which his students' grades were recorded."

I chuckled. "Some young fellow thinks to improve his marks. Isn't that a sound deduction, Holmes?"

My friend ignored me, leaning forward, his eyes bright. "Inspector Clark, be very precise. What was written or drawn on the chalkboard?"

The two policemen exchanged baffled looks. "Schoolboy nonsense," Clark muttered.

"What type of nonsense?"

"Why – there was a drawing of a figure being chased by a devil, and beneath it '*Restore the head or go to Hell.*'"

Holmes nodded. "Tell me of the burglaries."

"They have been shocking in their daring – the first was committed on 12 November, while the Ashwood family and their servants were all away, attending a special evening service at St. Agnes's. They returned to find everything in their home turned topsy-turvy. Someone slashed their pillows and beddings with a knife. There were feathers everywhere, and half the crockery and glassware were broken. Even the child's room was torn apart, his puzzles and toys strewn on the floor. And yet . . . ."

"Nothing was missing."

"Exactly. Of course, the lady was in a panic, because her jewel box was dumped on the rug, but with some sorting she soon found all her precious possessions. The same for the housekeeper, who owned some cameos that were dear to her. Things were in great disorder, but nothing was taken."

"And the second robbery?"

"Was even stranger. It was committed two evenings later at the home of Theodore Breslin, the village butcher. He is a widower, and lives alone with his son Jimmy in a very modest house. They both slept unusually sound that night, awaking to find everything in disarray the next morning. Jimmy's room seemed the most disheveled, all his clothes and books upon the floorboards. A collection of toy animals – little creatures made of rags, stuffed with cotton, playthings that had belonged to his beloved sister, who died recently from fever – were ripped to shreds. But nothing of value was taken."

"The toys were valuable," Holmes noted. "Of sentimental value to a bereaved brother." Inspector Clark shrugged his shoulders at this assessment.

"But they were of no real worth. It was on that night, I should add, that Black Ben was first seen."

"And who is he?" I asked.

"A figure of legend, a villager from three-hundred years ago who sold his soul to the Devil for riches, especially fine garb. The Devil tricked him, and now he wanders as a naked black shadow, darker than the night itself, unable to rest. It is said that if he touches you, grabs for your stickpin or watch, you will die. Foolishness, of course."

"Agreed – but who saw him?" Holmes asked.

"Andrew Quibley, and he is the village drunkard. He was pitched out of the King Henry pub at two in the morning, and was none too steady on his feet, but he swears he saw Black Ben slinking down the lane, an inky form with no face. Of course, he tells the story to everyone in the village, and after what happened at the Carters the next evening . . . ."

The inspector dropped his head. He snubbed out the cigarette which had burned to a long cylinder of ash in his finger. Gregson supplied him with another and his hand trembled as he lit it.

"This is the worst. Dr. Carter, our village physician, lives with his wife and his two children, Edith and Eddie, ten and fourteen years of age, in a fine home a half-mile beyond the station. The household retired at ten, but at two in the morning, the boy heard a noise and went downstairs. There he found his little sister dead on the parlor floor, strangled to death with the cord from the drapes."

Holmes closed his eyes. "And the room was ransacked?"

"The pillows on the parlor sofa had all been slashed, and some rugs turned back, but that was as far as the thief got before he was interrupted by the poor child. Yesterday, while the family was at Edith's funeral – "

"The villain completed his task."

Inspector Clarke winced. "Again, the house was overturned, but nothing was missing. This grows ever more perplexing, because Mrs. Carter has quite the collection of jewelry, and the doctor was known to keep large sums of money in the house."

Holmes rose from his chair. He pulled down his pipe, lit it, and gave a series of vigorous puffs.

"Inspector, I can hear the hesitation and trepidation in your voice. You haven't told me everything. You are holding back something, for fear it is a distraction."

"Reggie," Inspector Gregson prodded, "tell him all."

"But it is *foolishness!* A cruel child's prank, or perhaps the work of that idiot, Quibley. I'm half-a-mind to arrest him."

I could tell it was taking a supreme effort for Holmes not to throttle the inspector. At last, the man growled out an answer.

"I found words, scribbled in chalk, on the Carter's front door – '*Restore the saint or Black Ben will visit.*' Nonsense, but the scribbling would have caused a panic among the villagers. I immediately scrubbed it out with my sleeve."

Holmes groaned and collapsed back in his chair. "You would have done better to have come to me sooner, Inspector. Is there a train to Storley this evening?"

"The last one departs in less than an hour."

"I suggest that you be on it, sir. More than mischief is afoot in your town, and I dare not detain you any longer. Is there by any chance a lad in the school whose last name begins with '*D*'? Or '*E*'?"

"No *D*, but Anthony Evans and his family live next door to the Ashwoods."

"Telegraph ahead, set a guard for them. No, do not question. Their very lives may depend upon it."

"I only have two constables. It will be an expense. I will look like a fool."

"How much do you value their lives, Inspector?"

"Very well," Clark grumbled, his face still set in a scowl. He made me think of a petulant schoolboy, one refusing to accept his master's correction. "Will you come tomorrow and look into these matters?"

"Yes, by the earliest train."

Inspector Clark made his departure with a gruff and, to my ears, rather insincere thanks. Inspector Gregson lingered at our door as his companion plodded down the stairs.

"Your kinsman?" Holmes asked.

"No, only a chum from days when we walked a beat together. Reggie is a stalwart fellow, good for cracking heads and rousting drunkards, but promoted above his talents, I fear. Thank you for hearing him out."

"Holmes," I said, once our guests were visible walking down Baker Street. "You have clearly seen more in this strange business than I have."

"But not enough, I fear," Holmes muttered. "Surely you recognize the source of all the turmoil?"

I frowned. "We seem to circle back to the missing head of the statue."

"Indeed, it is the start of the villainy. Whatever Matteo concealed inside it – "

"Concealed?"

Holmes began to enumerate points upon his fingers. "Matteo arrives in the village, establishes himself as an artist in stone, and all is well. The statue of St. Agnes is damaged in the past, and he makes a repair without any consternation. But after Guy Fawkes night, when the statue is again decapitated, he panics. Why? He clearly has the talent to easily affect another repair and knows he will be paid for it, for he has already turned down a fee. But now his very sanity seems challenged. We must ask ourselves: What had he hidden in the statue's head, to be so distraught that the head had vanished?"

"Something valuable."

"*Exceedingly* valuable. Our thief, Black Ben, has now killed twice in pursuit of it."

"The specter?"

"Is no specter, but a burglar, clad all in dark attire, and perhaps relishing the idea that a village fable will work to his advantage. Common thievery isn't his aim. He wants the head returned."

"How does the schoolroom vandalism fit?"

Holmes began to pace. "Let us take this as our theory: Matteo Bruni didn't have whatever valuable object Black Ben sought until a year ago. At that point, he received it and, looking for a place to hide it, he caused the damage to the statue *himself*. Then, when he had the head in hand, made the repair, because it provided him a place of safekeeping for this treasure. But the villain caught up with him and demanded the loot. While begging for mercy, Matteo offered the theory that the head was taken by a prankster – the very theory Inspector Clark promotes. Matteo was killed, and our frustrated criminal seeks the prize in the homes of the schoolboys."

"The Devil drawn on the chalkboard, and the '*Restore the head*' instruction – these were warnings to the boys!"

"Precisely! Our fiend knew his culprit would understand. Whatever is hidden in that marble head, he has hopes it hasn't been found. If the head was placed back on the statue, he could retrieve the hidden object, and the burglaries would cease."

"Why take the tutor's book for his student's marks?"

"Simplicity itself, and an important clue. Our thief is a newcomer to the village, he doesn't know the names of village lads. Now, it's an elementary matter to track them, one by one, and search each dwelling until – "

A sudden and ferocious change came upon my friend. His face went white, his eyes wide. His pipe dropped to the floor.

380

"Holmes? Holmes! What is it?"

"I am a fool – A blind *fool*! Why didn't I ask? My God! How could I have missed it?"

"I don't understand! What – ?"

Holmes bolted for the door. He moved so fast that it was useless to chase after him, running off without his hat or his overcoat, despite the bitter gale that was blowing outside.

An hour passed before a cab rolled up to our door and I saw Holmes and Lestrade emerge. My friend was wrapped in a tartan blanket, and Lestrade, it appeared, was quite amused by his borrowed attire. The inspector laughed loudly as they entered our rooms, while Holmes headed straight to the fire to warm his blue-tipped fingers.

"You'd better keep a watch on him, Doctor!" Lestrade crowed. "He's a candidate for the madhouse if I ever saw one. I was tempted to drop him off at Bedlam instead of Baker Street."

"Thank you, Lestrade – that will do." Holmes whipped the blanket from his shoulders and tossed it at the inspector. "I can only hope your colleague in Storley will heed my advice. It seemed more likely he would if the message came through official channels."

Lestrade gave a mock-bow and made his exit. Holmes slumped into his favorite chair.

"I had hoped to find Gregson still on duty, but . . . you see how I fared."

"Holmes, I am completely in the dark! What were you trying to accomplish? I presume you sent a message to Clark?"

"I did. Watson, the thief wishes to inspire terror in the heart of the person who purloined the saint's head. One message was sent in the schoolroom, another on the Carters' door, though we don't know if that message became public knowledge, because the inspector so quickly erased it. But the names, Watson! What are the victim's names?"

"Ashwood . . . Breslin . . . Carter – the thief is going in alphabetical order!"

"As an outsider to the community, he has no sense of who might be most *likely* to have done the mischief. However, by working methodically, he hopes the person who holds the item will see the pattern and be terrified by it, intimidated into returning the head to its proper stone neck in the churchyard – along with whatever is hidden inside."

"But you already knew this," I said. "You asked Clarke about *D*'s and *E*'s."

"Yes, Watson. But 'Clark' would fall between 'Carter' and any name beginning with the letter *D* or *E*. I failed to inquire if the inspector had a child in the class . . . and he was too dull to intuit my point. My God, how I hope the official telegraph reaches him."

We boarded the train for Storley at five-thirty the next morning and reached the village at just after eight. Holmes had sent another telegram before we left the station, but said very little on the journey. As we stepped onto the platform, we were hailed by a tall, ruddy-faced constable.

"Are you Mr. Sherlock Holmes?" he asked.

"I am."

The man took off his hat and shook his head grimly. My friend, whose face had been anxious and drawn with distress throughout the journey, put his hand to a bench, as if needing the support.

"Not the family too?" Holmes whispered.

"No, sir. Last evening, just before eight, I received word from Inspector Clark to hire men to watch the Evans household. About an hour later, the message came for the inspector, direct from Scotland Yard. I was here with it when he got off the train. He . . . ."

The constable looked abashed. Holmes straightened.

"Go on, Officer . . . ."

"Morley, sir."

Holmes nodded. "Whatever has happened, Morley, it isn't your fault. You did as you were instructed. You couldn't have done more. How did the inspector react to the telegram?"

The young officer sniffled. "Inspector Clark tore it up. He called you a fool, and then he inquired as to who I had at the Evans' house. He approved of my choice, slapped me on the shoulder, and set off for his dwelling. That is the last time he was seen alive. Come, sir, I will take you to his house, where he was murdered."

The Clark home was a modest, two-story affair in the very center of the village. Morley admitted us with a solemn nod, and we were met by a dark-haired man in the hallway. He was clearly Carter, the recently bereaved doctor, for he carried his medical bag as well as a look of sorrow beyond what so many men of my profession wear.

"It was a clean shot, right between the eyes," he said, upon learning my friend's name and purpose. "Reggie didn't suffer. I would wager it was a derringer, or some other type of very small pistol, just like the one that did poor Mattteo Bruni in."

"What of the other residents?" Holmes asked.

"Timmy – that is his son – is the one who fetched me. His mother is upstairs, being watched by my nurse. It seems she was heavily drugged in some manner and is still senseless. The boy is in his room."

Holmes spent very little time with the body of the man who had, only hours before, been our guest in London. He confirmed Clark had been shot squarely between the eyes, and the bullet remained lodged in his brain. The room was somewhat disordered, several sofa cushions slashed, and drawers left open, with papers flung about. It appeared evident that the inspector had walked in upon the villain at work, and the fiend had instantly dispatched him, before Clark could react. Holmes turned and looked toward the staircase.

"This will require some delicate handling, I fear. Officer, if you don't mind, Watson and I shall conduct a private interview with the lad."

For just a moment, the constable seemed poised to object, but then nodded. I suspected the word had gone out to Scotland Yard, and soon a more important official might be in our midst. Holmes climbed the stairs, knocking softly on the boy's door.

The youth was a pale, slender lad of some thirteen years. His yellow hair was uncombed, his eyes red and swollen from weeping. Holmes sat on the side of the bed next to him. The boy rubbed a fist against his cheek.

"You're the gentleman Father went to see – the London detective."

"Yes, and I am sorry for your father's death. I had hoped to prevent it."

The boy shook his head. "It isn't your fault, sir. But it may be mine."

"You have done nothing wrong."

"Haven't I?"

Holmes frowned. "Tell me about yesterday, Master Timothy. Did anything out of the ordinary occur?"

"Yes . . . Mother said it was just a sad thing, not anything unnatural, and yet . . . it seems silly to even talk about it now, after what happened to Father."

"No matter how strange it may seem, it may have a bearing on this case. Tell me of it."

My friend had a natural and soothing manner with children, especially boys who were the age of his Irregulars. The youth nodded and began to speak.

"Yesterday morning, I found Champ dead in the back lot. He was my dog, sir, and quite old. When I cried out, Mother came down and saw me with him, and reminded me that he was like a very aged man, and it was his time – that I shouldn't grieve, but think of him playing in Heaven's fields, a puppy again. Mr. Holmes, I . . . I wanted to believe her, but there was foam on Champ's muzzle, and I saw a large bone in the corner, one I knew I hadn't thrown to him. I asked Father if it was possible that Champ was poisoned, but Father never so much as came into the lot to look for himself. He was too busy reading the newspaper and muttering about all the burglaries that had happened. Mother told me to hush, and together we buried Champ.

"I didn't feel like going to school, and Mother didn't make me. My friend Billy came by around two, to see if I was ill. When I opened the door, he was holding out a little waxed box."

"'This was on your step,' he said. 'I think it's chocolates! Annabelle must have sent them to you!'"

"She is your sweetheart?" Holmes asked. The boy gave a shy nod.

"There was no note with the box, but I couldn't imagine anyone else who would have delivered such a gift. I talked with Billy for ten minutes or so, and then he went away. I put the box on the kitchen table and went back upstairs to the book I was reading. Later, I came down, and saw that Mother was dressed to go out.

"'Since your father will not be home for supper, shall we have a treat?' she asked, and I agreed. We went to Mr. Kholi's little restaurant, for I am very fond of curry dishes, and it was already dark by the time we walked home. Mother asked me about the box, and I told her I thought it was candies from Annabelle. She opened it and gave a cry of delight, and asked if I would share them. I could hardly say no. She ate three or four candies, and then went off to bed."

"You did not partake?" Holmes asked.

"No sir. I had eaten too much curry, and it wasn't sitting well with me. I was afraid something sweet would make it worse. Mother was snoring in the next room, but I was up and down all night with my stomach. Once, I thought I heard a noise downstairs, but decided it was only the house creaking about me. I finally fell asleep and . . . then I heard something. A little pop or bang. At first, I thought I had dreamed it, but afterward I heard a clatter, like someone running out of the house. I hurried downstairs and . . . ."

Holmes gently laid his hand over the boy's. "You are a good and brave lad. You fetched the doctor and the constable. Your father would be proud of you for acting decisively."

"What is wrong with Mother?" Timmy asked, tears shining in his eyes.

"Your mother was drugged," I said, echoing the doctor's words. "Someone wanted her – and you – to sleep very soundly."

"Someone . . . not Annabelle," the boy said. He frowned, fitting the pieces together far more deftly than his unfortunate father had done. "The person who killed my dog – so no alarm would be raised – he killed Father too!"

The child looked to Holmes. Slowly, my friend nodded.

"Can you tell me where the apprentice to Mr. Bruni can be found?" Holmes asked.

"I know him, sir – he's a bit older than me. His name is Scotty Jenkins, and he's still working in the Bruni shop while everything is sorted. It's just down Baker's Lane."

"Go to your mother now," Holmes coaxed. "Be strong for her. There's a good lad."

The boy nodded and rolled his lips inward. Holmes spoke lowly to me as we exited.

"The child clearly knows more than he is telling. Time is our ally. Let us give him time to sort it through while we visit the apprentice."

Scotty Jenkins was tall, robust, and talented with his hands. He proudly showed us the tombstone he had been making for his mentor, an obelisk with vines creeping around it.

"Mr. Bruni was a good master," he said. "He was patient. He let me try my ideas, and never cursed at me when I made a mistake. I will miss him. I fear my lessons weren't complete when he died."

"How long have you been in Bruni's employ?"

"He came to the village some five years ago, and I was taken on as an apprentice two years afterward."

"Did you observe any change in him when the statue of St. Agnes was first damaged?"

The boy picked up his broom and slowly began to sweep up dust from his work.

"Anything you can tell me may help me avenge his death," Holmes coaxed. "There could be no greater honor to a kind master's memory than to bring his killer to justice."

The sweeping came to a halt, but the lad's gaze remained fixed to the floor.

"I said little because of Inspector Clark's manner – he was gruff with me, and asked if I had quarreled with my master. He asked me if I owned a gun. I suppose he had to ask but . . . I swear I had nothing to do with it!"

"But you had observed a change in Mr. Bruni – and would have mentioned it if the inspector hadn't frightened you?"

"Yes. Just a few days before the statue was first damaged, Mr. Bruni received a small package in the mail. I didn't see what was in it, but he began to curse and rant, and sent me home early. After St. Agnes lost her head, he fixed it, and I was glad he had the work, for it seemed to sooth him, and afterward he was himself again. But after Guy Fawkes Day, when the saint's head vanished, my master was piteous, weeping and wailing. I asked what I could do to help him, and he said there was nothing. That afternoon, he kept looking at the clock, and then he sent me away early, this time with my week's wages. I wondered later if he knew that death was coming for him, and it was his way of saying goodbye."

Holmes sat on a bench. "Do you recall his exact words, when he received the strange package?"

The lad half-smiled. "Mr. Bruni's English wasn't strong, and when he was passionate, he spoke in his native tongue. I know very few words in Italian, beyond names for tools and types of stone. I recall two phrases that he used repeatedly, but I have no idea of their meaning: *'lei diavolo'* and *'sangue del martire'*. As for what that means, you will have to ask the schoolmaster."

The words had an electric effect on Holmes. He rose from the bench, a new resolution sharpening his face. The hunter was on the scent.

"Fortunately, I have some small acquaintance with Italian. You have been most helpful, and I am in great hopes that your good master will shortly be avenged. Let me put one more question to you: Are there any other Italians or recently arrived foreigners in the village?"

The young man scratched his head. "No Italians, though I've heard a rumor that Lord Deaton has returned from his travels with a new . . . friend. A beautiful lady, said to be French, engaged to curate the fine pictures in his house. My sweetheart told me that bit of gossip. You know how women talk, sir. And this French lady came into the shop on Lord Deaton's arm just a few days before my master was killed. Mr. Bruni seemed quite – I am not sure how to describe it – in awe of her."

"A cup of coffee would not go amiss," Holmes said, as we strolled back into the heart of the village. "Let us take the seats in that pasty shop's window, where we can watch the passing scene and likewise be viewed by pedestrians."

I waited until we were settled, with warm mugs and delicious treats before us. My friend's gaze remained sharp, locked through the glass to the cobblestone streets.

"You have a clue?"

"I have vital information. I know who the thief and murderer is, and I know the object of such unholy lust that a villain would strangle an innocent child in pursuit of it."

"What?"

Holmes pulled out the paper Clark had provided. "Note the letters Bruni attempted to write, as he laying dying. I made the error of assuming he was spelling a name: *Leidiav*. Instead, he was writing a title – '*Lei Diavolo*' – or the '*She Devil*'."

A chill ran through me. "My God – she is real! I was certain she was a fiction."

"She is very real, and while her exploits have been exaggerated to sell sensational newspapers, she is known across Europe for her brazen thefts of gems from royal lovers. She is a chameleon, capable of changing her hair, her figure, her accent, and her role. Whether posing as an adventuress, an artist, or a chaste missionary lass, she worms her way into the heart of a nobleman and then makes off with a precious stone. Never more than one, but always a gem of remarkable value and reputation. Baron Sutter no longer possesses the 'Scottish Thistle', a table diamond once worn by Margaret Tudor, nor does the Duke of Amiens enjoy the 'Bonaparte Pearl' that graced the throat of the Empress Josphine. I could list half-a-dozen more, but now I know which item she is hunting – the *sangue del martire,* or 'Martyr's Blood'. It is – Hello! We have most welcome company."

Timothy Clark had entered the shop, holding hands with a pretty girl whose golden hair hung down her back in long braids. They were the picture of innocence and young love, but the youth wore a troubled expression upon his face.

"Master Timothy – and sure this is the lovely Miss Annabelle – ?"

"Xavier, sir," she offered, with a quaint little curtsey. I pulled up a chair for her as Holmes retrieved one for the boy. "My brother is Sebastian Xavier, who is in the class with Timmy."

Holmes and I exchanged a glance over their heads. Our villain would perhaps murder the entire schoolroom, if not stopped.

"Mr. Holmes," the youth said, in a rush, "I want you to arrest me."

"My word – whatever for?"

"Robbery, sir – the robbery that led to the death of Edith Carter, and Matteo Bruni, and good old Champ and . . . and my father. Sir, I am the one who stole St. Agnes's head. I suppose I deserve to hang."

"The Queen's Justice isn't so harsh to exact the death penalty for simple mischief," Holmes said. "Tell us what happened on the night of the Fifth of November."

"I was causing devilment – along with Billy and Sebastian. We had some firecrackers, and a bag filled with manure. We lit it on the schoolmaster's door. Then we fled and hid in the churchyard."

"How did you detach the statue's head?" I asked.

"It was by accident. As we ran into the churchyard, I tripped and stumbled into the statue. The head shook, then fell off and landed on the ground next to me. It gave me the idea for another lark. I gave the saint's head to Sebastian and told him to put it in Annabelle's room, on a shelf, to startle her when she woke up. We thought it might make her scream."

387

The girl proudly tossed her braids. "I didn't scream. The next morning I knew Sebastian had been naughty, so I hid the marble head beneath my bed. But sir, as I moved it, I heard a strange sound, a kind of rattling. I shook it hard, and this fell out."

She pulled a folded handkerchief from her coat and opened it. The item within left us breathless.

"Is it valuable, sir?" Miss Annabelle asked. "I thought it was only a bit of paste, like mother wears."

Holmes picked up the gem. The stone was oval and nearly the size of a robin's egg, but of a vivid red hue, so masterfully cut that its facets twinkled as if lit from within.

"It is very valuable," Holmes said.

"We thought it might be a game someone was playing," Timmy said. "A toy treasure hidden where no one would think to look. Some of the younger lads at school pretend to be pirates. I guessed we had stolen their loot. But then my father came home so angry about someone vandalizing the statue, and I thought it best to keep silent, for I didn't want a whipping." The boy began to choke. "Now I wouldn't care if Father whipped me!"

Holmes gently put a hand on the boy's shoulder.

"Did you see the words on the schoolroom chalkboard?"

"Yes, Mr. Holmes," he sniffled, "but I thought it was one of the older lads, trying to scare the teacher. I heard of the robberies and Black Ben prowling, but . . . I didn't put it together then that he was after this stone."

"What will you do with us?" the little girl asked, her eyes wide. "Then will we go to the gaol?"

"No, Miss Annabelle," Holmes assured her, as he rewrapped the diamond and slipped it in his pocket. "But I will put the real villain in a cell tonight."

"Three cheers for Sherlock Holmes!"

The village residents gave a trio of hearty shouts and sloshed a great deal of ale to the floorboards. My friend sat on the bar at the King Henry Inn and Public House, looking rather like a sovereign holding court. He had ordered a jeweler to set the red diamond on a cheap chain, and the man's eyes had nearly popped from his head as he did the work.

"Sir, I have never seen such a valuable stone. May I call my wife in to view it?"

"Yes, by all means – your wife and your servants as well! Give them all a good look," Holmes encouraged. Afterward, he strutted about town, with the diamond around his neck, bragging to everyone that his case had been solved, and inviting them to celebrate with him at the pub.

"There is nothing more to fear!" he shouted to his intoxicated admirers. "I have chased away the man who murdered good people, including your beloved inspector, in the quest for this fatal gem!"

At just that moment, I spotted a well-dressed pair entering the establishment. Holmes hopped from his perch and executed a bow, as the rest of the village folk made nods of deference toward their local nobleman. The dark-haired beauty on his arm sniffed in disdain.

"Lord Deaton, how good of you to come! I see Constable Morley delivered the message that you, as the representative of the Queen, would wish to hear."

"He did," the rotund old gentleman said while shaking Holmes's hand. "He told me that all the burglaries and murders were over a lost diamond."

Holmes held out the gem, making sure that the crowd could see it sparkle beneath the swaying lamp.

"They call it the 'Martyr's Blood', because it absorbed the lifeblood of Saint Agnes upon her execution, and therefore is blessed with miraculous properties. Of course, that is mere fable, but for centuries it was treated as a precious relic. It was last seen in the possession of Count Visconi of Naples, who gifted it to his paramour, just before the couple's private pleasure boat floundered off the coast of Capri."

"Remarkable! But how did it ever come to be lodged inside the statue's head?"

Holmes made a flourish with one arm. "I must keep certain matters in confidence – but I can safely say that I believe the stone was stolen by the thief, who was a conspirator in the sinking of the Count's vessel. Such a bauble," he added, with an unsteady bow, "would look much better around your throat than mine, Lady Deaton."

The nobleman laughed loudly while his female companion flushed in embarrassment. "Lord Deaton is a widower," the lady snapped. "I am merely the curator of his pictures."

"Oh, forgive me. I have imbibed too freely, Madame, and seem to have lost my manners. Perhaps I should be going. Watson, remind me – when must we leave for the train?"

"You are far too intoxicated to travel," I scolded. "I have acquired a room for you here."

"What? You aren't staying with me?"

"I have neglected the patients who require my attention long enough," I said, with a loud snort of disgust. "I will see you in Baker Street tomorrow."

"Very well. Another round for the house!" my friend shouted, to thunderous applause.

The clock had just struck two when Quibley staggered out of a friend's house and began to wander toward his own home. As he was rather intoxicated, he tumbled first over a barrel, then over his untied shoe, and finally over a loosened cobblestone. Laughing giddily, he leaned against a wall and began another chorus of "Danny Boy". Abruptly, the song died on his lips, for he saw Black Ben slithering down the sidewalk, melting in and out of the shadows. As the drunkard watched, the specter approached the King Henry Inn and threw a rope with a metal hook toward an open window on the upper floor. Quibley watched, astonished, as the dark figure tugged to test the rope's security, then began to climb it and disappeared inside the window.

Black Ben stepped down from the ledge, studying the room with a single bed, its occupant bundled beneath heavy blankets, snoring loudly. The chamber reeked as foully as the public house taproom below it. There was no danger the man in the bed would awaken. The intruder noted how nicely the gem, hanging from the bedpost on a gaudy chain, glittered in the moonlight.

The intruder had merely to grab the jewel, but a quick slicing of the sleeper's throat would add confusion to the case. The entire village had watched this fool brag. Everyone would be a suspect in his murder. By the time a new inspector was sent to sort it out, the killer would be safely on the Continent.

Like a lynx, the assailant sprang onto the bed.

Standing below, Quibley heard a scream.

"Careful, Watson! She bites!"

"Hurry up!" I shouted. The woman who'd climbed in through the window was much stronger than she appeared. She had already managed to stomp my left foot with her high boot, and now she was raking her nails on my arms so feverishly I was sure my jacket was shredded. It had taken our combined strength to seize her and wrestle her from the bed. Had she not been startled when her knife jammed inside the wooden throat of the bust of King Henry V – which we had borrowed from the pub's décor – she would easily have vaulted through the window and made her escape. Holmes at last managed to bind her hands and shoved her into the corner. Alerted from his post across the hall by the racket, Constable Morley burst into the room.

"You have the thief?"

"Thief, murderer, and attempted murderer," my friend said. The woman was clad in a single dark garment, much like an acrobat's costume. Her face was covered, except for her mouth and eyes, and her hair was buried beneath a stretchy cowl. Holmes yanked the dark mask from the intruder's face. "May I introduce the She Devil of Europe – known variously as Maria Tepes, Augustina Borzio, and Serenia Flores. Tell me, Madame: How exactly did you manage to lose the Martyr's Blood?"

The woman's eyes were dark, yet they glittered like two black diamonds on the pale canvas of her face. "I will tell you nothing."

"Allow me to speculate, then. A year ago, you hired a Bruni relation to assist you in scuttling the yacht owned by Count Visconi, the owner of the stone. Somehow, this Bruni acquired the gem, but soon realized the danger he courted by keeping it from you, so he mailed it to Matteo Bruni for safekeeping. He created the ruse to hide it inside the statue's head. It was but a momentary setback, and you eventually tracked down the recipient of the jewel. You spoke with him privately and gave him a choice – surrender the stone or pay with his life. But on the very night he went to retrieve it, his hiding place was pilfered – due to an impulsive childhood prank. He begged for mercy, swearing he would find whichever child had stolen it, but in a fury, you assassinated him. Days later, you stole the headmaster's book, and left a threat upon the school chalkboard. While the saint remained headless, you methodically and alphabetically began sacking the lads' houses, and murdering anyone who came between you and your quest for the stone."

"Do you know its value?" she hissed. "Do you realize how rare a red diamond is – much less one as old as antiquity? What is any peasant's life compared to that?"

Holmes folded his arms and nodded at the constable, whose face had turned as bloody as the diamond.

"My work is done, Officer. She is your prisoner now."

Readers of these tales often are curious as to their epilogues. The infamous She Devil – whose final alias, given in her guise as an expert of art, was Catherine LaRue – was tried and found guilty of the Storley village murders. Courts in Italy and France wished to bring her to justice as well, and the competing claims for who would eventually have the right to execute this cruel, calculating woman nearly caused a diplomatic incident. While nations squabbled, the lady made one last, daring attempt at escape. Managing to seduce a guard and gain her freedom, she stole a rowboat and set off across the Channel. The craft was found a day later, smashed on rocks near Dover. The lady's body was discovered nearby, a repulsive, bloated form being picked over by the scavengers of the sands.

Sherlock Holmes, I fear, never completely forgave himself for not inquiring as to whether Clark had a son. The inspector's death haunted him, but fate provided a way for Holmes to offer a gesture of respect to

Clark's survivors. The great gem called the Martyr's Blood was returned to the Visconi family. A few weeks after the adventure, Holmes showed me a letter and a cheque from that noble Italian house, expressing gratitude for his part in recovering the heirloom. I gave a low whistle at the amount.

"Will you be acquiring finer apartments?" I asked. "You could buy your own manor in the country!"

"I will never require a more distinguished domicile than this picturesque pile," Holmes said, "though it might be cheerful to one day to own a cottage and keep bees. No, Watson, I shall share this largesse – and make sure a promising but fatherless boy in Storley, and his pretty little sweetheart, have all they need to brighten their future."

# The Case of the
# Australian Atlases
## by Paul Metcalfe

It was a crisp mid-December morning in 1888, and I was breakfasting on my own. Holmes had gone out in the late afternoon of the previous day, working on a case. I had offered to accompany him, but he had informed me it was likely to be a long, cold night, and stealthy surveillance was the object of the outing, so for these reasons it was best that he operated alone. As he had not come down to breakfast, I assumed his night had been a late one and he had not yet arisen. I was thus a little surprised when, halfway through my kippers, I heard his brisk footsteps coming up the stairs, and moments later he appeared in the doorway, dressed as a common loafer, unshaven and looking not a little dishevelled.

"Good morning," he said cheerfully. "I've ordered some more kippers from Mrs. Hudson on the way in. Pour me a coffee, there's a good fellow. I trust you didn't lose too much money at cards last night?"

"No, indeed. I think I finished about four pounds to the good, so – " I stopped. "I'm sure it's obvious, but please explain how you know that I played cards last night. And please, don't say that it's elementary."

He chuckled.

"Very well. I knew by observing the fact that your shoes are drying in front of the fire, and by knowing your habits."

"Go on. I am still in the dark."

"Then let me enlighten you. Yesterday as I was leaving, you intimated that you would be dining at your club. I am aware that when you do this, you generally browse one or two periodicals while enjoying an after-dinner cigar and brandy, and then you make your way home by ten o'clock. Now, as I was out all last night, I know that it started snowing quite heavily just before midnight. In fact, upon my return to Baker Street just now, I noticed there is still some few inches of snow on parts of the pavement. Your shoes must have got wet in the snow as you traversed the short distance from the cab to our door. If you had arrived home before midnight, before it snowed, they would not be wet. On the few times in the past you have stayed at your club that late, it has always been to play cards, and I'm sorry to say, to lose. Therefore, my deduction that you lost at cards last night, but I am overjoyed to hear that I am wrong and you have come away a winner on this occasion."

"Yes, the cards fell in my favour for once. Now will you allow me to

393

make some deductions of my own?"

Holmes smiled. "Certainly."

"Last night, you solved the mystery of the dowager duchess and the missing silver tortoise, and the culprit was Johnson, the footman."

Mrs. Hudson chose that moment to enter with Holmes's breakfast, and frowned at his disreputable attire.

"Thank you, Mrs. Hudson," said Holmes. "I shall change quickly before I sit down to eat of your delightful repast. Now, you are entirely correct in your deductions. Pray tell, what led you to them?"

"Yesterday before you left, you said that your night's work would prove which one of the two suspects was in fact responsible – the footman Johnson, or Fletcher, her Ladyship's groom. You stated that if it was the former, you would have to spend the night watching from up a tree, and if the latter your night would be spent hidden in the stable. You don't appear to have any straw lodged in your clothing, but you do have some bark adhering to your right shin and a leaf in your left trouser turn-up. Thus, you have spent the night up a tree. You also ordered breakfast, and had a pleasant demeanour upon your arrival. Usually when a case is unsolved, you are irritable, and fret and smoke rather than eat, so I deduce that the case is therefore solved and Johnson is guilty. It is elementary," I said triumphantly.

"Bravo! I shall have to watch myself, or people with their problems will start beating a path to your door, not mine." He spoke jestingly, but I could sense he was pleased that I had applied his methods to good effect.

An hour later, Holmes had changed, shaved, and eaten, and was sitting staring into the fire, smoke rising lazily from his pipe. I was perusing *The Times*, when I suddenly became aware of footsteps on the stairs.

"Do come in, Inspector," Holmes said, raising his voice slightly, and Lestrade entered, though I could hardly identify him, so swaddled in coats and scarves against the cold was he.

"Come warm yourself, dear fellow," Holmes continued. "It is somewhat early in the day, but a sustaining brandy wouldn't go amiss, I feel."

Lestrade nodded gratefully and sank into the chair closest to the cheerful blaze. I pressed a glass into his hand, and he took a large swallow before speaking.

"Thank you, Doctor. Now I am fit to speak, I have a case where I would like your opinion, Mr. Holmes. It's murder, plain enough, a man's head crushed by a heavy blow, but there's an oddity in what was stolen, and I know you like all that is odd in matters of crime."

Holmes and I both leaned forward, expectantly.

"What is the odd thing?" I said.

Lestrade unearthed his pipe from his coat pocket, filled and lit it before answering. Holmes's brow furrowed at this delay.

"Have either of you heard of a publication titled *The Picturesque Atlas of Australasia*?"

We both shook our heads.

"What about it?" Holmes said shortly.

"It is a recent publication in three large volumes," Lestrade went on, reading from his notebook. "The murdered man, John Henry Colton, was a career soldier who spent most of his time in the Army serving in Australia. He retired at the rank of major some five years ago and settled down here in London, but he retained an interest in Australia and owned a small library of books about the country, including the atlas I have named. But why, gentlemen, would someone break into his house last night, murder him, and then steal only *one* of the volumes of this atlas, when all three were there for the taking?"

"Curious indeed," I observed.

"Nothing else was taken," interjected Holmes. "Just one volume of a three-volume set?"

"That seems to be the case, and I would be obliged if you would accompany me to the scene in Hampstead and take a look. I cannot find a single clue to the murderer."

"Indeed!" said Holmes, "Surely it isn't as bad as that. I have never known a murderer yet who didn't leave some indication, even of the slightest and most trivial nature, to his or her identity. But we shall see, for I am intrigued."

"I anticipated you would be, and have a growler waiting," said Lestrade, rising from his chair.

Five minutes later we were on our way to Hampstead. Holmes remained silent, puffing at his pipe, while Lestrade and I chatted about several inconsequential subjects. The weather was cold but clear, and snow still lay on the ground, thinly in some places but a foot deep in others. As we arrived and stepped out, Holmes asked, "What is the nature of Major Colton's establishment? Are there staff?"

"There is only a housekeeper who also cooks and cleans," replied Lestrade, "Mrs. McAndrew by name. There is a lad who comes in occasionally to help with the garden."

The house itself was a comfortably sized villa, set back from the road with a well-kept garden. The path to the front door was trodden slush, and I knew Holmes wouldn't find any footprints of use there. Obviously the path had been used by Mrs. McAndrew to raise the alarm. A constable or two had arrived, and when Lestrade had then been summoned and left to fetch us. Perhaps, I thought, the small lawn and garden would yield some traces.

We entered the hallway and saw a constable on guard at a doorway ahead. "All right, Jenkins," said Lestrade, "that will be all. See if Mrs. McAndrew will provide you with a cup of tea." The constable nodded and disappeared further into the house. "This is the study, gentlemen, and the body awaits within." He opened the door for us, and Holmes stepped forward, saying, "I beg you will wait here while I complete my examination. The less disturbance to the scene, the better my chances of finding any relevant data."

Holmes stood in the doorway for a time, his eyes sweeping the room, especially the carpeted floor. He then stepped inside, keeping to one side. Lestrade and I stood and watched as he approached the body carefully, the legs of which I could see projecting from behind a large mahogany desk in front of the window. He knelt beside the corpse for some minutes, then stood and examined the window sill with his powerful lens. He opened the window and looked out, then slowly traversed the room, measured some apparent marks in the thick carpet with his tape, ending up at a table upon which were piled some papers and envelopes, several stacks of general books, and two large tomes which I suspected must be the remaining two volumes of the atlas.

"I have finished." he said. "You may enter."

"What have you learned?" asked Lestrade. "I should be grateful if you would share any indications as the murderer."

"I would first like to see Mrs. McAndrew. Could you arrange it please, while I take a look around the house." And with that, he bustled out of the study.

Ten minutes later, Lestrade and I were sitting at the kitchen table enjoying the tea and scones that Mrs. McAndrew had provided when Holmes joined us, coming in through the back door.

"Ah, Mrs. McAndrew I presume," he said. "Pray seat yourself. I have a few questions for you, if you feel able."

"Certainly, sir. The inspector said you would. If I can help you clear up this terrible business, I will."

Mrs. McAndrew was a tall thin woman, her brown hair greying at the temples. I hope I didn't do her a disservice when I estimated her to be in her mid-fifties. She sat at the table facing Holmes and Lestrade, looking quite composed.

"Can I pour you some tea, Mr. Holmes?" she said.

"No, thank you. Now, what can you tell us about the events of last night?

"Very little, I'm afraid, sir. I made the major his supper and he dined about seven, as usual. He then went to his study, while I washed up and tidied the kitchen. Afterwards, I sat in here mending a pillowslip. I usually retire early, so at nine-thirty, I went to the study to ask the major if he needed anything before I went upstairs. He was seated at his desk writing, smoking a cigar. He didn't want anything, so I said goodnight. I didn't hear anything in the night. I awoke at six, and it was only when I took the major his usual tea in his bedroom at quarter past the hour that I discovered he wasn't there. Thinking he had arisen early for some reason, I went through the house looking for him. It was then I found him, in the study."

A tear crept down her cheek as she continued. "He was cold, so I knew he was dead. I was going to walk down to the police station, but just as I got to the gate, the baker's van arrived with our delivery, so I asked him to fetch the police, as he would be quicker. He agreed to do so, so I went back inside, locked the study, and waited in the kitchen until a sergeant and a constable arrived about fifteen minutes later. He was kind man, Major Colton, a pleasure to work for. I can't imagine why anyone would want to hurt him."

"Thank you. That is a very clear statement. Had he appeared nervous, or acted out of the ordinary lately?" Holmes asked.

"No, not at all. He lived quietly and had no friends outside his club, where he dined two or three times a week. He went out for occasional walks."

"Of which club was he a member?"

"It was the United Services Club, Pall Mall."

"What can you tell me about the Australian atlas on the study table? The third volume is missing."

"Yes I pointed that out to the inspector. He hadn't had it long. He had served in Australia for years, and liked to read about the country. It is strange that only the third volume has been taken. I don't think there is anything else missing."

"It wasn't a valuable book?"

"Not really. It was sold by subscription in monthly parts, which you could then have bound as your taste decreed and your budget allowed. It has taken I believe about two years to complete, and the third part hasn't long been back from the binders."

"Do you know which binder the major employed?"

"Yes, it was Pritchards."

Holmes was silent for a moment. "Thank you, Mrs. McAndrew. That will be all for now. It's possible I may have more questions later, depending where my inquiries lead."

She nodded, arose, and left.

"What do think?" I ventured.

"Her story is corroborated by the cigar stub in the ashtray, and a letter on the desk to his bank concerning an investment. His bed has been slept in, so he obviously retired sometime after nine-thirty when Mrs. McAndrew last saw him, having finished the cigar and the letter. And then, at some point before midnight, he was disturbed by a noise, and came downstairs to investigate.

"And then what happened?" asked Lestrade. "I'm inclined to think the stolen atlas is a blind of some sort, taken in haste to give the impression of an attempted theft which got out of hand, and to disguise the real reason for the murder. Surely nobody would want to steal just one of a three-volume set. Don't you agree?"

Holmes snorted. "There are several smaller, lighter, and more valuable items in the study than a folio-sized atlas, if a blind was the intent. No, the theft of the atlas was the reason for gaining entry. The murder was unintended, and forced upon the thief by his being discovered by Major Colton."

Lestrade looked a little nettled. "Is there anything else – any other theories you have?"

"The murderer is a right-handed person of about six feet, so probably a man – not many women are that tall. He picked the back door lock to gain entry, and made his way to the study. He was standing at the table, possibly with the missing volume of the atlas in hand, when he was surprised by the entry of Major Colton. The Major was then struck on the left temple with a cylindrical blunt instrument of approximately one-and-a-half inches diameter. This didn't kill him however, though no doubt he was stunned. The assailant then made for the window, which he had probably opened immediately on entering the room so as to facilitate a quick escape should it become necessary. The Major followed him around the desk and, after a short struggle, was felled by another blow, striking the back of his head on the desk as he fell. I believe this was the fatal injury.

"The footsteps visible on the carpet, the blood trail from the table to the window, the blood and hair on the corner of the desk, and the bruising on the Major's head are all conclusive. The murderer then escaped through the window in some haste, removing some of the paint from the sill with his boots as he did so. This all happened before midnight, as the snow on the path outside the window is pristine and, as Watson and I know, it started to snow around midnight." He looked at me with a slight smile as he said these last words.

"Well, if you're convinced the atlas is the key to this," said Lestrade, "and it isn't valuable in itself, then there must have been something inside it that had some value to someone – a letter perhaps. As it was newly arrived from the binders, I think I shall start there – Pritchards, she said."

"A good idea with some possible merit," said Holmes. "However, I have another lead I shall follow first. With your permission of course."

Lestrade knew Holmes too well, and needed his help too much to deny him. "Certainly, Mr. Holmes. Investigate as you see fit. You'll let me know how you get on?"

"Of course. Let's go."

We left Lestrade writing in his notebook and went outside to the street. "Where to now?" I asked, hailing a passing hansom. "What is this lead you wish to investigate?"

"United Services Club, my good man," said Holmes to the cabbie, answering my question, and we climbed aboard. "If I'm right about the atlas being the intended object of the raid on Major Colton's house," he continued as we set off, "then the murderer must have known Colton owned it. Therefore, I believe the killer was probably known to the Major. We have heard that Colton led a quiet life, with his only social circle at his club. Perhaps we can learn something there, from those who knew him. I must admit however, I'm still puzzled why only one volume was stolen."

"They're large and heavy books, and so a little unwieldy if one wanted to steal all three," I offered.

"True. Yet I feel certain if we knew why only the third volume was taken, it would lead us to the solution of this mystery." He knitted his brows and gazed out at the passing street life, remaining silent until we pulled up outside the United Services Club.

A sovereign ensured the cabbie would wait for us, and we then entered the imposing edifice, and Holmes asked to speak to the manager. We were ushered into his office, where an impeccably dressed middle-aged man came around the desk, proffering his hand. "I'm Mr. Godfrey Radcliffe, manager of the Club. A pleasure to meet you, Mr. Holmes. I've read of some of your cases in the newspapers. How can I help you?"

"We are here on a serious matter, sir." Holmes replied, "Major John Colton, one of your members, was murdered at his home last night, and we're here to learn what we may about his background, his habits, and his friends."

Radcliffe's face immediately fell, and he seated himself behind his desk, looking very distressed. "That is most – I mean, what a terrible thing to happen," he eventually got out. "How can I help?"

"How long had the Major been a member here?"

"Let me see – he applied and was accepted about four years ago, when he returned to this country from Australia. You are aware, no doubt, that Club membership is limited to men of the rank of major, naval commander, or higher, so he was eligible."

"How would you describe him? What sort of man was he?"

"I won't say he was popular. He was rather reserved, but convivial-enough with the other members. He was on speaking terms with most of them, and friendly with several, especially those who had spent time in Australia. He was always polite with me and the other staff – I think due to spending a long time away from this country and its, shall we say, conventional class attitudes?"

"Can you name any members with whom he particularly associated?"

"He dined with and played at billiards or cards most often with General Sir Grenville Fortescue, Colonel Arthur Barrington, and Major George Elkington. They had all spent time in the Australian colonies. The General had even been the Governor of one of them for a time."

"Are any of these gentlemen here now?"

"I know the General is presently holidaying at his Scottish estate. I'll check if the others are here lunching." He left the room, but returned after a minute. "Sorry, Mr. Holmes, but neither the Colonel nor the Major are here at the moment."

"Very well," said Holmes. "May I have their addresses, and the General's as well? I will need to speak with them."

"That would be a little irregular, but under the circumstances, I'll provide that information." He consulted a ledger and wrote the addresses on a slip of paper, which he handed to Holmes. "I hope this will help you in your search for Major Colton's killer," he said in a low voice. "What a tragedy!"

As we left the Club, my stomach reminded me that it was past my usual luncheon hour. "Holmes, what are your plans now? Will you visit Colton's friends immediately?"

He chuckled. "I will, as I'm not hungry. I have a different task for you though, after you have satisfied your inner man. I want you to go to the British Library and discover all you can about *The Picturesque Atlas of Australasia*. Is there anything about it that may bear on this mystery, I wonder?"

"I shall certainly find out all I can."

"Capital! We shall meet in Baker Street this evening and compare notes."

After consuming a steak-and-kidney pie and an ale at a local public house, I went to the British Library to fulfil Holmes's request for information about the atlas, and thence arrived back at Baker Street a little after the early winter sunset. I was thawing myself out in front of a crackling fire and drinking tea when Holmes returned, accompanied by Lestrade.

"The inspector was knocking on our door just as I arrived. Scotch all around, I think, then we shall see if we can throw some light on this problem with the results of our combined researches."

After we were settled comfortably with our drinks and pipes, Holmes started. "Inspector, do tell us what progress you've made."

"Very little on my own account, but I did find something out accidentally that I'm sure will interest and perhaps even astonish you."

"Indeed! Do go on."

"I first went the Pritchards bindery, as I told you I would. There I learned nothing of use. They had bound Colton's first two volumes as they were completed, and when the third volume arrived they bound it in the same manner: Red morocco, gilded title, *etcetera*. There was nothing out of the ordinary in the process, nor did anything unusual happen while the book was in their possession. So I went back to the Yard. And now here's the interesting part.

"I was taking tea with a colleague, Inspector Greenjohn, who deals with major burglaries, and telling him about this case – just to pass the time, you understand. When I mentioned the atlas, he stopped me and said, '*The Picturesque Atlas of Australasia*, you say? How curious. Six days ago, an army officer went on a trip to the north of England for two days and nights. He allowed his servants, a housekeeper and valet, the two days off to visit family, and so his house was empty. When the valet returned just before his master's arrival home, he discovered the house had been burgled, quite thoroughly. The items taken were some small paintings and bronzes, a selection of silver, some rare books, and about one-hundred pounds in notes. But I remember that on the list of stolen items provided by the owner was a three-volume *Picturesque Atlas of Australasia*.'"

Holmes raised his eyebrows. "Remarkable! Volumes of the same Australian atlas stolen from two places within a week. That cannot be a coincidence. But all three volumes were taken on the first occasion, and only one on the second. I shall have to speak to this burgled army officer – Who is he?"

"His name is Colonel Barrington, who – "

"Not Colonel Arthur Barrington, of Knightsbridge?"

"The same. But how did you know?"

"This is even more extraordinary, eh Watson? Two copies of the same atlas stolen in a week, from two friends who belong to same club? The game is definitely afoot!"

Holmes quickly gave Lestrade the results of our visit to the United Services Club. "I went to visit Major Colton's friends," he explained. "First, Colonel Barrington. He wasn't home, and his rather-surly valet declined to tell me where he was. When I said it was concerning an important matter and asked him where I might find the Colonel, he became rather quite rude – rather more rude than one would expect of a servant tasked with meeting his master's visitors at the door. I left my card and said I would call again tomorrow. I then visited Major George Elkington, who was actually born in the Victorian colony, and spent his first two decades in Australia. He then came to the land of his parents and joined the army, serving in the Indian Mutiny and the Second Afghan War. He retired six years ago, and is, I think, what he appears to be: A widowed, retired army officer who is active in his church and collects antique swords. Had I known about the theft of the Colonel Barrington's atlas then, I would have asked him if he owned a copy himself."

"As you say, Mr. Holmes, this is no coincidence. This atlas is at the heart of the burglaries and the murder, but where do we go from here?"

"A penetrating question, Inspector. But let us hear from Watson before we decide any plan of action. What did you learn at the Library today?"

I consulted my notes. "The atlas was published by an Australian company formed for the purpose, and obtainable by subscription for either five shillings per monthly part, or ten guineas in total payment. It is a beautiful publication. I have seen the Library's copy. The illustrations are numerous and all hand-engraved. There are perhaps not as many maps as you might consider in a work calling itself an atlas, but all the Australian colonies, New Zealand, New Guinea and some of the Pacific islands are represented. But there are also many essays on the history, geography, geology, native peoples, and the flora and fauna of these regions, and descriptions of places of unique beauty and interest. I'm assured by Askwith, the librarian with whom I spoke, that it's a publishing *tour-de-force* in all respects. However, I was unable to determine if any of this information helps our enquiry."

"It doesn't appear to, I agree, but we are none-the-worse for having complete information concerning the object of these two thefts. Thank you. Lestrade, I assume you would like to participate in an interview of Colonel Barrington tomorrow, so would you prefer to meet us there, or will you collect Watson and me on your way?"

Lestrade stood up. "I'll be here at – shall we say – ten?"

"Excellent. I must cogitate for a time now, so goodnight."

As Lestrade's footsteps diminished down the stairs, I said, "This case presents some extraordinary features."

"It is a pretty puzzle, I grant you, but I have little data as yet. We must hope the circumstances of the theft at Colonel Barrington's will provide us with more."

The next morning, Lestrade drew up in a carriage just before the hour

402

we had agreed, and we set off to Knightsbridge under a leaden sky that promised rain later. Upon our arrival, Holmes rapped on the door with his stick. A young man dressed in black, with a saturnine mien, answered. "It's Mr. Holmes again, isn't it?"

"And Inspector Lestrade of Scotland Yard," said the inspector, showing his warrant card.

The fellow bowed stiffly. "This way gentlemen, please. If you'll wait in the hall, I'll let the Colonel know you are here."

He said this in an almost insolent fashion, with a faint accent on the word "gentlemen" which implied he thought we were not worthy of the honorific. Holmes was right, I thought to myself – he does not possess anything like the necessary civility for a good servant.

Two minutes later, a tall dark-haired man in his forties, with a strong masterful face, came down the stairs.

"In here please, gentlemen," he said in a rich baritone, showing is into a room that obviously fulfilled the functions of library and study. After we had introduced ourselves and were all seated, he continued. "You are here investigating the murder of Major Colton, an acquaintance and fellow club member. I learned of his death at the Club last evening. It's a terrible thing. How may I assist you?"

Holmes looked at Lestrade, who nodded for Holmes to lead the questioning.

"How long had you known the Major? You met at the Club?"

"I have been a member there for over six years, and I met him there shortly after he joined. We discovered we had a common interest in Australia, both of having served there."

"When were you there, and in what capacity?"

He looked at Holmes for a moment. "I was there for five years in the 1870's, as a liaison officer between the British Army and the government of the colony of New South Wales."

"I see. Can you tell us anything which might help us? Had Major Colton confided anything to you which indicated he was in any financial difficulties, or trouble of any kind?"

"No, nothing at all. He had been his usual self. We played cards and billiards at the Club. We talked of current events, cricket, and Army life, as well as our time in Australia. He had been stationed in Victoria for many years."

"Now Colonel, I understand that several days ago while this house was empty, you were robbed of several items of substantial value, and some one-hundred pounds in notes? Is this correct?"

"Well, yes, but how does this relate to Colton's murder?"

"Because there is a common thread. The Major was also robbed, but he surprised the thief, and we believe he was killed so the thief could make good his escape. The only item stolen was the third volume of the major's copy of *The Picturesque Atlas of Australasia* – all three volumes of which you reported stolen during the burglary which occurred here."

The Colonel looked taken aback by this information. "How remarkable," he said.

"So you see why this intrigues us. You and Colton are both members of the same club, and are well-acquainted with each other. You both served in Australia, and now have had the same book taken from your possession. How did you come to own the Atlas?"

"For the same reason as Colton: We both had an interest in the country, but I also collect books, usually on the subject of militaria. Several more valuable books than the Atlas were stolen, as well as some silver and artworks. Are you of the opinion then, that the same person committed both burglaries and the murder?"

"I haven't made up my mind on that, but it is certainly possible. It's obvious the two events must be connected. Who knew that this house would be empty for the two days during which the theft occurred?"

"I told the Club I wouldn't be in during that period, and I suppose the baker and greengrocer were told by my housekeeper to hold their deliveries."

"Thank you, Colonel. Have you any questions, Inspector? No? Then we will bid you good day, sir. But I if I may have a few words with your housekeeper?"

"Certainly," said the Colonel. "Mrs. Abercrombie will be in the kitchen, no doubt." He showed us back into the hall and left us. Lestrade and I waited there until Holmes returned from the rear of the house. Was it my imagination, or did I detect a gleam in his eyes?

"What now, Mr. Holmes?" said Lestrade as we stood on the pavement outside the Colonel's house. "Is there anything in the Colonel's statement which helps us?"

"Perhaps one or two things, but I must investigate further before I may pronounce on their value to the case. What will you do now?"

"Well, it occurred to me that if there is someone going around stealing copies of this atlas, perhaps they have done so on more than the two occasions we know about. I thought I would check the burglary records with Inspector Greenjohn and see if this has happened before."

"Very well. I shall pursue other lines of enquiry."

After Lestrade had left in the carriage which brought us, Holmes said, "What did you think of the good Colonel?"

"A sound-enough chap. Perhaps he showed less emotion about the death of Colton than one might expect, but possibly they were only acquainted, and not the best of friends."

"He said one thing which interested me, and so did Mrs. Abercrombie. To elucidate some details of the Colonel's greengrocer's family, and his term of service in Australia, I'll need to travel alone to a particularly vile alley near the docks, and then Pall Mall."

"Are you sure you won't need me?" I said dubiously. "Vile alleys aren't generally safe."

"Your presence would only complicate matters. But thank you. I will be careful."

"And Pall Mall? You intend to visit the Club again?"

"I intend to visit a club, but not the United Services Club. I will see you back at Baker Street this afternoon." And with that he signalled a passing hansom and left me. I hailed the next one, and spent the journey back to our domicile trying to think how the Colonel's time in the antipodes and his greengrocer's family connected to the mystery, without any conclusions.

The rain arrived after lunch, a steady drizzle which started to ease as evening drew in. I was enjoying tea and crumpets when Mrs. Hudson knocked and entered, bearing an envelope on a tray.

"A telegram for Mr. Holmes, Doctor."

"Thank you, Mrs. Hudson." I looked at the envelope and was wondering if I should open it when Holmes strode in.

"Were your enquiries successful?" I asked eagerly.

"Yes, quite. But what's this? A telegram has arrived."

"Yes, just moments ago."

Holmes quickly opened the envelope and read the enclosure. "This case grows more and more fascinating. A third theft of this atlas has occurred!" He threw me the telegram, and I read:

*Another atlas stolen. Come at once.*

*Lestrade*

There was an address in the fashionable Belgravia district appended.

"A third atlas stolen! This is incredible. Surely it is the work of a madman!"

"No, there is method and intelligence behind these thefts. Let us make haste to Belgravia!"

We raced in a hansom to the address given, which turned out to be a large Georgian house in its own grounds. An elderly butler showed us into the library, where we found Lestrade pacing up and down in front of the fire. "Ah, here you are. And Doctor Watson. Perhaps there is now hope of

405

solving this mystery, which I confess has me completely baffled."

Holmes smiled. "I have a theory Lestrade, which will be confirmed or destroyed by two facts with which you can now furnish me. First, did the theft of the atlas from this house take place today, or at some time in the recent past – perhaps several days ago?"

"How did you guess? Yes, the owner has been away for two weeks. The theft was only noticed today upon the owner's return, but could have happened anytime while he was absent."

"You know I never guess," said Holmes sternly. "And second, were only two volumes of the atlas stolen, the first and second?"

Lestrade looked as if Holmes had suddenly appeared in a puff of smoke bearing horns and a pointed tail. "Again, you are correct," he stammered, "though how you could know is beyond my imagination."

"And the owner of this house is General Sir Grenville Fortescue, who returned today from his Highland sojourn. He's a member of the United Services Club, and and acquaintance of Major Colton."

"Indeed, sir," said a voice behind us. "This house is mine, and I have just come back from Scotland. But what do my club and Major Colton have to do with this burglary?"

We turned to see a tall man, obviously in his sixties but still with a fine physique, and with the air of one used to command.

"Sir Grenville," said Lestrade, "this is the detective, Mr. Sherlock Holmes, who is assisting me with this enquiry. And his associate, Doctor Watson."

"I have heard of you, Mr. Holmes," said the General, "but surely your powers and attention are wasted on a commonplace theft such as I have suffered?"

"You compliment me, Sir Grenville," replied Holmes, "but this burglary is only one in a series in which the very same atlas that was stolen from you was taken from others, and a murder has been committed in the course of one of them. Your friend and fellow club member Major Colton was killed trying to prevent the theft of his *Picturesque Atlas*, and we are endeavouring to ascertain why."

"Colton killed? How tragic. He was a good fellow, and I enjoyed his company. If I can help bring his killer to book, then I am at your disposal, gentlemen. Please be seated, and ask of me what you will."

"Thank you, General. Please tell us about how you came to own your *Picturesque Atlas*, and how you discovered it was missing."

"Certainly. Some years ago I was given the governorship of the South Australian colony. I spent five years in the position, and I grew to like the country. There are a lot of British people there, of course, but there is a growing proportion of the citizenry who have been born and raised there

406

for several generations in the century since it was established as part the British Empire. These Australians are a tough, hard-working, and industrious breed in the main, and more inclined to treat a man based on his deeds and actions rather than his position in society or his accidental birth into a noble family. I found this attitude refreshing, and I was sad when my tenure as Governor was over. I still retain an affection for the country and its people, so when some two or three years ago I learned of the proposed publication of the Atlas, I subscribed immediately, as did Major Colton and Colonel Barrington when I told them about it one evening at the Club. You are aware that it was published in monthly parts, and that it is only recently the final part was published?"

"Yes, we knew that," said Holmes. "I suspect that the reason only the first and second volumes of your atlas were stolen is because the third volume was at your binder?"

"True, Mr. Holmes. I sent it to them before I left for Scotland. No doubt it will be returned to me shortly. The other two volumes were on that desk there when I left, so I noticed they were missing as soon as I entered the library. Then I discovered the window had been forced, so I sent for the police. Nothing else appears to be missing."

"The servants heard nothing?" Holmes asked as he crossed to the window and examined the broken latch.

"Nothing. There were only three left here in my absence. The remainder accompanied my wife and me to Scotland. None of them have been in here in the last two weeks, save the maid to dust yesterday, and she didn't notice the broken latch. She wouldn't know what books were supposed to be here or if any were missing."

"Thank you, General, you have been most helpful. I think the solution to this mystery is within our grasp now. A few details to discover, and a trap to be set. Then, with any luck, we shall have our thief and murderer."

"That is indeed gratifying," said the old soldier as he escorted us to the door. "I wish you well, gentlemen."

As we left the General's house, Lestrade gave voice to my exact thoughts.

"You say you have almost solved this puzzle. Would you care to share the name of the guilty party, and on what evidence you assert his guilt?"

"Not at this juncture, as I don't yet have all the facts, only theories. And as you well know, theories will not convict anyone in a court. Would you please take Watson back to the no-doubt delicious supper Mrs. Hudson has prepared. I must seek my brother Mycroft's aid immediately to organise the trap of which I spoke." And with that he left us, striding swiftly down the General's driveway.

Holmes returned to Baker Street as the clock struck ten. "You wish to see the conclusion of this case no doubt?"

"Of course. I have followed it with great interest but little understanding so far. You have solved it then?"

"I believe so, but the evidence we need will not be available until tomorrow morning, if my plans come to fruition. Be ready by six, and we shall try to apprehend our atlas thief, murderer, and if I'm right, a threat to the security of the Empire."

"I see. So there is more to all this than the atlases. And the security of the Empire is where Mycroft comes into the picture."

"Exactly. Now let us get what slumber we may before our early rising will hopefully catch us our worm."

A hansom was waiting as we slipped out of the front door the next morning into a frosty half-light. We had dressed appropriately, however, and we were on our way the instant we climbed aboard. After a short journey the hansom stopped in front of a post-box and a laneway servicing the rear of a row of houses. We alighted from the hansom, which immediately rumbled off. Holmes grabbed my arm and pulled me into the lane, where I saw a muffled figure awaiting. "Lestrade!" I said, "You are joining us in the hunt then."

"Yes, Doctor," he said through chattering teeth "though let's hope it isn't a wild goose chase."

"Your constables are in place, Lestrade?" asked Holmes in a low voice.

"Yes, Mr. Holmes, as you directed: Two at each end of the street, and two also watching the rear of the house."

"Good. We shouldn't have too long to wait."

It was only about fifteen minutes later that Holmes tensed. "He's coming!"

There were several pedestrians on both sides of the street, including some coming toward us. One of them slowed as he reached the post-box, and as he reached inside his coat and pulled out an envelope, Holmes and Lestrade ran out, Lestrade grabbing the man by the wrist of the hand holding the envelope, and Holmes grabbing the other arm. I hurried up in time to hear Lestrade say, "I am Inspector Lestrade of Scotland Yard, and I have reason to believe that this letter contains information injurious to the British national interest."

Holmes plucked the letter from the man's hand and then pulled down the scarf muffling the features of their captive, to reveal the scowling face of Colonel Barrington's valet. "I have nothing to say," he spat out.

Two constables then ran up, and one them handcuffed the struggling manservant. "Take him away," Lestrade ordered.

Meanwhile, Holmes had opened the envelope, and after a quick glance said, "As I expected. We must now arrest his master."

Lestrade collected the two other constables on watch in the street, sending one of them to alert the others watching the rear of Barrington's house. We then approached the front and knocked. A plump, middle-aged woman answered the door. "Mrs. Abercrombie, nice to see you again," said Holmes genially. "Is the Colonel at home?"

"Yes sir, he's in the study. I'll let – "

"That won't be necessary," said Holmes, pushing past the confused housekeeper. "We'll just show ourselves in. We know the way." Lestrade, the constable, and I followed. Holmes opened the door to the study and we all trooped in.

Barrington rose up from behind the desk. "What is the meaning of this?" he snarled. "You can't just – "

"Yes, we can sir," said Lestrade evenly. "We have your valet and the letter he was about to post for you. I'm arresting you for the murder of Major John Colton. Other charges may follow."

The Colonel's eyes narrowed, and he half-crouched as he looked at the four of us. Obviously deciding that forcing his way past us was impossible, he stood up straight. "Beaten am I?" he said harshly. "Your doing, Holmes, I take it? It was the atlases that gave me away, I suppose, but I had to have them."

"I'd like to think I contributed materially to your demise, Colonel. And yes, it was the atlases. The third theft was intriguing. The first theft, of your atlases, put me on the track, and the second theft, when we became aware of it, confirmed it. Lestrade, after you have secured your prisoner in a cell, won't you join us for breakfast? I will then be happy to clear up any points which still mystify you."

"There are also one or two points I don't quite understand," I added drily.

Holmes laughed. "Indeed. Then let us go home and ask Mrs. Hudson for one of her best efforts, and then I shall enlighten you both as to how I solved the case of the Australian atlases!"

"As you rightly remarked," said Holmes when we had finished eating, "the first theft we heard about, of a single volume of a three-volume set, was curious. All three volumes were there for the taking, and there were also other more-valuable and more-easily transportable items available, if theft for monetary gain was the intention. You remember I said at the time that this indicated that the atlas, and only the atlas, was the object of the theft. But I was still puzzled then as to why only the one volume was stolen."

He spoke between puffs of his pipe, the debris of our hearty breakfast on the table between us. Lestrade took a sip of coffee. "Why did you let me waste my time going to the binders, while you went to Colton's club?" he asked.

"It wasn't like that, Inspector. I did think that there was more to be learned at the Club, but there was a chance that some clue might be found at Pritchards, so I was happy to let you follow that lead. No stone unturned. The United Services Club provided the names of Colton's closest associates and the fact that they had all at some point in their lives been in Australia. Since the stolen atlas concerned Australia, there was a connection there, if somewhat tenuous. I then visited Colonel Barrington, who wasn't home. His valet didn't impress me, but it isn't a crime to be rude. An interview with Major Elkington didn't raise my suspicions, but then we received the news that Barrington had also had his copy of the atlas stolen some days previous to the burglary at Major Colton's. These happenings were too coincidental and specific to be unrelated, but I still had too little data to form a theory. When we did see Colonel Barrington the next day, two things gave me pause."

"As I recall, you mentioned his greengrocer's family and his service in Australia."

"Correct. He stated that he had been a liaison officer between the Army and the New South Wales colonial government. In my experience, Army officers who 'liaise' between the Army and other agencies are very often in a particular branch of the Army."

"Intelligence!" I cried. "That's why you said you were going to another club in Pall Mall. You meant the Diogenes Club, to ask Mycroft if Barrington was an intelligence officer."

"Correct again. Mycroft confirmed that Barrington was not only an intelligence officer, but that he had lately worked on several top-secret matters. His record was exemplary. I had also found out from Mrs. Abercrombie that she had indeed told the baker and greengrocer to halt their deliveries for two days, and that the household supplier of fruit and vegetables was none other than Benjamin Fuller, a grocery establishment of excellent repute in the district."

"The name sounds familiar," I frowned.

"It should. Some weeks ago, Inspector Bradstreet asked me to find out anything I could about a newly formed and well-organised gang of house-breakers he had come across. You remember I set some of the Irregulars on to the task? They discovered that one of the gang members was Albert Fuller, eldest son of Benjamin Fuller and employee in his father's grocery business. So it was entirely possible that Albert had learned through his father that Barrington's house would be empty for two days. He supplied this information to his gang, who saw an opportunity to purloin most of the valuables from the house at some leisure. They did so, stealing Barrington's *Picturesque Atlas* along with other books, silver, artworks and cash. I confirmed this by looking through several windows of a warehouse near the docks, the headquarters of Fuller's gang, as discovered by one of the Irregulars a few days ago. There I saw the proceeds of several robberies, and Bradstreet will be cleaning up that little rat's nest today.

"However, Fuller's gang, being responsible for the burglary at Barrington's, meant that they wouldn't have known about, nor particularly wanted Colton's atlas. This inferred that instead of one person stealing two atlases from different owners, which was strange enough, there must have been two different thieves stealing the two atlases, an even stranger proposition. Who else would have wanted Colton's atlas, and only the third volume at that? I deduced it was someone who had just had their copy stolen – someone who knew Colton possessed the atlas, and someone who had already replaced the first and second volumes. So my suspicion rested on Barrington."

"So that's how you knew only the first two volumes had been stolen from Sir Grenville, and that they had been taken prior to theft at Colton's!" exclaimed Lestrade.

"Yes. He knew the General owned the atlas, and he knew he, his wife, and the majority of his servants were in Scotland. He decided to steal the General's copy, not realising that only two volumes were in the house, the third being at the binders. That is why he broke into Colton's a few nights later and took only the third volume he needed to complete the set. He didn't reckon on being interrupted, however, with the result we know."

"But why? Why the obsession with replacing his stolen atlas?

"The answer to that lies in the letter we took from Barrington's valet. His name is Jacob Whistler by the way, a convicted thief and general ne'er-do-well before finding employ with Barrington. After the theft of Sir Grenville's atlas confirmed for me that Barrington was our man, I had to flush him out and catch him red-handed. I went back to Mycroft and he arranged that Barrington should be sent for by his commanding officer immediately, and advised of a major change in the details of the latest secret government operation with which he has been involved. The change was fictional, of course, but we wanted to see if he would pass on the information to anyone. Lestrade, you have the letter?"

Lestrade took a sheet from his jacket pocket and handed it to me. It read:

411

*V175C1207*
*V188C140*
*V3645C215*
*V2421C2161*
*V1230C257*
*V2402C212*
*V3615C189*
*V2279C29*

"Obviously a code," I said. "Can you read it?"

"Yes. I knew how to break the code from seeing the letter when I took it from Whistler's possession. But Lestrade has done the actual work. He found the stolen atlases in Barrington's study, and by the using key to the cipher which I gave him, he has worked out the message before joining us. You see, each string of characters has a *V* and a *C* in it. When I realised the *V* is always followed by the numeral one, two or three, and that the *C* is always followed by the numeral one or two – "

"Volume and column," I interrupted. "The atlas has three volumes, and each page has two columns of text. The other numbers must be the page number and word number. Is this not similar to the code we came across earlier this year in the Birlstone case?"

"Yes. If you recall, an associate of Professor Moriarty named Porlock sent us the cipher, but then didn't tell us the book to be used to solve it. We had to use pure reason to obtain the solution, which turned out to be *Whitaker's Almanac.*

"In this case, the first word in the message is word 207 in column one on page 75 of the first volume. Barrington had to have a copy of the atlas in order to send and receive coded messages from his contact – hence his panic to replace it when his was stolen. It is a foolproof code which cannot be interpreted unless one knows the book you are using. Barrington had suggested to his contact they use the Atlas, as it was not a common book and he had it to hand. Obviously the contact has a copy as well. But as it was published by subscription, and therefore not available in bookshops for purchase, he was compelled to steal it."

I turned to Lestrade. "And what is Barrington's message then?" I asked. He handed me another sheet which read:

*Important change to Stuart Plan. Two-thousand pounds.*

"The amount named is the price of his treachery," said Holmes. "If this information wasn't a trap, and the contact had paid the sum, Barrington would have betrayed the secret and his country. Who knows

412

what secrets he has already betrayed? The Stuart Plan, whatever it may be, will now have to be changed or cancelled in case it has already been divulged by Barrington. I realised that Barrington would wish to inform his contact as soon as possible of his newly acquired knowledge concerning the Plan. Thus, our early morning surveillance of the nearest post-box to Barrington's residence. The was another post-box slightly farther away in the opposite direction, and two constables were assigned to watch it for Barrington, or more likely Whistler, who was well aware of his master's true occupation as a freelance agent and seller of his country's secrets."

"What of Barrington's contact?" I questioned. "Could he not be found through the address on the letter?"

"It is addressed to a large hotel in Paris, to be kept until called for. Mycroft will work with the French authorities and see what can be done. Are there any other points on which either of you are unclear?"

Lestrade stood up. "No, Mr. Holmes, you explained it all beautifully. You make it sound so obvious after the fact, but I have no problem admitting it was too deep for me. I thank you for your assistance in this case, and your country owes you a debt of gratitude."

I knew that Holmes disliked praise of any sort, and was indifferent to official recognition. The solving of the problem was its own reward for him. But he was gracious enough to reply.

"You are welcome to any credit, Lestrade. After all, you yourself did apprehend Whistler and his villainous master. As for our country – Well, I should not expect any reward for doing my duty as an Englishman."

413

## NOTES

Published in Sydney from 1886 to 1888, the three-volume *The Picturesque Atlas of Australasia* described Australia of that period with words and pictures, and was one of the most significant Australian cultural projects of that time. The books contained essays by writers and artists, academics and politicians, and over eleven-hundred steel and wood engravings, some of the finest anywhere in the world at that time. These were specially commissioned for the publication from leading Australian artists.

I'm proud to have a copy, and it's the pride of my collection

– P.M.

# About the Contributors

*The following contributors appear in this volume:*
**The MX Book of New Sherlock Holmes Stories**
Part XLIX: The True Sherlock Mr. Holmes –
England's Greatest Hero (1880-1888)

**Hugh Ashton** was born in the U.K., and moved to Japan in 1988, where he remained until 2016, living with his wife Yoshiko in the historic city of Kamakura, a little to the south of Yokohama. He and Yoshiko have now moved to Lichfield, a small cathedral city in the Midlands of the U.K., the birthplace of Samuel Johnson, and one-time home of Erasmus Darwin. In the past, he has worked in the technology and financial services industries, which have provided him with material for some of his books set in the 21st century. He currently works as a writer: Novelist, freelance editor, and copywriter, (his work for large Japanese corporations has appeared in international business journals), and journalist, as well as producing industry reports on various aspects of the financial services industry. However, his lifelong interest in Sherlock Holmes has developed into an acclaimed series of adventures featuring the world's most famous detective, written in the style of the originals. In addition to these, he has also published historical and alternate historical novels, short stories, and thrillers. Together with artist Andy Boerger, he has produced the *Sherlock Ferret* series of stories for children, featuring the world's cutest detective.

**Deanna Baran** lives in a remote part of Texas where cowboys may still be seen in their natural habitat. A librarian and former museum curator, she writes in between cups of tea, playing *Go*, and trading postcards with people around the world.

**Brian Belanger**, PSI, is a publisher, narrator, graphic designer, editor, and actor. In 2015 he co-founded Belanger Books publishing company along with his brother, author Derrick Belanger. His illustrations have appeared in *The Essential Sherlock Holmes* series, the *MacDougall Twins with Sherlock Holmes* series, and *Scones and Bones on Baker Street*. Brian has published a number of Sherlock Holmes anthologies and novels through Belanger Books, as well as new editions of August Derleth's classic Solar Pons mysteries. Brian continues to design all of the covers for Belanger Books, and from 2016–2023 he designed the majority of book covers for MX Publishing. In 2019, Brian received his investiture in the PSI as "Sir Ronald Duveen". More recently, he created the logo for the *ACD Society* and designed *The Great Game of Sherlock Holmes* card game. In July 2022, he played Sherlock Holmes onstage in "Yes, Virginia, There is a Sherlock Holmes" and "Sherlock Holmes Goes West". Brian has been narrating Belanger Books audio releases since April 2023.
*www.belangerbooks.com* and
*www.redbubble.com/people/zhahadun* and
*zhahadun.wixsite.com/221b*

**Stuart Douglas** is an author, editor, and publisher, and the creator of the Lowe and Le Breton Mysteries. He has written four Sherlock Holmes novels for Titan Books, and contributed stories to the anthologies *Encounters of Sherlock Holmes, Further Associates of Sherlock Holmes*, and *The MX Book of New Sherlock Holmes Stories*. He runs Obverse Books and lives in Edinburgh with his wife, three children, a dog named after Dusty Springfield and cat named after David Bowie.
Follow him on Bluesky: *@stuartdouglas.bsky.social*
and on Instagram: *@stuartamdouglas*

**Sir Arthur Conan Doyle** (1859-1930) *Holmes Chronicler Emeritus*. If not for him, this anthology would not exist. Author, physician, patriot, sportsman, spiritualist, husband and father, and advocate for the oppressed. He is remembered and honored for the purposes of this collection by being the man who introduced Sherlock Holmes to the world. Through fifty-six Holmes short stories, four novels, and additional Apocryphal entries, Doyle revolutionized mystery stories and also greatly influenced and improved police forensic methods and techniques for the betterment of all. *Steel True Blade Straight.*

**Steve Emecz**'s main field is technology, in which he has been working for about thirty years. Steve is a regular speaker at trade shows, and his tech career has taken him to more than seventy countries. In 2008, MX published its first Sherlock Holmes book, and MX has gone on to become the largest specialist Holmes publisher in the world with over 600 books. MX is a social enterprise and supports three main causes. The first is Undershaw, Sir Arthur Conan Doyle's former home, which is a school for children with special educational needs (SEN) that MX has been partnered with for a dozen or so years and raised over $135,000 for. Steve has been a mentor and Advisory Council member for the World Food Programme's Innovation Accelerator (based in Munich) for several years, and was part of the Nobel Peace Prize winning team in 2020. The third is Happy Life, a children's rescue project in Nairobi, Kenya, where he and his wife, Sharon, spent every Christmas at the rescue centre in Kasarani for a decade. They have written two editions of a short book about the project, *The Happy Life Story*.

**Mark A. Gagen** BSI is co-founder of Wessex Press, sponsor of the popular *From Gillette to Brett* conferences, and publisher of *The Sherlock Holmes Reference Library* and many other fine Sherlockian titles. A life-long Holmes enthusiast, he is a member of *The Baker Street Irregulars* and *The Illustrious Clients of Indianapolis*. A graphic artist by profession, his work is often seen on the covers of *The Baker Street Journal* and various BSI books.

**John Atkinson Grimshaw** (1836-1893) was born in Leeds, England. His amazing paintings, usually featuring twilight or night scenes illuminated by gas-lamps or moonlight, are easily recognizable, and are often used on the covers of books about The Great Detective to set the mood, as shadowy figures move in the distance through misty mysterious settings and over rain-slicked streets.

**Stephen Herczeg** is an IT Geek, writer, actor, and film-maker based in Canberra Australia. He has been writing for over twenty years and has completed a couple of dodgy novels, sixteen feature-length screenplays, and numerous short stories and scripts. Stephen was very successful in 2017's International Horror Hotel screenplay competition, with his scripts *TITAN* winning the Sci-Fi category and *Dark are the Woods* placing second in the horror category. His collection, *The Curious Cases of Sherlock Holmes*, is now at four volumes. His work has featured in *Sproutlings – A Compendium of Little Fictions* from Hunter Anthologies, the *Hells Bells* Christmas horror anthology published by the Australasian Horror Writers Association, and the *Below the Stairs*, *Trickster's Treats*, *Shades of Santa*, *Behind the Mask*, and *Beyond the Infinite* anthologies from *OzHorror.Com*, *The Body Horror Book*, *Anemone Enemy*, and *Petrified Punks* from Oscillate Wildly Press, and *Sherlock Holmes In the Realms of H.G. Wells* and *Sherlock Holmes: Adventures Beyond the Canon* from Belanger Books.

**Roger Johnson**, BSI ("The Pall Mall Gazette"), ASH, PSI, etc, is a member of more Holmesian Societies than he can remember, thanks to his eighteen years as editor of *The*

*Sherlock Holmes Journal* - a responsibility he has recently and gratefully passed over to Dr. Mark Jones. Roger founded and for thirty-two years edited *The Sherlock Holmes Society of London*'s newsletter, *The District Messenger*. For six years, it was edited by his wife Jean Upton, ASH, BSI, and is now in the safe hands of Holly Turner. At its 2025 Annual Dinner, Roger was awarded Honorary Membership of *The Sherlock Holmes Society of London*.

**Gordon Linzner** is founder and former editor of *Space and Time Magazine*, and author of four published novels and dozens of short stories in *F&SF*, *Twilight Zone*, *Sherlock Holmes Mystery Magazine*, and numerous other magazines and anthologies. He is a full member of the *Horror Writers Association* and a lifetime member of *Science Fiction and Fantasy Writers Association*.

**Bonnie MacBird**, BSI is the author of six critically acclaimed Sherlock Holmes novels for HarperCollins. They have been translated into fourteen languages and have been praised by *The London Times*, *Washington Post* , and *The Wall Street Journal*. MacBird read her first Sherlock Holmes story at age ten, and has been a fan since then. She's had a forty-year career in entertainment as a studio story editor, a screenwriter, a multiple Emmy winning documentary film producer, and a screenwriting teacher. She's also acted professionally and directs theatre. She lives in London with her husband, computer scientist Alan Kay, where she continues to write, as well as work in theatre.

**David Marcum** plays *The Game* with deadly seriousness. He first discovered Sherlock Holmes in 1975 at the age of ten, and since that time, he has collected, read, and chronologicized literally thousands of traditional Holmes pastiches in the form of novels, short stories, radio and television episodes, movies and scripts, comics, fan-fiction, and unpublished manuscripts. He is the author of over one-hundred-thirty Sherlockian pastiches, some published in anthologies and magazines such as *The Best Mystery Stories of the Year 2021* and *The Strand*, and others collected in his own books, *The Papers of Sherlock Holmes*, *Sherlock Holmes and A Quantity of Debt*, *Sherlock Holmes – Tangled Skeins*, *Sherlock Holmes and The Eye of Heka*, and *The Collected Papers of Sherlock Holmes* – seven volumes and more to come. He has won back-to-back first place fiction awards from *The Arthur Conan Doyle Society* (2023 and 2024) and from the Nero Wolfe *Wolfe Pack*. He has edited over 1,200 Holmes adventures and one-hundred books, including dozens of traditional Sherlockian anthologies, such as the ongoing series *The MX Book of New Sherlock Holmes Stories*, which he created in 2015 to promote traditional Canonical Holmes. This collection is now finishing at fifty-two volumes. He was responsible for bringing back August Derleth's Solar Pons for a new generation with his collections of authorized Pons stories, *The Papers of Solar Pons* and *The Further Papers of Solar Pons*. Pons's return was further assisted by his editing of the reissued authorized versions of the original Pons books, and then several volumes of new Pons adventures. He has done the same for the adventures of Dr. Thorndyke, and has plans for similar projects in the future. He has contributed numerous essays to various publications, and is a member of a number of Sherlockian groups and Scions, as well as *The Mystery Writers of America*. His irregular Sherlockian blog, *A Seventeen Step Program*, addresses various topics related to his favorite *Book Friends* (as his son used to call them when he was small), and can be found at *http://17stepprogram.blogspot.com/* He is a licensed Civil Engineer, living in Tennessee with his wife and son. Since the age of nineteen, he has worn a deerstalker as his regular-and-only hat. In 2013, he and his deerstalker were finally able make his first trip-of-a-lifetime Holmes Pilgrimage to England, with return Pilgrimages in 2015, 2016, and 2024, where you may have spotted him. Another Pilgrimage is planned in mid-2025. If you ever run into him and his deerstalker out and about, feel free to say hello!

**Paul Metcalfe** has been a librarian for twenty-eight years, starting in public libraries, but is now the librarian at a technical college in rural Western Australia. He has been a lifelong Holmes fan since reading the original stories aged twelve, and now enjoys many of the later pastiches and Holmesian nonfiction as well. In 2005, he made the semifinals of the ABC television quiz show *The Einstein Factor* with the Sherlock Holmes stories by ACD as his special subject. He thinks Jeremy Brett is the television Holmes *nonpareil*, he collects old books and antiques, and is a strong advocate of the use of graphic novels to encourage reading. This is his first work of fiction.

**Mark Mower** is a long-standing member of the *Crime Writers' Association, The Sherlock Holmes Society of London*, and *The Solar Pons Society of London*. His pastiche collections include *Sherlock Holmes: The Baker Street Case-Files, Sherlock Holmes: The Baker Street Legacy, Sherlock Holmes: The Baker Street Epilogue*, and *Sherlock Holmes: The Baker Street Archive* (all with MX Publishing). His non-fiction works include the bestselling book *Zeppelin Over Suffolk: The Final Raid of the L48* (Pen & Sword Books). Alongside his writing, Mark maintains a sizeable collection of pastiches, and never tires of discovering new stories about Sherlock Holmes and Dr. Watson.

**Will Murray** is the author of some 75 novels, including some 20 posthumous Doc Savage collaborations with Lester Dent, and 40 books in the long-running Destroyer series. Other Murray novels star the Executioner, Tarzan of the Apes, The Spider, Pat Savage and the Mars Attacks characters. His book, *Nick Fury, Agent of S.H.I.E.L.D.: Empyre* (2000) foreshadowed the 9/11 terrorist attacks. Murray has penned nearly sixty Sherlock Holmes short stories. Murray's Holmes short stories have been collected as *The Wild Adventures of Sherlock Holmes*, Volumes 1 through 4. His novelette, "The Adventure of the Vengeful Viscount", in which Tarzan of the Apes, otherwise Lord Greystoke, hires Sherlock Holmes to solve a mystery, was approved by both the Estate of Sir Arthur Conan Doyle and Edgar Rice Burroughs, Inc. Murray is the author of the non-fiction book, *Master of Mystery: The Rise of The Shadow*, which is an exploration of the famous radio and magazine character, and a sequel, *Dark Avenger: The Strange Saga of The Shadow. The Wild Adventures of Cthulhu* Vols 1 & 2 collect Murray's Lovecraftan short stories. For Marvel Comics, Murray created the Unbeatable Squirrel Girl with legendary artist Steve Ditko. Website: *www.adventuresinbronze.com*

**Sidney Paget** (1860-1908), a few of whose illustrations are used within this anthology, was born in London, and like his two older brothers, became a famed illustrator and painter. He completed over three-hundred-and-fifty drawings for the Sherlock Holmes stories that were first published in *The Strand* magazine, defining Holmes's image forever after in the public mind.

**Tracy J. Revels**, BSI, a Sherlockian from the age of eleven, is a professor of history at Wofford College in Spartanburg, South Carolina. She is a member of *The Survivors of the Gloria Scott* and *The Studious Scarlets Society*, and is a past recipient of the Beacon Society Award. Almost every semester, she teaches a class that covers The Canon, either to college students or to senior citizens. She is also the author of three supernatural Sherlockian pastiches with MX (*Shadowfall, Shadowblood*, and *Shadowwraith*), and most recently, the three-volume pastiche set, *Tales of Light, Tales of Shadow*, and *Tales of Darkness.* She is a regular contributor to her scion's newsletter. She also has some notoriety as an author of very silly skits: For proof, see "The Adventure of the Adversarial Adventuress" and "Occupy Baker Street" on YouTube. When not studying Sherlock, she can be found researching the history of her native state, and has written books on Florida in the Civil War and on the development of Florida's tourism industry.

**Roger Riccard**'s family history has Scottish roots, which trace his lineage back to Highland Scotland. This ancestry encouraged his interest in the writings of Sir Arthur Conan Doyle. He has authored the novels, *Sherlock Holmes & The Case of the Poisoned Lilly*, and *Sherlock Holmes & The Case of the Twain Papers*, which was featured at the Museum of London Sherlock Holmes Exhibit in 2015. In addition, he has produced dozens of short stories, and has now joined the Sherlock Holmes 60+ Club, having exceeded Sir Arthur Conan Doyle's number of original Sherlock Holmes stories. All of his books have been published by Baker Street Studios and can be found at his website: *www.sherlockriccard.com* He credits his success to the encouragement of his wife/editor/inspiration and Sherlock Holmes fan, Rosilyn. She passed in 2021, and it is in her memory that he continues to contribute to the legacy of the "*man who never lived and will never die*".

**Jane Rubino** is the author of *A Jersey Shore* mystery series, featuring a Jane Austen-loving amateur sleuth and a Sherlock Holmes-quoting detective, *Knight Errant, Lady Vernon and Her Daughter*, (a novel-length adaptation of Jane Austen's novella *Lady Susan*, co-authored with her daughter Caitlen Rubino-Bradway, *What Would Austen Do?*, also co-authored with her daughter, a short story in the anthology *Jane Austen Made Me Do It*, *The Rucastles' Pawn, The Copper Beeches from Violet Turner's POV*, and, of course, there's the Sherlockian novel *Hidden Fires*. Jane lives on a barrier island at the New Jersey shore.

**Brenda Seabrooke**'s stories have appeared in thirty-eight literary magazines, mystery anthologies, and magazines. Twenty books for young readers were published, and then two Sherlock's Dog books. She discovered that she liked writing about the world's greatest consulting detective and mysteries. Two collections of Sherlock Holmes stories were published by MX UK, and her stories have been included in "4 Best Mysteries of New England" (Level Best Books). She has received a grant from the NEA, a fellowship from Emerson College, and is an MWA runner-up. She has twice judged and once chaired Edgar mystery categories. Brenda is the former president of the Children's Book Guild of DC, a member of AG. *Viva* Holmes and Watson!

**Shane Simmons** is the author of the occult detective novels *necropolis* and *Epitaph*, and the crime collection *Raw and Other Stories*. An award-winning screenwriter and graphic novelist, his work has appeared in international film festivals, museums, and lectures about design and structure. He was born in Lachine, a suburb of Montreal best known for being massacred in 1689 and having a joke name. Visit Shane's homepage at *eyestrainproductions.com* for more information.

**Kevin Thornton** has, by his own count - and remember he's a writer, not an arithmetician – been in seventeen of these volumes, including this one. That's not a bad record, neither near the top nor the bottom, metaphor for his life mayhap. A middling student of English in South Africa, he was taught by two Nobel Literature Laureates to little noticeable effect, and has since been a soldier in Africa, a military contractor in Afghanistan, a forklift driver in Ontario, a bartender everywhere, and a logistician in Northern Alberta, which is, naturally, why he now works as a Communications Consultant for an Indigenous Nation of Cree, Denesuline, and Metis people. It has evolved into a good life, improved immeasurably by a tolerant, beautiful, and loving wife, two sons who smarter than they let on, and a Belgian Malinois with all of the energy of that breed and none of the intelligence. He lives in Northern Alberta, not quite in the North Pole, Santa Claus neighbourhood, but near enough for it to be a local telephone call. He is content.

A Sherlock Holmes fan since reading *The Hound of the Baskervilles* at about age twelve, **Tom Turley** has been writing pastiches since 2006. Most have appeared in previous volumes of *The MX Book of New Sherlock Holmes Stories*. All except the latest three have been collected in two books available from MX Publishing and Amazon. *Sherlock Holmes and the Crowned Heads of Europe* (2021) is a collection of four historical novellas that involve Holmes and Watson in the events leading up to World War I. The four stories are also available individually on Audible. As its title indicates, *Watson's Wives and Other Tales of Sherlock Holmes* (2023) focuses primarily on the Doctor's marriages. It likewise will soon be available on Audible. Currently, Tom is at work on a Sherlockian novel. A retired historian and archivist, he resides with his wife Paula in Montgomery, Alabama.

**DJ Tyrer** is the person behind Atlantean Publishing and has had fiction featuring Sherlock Holmes published in volumes from MX Publishing and Belanger Books, and an issue of *Awesome Tales*, and has a forthcoming story in *Sherlock Holmes Mystery Magazine*. DJ's non-Sherlockian mysteries can be found in anthologies such as *Mardi Gras Mysteries* (Mystery and Horror LLC) and *The Trench Coat Chronicles* (Celestial Echo Press), and on *Mystery Tribune*.
DJ Tyrer's website is at *https://djtyrer.blogspot.co.uk/*
DJ's Facebook page is at *https://www.facebook.com/DJTyrerwriter/*
The Atlantean Publishing website is at *https://atlanteanpublishing.wordpress.com/*

**Emma West** joined Undershaw in April 2021 as the Director of Education with a brief to ensure that qualifications formed the bedrock of our provision, whilst facilitating a positive balance between academia, pastoral care, and well-being. She quickly took on the role of Acting Headteacher from early summer 2021. Under her leadership, Undershaw has embraced its new name, new vision, and consequently we have seen an exponential increase in demand for places. There is a buzz in the air as we invite prospective students and families through the doors. Emma has overseen a strategic review, re-cemented relationships with Local Authorities, and positioned Undershaw at the helm of SEND education in Surrey and beyond. Undershaw has a wide appeal: Our students present to us with mild to moderate learning needs and therefore may have some very recent memories of poor experiences in their previous schools. Emma's background as a senior leader within the independent school sector has meant she is well-versed in brokering relationships between the key stakeholders, our many interdependences, local businesses, families, and staff, and all this while ensuring Undershaw remains relentlessly child-centric in its approach. Emma's energetic smile and boundless enthusiasm for Undershaw is inspiring.

**Marcia Wilson** is a freelance researcher and illustrator who likes to work in a style compatible for the color blind and visually impaired. She is Canon-centric, and has written many acclaimed stories about Sherlock Holmes and the Scotland Yard inspectors who knew and worked with him. Long unavailable, nine of these novels will be released by MX Publishing in Spring 2025, with more in preparation.

*The following contributors appear
in the companion volumes:*
**The True Sherlock Mr. Holmes –
England's Greatest Hero
Part L – (1889-1896)
Part LI – (1897-1901)
Part LII – (1902-1923)**

**Ian Ableson** is an ecologist by training and a writer by choice. When not reading or writing, he can reliably be found scowling at a clipboard while ankle-deep in a marsh somewhere in Michigan. His love for the stories of Arthur Conan Doyle started when his grandfather gave him a copy of *The Original Illustrated Sherlock Holmes* when he was in high school, and he's proud to have been able to contribute to the continuation of the tales of Sherlock Holmes and Dr. Watson.

**Mike Adamson** holds a Doctoral degree from Flinders University of South Australia. After early aspirations in art and writing, Mike secured qualifications in both marine biology and archaeology. Mike has been a university educator since 2006, has worked in the replication of convincing ancient fossils, is a passionate photographer, master-level hobbyist, and journalist for international magazines. Short fiction sales include to *Metastellar, Strand Magazine, Little Blue Marble, Abyss,* and *Apex, Daily Science Fiction, Compelling Science Fiction,* and *Nature Futures.* Mike has placed some two-hundred stories to date, totaling over a million words. Mike has completed his first Sherlock Holmes novel with Belanger Books, and will be appearing in translation in European magazines. You can catch up with his journey at his blog "The View From the Keyboard":
*http://mike-adamson.blogspot.com*

**Tim Newton Anderson** is a former senior daily newspaper journalist and PR manager who has recently started writing fiction. In the past six months, he has placed fourteen stories in publications including *Parsec Magazine, Tales of the Shadowmen, SF Writers Guild, Zoetic Press, Dark Lane Books, Dark Horses Magazine, Emanations,* and *Planet Bizarro.*

**Donald I. Baxter** has practiced medicine for over forty years. He resides in Erie Pennsylvania with his wife and their dog. His family and his friends are for the most part lawyers who have given him the ability to make stuff up just as they do.

**Derrick Belanger**, BSI ("The Board Schools"), PSI ("Albert, the Dove") is an award-winning author, publisher, and educator most noted for his books and lectures on Sherlock Holmes and Sir Arthur Conan Doyle. Derrick is co-owner of the publishing company Belanger Books, which published the first eBook editions of the original Solar Pons books by August Derleth. Derrick's work has been published in *The Baker Street Journal, The Sherlock Holmes Journal, The Strand Magazine,* and in *The Mysterious Bookshop Presents the Best Mystery Stories of the Year (2023).* Derrick is a board member of Dr. Watson's Neglected Patients, the Denver-based Scion Society. In January 2020, Mr. Belanger was awarded the Susan Z. Diamond Award in recognition of outstanding efforts to introduce young people to Sherlock Holmes, and in 2024, he won the Arthur Conan Doyle Society Doylean award in fiction for his short story, "The Joyce-Armstrong Confession". Derrick currently resides in Broomfield, Colorado. Find him at:
*www.belangerbooks.com*

**Mike Chinn**'s first ever Sherlock Holmes fiction was a steampunk mashup of *The Valley of Fear*, entitled *Vallis Timoris* (Fringeworks 2015). Since then he has written about Holmes' archenemy in *The Mammoth Book of the Adventures of Moriarty* (Robinson 2015), appeared in several volumes of *The MX Book of New Sherlock Holmes Stories*, and confronted the retired detective with cross-dimensional magic in the second volume of *Sherlock Holmes and the Occult Detectives* (Belanger Books 2020). He also had a non-Holmes story published in the Lovecraftian anthology *Sherlock & Friends: Eldritch Investigations* (Tule Fog Press, 2024).

**Martin Daley** was born in Carlisle, Cumbria in 1964. His thirty-year writing career has seen over twenty books and numerous short stories published. Inevitably, Holmes and Watson remain his favourite literary characters, and they continue to inspire his own detective writing. In 2010, Martin created Inspector Cornelius Armstrong, who carries out his police work against the backdrop of Edwardian Carlisle. With the publication of the first *Inspector Armstrong Casebook* (published by MX Publishing), Martin became a member of the Crime Writers' Association. Most recently, he published *The Selected Cases of Sherlock Holmes*. He lives with his wife Wendy, in Kirkcudbrightshire, in Southwest.

**Alan Dimes** was born in Northwest London and graduated from Sussex University with a BA in English Literature. He has spent most of his working life teaching English. Living in the Czech Republic since 2003, he is now semi-retired and divides his time between Prague and his country cottage. He has also written some fifty stories of horror and fantasy and thirty stories about his husband-and-wife detectives, Peter and Deirdre Creighton, set in the 1930's.

**Brett Fawcett** is a humanities and Latin teacher at the Chesterton Academy of St. Isidore in Sherwood Park, Alberta. He lives with his wife and son in Edmonton, where he is a member of The Wisteria Lodgers (The Sherlock Holmes Society of Edmonton). He vividly remembers the first time he finished reading the Sherlock Holmes stories in Grade 6, and has been a student of Holmesian literature and scholarship since then. He is also a frequent author of columns and articles on topics like theology, education, and mental health, as well as the occasional mystery story.

**Arianna Fox** is a triple-published and bestselling author, keynote speaker, actress, professional voiceover talent, award winner, book editor, and public figure whose passion is to motivate, educate, and entertain others through her work. From stories that connect with a modern audience to classically inspired works of literature, one of Arianna's foremost passions has always been writing. An avid Sherlockian and lover of all things Victorian, Arianna disliked reading for years until she read the first few paragraphs of *The Return of Sherlock Holmes* in a bookstore and immediately fell in love with classic literature and the intricate themes woven into its messages. As a whole, Arianna's ultimate goal is to empower others to achieve maximum success and keep their brain-attics well stocked.

**Mike Fox** is a CEO, entrepreneur, multi-award-winning filmmaker, director, producer, writer, designer, actor, voiceover talent, and all-around versatile creative professional. His professional work is known across the U.S. and has received numerous accolades and awards. As a filmmaker and director, Mike has produced three full-feature films, with over twenty-five Film Festival Awards, including several shorts and many commercials. With a unique flair for suspenseful storytelling, he derives much inspiration from the Sherlock Holmes universe, both of The Canon and adaptations. He was named Alignable's

"Business Person of the Year" four years in a row, and has been featured in several news and media outlets, along with a myriad of interviews on podcasts and more. Mike's goal is to impact, empower, and inspire through various forms of media. His professional work is known across the U.S., including having received numerous accolades and awards, including receiving the prestigious Delaware Press Association (DPA) several years in a row. He continues to speak, write, film, and direct to bring quality content to audiences.

**Paul D. Gilbert** was born in 1954 and has lived in and around London all of his life. His wife Jackie is a Holmes expert who keeps him on the straight and narrow! He has two sons, one of whom now lives in Spain. His interests include literature, ancient history, all religions, most sports, and movies. He is currently employed full-time as a funeral director. His books so far include *The Lost Files of Sherlock Holmes* (2007), *The Chronicles of Sherlock Holmes* (2008), *Sherlock Holmes and the Giant Rat of Sumatra* (2010), *The Annals of Sherlock Holmes* (2012), *Sherlock Holmes and the Unholy Trinity* (2015), *Sherlock Holmes: The Four Handed Game* (2017), *The Illumination of Sherlock Holmes* (2019), *The Treasure of the Poison King* (2021), and *Sherlock Holmes: Tales of Darkness* (2023).

**Dick Gillman** is an English writer and acrylic artist living in Brittany, France with his wife Alex, Truffle, their Black Labrador, and Jean-Claude, their Breton cat. During his retirement from teaching, he has written over twenty Sherlock Holmes short stories which are published as both e-books and paperbacks. His initial contribution to the superb MX Sherlock Holmes collection, published in October 2015, was entitled "The Man on Westminster Bridge" and had the privilege of being chosen as the anchor story in *The MX Book of New Sherlock Holmes Stories – Part II (1890-1895)*.

**John Linwood Grant** is a writer and editor who lives in Yorkshire with a pack of lurchers and a beard. He may also have a family. He focuses particularly on dark Victorian and Edwardian fiction, such as his recent novella *A Study in Grey*, which also features Holmes. Current projects include his *Tales of the Last Edwardian* series, about psychic and psychiatric mysteries, and curating a collection of new stories based on the darker side of the British Empire. He has been published in a number of anthologies and magazines, with stories range from madness in early Virginia to questions about the monsters we ourselves might be. He is also co-editor of *Occult Detective Quarterly*. His website *greydogtales.com* explores weird fiction, especially period ones, weird art, and even weirder lurchers.

**Arthur Hall** was born in Aston, Birmingham, UK, in 1944. He discovered his interest in writing during his schooldays, along with a love of fictional adventure and suspense. His first novel, *Sole Contact*, was an espionage story about an ultra-secret government department known as "Sector Three", and was followed, to date, by three sequels. Other works include seven Sherlock Holmes novels, *The Demon of the Dusk, The One Hundred Percent Society, The Secret Assassin, The Phantom Killer, In Pursuit of the Dead, The Justice Master,* and *The Experience Club* as well as three collections of Holmes *Further Little-Known Cases of Sherlock Holmes, Tales from the Annals of Sherlock* Holmes, *The Additional Investigations of Sherlock Holmes* and *The Hidden Enquiries of Sherlock Holmes.* He has also written other short stories and a modern detective novel. He lives in the West Midlands, United Kingdom.

**Paula Hammond** has written over sixty fiction and non-fiction books, as well as short stories, comics, poetry, and scripts for educational DVD's. When not glued to the

425

keyboard, she can usually be found prowling round second-hand books shops or hunkered down in a hide, soaking up the joys of the natural world.

**James R. Hawkins**, BSI writes: "I discovered Sherlock Holmes on my fortieth birthday, in Norman, OK. In high school, in Texas, I mainly read Ernest Hemingway and true-life stories set in exotic locations, like Alaska. I was inordinately interested in Eskimos.
I was born in Jacksboro, Texas, in 1944, the only son of Leon and Ruth Hawkins, owners of Hawkins Funeral Home, and little brother to Linda (1939) and Jane Hawkins (1940). My Dad wanted me to take over the funeral home, but I chose a life in music education, which took me to Oklahoma Baptist University in Shawnee, OK, and to the Eastman School of Music in Rochester, NY. With my vocal chops, I landed a place in The US Army Chorus in Washington, DC, during the Vietnam war, (1969-1973). Married in 1966, my wife and I struck out for Los Angeles to work on a doctorate in music at the University of So. California. From there, we moved to Norman, OK, where I was the music director at 1st Baptist Church in Norman before becoming the Youth, Adult, and Senior Adult Music Consultant for the Southern Baptist Convention in Nashville, TN (1985-1992). In 2001, I switched from music to aviation and joined that highly successful company, Southwest Airlines, where I held various positions, settling into the Flight Attendant job, retiring some sixteen years later in 2017. Since then, my life has revolved around Sherlock Holmes and the men and women who are Sherlockians, devotees of the detective "*who never lived, and so, could never die*". In 2018, I wrote about the man who influenced the most in my Holmes and Watson journey, John Bennett Shaw. The website I built for him caught the attention of many of The Baker Street Irregulars, who honored me with membership in their august body and shared with me the same investiture given to Shaw back in 1965, *The Hans Sloane of My Age.*"

**Liz Hedgecock** grew up in London, England (a train and a tube ride away from Baker Street), did an English degree, and then took forever to start writing. Now Liz travels between the nineteenth and twenty-first centuries, murdering people. To be fair, she does usually clean up after herself. Liz's reimaginings of Sherlock Holmes and her Victorian and contemporary mystery series are available in eBook and paperback. Liz lives in Cheshire with her husband and two sons, and when she's not writing you can usually find her reading, messing about on social media, or cooing over stuff in museums and art galleries. That's her story, anyway, and she's sticking to it.

**Paul Hiscock** is an author of crime, fantasy, horror, and science fiction tales. His short stories have appeared in a variety of anthologies, and include a seventeenth-century whodunnit, a science fiction western, a clockpunk fairytale, and numerous Sherlock Holmes pastiches. He lives with his family in Kent (England) and spends his days taking care of his two children. You can find out more about Paul's writing at: *www.detectivesanddragons.uk.*

**Christopher James** was born in 1975 in Paisley, Scotland. Educated at Newcastle and UEA, he was a winner of the UK's National Poetry Competition in 2008. He has written three full-length Sherlock Holmes novels, *The Adventure of the Ruby Elephant*, *The Jeweller of Florence*, and *The Adventure of the Beer Barons*, all published by MX.

In the year 1998 **Craig Janacek** took his degree of Doctor of Medicine at Vanderbilt University, and proceeded to Stanford to go through the training prescribed for pediatricians in practice. Having completed his studies there, he was duly attached to the University of California, San Francisco as a Professor. The author of over two-hundred medical monographs upon a variety of obscure lesions, his travel-worn and battered tin dispatch-box is crammed with papers, most of which are records of his fictional works. These include several collections of *The Further Adventures of Sherlock Holmes*: *Light in the Darkness*, *The Gathering Gloom*, *The Treasury of Sherlock Holmes*, *The Travels of Sherlock Holmes*, *The Chronicles of Sherlock Holmes*, *The Histories of Sherlock Holmes*, *The Acts of Sherlock Holmes*, and *The Assassination of Sherlock Holmes* – as well as two Dr. Watson novels (*The Isle of Devils* and *The Gate of Gold*), the complete and expanded *Adventures* and *Exploits of Brigadier Gerard* (*Set Europe Shaking* and *A Mighty Shadow*), and two non-Holmes novels (*The Oxford Deception* and *The Anger of Achilles Peterson*). His short stories have been published in several editions of *The MX Book of New Sherlock Holmes Stories, Part I: 1881-1889* (2015), *Part IV: 2016 Annual* (2016), *Part VI: 2017 Annual* (2017), *Part VIII: Eliminate the Impossible* (2017), *Part XI: Some Untold Cases* (2018), *Part XVIII: Whatever Remains Must be the Truth* (2019), *Part XXIII: Some More Untold Cases* (2020), *Part XXV: 2021 Annual* (2021), *Part XXXII: 2022 Annual* (2022), *Part XXXVI: However Improbable . . . .* (2022), and *Part XXXVIII: 2023 Annual* (2023). Other stories have appeared in *Holmes Away From Home: Tales of the Great Hiatus* (2016), *Tales from the Stranger's Room 3* (2017), *Sherlock Holmes: Adventures Beyond the Canon* (2018), *Sherlock Holmes, A Year of Mysteries – 1881* (2021), and *Sherlock Holmes: Stranger than Fiction* (2021). He lives near San Francisco, California with his wife and two children, where he is at work on his next story. Craig Janacek is a *nom-de-plume*.

**Steven Philip Jones** has written fiction novels for adults and young adults, comic books, graphic novels, radio scripts, non-fiction, and advertising pieces. His Sherlock Holmes pastiches include the novel *The Adventure of the Coal-Tar Derivative* from MX Publishing and the radio dramas "The Adventure of the Petty Curses" and "A Case of Unfinished Business" for Jim French Productions' *Imagination Theatre*. He currently makes his home with his family in northern Utah.

**Naching T. Kassa** is a wife, mother, and writer. She's created short stories, novellas, poems, and co-created three children. She resides in Eastern Washington State with her husband, Dan Kassa. Naching is a member of *The Horror Writers Association*, *Mystery Writers of America*, *The Sound of the Baskervilles*, *The ACD Society*, *The Crew of the Barque Lone Star*, and *The Sherlock Holmes Society of London*. She works in Talent Relations at Crystal Lake Publishing and was a recipient of the 2022 HWA Diversity Grant. You can find her work on Amazon.
*https://www.amazon.com/Naching-T-Kassa/e/B005ZGHTI0*

**Susan Knight**'s newest Mrs. Hudson novel is *Death in the Harem* (October 2024, MX publishing), in which Sherlock Holmes and Dr. Watson enlist their landlady's help in solving a series of murders at the court of the Sultan of Turkey. Susan has written four previous Mrs. Hudson books, starting with a collection of short stories, *Mrs. Hudson Investigates* (2019). This was followed by the novels, *Mrs. Hudson Goes to Ireland* (2020), *Mrs. Hudson Goes to Paris* (2022) and *Death in the Garden of England* (2023). She has also contributed to many recent MX anthologies of new Sherlock Holmes short stories and enjoys writing as Dr. Watson as much as Mrs. Hudson. Nine of these stories have been included in *The Strange Case of the Pale Boy and Other Mysteries* (MX, 2023), and another story, *The Case of the Reluctant Footman*, has been released on Kindle Unlimited as Volume 7 of its *Discoveries* series (2025). She is the author of two other non-Sherlockian story collections, as well as three novels, a book of non-fiction, and several plays, and has won several prizes for her writing. She lives in Dublin, Ireland.

**John Lawrence** served for thirty-eight years on personal, committee, and leadership staffs in the U.S. House of Representatives. A visiting professor at the University of California's Washington Center since 2013, he is the author of *The Class of '74: Congress After Watergate and the Roots of Partisanship* (Johns-Hopkins, 2018) and *Arc of Power: Inside the Pelosi Speakership 2005-2010* (Kansas, 2022). His collected "history mystery" Sherlock Holmes pastiches have been published in *The Undiscovered Archives of Sherlock Holmes, The Further Undiscovered Archives of Sherlock Holmes*, in numerous volumes of *The MX Book of New Sherlock Holmes Stories*, and in Belanger Books' *After the East Wind Blows*. His novel, *Sherlock Holmes: The Affair at Mayerling Lodge* was published in 2023. He blogs at DOMEocracy (johnalawrence.wordpress.com). He is a graduate of Oberlin College and has a Ph.D. in history from the University of California (Berkeley).

**Steve Lockley** is responsible for around 100 short stories and 20 novels, though not all under his own name, including contributions to a couple of Doctor Who anthologies and a novel based on the TV series *Ghost Whisperer*. He has also written several Sherlock Holmes stories, including an appearance in *Encounters of Sherlock Holmes* (Titan Books), and another due to appear in a future issue of *Sherlock Holmes Mystery Magazine*. Steve's work as both writer and editor has been shortlisted several times for British Fantasy Awards. He lives in Swansea and hates writing about himself in the third person.

**David MacGregor** is a playwright, screenwriter, and novelist. His plays have been performed from New York to Tasmania, and his work has been published by Dramatic Publishing, Playscripts, and Theatrical Rights Worldwide (TRW). He adapted his dark comedy, *Vino Veritas*, into a feature film, and several of his short plays have also been adapted into films. He is the author of three Sherlock Holmes plays: *Sherlock Holmes and the Adventure of the Elusive Ear, Sherlock Holmes and the Adventure of the Fallen Soufflé*, and *Sherlock Holmes and the Adventure of the Ghost Machine*. He adapted all three plays into novels for Orange Pip Books, and the novels have also been translated into Italian by Mondadori Publishing. In addition, he wrote the two-volume nonfiction *Sherlock Holmes: The Hero with a Thousand Faces*, which traces the evolution of the character over three centuries. He teaches writing at Wayne State University in Detroit. His website is: *david-macgregor.com*

**David Marcum** *also has stories in Parts L, LI, and LII*

**J. Lawrence Matthews** has contributed fiction to *The New York Times* and *NPR*'s *All Things Considered* and is the author of *One Must Tell the Bees: Abraham Lincoln and the Final Education of Sherlock Holmes* (East Dean Press, 2021). The first novel to bring Sherlock Holmes together with Abraham Lincoln during the American Civil War, *One Must Tell the Bees* was called "*beautifully written and immediately engaging*" in the summer journal of *The Sherlock Holmes Society of London*. Matthews is at work on the sequel, which takes Sherlock Holmes to Tibet in 1891 for Holmes's encounter with the 13th Dalai Lama. He resides in Naples, FL, where his favorite breaks from writing are travel, book club meetings with his readers, visits from children and grandchildren, and, when the house gets a little too quiet, playing the drums.

**John McNabb** is a Welshman and an archaeologist, and a proud member of *The Sherlock Holmes Society of London*. He has published academic analysis of aspects of Conan Doyle's work, as well as its broader context. Mac also has a long-standing interest in

Victorian and Edwardian scientific romances and the portrayal of human origins in early science fiction.

**Adrian Middleton** is a Staffordshire-born independent publisher. The son of a real-world detective, he is a former civil servant and policy adviser who now writes and edits science fiction, fantasy, and a popular series of steampunked Sherlock Holmes stories.

**Paul W. Nash** is a librarian, bibliographer, and printing historian. He has worked at the Royal Institute of British Architect's Library in London and the Bodleian Library in Oxford, and is currently editor of *The Journal of the Printing Historical Society*. He writes fiction and composes music as a relaxation.

**Orlando Pearson** is an accountant. He commutes into London by day and communes with the spirits of Baker Street by night. He was born a short rather than a long shot away from 221b. He is the creator of the series, *The Redacted Sherlock Holmes*, which runs to eight collections of short works, two novels, and a book of plays. A new collection of short works is appearing later this year and a Mycroftian novel will come out in 2026. These accounts of real events were redacted one-hundred or so years ago at the time The Canon was being published. The liberality of modern times means we can now read of Holmes's exposure of the rigging of the home-insurance market, his identification of an alternative claimant for the British throne, and his investigation into someone even better known than himself who rose from the dead. Orlando's profile can be found at:
*https://www.amazon.co.uk/Orlando-Pearson/e/B07DWP857S/ref=dp_byline_cont_book_1*

**Tracy Revels** *also has stories in Parts L and LI*

A professional author since 2007, **Josh Reynolds** has over thirty novels to his name, as well as numerous short stories, novellas, and audio scripts. Born and raised in South Carolina, he now resides in Sheffield with his wife and daughter, as well as a highly excitable dog and something he hopes is a cat. A complete list of his work can be found at *https://joshuamreynolds.co.uk/*

**Roger Riccard** *also has a story in Part LII*

**Dan Rowley** practiced law for over forty years in private practice and with a large international corporation. He is retired and lives in Erie, Pennsylvania, with his wife Judy, who puts her artistic eye to his transcription of Watson's manuscripts. He inherited his writing ability and creativity from his children, Jim and Katy, and his love of mysteries from his parents, Jim and Ruth.

**Andrew Salmon** has won several awards for his Sherlock Holmes stories and has been nominated for the Ellis, Pulp Ark, Pulp Factory and New Pulp Awards. He lives and writes in Vancouver, BC. His novels include: *Fight Card Sherlock Holmes: Work Capitol, Blood to the Bone*, and *A Congression of Pallbearers* (collected in the *Fight Card Sherlock Holmes Omnibus*) *The Dark Land, The Light Of Men*, and *Ghost Squad: Rise of the Black Legion* (with Ron Fortier) and his first children's book, *Wandering Webber*. His work has also appeared in numerous anthologies covering multiple genres. His tales from the award winning *Sherlock Holmes Consulting Detective* series were collected in *Sherlock Holmes Investigates*. *Ace of Devils*, the second novel in the Eby Stokes series featuring the female pugilist turned Special Branch agent, is out now and he's working on the third book, as well as a myriad of other projects. To learn more about his work check out: *amazon.com/Andrew-Salmon/e/B002NS5KR0*

**Geri Schear** is a novelist and short story writer. Her work has been published in literary journals in the U.S. and Ireland. Her first novel, *A Biased Judgement: The Diaries of Sherlock Holmes 1897* was released to critical acclaim in 2014. The sequel, *Sherlock Holmes and the Other Woman* was published in 2015, and *Return to Reichenbach* in 2016. *Great Warrior* was published in 2024. She lives in Kells, Ireland.

**Peter Shumway** is a retired computer professional residing in Pennsylvania with his wife, Patty. They have been married forty-one years and have two daughters and four grandchildren. In the early 1970's, Peter performed magic with Bill Baker's World of Magic, John Bundy's Magic Concert, and traded secrets with David Copperfield when they were teenagers. Peter read the original Sherlock Holmes stories while in college in 1979, and has enjoyed rereading them many times since. He published his pastiche *Sherlock Holmes and The Kiss of Death in* 2005 and *Gullible's Journey* in 2023. When he was offered the opportunity to write a short story for the MX Series, he picked up his pen yet again.

**Shane Simmons** *also has a story in Part LII*

**Robert V. Stapleton** was born and brought up in Leeds, Yorkshire, England, and studied at Durham University. After working in various parts of the country as an Anglican parish priest, he is now retired and lives with his wife in North Yorkshire. As a member of his local writing group, he now has time to develop his other life as a writer of adventure stories. He has published a number of short stories, and he is hoping to have a couple of completed novels published at some time in the future.

Award winning poet and author **Joseph W. Svec III** enjoys writing, poetry, and stories, and creating new adventures for Holmes and Watson that take them into the worlds of famous literary authors and scientists. His *Missing Authors* trilogy introduced Holmes to Lewis Carroll, Jules Verne, H.G. Wells, and Alfred Lord Tennyson, as well as many of their characters. His transitional story *Sherlock Holmes and the Mystery of the First Unicorn* involved several historical figures, besides a Unicorn or two. He has also written the rhymed and metered Sherlock Holmes Christmas adventure, *The Night Before Christmas in 221b*, sure to be a delight for Sherlock Holmes enthusiasts of all ages. 2024 saw the publication of *Sherlock Holmes for Letter or Verse*. Joseph won the Amador Arts Council 2021 Original Poetry Contest, with his Rhymed and metered story poem, "The Homecoming". Joseph has presented a literary paper on Sherlock Holmes/Alice in Wonderland crossover literature to the Lewis Carroll Society of North America, as well as given several presentations to the Amador County Holmes Hounds, Sherlockian Society. He is currently working on his first book in the Missing Scientist Trilogy, *Sherlock Holmes and the Adventure of the Demonstrative Dinosaur*, in which Sherlock meets Professor George Edward Challenger. Joseph has Masters Degrees in Systems Engineering and Human Organization Management, and has written numerous technical papers on Aerospace Testing. In addition to writing, Joseph enjoys creating miniature dioramas based on music, literature, and history from many different eras. His dioramas have been featured in magazine articles and many different blogs, including the North American Jules Verne society newsletter. He currently has fifty-seven dioramas set up in his display area, and has written a reference book on toy castles and knights from around the world. An avid tea enthusiast, his tea cabinet contains over five-hundred different varieties, and he delights in sharing afternoon tea with his childhood sweetheart and wonderful wife, who has inspired and coauthored several books with him.

**William Todd** has been a Holmes fan his entire life, and credits *The Hound of the Baskervilles* as the impetus for his love of both reading and writing. He began to delve into fan fiction a few years ago when he decided to take a break from writing his usual Victorian/Gothic horror stories. He was surprised how well-received they were, and has tried to put out a couple of Holmes stories a year since then. When not writing, Mr. Todd is a pathology supervisor at a local hospital in Northwestern Pennsylvania. He is the husband of a terrific lady and father to two great kids, one with special needs, so the benefactor of these anthologies is close to his heart.

**DJ Tyrer** *also has a story in Part LI*

**Peter Coe Verbica** lives in the redwoods of Northern California. He grew up on Rancho San Felipe, a cattle ranch, where he learned the value of a strong work ethic. He obtained a BA from Santa Clara University, a JD from Santa Clara University School of Law and an MS from the Massachusetts Institute of Technology. Readers can find ten of his short stories in *The MX Book of New Sherlock Holmes Stories* anthologies, edited by David Marcum. These include "The Disfigured Hand", "The Magic Bullet", "The Adventure of the Matched Set", "The Musician Who Spoke from the Grave", "The Dutch Imposters", "A Ghost in the Mirror", "The Deceased Priest", "The King of Spades", "The Hyde Park Blackmailer", and, most recently, "The Ambassador's Dilemma". An additional seven stories, including "The Lucky Strike", "The Mystery of the Five Keys", "The Man Who Didn't Smoke", "The Noble Heart", "The Curious Case of the Bald Prince", "The Lost Uncle", and "Death at Hampton Court" can be found in *The Missing Tales of Sherlock Holmes*. Mr. Verbica is the author of non-fiction articles as well, including "Rise of the Rothschilds: A Legacy of Lessons", featured in *Opportunity Now Silicon Valley*, "We are thinking about . . . Artificial intelligence and trading platforms" featured by Silicon Private Wealth, and "The Divine Leaven of Self-Sacrifice (written in honor of Lenah Sutcliff Higbee)" presented at the Mast Stepping Ceremony of *USS Lenah Sutcliff Higbee* (DDG-123). His free verse works, such as "Small Mound of Stones", "A Visit with Quentin", "Dreams of a Burning Man", "The Locusts", "Visitor 231", "A Thanksgiving Lesson", "Small Miracles", "Brazil", Gold", "Fear of Long Words", "Speak Easy", "Heaven", "The Home Which Dreams", and scores of other pieces appear in various anthologies and books across the globe. The author has also served as moderator and host of a popular speaker series, featuring the former CTO of the US Space Force; Deputy Director of the National Intelligence Agency on cybersecurity; the former US Ambassador to Ukraine on Eurasian security issues; the former US Ambassador to Thailand on US-China relations; a former USN Rear Admiral on the importance of civility in society; an expert on US tax law regarding proposed changes, and other speakers of merit, including the preeminent publisher of Sherlock Holmes-based fiction. Mr. Verbica currently serves as a Managing Director and Principal of Silicon Private Wealth, a Registered Investment Advisor where he helps "clients achieve their dreams through prudent and personalized investment planning." He won a top-two slot in the primary election for Board of Equalization in the State of California. He has served as President, Vice-President, and Chair for numerous non-profit local and statewide non-profit and political organizations' boards. For more information, please visit:
*www.peterverbica.com*

**I.A. Watson** has written over fifty Sherlock Holmes stories, and is always surprised that there are still new things for The Great Detective to do, which is a real testament to the genius behind Doyle's most famous creations. His most recent Holmes activities though were in providing extensive notes for a talk about the character in a New York public library, which was quite a different creative challenge. In addition to the novel *Holmes and Houdini*, the anthology *The Incunabulum of Sherlock Holmes*, and the forthcoming *The Paralipomena of Sherlock Holmes*, I.A. Watson has provided entries to all twenty of the *Sherlock Holmes Consulting Detective* books, to about the same number of MX volumes, and another dozen or more in other eccentric places. In his spare time he produces other novels such as *The Death of Persephone*, *The Labours of Hercules*, *The Legend of Robin Hood*, *Women of Myth*, *The Transdimensional Transport Company*, and *Vinnie de Soth, Jobbing Occultist*. It is perhaps not traditional to use an "About the Author" paragraph to offer thanks, but I.A. Watson would like to dedicate this "About the Author" piece to Mr. David Marcum for his astonishing accomplishment with the MX Holmes series, and his tireless enthusiasm as one of the stoutest Holmesians. A full list of I.A. Watson's publications is available at:

 *http://www.chillwater.org.uk/writing/iawatsonhome.htm*

**Ashley Williford** writes: "This is my first Sherlockian publication. I am a devoted Sherlockian and Ravenclaw and a member of my local Sherlockian scion society. *The Giant Rats of Sumatra* in Memphis, Tennessee. I have a hilarious three-year-old boy, Williford "Will" Roney, as well as two goldendoodles, Albus Percival Wulfric Brian Dumbledoodle (eight) and Merlin Aberforth Dumbledoodle (six). I am an Adult-Gerontological Acute Care Nurse Practitioner with a Doctorate in Nursing Practice, and I specialize in critical care. My favorite of my many hobbies include writing Sherlock adventures, hand embroidery, puzzles, games, reading, starting flowers from seeds only to abandon them after sprouting, and listening to absolutely everything Steven Fry narrates."

**Marcia Wilson** *also has stories in Parts L and LI*

**DeForeest Wright III** has a day job as a baker for Ralphs grocery stores. It helps support his love for books. A long-time lover of literature, especially of the Sherlock Holmes tales, he spends his time away from the oven hunched over novels, poetry, anthologies, or any tome on philosophy, mathematics, science, or martial arts he can find, sipping an espresso if one is to hand. He writes prose and poetry in his off hours and currently hosts "The Sunless Sea Open-Mic: Spoken Word and Poetry Show" at the Unurban Coffee House in Santa Monica. He was glad to team up writing with his father.

**Sean Wright**, BSI makes his home in Santa Clarita, a charming city at the entrance of the high desert in Southern California. For sixteen years, features and articles under his byline appeared in *The Tidings* – now *The Angelus News*, publications of the Roman Catholic Archdiocese of Los Angeles. Continuing his education in 2007, Mr. Wright graduated from Grand Canyon University, attaining a Bachelor of Arts degree in Christian Studies with a *summa cum laude*. He then attained a Master of Arts degree, also in Christian Studies. Once active in the entertainment industry, and in an abortive attempt to revive dramatic radio in 1976 with his beloved mentor, the late Daws Butler, directing, Mr. Wright co-produced and wrote the syndicated *New Radio Adventures of Sherlock Holmes*, starring the late Edward Mulhare as the Great Detective. Mr. Wright has written for several television quiz shows and remains proud of his work for *The Quiz Kid's Challenge* and the popular TV quiz show *Jeopardy!* for which the Academy of Television Arts and Sciences honored him in 1985 with an Emmy nomination in the field of writing. Honored with membership in The Baker Street Irregulars as "The Manor House Case" after founding The Non-Canonical Calabashes, the Sherlock Holmes Society of Los Angeles in 1970, Mr. Wright has written for *The Baker Street Journal* and *Mystery Magazine*. Since 1971, he has conducted lectures on Sherlock Holmes's influence on literature and cinema for libraries, colleges, and private organizations, including MENSA. Mr. Wright's whimsical *Sherlock Holmes Cookbook* (Drake), created with John Farrell, BSI, was published in 1976, and a mystery novel, *Enter the Lion: a Posthumous Memoir of Mycroft Holmes* (Hawthorne), "edited" with Michael Hodel, BSI, followed in 1979. As director general of The Plot Thickens Mystery Company, Mr. Wright originated hosting "mystery parties" in homes, restaurants, and offices, as well as producing and directing the very first "Mystery Train" tours on Amtrak, beginning in 1982.

# The MX Book of New Sherlock Holmes Stories

*Edited by David Marcum*
(MX Publishing, 2015-2025)

*"This is the finest volume of Sherlockian fiction I have ever read, and I have read, literally, thousands."* – Philip K. Jones

*"Beyond Impressive . . . This is a splendid venture for a great cause!"*
– Roger Johnson, Editor, *The Sherlock Holmes Journal*,
The Sherlock Holmes Society of London

*Part I: 1881-1889; Part II: 1890-1895; Part III: 1896-1929*

*Part IV: 2016 Annual*

*Part V: Christmas Adventures*

*Part VI: 2017 Annual*

*Eliminate the Impossible*
*Part VII: (1880-1891); Part VIII: (1892-1905)*

*2018 Annual*
*Part IX: (1879-1895); Part X: (1896-1916)*

*Some Untold Cases*
*Part XI: (1880-1891); Part XII: (1894-1902)*

*2019 Annual*
*Part XIII: (1881-1890); Part XIV: (1891-1897); Part XV: (1898-1917)*

*Whatever Remains . . . Must be the Truth*
*Part XVI: (1881-1890); Part XVII: (1891-1898); Part XVIII: (1898-1925)*

*2020 Annual*
*Part XIX: (1882-1890); Part XX: (1891-1897); Part XXI: (1898-1923)·*

*Some More Untold Cases*
*Part XXII: (1877-1887); Part XXIII: (1888-1894); Part XXIV: (1895-1903)*

*2021 Annual*
*Part XXV: (1881-1888); Part XXVI: (1889-1897); Part XXVII: (1898-1928)*

*More Christmas Adventures*
*Part XXVIII: (1869-1888); Part XXIX: (1889-1896); Part XXX: (1897-1928)*

*2022 Annual*
*Part XXXI: (1875-1887); Part XXXII: (1888-1895); Part XXXIII: (1896-1919)*

*"However Improbable . . . ."*
*Part XXXIV: (1878-1888); Part XXXV: (1889-1896); Part XXXVI: (1897-1919)*

*2023 Annual*
*Parts XXXVII (1875-1889), XXXVIII (1889-1896), and XXXIX (1897-1923)*

*Further Untold Cases*
*Part XL: (1879-1886), Part XLI: (1887-1892) and Part XLII: (1894-1922)*

*2024 Annual*
*Parts XLIII (1874-1888), XLIV (1889-1897), and XLV (1898-1917)*

*Occupants of the Canonical Realm*
*Parts XLVI (1861-1889), XLVII (1890-1898), and XLVIII (1899-1924)*

*The True Mr. Holmes: England's Greatest Hero*
*Parts XLIX and L (18XX-18XX) and (18XX-19XX)*

# The MX Book of New Sherlock Holmes Stories
## *Edited by David Marcum*
### (MX Publishing, 2015-2025)

437

# An Investees' Anthology
### *Edited by David Marcum*
(MX Publishing, 2022)

Selected Contributions to
*The MX Book of New Sherlock Holmes Stories*
by Members of
*The Baker Street Irregulars*

*All royalties from this collection are being donated
for the benefit of the preservation of Undershaw,
a school for special needs students located at
one of the former homes of Sir Arthur Conan Doyle*

Stories, Forewords, and Poems in this volume
have previously appeared in Parts I – XXXVI of
*The MX Book of New Sherlock Holmes Stories*

*Featuring Contributions by:*

Mark Alberstat, Marino C. Alvarez, Peter Calamai, Catherine Cooke, Carla Coupe, David Stuart Davies, John Farrell, Lyndsay Faye, Sonia Fetherston, Jayantika Ganguly, Jeffrey Hatcher, Roger Johnson, Leslie S. Klinger, Ann Margaret Lewis, Bonnie MacBird, Stephen Mason, Julie McKuras Nicholas Meyer, Jacquelynn Morris, Otto Penzler, Christopher Redmond, Tracy J. Revels, Steven Rothman, Nancy Holder, Mark Levy (and Arlene Mantin Levy), Nicholas Utechin, and Sean M. Wright (and DeForeest B. Wright, III)

## MX Publishing

**MX Publishing** is the world's largest specialist Sherlock Holmes publisher, with over six-hundred titles and over two-hundred authors creating the latest in Sherlock Holmes fiction and non-fiction

The catalogue includes several award winning books, and over four-hundred-and-fifty have been converted into audio.

MX Publishing also has one of the largest communities of Holmes fans on Facebook, with regular contributions from dozens of authors.

www.mxpublishing.com

@mxpublishing on Facebook, Twitter, and Instagram